SPECIAL MESSAGE ‖‖‖‖‖‖‖‖‖‖‖‖‖‖‖‖‖
KT-500-496

THE ULVERSCROFT FOUNDATION
(registered UK charity number 264873)
was established in 1972 to provide funds for
research, diagnosis and treatment of eye diseases.
Examples of major projects funded by
the Ulverscroft Foundation are:-

- The Children's Eye Unit at Moorfields Eye Hospital, London
- The Ulverscroft Children's Eye Unit at Great Ormond Street Hospital for Sick Children
- Funding research into eye diseases and treatment at the Department of Ophthalmology, University of Leicester
- The Ulverscroft Vision Research Group, Institute of Child Health
- Twin operating theatres at the Western Ophthalmic Hospital, London
- The Chair of Ophthalmology at the Royal Australian College of Ophthalmologists

You can help further the work of the Foundation
by making a donation or leaving a legacy.
Every contribution is gratefully received. If you
would like to help support the Foundation or
require further information, please contact:

THE ULVERSCROFT FOUNDATION
The Green, Bradgate Road, Anstey
Leicester LE7 7FU, England
Tel: (0116) 236 4325

e: www.ulverscroft-foundation.org.uk

THE DISTRICT NURSES OF VICTORY WALK

Alice Lake has arrived in London from Liverpool to start her training as a district nurse, but her journey has been far from easy. Her parents think that she should settle down and get married, but she has already had her heart broken once and isn't about to make the same mistake again. Alice and her best friend Edith are based in the East End, but before they've even got their smart new uniforms on, war breaks out and Hitler's bombs are raining down on London. Alice must learn to keep calm and carry on as she tends to London's sick and injured, all the time facing her own heartache and misfortune while keeping up the spirit of the blitz . . .

ANNIE GROVES

THE DISTRICT NURSES OF VICTORY WALK

Complete and Unabridged

MAGNA
Leicester

First published in Great Britain in 2018 by
HarperCollins*Publishers*
London

First Ulverscroft Edition
published 2020
by arrangement with
HarperCollins*Publishers* Ltd
London

The moral right of the author has been asserted

A catalogue record for this book is available
from the British Library.

ISBN 978–0–7505–4806–9

Published by
Ulverscroft Limited
Anstey, Leicestershire
Set by Words & Graphics Ltd.
Anstey, Leicestershire
Printed and bound in Great Britain by
T. J. International Ltd., Padstow, Cornwall

This book is printed on acid-free paper

Acknowledgements

Many thanks to the redoubtable Teresa Chris, and for the invaluable encouragement and support from editor Kate Bradley and copy editor Pen Isaac. Also to the staff of the Queen's Nursing Institute, especially Matthew Bradby and Christine Widdowson.

1

'Are you sure this is the right way?' asked Edith, putting her hand to her head as the early summer breeze threatened to blow her nurse's hat into the dusty road. 'Wasn't it meant to be five minutes from the bus stop? I bet we've walked for longer than that. My feet are killing me.'

Alice checked the piece of paper again. 'I can't see where we could have gone wrong. Anyway, Edie, we haven't been walking for more than a few minutes. Don't take on so.' She looked down at her colleague with good humour — Edith barely reached her shoulder. 'Let's go to the next corner and see if we can spot it from there. If we see anyone we can ask.'

Edith grimaced but, left with little choice, gamely picked up her case once more and followed Alice, whose longer stride meant she was always slightly ahead. In her other hand she carried her precious nurse's bag. The rows of terraced houses they passed all looked the same, three storeys high if you counted the big basements, with bay windows and steep stone steps, but narrow-fronted, built to fit a lot of people into a small space. They didn't have much in the way of front gardens, just an area where you could leave dustbins or reach the

1

basement door. Still, Edith told herself, it wasn't as grim as the street she had grown up in, on the other side of the river in south London. This was bright in comparison. It wouldn't be too bad at all.

Alice came to a sudden halt and Edith nearly smacked into her. The taller young woman pointed at a street sign. 'There we are. Victory Walk.'

Edith looked up, pushing one of her stray dark curls out of her eyes. Try as she might they would never do as she wanted, and she'd been in trouble with her previous matron because of that — and for numerous other reasons as well. 'So it is. Victory Walk. Suppose it was named after we won the Great War, though I bet the houses were built ages before that. Are we at this end?'

Alice looked at the houses on the corners. 'No, I don't think so. They said it was a bigger house and we'd know it straight away. Must be further along.'

Edith groaned as her shoulder protested at the weight of her case.

Alice smiled in sympathy. 'Buck up, Edie. Not far now.'

'Easy for you to say, with your long legs,' Edith grumbled, but picked up her case once more. 'I'm sure it's further than five minutes . . . '

'It won't be. Not when we aren't carrying these great lumbering things,' Alice pointed out. 'We'll be on and off those buses in a jiffy. You can get to the West End as quickly as you like on your days off.' She paused as they got to the other end of the short road. 'Here we are. They were right, there's no mistaking it.'

Both young women set down their cases and nurses' bags and stood to take in the first sight of what would be their new home, and also the base for their work. It was in the style of the rest of the street but felt grander, being double-fronted, standing a little taller than the buildings around it, and there were attic windows too. The sign above the immaculate front door left no room for doubt that they'd found what they were looking for: 'North Hackney Queen's Nurses Association'. This was why they'd taken the bus to the east side of the city, and then up Kingsland Road, with its busy mix of shops, cafés, factories and cinemas. This is where they would live for the foreseeable future and from where they would go out into the local community as district nurses. Alice found she was tracing with her forefinger the shape of the Queen's Nurse badge that she wore on a cord around her neck.

For a moment her nerve failed her. Would she be good enough? Would she live up to the trust of her tutors and the expectations of her patients? She'd trained for years, first as a general nurse in a hospital, then on the specialist course to become a district nurse, but there had always been someone else there to guide her. Now she would be out there, on the district as it was called, on her own, in her patients' houses rather than on wards, relying on her own skill and judgement to cope with whatever was thrown at her. Would she be able to do it?

Edith, who often relied on her friend to take

3

the lead, now stepped forward. 'Come on then. Let's see what this place is like on the inside. Hope we get rooms on the top storey.' She glanced up at Alice. 'We'll be all right, just you see.'

'Of course we will.' Alice gave herself a mental shake. 'They wouldn't have passed us otherwise.' And with that she picked up her heavy case for what she hoped would be the last time for a very long while, strode up the steps and rapped sharply on the glossy navy paint of the door.

★   ★   ★

The difference between the bright daylight and the gloom of the corridor made them blink, and Alice at first almost didn't see the young woman who let them in. She swiftly led them down the dim hallway and up a set of stairs, turning and opening a door, with a shy murmur of 'she's been expecting you', before vanishing again. Sunshine flooded in through a large window, falling on a sturdy but well-worn wooden desk covered in cardboard folders, with an equally solid-looking wooden bookcase behind it. Alice had just enough time to notice the familiar spines of textbooks she had studied when a student nurse before a bustling woman in uniform shot across from the far corner of the room and started speaking at top speed. Her hair was red as copper, her face was sprinkled with freckles and she was even shorter than Edith. Alice had the distinct impression that here was somebody who hardly ever sat still — keen energy radiated from her as she waved them inside the office.

'Come in, come in. Make yourselves comfortable. Nurses Lake and Gillespie, I take it?' She looked at them brightly.

'Y-yes,' Alice stuttered, momentarily taken aback by the woman's strong Scottish accent. 'I'm Alice Lake.'

'Then you must be Edith Gillespie,' the woman said, sounding delighted as she took them across to the slightly faded sofa on the far side of the room. 'I'm Fiona Dewar, and I'll be your superintendent. Sit, sit and take the weight off your feet, there'll be time enough for standing very shortly. Take every opportunity for a nice sit-down in this business, that's what I say, because who knows when you'll get another chance? You'll be rushing around soon enough, I'll be bound.' She took her seat behind the desk and pulled one of the folders towards her. 'Gladys will bring us a cup of tea, that's the young lady who let you in. She doesn't say much to start with but you'll get to know her all the same, I'm sure. So, now, your previous matron has said some very impressive things about you, Miss Lake.' She turned a page in the file. 'Most promising. You weren't inclined to go back to your home town, then?' She looked up and, although her grey eyes were kind, Alice realised they missed nothing.

Hastily she cleared her throat. 'No, I did my specialist training in London and I grew to like it. Besides, it means I can work with Edith, we work well as a team.' She smiled at the

5

superintendent, hoping there would be no further questions in this delicate area. She had no intention of revealing her real reason for staying away from Liverpool. That was her own private business, and it would stay that way if she had anything to do with it.

Edith beamed and the superintendent turned her gaze towards her. 'Ah yes, Miss Gillespie, it's always good to have a friend to hand, especially when you're in a responsible profession like nursing.'

Alice winced a little as yet again the older woman had homed in on a sensitive issue. Edith took her responsibilities very seriously — for as long as she was on duty. After that she took having fun very seriously as well. Alice suspected their former matron might well have made a note to that effect.

Edith sat up straight against the slightly sagging cushions of the sofa. 'Yes, Miss Dewar. I know we won't go round in pairs but we always found it useful to help each other out when we were studying, testing each other, that sort of thing.'

Fiona Dewar nodded sagely. 'Indeed. That shows commendable dedication. And we don't stand on ceremony here, girls. You may call me Fiona, unless it's in front of patients or doctors. It may surprise you to learn that I'm not vastly older than you are.'

Alice made a valiant attempt not to let her astonishment show on her face. Their previous superiors would have never, ever have relaxed the tradition of formal titles. Besides, she had thought Fiona Dewar must be at least twice her own age — but then, looking more closely, she saw that she was wrong. Perhaps the superintendent was in her late thirties; but knowing she was at such a senior level had made Alice assume she must be even older. 'No, of course not,' she managed to say, as Edith was clearly unable to utter a word.

The superintendent beamed again. 'I'm delighted you've both decided to join us. I know the borough's main branch is a bit more central, but we like to think we keep a welcoming house here.'

Alice shifted in her seat. 'We saw that you had vacancies for two nurses and so we thought we could stick together.'

Fiona nodded again. 'That sounds very sensible. So, I'm sure you're well prepared for your new positions and you'd never have passed the exam if you weren't, but all the same . . . ' She sat back a little, clasping her hands. 'It will be different to what you've been used to working in a hospital. Of course you are still under the medical direction of a doctor — you won't be expected to dispense medicine for any patient except in emergencies, and I'm happy to say that our local GPs all appreciate the hard work we district nurses do. All the same, you will be required to show initiative and to take every opportunity to promote good health and hygiene to every family. Prevention is better than cure.' Her eyes gleamed and Alice and Edith smiled in agreement.

'Always remember, you are guests in the

patients' homes.' Fiona's face grew serious. 'We never, ever judge our patients on account of their creed or degree of poverty. I regret to say that you will have plenty of dealings with the various officials who oversee public assistance, as many households around here can't pay into provident schemes. Yet they are all equal when it comes to treatment.'

'Of course,' said Alice hurriedly, inwardly wondering how bad it might be. She knew all about poverty in theory — but she'd never gone without herself.

'So, ladies, may I safely presume that you can ride bicycles?'

'Yes, I been doing that since I was a kiddie,' Edith assured the woman.

Alice inclined her head towards her friend. 'I can manage a bike too.' She'd never been allowed one as a child; her parents had thought it was too dangerous an activity for their beloved only daughter. 'I learned when I was a student nurse. When we were working shifts it was the only reliable way to get around.'

'Quite so,' Fiona Dewar said approvingly. 'We are fortunate to be well connected with public transport here, as you must have found out earlier, but when visiting your patients you will have to do so by bike. There's no bus or tram that will get down some of our narrower streets. Do I take it that neither of you are familiar with this part of London?'

Both nurses shook their heads.

'Oh, it's a wonderful place to work.' The superintendent spread her hands in front of her.

'You'll never be bored for a minute. We have unemployment around here, of course, and some of our local citizens do live cheek by jowl, you might say, and so we have to be extra vigilant against the spread of disease. There was an outbreak of typhoid down in Shoreditch at the beginning of the year, terrible business. Over-crowding makes it worse. But then, you knew all that before you qualified, didn't you?'

Alice agreed somewhat nervously. It was one thing to learn such things as a part of a course, quite another to be brought face to face with the facts. Still, if she'd wanted an easy life she could have gone back to Liverpool. Although that would have been difficult in other ways.

'It can't be any more overcrowded than where I grew up,' said Edith matter-of-factly. 'We were seven of us children in a two-bedroom house and that was better off than some of our neighbours. You just got on and made the best of things.'

'That's the spirit,' said Fiona.

Alice glanced at her friend. She knew it hadn't been as simple as that. But that was Edith's story to tell.

There was a nervous knock at the door and the young woman who'd let them in tentatively balanced a laden tea tray as she stepped across to the desk. She didn't meet their eyes, but kept her gaze towards the floor and her mousy brown hair fell forward, obscuring her pale face.

'Thank you, Gladys,' said Fiona, as Gladys scooted out again. She poured three cups from the pot. 'I wouldn't like to give you the impression that you'll be waited on hand and

9

foot here. This is purely because it's a special occasion, to welcome you to your new home.' She glanced up as she passed the cups across the desk. 'We see to ourselves most of the time when it comes to cups of tea or that sort of thing. There are three meals a day served downstairs on the lower ground floor, all provided by our esteemed Cook, and you will of course maintain your own rooms in spick-and-span order. We must value hygienic practices at all times.'

'Of course,' Alice agreed hurriedly. It was what they'd been used to, after all. She gratefully sipped her tea, realising that her last cup had been at an unearthly hour that morning, and felt like a long time ago.

'Our district room is on the ground floor — you'll have passed the door to it on your way in,' Fiona went on. 'I must warn you that, although we are by and large a friendly establishment here, any nurse who leaves that room less tidy than she found it will incur immediate wrath. There can be absolutely no exceptions. I trust I need say no more about that most vital rule.'

Alice hastily swallowed her tea and nodded vigorously. The district room was where all supplies and equipment were kept, with which each nurse replenished the contents of her own Gladstone bag that went everywhere with her. To fall foul of the superintendent's rule would be to risk another nurse being unable to find something important, possibly in an emergency. That could never be allowed to happen.

'Yes, Fiona. I mean no,' added Edith.

'Good,' said the superintendent, setting down her cup of tea on its serviceable saucer. 'All finished? Excellent. Now, follow me. I'm afraid you'll have to hit the ground running as we are extremely busy right now. Which is why we're so glad to recruit the pair of you together, of course. You'll be needed just as soon as you've had a moment to catch your breath. Someone will bring up your big cases, but please take your bags. I'll show you to your rooms. You're on the top floor, so I hope you've got good legs. Well, if you haven't already, you soon will have.'

Alice and Edith exchanged a glance as they obediently followed the diminutive superintendent. Their previous matron would sooner have died than make a comment about their legs. Clearly things were very different around here, and Alice had the distinct impression that, whatever else they were in for, it wasn't going to be boring.

2

Alice had barely had time to unpack and settle herself in a Spartan but immaculately clean attic room when her first callout came. A young mother was worried about her baby, who seemed to be running an unusual temperature. One of the local doctors had referred her to the district nurses — could somebody come that afternoon?

The message reached Alice just as she'd found her hairbrush and managed to give her hair a quick tidy as she peered into the small mirror perched on top of the chest of drawers. When not pinned up under her uniform hat or cap, her dark blonde locks reached to her shoulders in natural waves, but it was rare for her to wear her hair down. She was settling it back into its usual neat bun when there was a knock on her door.

'Come — ' she began, but before she could even finish her sentence, in burst a young woman in nurse's uniform, big blue eyes gazing at Alice with frank curiosity.

'Are you Miss Lake? I'm Mary Perkins and I've got the room at the end of this corridor,' the new arrival announced. 'Sorry, you're needed already. Only this minute got here, haven't you? I've been here for two months so I can show you the ropes. We'll get to know each other properly later, but if your bag is all ready to go, you'd better come with me.'

'I'm Alice,' said Alice, grabbing her bag, which

she'd prepared in advance, and reaching for her navy coat. 'But I haven't got a bike yet.'

'Not to worry, it'll be around the side, they always are,' said Mary Perkins, who Alice judged to be about Edith's age, a couple of years younger than herself. 'This house is a doddle to find, and you'll be going there often if I'm any judge, and I can tell you right now I'm pretty good at guessing these things.' She set off at a great pace and it was all Alice could do to keep up as her new colleague dashed along the narrow attic corridor and down the main set of stairs.

'No running! Nurse Perkins, is that you?' came a grim voice from the storey below.

'Bloody old busybody,' Mary muttered under her breath, but she did at least slow to a fast walk. 'Have you met Gwen yet? No? Well, you soon will. She's Fiona's deputy, but don't pay her any mind. Look, this is the way to the side door, it'll save you time. That's the district room, and that's the drying room for your cloak when you've been out in the rain, but you can see all that later.' She ducked around a corner and led Alice out into a sunny yard.

Alice realised that — as it was on the corner of the road — the nurses' home had a large area to the side. One wall had been turned into an informal bike shed, with a light timber roof balanced on the top ridge, and a makeshift rack propped so that a dozen or so cycles could be stored beneath it. Mary made her way along and paused at the end. 'These are the spare bikes — one for you and one for the other new nurse.'

'How can you tell? They all look alike,' Alice wondered.

'We all put something on our bike to show it's ours. We're not meant to but we do.' Mary pointed to a bike at the far end. 'See the one with the bit of blue ribbon around the bell? That's mine. Silly really, but when I was walking out with this chap, he said I looked lovely in blue because it went with my eyes, so I got myself some ribbon to trim my hat, and that was what was left over. Turns out the ribbon lasted longer than he did.' She shrugged, not overly concerned. 'I say, have you got a chap?'

Alice took a step back. She wasn't accustomed to such direct questions from someone she'd only just met. 'No,' she said shortly and then, realising it sounded rude to be so abrupt, 'I haven't had time, after studying so hard. Anyway, I didn't spend all those years training just to give it up to get married.'

'Quite right,' said Mary. 'Only I wish they weren't quite so strict about the rules. In by ten o'clock, no men on the premises, there's hardly any fun to be had. Still, if you aren't bothered about that then that's all right.'

Alice thought that Edith would find a way around the restrictions within the week, if her past history was anything to go by. But she didn't offer that piece of information to Mary. Instead she asked, 'Where am I going now?'

'Jeeves Place,' said Mary. 'It's hard to miss. You go back the way you'd have come this morning as far as the high road. Go straight over — that's Jeeves Street. The road one further down, parallel to it, is Jeeves Place. Easy. Number nine. Patient's name is Kathleen Berry, well, that's the mother. Not sure what her baby's called.'

'I expect I'll find out soon, then,' said Alice, placing her leather bag in the basket of the bike and pushing it carefully towards the side gate. 'Wish me luck. If I'm not back by teatime, send out a search party.'

'Will do.' Mary waved cheerfully and her lively rich brown curls bobbed around her face.

★ ★ ★

Kathleen Berry tried to shut out the sounds of her baby son's screaming. She'd tried picking him up and carrying him around, changing his nappy, offering him cold water, feeding him herself, taking him outside, bringing him back in. Nothing helped and now he was working himself up into a proper state. He lay in his makeshift cot, waving his fists in the air, his face an angry red. She didn't know what to do. She hoped the nurse would get here soon. She was so frightened.

Her mum had told her not to have anything to do with Ray Berry, that he was a feckless charmer who'd love her and leave her. Kathleen had defended him staunchly. He'd never treat her like that, her mother was just listening to the gossipy old women who had nothing better to do than spread cruel rumours that were without foundation. They were just jealous because they weren't young any more and had probably never had the attention of a man as good-looking as her Ray. She knew he'd do right by her.

And Ray had — she had his ring on her finger to prove it. No matter how tough things got she was never tempted to pawn it — it was too precious to her, it stood for everything they'd promised to each other. He'd done his best to provide for her but it hadn't been easy. People were too quick to believe the gossip and he found it hard to get regular work. One day he'd told her he was going down the docks to see if anything was to be found there, and that had been the last she'd seen of him. One of his mates had dropped round to say he'd signed up for a merchant ship and had set sail that very day. It was too good a chance for him to miss.

Kathleen knew he'd be back, but the trouble was he hadn't sent home regular wages. She was never sure what she would get, if anything at all, but she hated to ask anyone for help. She hadn't known for certain that she was pregnant before he left — she didn't want to get it wrong and so she'd waited to tell him. He'd set sail without realising he was soon to become a father.

Now she was stuck with little Brian in this rundown house, which was all she could afford, although if truth be told she couldn't really even do that. She didn't even have the whole place to herself — she had the ground floor, with its badly lit front room, cramped kitchen and even more cramped back kitchen, with its doorway into the back yard where there was an outside privy, shared by several families. Upstairs lived the Coynes, who trampled around on the bare

16

boards with no regard of her need to sleep. Then again, they heard Brian's cries all day and night as clearly as she did.

'Shush, shush,' she said, trying to keep the desperation out of her voice. 'Mummy's here. The kind nurse will come soon, she'll make everything better, just you wait and see.' She fervently hoped this was true. Wearily she leaned over the baby and took him up into her arms again, noting that he was still far too hot. 'Mummy's going to stand in the door with you, see if that cools you down.' She shoved open the flaking front door and leant on the creaky frame, grateful for the light breeze to fan their faces, even if it blew rubbish down the narrow street. Bits of old newspaper tumbled by. She was so tired she could have slept standing up, if she didn't have little Brian to look after.

Brian's cries gradually turned to sad whimpers, but she knew it was because he was too tired to cry lustily any more rather than because he felt better. Anxiously she pressed her hand to his forehead. No, still hot. It wasn't right. Why was he like this? Was it something she'd done, or hadn't done?

Kathleen bit down on her lower lip. It wouldn't help if she went to pieces. It wasn't as if she had many people to turn to. Her mother would say it served her right for marrying that good-for-nothing. Besides, her mother had four other children to see to, and three more grandchildren to fuss over. Kathleen knew she was a fair way down the list of her mother's priorities. Sometimes she wondered if she'd been

17

switched at birth as she couldn't remember a time when she and her mother had got along. They were just too different, even before she'd met Ray. She knew she was quieter, more serious than her mother, who had a loud voice and coarse laugh. Her other siblings had had no such problems, and Kathleen had ended up distant from all of them as a result. She had one good friend who lived on the next street but she couldn't expect her to be round every time something went wrong — which seemed to happen more and more. 'It's just you and me, Brian,' she breathed, feeling better for admitting the frightening truth. If only Ray were here.

She wasn't sure how long she'd been standing there when there was a rattle of wheels behind her. Turning, she saw it was a tall figure in a navy cloak on a bike that had seen better days. There was no mistaking the woman's hat though. It was the nurse, at last.

'Mrs Berry? I'm Nurse Lake. Alice Lake.' Alice dismounted from the bike and propped it against the house, pausing to take the Gladstone bag out of the basket. 'Hope I haven't kept you waiting too long.'

Kathleen could have cried with relief. 'Come in, come in,' she said, stepping back inside the house with its meagre furnishings. She perched on a wooden chair, Brian in her arms, and left the one decent armchair for Alice.

Alice took it, noticing that the cushions were faded and frayed, but had been carefully mended. The young mother before her wasn't far off her own age, she guessed; maybe a couple of

18

years younger. But her face was creased with lines of worry and she looked as if she hadn't slept properly for a very long time. 'Well, Mrs Berry, what seems to be the trouble?'

'Oh, it's Brian here.' The words came tumbling out now. 'He's ever so hot, he's been like this since yesterday, and I can't calm him down. I don't know what it is. You don't think . . . you don't think . . . ' She could barely form the words to name her deepest fear. 'Could it be typhoid, Miss? They had it down Shoreditch way. Took them awful bad, it did, and people died and everything. I couldn't bear for it to be typhoid, not my Brian, he's only four months old . . . ' She hated to cry in front of anyone, let alone a stranger, and hastily cuffed away a tear that she could not hold in.

Alice recognised that her first task would be to reassure the mother. If she were anxious then her baby would surely pick up on this and react badly. All the way over here on the short journey she'd been wondering what she would do or say, but now her training kicked in.

'I'd be very surprised if it is typhoid,' she said immediately. 'But why don't you let me take a look? How about you put him to lie here on this cushion and we can see what signs of illness he has.'

'He's dreadful hot, Miss.' Kathleen set the small body on the cushion and, true to form, Brian started up his piteous screaming again.

'Oh, young man, what can we do for you, eh?' Alice gently laid her hand on his forehead and agreed that he was indeed very hot. She reached across to her bag. 'I'm just going to pop this thermometer in his mouth. There, that's not so bad, is it?' The baby stopped crying in surprise at the sensation of the cool thermometer. Alice carefully checked the time and withdrew it. 'Yes, you're right, it is a little high, but not as high as we'd expect for a case of typhoid.' She next checked his pulse and breathing, as the first thing the doctor would look for in her report was his TPR: temperature, pulse, respiration. She then pulled up his little shirt and observed his abdomen. 'Well, there's no telltale rash. Those two things make me doubt it's typhoid, Mrs Berry. Tell me, have you been to Shoreditch recently?'

Kathleen had sagged against the hard back of the chair as Alice had assessed her child, but now perked up as her biggest fear was allayed. 'Oh no, Miss. We've got no call to go down there. Leastways, my Ray's got a brother down that way but we don't see him regular. They wasn't close, you see.' She sniffed. 'It's just . . . you hear these things . . . I didn't know where to turn . . . '

Alice made a decision. 'Mrs Berry, may I make a suggestion? You take a seat in the comfy chair and I'll make us both a cup of tea. Through there, I take it?' and before the exhausted young mother could object, she slipped through the connecting door to the back of the house.

She'd wanted to observe the state of the rest of the place. She knew only too well that typhoid flourished in conditions of poverty which so often led to over-crowding and a lack of hygiene.

20

But here, although money was so evidently painfully short, everything was scrubbed and tidy. What food and drink there was, was covered and protected, and therefore far less likely to be a source of contagion. Somehow the frazzled young woman managed to maintain a clean house, even with a demanding small baby.

Alice opened one of the two wooden cupboards and found the tin of tea leaves, which was easy as there wasn't much else on the warped shelves. She set the kettle to boil and found a small amount of milk in a bottle beneath a pottery cooler. She sniffed it dubiously but it was fresh. There was a collection of slightly chipped but matching cups hanging from hooks beneath a wooden rack holding plates from the same set. Alice wondered if they had been a wedding present, as she cautiously unhooked two cups.

She put the tea things on a tray and then filled a dish of cool water from the one tap in the back kitchen, adding a tea towel she found in the drawer under the sink. Then she carried everything through.

'Why don't you pour, Mrs Berry, and I'll sponge down the boy.' She knelt beside the little figure and gently dipped the towel in water and wiped his hot face very carefully.

'Call me Kathleen, do, Miss. I'm so grateful you came round,' Kathleen said, her hands shaking a little as she filled Alice's cup. 'If it's not typhoid, do you know what's wrong with him?'

Alice smiled reassuringly. 'Has he been mixing with anyone who's got a cold? Babies often show a high temperature when you or I would just feel a little under the weather.'

Kathleen thought for a moment. 'He might have, Miss. My friend's brother had to pull out of a match last week as he was took bad but then he was right as rain by the weekend. Could that be it?'

'It could be something as simple as that. Keep him warm, wipe his face with a cool cloth and give him plenty of fluids.' Alice looked appraisingly at the young woman. 'You are feeding him yourself still, I assume?'

Kathleen nodded.

'You might want to consider a supplementary feed, such as Cow and Gate,' Alice suggested gently.

'Oh no, Nurse. Our family don't hold with that. Mother's milk is best, that's what they say.' Kathleen knew she could never afford any alternative.

'Well, you've got to make sure that you keep your strength up, that you're taking in enough nutrition to make good milk.' Alice had noticed the baby was on the scrawny side and suspected the mother was scrimping on meals. She didn't have a spare ounce of fat on her. 'Is it just the two of you here?' She had registered the wedding ring on the young woman's hand, but also the narrow single bed pushed against the back wall and the clothes rail with a few well-worn frocks on it but no men's items.

Kathleen's head came up. 'My Ray's away on a merchant ship, Miss. He'll be back soon and then he'll see us right. It's just he can't always tell us where he is or when he'll be back, letters take so long, though I always try to keep him up to date with our news. I'm keeping the place nice for when he returns. I'll be able to pay you then.'

Alice glanced down. She hated the moment when the subject of money was raised, and had already presumed that Kathleen would fall into the bracket of those too poor to afford to pay, and who would therefore be treated for free. But it was a thorny issue. Everyone had their pride, and just because cash was short didn't mean Kathleen wanted to be a sympathy case. Alice fixed her gaze on the rag rug on the bare floor, which had been skilfully made, even if not very recently. 'You might be eligible for extra milk from the local authority. You can drink it yourself and also dilute it for your baby.'

Kathleen visibly recoiled at the notion of receiving a handout. 'That won't be necessary, Nurse.'

'No need to worry about that just now,' Alice said hastily. 'You let us know when your husband comes home and we can maybe talk about it then. But in the meanwhile, you mustn't hesitate to call for us again if the boy doesn't improve or goes down with something else.' She looked directly at Kathleen. 'The best way to keep your child well is to make sure you stay healthy yourself, Mrs Berry. Kathleen.' She paused to let her words sink in. 'And that means eating well. I know it's not always easy to find the time when you are busy but you have to remember to do so.'

Kathleen flushed. Of course she'd been

missing meals. There wasn't the money to eat properly every day, but she was damned if she'd admit that to the kind nurse.

* * *

Alice had finished her tea and was making ready to leave when there came a knock at the door and a young woman came in without waiting for Kathleen to answer. In the dim light the first thing Alice noticed was her hair — there was so much of it, partially pinned up but most of it falling down around her shoulders, wind-blown and untameable. 'Thought you were coming round?' she demanded, and then stopped in her tracks. 'Sorry, didn't realise you had company.'

Alice stood. 'I was just leaving. I'm Nurse Lake, Alice Lake.'

Kathleen hurriedly stood as well. 'Oh, Mattie, Brian was took bad and I clean forgot. I'm sorry, I hope your ma didn't go to no trouble . . . '

'Don't be silly.' Mattie took one look at her friend who was all of a fluster and went and gave her a big hug. Then she turned to Alice. 'You're not going on my account, are you?'

'No, no, I was on my way anyway,' Alice assured her. 'I've taken a look at Brian and I'm sure he's in no danger. He just needs good care and plenty of rest.'

Mattie nodded. 'Glad to hear it. I'm Mattie Askew, by the way. I've got a baby Brian's age so I know what it's like, don't I, Kath? Only I live at me ma's while my Lennie's away, so I got

24

someone to help me out and look after her now and again.'

Kathleen breathed out. 'Your ma's a diamond, Mattie. She's been good to me an' all. I don't know where I'd be without her, that's the truth.'

Alice picked up her bag. 'Well, I'm glad to see you've got a good friend, Kathleen. A trouble shared is a trouble halved, that's what they say.' She moved towards the door.

'Works both ways,' Mattie said staunchly. 'When my Lennie joined up I was in a proper tizz, and Kathleen looked after me then. He always wanted to go into the army but when he went ahead and did it I didn't know what to do. It was Kathleen what stopped me running after him and making a fool of myself.' She grinned at her friend with affection. Alice saw Kathleen in a different light, not a poverty-stricken young woman panicking about her child's health, but a steadfast friend who could be relied upon. It was a good lesson to learn on her first real visit as a district nurse. People had different sides and you couldn't presume that you understood every-thing about them on one short visit.

'I'll say goodbye, then,' she said. 'Don't hesitate to call on me again, Kathleen. Remember what I said earlier.'

'I will. I reckon he'll be right as rain now,' said Kathleen, stepping towards the door to see Alice out. 'Thank you, Nurse. You've set my mind at rest and I'm really grateful.' She stood at the open door as Alice lifted her Gladstone bag into the wire basket of her bike and set off.

Mattie took a look at Brian and carefully

25

placed her hand on his small forehead. 'He is a bit warm, isn't he? What did she think it was?'

Kathleen came back inside and shook her head ruefully. 'He's better than he was. She sponged him down ever so gently and he settled at last. He was ever so hot this morning, and I thought . . . I thought . . . ' She could barely form the word as the fear leapt up inside her once more, but she forced herself to stay calm. 'You know. Like down in Shoreditch. I thought it had come here and he'd got it.'

'Oh, Kath.' Mattie knew exactly what her friend was thinking, and if she were honest she'd worried about it herself, even though she rarely went anywhere near the area. 'It won't be that, really it won't.'

'I know that now.' Kathleen composed herself again. 'She said he probably had a bit of a cold and that babies his age can get a temperature where you or me wouldn't have more than a bit of a sniffle.'

'Probably got it off our Harry.' Mattie shifted uncomfortably. 'I'll kill him. I said to stay away from the little 'uns but he can't resist them. He was picking up your Brian and playing with him a few days ago, wasn't he?'

Kathleen nodded. 'Don't blame him though, Mattie. I'm glad he plays with them. Brian likes it, you can tell. Does him good to get a cuddle from someone apart from me. Not all men like to do it, so don't you go stopping him.'

Mattie knew what Kathleen really meant. 'Still no word from Ray, then?'

Kathleen shook her head. 'He can't send word

if he's halfway to Canada, can he? Stands to reason, that does. I don't expect to hear nothing till he's back in port, and who knows when that'll be?'

'Who knows,' Mattie echoed loyally, keeping her true feelings out of her voice. She wouldn't trust Ray Berry as far as she could throw him which, given that he was six foot tall and she was a shade over five foot two, wouldn't be far. She knew Kathleen loved him with a fierce and unstoppable passion, which meant she never complained about being left high and dry with a baby to look after on hardly any money. She herself wouldn't have put up with it. But then, her Lennie sent home a portion of his wages regular as clockwork, and wrote letters every time he could. He was desperate for news of his baby daughter. He and Ray were as different as chalk and cheese.

'You going to come back with me, then?' she asked now. 'Bring Brian — if he's got what Harry had then we'd all have caught it by now if we were going to. Ma's made a big pot of stew and says it won't last, and she'll be furious if I don't bring you home with me.'

Kathleen briefly shut her eyes. She knew she was a bit of a charity case, and didn't want to presume on Mattie's mother's kindness. All the same, her mouth was watering at the thought of her stew, and Nurse Lake had been very clear: she had to eat well to keep Brian in good health. She really didn't have much choice.

'I'd love to,' she said.

3

Edith was deep in conversation with Mary Perkins when Alice returned, a little shaky after the ride on the unfamiliar bike.

'Come and have a cup of tea,' Mary said at once. 'I know what it's like to ride that boneshaker. You'll want a good sit-down to recover.' She got up to boil the kettle and refresh the pot that she and Edith had already started. They were in the big room on the lower-ground floor, which was comfortably if slightly shabbily furnished to function as a combined dining and common room, next to the handy service room with all that thirsty nurses could need, as each had their own cupboard for drinks and snacks as well as a communal iron and ironing board. Light poured in through the big windows, and Alice could see the bike stand through one of them.

'Don't mind if I do,' she said, collapsing onto a wooden carver chair, the seat of which was softened by a big patchwork cushion. 'I found my way there and back all right though. I'm slowly getting my bearings.'

Mary set a cup and saucer in front of her. 'There you are. What was it like? Was the baby very sick?'

Alice sipped the welcome tea and thought for a moment. 'No, not really. Well, he had a temperature but I'm pretty sure it was nothing to worry about. It's just that the real reason for concern is he's undernourished, and we can't do much about that unless the mother lets us.'

Edith looked at her. 'Remember, they warned us about that in our lectures. You can't save everyone, Alice, even though I know you want to.'

'I know, I know.' Alice was only too aware that she had a tendency to get drawn in. It was the only fault that her previous matron had noted. She'd been ticked off for not maintaining a professional barrier, and told in no uncertain terms that it would do nobody any good — not the patient and not her. 'Really, Edith, you needn't worry. I'm not about to go round there and start taking over. It's just — well, the mother was trying her best, you could see it in the way she kept the place, but she had next to nothing. She can barely feed herself, let alone the baby.'

Mary raised her eyebrows. 'Like I said, you'll be back, I'll put money on it. A penny it's within the fortnight. What do you say?'

'I . . . I don't really bet,' Alice said, secretly shocked. She had been raised to think of gambling as a sin, and yet here was Mary blithely offering to put money down on a patient getting sick again. It didn't seem right, but she didn't want to appear too disapproving on her first day.

'Oh, Alice doesn't like a flutter but I do.' Edith's eyes gleamed. 'Just you wait till I have my first case.'

'Didn't you get called out today, then?' Alice asked.

'No, I've been unpacking and making myself

familiar with where everything is around here,' Edith explained. 'Nearest bathroom, quickest way down the stairs, who sleeps where, that kind of thing. Met a few of our colleagues and heard all the stories about which doctors are easiest to work with and which try to palm you off with patients they don't want to deal with. Tested out which of the chairs down here are the comfiest.'

Alice nodded. 'Have you been outside?' She had a very good idea of what Edith had been on the lookout for.

'I might have.' Edith rolled her eyes. 'There's a solid tall fence to the side but the one at the back is a bit rickety.' She grinned.

Alice said nothing but sent a silent message to her friend to go no further. Neither of them knew Mary well enough yet to share what Edith was up to, but Alice was sure she'd been checking for ways in and out after curfew. She'd done the same at their last place, working out where the rotten fence posts were and pushing in that way if she hadn't got back in time. Alice didn't exactly approve, but she wasn't going to land Edith in hot water if she could help it.

Mary remained blissfully ignorant of what was going on under her nose. 'I got called out just after you left. One of the girls who works in the gas-mask factory had run a needle through her hand, but hadn't done anything about it. She stayed off work but only thought to tell the doctor once the wound started puffing up. Should have disinfected it immediately but too late now. Anyway I cleaned it and dressed it and she should be all right, but it'll take her twice as long to heal than if she'd had it seen to at once.' She shrugged.

'Gas-mask factory?' Edith sat up in her hard-backed chair.

'Yes, it's not far from here. Used to be a furniture factory but now it turns out all those ghastly masks in case there's a war. Which there won't be,' Mary said confidently, draining her cup.

Alice looked up. 'Are you sure? There are lots of people who'd disagree with you.'

Mary nodded. 'Oh, of course. Mr Chamberlain wouldn't declare war, that's tosh. He'll keep us safe, there's no question of it.'

Alice swallowed slowly. She wondered how her new colleague could be so definite in her views when all around quiet preparations were going ahead in case the worst came to the worst. This very morning they had seen many kerbstones painted white to stand out if the city was in blackout, and from the top deck of the bus they had glimpsed skylights painted black to hide any lights beneath them. 'So why are they making gas masks?' she asked.

'It's just a precaution,' Mary said breezily. 'I expect they'll go back to making toys or whatever those factories did until recently. Give them a few months and all the panic will be over. I'm not going around wearing a gas mask, I can tell you that right now. It's bad enough trying to keep my hair in order as it is.'

'Yes, they aren't really designed with fashion in mind,' said Edith, trying to make light of it while keeping an eye on Alice. She knew her friend followed public events with keen scrutiny, and had little patience with people who buried their heads in the sand. Would Alice start an argument now? Normally she was the most level-headed person around, but she had been known to grow hot under the collar about world affairs.

Alice held her tongue, but Edith could see it was an effort. 'Well, all I can say is there are lots of Canadian and American servicemen in town, so I shan't complain.' She smiled at the memory of the last time she'd been out dancing.

'Edith, you are dreadful,' said Alice, but without malice. 'Mary, pay no attention to her.'

'Oh no, I completely agree,' Mary said. 'They're so smart, aren't they? And I do like their uniforms. Especially the Canadians. They're so straightforward; you haven't got to go through the usual palaver about who their families are or if they've gone to school with your brothers.'

Edith nodded dubiously. She didn't usually have to worry about that sort of thing, especially as all her brothers had done their best to avoid school whenever possible. 'Lots of them are good dancers,' she said.

'Aren't they just? And they aren't shy to ask you onto the dance floor,' Mary said with growing enthusiasm. 'We'll have to put them to the test the next time our shifts allow. We'll have such fun. Long may they stay over here.'

There was a sound from the door, a gruff cough, and an older woman appeared in a highly starched nurse's uniform.

'That's enough of such frivolous talk, Nurse

32

Perkins,' she said, her expression lined with severity, her cardigan buttoned tightly all the way up to her throat. 'You might think war is just an excuse for dancing with young men, but I can tell you right now it is no laughing matter. Besides, you owe it to your training to put your profession first and not to lower our standards. Kindly bear that in mind.' She let her gaze rest on each of them in turn before abruptly swirling around, leaving them open-mouthed.

'Who was that?' asked Edith after a moment.

Mary pulled a face. 'Gwen. You heard her earlier. She's been here for ever, and is as old as the hills. Well, as you saw. She disapproves of everybody and everything and her pet hate is anyone enjoying themselves. As she's Fiona's deputy, she's always telling us off for something. Bet she hasn't been out dancing for years. Well, that's not my fault.'

Edith grimaced. 'That's too bad, but I can tell you right now, I think we deserve a bit of fun in our time off. Don't get me wrong, I love being a nurse and I work hard, but everyone is entitled to a spot of recreation now and again. Isn't that true, Alice?'

Alice paused. She'd caught a look in the older woman's eye that made her wonder why she was so sharp, so judgemental. Still, it couldn't be much fun watching young nurses arrive, full of life and energy, if you were older and more set in your ways.

'You go on out and enjoy yourselves,' she said. 'I'm no good at dancing. I'd rather stay in with a good book, if you want the truth.'

'Oh, I'm sure that can't be so!' Mary exclaimed. 'Look at you, you'll be bombarded with offers to dance. We'll have to take your rejected suitors.'

Alice smiled gamely but her heart wasn't in it. She had no intention of going dancing, with Mary or anyone else. She used to do it with a light heart but that was before. She was no longer that carefree young nursing student. Life had seen to that.

* * *

As soon as Mattie and Kathleen opened the door the steam hit them. Delicious wafts were coming from the kitchen and they could hear Mattie's mother singing at full volume, unaware that anyone had come in. 'My old man said follow the van,' she sang, slightly off-key.

Mattie grinned. 'Come on through, then we can put Brian down with Gillian.' She led the way down the short corridor to the big kitchen, three times the size of Kathleen's, where little Gillian was tucked into a cot in the corner and her grandmother stood at the range, her sleeves rolled up and her face red with the heat from cooking.

'Kathleen Berry! And there was me thinking you'd got a better offer.' The older woman put down her big wooden spoon and strode across to greet her guest. 'You need feeding up by the looks of you. And how's the boy?' She peered at the little bundle in Kathleen's arms. 'Has your Auntie Mattie brought you round for your tea?

He's a proper little darling, just look at him.'

'Thank you, Mrs Banham,' said Kathleen, who still found Mattie's mother overwhelming even though she'd known her for years. 'It's kind of you to have us.'

'Nonsense, what else am I going to do with all this stew? It would be a crying shame for it to go to waste,' Flo Banham insisted, returning to her bubbling pot.

'I'm sure Joe and Harry could finish it off,' Kathleen said, knowing that Mattie's brothers had hollow legs, particularly when it came to their mother's cooking. She carefully tucked Brian into the opposite end of the big cot, which had held generations of Banham children, and had plenty of room for two small babies.

Flo Banham tutted. 'There will be plenty to go round. I went down Ridley Road and the butcher let me have this cheap as he was expecting a new delivery. Practically begged me to take it off him, he did.' She gave the stew one more vigorous stir and then put on the lid. 'There, we'll let that simmer away for a while and then it'll be ready by the time the boys get back.'

Mattie grinned. Her brothers hadn't been boys for a long time but their mother always called them that, as if they still needed cosseting and looking after. She used to think that was funny but now that she had Gillian, she understood it better. She couldn't imagine ever not wanting to take care of her. She looked over the side of the cot at the little girl, fast asleep, her soft baby hair spread out on the little pillow. 'Has she been good?' she asked her mother.

'She's been a little angel for her granny,' said Flo, coming to join her daughter to gaze down at the youngest member of the family. 'She's far quieter than you ever were, Mattie. You used to burst into tears every time I put you into your cot. I had to tie you in a sling so I could carry you round while I did my housework.'

'Must be why I'm so good at it now,' said Mattie cheekily, rolling her eyes. She'd heard it all before.

Kathleen sat down in the rocking chair with a sigh. She was tired out by the worries of the day and because Brian had kept her awake for much of the night, but it was comforting to hear Mattie and her mother gently bickering. After a few moments she felt herself nodding off and, although she fought to stop it, the warmth of the room soon had her falling into a light doze. That came to an abrupt end when the front door banged and loud voices filled the air. Mattie's brothers were home.

Kathleen jolted upright, shaking her head to clear it, as Joe and Harry strode into the kitchen. Neither was surprised to see her there. Harry flung his jacket at a stool beside the back door, but his mother caught him.

'You just put that back in the hallway where it belongs, Harry Banham,' she scolded. 'A place for everything and everything in its place — how else are we going to manage, can you tell me that? If Joe can remember then I don't see why you can't as well.'

Harry rolled his eyes but went to do as he was

36

asked. 'Won't do any harm, it's only a jacket,' he protested, his voice echoing back down the hall.

'It's cluttering up my kitchen, that's what it's doing. If we all did that there'd be no room to cook.' His mother wasn't going to let him get away with anything. Harry was always trying his luck, trying to wind her around his little finger, but she'd had years of practice at resisting his easy charm.

Joe snorted, settling himself down at the well-scrubbed old wooden table, fishing the evening paper out of his back pocket. 'Hello, Kathleen. Brought little Brian round to see Gillian, have you?'

'Yes, they're both in the cot,' Kathleen began, before Harry burst back in and made his way over to that corner, making eager noises.

'How are my two best playmates?' he said in a singsong voice, and Kathleen looked up in alarm.

Mattie saw and intercepted her brother. 'Leave them to sleep, Harry,' she said firmly. 'Brian's been up half the night and given Kath the runaround — all because he caught your cold. Poor little mite can't fight it off like you can. He needs his sleep.'

Harry slunk away, chastened but not for long. 'I'll teach him to fight once he's big enough though. I'll take him down the ring when he can walk, Kath, see if he likes it. It'd be the making of him.'

Kathleen shook her head. 'I don't know if I hold with all that boxing, Harry. I know you're good at it but it always looks awful rough.'

Harry strutted across his mother's rag rug. 'It'll turn him into a real man, Kath. Go on, say you'll let him try.'

'Plenty of time yet,' said Flo, wiping her hands on her faded apron. 'Give the little fellow a chance to make up his own mind, and don't be bothering Kathleen about it all the time.'

'And look what it's done to you,' Mattie added. 'Knocked what little sense you ever had clean out of your head.'

Harry folded his arms. 'You won't say that when I bring home the shield. I'll have all the big promoters after me once I start winning big time. It won't be long now, then you'll have to fight your way to your own front door, the crowds'll be out there shouting for me to sign their autograph books.'

Mattie shook her head. 'Says you. That'll be the day. More likely someone'll bust your nose, then you'll be all upset that your beauty's ruined.'

Harry couldn't help but turn to the mirror over the mantelpiece to check his face. He was good-looking and he knew it, with oak-brown hair that was thick enough to be the envy of all the girls he knew — and he knew a lot. So far, despite having been a keen amateur boxer for several years, his looks hadn't been ruined and he'd kept his unmarked profile. 'You're just jealous,' he said, ruffling Mattie's hair because he knew it annoyed her.

'Gerroff,' she protested, swiping at him.

Joe cleared his throat, well used to breaking up arguments between his two younger siblings.

'Give it a rest, you two. Let me read the paper in peace.' He turned his attention back to the headlines, even though they didn't make for cheerful reading.

'Kath had the nurse round to see Brian today, you'd made him so poorly,' Mattie said, goading her brother once more.

Harry's face fell. 'Really, Kath? Was he that bad? I'm sorry, I didn't realise. You know I'd never do that deliberately.'

Kath nodded. 'I know. He's just got a bit of a cold, that's probably all it is, but he was so hot and I couldn't get him to settle. Anyway, the nurse was very kind. I think she's new, I haven't seen her before.'

'There, see, Mattie, if you'd stayed on at school like your teacher wanted you to, you could have been a nurse too,' said Harry.

Mattie tossed her head, and the remaining hair in her bun fell out and tumbled to her shoulders. 'Leave it out, Harry. You know what it's like as well as I do. They don't let you do nothing in those nurses' homes, it's worse than being in school. I'd never have been able to marry my Lennie and then we wouldn't have Gillian, and then you'd be sorry.'

Harry shrugged. 'Suit yourself. I reckon they're all hoity-toity anyway.'

Kathleen felt obliged to defend Alice. 'This one wasn't. She didn't speak all posh like some of them. She wasn't that much older than me neither. She was lovely and kind to Brian and she made me a cup of tea. I felt better for seeing her and that's the truth.'

Flo put a gentle hand on the young woman's shoulder. 'Don't you let that Harry wind you up. I'm glad the nurse could help. That's what we pay into the provident scheme for, after all.'

Kathleen's face flushed red in embarrassment, knowing she couldn't afford to be part of the scheme, but Mattie came to her rescue. 'Kath's right, this one wasn't hoity-toity. She spoke normal — she's not from round here though. Anyway, that didn't matter. If Gillian gets taken poorly I'm going to ask for her specially.'

'I don't think they let you do that,' warned Joe from behind his paper with its picture of Neville Chamberlain on the front.

'Well, they might. If they do I'm going to tell them I want Alice Lake,' said Mattie firmly. 'You can say what you like, Joe. I'm going to try, but touch wood I don't have to.'

Harry immediately touched his sister's head, and was swiped away once more.

Joe sighed and folded the paper in half, laying it on the table. 'I don't like the sound of this,' he said quietly, tapping one of the articles. 'They're gearing up for something big, that's what it feels like.'

'Oh, don't be like that, Joe,' said Mattie. 'It's all a big fuss over nothing, I bet.'

Joe shook his head, and his mother caught his expression. Normally she'd be the first to encourage everyone to look on the bright side, but her eldest's face gave her pause. She was increasingly coming to respect his views. Joe was the one who'd buckled down to his lessons and got a scholarship to the technical college, a rare achievement for a boy from Jeeves Street. He knew what he was talking about. Mattie could have done well at school if she hadn't had boys on the brain, and Harry had only ever shown interest in boxing. But her Joe — she was quietly extremely proud of her firstborn. He was going to make something of his life — if this threat of war didn't get in the way.

Now she busied herself stacking plates beside the stove. Worrying about the future wouldn't change it. What mattered to her were the people in this room right now — her children and the friend who was almost a member of the family, along with the precious babies. Only one person was missing, and footsteps outside the back door heralded his arrival.

Stanley Banham pushed open the door and inhaled the delicious smell of his wife's beef stew. 'That's something to come home to!' he exclaimed, going across to peck her quickly on the cheek, as he wasn't given to big shows of affection.

Flo Banham beamed. Now all was right in her world. She just hoped it would stay that way.

4

Gwen wove her way along the busy street, automatically dodging the boys running messages for their employers, the housewives shopping for food, the small children too young to go to school. Her mind was whirling and she longed for the peace and quiet of her room at the nurses' home to think about what she'd just heard.

She'd met up with her old friend Miriam for a cup of tea in a café just off Kingsland Road. Miriam, as always, was immaculately turned out, far more fashionable than Gwen had ever been, even when she'd been young and cared about such things. Miriam's smart navy suit with wide white-trimmed collar put Gwen's serviceable old brown jacket to shame.

However, Miriam had looked troubled and Gwen soon found out why. Miriam's husband ran an upholstery factory not far from the café, and for years the business had been growing steadily. Now there was a change in the air, and unrest among some of the people working there. 'It's that Oswald Mosley, he stokes them up,' Miriam complained. 'He tells them it's the Jews who are behind the threat of war, that it's all our fault. Damn the man. You know his followers are doing disgusting things, pinning pigs' heads to the synagogues, defacing our shops. It's made Jacob really worried. Now, when he goes to business meetings, he says some of his former contacts ignore him.'

'Mosley's lot talk about peace though,' Gwen pointed out.

'Gwen!' Miriam had been shocked. 'You're never telling me you agree with the Fascists? If you do, you're not the woman I thought you were.'

'No, no, of course not,' Gwen said hurriedly. 'It's just that I can't bear the thought of another war. You know what it's like, you lived through the last one.' She sighed. 'I want to believe there's hope that it won't happen. Surely there's still a chance?'

Miriam had raised a beautifully shaped eyebrow at her friend. 'And if you believe that, Gwen, then again, you aren't the woman I thought you were.'

They had changed the subject, turning to news of Miriam and Jacob's son Max, who was in New York, partly for business and partly taking advantage of the chance to see the world. 'I think he's met a girl,' Miriam confided. 'He won't say much — he never does. But a mother can tell.'

Gwen had nodded sagely, even though she had no children of her own.

Now she strolled slowly back to Victory Walk, her unease increasing with every step. She wanted so badly to hope that there wouldn't be another war. What had happened twenty-five years ago had been unbearable and she didn't think she could go through it all over again. She glanced at the street sign, thinking that it would be a hollow victory indeed if it was all to start up once more. But she was a realist, not a dreamer, and Miriam's words had confirmed her growing fears. Miriam wasn't given to despair; her own life had taught her to make the best of things. So if she was gloomy about the future, Gwen took it very seriously.

She valued her time with her friend. It was a respite from the hard daily work of a nurse, and also it was wonderful to chat with somebody her own age. Fiona Dewar was sensible and kind, but as superintendent of the busy nurses' home she rarely had a moment for a casual chinwag. Gwen sighed. She couldn't blame the other nurses for being young — after all, she herself had once been their age. But she could blame them — or at least some of them — for their silliness.

That Mary Perkins for a start. Heaven only knew how the girl had managed to qualify as a nurse. She had no common sense at all. To be fair, Gwen could see that she was good with her many elderly patients, warm and friendly. But she was as daft as a brush. She seemed to believe whatever anybody told her, whether it was likely to be true or not. How on earth had she ever passed her exams?

Then there were those new arrivals. Gwen prided herself on being a good judge of character and she could sense that Edith Gillespie had trouble written all over her. As yet she'd done nothing, but then she'd only been at the home for a week. Gwen decided to keep a very close eye on that one. She didn't like disruptive influences in the home — that meant everyone was on edge and therefore didn't work as well. That in turn might mean one of them could make a mistake, possibly a fatal one. She couldn't allow that.

She was less sure about the other young woman, the taller one with the dark blonde hair. She was much harder to read. So far she'd shown herself to be competent and steady. Fiona had let slip that she had outstanding references. However, she gave very little away. She hadn't shown any tendency towards flightiness, but that didn't mean it wasn't lurking there underneath. Gwen decided to keep a close eye on her as well, just in case. You couldn't be too careful in this profession.

Pushing open the door to the nurses' home she was greeted with a whoop of joy from somewhere on the lower-ground floor, probably the common room, and then there was a loud burst of laughter. Two seconds later Mary Perkins and that new girl, Edith, came skidding out into the corridor, hastily turning their run into a walk when they saw her glowering at them from the front porch.

'I'm glad to see you are enjoying yourselves,' Gwen said firmly, 'but I must remind you that there is to be no running along the corridors. What if someone were to come down the stairs, possibly carrying something sharp?'

Mary Perkins nodded. 'Of course. We were just pleased to find out that we've got the same free time this week.'

Gwen moved to one side to let them past. She

doubted the pair would be spending their leisure hours studying together, or doing anything useful. She closed her eyes briefly. She really mustn't condemn them out of hand, and yet she reckoned they didn't have two ounces of brain cells to rub together between them.

★ ★ ★

'Oooh, look, they're definitely Canadian.' Mary perched on her stool to one side of the Paramount's dance floor, eyeing the crowd. She nudged Edith, who was looking the other way, trying to catch a glimpse of herself in one of the mirrors.

'Careful! You nearly had my ginger beer.' Edith adjusted herself on her stool. She knew it was a mistake to wear a white frock out dancing, it showed every smudge and spill, but she couldn't resist showing it off. It had a tight waistband, full skirt and deep stiff collar, and she reckoned it was her best chance of looking suave and sophisticated. Being so short, she often felt like a schoolgirl. The downside of this frock was the pressing need to avoid anyone who might knock over a drink on it. Such as Mary.

Mary herself had piled her hair high and wore an equally arresting dress in turquoise silk, designed to draw attention to her curves. It was drawing the attentions of the Canadians right now, and two broke from their group and made their way over.

'Excuse me, ladies, but would you care for a dance?' asked the taller one, and Mary immediately jumped off her stool. Edith took in his friend, a pleasant-enough seeming young man, slightly more bashful but evidently keen to hit the floor. 'Shall we?' she said, carefully putting her glass on a small side table.

'Gosh, you're a good dancer,' Mary said after the Canadians had reluctantly retreated in order to catch their breath. 'I can see you've done this before.' The loud hum of many young people enjoying themselves almost drowned out her voice.

'I have, though I didn't come here very often,' Edith admitted. 'Tottenham Court Road was too far from where I grew up, and we trained in West London so it was usually the Hammersmith Palais. That's too far from Dalston though. Anyway, you're not so bad yourself.'

'That nice pilot was very sweet and said all the right things, but actually he had two left feet. I had to do all the work while making him think he was leading me.' Mary sighed. 'Why is it some grown men can't count to four? It's not hard.'

'I hope he's better at numbers when he's navigating,' Edith giggled, swigging the last of her ginger beer. Then her face fell. 'Talking of numbers, have you seen the time? We've well and truly missed curfew.'

Mary shrugged. 'We knew we probably would.'

Edith looked guilty. 'Yes, but Alice will wait up. It's not fair on her. We'll have to go. What a shame, here come those pilots again. You explain to them we must be off and I'll go and queue at the cloakroom.'

Mary nodded reluctantly. 'All right, although

we might as well be hung for a sheep as a lamb. I don't want to upset Alice, though. You fetch my cream jacket and I'll let these nice young men down gently, and won't tell them it's because one of them can't dance for toffee.'

★   ★   ★

Edith and Mary crept carefully along the back fence of the nurses' home, having just caught the last bus. The ground behind the home was uneven and tricky to navigate in their dancing shoes, which made Edith want to giggle. She knew that would be a bad idea. It was a warm evening and some of her fellow nurses might have kept their windows open, which would surely mean they would hear every unusual noise.

'Ouch!' Mary grabbed on to Edith's arm as she nearly twisted her ankle. 'That was lucky, I thought I was a goner then. That will teach me to wear heels. I could take them off but these stones will rip my stockings to bits.'

'Shh, keep it down,' Edith hissed. 'We're nearly there.' She felt along the fence, testing each panel by gently pushing it, until she found the spot she was searching for. With a little creak it gave way, exposing a gap just wide enough to squeeze through. Carefully she gathered her skirt and hoiked it up so she wouldn't rip the seam. 'Mind that nail, don't want to damage your lovely silk frock.' She gave a final wriggle and was through.

Mary struggled to fit through the gap, cursing the curves that had brought her so much admiration during the evening. She finally made it, but there was a splintering noise as the adjacent panel gave way. 'Now what?' she asked.

'Shhh. Not so loud. I left one of the common-room windows open just a little and asked Alice to check nobody had shut it before she went to bed.' Edith made her way across the back yard and approached the casement. 'This is it. I hope she didn't wait up for us.'

Slowly she edged the sash upwards, making sure not to let it squeak in its frame, and then pulled herself up and over the window ledge and into the common room. 'Here, take my hands, I'll pull you up,' she whispered, not knowing how agile Mary was. Excelling on the dance floor didn't mean she would have the strength to climb in through a window.

Mary gratefully accepted the help and struggled to reach the windowsill, using all her strength to make it over the threshold. 'Gosh, that was harder than I thought,' she admitted, sinking down onto the nearest chair in the dark room. The streetlight from the side road illuminated the sofas and the dining tables, all neatly laid and waiting for the following morning's breakfast.

Slowly it became clear there was a tall figure standing by the entrance to the service room, half hidden by the deep shadow. 'Alice? Is that you?' Edith called as loudly as she dared.

The figure came swiftly forwards; the hair was scraped back in a severe bun, not falling in long waves, and too late Edith realised her mistake. 'Nurse Gillespie, Nurse Perkins,' snapped Gwen.

'What is the meaning of this? Not only have you broken the rule of curfew, which is there for a very good reason, namely your own protection, but you are also utterly incompetent. If you intend to go sneaking around at night, you might consider your clothing. That dress and that jacket make you stand out like beacons. Clearly you don't mind missing your sleep but I do. You will report to me before breakfast in the morning.' With that she turned briskly and strode out, leaving Edith and Mary with a cold feeling of fear in their stomachs.

★   ★   ★

'Was it awful?' Alice asked in sympathy when Edith finally took her place at the table for breakfast. There was very little left, but Alice had saved some toast for her friend and persuaded Gladys not to put the butter and marmalade away.

Edith's shoulders slumped in dejection. 'It wasn't very nice. She hauled us both over the coals. There wasn't much we could say as we were caught red-handed.' She brightened a little. 'Still, I convinced her that you weren't part of it. I stupidly said your name when I climbed in and Gwen was sure you were down here somewhere up to no good, but I just said I thought she was you because you're both tall.'

Alice pulled a face. 'That's kind. I did check the window for you, though, so I'm guilty too. Should I tell her — will that make her less cross?'

Edith shook her head vehemently. 'No. Absolutely not. It won't achieve anything useful; it'll just make her mistrust you as much as she does Mary and me, which you don't deserve seeing as you didn't go out dancing but stayed in with your book. And anyway . . . ' She took a big bite out of her toast ' . . . you'd only get in the way. Me and Mary have got to clear out the district room, wash the whole place down with Dettol — shelves, cupboards, walls, the lot — and then put it back together again. Two's plenty for that. Oh, and we're grounded for a week.'

'That's tough luck.' Alice grimaced, sorry for her friend. 'But was it worth it? Did you enjoy yourselves?'

Edith gave a cheeky grin. She was rarely depressed for long. 'It was. You should see the Paramount. It's packed to the rafters with people who want to dance, including some very friendly Canadians. I didn't really fancy mine but he was good for a few spins on the dance floor and he bought me a ginger beer. So yes, it was worth it.'

'You are impossible.' Part of Alice thought she should disapprove of her friend taking such a risk but the other part knew how much Edith enjoyed a night out.

'Not at all. It was good clean fun. Maybe you'll come along next time?'

Alice's expression closed down. 'Maybe,' she said cautiously, in the tone of voice that Edith knew meant 'no'.

5

'Go on, Alice. Say you'll come,' begged Edith. 'It's a lovely day. You'll enjoy yourself once you're there.'

Alice hesitated. It was rare that they both had the afternoon off together, and there was no denying it — the sun was shining, and only a light breeze disturbed the leaves of the trees outside. Edith's long, dull week of being grounded had at last come to its end, and to give her her due, there had been little in the way of complaining, even if she had reeked of Dettol for days on end. A concert in Victoria Park might take Alice's mind off all the sombre news she'd been hearing on the wireless about the threat of conflict in Poland, even though she'd planned to spend the afternoon catching up with those newspapers she hadn't had time to read during the past week. 'All right,' she said, suddenly making the decision. 'Why not? Did you say there would be a band playing?'

'Yes, there's a bandstand and we'll head for that. Mary said she'd make a picnic,' Edith explained.

Alice hadn't realised Mary had the afternoon off as well.

'The more the merrier,' Edith went on, catching the look of hesitation on her friend's face. 'She hasn't been out all week either. Besides, her mother has sent her some fruitcake and she said she'd bring it. I'll bring some lemonade.'

'The shop on the corner had some lovely apples when I went past yesterday,' Alice remembered. 'I'll buy some of those, shall I? They'll go well with fruit-cake.'

'Shall I make some sandwiches?' Edith offered. 'Just a few. We don't want to get hungry, do we? I'll see if Mary can fit it all in her wicker basket.'

*   *   *

Alice stretched out luxuriously beneath the shade of the big tree. The sun had been hot on their faces as they'd sat close to the bandstand, and now that the music was over they'd taken refuge, Edith unpacking the picnic as Mary spread out a red and white checked cloth. From all around came the sounds of children playing, and people were strolling by in all directions. Others were settling on the grass with their own picnics. Everyone seemed to have had the same idea.

Mary produced three tin mugs with a flourish. 'Look what I found. They were in the back of a cupboard in the service room.'

'Then we won't even have to swig from the bottle,' smiled Edith. 'We'll be all correct and proper.'

'I should hope so,' said Alice, propping herself up on one elbow. 'What if any of our patients were to see us? Can't let the side down by swigging from a bottle in public.'

Mary grinned, pitching up the sleeves of her lilac cardigan before laying the mugs on the checked cloth. 'I'll drink to that. Edie, can you pop open that lemonade?'

Edith obligingly did so, with a loud fizz as the stopper came loose. Several heads turned nearby to see what the noise was.

Alice held each mug while Mary poured, but Edith's attention was caught by one of the groups who had looked round at them. She shook her hair a little before returning her gaze to the drinks.

'Here you are,' said Alice, passing her a mug. 'What's up?'

'Oh, nothing,' said Edith, over-casually. 'Don't look now, but I think that man over there is looking at us.'

'What man?' asked Mary, turning round at once.

'Mary! Now he'll think we're interested,' Edith tutted. She deliberately cast her gaze upwards into the branches. 'Do you reckon that's a blackbird up there, Alice? I can't quite see.' She made a show of peering into the foliage, shading her eyes with her hand.

'Do you mean the fellow in the green shirt?' Mary asked. 'Sitting with several other people and a baby?'

'Maybe. I didn't really notice the details,' said Edith unconvincingly.

Alice took a sip of her lemonade and waited for what would come next. Sure enough, in no time at all a male voice sounded from behind them.

'Good afternoon, ladies,' said the voice, and one glance revealed that it was a man in a green shirt. 'I couldn't help noticing you don't have a bottle opener. Would you like to borrow ours?'

Edith smiled up at him. 'Thank you, but we don't need one. Anyway, we've only brought the one bottle of lemonade.'

The man nodded and Alice had to admit that his looks were eye-catching. He had a handsome face, hair like polished oak, and with his sleeves rolled back and his tie-less collar undone, she couldn't help but notice he had very well-developed muscles. Edith clearly liked what she saw, because she shifted around, rearranging her flared skirt with its colourful patches of bright flowers, and arched her neck at him. 'Still, thank you for asking. It's very hot today, isn't it?'

'It is.' The man was smiling back, his eyes dancing with merriment as he took in Edith. 'Can I offer you ladies something a little stronger? My brother's brought some beer with us and we won't finish it all.'

'Oh no, really we don't — ' Alice began, but Mary's reply was louder.

'That's very kind. We could mix it and make shandy. Maybe you'd like some too?'

The man in the green shirt nodded. 'That's a good idea. Why don't you come over and join us?' He pointed across to the group he had just left: a man of similar age to himself, and a woman with her back to the rest of them, clearly holding a young baby.

'I don't know . . . ' muttered Alice, who had been perfectly comfortable under the tree.

55

'Oh go on, Alice,' said Edith, gathering up her skirts and delicately making sure her lemonade didn't spill against the tree roots. 'What harm can it do? We haven't made many new friends apart from the nurses since we moved here. Maybe they can tell us about the area, give us some local tips.'

'All right, all right.' Alice could tell when Edith had set her heart on doing something, and it was usually pointless to resist. 'Give me a moment. Let me tuck our bottle back in the basket and prop it up with the cloth.' She arranged the bottle so it wouldn't empty itself over the grass when moved, and got to her feet, trailing across behind the others the short distance to the man, woman and baby.

She'd missed the first introductions, although it wasn't hard to see that the other man was related to the first. He wasn't as strikingly good-looking and his hair was darker, but he had similar features. His expression was pleasant but warier. Alice had the clear impression that he wouldn't have invited a party of strange women to join his family group on the slight pretext of sharing a bottle opener, but he seemed friendly enough. Then the woman turned around properly and she realised she knew her.

'It's Nurse Lake, isn't it?' said the young woman, kneeling up and placing her baby on the ground in front of her, where there was a pale yellow knitted blanket. 'Alice?'

'Mattie! How nice to see you,' said Alice, swiftly recognising her first patient's friend. 'Is this your baby? Isn't she a little beauty?'

56

'Yes, this is Gillian,' said Mattie, beaming with pride. 'And these are my brothers, Harry and Joe. Looks as if you've already met Harry.' She pulled an affectionate face. 'This is the nurse I told you about a few weeks ago, the one who came to see to Brian after you gave him your cold, Harry.'

Harry stuck out his hand. 'Pleased to meet you. Mattie told us all about you. Are you all nurses, then?'

'We are,' said Edith. 'So you can believe us when we say that it's very important not to get too thirsty on a hot day.'

'And is shandy an acceptable medicine?' asked Harry, eyes bright with mischief.

'It is.' Edith nodded seriously.

Alice turned back to Mattie. 'And how is little Brian now? I haven't heard from Mrs Berry again, so I assumed he was better, but you never know.'

Mattie shifted a little so that Alice could sit down beside her. 'He's much better. They almost came with us today but then Kathleen had to go to see her mother about something or other. She said he had a bit of a temperature for a few days after you saw him and some sniffles, but it didn't last long. He'll be all right.'

'Good.' Alice was relieved. 'And your friend? Kathleen? How is she? It must be so tiring, looking after a baby on her own, especially when he's sick.'

Mattie pursed her mouth. 'Well, she's as right as can be expected when her husband's buggered off and left her with hardly a penny. He thinks she can live off air alone. No wonder she's so thin. My mother feeds her up as much as she can, but Kath's got her pride.' She suddenly came to a halt. 'Sorry, you probably don't want to know that sort of thing.'

Alice shook her head. 'Don't worry, she told me something of the sort when I was there, and I could see she was underweight, and so was Brian.'

Joe sat up and looked at his sister. 'Mattie, I don't think you should say things like that about your friend. She's not here to defend herself.'

Alice leant back a little at the tone of his voice, but Mattie wasn't deterred.

'You weren't there to see how upset Kathleen was, Joe. She was much better by the time you got home, and Brian was on the mend because Nurse Alice was kind to him. I'm only saying what anyone can see for themselves.'

Joe's frown deepened. 'It's her business though, Mattie. You wouldn't like it if anyone talked about you behind your back or said things about Gillian.'

'I should hope not!' Mattie tugged at her collar to loosen it. 'It's not the same, is it? Lennie gives me plenty to live on and Gillian is healthy as a horse.'

'Really, I don't want to upset anyone,' said Alice hurriedly, feeling caught in the middle.

'That's enough, now, Mattie,' Joe said, though he looked directly at Alice who felt the weight of his disapproval. 'I'm sure Kathleen wouldn't thank any of us for airing her dirty laundry in public.'

58

So that's what he thought, Alice realised, that she went around gossiping about her patients. 'I can assure you . . . ' she began, but he looked away.

'I'm sure you acted for the best,' he said, and then moved so that he was on the other side of the group, leaving Harry, Mary and Edith in the middle, mixing their shandies.

Alice felt a warm anger flushing her cheeks but was determined to hide it. Who did Joe Banham think he was, accusing her of something like that?

'Want one?' Mary asked Alice.

Alice almost had to grit her teeth. 'No, that lemonade was enough, thanks.'

'Mattie, how about you?' Mary offered.

Mattie shook her head ruefully. 'I'd better not. I'm feeding Gillian and some folks say it don't do her any good.'

Trying to shake off her annoyance, Alice nodded in approval. She'd come across plenty of mothers who thought nothing of having a drink while feeding their babies, but she agreed that it wasn't good for them.

'Then I'll take you back, Mattie,' said Joe, getting to his feet. 'Those buses will be getting crowded now these crowds are thinning out. You might as well come back with me and let Harry and his new friends get on with it.'

Mattie pulled a face but agreed. 'I wouldn't mind staying a bit longer, but I can always do with a hand, what with the pram and everything.' She nodded towards where a big silver pram was parked under a neighbouring tree. 'Bye then,

Alice. Thanks again for looking after Kathleen like that. We won't forget it.'

'Only doing my job,' smiled Alice, but she felt slightly resentful that Joe could just end the conversation so abruptly — and sounding so self-righteous, too. Who did he think he was, to pass judgement like that? She could feel herself blushing at the injustice of it but she held her tongue. She didn't really know these people, after all. It wasn't her place to cause trouble, and she'd probably never see him again anyway.

Mattie and Joe set off towards the pram and Alice pulled herself closer to the others, accepting a top-up of lemonade and a piece of fruitcake. She wasn't going to let the incident ruin what had been a lovely afternoon. Poor Mattie to have such a killjoy of an older brother.

★   ★   ★

Joe Banham fumed silently as he stood on the lower floor of the crowded bus, having made sure Mattie got a seat and the pram was safely on board. It wasn't just the press of people, or the heat, or the fact that some of their fellow passengers had clearly had more than a single mug of shandy while out enjoying themselves that afternoon. He was used to all that. No, it was the way that nurse had looked at him. It had made him uncomfortable and he didn't know why.

He'd been surprised that the nurse Mattie had spoken so highly of had turned out to be so willing to listen to gossip. He had thought

60

someone in such a profession would be above that sort of thing. Didn't they have standards, a code of conduct or suchlike? Should he report her? No, he was being stupid, it wasn't as bad as that — and yet, he'd reacted to her expression and the few things she'd said in a way that disturbed him. He could tell that she disapproved of him as well. Mattie had said she wasn't hoity-toity like some of them but he wasn't so sure. She probably thought she was above him and his family. Plenty of nurses came from good backgrounds and Alice Lake had probably been raised to have the best of everything; a far cry from growing up on Jeeves Street. Well, he was having none of it. He'd worked extremely hard to get his scholarship and had passed his exams at the technical college with flying colours. He was second to none and he wouldn't stand for some toffee-nosed nurse looking down at him. She had no right. Just because she had a smattering of new freckles on her nose and bright blue eyes, she probably thought she could get around anybody. Well, it wasn't going to work with him.

He brought himself up short. He hadn't realised he'd noticed those details about her — they'd only been sitting together for a matter of minutes when it came down to it. It was silly to get worked up about such a small incident on what had up till then been a fine day out. Mattie often found it difficult to get anywhere beyond walking distance if it meant manoeuvring the pram onto public transport and he'd been pleased to help his sister. The trip had been worth it for that alone. He was damned if he would let thoughts of that blonde nurse ruin the occasion.

6

'A word, Alice, if I may.' Fiona Dewar popped her head out of her office doorway just as Alice was walking by. Alice wondered how she did it — was it just luck, did she already recognise her footsteps, or was the superintendent even smarter than they thought? Alice quickly racked her brains for anything she might have done wrong over the past few weeks. Surely she wasn't going to be blamed for helping Edith and Mary defy the curfew? That was all over and done with.

'Nothing to worry about,' Fiona Dewar said, catching the change of expression on the young nurse's face. 'I have something I wish to speak to you about, that's all. Take a seat, do.' She herself sat down behind her desk, quickly restacking a pile of papers out of habit.

Alice did as she was asked, her mind racing. She touched her Queen's Nurse badge at her throat, as she often did when anxious.

'Well, now.' Fiona sat back in her chair. 'We have been approached by a local primary school — St Benedict's, maybe you know it? Just on the other side of Kingsland High Street. You'll have cycled past it, I'm sure.'

Alice frowned and then nodded. 'Yes, I know the one. A big brick building, not far from the market.'

Fiona beamed. 'Got it in one. It's just opposite the entrance to Ridley Road but along a bit. If you haven't done so already, you'll most likely be treating some patients who attend there.'

Alice nodded again. 'I don't think I've done so yet.' Then she stopped. 'No, wait, I have treated the younger brother of one of the pupils there. From one of those really crowded terraces behind the High Street. I went there last week.'

★ ★ ★

The house had been almost falling down around their ears. Alice had had to strain her eyes to work out who was human and what was furniture, the light was so dim in the front room, despite the sunshine outside. The referral had come from Dr Beasley, often called Beastly Beasley by some of the nurses behind his back, as he didn't seem to possess an ounce of compassion. Mary could do a horribly realistic impersonation of him. Alice wasn't surprised that he had failed to warn her of the depths of this family's situation. It was the most dire she had yet come across.

The patient was hardly more than a baby but already he was showing signs of rickets. Alice had struggled to know what to say to start with. The little boy was sweating, restless, and when she gently touched his limbs he recoiled as if it caused him pain.

'He always does that, Nurse,' said the mother, as she tried to restrain a slightly older child — a girl, Alice thought, but in the murk it was tricky

64

to tell. 'He wouldn't crawl nor nothing. His dad says he's just lazy.'

Alice hadn't been able to prevent her eyebrows from rising. 'I'm not sure that's right,' she said as steadily as she could. 'It could be a symptom of rickets. Do you know what that is?'

'Oh, that.' The mother paused. 'Yes, me granddad's sister had it, made her short as anything. I hope that isn't what Frankie's got, poor little mite.' She turned to shoo away the girl. 'What can we do for him, Nurse? It's horrible to see those what's got the bandy legs. The other kids won't half take the mick. I don't want that.'

Alice had sighed. The textbook answer would be: keep him outside in the sunlight as much as possible, without putting weight on his legs. There was as much chance of that as teaching him to fly, as there was scarcely room to swing a cat between the rows of the terrace, and the back yard stank from the privy shared between all the houses. Then she should suggest improving the child's vitamin intake with bone soups, fresh pasteurised milk and green vegetables, especially spinach. That was unlikely to happen either.

This was an occasion to resort to the authorities. Taking a deep breath, Alice plunged in. 'In that case,' she said, 'I strongly recommend you take Frankie to the Infant Welfare Clinic and they will be able to refer you for assistance. He needs a special diet while there is still time. Don't delay, but don't despair either. We can help his bones to grow more normally, but not on what he's eating at the moment.'

Frankie's mother had balked at that but then she had nodded. 'All right. I don't hold with going to the welfare for nothing, but if it's his only chance . . . '

'It's a very good chance,' Alice had answered immediately, determined to drive the point home. And, she thought to herself, I'm going to contact the Sanitary Inspector for once. There's overcrowding and filthy living conditions and then there's this. Whoever is renting this out as a family home needs reporting.

★ ★ ★

'Ah yes. I heard about that,' Fiona said now. 'Well done.' The superintendent clasped her hands together on her desk and went on: 'St Benedict's are concerned about instilling good habits of hygiene in their pupils. Sadly we can't assume that parents have the time or knowledge to teach the children as well as might be desired.' She looked Alice directly in the eye. 'You'll already have noticed that the homes around here have widely different facilities available. Some have indoor bathrooms with running water. Some make do with a tin bath hung on the scullery door and an outside toilet but have running water indoors nonetheless. Some don't even have that. As I believe you saw for yourself only the other day.' She paused and sighed. 'When you have a family consisting of several generations under one small roof, teaching each child how best to brush their teeth is seldom a priority. And very few of them can afford a trip to the dentist.'

'No, I suppose not,' said Alice.

'That's where we come in,' Fiona announced. 'Or, more precisely, you, Alice, if you are willing to take on this service.'

'Me?' Alice was taken aback. 'What would I have to do? I'm not sure . . . I mean, I know how to clean my teeth, but I'm not an expert or anything . . . '

'No, no, I'm not expecting you to be,' Fiona said reassuringly. 'We don't want a stranger scaring the little ones. We want someone who is good with children and I've noticed that you are. Word gets around, you see. So, what they'd like you to do is go into the school and show the children how to do it, maybe one class at a time, so that you can keep a good eye on how well they're doing. They'll bring in their own toothbrushes — or the school might see to it quietly that they all have one. I'm going to approach a local wholesaler to ask if they can let us have toothpaste or toothpowder cheaply or even for free, as a goodwill gesture. Some families make their own toothpowder, but you can't guarantee what's in it half the time.'

'I see,' said Alice, shuddering inwardly, and realising yet again how lucky she'd been in her upbringing in this small but vital matter — always having a new toothbrush and constant supplies of proper toothpaste.

'Excellent,' said Fiona briskly. 'Well, no time like the present. They're expecting you this afternoon.'

'This afternoon?' Alice echoed in surprise.

'Yes indeed. Leave it much longer and the

67

children will be on their school holidays. We need to get good habits well ingrained before that. Of course the toothpaste won't have arrived from the company, but you can demonstrate what to do so they know in advance.'

'Oh,' said Alice, because she couldn't think of anything else to say. Really, there wasn't much to say when you were swept up in Fiona's efficient whirlwind.

'That gives you a couple of hours to think about what you'll say and to cycle over there. Ask for Miss Phipps. Best take your own brush with you, so you can show them exactly what you mean.' Fiona beamed. 'And you can tell me all about it later,' she added, standing as she did so. The interview was evidently over.

★   ★   ★

St Benedict's was a big Victorian building with a playground at the front, large windows overlooking the entrance and the main road beyond. Alice could hear the hum of children's voices as she approached, swinging her legs off the boneshaker bike which she'd now got used to, and sliding it into a purpose-built bike rack to the side of the yard.

Before she could even look for a bell or door-knocker, a woman came out to greet her. 'You must be Nurse Lake! Do come in,' she said, in a voice Alice could easily believe would command a room of six-year-olds. 'I'm Janet Phipps.'

'Pleased to meet you,' said Alice, shaking the woman's hand, and noting that she was older

68

than her by a few years but not as old as Fiona. She wore horn-rimmed glasses and had a smiling, red-cheeked face, and was dressed very neatly in a slim cotton skirt and lemon twinset. She wore absolutely no jewellery, and Alice wondered if that was because it would be too easy to snag on little children's clothing or hair.

Janet Phipps led her into the building, with its distinctive school smell, and into a classroom full of small faces all turned in curiosity towards the door. 'Our youngest class,' Janet explained. 'As they go home earliest we thought it best you started with them. Now, say good afternoon to Nurse Lake.'

'Good afternoon, Nurse Lake,' most of them chanted, although a few looked confused, apprehensive or sullen. One little boy in an unravelling grey jumper was concentrating too hard on picking his nose to say anything, and Janet Phipps gently admonished him while bringing Alice to the front of the class.

'Now, did we all remember to bring our toothbrushes?' the teacher asked. 'Here's mine.' She brought a red-handled one out from her skirt pocket. 'Wave them in the air if you remembered.'

'Please, Miss, I ain't got one,' said a tiny girl with fair ringlets, sitting directly in front of the boy with the unravelling jumper.

'My gran says they're bad for you,' added the girl sitting beside her, with a mutinous face.

Janet Phipps shook her head. 'Those of you who don't have one yet, just watch and try to remember what Nurse Lake says. We'll make sure you all have them when she comes next and you can show her what you've learnt. Yes, Pauline, even you. You want to have nice white teeth when you grow up, don't you?' Turning to Alice she muttered, 'The child's gran hasn't got a tooth in her head, but that's all right as she mostly drinks gin. However . . . '

Alice tried not to show her surprise, and realised that she might get on very well with Janet Phipps in the future. But now, she concentrated her attention on the job in hand. Taking out her own brush, she smiled at the classroom of young faces, and began.

★ ★ ★

'That was harder than I thought,' Alice confessed later, having talked to three separate classes one after the other. 'It's not so much showing them what to do: that's simple and they're keen to learn.'

'They are at that age,' Janet agreed. 'Was it hearing how many of them didn't have running water, or toothbrushes at all?'

Alice shrugged. 'I've been to plenty of houses around here now, but all the same it hits you sometimes. I've never lived anywhere where I couldn't simply turn on a tap for water. It makes you forget how different it is if you don't have that.'

Janet Phipps nodded in sympathy. 'Yes, and when the very little ones come here to begin with, sometimes we have to teach them how to wash their hands. It was good that you mentioned that today. Then they'll know it's not just me who goes on about how important it is.'

Alice pushed open the front door to the playground and lifted her bike from its rack. 'I'll make sure to say that again next week.'

Janet smiled. 'They'll look forward to your visit. As shall I. Maybe you'd have time for a cup of tea afterwards?'

Alice smiled back. 'That would be lovely.'

Pushing her bike back to the main road, she decided to wheel it through the market, tempted by the thought of all the sights and smells. Summer was now here and the vegetable stalls were full of colour, with the stallholders shouting out as she went past. As the nurses had their meals together at the home, Alice didn't need to buy anything, but her eye was caught by a cleverly arranged pile of pears, their bright skins shining in the sunlight. Suddenly she could imagine the taste of them and on impulse she went over to the stallholder. 'Get yer vitamins here, Nurse!' he shouted. 'These'll put hairs on yer chest.'

'I hope not,' said Alice, raising her eyebrows. 'May I have half a dozen?' She waited while he put them into a paper bag, and drew out her purse. She imagined how pleased Edith and Mary would be when she produced them later, and maybe she'd give one to Fiona too.

Looking up after carefully placing the bag in her wire basket, she thought she saw a familiar figure — was that Mattie in the distance, with her wild hair? But the figure moved into the shadow cast by an awning and disappeared,

71

while Alice wasn't close enough to call out. The sight of the young woman, whether it was Mattie or not, made Alice recall the picnic after the band concert in Victoria Park, and the way her older brother had spoken. It still rankled when she thought about it, the unfairness of it. She shook her head and reminded herself it didn't matter. The only thing was, Edith had hinted how much she had liked Harry and it had been pretty clear he'd been attracted to her. Edith hadn't mentioned him since but Alice knew her friend was not one to let such an opportunity pass her by.

★ ★ ★

For the second time that day, Fiona Dewar opened her office door just as Alice was passing, almost as if she'd been waiting for her. 'How did it go?' she asked, beckoning her in.

Alice took the same chair as before. 'Very well, I think,' she said, offering Fiona a pear as the superintendent returned to her desk.

'Why, thank you. I don't mind if I do.' Fiona took the fruit and set it to one side for later. 'So, do you think your visits will be of use to the children? Will you be happy to go back next week?'

Alice nodded. 'They're good as gold, or at least most of them are. They listened to what I said, and it will be better when they all have the brushes and toothpaste. It breaks your heart to see some of them not knowing what I'm talking about.'

'But you didn't show it,' said Fiona briskly.

'No, I wouldn't do that. That would make them feel worse, wouldn't it.' It came out as a statement, not a question.

'Quite right,' the superintendent agreed. 'We are here to help alleviate the difficulties of poverty in whatever practical ways we can, not to blame our patients for it, above all not the children. They can't help which households they are born into. I'm glad to hear it was a success. It might be that it will be important to have close bonds with local schools in the near future.'

Alice raised her eyebrows but wasn't sure what lay behind the superintendent's words.

Fiona realised her hint had not hit its mark. 'I hear you are a keen reader of the newspapers, Alice,' she said. 'That can only mean you are fully aware of the storm that is about to break very soon. You will have seen the preparations taking place already, with the trenches dug around all municipal open spaces and the factories changing use. I wish it were not so, but I see no point in burying our heads in the sand.'

'You mean war,' said Alice flatly. The words fell like lead.

'Indeed.' Fiona took a sharp inward breath. 'Best to be prepared, as far as that is possible. There are plans in place to get children away from the most obvious points of attack, and it's fair to say we are living slap-bang in the middle of one of them. We don't have the details yet but, if it comes to it, it will be far better for them to be seen off by a friendly face than an anonymous stranger. That will help them leave in less distress

73

and settle more quickly wherever they are sent.' Her eyes fell to her desk. 'Anyway, that's the theory. We shall see. And it might not come to that. We can always hope.'

'But you don't seriously think war can be averted?' Alice asked her.

Fiona looked up again. 'Quite honestly, no. So, Nurse Lake, please get to know those children over the next few weeks, and make sure they think of you as a figure of authority they can trust. Yes, it's important that you teach them the rudiments of personal hygiene. But in fact, you will be doing far more than that. When it comes to separating a child from its parent, it will make all the difference if there is somebody in charge whom they recognise. We should not fool ourselves. This could happen very soon. So, time is of the essence.'

* * *

Alice sank down on her bed in a confusion of emotions. The conversation had hit her hard. As the superintendent had pointed out, she knew from the papers, from local gossip and the evidence of her own eyes what was probably waiting around the corner, but to hear it spoken aloud by someone she trusted made it all too real. Part of her wanted to run away and hide somewhere, but she was conscious of the extra responsibility Fiona had just placed upon her. The superintendent thought she was worthy of such a task, should it come to it. That left her with little choice; she had to be ready to step up to the mark. If the children were going to be separated from their homes and loved ones, they had to suffer as little as possible — there was no question about that.

And how would the war affect her family, and all the people she had grown up with or met while training? Despite herself, her mind flicked to the one place she tried so hard to stop it from going. To the place where she held the memory of the young doctor who had once meant so much to her: Mark. The man she'd loved so fiercely, and who she had fervently believed had loved her back with equal passion. The man who had sworn they would never be parted, whatever life had in store; that they'd be together through thick and thin. What would he have said if he was here now, sharing her dilemma and sense of imminent danger? But he would never share anything with her again. He was lost to her and she had to bear it, somehow. Of her current circle, only Edith knew. Well, her parents did of course — and she knew they quietly thought she should forget him and move on in her life. She couldn't bear that either.

There was a knock on the door and Edith burst in. 'Thought I heard you come back. How did it go? Are you off duty now? I've just done my last call of the day. A poor old lady down Boleyn Road needed her dressing changed. She would have kept me chatting all day but I couldn't take her last biscuits, it wouldn't have been right.'

'Have a pear instead.' Alice opened the paper bag.

'Oooh, I knew it would be worth dropping in,' said Edith, snatching one quickly. 'Now guess what my news is.'

Alice rolled her eyes. 'No idea.'

'Well, now.' Edith settled herself on her friend's bed, looking pleased with herself. 'Remember those brothers from the park?'

'From the picnic, you mean?'

'Of course, do we know any others? Yes, from the day of the band concert. You know the one in the green shirt, the handsome one with the deep brown eyes?'

'I remember the shirt. Can't say I noticed his eyes.'

'I did. Anyway, he's only gone and asked me to go to the pictures with him.'

Alice sat up straight. 'Has he? How did he do that?'

Edith looked a little sheepish. 'He came round here with a message for me.'

Alice gasped. 'He shouldn't do that. You're only meant to leave messages if you need the attentions of a nurse.'

'Seems he does,' said Edith with a wicked grin. 'Anyway it was all right, it was Mary who opened the door, and of course she recognised him. Actually I think she's a bit miffed he asked me and not her. But she'll get over it.'

'What did you say?' demanded Alice.

Edith gave her a straight look. 'I said yes, of course.'

7

Edith talked about nothing else for the rest of the week. Alice wondered if she even noticed what her patients said to her; when Alice asked her how the old lady on Boleyn Road was coming along after several repeat visits, Edith simply shrugged and said 'all right'. When a postman fell off his bike and Edith was first on the scene, she barely commented on it, despite it being the most exciting thing to happen for ages. They'd had to draw the details out of her one by one.

'Where's he taking you?' Mary asked, excited for her friend and gamely putting aside her envy at not being picked. It was Friday morning and they were eating breakfast.

'He didn't say. But if he gives me the choice, I'm going to suggest *Jamaica Inn*. It's meant to be all moody and romantic. It's on at that new Odeon on Hackney Road, so we won't even have too far to go. He could walk me home,' Edith said dreamily.

'Sounds as if you've got it all planned,' said Alice. It wasn't that she begrudged her friend an evening out, but since it had been the sole topic of conversation for days she was getting fed up.

'Oh, don't be like that, Al. I bet you've wanted to see that film as much as I have. Shall I ask him if his brother wants to come along and we could make a four?'

Alice tightened her jaw. 'I don't think so.'

77

'No, can't say I blame you,' said Mary. 'He was a bit serious, wasn't he? And not as good-looking either.'

'Right, I won't bother then,' Edith told her friend. 'Don't say I never do anything for you, though. What do you think I should wear?'

'How about that flowery skirt you wore to the picnic?' asked Mary, buttering her toast. 'Pass the marmalade, Alice, would you?'

'Oh no, I couldn't do that. It will have to be something different,' Edith insisted. 'What about my blouse with the puff sleeves, Alice? You know, I got it cheap late last summer in the sales, then it got too cold to wear it.'

'Perfect,' said Alice. 'And you've got those sandals in cherry red that will go with its pattern. It was meant to be.'

'Yes, that'll be just right.' Edith all but hugged herself in anticipation. 'Only today's shift and then it'll be time to see him. I can't wait.' She took a spoonful of porridge and ate it slowly.

'Aren't you going to finish that?' Mary demanded, always on the alert for any extra food. 'Cos if you aren't . . . '

'You have it, I've got butterflies in my tummy already,' said Edith, getting up and sliding her chair back under the table. 'Right, I'll see you two later before I go.'

'That's if there aren't any last-minute emergencies,' said Mary cheerfully, digging into the porridge, but Edith was already halfway across the room.

★ ★ ★

'Right, that's it, that's me finished for the day.' Alice slung her Gladstone bag down by the table in the dining area. 'I'm parched. I was so busy all day I hardly had time for a cup of tea.'

'I'll put the kettle on,' Edith offered. 'Then I'll be off. I was lucky, my last visit was terribly quick. A toddler had burnt himself but the grannie was so fast at getting his arm under running water that I barely had to do anything. She and the kiddie's mother knew exactly what was for the best. She was getting ready to bathe his arm with tea — that's said to help you know; all that tannin in it.'

Alice reached for a cup. 'Funny, isn't it, how some families are so well equipped and others have nothing.' She thought for the umpteenth time of Kathleen Berry, in many ways so alone, and all the children of St Benedict's with no running water in their homes. Little Frankie, with hardly any light. 'That blouse looks good on you, Edith. And with those sandals too.'

'I'm pleased it still fits.' Edith primped her hair in the reflection of the window. 'I'm going to bring my white bolero in case it turns cold later.'

'Good idea,' Alice began, but was cut short when Gladys came in, her expression an agonised mixture of shyness and urgency.

'Please, Miss. Nurse Gillespie. They need yer.'

Edith gasped in alarm. 'Me? Are you sure it's me they need? I've done my shift, Gladys, there's been a mistake.'

'No, Miss.' Gladys twisted her hands. 'It's that postman what you saw before, he's been took bad again, and they said you was to go cos you knew him and what happened.'

Edith could have stamped her foot in frustration. 'Not tonight, why did it have to be tonight? Harry will turn up and you or Mary will have to say I couldn't make it. Then he'll get all cross and he might even take Mary instead — I could tell he liked her, just not as much as me . . .'

Alice took her friend by the shoulders. 'Don't be silly. I'll go. You told me all about the accident. He's probably tried to do too much too soon. Just give me the address and I'll go. There won't be much they can say about it if I simply turn up instead of you.'

Edith looked up at her friend in relief. 'Would you really, Alice? But you're exhausted, you said so.'

'Doesn't matter,' said Alice, reaching once more for her leather bag. 'I've had half a cup of tea, and if it's close by, it most likely won't take long. You go on, then we can say you'd already left before the message came. As long as he sees someone, it won't matter which nurse it is. Sorry, Gladys, that's a bit confusing, isn't it? But I'm happy to go. I'll be off now.'

'Suppose so, Miss. Nurse Lake,' said Gladys dubiously, her lank hair almost covering her eyes.

Edith impulsively hugged her friend. 'I owe you for this.'

'You do,' said Alice. 'Have a lovely evening, and don't do anything I wouldn't do.'

★   ★   ★

The house was easy enough to find, and Alice reckoned it was almost exactly halfway between St Benedict's and Jeeves Place. The door was open, and she propped her bike up on the tiny strip of paving stones serving as a front garden, before knocking and going inside. Her uniform made her instantly recognisable, and the woman leaning over the sofa in the tiny parlour stood up to give her room.

'Thank you for coming, Nurse. We're mighty glad to see you. I'm his next-door neighbour, and I heard Ernie cry out. I come round at once and found him here like this.' The woman in the faded print apron wiped her hands nervously on her sleeves. 'Will he be all right, Nurse?'

Alice moved closer to the man on the sofa. 'Mr Leagrave? Ernest, may I call you that? I'm Nurse Lake. I'm a colleague of Nurse Gillespie and she's told me all about you.' She spoke quietly and firmly, to reassure him and also to judge his reactions. Was he alert or confused? She dreaded that he'd developed concussion from the accident.

Ernest Leagrave slowly moved his head round so he could see her properly. He was half lying, half sitting, propped against a pair of worn cushions. 'You ain't the one what looked after me before,' he said, and though his voice was querulous there was no trace of confusion there.

'No, I'm not. She'd finished her shift. I trained with her so I'm qualified to look after you just the same.' Alice gave him a broad, steady smile. 'Why don't you tell me about what happened today?' She noticed a footstool with a woven

81

wicker top and drew it closer so that she could sit on it and look into his eyes on the same level.

'I just took a funny turn. I said to my wife, you go and see yer sister like you was going to before I had my bit of trouble. Ain't no need for you to stay home and look after me. Then I thought as I might as well go to work cos I was feeling so much better — but I had a funny turn. Me neighbour come in and help me and then sent for you.' He fell back against the cushion as if worn out.

Alice took his pulse and temperature, and assessed his breathing, then leant back. 'What did the doctor say after you had your accident?' she asked.

'Oh, doctors.' The man, who was probably in his fifties, gave a snort of contempt. 'Nobody would ever get anything done if they was to listen to doctors. Stay in bed, take it easy, all that rubbish. I don't pay no attention to them.'

Alice noticed the neighbour moving towards the door, mouthing, 'I'll be next door if you need me', clearly eager to get back to her own business. Alice was glad — that meant there would be no one to witness the telling off she felt obliged to give her patient.

'Now, Mr Leagrave,' she began, quietly but firmly, aware that here was a man of definite opinions. The problem was, if he kept to them, he'd be putting himself in danger. Gently but insistently, she explained this to him. 'The doctor didn't advise you to rest because he couldn't think of anything else,' she finished. 'He said it because it was what you need to do. And

82

now, look what happens when you go against that. So you had better promise me you'll rest like he told you.'

Ernest Leagrave looked too worn out to argue, but nodded. 'Yes, Nurse. I see that now.'

'Good.' Alice sat back. 'Rest really is the best medicine. Then you'll be able to return to work sure as eggs is eggs.'

'That's what I want, Nurse. I hate sitting around on my arse doing nothing,' Ernest confessed. 'I never was one for doing nothing. Just ask anyone who knows me.' He nodded to a shape behind him, and Alice realised someone else had come into the room, so quietly she hadn't heard them. 'Here's my colleague from the GPO, he'll tell you. Isn't that right, Joe?'

'Oh, I don't doubt it,' said Alice comfortingly, and then did a double take when she saw who the newcomer was, recognising Joe Banham, the man who'd treated her curtly when she'd met him at Victoria Park with Edith. She swallowed hard. 'Good afternoon, Mr Banham. I didn't realise you'd come in.' She stood. 'I was just leaving.'

'I've been here for a few minutes, you seemed engrossed in your work and I didn't want to interrupt.'

Alice was flummoxed knowing that Joe had been quietly watching her while she treated his friend. There was a smile in his eyes that she didn't remember from their last meeting.

'What about payment, Nurse? I want things done proper,' Ernest insisted.

Alice waved his suggestion aside. 'No, no, Mr

Leagrave. You pay into the scheme and, besides, I haven't done anything except talk.'

'Made me feel a good deal better though, Miss,' he said stoutly. 'You're a tonic to behold, you are. You and that friend of yours, you tell her thanks again from me.'

'I will, thank you,' Alice said, picking up her bag and making for the door, avoiding eye contact with Ernest's visitor.

'I'll see you out, Miss Lake,' said Joe Banham. 'Give me one moment, Ernie, and I'll be back.' He slipped out behind Alice as she went through the front door and into the narrow ribbon of a garden.

'Really, there's no need,' she said. 'You go and see your friend. Just don't tire him out or let him do too much — that's what's brought him to this state to begin with.' She spoke with more asperity than she'd intended, but somehow this man got under her skin. Especially as there wasn't much room in this tiny garden.

'I know,' Joe said, and there was no disapproval in his voice this time. 'I heard what you said to him just now. I wanted to thank you for being so straightforward — Ernie's a good bloke but stubborn as they come.' He paused, then gave a half-laugh. 'I think I owe you an apology, Miss Lake.'

'Really, Mr Banham?' She raised an eyebrow, turning to face him full on.

He nodded. 'Here am I doing the very thing I blamed my sister for, talking about a friend behind their back. So I'm sorry. I can see how good you are with patients now. I got the wrong idea before. Just being over-protective, that's all. Kathleen's been unlucky.'

Alice didn't know what to say for a moment, it was so unexpected — first to bump into the man again and then to hear this. 'Well, thank you,' she managed, trying to put aside the quiet fury she had felt at the time. 'I'm only doing what is best for the patients — I'd never do anything else. It's not gossip if you're telling me something that will help them.'

'No, I understand now.' He straightened. 'Anyway, I hear my brother is taking your friend to the pictures this evening.'

'So I believe,' said Alice, not wanting to get drawn in. She still wasn't sure if she could trust him.

'*Jamaica Inn*, possibly,' Joe went on.

'Possibly.' Alice couldn't see what business it was of his. 'Personally I think I'd prefer the book.'

'Yes, you can't beat a good book,' Joe agreed, his eyes lighting up.

Despite herself, Alice responded. 'Exactly.'

'Tell you what,' he said. 'I'm a member of the Billet Library in Upper Clapton. Shall I see if they've got it? That's if you haven't read it?'

Alice was taken aback both by the turn of the conversation and the offer, but couldn't see how to say no and not sound rude. What harm could it do to accept? Perhaps she had been wrong about the man. He'd admitted it, so she should be able to acknowledge it as well. 'Thank you,' she said. 'That would be kind. I haven't read it yet.'

'You should join the library if you like books,' he went on, warming to his theme. 'It's a subscription one but it gets all the latest titles. If you're interested, that is. It's not far, you could cycle there.' He looked dubiously at the boneshaker.

'I might,' said Alice, not wanting to commit to anything. 'If I have time.'

'Oh, of course.' Joe seemed to take that as a dismissal. 'Well, I'd better be getting back to Ernie. See if he needs anything. Goodbye, Miss Lake.'

Alice began to push her bike, aware of a strange feeling as she squeezed past him in the narrow space. 'Thanks again.' She looked at him as he turned to go. He had very deep brown eyes. She remembered the anger he had provoked, how intense it had seemed, and still wasn't quite sure what to make of him. 'Goodbye, Mr Banham.'

★　★　★

'Alice! Alice! Are you awake?'

Edith crept into her friend's room, guided by the light of the streetlamp outside.

'What? What's happened?' Alice woke up in confusion. 'Edie, is that you? Is something wrong? Whatever time is it?'

'Yes, it's me. Nothing's wrong, don't worry,' hissed Edith, skirting around the question of what time it was. 'I just got back. Sorry, did I wake you? I thought you might still be up reading or something.'

'No, but it doesn't matter.' Alice rolled over

86

and sat up, rubbing her eyes. 'How did it go?'

Edith sat down on the bed in front of her friend. There was enough light for Alice to see how animated she was. 'It was lovely. It was the best evening I've had for ages. Much better than dancing at the Paramount. He's really nice, Alice, really nice.'

'Good,' said Alice, who was used to Edith's conquests. Even so, it was unlike her to be so enthusiastic quite so soon. 'So what did you do?'

'He met me at the bus stop and we went to the cinema. He bought me an ice cream. He was a proper gent while the film was on, didn't try anything on or nothing.'

'What was the film like?'

'Oh, it was scary, a girl gets trapped in a remote inn full of smugglers — '

'Don't tell me the whole plot, I might read the book soon,' Alice interrupted.

'All right, keep your hair on. You did ask. Anyway it was a great yarn, you'd like it. It was romantic, too, but I shan't tell you why or it'll spoil it. He did hold my hand a bit at the end.'

'The film must have finished ages ago,' Alice said. 'What happened then?'

'We went for fish and chips. He bought them, he's very generous. Then we went to the pub to meet some of his friends.'

'Edie, have you been drinking?' Alice was wide awake now. 'With someone you hardly know?'

Edith shifted a little. 'Don't worry, I only had lemonade. I'm not daft. He introduced me to his friends and they all seemed to like me. He's a boxer, you know.'

'A boxer?'

'Yes, just amateur for now, but he thinks he's going to make it big.' Edith nodded. 'Imagine! He could be famous. He's already been in the local paper. This is just the start, he says.'

'Goodness.' Alice didn't know much about boxing and wasn't sure what to say. It sounded like a dangerous hobby.

'Then he walked me all the way home. We couldn't stop talking. You know sometimes you run out of things to say to someone — well, it wasn't like that at all. You'd like him, Al. He knows lots of stuff.'

'Maybe,' said Alice.

'I said we'd meet him, you and me and Mary, and he'll bring along his friends.'

'I don't know . . . '

'Oh, don't be a spoilsport, Al. You'd have fun. You can't hide away with your books for the rest of your life. Not after Mark and everything . . . '

Alice pushed back her hair behind her ears. 'I'm not hiding away. I just like a nice night in with my books. We'll see. I'm sure Mary will go out with you. Anyway, how did you get back in? Isn't it after curfew? Oh, Edie, not again!'

Edith shook her dark curls. 'No, no, it's fine — I was just in time. About thirty seconds to go, I reckon. I was very careful. Even so, I crept along so I wouldn't wake Gwen or Fiona. So it's all turned out fine.'

'You were lucky though.'

'That's me,' said Edith confidently. 'Look, I'll leave you to sleep.'

'Don't you want to know about your patient,

the postman?' Alice wondered.

'Tell me tomorrow. Night night.' Edith slipped out of the room as quietly as she'd come in.

Alice was left to try to get back to sleep, noting that Edith hadn't asked what sort of evening she'd had. But then, she hadn't tried to tell her. Maybe she should have mentioned meeting Joe, and his offer to find her the book. Then again, perhaps she'd keep that to herself for the time being. It was hardly the same thing. And she couldn't quite explain the sensation that thinking of him gave her — no longer anger, or righteous indignation, but something not quite describable either.

8

Kathleen woke with a start and for a moment couldn't work out what the noise was. She tried to make out the time on her battered old enamel alarm clock, but it was barely dawn and still too dark to see. The banging was coming from the front door. Still foggy from sleep, she swung her legs out of bed and pushed her feet into her well-worn slippers. She had to stop the banging before it woke Brian. He'd taken ages to get off last night and an early wake-up was the last thing he needed.

'Kathleen! Open up!' came a voice.

For a moment she was seized with terror. Last week a man had come to the door, banging on it just like this. It had been in the middle of the morning, as she was thinking about going to the market to see if there were any bargains; perhaps some rolls at the bakery left over from the day before that would be all right for toast. The man's voice had been aggressive and she had instinctively ducked out of sight in case he tried to look through the window. Most people would have given up after a minute, assuming nobody was in, but this man had just kept on, then shouted, 'I know you're in there' very loudly, enough to annoy the Coynes upstairs.

Mrs Coyne had come to the window. 'What's all the bleedin' fuss about?' she had demanded.

'Where's your neighbour?' the man had shouted back.

'How the hell should I know? I'm not her bleedin' keeper, am I?'

There had been the sounds of shuffling feet as the man had indeed gone to peer through the window. Kathleen had crouched, trembling, against the wall beside the bed, praying the noise wouldn't wake Brian.

'Well, you tell her next time you see her that she's behind with the rent and the landlord won't stand for it. She's got a week to make up the shortfall or she's out,' the man roared up at Mrs Coyne.

'Tell her yerself, I ain't doin' your dirty work.' She had slammed the window.

Kathleen had sent up a prayer of thanks. Usually the Coynes were the first to complain if she made too much noise or left baby clothes dripping for too long outside, but they didn't like the landlord any more than she did.

A minute or so later, an envelope fluttered through her letterbox, addressed to her in an angry scrawl. Then there had been the sound of retreating footsteps. She had waited a further ten minutes before she felt safe to move to retrieve it. With shaking hands she tore it open, to find what she had feared: a demand to pay her rent arrears in full by this time next week or she'd be evicted. She had no way to find that amount of money. She could barely afford stale bread.

Dismayed, she'd forced herself up and made a cup of weak tea before collapsing at the little table. She knew she had to think, to plan, but no

91

ideas came. Short of a miracle, or Ray sending some money, which was even more unlikely, she was done for.

She had no idea how long she had sat there like that, when there came another tap at the door, this time followed by a familiar voice, a friendly one.

'Kath, you in?'

Kathleen sighed in relief and went to open the door. It was her old school friend, Billy Reilly. He worked down at the docks and occasionally did early or late shifts so he was free in the daytime. Now and again he would drop by, just for old times' sake. She always loved to see him as he seemed to know what to say to cheer her up.

'All right, Kath? How's the nipper?' Billy came in and then took in the expression on her face. 'Kath, what's up? You look like you seen a ghost.'

Kathleen hurriedly shoved the envelope in her patch pocket and ran her other hand through her hair, trying to appear normal. 'Nothing, Billy. Nothing at all. How are you? Care for a cuppa?' She spoke as brightly as she could. There was no way on this earth that she would admit to anyone how much money she owed. She went through to the tiny back kitchen to boil the kettle, gritting her teeth with the effort of not showing her despair.

Billy had always been kind to her at school, although they hadn't known each other very well as he was in the year above her. He'd stayed friends with the Banhams, which meant she saw more of him, and they'd become friendlier. Then she'd met Ray, and everything else had taken second place.

She recalled one incident when she and Ray had been courting for a few months and he'd agreed to go to the pub with her old friends. Afterwards he'd been strangely quiet, his face tight with suppressed emotion. Finally she could bear it no more and asked what was wrong.

'What's the story between you and Billy?' he had demanded.

She'd been taken totally by surprise. 'Nothing. There's no story. We was at school together, just like the rest of them.'

Ray had huffed in disbelief. 'I don't like the way he looks at you. You been leading him on or something?'

'What? Billy? He's a mate, nothing more,' she had protested, sensing a side to Ray she hadn't seen before. She'd known he could be very protective. But she hadn't realised he could be jealous.

'You make sure that's all it is,' he had snarled, gripping her arm and lowering his face close to hers, and for a moment she thought he was going to turn on her. Then he had smiled his usual charming smile and the dark moment passed. 'There's only one man for you, Kath, and that's me. You don't need no other,' he had said, slinging his arm around her shoulder, and she had looked up at him and smiled back in delight, because she believed he would look after her and love her.

She shook her head. That had been a long time ago now.

The familiar ritual of making a pot of tea had calmed her, and by the time she'd brought it through to Billy, her hands were steady again.

He'd stayed for a while to make small talk, producing a little rattle he'd picked up 'for next to nothing' and waving it at a now fully awake Brian, who had waved his arms back. Kathleen had beamed in pleasure, watching another stage of her baby learning how to reach for an object, loving his big smile.

'Heard from Ray recently?' Billy had asked.

Kathleen shook her head. 'It's been a while. He'll be in the middle of the Atlantic, he can't always be sending letters home.' It was what she always said to others; what she told herself. Working on board a ship wasn't like any other job. There were bound to be long periods when he was out of contact.

'Kath, don't take this the wrong way,' Billy had said, frowning a little so that the freckles on his nose stood out more than usual against his pale skin, 'but I had a bit of a win on the gee-gees at the weekend. If he is stuck out on the high seas and can't send money back, I'll lend you some.'

'Billy, no. There's no need,' she said at once.

He knew her too well though. He pushed back his dark curly hair, tamed with Brylcreem, and glanced downwards in embarrassment but stuck to his guns. 'It's a loan, Kath. Not a present. Just a bit to tide you over, till he reaches port. What am I going to do with it? Ma sorts all the food out, and I'm not much of a drinker. If you don't want it, take it for the nipper. Buy him something nice. Come on, Kath, there's no harm in it.'

He'd hit her vulnerable spot. She couldn't resist the idea of making Brian warm and safe. Shutting her eyes briefly, she looked at her old friend. 'All right, Billy, if you're sure — and it's just a loan, I'll pay you back,' she said quietly, and he had given her such a smile it was almost as if it was her giving him a loan, not the other way around. She wouldn't buy anything big for Brian or herself though, this would have to go on the rent and food, and besides, Ray wouldn't like it if he found out.

The rapping on the door was louder now, snapping Kathleen back out of her reverie and bringing her back to the present. She shuffled to the door. 'Hang on,' she hissed. 'Who is it?'

'Kathleen!' The voice was insistent but cheery. 'Don't you want to see me?'

Suddenly she was fully alert. There was only one person who spoke like that. Eagerly she turned the key and unlocked the door, its paint flaking as she did so. As swiftly as she could, she tugged the door open.

'Ray!'

All her doubts about her husband flew from her mind as she took in the sight of him, backlit by the grey summer dawn. He was so tall, so well-built, and his arms were open. She flung herself at him, holding him as tightly as she could, and he hugged her to his broad chest, murmuring into her hair.

They stood there for some moments before a noise came from the rooms upstairs. 'Come inside, we'd better not wake the neighbours,' Kathleen said, hurriedly leading him in.

'What do we care?' Ray said, clasping her to him once more. 'Nosy old buggers can just mind their own business. I've come to see my wife, I've a right to make a bit of noise.'

'Sit down, take the weight off your feet. Are you tired? Did you come straight from the ship? Oh, Ray, you could have sent me word. Then I'd have got some food in, made a bit of an effort . . . '

'Never mind all that,' said Ray, nuzzling her neck. 'I come as soon as I could, Kath. You don't know what it's like, being away from you all that time. We'll worry about all the rest later.'

She held him close for a moment longer and then looked up at him. 'Don't you want to see Brian? Your son? He's the spit of you, he is.'

Ray stroked her neck, her shoulders, and his hands moved lower. 'Oh I do, I'm dying to see him. But later, Kath. First I want to see you. All of you.' He pulled her towards the unmade bed, his breathing growing heavy.

'Oh Ray.' She let herself be edged across the room. 'As long as we don't wake him . . . '

'We won't wake him,' Ray said easily. 'Don't you want to show me how you've missed me, Kath? I've missed you, I don't mind telling you, and I've thought about nothing else. That's right, you lie down there . . . '

Kathleen did as he asked and opened herself up to him, torn between her delight at Ray's sudden arrival and her anxiety about her son. Then her husband was on top of her and she forgot all about everything except having him home again, where he belonged.

★ ★ ★

Flo was scrubbing her front doorstep when she heard footsteps behind her. She felt caught out, as normally she'd get this chore out of the way earlier in the day, and then nobody passing by could accuse her of not taking care of her house. But the morning had been busy and she'd only now found the time. She hoped it wasn't one of her more quarrelsome neighbours. Mrs Dennis down the street, for instance. It was all very well for her; she didn't have three grown children and a grandchild sharing her house. It was easy for her to keep an immaculate home.

Flo shifted around and saw that she had no reason to worry. It was only Kathleen, with little Brian. 'Hello,' she called as the young woman approached. 'Have you come to see Mattie? She's inside, feeding Gillian.'

'Hello, yes, thank you.' Kathleen seemed all of a fluster.

Flo looked at her keenly. 'Everything all right, Kathleen? Brian's not took bad again, is he?'

Kathleen beamed in happiness. 'Oh no, Mrs Banham. No, nothing's wrong, far from it. You'll never guess.'

Flo eased herself up to her feet to give her aching knees a rest, shaking her dripping scrubbing brush. 'What is it? Out with it, you can't keep a secret round here.'

Kathleen's face lit up with an inner glow of

happiness. 'It's Ray, he's back. He just got back early this morning. I can't believe it, he didn't write to warn me or nothing, just got home as soon as he could.'

Flo raised her eyebrows. She hadn't been the only one to suspect that Ray Berry would never be seen around these parts again. But she had no wish to dampen his young wife's joy. 'Well, that's a turn-up for the books,' she said instead.

'Isn't it? So I thought I'd come and tell Mattie . . . and maybe ask if she can see to Brian for a few hours.'

Flo nodded understandingly. 'You've got a lot of time to make up for, I can see that. I'm sure she won't mind, and if not then I'll look after him, little angel that he is.' She went over and looked at the little boy's sleeping face. 'So he's finally met his daddy, then?'

'Oh yes. Ray's pleased as punch,' Kathleen said, skirting over the somewhat awkward moment earlier when Ray had woken up, and wanted to make love again just as Brian started crying for his feed. Yet it was only to be expected — Ray wasn't used to the ways of a small baby. It was perfectly normal for him to be a bit cross. He'd grow to love the baby as much as she did in time. He was as proud as anything, she could see that.

'Of course he is,' said Flo. 'Who wouldn't be delighted to have a son like this? You take him in to his Auntie Mattie, and while you're in there help yourself to some scones. I made them fresh earlier. Take a couple for Ray as a welcome home present.'

Kathleen's eyes lit up. 'Oh I will. Thank you. He'll love that.' She went through the front door, carefully avoiding the step where Flo had just scrubbed. Turning from the hall she could hear the familiar sound of Mattie bickering with one of her brothers. From the measured tone of his replies, it was Joe.

' . . . because you always think you know what's best and you don't,' Mattie was complaining as Kathleen walked into the room. 'Oh, hello, Kath. Didn't hear you come in.'

'Your mum was outside so I didn't have to knock,' Kathleen explained breathlessly. 'Mattie, guess what happened this morning. I can't believe it, I've waited so long. Ray's back, how about that?'

Joe had been taking a sip of his tea and almost sputtered it out. 'Ray? Your Ray?'

'Well, of course,' said Kathleen, affronted. 'Why say it like that, Joe? I was surprised, I know, but he didn't have time to send a letter. He just wanted to get back to see me as soon as he could. And Brian, of course.'

'Of course,' said Joe. 'I didn't mean anything by it, Kath. I was just taken aback, that's all.'

Mattie rose and put Gillian into the cot. The baby whimpered a little but then settled without a fuss. 'Yes, where's he been all this time, Kath? Has he said?'

Kathleen pulled out a wooden chair and sat down opposite Joe, while balancing Brian on her knee. 'He's been everywhere! He signed on with a merchant ship like he said he was going to. He's been mostly going between Canada and

Liverpool, on those big ships what bring the timber across. He says it was back-breaking to begin with but you get used to it. Lots of fresh air too. Not like the factories round here, he says. He's been working ever so hard, all the hours God sends.'

Mattie frowned. 'So if he's been in Liverpool, why didn't he come home? Or at least write more?'

Kathleen shifted in her chair. She'd wondered the same thing, but Ray had put her mind at rest. 'He never had the time. They dock one day and then they either leave again the next or you're put on a different ship that's leaving beforehand. Barely had time to get his land legs, he said. And he hates writing — he never was one for his letters. He's clever, mind, but he doesn't write very much. His brains are quicker than his hands, he says.'

Joe took a fresh sip of tea before replying. 'Right. So that's all there was to it, then.'

Kathleen frowned. 'Of course. Don't be so suspicious, Joe. Just because you're good with writing everything down and passing exams doesn't mean everyone's the same.'

Joe put down his cup and got to his feet. 'Don't you start. I've had all of that from Mattie today already.' But he said it with affection.

'Don't go on my account . . . ' Kathleen began.

'I'm not. I've got to get to the library and back before the football starts,' he said, pushing back his chair and heading for the door. 'Glad to hear he's back in one piece, Kath. Maybe I'll see him down the pub soon.'

'Maybe.' Kathleen's smile faltered a little; she wasn't sure how long Ray was going to be around for. He'd managed to avoid giving her a direct answer when she'd asked earlier. 'Bye, Joe.'

Mattie waited until her brother had gone before turning to her friend. 'Well, go on. Tell me everything. Where is he now?'

'Home, asleep,' said Kathleen. 'Look, I'm here to ask a favour. Could you mind Brian for a bit this afternoon? Just so I can have some time alone with Ray, you know.'

Mattie's face creased into a broad smile. 'Oh I know. Or I can guess.' Then she grew serious once more. 'Doesn't Ray want to get to know Brian, though? His own little boy? It broke Lennie's heart when he had to say goodbye to Gillian after his last leave. He wanted to spend every moment with her.'

'Oh, Ray's the same,' Kathleen said hastily. 'But Gillian's so good, she sleeps so well, whereas Brian's liable to wake up at the least noise. My Ray's got to get his rest in a proper bed while he can.'

Mattie nodded doubtfully. It was just one more way in which Ray and Lennie were chalk and cheese. She knew which she preferred. Still, Ray wasn't her husband, and if Kathleen thought it was fine to hand her son over a mere matter of hours after his father finally met him, then it wasn't her concern. 'It's no trouble at all,' she assured her friend. 'Just pop him at the opposite end of the cot to Gillian as usual. I'll be here

101

most of the time and, when I need to go to the market, Ma will see to him.'

'Or I will,' said a voice from the doorway. Harry's silhouette appeared, then he came all the way into the room. 'Morning, Kath.'

Mattie erupted. 'Morning! Afternoon, near as. What did you get up to last night that you slept in so late? I had to go down the bicycle shop with Dad because you weren't up on time. You promised you'd help him when he said he'd fetch their replacement tyres, but you wasn't around after breakfast. Hope it was worth it, whatever you were doing.'

Both Mattie and Kathleen turned their attention to Harry's face, which was grinning unashamedly.

'You were with a girl, weren't you?' said Mattie.

'Might have been.' He shrugged.

'Harry Banham, you sly thing, you were. Who was it? Anyone we know?' Kathleen was on to him at once.

'Not telling you. Look at the pair of you, why would I tell you anything? You'll rip whatever I say into pieces.' He made his way to the breadbin. 'Any chance of toast?'

'You don't deserve any, missing breakfast like that . . . ' Mattie began, but Kathleen stood up.

'I'd better go. Your mum said I could take some scones for Ray. Is that them over there?' Kathleen went to the battered old biscuit tin and lifted the lid.

'Put them in that tea towel there,' said Mattie, jerking her head towards a red and white checked towel hanging beside the window, at the same time as Harry exclaimed, 'Ray? Did you say Ray?'

'You tell him,' said Kathleen, bundling up a few scones. 'I'm needed back at home.' She raced out, a big smile on her face.

Harry turned to face his sister.

'Ray's back?'

Mattie shrugged. 'Looks like it. She's happy as can be, Harry, so don't you go saying nothing.'

Harry looked wounded. 'I haven't. I wouldn't. But all the same, come off it, Mattie, you think the same of that scumbag as I do. What sort of man leaves his wife to practically starve without a word of comfort for months on end? Has he just swanned back in as if he'd never been away?'

'Apparently.' Mattie raised her hands. 'I don't know much more than you do. She's only been here five minutes. He got in this morning, came round early.'

Harry shook his head. 'Where's he been then? Cos I know for a fact that no ships got in yesterday or were due this morning. I saw Billy Reilly in the pub last night, and he happened to mention it. He gets extra if he unloads cargo down the docks at weekends.'

'Maybe he didn't dock here. She said he'd been on the Liverpool run. Maybe he docked there and travelled down.'

'On a train that got in early this morning? Come on, Mattie. You wasn't born yesterday.'

'Maybe he got a lift. Look, I don't know. There's no point throwing all those questions at me. I don't trust him any more than you do, but she married him, Harry. We can't do nothing about that.' She glanced across the room to where Brian was now slumbering peacefully in the far end of the big cot.

'Good job Billy didn't know about this last night,' Harry observed.

'Crikey, I forgot. He used to hold a candle for Kath, didn't he.'

'Fat lot of good that did him,' said Harry, cutting a slice of bread. 'Decent man he is, too. Unlike some we could mention.'

'We can't do nothing about it,' Mattie repeated sadly. 'Cut me some while you're at it, would you? I got to top up my energy, after I been doing all your chores this morning.'

For once Harry didn't argue. On the one hand it was none of his business what Kath did. She was a grown woman who could make her own decisions. Yet, like the rest of the family, he was very fond of his sister's best friend and he had felt uncomfortable these past months watching her struggling to keep herself and Brian healthy and properly fed. Not to mention the fact that his own friend, Billy, had at one time been very fond of her, but had been pipped to the post before he'd managed to screw up his courage to ask her out. So, whatever way you looked at it, he felt that Ray's return was anything but good news.

9

'Sorry, Miss!' The little girl wiped her nose with the back of her hand as she gazed up at Alice. She'd run around the corner without looking and gone straight into Alice's legs, but as she was so small there wasn't much harm done.

Alice looked down at her and recognised the features, even though they were grimier than on a school day. 'It's Pauline, isn't it?' she asked.

Pauline nodded solemnly. 'You're the nurse, ain't you? But you ain't got your uniform on.'

Alice laughed. 'I don't wear it all the time, you know.'

'But you're still a nurse? Even when you wear a pretty frock?'

'Of course I am. But I'm not on duty — I get Sunday evenings off. Isn't it a bit late for you to be out? Are you on your own?' Alice asked, concerned for the little girl. Surely it was the child's bedtime. Alice had been to evening service at the local church, feeling the need for the comfort of familiar hymns.

Pauline stared at her as if she was mad. 'I'm not a baby. Ain't my bedtime for hours yet,' she said. 'I had to go and get Gran's fags.' She held up a paper bag.

Alice tried not to look shocked. 'Do you buy them from the shop?' she asked, thinking there wouldn't be one open.

'Nah, the pub. They know me in there,' the little girl assured her. 'They know what sort she likes, see. Gran'll go in there tomorrow and settle up with them, but she's mindin' me little brother this evening so I had to go and fetch them.'

'I see,' said Alice, making a mental note. 'How are you getting on with brushing your teeth?' She remembered the child had said that Gran didn't approve of toothbrushes.

'Very well, thank you for asking,' Pauline said politely. 'I brush 'em every night now. But I got to hide the toothpaste from me little brother cos he tries to eat it.'

'Yes, you'd better not let him do that,' Alice said hurriedly.

'Will it poison him, Miss?' Pauline asked curiously.

'No, nothing like that. It just won't do him much good. Besides, it would be a dreadful waste,' Alice pointed out. 'And we don't want that, do we?'

'No, Miss.' Pauline shuffled her feet. 'I got to be goin' now. Gran don't like to be kept waitin' for her fags.'

'Of course.' Alice nodded solemnly. 'I shall see you at school later in the week, then.'

'Bye, Miss.' Pauline sprinted off, one sock falling down as she did so.

Alice stared after her for a moment, pulling her cardigan more tightly around her shoulders against the evening chill. She wondered what sort of home the child had. Whatever the condition of it, it didn't seem to dampen her spirits. Perhaps she would have to leave it soon anyway, with the planned evacuation of young children. Alice shook her head. She didn't know why she'd been so strongly drawn to go to church that evening; she'd got into the habit of going with some of the other nurses to the morning service, but something about the overwhelming likelihood of war had propelled her out again, seeking some kind of solace. But there was little to be had. For once, the singing and the familiar responses hadn't worked their magic, and even the fading golden light of what had been a hot summer day was making her despondent. The congregation had talked of little else but war as they made their way out though the churchyard.

Then again, she had an interesting book to read later. Joe had made good on his promise. When she'd got back to the nurses' home after the morning service, there had been a brown paper parcel waiting, with her name written on it in clear copperplate. She'd slipped it inside her handbag before any of the others could notice, and once upstairs in the privacy of her room, she'd torn off the paper — carefully, as she didn't like to waste it — to reveal a copy of *Jamaica Inn*. There was no note, but she knew who it was from all right.

She wasn't sure why she still hadn't told Edith about it. Her friend was Catholic, so didn't go to the same church, and hadn't seen Alice's swift move to hide the book in the bag. Edith would never have missed such a thing, and Alice knew she was off the hook for the time being. She told herself that the reason behind her reluctance was that she didn't want to spoil Edith's excitement about Harry. This way, Edith wouldn't have to share the limelight. But she knew her friend would be delighted if Alice received a gift from a man — even if it was purely out of a common interest in books, with nothing remotely romantic behind it. Alice sighed. It was all too complicated. She'd tried to explain to her friend why she wasn't interested in men after Mark, but Edith was keen to see her find romance, or at least have some fun.

She was married to her profession, she reminded herself. It was a path she'd chosen, and nothing must interfere with her dedication. It was important work, she'd trained for years, and she was good at what she did. There was no room in her life for distractions. Edith and Mary and the others might dream of finding a man and giving up nursing, but she had no intention of ever letting that happen to her.

Although that didn't mean she couldn't enjoy *Jamaica Inn*. She'd make a start on it tonight; she'd have to get it back to Joe in good time, as it was only out on loan. She smiled to herself. There was no harm in a friendship, and that was all it was, all it could ever be. She deliberately didn't think about how she'd first reacted to him, the anger beyond what the insult merited. It would be nice to have someone to talk about books with. None of her fellow nurses at the home shared her interest, or to nothing like the same degree. It was one of the main things that made her tick, and it was only common sense to become friends with anyone who felt the same way.

★　★　★

'I said, get rid of it!' Ray was tense with fury, his eyes staring at his wife, every muscle taut.

'He's not an 'it', he's your son!' protested Kathleen.

'Is he? You sure?' He grabbed her by the wrist.

'Of course he is! You know he is! Everyone says he looks just like you!' she cried, bewildered at how the evening had suddenly turned into an argument, stung by the unfairness of the accusation.

'If I find out you was fooling around, there'll be trouble,' he warned, gripping her wrist harder.

'I never!'

'Look at his dark hair. Same colour as your old mate's, is it? That Billy?'

'You got dark hair, Ray! His hair is like yours! I never been anywhere near Billy.'

'Good, cos you're my wife and you'll do as I say,' he snarled. 'And I'm saying get rid of it. Every time I come near you that bloody creature starts screaming, like it don't want me to touch you.'

'He's just a baby! You can't be jealous of a baby!'

'Jealous, am I? What have I got to be jealous of?' He pulled her face close to his and his spittle struck her on the cheek.

'I . . . I . . . ' Kathleen knew she'd somehow said the wrong thing but couldn't think how to put it right. This reunion that she'd longed for so badly for so long had gone horribly wrong, and now Ray was livid, all because little Brian needed his feed.

'Take it round to your mates' house.'

'I . . . I can't. They've had him most of the weekend . . . '

He twisted her wrist and she cried out in pain, which made Brian scream even louder.

'What sort of friends are they, then? Don't they understand I'm back and want to have my rights?'

'Just let me feed him, then he'll be quiet,' she managed to say, but it came out faintly as she was in so much pain.

'You only think about that bloody baby, you don't think about me at all. What about my needs, eh? Try putting them first for once. You're my wife, it's your duty.'

'I will, I will, just let me feed him,' she begged, but it was no good.

He twisted her arm behind her back and she almost collapsed with the pain. 'Is that what you want? To feed him and not do your duty by me?' he snarled into her ear. 'Is he more important than me?'

'No, no, but he doesn't understand . . . '

'But I understand, Kath. I understand all too well. That little scrap of bones means more to you than I do — me, your own husband. Don't matter that I haven't seen you for months, or that I brought you back my wages.' With his free hand he reached into his trouser pocket and pulled out a bundle of notes. 'There you are then. That's all you wanted, wasn't it.' He flung them onto the floor where they fluttered in the draught from the open window.

'No, Ray, please, no . . . '

'I'm keeping back a few shillings for myself if that's all right with you,' he said, pulling her arm still tighter. 'If I'm not welcome here, I'm going down the pub, where at least I know I'm wanted.'

'No, Ray, stay here with me, you only just got back,' she cried.

'With a snivelling woman and a screaming baby? What, do you think I'm stupid or something?' He flung her from him and turned for the door, not caring that the force with which he'd thrown her had sent her straight to the floor.

Kathleen lay very still and everything went black.

★　★　★

First thing on Monday morning, Mattie hammered on the door to the nurses' home.

Gwen opened it, staring at the wild-haired young woman who was gasping for breath.

'Yes? Is there an emergency? You appear to have been running,' she said.

'Please,' Mattie got out, 'please, is Nurse Lake here? Alice Lake? We need her. My friend . . . '

Gwen frowned. 'This is highly irregular. You should have whichever nurse is on duty and available. The referral should be via a doctor or hospital.'

Mattie nodded. 'I'm sorry, I know, but is Alice on duty? Can she come? My friend . . . my friend trusts her, you see.' She gulped. 'She'll know what to do.'

'All nurses will know what to do,' Gwen said sternly.

Mattie screwed her eyes tight shut and opened them again. 'I'm sorry. I know. It's just . . . my friend knows her and Alice has been there before and I don't know if she'll see anyone else; she's so upset and she didn't want me to come here and fetch anyone to see her but she's in a bad way and I just know Alice will know what's best.' She drew breath. 'I'm sorry.'

Gwen pursed her lips but relented. 'Very well. Wait here.' She went back inside, leaving the door ajar. Mattie leant against the wall, hoping she'd done the right thing.

It seemed an eternity before she heard footsteps from along the corridor and Alice appeared at the door, adjusting her collar and patting her hair, obviously only just ready to come on duty.

'Alice! Thank God. I thought that old battleaxe wasn't going to fetch you,' Mattie said. 'Come quick, something awful's happened to Kathleen.'

Alice gasped. 'Whatever is it? Wait a moment, tell me what you can, then I'll cycle over there. Is she at home?'

Mattie wrung her hands. 'I found her this morning. I went over with some of Ma's gingerbread cos I know she likes it, and there she was, lying on the floor, her arm all funny and

Brian crying cos he hadn't been fed.'

'Was she unconscious?' Alice asked.

'She sort of came round when she heard me. She was moaning and groaning, but she could speak. She was all white in the face, it was terrible, so I came straight for you. She won't see nobody else.'

Alice frowned. 'Had she tripped over or something?'

Mattie's expression grew dark. 'She says she fell. That's what she told me. But, Alice . . . ' Mattie's face twisted in misery. 'She'll tell you that as well, I bet. But she didn't — she didn't fall. It was that bastard Ray. Her husband.'

★ ★ ★

Alice arrived ahead of Mattie, as she'd cycled as hard as she could. She swung off her bike and grabbed her nurse's bag, knocked on the front door and let herself in without waiting for a reply. The front room was dark as the curtains were still closed. Alice went to the window and pulled them back so that she could see what she was doing.

Kathleen let out a faint whimper at the sudden daylight. Alice turned to find her patient propped in the armchair, leaning over at a strange angle, trying to feed her baby using only one arm. The other hung uselessly by her side.

'Kathleen.' Alice went to the woman's side and crouched down. 'It's all right, I'm here to help you. Your poor arm. Here, let me take Brian for a bit, he doesn't look very comfy like that.' In truth

113

she was worried the baby would fall from his mother's lap and hurt himself on the hard floor. Kathleen surrendered the child with barely a protest and Alice held him gently against her shoulder as he grizzled and then grew calmer. 'There, there, that's right. We'll just put you in your cot while I look at Mummy.' Carefully she laid the baby on the thin mattress, and waited a moment for him to settle. Then she turned her attentions back to her patient.

Kathleen wouldn't meet her eyes. 'I told Mattie not to bother,' she whispered. 'I'll be all right, it's nothing. You didn't need to come.'

Alice pulled a wooden chair across the room and sat on it, opposite her patient. 'Kathleen, that's not true, is it? I think I did need to come. Mattie was right to be worried. Here, let me see you properly. Can you move your arm?' Kathleen tried to do so but her face contorted with pain. Then a shaft of sunlight hit her and Alice just managed not to gasp out loud. One side of the young woman's face was livid with bruising. The colours matched those around her swollen wrist.

'Oh, Kathleen.' Alice's heart went out to her but she knew sympathy was only part of what was needed. Somehow she had to make her more comfortable and treat the arm so that Kathleen could use it fully again as soon as possible. 'Can you tell me what happened?'

Kathleen twisted her face away. 'I fell,' she said blankly.

'You fell? But your wrist . . . '

'I fell and hit my head, and landed on my wrist. My arm got stuck under me,' Kathleen insisted. 'I was stupid, it was my fault. I tripped and fell.'

Alice wasn't at all convinced. 'Let me see your wrist. I'll be very gentle.' She slowly lifted it so that it rested on her lap, and as the sunlight fell fully on it she could see the impressions of fingers, marking the pale white skin. Even if she'd believed the woman before, she certainly didn't do so now.

'I'm going to bathe your wrist to help the swelling and then I shall bandage it, as it's not only bruised but cut too,' she told her. 'Then I'll bathe your face and assess what else is wrong with your arm.' Calmly she rose and moved to the back kitchen, now familiar to her, and set the kettle to boil. Mattie arrived just as she was making a pot of tea, reaching for the sugar as well, to help with the patient's shock.

'Here, Mattie, would you mind making us all some tea?' Alice asked, glad that Kathleen had such a loyal friend. 'I'll just bring through this bowl of warm water.' Steadily she went about her business, trying to cause as little pain as she could while still ensuring the treatment was accurate and effective. Kathleen made barely a sound, stoically enduring what Alice could see must be uncomfortable at best and downright agony when she had to move the damaged arm.

Finally she was satisfied that she had done as much as she could for the young woman, and sat back on the wooden chair. Kathleen sipped the sugary tea, her hand shaking, and her teeth chattered against the china. Alice leant forward and helped her set the cup down again. 'Now,

Kathleen, can you tell me again what happened?' she asked quietly. 'It's my duty to try to make sure you are safe and that your injuries don't become worse; can I be sure of that when I leave here?'

Kathleen stared miserably down at the floor. 'I'll be more careful. That's all.'

Alice shook her head. 'Will that really be enough, Kathleen?'

'It won't happen again,' said the young woman. Her voice was dull but there was a stubborn tone to it that Alice could not miss.

'You know you can tell me anything and I won't repeat it,' she pressed. 'It's confidential — anything you say to me need not go any further. You can tell me whatever you like.'

'Ain't nothing to tell,' Kathleen maintained. 'I fell, just like what I told you. Like what I told Mattie.'

'Yes, but — ' Mattie began.

'That's all there is to say,' Kathleen interrupted. 'It won't happen again neither. So you needn't worry. I'm all right, really I am.'

Alice rose, unwilling to leave her patient without hearing exactly what had brought her to this state, but realising there was little to be gained by challenging her directly. She knew there would be other calls to make this morning, more sick patients to see, all equally in need of medical attention. Yet her heart was sore with the knowledge that this young woman was suffering because of her violent husband who'd got away scot-free.

'I'll leave you both, then,' she said heavily. 'I'll

116

be back tomorrow to check on your progress, Kathleen. Mattie, if there's any change, you know where to find me.'

Mattie walked with her to the door and stood just outside while Alice fitted her leather bag into the front basket of the bicycle. 'She won't change her story,' she said in an undertone.

'And we can't make her,' said Alice resignedly. 'But you will let me know if he does it again, won't you?'

Mattie shrugged. 'I reckon he's scarpered. Did you see all that money in the corner? I bet that's his wages. At least he's left her with something useful. What a coward. I'll get Harry to ask around; someone'll know where the bastard has gone to.'

'Will you stay with her?' asked Alice. 'She'll struggle to look after herself, let alone Brian, with only one arm.'

Mattie stood up straighter. 'Of course. I can take the baby round for Ma to see to and then I can get some shopping in for Kath. I can set the place a bit straighter too — looks as if she wasn't the only thing that fell over. I won't take her round to our house, though — not when she's looking like that. She won't want anyone else to see. Besides,' her voice dropped even lower, 'if my brothers see what that snivelling excuse for a husband has done, they'll hunt him down and kill him.'

10

Flo Banham prodded the potatoes with a knife, but they weren't yet done. She decided to get on with something else while she waited. A watched pot never boiled and watched potatoes never cooked properly. It was one of those facts of life. She began to sort through a large pile of clean laundry, folding clothes and pairing socks, as her thoughts wandered. Harry was up to something, she could just tell. He had that look on his face and a mother always noticed these things. She'd bide her time and then worm it out of him, whatever it was.

The back door opened and she almost jumped as Stan came in, dusting off his jacket and wiping his feet on the old coir mat.

'You gave me a surprise, you did!' she mock-scolded him. 'I didn't expect you for ages yet.' She frowned. 'Is everything all right?'

Stan nodded, but looked a little sheepish. 'Sorry to take you by surprise.' He came across to where she stood and gave her a quick kiss. 'Here, put that down for a minute. I had something to do this afternoon and thought I'd come home directly afterwards. Not much point in going back to work now.'

'Stanley Banham, what have you been doing?' Flo was worried now. 'You better tell me what you mean, and sharpish.'

Stan went to sit down at the kitchen table and she followed suit.

'The thing is,' he said, 'I been looking at all those notices in the paper and they're saying that not enough people have come forward to be ARP wardens. They been naming the roads where nobody's stepped up to the mark. All these people living cheek by jowl, and not one of them says they'll do it. I thought to myself, that can't be right. I mean, I hope it doesn't come to it, but if we do go to war then we'll need to be organised against air raids. Then I said to myself, Stan, my lad, you can't just sit there with your feet up and complain when you aren't doing anything about it. So I been and signed up as an ARP warden. There. I've said it.' He spoke confidently but he was eyeing his wife anxiously. He loved her dearly and didn't want to hurt her and yet he'd sensed that if he'd spoken about this beforehand she might have talked him out of it. Even after all these years, he could never quite predict how she would react.

Flo's face relaxed. 'I thought you had bad news, Stan. My heart was beating fast there for a minute.' She sighed. 'I wish you didn't need to as well, but I think you gone and done the right thing. That's brave of you, that is.' She reached forward and took his big hand in her smaller one, worn into calluses by years of hard work. 'You better tell me what it'll all mean. Will you be in more danger than the rest of us?'

Stan shook his head. 'I don't think so. I'll have to make sure everyone toes the line when it comes to air-raid precautions. It will mean I

119

won't be home quite as much, but you'll have Joe and Harry to see to things.'

They exchanged a look. Both knew what had happened to men of Joe and Harry's age in the Great War. Stan had been called up when he was about Joe's age and he never wanted to go through anything like that again. He'd been one of the lucky ones; he'd survived the fighting and even managed to get home on leave several times. Harry and Mattie had both been conceived on his all-too-brief breaks from the Front. He knew how stoic Flo had been, left behind to cope with small children, never certain if she'd see him again. He didn't want that for their sons; he hadn't fought for his country only for his children to have to endure the same thing all over again. Yet there was little he could do about it.

Flo glanced away. 'You do what you think is best,' she said steadily. She swallowed hard and then looked him in the eye once more. 'You make me proud, you do, Stanley Banham. You don't sit around letting everyone else do the work. I suppose I better start thinking about what I can do as well.'

Stan smiled. 'That's the spirit, love. I'm glad you see it like that. Not every wife would.'

'Of course I do!' Flo was indignant. 'You got to do what you think is right, to keep us all safe.'

Stan stroked her hand. 'One thing we got to consider is how to protect our house.'

'Our house?' Flo put her other hand to her throat. This house was her pride and joy, her sanctuary, the home in which she had brought

120

up her brood of children and now her precious grandchild. She could not contemplate how they would manage without the familiar four walls. It was nothing fancy, and a bit worn at the edges, but everything in it had been put together with love and care for the family. It was a bit of a tight squeeze now Mattie was back again and the boys had to share the biggest bedroom, but nobody really minded. She was damned if Hitler was going to damage her house.

'We got to think about the windows. We'll need blackout blinds,' Stan said. 'Best be getting on with it right away as everything is bound to get scarce once the word gets out. Material will be dear, you can bet on it. And we need to put strips of sticky tape across the windowpanes in case there's a bomb blast.'

Flo shivered, but she knew he was right. She gave a little sigh of regret, as she loved looking out of the kitchen window at the small back garden, the flower pots filled with geraniums and petunias. Now she'd have to peer at them around the tape. But it was a small price to pay.

'You're right as ever, Stan. I'll get down the market tomorrow and see what they got.' She stood up. 'Now you'll have to excuse me, as those spuds must be done by now and I don't want the pan to boil dry. Blackout blinds will have to wait until I've fed you lot.'

* * *

'Alice, are you sure you don't want to come with us?' Edith asked, for the twentieth time that

Friday. 'You won't feel like a gooseberry, honest. Harry's bringing several of his friends along.'

While that might have made all the difference to any of the other nurses, it had the reverse effect on Alice. 'No, really,' she said. 'I've still got the final few chapters to read of my book. You go on and have fun. Mary's dying to go.'

'I know, but it's not the same without you there,' Edith said. Her eyes were dark with concern for her friend. 'You are going to come out at some point, aren't you, Al? I'm going to keep asking until you do.'

Alice laughed. 'I'd realised that. But not tonight. I'm shattered, for a start. I haven't stopped for a moment since that callout first thing Monday morning.' She pulled a face as she remembered the state of poor Kathleen. She'd been back on the Tuesday to check that all was well and fortunately she'd heard no more from Jeeves Place since then. She had therefore assumed that the young woman was recovering, but still half expected Mattie to reappear at any minute. 'What are you wearing tonight?'

Edith leant against the window frame in Alice's room. 'I thought I'd go in my red sandals again — they brought me luck last time. Maybe my cream dress with the cap sleeves. It's warm out today.'

'I've got a red and white scarf you could borrow,' Alice offered, suddenly remembering. 'I haven't even unpacked it since we moved in. That would go well, wouldn't it?'

Edith's face lit up. 'It would. I know the one. Oh, Alice, don't you mind?'

'Not a bit,' said Alice. 'You go off and get ready or Mary will be left hanging around.'

★ ★ ★

Mary hung on to Edith's arm, swinging her shoulder bag with her other hand. 'Do you think he'll be there already?' she asked.

'I'm sure he will,' said Edith, trying to conceal just how much she was looking forward to seeing Harry Banham again. She had planned to play it very cool, but her heart was hammering in her chest. Calm down, she told herself. You hardly know him. All the same, every nerve zinged with anticipation.

As they rounded the corner of Victory Walk she could see him waiting at the bus stop and her breath caught in her throat. He really was quite astonishingly good-looking, and the evening sun was glinting on that gorgeous oak-brown hair. As they drew closer he heard them and looked up, giving her a wide smile.

Steady on, she reminded herself, he's smiling at Mary too, so he probably looks like that at everyone. Yet something told her his expression was because she was there. 'Hello, Harry,' she said, smiling back at him, but not too eagerly — although that was an effort. 'You remember Mary, don't you?'

'Course I do,' he said, holding out his hand, which Mary shook with a wide grin of her own. 'Pleased you could come, Mary.'

Mary gave a little laugh and tossed her hair back over her shoulder. She had taken care with her appearance tonight, Edith noted — she'd brought out another silky dress with a tightly belted waist which showed off her curves, her favourite sort of dress for going out.

'Where are you taking us, Harry?' she asked, glancing up at him through her eyelashes.

'Well, ladies, I thought we'd go to the Duke's Arms,' he said. 'There's a garden out the back so you won't feel out of place. Do you know it?'

'No, I don't know much around here yet,' admitted Edith, but Mary said, 'I've been there before and it was very friendly. What a good idea, Harry.'

He ushered them down the main road and then off on a side street, which opened out into a wide road of tall terraced houses, their windows reflecting the evening sunlight. Window boxes full of bright flowers stood on the ledges and by the front steps. Towards the far end of the road, on a corner, they could see the painted sign of the Duke's Arms, swinging in the light breeze. Sounds of laughter floated out from the open door.

'Here we are, ladies.' Harry waved them in to the front bar, which was full of people celebrating the start of the weekend, mostly men in working clothes. A few women, nearly all older than the nurses, turned to look at the new arrivals, and several appeared to know Harry, who waved at them as he escorted Edith and Mary through to the garden at the back. It was little more than a big yard with tables and chairs dotted about, but there was clearly a keen gardener in charge, as the fences were covered in climbing plants and the sweet scent of honeysuckle filled the air, mingling with the hoppy aroma of the beer. There were more pots full of flowers, bright nasturtiums and busy Lizzies.

'Oh, this is very nice,' breathed Edith. Although she had no objection to public bars, she knew Alice would frown at the idea. But even her more particular friend could not have found fault with this.

'Glad you approve,' said Harry, as his hand lightly brushed the top of her arm. 'What can I get you to drink?'

'Shandy, please,' said Edith at once.

'Yes, me too,' said Mary.

Harry patted the shoulder of the man standing with his back to them. 'Joe, look after these two ladies until I return. You know them already — Edith and Mary.'

Joe turned around and politely said hello. Edith was struck again by how much he looked like his brother, and yet he didn't. Harry was in a blue shirt, with the sleeves rolled back and his tie loosened to the point where it was about to come undone. Joe was in a far more traditional white shirt, with a barely loosened dark tie, and his expression was friendly enough but somehow reserved at the same time. She could see that their eyes were very similar, and yet Harry's were full of energy whereas Joe's were deep and shrewd. Edith said 'hello' back brightly but she knew which brother she preferred.

'And this is our friend Billy,' Joe said, as another man came over to join them.

Edith observed how Billy was a little shorter than the Banham brothers, with black hair and eyes of grey-blue. 'Pleased to meet you,' he said, shaking their hands. 'Pardon me, ladies, I haven't had time to use my hand cream today and I know my grip's a bit rough.' He grinned to show he was joking but it was true — his palms were like sandpaper, Edith noticed. 'I work down the docks and there ain't nothing you can do about it.'

'I bet it's busy down there at the moment,' said Edith.

'You're telling me. I didn't think I was going to get here at all at one point, and I been down there since breakfast.' Billy didn't sound too sad about it though. 'And where do you work, girls? Or are you ladies of leisure?'

'We're nurses,' Mary said.

'Oh, nurses!' Billy's smile was even wider. 'Which hospital? My old ma used to clean up the Mothers in Clapton, that was before her knees gave out.'

'We're district nurses,' Edith explained. 'We do our basic hospital training and then we specialise, so we can go into people's homes and treat them there.'

Harry nodded in approval as he returned, bearing a tray of drinks. 'Here you are — shandies for you and a pint of the landlord's finest for me.' He raised his glass. 'Yes, that's how we met. Edith's friend came to help Kathleen, and Mattie got talking to her. Then we happened to bump into each other down Vicky Park. Small world, eh?' He took a long draught

126

of his beer. 'Ah, nectar. You don't know what you're missing, Edie.' He grinned at her and again she felt it was a look he kept just for her.

'Ah, was that you what did that?' asked Billy, turning to Mary.

'No, it was another of us from the same home — she's called Alice,' Mary explained.

'She didn't fancy comin' out with you tonight, then?' Billy asked.

Edith laughed. 'No, she's happier staying in and finishing her book. That's how she likes to spend her time off.'

'Takes all sorts,' said Billy, lifting his glass to his mouth.

Joe inclined his head. 'Which book would that be?' he asked, a small smile on his face.

Edith looked at him and tried not to show that she thought that was a very odd question. 'Well, I'm not sure. She reads so many. No, hang on — it's that one we went to the film of, Harry. The one with the smugglers — *Jamaica Inn*, that was it.'

'Oh.' Joe nodded. 'I've heard it's very good.'

'Couldn't tell you, but the film was riveting,' said Harry, his gaze on Edith even though he was speaking to his brother. His expression told her he was remembering holding her hand at the end. 'It's a dire warning not to get caught out on the remote moors on your own.'

'Oooh, I wouldn't dare,' said Mary and pretended to shudder. 'I'd be scared.' She glanced hopefully at Joe but he hadn't noticed.

He was glancing round at the other people in the beer garden, which was filling up with more and more workers, some obviously arriving straight from the nearby factory. Two women came in, pulling wide scarves from their hair, shaking out the dust. They were groaning theatrically, flapping the material. Joe acknowledged them with a nod and they came over.

'Hiya, Joe. How are you?' asked the taller one, a redhead. Then she turned to Harry. 'Well, well, look who it is. Haven't seen you for ages, Harry. Where've you been hiding yourself?'

'I'm in training,' he said, grinning and flexing the muscles of the arm not holding his beer. 'I can't be out gadding around, not with my busy schedule. Tonight's an exception.'

'Oh, and what's that in honour of?' the redhead purred.

Edith bridled a little, sensing that the woman would take over the conversation with the slightest encouragement.

'Oh, I promised to show Edith here the local pub,' Harry said easily, putting a light hand on her waist to bring her forward into the conversation. 'She's yet to become familiar with the bright lights of Dalston.'

Edith felt a rush of gratitude towards him and recognised that she didn't have to worry. 'Yes, that's right,' she said to the redhead. 'I moved here back at the beginning of June but haven't been to many places yet. Did you just come straight from work? Is that near here?'

The woman turned with a friendly look. 'That's right, I make boxes for gas masks,' she said. 'We used to do boxes for toys, but what with the coming war and all that . . . Look at me, all covered in dust from the cardboard, no matter how I try to get rid of it. It's an infernal nuisance. But we've got to keep the production lines running, we're even doing a shift tomorrow.'

'I don't mind, it'll help me pay for my wedding,' said the shorter woman. 'I'm Peggy and this is Clarrie. Oh, hang on, there's Pete over there. He hasn't seen me, excuse me a mo.' She edged her way past a group that had just come in and made her way to a tall, athletic-looking young man in a brown jacket, tapping him on the shoulder. He swung around and gave her a big hug.

'That's Peggy's intended,' said Clarrie in explanation. 'She puts her name down for every extra shift available — weekends, evenings, the lot. He's just as bad. They're planning an autumn wedding so they need every penny they can get.'

'Isn't that romantic,' breathed Mary. 'I'm sure I'd be the same.'

Edith bit back the remark that first sprang into her head, which was that Mary had told her about her parents and where they lived in Surrey, leading Edith to surmise that they weren't short of a bob or two. She doubted very much that Mary would ever have to work extra shifts, come the day that she got engaged. But she knew it would hurt her friend to mention it and so she just nodded.

Looking across the garden, she could see Peggy in earnest conversation with Pete. It looked as if she didn't like what he was telling her. He was leaning forward and everything about his posture was intense, whereas Peggy was growing more and more dismayed. Billy noticed the direction of Edith's glance and looked over at the couple as well. He caught Pete's eye, and Pete promptly beckoned him over.

'Scuse me, ladies,' he said, taking his drink and heading across to the couple.

'Well, he's in a hurry,' said Clarrie carelessly. 'Maybe something I said? He's not usually so keen to scarper. Well, never mind, do you work in a factory round here as well?'

'Oh, no,' Mary replied, and started to explain again what district nursing entailed.

Harry nudged closer to Edith. 'Seems as if we haven't had a chance to talk all evening,' he said quietly. 'I hope you don't mind. I wanted you to meet my friends.' He held her gaze and his dark brown eyes were full of warmth. 'I've known most of them for years.'

Edith looked up at him, and couldn't help smiling. She lost all thought of playing it cool. 'I like them,' she said happily. 'Thank you for the shandy too. You're very generous.'

'Think nothing of it,' he said, taking her free hand, but discreetly, so she wouldn't be embarrassed. 'Would you like another? It's thirsty work, meeting new people.'

'Maybe later.' She relished how warm his hand was, how big it was compared to hers and how safe it made her feel. She gently squeezed it, and felt a delicious sensation go through her as he squeezed hers back.

130

'They're bound to like you,' Harry assured her. 'Don't pay any mind to Clarrie, she's always teasing me. We were at school together when we were little and she started then. Nothing's changed in all the time since.'

'I've got friends like that, back in south London,' Edith admitted. 'What did you mean when you said you were training? Did you mean for the boxing? When's your next fight?'

Harry nodded. 'Yes, and I meant it when I said I hadn't been out much recently. Just with you.' He winked. 'I've got a big bout coming up in a few weeks. I missed my last one cos I had a really bad cold and there wasn't no point in even showing up. So there will be a lot riding on this one.' He stopped, suddenly almost shy. 'Would you come to watch me? Do you like boxing? You could cheer me on.'

Edith was briefly at a loss for words. It felt like he was asking her something important, that how she answered would mean a lot. 'Well . . . I don't know because I've never been to a fight,' she confessed. 'But I'd like to cheer for you, Harry. You'd be bound to win. I bet you're really good.'

He beamed with pride. 'As a matter of fact I am. I wouldn't ask you otherwise. I been doing it for years, and it's been a hard slog, but I'm getting better all the time now. I haven't lost for ten fights, not since I took on someone who'd won the area shield. He was good but I reckon I'm up to his standard now.' As he spoke Edith could tell how much he loved the sport and the pleasure he took in his progress.

'As long as you don't get hurt,' she said, half

131

jokingly but with an edge in her voice, as that was exactly what she feared.

'With you there watching? No chance,' he laughed. 'You'll be my lucky mascot. I'll be unbeatable if you come along to watch, just you see.'

'Sounds as if I'd better, then, or else you're at risk of injury, and as a nurse I can't have that,' said Edith smartly, her eyes dancing even though part of her still dreaded him being hurt.

Billy had come back across to them as they talked and now he gave Harry a significant look. 'Can I have a quick word?' he asked, a note of urgency in his voice. 'Sorry for interrupting,' he added, making an apologetic face at Edith.

'No, no, not at all,' she said, slightly piqued to have the moment broken so soon. She sipped her shandy as Harry stepped away a little to have a quick conversation with his friend.

'Right,' she heard him say. 'Let's do it, then.'

'Shall we take Joe?' Billy asked.

'No, he needs to stay here with the ladies. You, me and Pete will sort it out.' Harry's face had completely changed. A look of fury had come across it and his body had gone rigid as he drained his pint then plunged his hands into his pockets. Swiftly he drew his brother to one side and spoke softly into his ear. She couldn't see Joe's face to gauge his reaction.

★ ★ ★

Joe blinked once to take in what Harry had said and then pinched the fold of skin between his

132

eyebrows. 'You're kidding, right?'

Harry reared back. 'I am not bloody kidding. Someone's got to put a stop to this, you must see that. The man's a right bastard, we all know it, and he can't get away with this.'

'That's not the point,' said Joe, urgent now. He knew what his brother was like, all act now and think later. 'The risk is you make it worse. You beat him up, get caught, and Bob's your uncle, it's you who gets into trouble. How's that going to help?'

'We won't beat him up. Not really. Just give him a fright. Enough to put the wind up him, stop him doing it again.'

Joe looked his brother straight in the eye. 'You sure? I know what you're capable of. You hit someone and that's it, lights out.'

'Joe, I promise. I'll let the others do most of it, we'll just rough him up a bit. I'll stand there and keep them in order, but if he sees me he knows I can floor him with one punch.'

'That's exactly what I meant,' Joe pointed out.

'Not that I will.'

'See that you don't. For God's sake don't make things worse for Kath than they already are. She may not even thank you for it.'

Harry pursed his lips. 'But we're doing it for her. To protect her.'

Joe gazed skywards. There was no stopping this, he knew, despite the perils of someone coming between a man and his wife, but he had to make Harry understand that he couldn't allow his little brother to get on the wrong side of the law.

'Come on, Harry,' called Pete, making to leave.

Harry turned. 'I got to go.'

'Remember what you promised. Don't make it worse, Harry.'

'I won't.' And he was heading back over to Edith.

★ ★ ★

The daylight was fading now but — even with what was left of the sun behind him — Edith could tell Harry was very angry as he came back towards her. 'Listen, I'm sorry, but something has come up that needs taking care of,' he said. 'You wait here with Joe and I'll be back in no time. But I gotta go. See you very soon.' He leant in and swiftly kissed her cheek before hurrying out of a back gate she hadn't even seen was there, immediately followed by Billy and Pete.

11

Edith couldn't fault Joe's manners. He bought another round of drinks and assured them that it was nothing to worry about and the other men would be back in no time. Mary had accepted this at face value, and seemed to have forgotten her former opinion of Joe as uninteresting, as she tried hard to get him to flirt back with her. When that failed, she turned to Clarrie and Peggy, asking them all about the factory and quizzing Peggy about her wedding plans.

It was only when Mary said she had to powder her nose and persuaded the other two women to show her where to go that Edith had a chance to press Joe for the truth.

'You might as well tell me,' she said, her eyes wide with concern. 'I wasn't born yesterday — I can see something's up.'

Joe sighed. 'All right. You're right, we just heard some news.' He shifted uneasily. 'How much has Alice told you about our friend Kathleen?'

'Well, I know she's the reason we know you at all,' said Edith. 'Then at the start of this week Alice got called to her house because she said she'd had a fall. But Alice didn't believe that was what had really happened.'

Joe shrugged. 'That's what she's maintained all this week, but we know that's not the case. Mattie saw her that morning — she's no fool.

135

She said Kath had marks on her wrist from where she'd been grabbed or dragged. Kath's husband turned up on Saturday morning, apparently as if nothing was wrong; as though he hadn't left her for months with hardly any money or letting her know how or where he was. Mattie and Ma looked after the baby most of the weekend. Then Monday morning, she looks in a state and he's scarpered. Draw your own conclusions.'

Edith nodded sadly. 'That's pretty well what Alice thought — the injuries weren't consistent with Kathleen's story, but fitted being pushed around by someone else.'

'Usually she's in and out of our house all the time, but we haven't seen her all week,' Joe went on. 'Mattie's been going over there instead. She said she didn't want us to see her in that state, but Harry's been asking around, seeing if he can get word of where Ray went. Nobody had seen hide nor hair of him, certainly not down the docks, or Billy would've known. I might as well tell you, Billy used to be sweet on Kathleen so he was spitting blood when he heard.'

'So that's why he was in such a rush,' said Edith, abruptly losing her taste for her shandy. She put her glass down on the nearest table.

'Anyway, someone at Pete's workplace told him that Ray would be at the Dog and Whistle this evening, so they've set off to find him,' Joe explained. 'I warned them not to do anything stupid. It's all well and good trying to help Kathleen, but I don't want them putting themselves at risk. That will have the exact opposite effect. I said they'll have to stick to pointing out to him that he won't get away with it again.'

Edith could hear the doubt in his voice. 'But if Billy's angry and Harry's ready for a fight . . . what if they get hurt? What if the police get called?'

'You don't call the police to the Dog and Whistle,' said Joe. 'It's not that sort of place. Don't you worry about Harry, he can take care of himself. It's just not how I like to go about things. Ray's a cowardly bully but there are ways and means.'

Edith nodded. Where she grew up, nobody would have thought of calling the police, either. You sorted out your own problems. All the same her stomach churned with anxiety. 'What can we do?' she asked, quietly now as out of the corner of her eye she could see Mary returning with the other two young women.

'Nothing,' said Joe bluntly. 'We wait here. Drink up, Edith, put a smile on your face and maybe it'll all be fine.'

★　★　★

Alice sat back against her pillows, setting down her book. She'd finally turned the last page, although she'd deliberately made it last all evening, getting the very most from it. She could see why Edith would have enjoyed the film — the stirring story, the dramatic settings. She'd loved it, all the more so because she secretly suspected it wouldn't have been Joe's cup of tea at all. Still, this meant she could return it to him tomorrow so he could take it back to the library in the coming week. She smiled at the thought of seeing him again, then stopped herself. What was she doing, thinking of him late into the evening?

Her thoughts turned to the conversation she'd had with Janet Phipps when she'd visited St Benedict's earlier in the week. She'd ruefully told the teacher about her encounter with Pauline and Janet had laughed. 'Yes, that sounds like the Gran we know,' she said. 'Still, at least Pauline's got her. The mother isn't around much, so I believe.'

'That's a shame,' Alice had replied, nibbling on a shortbread that Janet had provided from her own batch.

'Her little friend has the opposite problem — her mother hates to let her go and always waits at the school gates for ages,' Janet had gone on. 'You know, little Dotty, with the ringlets? I'm sure I shouldn't say it but her mother absolutely smothers her. How we're going to get her to stand on her own two feet I really couldn't say. I dread to think what will happen if the class is evacuated.'

'Do you really think they will be?' Alice asked, remembering Fiona Dewar's warnings.

Janet had set down her cup and saucer and stared out of the classroom window into the deserted play-ground. 'Yes, she said. 'I should say it's inevitable. And soon. All those careful plans will have to be executed to the letter to keep those children out of harm's way.'

Alice turned over, feeling the coolness of the

pillow-case on her cheek. Such a lot had happened since they'd first arrived at Victory Walk. It wasn't even that long ago, only early June, and yet it felt like ages. She and Edith had adapted to the work and started to get to know who was who in the local community — the nice doctors, like old Dr Patcham, the others like Beastly Beasley. The nearby shopkeepers, like the one who knew which paper she bought and who would now keep one back for her if she was running late and they were liable to sell out. The teachers and pupils at St Benedict's. Above all, the many and varied patients.

She felt increasingly confident in the work. If she was honest, some of it wasn't what she had expected; the huge numbers of households living in poverty was something she'd known about and had seen to an extent at home in Liverpool, but to see it up close was a different matter. The sheer difficulty of giving advice on health and hygiene when there was barely access to running water for so many patients; it stretched her ingenuity to its limits. Then again, she'd been prepared to see regular cases of diphtheria, and yet for all its difficulties the borough had managed to limit cases of that horrible disease. It made her feel her work was worth it, and if she kept up the message that prevention was better than cure and led by her own example, then things would slowly get better. Yet when the war came . . . Sighing, she tried to settle to sleep, knowing that worrying wouldn't help.

★ ★ ★

The next hour passed agonisingly slowly as Edith pretended to join in the conversation and look as if she was enjoying herself while she waited for Harry to return. Every second seemed to last for an eternity. All around her people were chatting and laughing, just like on any other Friday night. Mary was getting on famously with Clarrie and Peggy, who didn't seem to be particularly worried about the absence of the men — even though Peggy at least must have had a fair idea of why they had left. Edith wondered if it was perhaps because she was a nurse and had seen all too often at first hand the damage a street fight could do. She could tell Harry would be well able to look after himself, but all it took was one lucky punch from his opponent . . . she tried not to let her thoughts wander down that track.

At last there was a commotion from the direction of the back gate. Edith looked across to see Pete, his tall frame clearly visible above the crowd, his face clearly bearing new scratches even from this distance and in the dim streetlight. The crowd parted to let him through and he instantly sought out Peggy, who whirled around at the sound of his voice. He was followed by Billy, also bruised and bloodied, walking a little stiffly but grinning from ear to ear. Finally Harry appeared, his blue shirt smeared with blood and his knuckles red, but his eyes gleaming.

'Harry.' Edith couldn't hold back her worry. 'Are you all right?'

He smiled and she could see he was glad she'd been concerned for him. 'More than all right,' he

140

said. 'We found the bastard, scuse my language, and we sorted him out good and proper. He won't be hurting Kathleen again, the filthy coward. Not now he knows we're on to him.'

'But your hands,' Edith protested. 'And your shirt, it's got blood all over it.'

'Not mine,' said Harry grimly. 'He didn't get a chance to lay a hand on me. He's not fast enough, doesn't know the moves like I do.'

'What about Pete and Billy?' she asked. 'They look as if they've been in the wars.'

Harry shrugged a little. 'It might look like that but Ray's come off much worse, believe me. They aren't hurt, or not really. They'll be fine tomorrow. Pete's got Peggy to kiss him better and that'll work wonders.'

Edith shook her head. 'Harry Banham, what can I say? You take off like that and now you're back here telling jokes . . . '

'Hey.' He caught her hand in his. She looked down and could see the wounded knuckles. 'You weren't really worried, were you? I didn't mean to frighten you. We had to do it; we couldn't let him get away with hurting Kath like that.'

'No, I know.' Edith realised that if she wasn't careful she might cry. The effort of hiding her anxiety inside for most of the evening was beginning to tell. 'It was the waiting around, that's all.' She shivered.

'Are you cold?' he said at once. 'You must be, you've been standing out here with only that cardigan thing to keep you warm. Shall I walk you home?'

'It's not closing time yet, don't you want to go

141

into the pub?' she asked.

He gave her a rueful grin. 'No, I might give that a miss. Someone's bound to see my shirt and get the wrong idea.'

Edith nodded. She didn't want him to get into trouble, not now he'd returned without any major injury to himself. She also realised that Mary would walk home with them and they'd lose any chance to have a moment to themselves. 'You came in by the back gate,' she said. 'Where does that lead?'

As if following her thoughts, Harry nodded. 'It opens onto an alley, at the back of some gardens. Come, I'll show you.'

Quietly they made their way past the others in the beer garden and out of the gate, until they were standing on a narrow path that ran beside a set of railings, under a tree which filtered the streetlight and the light from the moon which had now risen. She could make out the shape of his face, partly covered in shadow. He drew her to him.

'Mind the blood,' she whispered, but she didn't really care. It was all she wanted, to be in his strong arms, feeling safer than she'd ever known, and sensing somehow that this was where she belonged. They stood there while the shapes thrown by the moonlight changed, the lawn on the other side of the railing now glistening with dew, a few birds calling. He breathed into her hair and stroked her back through the thin bolero and cotton of her cream frock. 'I didn't want you to worry,' he repeated. 'I never want to make you upset, Edith. I'd do anything not to do that. I just want you to be happy.'

She rested her head against his chest, which was warm through the blue shirt. 'You make me happy,' she murmured. 'You do, Harry Banham.' She held him tight around his waist and thought how well he fitted, how well their bodies suited each other. She sighed, knowing she had to get back, wishing this moment could last for ever.

'Ready to go?' Again he seemed to read her thoughts.

'I'd better.' She looked up at him in the moonlit shadows and he bent to kiss her gently, and then more passionately, before eventually she broke away, a little breathless.

'Come on then.' He smiled and held fast to her hand.

'We'd better fetch Mary,' she said, not wanting to leave her friend to make her own way home.

'Of course,' he said gallantly, pushing open the back gate to the beer garden and waving at their group.

They hastily said their goodbyes and headed back down the terraced street, Edith mindful of the ten o'clock curfew. They might just make it. She'd taken the precaution of leaving a lower window slightly open in case they had to climb in, but it was so much easier to go in the usual way, especially as there were two of them. She felt as if she'd had enough excitement for one night.

Mary chatted on, oblivious, and Harry made all the right noises in the right places, as if he were listening to every word she said. Edith was sure he wasn't. She felt as if every nerve of his being was attuned to her, just as every cell of her body was alert to his every movement. Something had irrevocably changed in her and it was because of him. Walking along the darkened streets, she knew that whatever happened in the future, in some deep way that she could not quite name, she was now connected to Harry Banham, wherever that might take her.

12

'You cut it very fine yesterday evening, Miss Gillespie,' said Gwen at breakfast the next morning. 'You seem to be making a habit of it. Don't think I haven't noticed. One further transgression and you're in even deeper trouble than before.' She gave Edith a sharp look. Edith, who'd had very little sleep as she'd been so wound up by yesterday's events, just shrugged. Gwen could have no formal cause for complaint as she and Mary had come through the front door at three minutes to ten, trying not to make any noise as they did so. Gwen obviously had extremely acute powers of hearing.

Alice, at Edith's side, wasn't sure what had happened, as she'd fallen asleep before her friend came home and for once Edith hadn't gone straight in to wake her. She just smiled politely as she set her tray down and waited for the older woman to pass by. Gwen stacked her used plate and cutlery ready to be washed and left, shooting another look at Edith over her shoulder.

'What was all that about?' Alice demanded as soon as she had vanished through the door.

'She's making a fuss over nothing as usual,' Edith said, spreading marmalade on her toast. 'You'd be proud of me, Alice. We got back just in time. So, she can't complain. We were quiet as

145

mice and stone-cold sober, models of good behaviour in fact.'

'Really?' Alice wasn't convinced.

'Well, nearly.' Edith flashed a grin. 'It was quite an evening.'

'How?' Alice took a bite from her own toast, and listened as Edith explained. Somehow she wasn't surprised, even though she felt very uneasy about Harry and his friends taking matters into their own hands like that. As a Londoner, part of her understood the urge to protect someone they thought of as one of their own, while the other side of her recoiled from the violence. 'And Joe was in the pub with you, did you say? He didn't join in?'

'No, he stayed with us,' Edith said. 'Why, do you think it makes him a coward? I don't think that was it at all. Harry said he thought it was a big risk and they could make things worse if they weren't careful. He's probably more sensible, to be honest.'

'No, I don't think he's a coward,' Alice said.

'But you don't know him that well, do you?' Edith asked. 'You only met him that one time in the park . . . that's right, isn't it?' She came to a halt at the look on her friend's face. 'Alice, is there something you haven't told me?' Her expression darkened.

Alice shifted awkwardly in the hard-backed chair. She'd chosen to say nothing about the book because there was nothing much to say, but now she realised that by not mentioning it at all it seemed as if she was hiding something — the very opposite of what she'd intended. 'It's not

146

really anything,' she said hurriedly. 'I met Joe again when I was visiting a patient, the postman — you remember? It turns out he works with Joe, who came over to see how he was. He said he'd lend me a book, which he sent round. That's all. There's really no more to it.'

Edith frowned. 'Then why didn't you say? Here am I, meeting up with Harry, and all the while you've been seeing his brother behind my back. Now I feel like a complete fool. He even asked after you last night — asked what you were reading! He knew all the while and he's going to think I'm an idiot. Thanks a bunch. Some friend you are.' She pushed her plate away, the toast only half eaten.

'Edie! Don't be like that.' Alice's voice was full of regret. 'Honestly, I'm not seeing him — not like that. He's not sweet on me or anything. He just lent me a book. It was only because he knew Harry had taken you to see the film. We'd probably never even have mentioned it otherwise.'

Edith looked sceptical, unsure whether to believe her friend or not. If it had been anyone else, the whole thing would have sounded unlikely — a man didn't go round putting himself out like that if he didn't like the girl in question. But Alice was usually honest to a fault, and Edith knew all too well that she genuinely had little interest in finding herself a young man. She'd been hurt too badly before. She sighed. 'But you could have told me. It seems very odd otherwise.'

Alice nodded miserably. 'I can see what you

mean now. I didn't mean it to look that way. It's just you were so very keen on Harry, I didn't want to make it seem as if I had someone too. It's nothing like the same thing. You do still like him, don't you?'

Edith sighed in turn, picked up her knife and turned it around before putting it back on her plate. 'Yes. Even after last night — well, almost especially after last night.' She raised her gaze to meet Alice's. 'When I knew he'd gone after Ray and that there was a chance he'd get hurt, or picked up by the police, or something — I couldn't bear it. I've never felt like that before. I can't stand the thought of anything happening to him. Does that sound daft? He's not just some fellow I've met in a dance hall and had a bit of fun with. It's different with him.' She blushed. 'It's as if we belong together.'

'Oh, Edie.' Alice's heart went out to her friend. 'Does he feel the same? Have you told him?'

Edie made a little face. 'I've only just got to know him. I don't want to seem too serious too soon. That puts a man off, we both know that. But I think he likes me.' She blinked. 'I just want the time to get to know him better. He's asked me to go to see him boxing in a few weeks.'

'A proper match, you mean?'

'Yes, he says I'll be his good-luck charm. Do you think I should go? Will you come too?'

'Maybe Mary would enjoy it more,' said Alice diplomatically. It wasn't a sport she enjoyed. 'As for whether you should go, that's up to you, isn't it? If you want to go, then go.'

'I think he'd like me to be there,' said Edith, uncharacteristically shy.

Alice took another quick mouthful of toast. 'Then you should go. If the thought of watching him hitting someone else and getting hit back doesn't put you off.'

Edith laughed. 'I know you don't like it. But at least with a proper match there's a referee and everything. It can't possibly be as bad as knowing he's gone looking for a fight in the street and anything could happen.' She shuddered.

'But he's back in one piece,' Alice reminded her. 'Don't think about it any more, Edie. It's upsetting you.'

Edith nodded. 'Oh, Alice. I don't want him to be hurt. He's special, he really is. Are you sure you won't come to watch him? Promise me you'll at least think about it?'

Alice hesitated, and then reluctantly nodded, realising that her friend had fallen hard for this young man. This was going to be different. She wondered if it would change their friendship, but it was too soon to tell.

'He seems like a nice man,' she said seriously. 'But, I'd best be off now. Look at the time — I'm late already.'

'Late?' echoed Edith. 'For what?'

Alice grinned. 'I've got a book to return.'

★ ★ ★

Harry raised his arms in triumph. It was the best moment of his life — his biggest win, in front of

149

his largest-ever audience. Everyone was roaring his name, stamping and clapping, and out of the corner of his eye he could see Edith, along with her friends Alice and Mary. It added an extra-special something to know she was there, cheering him on. His heart swelled.

'Congratulations.' Now the officials and dignitaries were in the ring, all keen to shake his hand, give him praise and accolades. He greeted them in turn without taking in their names. That must be the mayor — he wore a large gold chain of office. The lights and the noise were dazzling. Harry knew he should be feeling exhausted after the tough fight but he was riding on a wave of euphoria. He never wanted this moment to end. It was what he'd trained for, making all the early starts and weekend workouts worthwhile. He was about to hit the big time, if he played his cards right.

Still buzzing with the excitement and adrenaline, he allowed himself to be led backstage, to where still more men crowded around, eager to congratulate him. The photographer from the local paper was there and snapped him with the mayor. The president of the local club came to stand beside them and there were more photographs. It took a long time for the uproar to subside, as the dignitaries were ushered back into the main hall, and the people slowly thinned out. He glimpsed Joe making his way through the door and across to him.

'Well done.' His brother gave him a bear hug. Joe of all people knew the work that had gone into this, all the nights in the pub Harry had turned down, the family occasions he'd missed, been late for or left early. 'You deserved to win. The other fellow was tough but you were better.'

'I was, wasn't I.' Harry knew this was true. The right man had won on the night, and it was him.

'Aren't you dying to sit down and have a drink?' Joe asked. 'I would be.'

'No,' Harry protested. 'Not yet. I couldn't sit still if you paid me. Where are the girls? Where's Edith?' He looked around as if she might have come in without his noticing.

Joe laughed. 'What, do you think she's in here with you all sweaty and horrible?'

Harry looked down at his torso and shook his head. 'No, you're right, of course not. This is no place for ladies. You haven't left them alone out there, have you?'

'Don't worry, Billy's with them,' Joe reassured him. 'If you get changed then you can soak up their admiration in person. Hurry up, aren't you meant to put on something warm after all that?'

'Don't fuss.' Harry couldn't help but notice that Joe was still acting like the big brother who had had a lifetime of being told to look after his siblings. Old habits died hard — even when the younger brother had just won a major boxing championship and was taller and in far better shape. 'I won't catch my death of cold, you don't have to worry. You can pass me that towel if you're that bothered.'

Joe reached for the huge towel that hung on a hook on the back of the door. As he lifted it off, the door began to swing open again and a man who was maybe in his late thirties, dressed in army uniform, came in.

'Congratulations, Mr Banham.' The man strode confidently forward, arm outstretched, and shook hands with Harry. 'That was as impressive a display of prowess as I've ever seen, I don't mind admitting.'

'Thank you,' said Harry, draping himself in the towel, wondering what this man wanted.

'I used to box myself a bit, and I can see you're very competent,' the man went on. 'There are plenty of talented young men who can land a punch but you fight with your brain as well as your body. It's surprisingly rare, and you're not very old, are you?'

'Twenty-one,' said Harry.

'Still plenty of time to improve even further, then,' said the man. 'I'm so sorry, I haven't introduced myself. James Ingham. Major James Ingham.'

Both brothers stared at the details of the uniform, suddenly aware of the stature of their guest. Joe recovered first.

'Joseph Banham, older brother of the champ here,' he said, offering his own hand.

'You must be very proud,' said Major Ingham. 'Don't let me interrupt you — I can see I've come in at a bad moment.'

'No, not at all . . . ' Harry began.

'You need your time to gather yourself after a bout, I know that only too well,' the major went on. 'Don't underestimate the body's need for that. You take your time but I should like to buy you a drink in the bar afterwards, if you'll allow me. Both of you, that is. And any special guests you might have,' he continued smoothly, as if this was only to be expected. 'I'll wait for you there.' He turned and left the room before either of them could object.

Harry was thinking. 'Ingham . . . James Ingham . . . and he's what, fifteen or more years older than me . . . God, Joe, you know who that is, don't you?'

Joe shook his head. 'He's a major in the army, he told us that much.'

Harry looked to the ceiling. 'It's only bleeding Jimmy Ingham. He was inter-services champion about ten years ago. He's boxing royalty. Joe, that was Jimmy Ingham, I can't believe it.'

'And he thought you were good,' said Joe. 'Even better, he wants to buy us a drink. Come on, get your skates on. You can't go out there and mix with the great and the good if you're all sweaty with your hair sticking up, and anyway Edith will be wanting to congratulate you.' He gave his brother a wink.

Harry grinned. 'You might get a smile yourself off her mate, Alice, thanks to me. You'd like that, wouldn't you, Joe?'

Joe playfully punched his big little brother on the arm. 'Mind your own business and don't be cheeky. C'mon, let's get out there, before some other spivs get there before us.'

⋆ ⋆ ⋆

Edith's eyes shone with pride at Harry's achievement. It was as if he'd done it just for her,

153

even though she knew that wasn't really true. Still, he'd been adamant he wanted her there and she felt that might have just made the difference. She hadn't known what to expect of the fight itself and at first she'd been nervous, flinching every time his opponent had landed a punch on Harry, worried he'd be permanently hurt. Yet, as the bout had gone on, she could begin to appreciate how good he was, how fast his footwork, the sheer power in his arms. She felt a keen sense of delight that those were the arms which had held her close, shielding her from the outside world.

Billy led the three young women over to the bar area in response to the message he'd just received. 'Through here, ladies,' he said gallantly, making way for them to pass unimpeded. Mary gazed around, fascinated, her arm linked through Edith's, basking in the reflected glory of being part of the new champion's inner circle. She'd put her hair up for the occasion and put on her best summer coat, over a dress with a deeper neckline than she usually wore. She was pleased to see she was attracting plenty of notice.

Alice followed slightly behind, feeling awkward. It wasn't the sort of place she could be comfortable in, and yet she could see that Harry was good. Possibly more than good. She could sense how proud Edith was of him, and Joe too, even though she hadn't had much of a chance to speak to him yet. During the fight it had been too noisy, and afterwards he had been swept up with all the crowds trying to talk to his triumphant brother.

Billy was about to escort them to a small table covered in a maroon velour cloth, when there was a commotion from the opposite side, followed by clapping, as Harry came into the area, followed by Joe. Edith instantly sprinted across and flung her arms around him. Harry picked her up and twirled her around, his happiness complete, as the photographer took yet another set of pictures.

Major Ingham indicated that they should all join him at the larger table where he had installed himself, along with another man in army uniform. 'Well done again, Banham,' he said, slapping Harry heartily on the back. 'And may I ask who is your very beautiful friend? I beg your pardon, friends?'

Harry introduced Edith, Alice and Mary, then took a seat in between Edith and the major.

'Some champagne, I think,' said the major. He waved to the barman, who had obviously been prepared; he hurried over, carrying a tray, on which he'd balanced an ice bucket containing a glistening green bottle and an assortment of fluted glasses.

Edith eyed it in amazement, but Mary nodded as if she was rather more used to such goings-on. 'Don't mind if I do,' she said as the other officer popped open the cork.

Harry accepted a glass, as it would clearly have been rude not to, although for two pins he'd as soon as had a pint of bitter. Joe exchanged a look with his brother, evidently wishing the same, but he too accepted a flute and raised it. 'To Harry,' he said.

'To Harry,' everyone echoed, and Harry beamed in appreciation, one arm around the back of Edith's chair.

Mary turned her smile on the officer who'd opened the bottle and began to charm him, while he seemed only too happen to listen.

Joe, who had wondered if this might turn out to be an awkward occasion, breathed a low sigh of relief. He'd had champagne exactly once before in his whole life, and he suspected Harry had never tried it. He was pretty certain Billy hadn't either, although their old friend was slugging it back as if there was no tomorrow and the officer had already topped him up. Mary was perfectly at home, but then, Joe had clocked her accent on their first meeting and could assume she had been brought up in a very different social circle to that of Jeeves Street. He looked down the table at Alice, who was tentatively sipping at her glass, hardly drinking anything. He hoped he could catch her eye . . . Joe guessed this wasn't the sort of night out she was normally used to and was keen to talk to her, to put her at her ease, though she and Edith seemed to be enjoying themselves. Joe supposed that as nurses they were accustomed to meeting all kinds of people and instantly establishing a rapport so maybe she didn't need to be put at ease. It wouldn't do to be shy and bumbling if you had to persuade a patient what was in their best interests and had only a short time in which to do it. At that moment, Alice looked down the table towards him and saw him looking at her. He smiled and mouthed, 'Are you all right?' at her and she shrugged and nodded, returning his smile with a wry one of her own.

Reluctantly, he turned his attention back to the conversation.

' . . . in the event of war breaking out in the near future,' the officer was saying earnestly.

'Oh, surely not!' Mary exclaimed. 'It's too bad. I can't believe that's really going to happen.' Her hand flew to her throat.

Joe suppressed a groan, as everyone else looked at Mary in sad amazement. Did she really think that it could still be avoided? Joe's limited knowledge of the young woman had taught him that she was a perpetual optimist, not exactly switched on when it came to current affairs — unlike Alice, who he'd swiftly realised followed them obsessively, or, by the looks of it, Edith, who might not come across as the studious kind but was proving herself to be very quick on the uptake in all manner of ways.

'I would love to agree with you, my dear,' said the major, his serious grey eyes resting on Mary, 'but I am afraid it is merely a question of when, not if. We would do well to make what preparations we can, with what little time is left to us before it all begins.'

Mary paled and bit her lip.

Major Ingham turned back to Harry. 'This brings me to one particular reason I wanted to speak to you,' he said. 'Forgive me for being so direct but, as I just said, we might not have the luxury of time. Have you thought what you will do once hostilities are underway? Have you joined any of the reserves?'

Harry shook his head. 'Not yet, but I won't chicken out if it comes to it,' he said. 'I want to do my bit. I hate that Hitler, and those followers of his who've been running all over the East End and stirring up trouble. We catch any of those on our patch, we throw them out of the pub.'

The major nodded, as if he'd expected nothing less. 'Then you'll probably have worked out that there is likely to be conscription of one kind or another. You' — he gazed at Harry, Joe and Billy in turn — 'are just the sort of young men who'll be in demand. If you act now, you stand a better chance of getting a choice in what you do, rather than being forced into a situation that doesn't suit you.'

Joe cleared his throat. 'What do you mean, exactly?' He met the major's eyes and didn't back down.

The major clasped and re-clasped his hands, which rested on the deep red tablecloth. 'I suppose what I'm trying to do is get my bid in before anyone else does, or at least with regard to your brother. You, Harry,' and he swivelled around again, 'are a genuine talent in the boxing world and I'd hate to see that go to waste because you are called up to serve your country.'

Harry bridled. 'I just said, I intend to serve if it comes to it. I won't ask for a way out just cos I'm a boxer.'

'No, no, that's not what I had in mind,' said the major hurriedly. 'You may know that I was inter-services champion myself when I was not much older than you. You may also know that the army produces most of the champions in that competition. That's not to say that the Air Force and Navy don't have good coaches, or that they don't take boxing seriously — but if I say so myself, the army does it better. You may want to take that into consideration.'

Harry took a slow sip from his glass. This wasn't how he'd expected the evening to go. He glanced down at Edith, who had an alarmed expression on her face. She fiddled anxiously with the stem of her flute and looked swiftly away, and already he knew her well enough to understand this was because she didn't want him to see she was afraid.

'Harry,' said Joe, 'we can't make any sudden decisions. What the major has to say is valid but we have to talk to Ma and Pa.'

'Of course,' said the major. 'Don't rush into anything — but don't leave it until it's too late, either.' He reached into his pocket. 'Here's my card. I've written an address on the back. If you do decide to take my advice, go to that recruiting office and explain I have sent you. I'm sure your local office is very efficient but, if you do sign up with us, I want to know that I can personally oversee your progress.'

Harry blinked slowly as he tucked the card into his own pocket. To be under Jimmy Ingham's wing — that was more than he could ever have hoped for. He hadn't really thought about signing up yet, but it made sense in many ways. He didn't mind his current job, in the local hardware store, but he only worked there to give himself lots of time for boxing. It wasn't exactly a reserved profession and nor was it something he wanted to continue for the rest of his life.

'I want to talk it over with Edith too,' he said, squeezing her hand.

Edith's chin went up. 'You must do what you think is right, Harry,' she said with just the smallest shake in her voice. 'I'll be proud of you whatever you do. You're a brave man, I knew that already, but you showed us all this evening. I'll support whatever decision you make.'

Joe nodded, impressed by this young woman who'd so recently come into his brother's life, but who was showing herself to be mature beyond her years. Again, he brought himself up short. As a nurse, she must have seen things that most women her age would have known nothing about. Also, if it came to war, she'd be in the thick of it. Mary, meanwhile, looked as if she might cry at any moment.

He glanced along to where Alice was sitting. She'd calmly listened while all of this was going on and Joe was struck again by her poise and demeanour. Watchful and unruffled. She was the sort of person this country would need when the going got tough, he thought. He'd seen her only once since she'd returned the book, and that was just briefly, but what she'd said had stuck in his mind. She'd been with her teacher friend, Janet Phipps, and he'd bumped into them on what turned out to be the last day of the school term. Alice had told him that all the parents had just been given a letter, asking them to listen for announcements on the radio that would tell them when the children needed to be evacuated. She and Janet had prepared a plan for the junior

160

classes of St Benedict's. Mary might not want to believe it, but people all around her were getting ready for war.

Edith swallowed a gulp of champagne and quietly prayed that it would give her courage. She'd been so proud of Harry when he'd won, and for a wonderful few minutes she'd entertained the idea of another kind of life — being feted as the girlfriend of a champion, her picture in the papers, going to parties and having one long good time. Already that bubble had burst. Reality was staring her in the face. War was coming, but Harry would fight for his country just as hard as he'd fought in the ring. Maybe this way he could do both. She had to be glad that he'd been given the chance to make that choice.

She didn't want to think about what it would be like without him, waiting to hear how he was, what he was doing, if he was unhurt, or even if he was still alive. It had been bad enough for that hour or so in the pub garden. How much worse would it be to endure months of not knowing? She clenched her jaw, trying not to give way to her emotions. She'd only known Harry for a couple of months but it was as if he'd always been there, an essential part of her existence. Now she was just going to have to learn to be apart from him. It wasn't fair. But she couldn't break down and show her disappointment now. It was the night of his triumph: he was her hero, and she had to remember that, hang on to it, whatever the future was about to bring.

13

September 1939

'Pinch, punch, first of the month,' said Fiona Dewar brightly as she joined Gwen at the breakfast table. They were the only ones down so far. The dawn had not long broken and the birds could still be heard calling outside in the trees at the back of the yard.

Gwen looked up. 'You're very cheerful today.'

Fiona tipped her head to one side. 'No point in being gloomier than necessary, Gwen. There'll be enough of that to come. It's down to us to buoy our spirits up, and we must set an example to our younger colleagues.'

Gwen spooned up some porridge. 'I wonder how they'll cope,' she said. 'It's going to be the biggest test of character any of them will ever have faced. I worry about them — I have some serious doubts where a few of them are concerned.'

Fiona looked kindly at her old friend. 'You don't need to worry, or at least not yet. Worrying before the event never changed anything, you know that as well as I do.' She buttered her toast. 'Better make the most of these everyday luxuries, hey? I do like my toast smothered in this stuff.' She took a big bite.

'Miriam's told her son to stay in America,' Gwen said. 'I think she's trying to organise an escape plan if it becomes necessary. She's already got a family staying in her spare rooms — they've come over from Austria and can barely speak a word of English.'

'The poor things.' Fiona's expression changed from lively to sad and then to resolute. 'She's doing the right thing. It doesn't hurt to plan. We will all need our organisational skills soon.'

Gwen ate her food thoughtfully. 'Should we think about offering first-aid training to the general public? That might be reassuring for them — and it could help to keep some of our flightier young colleagues in check.'

Fiona couldn't help laughing. 'Oh really, Gwen. Sorry, no, that's a good idea, but they aren't a bunch of schoolgirls, you know.'

'No?' Gwen raised her eyebrows. 'You do know that Edith Gillespie has only just returned before ten o'clock on a number of occasions, having been caught flagrantly breaking curfew with that Mary Perkins a matter of days after arriving. Those two lack discipline, no two ways about it.'

'Oh, surely not.' Fiona set down her last slice of toast. 'There have been no complaints about their professional conduct, have there? In fact the reverse. They are both assets to our establishment, I'd say.'

'That's as maybe,' said Gwen darkly, 'but it's a breach of discipline all the same. If they are missing their sleep they will find their ability to concentrate is affected. That's a fact.'

Fiona sighed. 'I realise they shouldn't be defying the curfew, but all the same, as long as they aren't making mistakes in their work, then I'm inclined to let them have their fun while they can. Edith was in the paper last week, wasn't she, with that new local boxing hero? Good-looking chap, I'll say that much. Bit of a catch, you might say.'

Gwen gave her colleague a level look, as if to indicate she herself would say no such thing.

'I'd better get cracking.' Fiona stood up. 'Plenty of letters to attend to first thing. Do tell Gladys I'll need her to go to the post office if you see her, won't you? I'm going to be rather busy.'

Gwen raised her eyebrows as she swallowed more porridge.

Fiona nodded. 'Today's the day. I have to find Alice Lake and then we have to organise the evacuation of St Benedict's. Trains are leaving Hackney Downs at noon.'

⋆   ⋆   ⋆

Alice gazed along the platform, trying to gauge how many children had yet to be recorded on her clipboard. They ranged from the very smallest in the reception class up to young teenagers, the big brothers and sisters of the pupils she had met. There were mothers who had very young children, who had chosen to accompany them to wherever they were being sent — somewhere safer than London's East End. A few were carrying babes in arms. All had the regulation gas masks in their carriers, and most clutched bags of belongings.

Alice was impressed that so far most of them,

164

mothers and children alike, had managed to stay calm, even though it must have seemed overwhelming and frightening to the very little ones. It was hard enough to explain to the older children. Some clearly thought it was a great adventure, holding their paper bags of food as if they were off to a grand picnic. Others cowered behind adults or their friends, unwilling to show how upset they were, but unable to make a game of it.

Janet Phipps bustled along to where Alice stood. 'How are you doing?' she asked, her customary calm demeanour just about still in place.

'Not too bad,' said Alice, hoping her confidence wasn't misplaced. 'I've got all the names as far down as that bench there. I'm just about to take the last ones.'

'Good,' said Janet. 'There are some faces missing, though. I'm sure of it.'

'How can you tell?' asked Alice.

'You get used to it when you've been teaching big groups as long as I have,' Janet assured her. 'Ah, here comes trouble. Mrs Barnes is on her way over.'

'Who is that?' Alice asked.

'Dotty's mother,' Janet said out of the corner of her mouth as the woman approached, and sure enough Alice caught sight of the familiar little figure with blonde ringlets holding on to the woman's coat-tails. When the girl noticed her, she ran across, waving.

'Look, Mummy, it's the nurse,' she called, as Alice crouched to speak to her.

'Hello, Dotty. I see you've got your gas mask, just like you were asked to,' Alice said, observing that the mask in its container was almost the same size as the child's body, she was so small.

Mrs Barnes was highly agitated, much more so than her daughter. 'Miss Phipps, Miss Phipps,' she began, her voice straining with anxiety. 'You've got to tell us, where are we going? How do we know we'll be safe? Should we really go? What's best for the children? I can't put Dotty in danger, I just can't.'

Janet took a quick inward breath and turned to face the panicking mother. 'Now, Mrs Barnes. There's really no need to worry. We've got it all in hand.'

'No need to worry!' echoed the woman in disbelief. 'Why else would all the children be lined up like this? There's every need to worry, it stands to reason. My Dotty's sensitive, she doesn't like crowds, you see.'

Alice thought the little girl was coping very well, watching everything unfold with interest and showing no signs of hating the crowd. Perhaps she was used to seeing her mother in a tizz.

'We'll look after Dotty,' Janet began, but Mrs Barnes interrupted.

'I'm not letting her go anywhere without me. I'm staying right by her side. She's never spent more than the length of a school day away from me and she won't cope. I'm going too, wherever it is you're sending us.'

Janet nodded, acknowledging that as Dotty was so young her mother would be entitled to go

166

with her, but wondering in reality who it was who would be unable to cope. She felt obliged to test the waters.

'Now that's very commendable, Mrs Barnes, but rest assured Dotty will be looked after very well, and you shouldn't feel obliged to come, particularly if your husband needs you at home.'

'Obliged!' The woman's face flushed red. 'That's got nothing to do with it! My Dotty is the most precious thing in my life and I can't trust anyone else to look after her, not even for a day. You could be sending them off to anybody. They might have no idea of how to look after children. Dotty gets bronchitis; I can't rely on any old Tom, Dick or Harry to know how to care for her.'

'Don't distress yourself, Mrs Barnes,' Janet said, realising there would be no separating them. 'We don't want Dotty to become upset, now do we? You can certainly go with her if you feel that is the right thing to do.' She paused. 'Have you everything you need with you?'

The woman bridled. 'Of course. What sort of mother do you think I am? We got everything the government said — two pairs of socks and knickers, spares of everything, enough food for a day.' She held up her bag. 'And we didn't drink much this morning specially, on account of not knowing when we can go to the you-know-what.'

'Very wise,' said Janet. 'Now I must move on, but, Nurse Lake, can you make a note that Mrs Barnes is to accompany her daughter?'

Alice watched as her friend made good her

167

escape from the desperate mother. She straightened up so that she could speak to the woman face to face. 'It's all in hand, Mrs Barnes. We've been preparing for this eventuality for weeks. I hope you packed your toothbrush, Dotty?'

Dotty beamed up at her. 'Of course, Nurse. I been practising with it just like you said, and using that powder stuff.'

'Glad to hear it,' said Alice, and blessed Fiona Dewar's foresight in placing her at the school. Now the little ones accepted what she said and trusted her — even if their mothers didn't. 'We had better stand further away from the platform edge as that looks like our train about to pull in.'

Mrs Barnes immediately picked Dotty up and hurried to the far side of the platform, and Alice followed, as she still had to note down the mother's details.

'Where's Pauline?' the little girl suddenly asked.

Alice ran her eyes over her lists. 'I'm afraid I don't know, Dotty. I haven't seen her this morning.'

For the first time, the little girl was uneasy. 'She's got to come. She's my best friend.'

Alice sighed. 'I know, Dotty. You always sit next to each other, don't you? Don't worry, though. One of the teachers might have ticked her off on another list instead. She might be here but there are so many people we just can't see her.'

'You don't want to worry about that girl; she'll take care of herself,' sniffed Mrs Barnes dismissively. 'Her mother's no better than she

168

should be, and the girl's a bad influence. I don't like you sitting next to her, Dotty, and you know that very well.'

Dotty was now looking upset. 'She's not a bad inf . . . inf . . . what you said. She's funny and kind. I don't want to go without her.'

Alice frowned. This was exactly the sort of thing she dreaded — families and friends being separated, either by choice or by accident. From what she had heard of Pauline's mother and gran, it seemed unlikely either would turn up with the little girl. However, it was not her place to say so.

She knew she had to keep both mother and daughter as calm as possible. Given the press of people all around, she knew it would be all too easy to start a mass panic. It was a wonder that things had gone so smoothly so far. 'Look, why don't you two take a seat in one of the carriages,' she suggested. 'I'll mark down that's what you've done and then if I see Pauline I can tell her where you are. How about that, Dotty?'

The little girl nodded dubiously, twisting her hair around her finger in the way she always did when she was nervous. 'Yes, Nurse.'

'That's a good girl. Chin up,' said Alice boldly. 'I know you'll be sensible, Dotty, because you're a big girl now. You can look after Mummy, can't you?'

'Yes, Nurse,' Dotty agreed quietly. 'Please find her though.'

'I'll do what I can,' Alice promised, but couldn't help thinking that it would be a futile quest. The platform was getting more crowded

169

by the minute, and now people were beginning to jostle to get onto the train. She couldn't spend any more time with these two; she had to ensure everyone who needed it got a seat and that there were no accidents.

Steadily and methodically, she opened doors, helped struggling young mothers into the train, gently restrained two small boys from fighting and retrieved a lost gas mask for one of the very confused toddlers, who wanted to stand still sucking his thumb while chaos reigned all around. Alice recorded the last of the names, tallying them against the class sizes, adding in older or younger siblings, noting who had accompanying adults with the family group or any particularly young children travelling alone. Finally, just in time before the train was due to depart, she was confident that nobody had slipped through the net.

Despite her best efforts, though, there was no sign of Pauline.

★ ★ ★

Edith returned from her shift that afternoon and immediately went to look for Alice. It had been an unsettling day, with every family on edge, trying to decide whether to evacuate their children or not. An anxious mother with four children under ten had asked Edith for advice and she felt very under-qualified to offer any. How could she order a parent to send their children into the unknown? She had tried to be logical. Was there a safe place to act as a refuge room in case of a gas attack? Where would the family go if there was a bombing raid? She had helped the woman weigh up the odds, without pushing her either way, but had been relieved when the decision to evacuate all four was finally made. The house they lived in, just off Kingsland Road, looked barely strong enough to withstand a high wind, let alone a Nazi bomber. Even so, that wasn't what was upper-most in Edith's mind.

'There you are.' She found Alice getting changed out of her uniform and into a cotton frock with bias binding edging around the collar and cuffs. 'That's nice, is it new? When did you find the time to go shopping?'

Alice laughed as she hung up her uniform, pulling out the creases so it would look fresh for her next shift. 'My mother sent it. She included two cardigans as well, one for summer and a heavier one for autumn. Wasn't that kind?'

'Lucky you.' Edith knew her own mother wouldn't have had the money for such a gift, nor would she have ever considered it necessary. She fingered the lighter cardigan, in a soft grey. 'Al, are you busy? I mean, after you've put this away? Do you want to come for a walk?'

Alice shrugged. 'I could do. Why, is something up?'

'I could do with a bit of a chinwag,' said Edith. 'We don't have to go far. Maybe over to the Downs via the back road.'

Alice picked up the grey cardigan and put it on. 'Might as well try this out for its first airing, then. As it happens I've spent most of the day

171

over there, at the station.'

'How did it go?'

'I'll tell you about it as we walk,' said Alice, who had spent the last half-hour recounting all the details to Fiona Dewar. The superintendent had made notes all the while, so that if they ever had to do such a thing again, they would be able to improve.

Edith sighed as they descended the front steps. 'Do you want an apple?' she said, reaching into her bag. 'Here, have the red one.'

'Thanks, I was so busy I missed lunch.' Alice took a grateful bite. 'So, what's happened? Did you have a bad visit or something?'

Edith stared ahead, taking in the trees along the road, their leaves just beginning to lose their colour, without really seeing them. The street was unusually quiet — there were very few children around. Often there would be a group of schoolboys kicking a football about, or some girls skipping with ropes, inventing complicated games on the pavement. Now it was nearly empty.

'No, or nothing really horrible,' she said. 'Lots of parents asked me if they'd done the right thing sending their children away or, in some cases, keeping them behind. One family was particularly tricky. But that's not it — well, it's not why I wanted to speak to you. I managed to meet Harry in a café for lunch. He's gone and done it. He's signed up.'

Alice nodded slowly. 'You did say he was seriously thinking about it.'

Edith tipped her head back and stared at the

172

clouds scudding by. 'I know. After the fight he talked about nothing else. It's not that it's a surprise — I don't blame him at all. It's just . . . well, it's real now. He's going to be leaving, and everything will change.'

Alice slipped her arm through her friend's. 'He's doing the right thing though. You said yourself, this way he can serve his country and carry on boxing.'

Edith slowed down, practically to a halt. 'Yes, if it's got to happen then this is the best way. I just don't want him to go. Or part of me does. The other part feels . . . as if I've had a limb cut off. I know I'm being selfish, and I've only known him a short time, but all the same . . . ' She paused and swallowed hard. 'I want him to stay here, and not get hurt, and look after me. But I also want him to fight and be a hero. Does that sound daft?'

Alice squeezed her friend's arm. 'No, not at all. It was the same for some of the parents today — they knew it made sense to send their children away and yet they couldn't bear to part with them. There were lots of tears on the platform. It was terribly sad, and yet some of the children were so brave, not breaking down, the older ones trying to look after the little ones. I tell you what, Edie, I'm exhausted.'

'No wonder.' Edith gave a small smile. 'I bet you were good, though, Al. You'd have kept a level head and reassured them all.'

'I tried,' said Alice ruefully. 'Not sure how well I succeeded. They all got safely on the train, though. Then there were all the parents left

behind after they'd waved their children goodbye
— that was hard to watch.'

'Must have been.' Edith looked sadly ahead.
'It's no fun being separated from those you love.'

'No.' Alice threw the apple core onto the grass
as the Downs opened out before them. 'It isn't.'

'Sorry, I didn't mean to dig all that up again,'
Edith said, kicking at the long grass.

'Think nothing of it. I don't any longer, it was
all ages ago,' Alice said stoutly, making sure her
friend couldn't see her face.

'Good.' Edith began to wander across the
grass, her hands now firmly wedged into her
skirt pockets. 'Oh, and another thing. Joe's
thinking of joining up too.'

Alice cocked her head. 'Is he? I haven't seen
him since the boxing match so I hadn't heard.'

'Yes, but I don't know when, or to what
branch of the Forces or anything. Now I come to
think of it, Harry mentioned his brother wanted
to see you — some other library thing I expect.'
Edith turned back to her friend. 'He'll be in
Percy's café tomorrow lunchtime; he often goes
there on a Saturday. You're free, aren't you? You
should go down there, it's only along Kingsland
Road, find out what his plans are.'

'Thanks,' said Alice. 'I might.'

'Good,' said Edith, 'cos I said you would.'

Alice groaned. 'Thanks a bunch.' She walked
alongside her friend for a few paces. 'So . . . does
that mean you love Harry, then? Is that what you
just said?'

Edith blushed. 'I suppose so. I haven't said so
to him. It's all too soon, isn't it? But in my heart

174

I'm sure I do. I know I've changed since I met him, I feel totally different about everything. Oh, Alice.' She stopped and gazed at her friend. 'Yes, he's the one for me all right. I've never felt like this before, and I'm pretty certain he feels the same about me. It's the way he looks at me and the way we laugh at the same things, or know what the other one is thinking. That's love, isn't it?'

Alice shrugged. 'I suppose so. Edie, I'm really happy for you. He's a good man. And he's brought out the best in you, anyone can see it. You aren't wild like when I first met you. That must mean something, mustn't it? But he's a lucky man.'

Edith broke into a huge grin. 'He is, isn't he? He should be bloody grateful, that's what.' Suddenly she threw her hands wide and turned around on the spot, gazing up at the sky. 'You know what, I could shout it out loud.'

Then, as Alice started to laugh too, and protest that people would be watching, Edith twirled even faster.

'I don't care if they stare! Edith Gillespie loves Harry Banham!' she shouted as loudly as she could, scaring the birds in the top branches and making several people on their way home from work glance their way. 'Edie loves Harry! And she doesn't care who knows it!'

★ ★ ★

Alice woke later than usual the next day, safe in the knowledge that she wasn't on shift. She still felt worn out from the day before, and thought not for the first time that while their work was often physically demanding, it was the emotional toll that was the worst aspect. Now that she'd mastered the boneshaker, her daily round was not so bad, but the responsibility often weighed heavily on her shoulders. On the other hand, she now had to factor in a few extra minutes each day for stopping to chat to people around the district who she'd got to know over the past three months, whether patients, members of their families, or just those she bumped into regularly.

It was hard to be downcast on a sunny day, with no shifts to do, and the sight of the trees opposite throwing their shadows on the curtains. She shoved back the bed covers and went to the window, pulling the curtains wide open and throwing the sash up as far as it would go. Peering out she could see Gwen on the pavement beneath, talking to a woman with dark wavy hair in a beautiful smart charcoal suit. They were deep in what looked like a very earnest conversation. Gwen indicated that they should move and the pair of them began walking along Victory Walk towards the main road.

Alice slipped down from the windowsill and turned to her wardrobe. She might as well take advantage of her mother's presents and wear her new cardigan again, maybe this time with a skirt and blouse. Her dark green skirt would show off her figure, and she was sure she looked trimmer than when she'd first arrived here. Then again, she wasn't dressing for a date, she reminded herself sternly. It was meeting a friend for lunch, nothing more.

Down in the canteen, as she poured herself a cup of tea, she noticed Edith and Mary sitting at a table in the corner. Mary was done up to the nines considering it was Saturday morning. Her hair was swept up and held in place with a tortoiseshell clasp. Her blouse was tightly fitted, with a plunging neckline, and she wore a gold locket around her neck. Alice could see she had on smart high heels.

'Goodness, what's the special occasion?' she asked, sitting down to join them.

Mary glanced demurely down at her breakfast, her hands clasped in front of her. 'I'm only going out for lunch.'

Edith made a face. 'Now, Mary, we know it's a bit more than that.'

'Must be a very special lunch,' Alice observed, thinking her own preparations paled in comparison.

'Go on, you tell her,' Edith urged.

Mary pursed her lips, which Alice now noticed bore a trace of pale pink lipstick. 'You know when Harry won his big match,' she said, 'and he met Major Ingham? Well, do you remember that the major brought along one of his fellow officers, and we got along like a house on fire? Now he's got in touch to ask me to lunch. Isn't that nice?' She looked up and it was clear from her eyes that she thought it was more than nice.

'I say, that's rather good,' exclaimed Alice. 'And does he have a name, this fellow officer? I don't know if he told us, or if he did I don't recall it.'

'He does,' said Mary. 'Charles Paynter. Captain Charles Paynter.'

'Oooh, a captain!' said Edith. 'You've done well there, Mary. I must admit I was too busy listening to what Major Ingham had to say to take much notice, but I do remember he seemed very polite, very smart. Didn't he have blond hair?'

'Yes, and very blue eyes,' said Mary, pleased with herself. 'He's quite a bit taller than me, though not as much as Harry. He seemed like a real gent.'

'Where are you going?' Alice asked, intrigued.

'Oh, to a restaurant he knows in the West End. He's meeting me at Fortnum's and we'll go on from there. So I thought I should dress up and look the part.' She brushed down her skirt, to get rid of the crumbs.

'Very nice,' said Edith, who had never been to Fortnum & Mason, despite living in London all her life.

'What are you doing today, Edith?' Mary asked.

'I'm helping Fiona sort out the district room,' she said. 'Lots of new supplies arrived this week and she couldn't spare anyone to help unpack them. So I said I'd do it. Might as well take advantage of the fact I know every nook and cranny of the place from when I had to clean it.'

Alice privately thought that the old Edith would never have volunteered to do any such thing.

'I think that's very noble of you,' said Mary

warmly. 'Well, I'd best be off — I don't want to keep Charles waiting. Toodle pip.' She pushed back her chair and headed out of the room, pausing at the door to turn and give them a little wave.

Alice and Edith exchanged a look.

'She didn't even ask why we had such a big delivery of fresh supplies,' Edith remarked. 'She's in a world of her own, that one. She still thinks nothing's going to happen.'

Alice sighed. 'Ah, let her go. What one nurse thinks won't change anything.'

★ ★ ★

Percy's café was already nearly full when Alice pushed her way in through the glass door. She glanced around the tiled room, heavy with tobacco smoke, the air full of the smell of frying eggs and bacon. For a moment she couldn't see him, but then she caught sight of the distinctive Banham hair, thick and wavy, and Joe was standing up at his table to wave her over. He pulled out her chair for her, which made her smile.

'Thank you,' she laughed.

'Welcome to the best café in Dalston,' said Joe, mock-seriously. 'If you like bacon sandwiches, that is.'

'As it happens, I do,' said Alice. 'I can never make them so that they taste the same as in a good café.'

'You probably cut the bread too thin,' suggested Joe. 'That's a cardinal sin around here.

179

Your HP Sauce will soak right through.'

'HP Sauce? I like mine with mustard,' Alice told him without a trace of a smile.

Joe threw up his hands in horror. 'If I'd have known that, I'd never have asked you to meet me. I had you down as a lady of good taste, but now I see I'm mistaken.'

Alice pulled a face. 'Edith is worse. She likes both.'

'What, both at the same time?'

'Believe it or not, yes.'

Joe shook his head. 'I'd better tell Harry. My brother goes round mooning over your friend but he doesn't know this vital fact about her, does he? The sooner I tell him the better, or else he'll have his heart broken. So you got the message, then? I wasn't sure he'd remember to pass it on, to be honest.'

Alice nodded. 'Well, obviously, yes — I'm here, aren't I?' She paused in her teasing as a man in a tightly wrapped white apron swung by their table, carrying a notepad.

'What'll it be, Joe — the usual?' he asked. 'And what about your friend?'

Joe looked queryingly at Alice.

'Bacon sandwich, please,' she said. 'And a cup of tea.'

'Two bacon sandwiches, two teas,' the man said, writing swiftly in the book, and then disappearing back behind the steamy counter.

'Good choice,' said Joe. 'So . . . I thought I'd tell you about my plans. Rather than you hearing about them second-hand from Edith and Harry, that is.'

Alice nodded. 'She said something about you enlisting.'

Joe inclined his head. 'That's right. Harry got me thinking — you know, getting in there early before you don't have a choice. I thought I'd sign up for somewhere that could use my skills.'

'Good idea,' said Alice. 'What skills are those? What sort of things do postmen have to learn?'

Joe looked puzzled. 'Postmen?'

'Yes, postmen.' Now it was Alice's turn to look puzzled. 'Isn't that what you are? A postman?'

For a moment Joe's expression was still one of bafflement, but then he started laughing. 'Postman? No, no, I'm not a postman. Not that there's anything wrong with being a postman, it's just . . . ' He recovered himself. 'No. That's not what I do.'

'Oh?' Alice was confused. 'But when I came to treat your colleague — what was his name? Ernest; he was a postman. And you work together, don't you? So I just assumed you were a postman.'

'Ah.' Joe smiled as the penny dropped. 'I see now. Of course. Yes, he's a postman, and we are colleagues, but that's because I work for the GPO. I'm an engineer.'

Alice looked away, mortified. 'I'm sorry. I didn't realise.'

Joe was on the point of asking why she'd made the assumption; whether it was because she'd presumed that nobody from Jeeves Street would have managed to qualify as an engineer, but he decided that would be unfair. It was how Harry would have replied, and in truth maybe he would have done the same a few months ago. He recalled Harry's remarks about hoity-toity nurses. But Alice had made a genuine mistake — anybody might have thought the same. Also, it hadn't stopped her coming here today, whether or not she thought he was a postman.

'Well, the thing is, I'm quite highly trained already, so I thought it might come in handy somewhere,' he said. 'Such as the navy. I went and spoke to someone at the recruiting office and they agreed, so that's what I'm going to do.'

Alice met his gaze. 'That's very brave, Joe.'

Joe shrugged. 'Thanks, but it isn't anything special really. At least all that studying won't have gone to waste, and I can learn new ways of using all the stuff I learnt.'

Alice thought it was admirable how he looked on the bright side. Surely what he really wanted to do was to stay exactly as he was — he had seemed so content with his family, in his role of big brother, looking after them all. Yet that wasn't likely to be an option. He'd made the best of the situation facing him.

'I hope you do,' she said. 'Who knows what you'll end up working as? Anything could happen. That's good, isn't it?' She said it almost as a way of convincing herself.

'Yes, a change is as good as a rest and all that.' He raised his eyebrows. 'Not sure how much time I'll have for reading, though. I was wondering, do you want to take over my subscription for the lending library?'

Alice's expression brightened. 'Do they let you do that? I haven't got round to applying myself

182

— I meant to but somehow never found the time. Yes please.'

Joe nodded. 'I'll check with them. Don't see why not. Oh look, here's our lunch.'

Two enormous bacon sandwiches came into view, almost obliterating the man carrying them.

'See what I mean? The best in town,' said Joe, pulling back his shirtsleeves in anticipation. 'Here you are, mustard or HP or a bit of both.'

For a few minutes they fell silent as each of them devoured their enormous sandwich, the meat crispy and perfect inside the big doorsteps of fresh bread. Finally Alice put down her last crust and licked her lips.

'That was delicious,' she proclaimed, delicately wiping the grease from her hands. She'd tried to be ladylike and use a knife and fork, but had given up the attempt after noticing Joe barely bothered, but simply picked up his sandwich and bit into it. 'You were right.'

'Even down to the HP?'

'Maybe not that right.'

'Don't they feed you at that nurses' home then?' he asked. 'You put that away with no problem. Have they been starving you or something?'

'No, but they don't give us anything like that,' Alice admitted.

Joe tutted. 'That reminds me. I almost forgot. Ma asked me to tell you and Edith to come for Sunday dinner tomorrow. You're not on duty, are you?'

Alice laughed. 'Tell us? What if we had a better offer?'

Joe looked affronted. 'That isn't possible. Ma's roasts are famous around here. You don't say no — you'd be mad to.' He grinned but seemed a little less sure of himself. 'She wants to meet Edith, of course, as Harry's talked of nobody else since he admitted he'd been walking out with her. Ma is keen to see what the fuss is about — that's why he tried to keep it a secret for a few weeks, but of course she knew something was up. Then he said she'd got a friend and I said I knew you too, so she's decided you're both to come. If you want to, that is. Don't you want to?'

Alice decided to put him out of his misery. 'Thank you. I'd love to — it's very kind. I'm sure Edith will want to as well. She'll have had enough of tidying and restocking the district room by then. Please thank your mother for us. Can we bring anything?'

'Just yourselves,' Joe said. 'Come early, then you can meet everyone properly before we all sit down to eat.'

'If I go to the nine o'clock service I can be there by, what, quarter to eleven,' said Alice. 'Edith usually goes to morning mass, so that would be perfect.'

Joe beamed. 'That's that agreed, then. Now, how about some treacle sponge and custard?'

'You're on.' And Alice found she was beaming too, though she couldn't quite work out why.

14

Kathleen reached into the makeshift cot to lift Brian up and into the new pram. At least, it was new to them. She'd got it second-hand from the market, at a good price because it was so battered around the chassis, but she didn't care. Mattie had brought round a not quite empty tin of white paint and a couple of Stan's brushes, and the two of them had covered over the worst of the marks. The springs were still sound and that meant the little boy could be pushed around in comfort, which was all that really mattered to Kathleen. 'Aren't you growing big!' she exclaimed as he opened his eyes and gave her the special smile that melted her heart every time she saw it.

That was the other reason she had been so delighted to find the pram. Now she had the lump sum of Ray's money, she'd been able to feed herself much better, which meant Brian was feeding better too. She'd begun trying him on a few solids. He was catching up on all the growth he'd missed in his first months and carrying him was becoming quite tricky, especially if she had heavy shopping too. He loved the pram, though, and now he waved his arms with pleasure as she put him in it. 'Off for a ride!' she told him. 'Off to see Auntie Mattie and Gillian and all the family.'

From the tiny kitchen she brought out a small

sack of potatoes and carefully placed it on the wire shelf under the pram. Now that she was in a position to buy food like anyone else, she wanted to pay back the people who had looked after her when she was all but a charity case. Mattie had said they would be a big group sitting down for Sunday dinner and Kathleen was keen to contribute. 'There we are, all ready,' she sang, as Brian wriggled around trying to see what was going on beyond the sides of his pram.

Kathleen swung the handle and manoeuvred it through the front door, a tricky move but one she had now perfected. She felt lucky that her wrist had healed and that the bruises along her arm and face had cleared up. Nobody looking at her now would know what had happened. If her injuries had been any worse she'd have been trapped, unable to get out with her baby. There was much to be thankful for.

She usually tried not to think about Ray and what he had done to her. Part of her still missed him and longed for him to return, but the other half was glad he wasn't there to hurt her any more. She wanted things to go back to how they were before, when he was courting her and so charming and attentive, making her heart sing with the certainty of his love for her. She couldn't bear the fact that those days were gone forever, and wanted so badly to be able to love him again. Yet she also feared his hostility towards his son and dreaded him trying to hurt Brian too. It was all very well for her; she'd chosen her husband and nobody had forced her to marry him — the very reverse. Brian had done

186

nothing to hurt Ray and yet the man seemed to hate the baby, no matter what. She wondered where Ray was now. For the sake of their child's safety, she had to hope he was nowhere nearby.

★ ★ ★

Flo set the kettle to boil and surveyed her preparations. She'd haggled as hard as she knew how with the stallholder as he was packing up yesterday afternoon, certain that was the best time of day to secure a bargain, and had been rewarded for her perseverance with a nice big chicken. It was now in the roasting pan, surrounded by peeled vegetables. She nodded in satisfaction as she lifted it gingerly into the warmed oven. It was almost too big to fit, but a little skilled balancing and shifting saw it go in without spilling so much as a carrot.

Next she put the marrowfat peas on to boil, having soaked them overnight. They would fill everyone up nicely. That would just about leave room for some Yorkshire puddings on the side.

Flo was bursting with curiosity about the two new guests. Harry had tried to keep his feelings for Edith hidden, but he hadn't managed it for long. She was used to her youngest's successes with the opposite sex and usually turned a blind eye to what she suspected he was up to, but she had never known him to be so taken with a girlfriend. Usually he joked about it, but now he was quieter, more intense. She was dying to see what sort of woman could have this effect on her popular son.

She was bringing her friend, the one Mattie and Kathleen had first met when Brian was sick. Flo nodded to herself. It was always handy to know a nurse or two. She was proud that she'd raised her three children relatively unscathed, tending them through the usual ailments of measles and chickenpox, but she knew her knowledge was limited. They'd all been worried for Mattie when she'd caught a bad case of flu when she was a schoolgirl. People died of it. There had been no lasting ill-effects, but Flo never forgot the fear and sense of sheer hopelessness that had invaded her before the fever broke. She fervently hoped Gillian would never cause them such worry.

The back door banged and Mattie came in, baby on her hip. 'Is Kath here yet?' she asked.

'Not that I know of,' said Flo, wiping her hands on her faded apron. 'How's my gorgeous granddaughter?' She bent to smile at the little girl. 'They're getting too big to share that cot in the corner, Mattie.'

Mattie went across and put her daughter down in it, whereupon the baby sat up and peered through the wooden bars. 'Brian will have to stay in his pram,' she said. 'It's warm enough to put it in the back garden if we're too crowded. Shall I fetch more chairs?'

Flo considered their arrangements. She had opened up the drop leaves of the kitchen table and brought in the small table which usually stood beneath the window in the parlour.

'You might bring down that wooden stool from your bedroom,' she said.

Mattie made a face. 'I've got it piled up with the last lot of ironing,' she protested.

'Haven't you put that away yet? I did that two days ago,' Flo scolded. 'You'll just have to move it. We'll need that stool. It can go on the end there. Thank you, love.'

Mattie scowled but went off to do as she was asked.

Harry came into the room as his sister was leaving. 'All set?' he asked.

Flo laughed. 'Since when were you so anxious about a Sunday dinner? I've made a few before, you know.'

Harry grinned reluctantly. 'I know. It'll be a treat, as always.'

'Course it will.' Flo grew serious. 'I won't let you down, son. I can see how much this means to you.'

Harry shuffled and looked away. 'I just want her to like us. And you to like her.'

'Come here.' Flo opened her arms. 'You aren't too old for a hug from your old ma. Don't you worry. Everything will be fine. I brought you up to have good taste, didn't I? If she's the one you've chosen, she's bound to be all right.'

'Well, I haven't said that to her,' said Harry, pulling away. 'I haven't known her very long.'

Flo regarded him steadily. 'You'll know when she's the right one, long time or not,' she said. 'You simply listen to your heart, my boy. I'm not saying you have to rush things, specially what with you enlisting. You take your time. Just don't deceive yourself.'

Harry nodded, embarrassed at his mother

saying such things to him. 'Thanks, Ma.' He moved to the door. 'Sounds like somebody now . . . oh, it's Kath. Shall I help you with the pram?' he called into the corridor.

Flo glanced at the clock on the wall. Twenty-five to eleven. Plenty of time to get everything done. She took the teapot from the dresser shelf and poured a little warm water into it. Kath might appreciate a cup, and the nurses too, once they got here.

Mattie reappeared with the stool, followed by Kath with the pram, which the two of them shunted out into the back garden in the early September sunshine, placing it so that they could see Brian and he could see them. Kath pulled out the potatoes and carried them over to the oven. 'Here, Mrs Banham, I brought some extras,' she said shyly.

'Bless you, Kath, you didn't need to do that,' said Flo, realising the effort it would have taken the young woman to have pushed them round along with the increasingly sturdy Brian. 'I've put ours in already — but it won't hurt to have some spare just in case.'

Kath beamed with pleasure at having been able to contribute for once.

There was a sound from the front door but before either of them could respond they could hear swift footsteps in the corridor, which Flo guessed was Harry running to get there first. Then the kitchen door swung open as he ushered two young women into the room.

Flo looked up and almost caught her breath at the expression on her son's face. 'Ma,' he said, his eyes as bright as she had ever seen them. 'This is Alice Lake . . . ' The taller of the two stepped forward and shook her hand ' . . . and this is Edith Gillespie. Edie.'

Flo immediately noticed the girl's dark, curly hair and lively eyes as she shook her hand too. She was smartly turned out but not too showily, Flo thought approvingly, registering the neat trim of her freshly pressed dress and polished shoes, not too high-heeled, but with enough to give her a little boost — she wasn't anywhere near as tall as her friend. 'You're very welcome,' she said warmly. 'Pleased to meet you both.'

'Thank you for inviting us,' Edie said.

Alice produced a tin. 'We brought an apple tart — I hope that's all right,' she said.

'You shouldn't have. That's very kind.' Flo took it from them and decided they seemed like sensible, polite young women, as might be expected if they had qualified in their chosen profession. 'We'll have some tea, shall we?'

As she was busying herself with the teapot, Joe and Stan came in. Flo was about to offer them a cup each but Stan got in first.

'There's to be an important announcement on the wireless at eleven fifteen,' he said, with a tone of authority he rarely adopted, but which Flo knew to take seriously on the rare times she heard it.

'Eleven fifteen? Then we've only got a few minutes,' she said, hastily pouring the tea. 'Here, you'd better sit down. Alice, Edie, you take the comfy seats, you're our guests. Joe, get that wireless tuned in, will you? He's much better at

191

it than any of us,' she explained to the girls as they took their places on the sofa.

Harry stood protectively behind Edie as Joe coaxed the wireless set into action and the measured words of the newsreader boomed out. Alice found she was watching him anxiously, even as her hand gripped the fabric of the armrest. Edie cast Harry an imploring look.

They all fell silent, even Gillian and Brian from his pram, as the prime minister began to speak. The solemnity of the occasion took their words away. Finally the waiting was over; the country was now officially at war with Germany.

Flo found she was holding her breath. The speech confirmed all her worst fears; it was happening again. This time her two precious sons would be swept up in it, and there was little she could do to save them. They were grown men; they had to face the forthcoming dangers for themselves. She turned to Mattie, who had gone over to the cot and was gently stroking Gillian's head. Somehow they would have to keep the youngest ones safe.

'What do we do, Stan?' she asked quietly.

Stan came across and set his hands on her shoulders. 'We do what we've been doing,' he said steadily. 'You've already made blackout blinds. I'm going to put in an Anderson shelter in our garden — we've got just enough space, and you boys can help me before you go to wherever you'll be going to.' Joe and Harry nodded, knowing it was their duty to help their parents make the family home as safe as possible. 'Meanwhile, we aren't going to let

Hitler get in the way of one of your roast dinners. We'll carry on as normally as we can unless we're forced to do otherwise.'

'Right, then let's get on with it.' Flo went back to the oven to check that all was well, the aroma of roasting chicken becoming stronger by the minute.

Stan began to talk to Edith, prompted by Harry, and Alice slipped away from them to have a word with Joe.

'Are you all right?' he asked with concern.

Alice gave a little shrug. 'It feels strange, now that it's been said out loud, but it's what we've been waiting for all summer, so in a way it's a relief.'

Joe acknowledged this with a sigh. 'Yes, it does sound odd, but that's how I feel too. Now nobody can say we were making a fuss over nothing. I know I'm doing the right thing, more than ever.'

'I'm glad you decided beforehand,' said Alice quietly. 'I bet lots of people are panicking and rushing into things right now. You know what you want to do and the best way to do it.'

'What about you?' he asked, worry in his eyes. 'Is the nurses' home protected?'

Alice laughed. 'Our superintendent has seen to it that we're all stocked up with material for blackout blinds. There's also a big basement under half of the building and she's been quietly making plans to equip it as a refuge room. We should just about all fit in, though it won't be exactly luxurious. Several of the other nurses have started carrying around good-luck charms.

Mary's got a rabbit's foot but I always feel sorry for the poor rabbit. Edith used to have a shamrock but I don't know if she's still got it. Her Irish grandmother gave it to her when she was little and she's kept it for years.'

'Maybe they're easier to come by than four-leafed clovers,' Joe suggested.

'Perhaps. I'd sooner have a leaf than a bit of an animal,' Alice admitted. 'In any case, I'd put more faith in a well-stocked refuge room.'

'That sounds like a good idea.' Joe was glad the women would be safe. He didn't like the thought of leaving Alice unprotected in a city at war.

'I can't say I'm looking forward to using it, but I'm sure we will cope,' Alice said confidently, partly to reassure herself.

'I'm sure you will,' Joe replied, 'it's what you nurses are known for, isn't it?'

'It certainly is . . . ' Alice was just beginning to work out a smart response though the tender look on Joe's face as he spoke to her made her pause, but before she could respond a loud wail suddenly filled the air, drowning out their conversation. She turned around in confusion and was met by several other equally dismayed faces.

'What's that?' mouthed Edith.

Flo dropped the lid to one of the saucepans in shock, but its din could hardly be heard.

Stan took charge. 'Air-raid warning,' he shouted.

'Air raid?' Kathleen stuttered. 'What . . . what do we do? Where do we go?' She cast around frantically and then dashed into the garden to fetch Brian, snatching him out of his pram and hugging him fiercely as she brought him indoors. His cries added to the sinister wailing.

Stan briefly shut his eyes. This was the nightmare he had dreaded — being caught unprepared. He should have got his sons to help him dig the shelter sooner, but he'd held out in the hope that there would be a last-minute solution. Now he could only keep his fingers crossed that they'd all still be around to do it as soon as this was over. He made his decision.

'We do nothing,' he said steadily in a brief lull in the noise. 'It will be a drill; it's too soon for Germany to have sent a proper bombing raid. We don't run into the streets and panic. We stay inside and have our dinner just like we planned.' He gave Flo a significant look and she promptly started her final preparations, removing the warmed plates from the bottom of the oven, checking the Yorkshire puddings. She held up a hand with three fingers out.

'Ready in three minutes,' she mouthed as the noise increased again, beckoning to Mattie for help. Edith got up to help as well but Flo frowned and shooed her off. Still, she was pleased that Harry's girl had made the offer. It showed she had been brought up properly.

Hesitantly they all took their seats around the extended table, Harry having the stool at the end, and Kathleen balancing a grizzling Brian on her lap. Flo served up and Mattie passed the plates along, then placed the tray of Yorkshires in the middle for everyone to help themselves. The

195

noise abated as they began to tuck in.

'Takes more than a declaration of war to ruin your roast, Ma,' said Joe, eagerly shovelling forkfuls of peas into his mouth.

'This is lovely, Mrs Banham,' exclaimed Edith, slicing through her chicken. 'We don't get food like this at the nurses' home, do we, Alice?'

'We certainly don't,' Alice agreed, spearing a carrot and potato in one go. 'You are spoiling us and we're very grateful.'

'I'm sure you deserve it,' said Flo staunchly. 'We need to keep you nurses well fed. Who knows what you'll have to help out with now? Stands to reason you'll need all the energy you can get.'

'Ma's right,' said Harry with a glint in his eye. 'Can't have you girls getting tired out before the action's even started, can we?'

'Harry, behave yourself,' said Mattie sternly, dodging as he reached out to tousle her hair.

'Now, now, not at the table. Honestly, how old are you two?' Flo pretended to be cross but she couldn't keep it up for long.

Mattie pulled a face and took another bite of chicken, but inside she was in turmoil. What would this mean for Lennie? He hadn't had leave all summer as it was. Would she see him again before he was called off to fight — or, even worse, would she see him again at all? Suddenly there was a lump in her throat and the chicken didn't seem so tasty after all.

Flo caught her daughter's expression and realised what she was thinking. She reached under the table and discreetly took her hand.

196

'He'll be fine, love,' she said softly. 'It's what he's trained for, remember? Why don't you write to him when we've finished eating and say you're proud of him, build up his spirits a bit.'

Mattie gulped and then nodded. 'I am an' all. But I want him to come home and see me and Gillian. She'll forget what he looks like if we aren't careful.'

Flo cocked her head. 'Gillian will be fine. She'll appreciate him even more when she's a bit older. I'm sure they'll give them leave, love. Meantime, you eat up your food and keep building yourself up for the days to come.'

Mattie nodded, even though her heart was heavy, knowing that her mother made sense.

Edith smiled to herself at Harry's teasing his sister, and decided that she could feel at home here. His parents were welcoming and friendly, as he'd assured her they would be, but you could never tell such things in advance. Mothers could be very protective of their sons and she had dressed with care, wanting to make the right impression. Not for her the low necklines and tight waistbands favoured by Mary Perkins. Just as well, she thought, she'd never have managed the roast chicken if she'd worn her most fitted skirt. There was still the apple pie to come as well.

Harry glanced across at her and gave her an encouraging look. He was pleased with how it was going, or at least the way his parents had reacted to Edith. He was glad; now that he would definitely be off to war he wanted to know that she'd have someone looking out for her. He knew that she and Alice were as close as sisters, but sometimes you needed the advice of someone who'd been alive for longer. He wanted the comfort of knowing that if anything dreadful happened, his parents would help her.

Joe caught the exchange of glances between his brother and Edith. Who would have thought it — Harry bringing a girl home. He had no illusions about his brother's reputation with women, and had assumed he'd go on happily playing the field for many years yet. Although it was very early days, surely this signified something. He could see Harry treated her differently to any of the girlfriends he'd had in the past — not that many had been around for long enough even to meet Joe. At first he'd thought Edith flirty and silly, but that was just her outward demeanour. He could see she had a core of steel underneath the smiles.

As for her friend, Alice . . . well, he had to admit he'd totally misjudged her. She was an intriguing woman, all right — but there was a wall of reserve he hadn't even begun to break down. If circumstances had been different . . . but they weren't. He got the strong impression that all she wanted was friendship and — given that he could soon be deployed anywhere — maybe that was all he should try to offer. He'd liked being around her, and he would have to put aside the underlying draw he felt towards her, something that had sparked off the first time they'd spoken and he'd got so angry so quickly. Maybe it wasn't anger he'd sensed — but whatever else it was could be of no use now.

Edith broke her glance with Harry to notice that everyone had now finished, with nearly every plate wiped clean. She got up and began to gather the crockery and cutlery, despite Flo's protests: 'Sit down, Edith, you're our guest.'

'Well, you did the cooking and Mattie helped, and so I reckon it's my turn to do something,' Edith replied, standing her ground. Alice rose and began to pass used plates along the extended length of the table, so that Edith wouldn't have to reach across people.

Only when they'd cleared the table did they agree to sit down, as Flo brought out the warmed apple tart. Mattie vanished into the back kitchen and reappeared with an earthenware jug of cream, which she set in the middle of the table. 'And don't you go taking it all,' she said to Harry, before he could even reach for it.

Before Flo could cut into the fragrant pastry, another loud noise started, and this time Stan visibly relaxed. 'It's the all clear,' he told them, relief flooding his voice. 'We don't have to worry. We're safe now for the time being.'

'Good, because I don't want this tart to go to waste,' said Flo forcefully. 'Eat up, everyone. We don't know what's in store for us in the future, but let's make the most of the next five minutes.'

15

It was early evening when Alice and Edith left Jeeves Street, knowing they should get back to the home in good time so that they'd be fresh for their rounds in the morning, but reluctant to go nevertheless.

'I'm so full I can scarcely move,' Edith admitted as Harry helped her on with her coat. 'You must thank your ma again for me, Harry.' He led her through the front door and on to the pavement, where he turned to give her a quick kiss on the forehead. He was keenly aware that neighbours might be watching and didn't want to cause her embarrassment.

'She loved having you here,' he assured her. 'We all did. Both of you,' he added as Alice stepped through the front doorway too.

'I'm glad I was with you when we heard the announcement,' Edith said seriously. 'At least we know where we stand now.' She reached up and gave Harry a quick kiss before forcing herself to break away from him. 'See you Wednesday, then.'

'Wednesday,' he agreed, waving to them as they walked towards the main road. He couldn't help appreciating Edith's figure in her neat light coat as she turned her back. Alice was more elegant, he supposed, but she couldn't hold a candle to his Edie.

Alice tucked her arm into Edith's as they reached the other side of the high road. 'That went well, didn't it?' she said.

'Apart from the fact we're now at war with Germany,' Edith said tartly. 'You know when you worry about all the things that could go wrong when you first meet your chap's parents? Didn't imagine it would be that, did I?' She shook her head. 'But no, you're right, they are lovely.'

'I think they thought the same about you,' Alice said. 'It's funny, isn't it, Joe's so like his father and Harry is more like his mother. They all seem so close.'

Edith sighed, thinking of her own big family, who somehow never managed that welcoming atmosphere. She was pretty sure her mother would have immediately sat Harry down and quizzed him about how much money he made. Stan and Flo had been open and affectionate but hadn't interrogated her in any way — although she'd been aware that Mrs Banham had been covertly sizing her up most of the afternoon. 'Harry's ma said I could go round there even when Harry gets sent away,' she said.

'You should, especially if there's food on offer,' Alice replied at once. 'I haven't had a roast like that since . . . well, since the last time I was with my parents.' Her thoughts flew to Liverpool, and she realised she hadn't been back since Easter. Her mother and father would be worrying about her now war had been officially announced, and although they lived a fair distance from the main dockside area of the city she recognised with a sinking feeling that they were by no means safe either.

Edith shot a sharp glance at her friend. 'Do

you think you will go home for a visit?' she asked. 'I'm sure Fiona would give you time off, she'll understand. We're all entitled to a month's holiday a year and you have hardly used any, have you?'

Alice straightened up. 'I don't know. They'll probably be more concerned if I hurry up there — they'll assume something's wrong.'

'Well, we have just gone to war with Germany,' Edith pointed out.

'No,' Alice replied decisively. 'My place is here, as this is where I'll be needed. That has to come first. I'll write to them when we get back.'

'Up to you,' said Edith, able to read between the lines and understand what Alice really meant. She didn't want to go back to Liverpool, as her parents would want to see that their daughter had put Mark firmly behind her and Alice wasn't ready to do so quite yet. 'I might try to get a day off to go to see my ma and the younger ones. Just in case she's at all worried — although she won't be.'

Alice nodded, knowing that Edith was probably right. Her mother was too busy to fret over her older children; she regarded Edith as a fully independent adult who needed nothing more than a hurriedly scribbled card at Christmas.

'Nurse!' A small voice cut through her thoughts. 'Oy, Nurse! It is you, ain't it?'

A little figure dashed out from a side road and stood before them, followed by a much slower stooping one.

It took Alice took a moment to snap out of

daydreaming about families, wondering if something had happened — an accident due to the air-raid warning, perhaps. Then she recognised who it was.

'Pauline!' she exclaimed. 'Fancy seeing you here.'

'That's cos I only lives over there,' Pauline answered, pointing back along the side road. 'Not far to go for school, see.'

Alice nodded. 'I can see that. Although most of your school friends aren't here any more, are they? They were all evacuated on Friday.'

Pauline sniffed. 'I didn't want to go with them though. Me gran don't hold with all that. Do you, Gran?'

The stooping figure drew level with them and peered up at Alice with suspicion.

'This is me gran,' Pauline said, remembering her manners.

'Pleased to meet you.' Alice held out her hand but the old lady didn't do the same.

'And who might you be?' she demanded instead.

'Alice Lake. I'm a nurse, and I have been to St Benedict's several times this last term,' Alice explained, noticing that Janet Phipps, the teacher, had been right — the grandmother had hardly any teeth.

'You're the one what gave our Pauline the notion that she had to use a toothbrush,' the old woman snapped, pointing her finger accusingly. 'You're wasting your time, Miss. We never had any truck with such things and we've done all right. My old ma, God rest her soul, lived to be ninety-two and she never so much as set eyes on one. So don't you go bothering us with such newfangled pieces of nonsense.'

'It's entirely up to you, but we do encourage — ' Alice began.

'Stuff and nonsense,' Gran proclaimed, and both Alice and Edith noticed she smelt distinctly of gin.

Pauline hopped up and down. 'We got to get back, we left me brother on his own,' she told them.

Alice's eyebrows shot up, as she remembered Pauline's brother was even younger, but Gran didn't seem to be worried. 'He'll be all right, he never come to no harm before,' she said. 'Still, you and him are best off with me rather than being sent away to God knows who living in a field somewhere.'

'I'm sure all evacuated children are sent to perfectly good houses . . . ' Alice protested, but Gran was having none of it.

'Sent away from all they know, with cows and pigs and God knows what,' she went on. 'Poor little mites. My grandkids are Hackney born and bred, they're Londoners through and through. They ain't going nowhere. We'll stick it out together. That old Hitler ain't going to break up our family, I can tell you that for nothing.'

Alice sighed. 'Well, it's not compulsory, but if you ever change your mind . . . '

'We won't,' Gran snapped. 'Come on, Pauline, stop your dallying, you got work to do once you get home.' She took the little girl by the elbow and marched her away. Pauline didn't seem at all bothered but twisted around and waved.

'Bye, Nurse,' she called.

Edith let out a big breath as the pair disappeared around another corner. 'There's gratitude,' she remarked.

'What can I do?' Alice asked hopelessly. 'That child is bright as a button but what hope will there be for her if she grows up with a woman like that?'

Edith shrugged. 'All you can do is keep an eye out and let her know that, if there's any trouble, she can always come to you. She clearly trusts you, that much is obvious.'

'I suppose so.' Alice began walking slowly towards their home as Edith strolled beside her. 'I can't make it right for everyone. Not all at once anyway.'

'Exactly,' said Edith. 'We've got quite enough to worry about after today without you taking up the cause of one little girl, Alice. Now let's get back before the light fades any more and Fiona makes it worse by putting up all the blackout blinds.'

★ ★ ★

Mary was waiting for them once they got in, distraught. 'I can't believe it,' she said over and over again, as all three of them crowded into her room on the top floor at the end of the corridor. Mary had made it feel like home by adding velvet cushions and lots of silver-framed photographs of her parents and brothers. There was hardly a surface that wasn't covered in them.

They even crowded along the shelf where she kept her cosmetics and favourite Evening in Paris perfume. 'It can't be true, it's like a nightmare.'

Alice patted her shoulder, trying to comfort her, but it was no use.

'They'll all be in such danger!' she wailed. 'Charles is so brave, he's bound to head straight into the worst of it, and then what will I do?'

'You'll manage, we all will,' said Edith, keeping her voice steady but feeling slightly put out. Mary had barely met Charles, and certainly hadn't got as far as meeting his family. She herself was entitled to give way to despair far more because she would soon be separated from Harry, but she had no intention of doing so — not in front of anyone anyway.

'Will we?' Mary gulped, her eyes red from crying. Her tears had splashed down the front of her good silk blouse and made a random pattern.

'Of course,' said Edith stoutly. 'It's what we've been trained to do. We can have a good cry up here amongst ourselves but we can't show despair to anyone else, all right? And above all not to Charles.'

'Or Harry,' said Mary, belatedly remembering where Edith and Alice had been all day.

'Exactly,' said Alice, sensing that brisk decisiveness would be of more use than joining in with the weeping and wailing. 'We'll be needed more than ever and we have to show a united front. That's what's expected of us. We're not silly girls, to go giving in to moments of despair. We've got to show a bit of backbone.'

'Right.' Mary gulped again and reached for her handkerchief. 'Yes, I do see that. It's just such a shock. I never thought it would come to this, I was so sure the government would come up with a way of keeping the peace.'

Alice shook her head sadly. 'It's gone too far for that, Mary. You must see that there really wasn't much choice after what Hitler's done. Now we have to make sure we're ready. Have you got your blind sorted out?' She glanced towards the attic window, through which the sunset could be seen.

'N . . . not yet,' Mary admitted. 'I'm useless at sewing. Never could thread a needle.'

'Blimey, Mary, how do you ever manage with syringes for your diabetic patients?' Edith wondered.

Mary tilted her head. 'Well, that's different. I can do that, of course. But sewing . . . no, never could get the hang of it.'

'We'll help,' Alice told her. 'We don't want the local ARP warden coming round and getting us into trouble.'

'Specially as it's quite likely to be Harry's dad,' Edith cut in, eyes dancing.

★   ★   ★

Alice found she couldn't sleep, despite encouraging Mary to keep her spirits up and not give way to despair. She was restless, beset by thoughts of what could happen. She'd enjoyed the day so much, and was impressed by the courage of

Harry and Joe. She hoped she'd see him before he left; he'd offered her the library subscription, after all. Wearily she gave up the hope of easy sleep and made her way downstairs for a late cup of cocoa.

There was a light on in the service room — somebody else was having trouble sleeping, not surprisingly. Alice started when she saw who it was.

'Gladys,' she said. 'Are you all right?' When she came to think about it, she hadn't even realised the young woman slept on the premises. She'd formed the impression she arrived early and left late to return to somewhere nearby, as they all knew Cook did.

Gladys jumped and nearly dropped the cup she was holding.

'Oh, Miss . . . sorry . . . It's just that I wasn't expecting to see nobody.'

'That's quite all right. Here, let me wipe that,' Alice offered. 'Couldn't you sleep either?'

Gladys set down the cup containing what remained of her Ovaltine and hung her head. 'I couldn't, Miss. Me thoughts keep goin' round and round.'

'No wonder.' Alice turned to her cupboard and lifted out the cocoa powder and sugar. 'We're all going to be a bit like that for a while, I expect. It's a big change, even though we've been preparing for it for so long.'

Gladys nodded and bit her lip. She looked as if she couldn't decide what to say next. Then she took a deep breath and her words all came rushing out at once.

'Tisn't that, Miss. Or it is, but not exactly. See, I been thinking. I loves it here, I really do, it's like me 'ome.'

Alice nodded, trying to work out what was at the root of the young woman's agitation.

'I love bein' with you and the others, and hearin' all the stories about what you do when you're on the district.' Gladys rubbed her forehead as if she had a headache coming on. 'I learn heaps when you all talk to each other, I do. I know how to dress a wound, and what to look for when a baby gets sick, and old people what get pneumonia and everything.' Her face grew determined. 'You know what, Miss? I want to be a nurse too. There, I've said it.'

Alice's eyes widened but she nodded. 'Well, that's a good thing, Gladys. I expect the country will need many more nurses in the times to come.'

Gladys reddened. 'But I can't, Miss. I just can't.'

Alice stirred the cocoa powder and added some sugar with a little milk before pouring on the hot water she'd been boiling while they spoke. 'Is it because of your family, Gladys? I won't repeat it if you'd like to tell me.'

'No, Miss. Or yes, sort of.' Gladys groaned. 'See, when I was younger, me ma had so many kids that she couldn't look after them all and I was the eldest so I stayed home and fed them. So I never went to school much.' Her expression turned to one of great shame. 'Miss, I can't read.'

Alice had to take a moment to rein in her

shock. Even though she knew plenty of people couldn't complete their schooling, and Gladys's situation was not unusual, it still came as a surprise to her. She had been raised to respect education and to stay at school for as long as she was able, and everyone she knew had done the same. Edith was the only person she was close to who had had to fight to stay on and study in the face of family opposition.

'Well, that's a pity,' she managed, realising what it must have taken for Gladys to admit such a thing.

'Yes, I wish I could, cos I know I'm missing out,' Gladys went on, unstoppable now the floodgates had opened. 'I ain't stupid, I know that, even though teachers said I was when I was little cos I didn't go to class very often. I can remember things. Then I heard on the wireless about the, the . . . Civil Nursing Reserve, that was it. Where you're like an extra and don't have to stop working or go away to study or nothing.'

Alice nodded in sympathy. 'But you still have to study. You need to go to a course of lectures, for a start.'

Gladys hung her head. 'That's just it, Miss. I could go, and having heard all you nurses talking about it I'm sure I'd remember. But I couldn't write down what they told me or nothing. I'd never be able to study at home or do an exam.'

Alice nodded slowly. She had never really thought about how much her job relied upon being able to read and write; it was something she had always taken for granted. 'We always have to write accurate reports after every visit,'

210

she said, half to herself. 'We have to leave notes for the doctor, or take written instructions from him. We have to be able to read the packets, and catch up with the latest news in our magazines.'

'That's just it, Miss!' Gladys cried. 'There are so many things I can't do, and yet I know I'd be good at it, I know it!' She buried her head in her hands and her shoulders shook as she wept in frustration.

For the second time that evening Alice found herself comforting someone. She recognised the best thing to do was to wait for Gladys to let it all out. She sensed the younger woman had been holding this in for a long time and the announcement of war had brought it to a head. Slowly, as she rubbed Gladys's shoulders, a plan formed in her mind.

Finally Gladys grew calmer.

'Here, why don't I make you some cocoa,' Alice offered. 'I'm going to have a bit more.' Her first cup was now cold, only half finished.

'Thanks, Miss.' Gladys gave a final sniff.

Alice busied herself with the preparation of the comforting drink as she worked out exactly what to say. She didn't want to hurt the young woman's pride, but then again, she reasoned, Gladys had trusted her enough to confide her shameful secret. So she had to say something more than 'there, there'.

'Here you are.' She pushed a cupful across the wooden counter. 'You'll feel better after that, everyone does.'

'Thanks, Miss,' Gladys said again.

Alice took a deep breath, wondering what she

was letting herself in for. She didn't want to promise something that she couldn't complete, and yet she could not walk away and do nothing. 'I could help you, you know,' she said.

The other woman's head went up, her eyes ablaze. 'Really?'

Alice nodded. 'I mean, I'm not a trained teacher or anything, but I've spent the last term going into a school. While I was waiting to take my turn at speaking to the children, I could see how the real teachers went about helping the pupils to learn to read.'

'Gosh, Miss.' Gladys's eyes were on her now.

'I can't guarantee it, but I could ask one of the teachers who's my friend if she could lend me a textbook,' Alice went on, the plan forming in her mind as she spoke. 'Look, why don't we sit down tomorrow after I've finished my rounds and I can see how much you remember, then I can ask her for the right sort of book. Are you free then?'

Gladys nodded vigorously. 'I will be, Miss. I got to make tea for everyone but then I can stay after, cos I worked late tonight. I'd be ever so grateful.'

'Are you walking home now?' Alice asked, suddenly alarmed, aware how dark it was and how late.

Gladys looked sheepish. 'No, Miss. When I'm here this late I kips down in the basement. Where you're going to have your refuge room. Fiona knows but she said not to tell, as it's not really allowed. But otherwise I can't do me work.'

Alice gasped, realising the extent of Gladys's dedication, and how little they all knew about this daily presence in their lives. 'Well, that shows your commitment,' she said. 'Good. What we'll do is have a cup of tea together tomorrow and begin then. Oh, and Gladys.' She paused.

'Yes, Miss?'

'You've got to stop calling me Miss. Call me Alice.'

16

'Come on, Joe, you can dig faster than that.' Stan stood with his hands on his hips, observing his two sons. He was fiercely proud of them, both in the way they had matured as young men and because they had immediately signed up for the conflict that was to come. That didn't mean he had to be soft on them though. 'We've got to get this done before you go.'

Joe stepped out of the trench that he'd dug in what he thought was double-quick time and came to stand beside his father, taking a breather. He wiped his brow with the back of his forearm. 'Only if I have another cup of tea,' he hinted. 'And some of Ma's Bakewell tart. Then I'd be even faster.'

'You'll get your reward at elevenses, same as the rest of us,' Stan told him. 'Otherwise it will be unfair on Harry. Won't it, son?'

Harry was making such a clatter dragging the corrugated sheets that he hadn't heard a word of the exchange. 'What's that?' he asked, coming to a halt. Stan repeated what had been said.

'Sooner I'm finished the better,' Harry said. 'I've got to look my best for this evening.'

Joe nodded in acknowledgement. 'Can't keep Edith waiting, especially as it might be the last time you see her for a while.'

Harry had received his notification and had to report to a base in Northwest London on Friday, prior to being trained somewhere as yet unspecified. But it was unlikely he'd be anywhere within easy reach of the nurses' home, so evenings out with Edith would have to be shelved after tonight.

'I want her to remember me as my handsome self, not covered in sweat and grime like this,' Harry told his brother, looking down in dismay at the state of his old work shirt.

Stan snorted. 'You're going to have to get used to a bit of dirt wherever you're going, my lad. The army won't think twice about asking you to get covered in mud.'

Harry shrugged. In a way he was quite looking forward to it. He was certain he was in better physical condition than anyone else he'd be training alongside, and then there was the promise of boxing to keep him at peak fitness. He had no doubts that he would excel at whatever was asked of him.

Two hours later and the shelter was close to being finished, in no small way thanks to the extra fuel from Flo's tart, banana bread and several fruit scones. Harry was just about to ask when it would be time for dinner when there was a squeal from inside the house, floating shrilly through the open back kitchen window.

'Lennie! It's Lennie!'

Harry, Joe and Stan looked at each other and, as one, wiped their hands and faces and strode inside.

* * *

The kitchen was dim compared to the brightness of the garden, but there was no mistaking the man who had just walked in — also because Mattie was hugging him tightly, face revealing her delight and surprise. 'Look who it is! And he never said nothing!'

Lennie gently broke free from his wife's embrace and shook hands with his two brothers-in-law and father-in-law. 'Just got back from me latest training and they give us four days' leave. Four days! So I didn't hang around, I was on that train fast as you could say knife.' He beamed.

Lennie was shorter than Joe, Harry or Stan, and stouter, for all his army training. His face was round and his hair cut short, but his eyes were sparkling and bright green-grey. He'd always had a kind expression but now he was the picture of happiness, the hero returning to his family. 'Where is she?' he asked, his gaze raking the room. 'Where's my little star? Where's Gilly?'

'Ma took her upstairs for a nap,' Mattie said, patting her hair, which had come even looser than usual and was now falling all about her shoulders. 'I'll just fetch her.'

'You stay here with Lennie, I'll go,' said Harry, disappearing out of the kitchen door, knowing his sister wouldn't want to let her sorely missed husband out of her sight for one precious minute.

'Don't get her muddy from your filthy shirt,' Mattie called after him, but really she didn't mind a bit. What was a spot of dirt compared to the thrill of having Lennie home again?

216

'Honestly, he dotes on that girl, and on Kath's baby too,' she said, shaking her head in mock-despair, but enjoying her child's popularity.

Lennie took a moment to look around the familiar room, observing the small differences that had appeared since he'd last been home, way back at the end of spring. The most obvious one was the big blackout blind, rolled up at the window. He nodded in approval. He might have known Stan and Flo would ensure everyone would be safe in their home.

Joe inclined his head towards the garden. 'You're just in time to see our handiwork. One Anderson shelter, exactly as prescribed.'

Lennie looked out. 'Is that going to hold you all?' he asked dubiously.

Joe shook his head. 'We won't all be here. Harry leaves the day after tomorrow, and I expect to get my details next week. I'm heading for the navy, he's going into the army.'

'Good man,' said Lennie approvingly. 'I can give him some tips, tell him what's what.'

'Tell who?' said Harry teasingly, reappearing with the little girl in his arms. 'Here she is, Lennie.'

'Careful, you'll find she's a bit bigger than when you last saw her,' fussed Mattie as Harry passed his niece over to her cooing father.

'Oh, hasn't she grown!' Lennie's face was a picture as he held his beloved daughter, who was still half asleep. However, since she was used to being passed around to different adults, all of whom showered her with affection, she didn't

217

consider it worth stirring to protest.

Lennie gazed at the child with pride, hardly able to believe that this was the little baby he'd last seen only a matter of months ago but who had now doubled in size.

'She can sit up, she's starting to crawl and pull herself up and she gets into everything,' Mattie warned him. 'She'll try to talk too but so far she just makes nonsense noises. It's so funny. When we put her and Brian on the rug together they carry on a conversation of burps and giggles. We used to put them one at each end of the cot, but they don't fit no more.'

Stan cast his eyes to the sky outside and cleared his throat. 'Joe, Harry, just another hour will do it but I reckon it's coming on to rain. As Lennie will be here for a few days — you will, won't you, son? — can I have just a bit more of your time and we'll get that shelter finished.' He didn't wait for their agreement but headed outside, followed by his two sons.

Mattie and Lennie sank onto the sofa, arms around each other, encircling Gillian.

'Oh Lennie, I'm so glad you're back,' she breathed. 'I was worried you'd be sent away without me seeing you again. I couldn't have borne that.' She rested her head on his shoulder.

'As if I could go without seeing you.' He stroked her back. 'I got your last letter, you know, just as I was closing my kitbag. Almost made me blub, it did. You two are the most precious things in the world, you know that.'

'And you're the most precious people to me too,' said Mattie, holding back tears of joy mixed with relief. 'I know you're going to go away to fight again, Lennie, and I know you're properly trained and good at it, but I needed to see you, just to know you're real.'

'Course I am. But I know what you mean.' Lennie sighed. 'Look, I'm sure you've discussed this with your ma, but do you think you should be here — in London, I mean? Haven't most of the kiddies been evacuated?'

Mattie gave a small sniff, and pulled back so that she could look at her husband. 'Course we have.' She paused. 'I don't know, Lennie, it's so hard to tell what's for the best. I only want Gillian to be safe, you know that. I talked about it with Kath too — there's only her to protect Brian, we can't rely on that scumbag Ray to do anything.'

'No, it fair made my blood boil when you told me what he done to her,' said Lennie with feeling.

'Well, we thought maybe we should both go and take our babies somewhere. But what if something was to happen to Ma once we'd gone? Who would I come back to?' Mattie's face crinkled with distress at the very idea. 'We weighed it up and decided we'd take our chances here. Look, we got the shelter now. And this room's only got the one window facing the garden, it's sheltered, and we can all share the cooking and everything . . . ' She trailed off. 'It's like I said, we don't know for certain, but we reckon it's best to stay. At least for now.'

Lennie regarded his wife, his heart turning over that she'd had to face such a decision on her own without him there to support her. He knew her family were close and would do anything for them, but sometimes he found it hard to be away from her even though it was for the best of reasons. He pulled her to him again and could feel her heart beat through her thin cotton blouse. 'You got to do what you think is right,' he said, 'but if you change your mind, you'll tell me, won't you? I just want to know you're safe. I couldn't bear it if anything happened to Gillian and you.'

* * *

Billy Reilly sat on the barstool and stared morosely into his pint. He'd never been one for lunchtime drinking but today was the exception. The rest of the Duke's Arms was nearly empty, apart from a few older hardened drinkers, and he knew it would be because men of his age would be preparing to enlist or maybe had already done so. Harry had already gone. They'd shared a pint in here only two nights ago to send him on his way. Billy had confided in his old mate what he intended to do.

'I fancy my chances in the army too,' he said. 'I just been listening to what Lennie was saying and it sounds like a grand life. I know I won't be doing stuff like you, what with the boxing and everything, but I reckon I could do my bit that way.'

Harry had slapped him on the back. 'Good for you, Billy. But you could stay on at the docks, couldn't you? They'll need them to keep going.'

220

Billy had shaken his head. 'Yeah, I could, but so could lots of the old blokes. They don't need me there as much as the army does. New blood and all that.' He'd flexed his biceps, which weren't as impressive as Harry's, but were still testament to the heavy work he did, day in, day out.

Now Billy groaned and raised his glass. He'd been full of optimistic bravado, so keen to join up as all his friends were doing. He'd had secret hopes of coming home a hero. Look at the way everyone was all over Lennie, and he hadn't even seen any fighting yet. But now he knew his dreams were finished before they'd started. He drained his glass and waved at the barman to order another.

He realised he was swaying a bit and took his fresh pint over to a table. He didn't want to fall off his stool and be subject to even more ridicule than he was sure he'd receive once the news got out. The polished wood of the table's surface reflected the outline of his upper body as he slumped in utter dejection, gazing miserably out of the window to the street beyond. Hardly any kids about — strange for a weekend, but he supposed they'd all gone off to Hertfordshire, or Bedfordshire, or wherever the trains had taken them. Poor little mites, separated from their parents and all they knew.

'Billy! What are you doing in here this time of day?'

Billy blearily looked up. Someone was striding towards him. It was Joe. Billy groaned. It wasn't that he didn't enjoy Joe's company — usually they got on like a house on fire. But Joe was about to go off and join the navy, where they'd no doubt be delighted to make full use of someone who everybody knew had a good brain. He'd be a hero soon too. That just left Billy on his own, with never a chance to make his mark.

'All right, Joe?' he managed.

Joe pulled out a wooden stool and sank down on it. Even at this level, he towered over Billy. 'Don't usually see you in here this early,' Joe commented.

Billy grunted. 'I could say the same for you. Thought you usually went to Percy's café this time of the week.'

Joe nodded. 'I do. I'm on my way there now — I promised Alice I'd transfer my library subscription over to her and I said I'd see her there. But I was passing by and thought I saw you through the window. So I dropped in to see how you were. How did it go yesterday?'

Billy looked at his old friend steadily for a moment and then turned away. He didn't know if he could bear the shame of admitting what had happened at the recruiting office. Yet he didn't see how he could get out of such a direct question, and besides, people were bound to find out one way or another. It might as well be Joe who he told first. He was probably the kindest and most understanding of their gang of friends. All the same, his shoulders sagged in defeat as he prepared to confess.

'I didn't get in,' he muttered, still not meeting Joe's eyes.

Joe grimaced. 'What do you mean, you didn't

get in? Fit fellow like you, I'd have thought they'd have snapped you up straight away.'

'Well they didn't.' Billy rubbed his hand over his face. Then he turned back to Joe. 'Failed the medical, didn't I?'

'You?' asked Joe in astonishment. 'But you're fit as a flea, you never have days off sick, you're lifting heavy goods down the warehouse day in, day out — '

'Don't make no difference,' Billy cut in. 'It's not my lack of strength that's the problem. It's me feet. I got flat feet.'

'Oh.' Joe didn't know what to say. 'That makes a difference, does it? I never thought about it . . . '

'Seems like it does,' Billy said dully. 'I can't march, apparently. I'll hold everyone back. You'd have thought I could have done other stuff, you don't need your feet to fire a gun, but they weren't having it. I argued like mad but they didn't like that. They sent me packing.'

'Billy, I'm sorry to hear that.' Joe realised what a devastating blow this would be for his mate. 'You can carry on down the docks though, can't you? They'll need you there.'

'That's just what me ma said,' snapped Billy.

'All right, I was just saying.' Joe leant back.

'No, I'm not having a go, it's just that if I'd wanted to stay on the docks, I wouldn't have bothered going to enlist,' said Billy, cross with himself that he'd antagonised his friend but unable to stop himself. 'They all know I was going to do it and now, on Monday morning, they'll start asking and I'll have to tell them what's wrong. I'm useless, a dud, all cos of my stupid feet.'

Joe patted him on the shoulder. 'Don't take on, Bill. It doesn't make you useless, just that you can't be in the army. You could do things at home.'

'Like what,' Billy said, looking down at his hated feet.

'Dad says they'll need many more ARP wardens, and they can't all be old gaffers. They'll have to lift casualties and move around fast if it comes to it. Or fire watching — we know the docks and round here will be a target if it comes to it.'

'Suppose so.'

'It's true, I'm not making it up to make you feel better.' Joe got to his feet. 'Sorry, Bill, I got to go.'

Billy looked up at his tall friend as he stood. 'Quite right, can't keep the lovely Alice waiting.'

'It's not like that,' Joe said, slightly embarrassed, buttoning his coat.

Billy scoffed, but knew there was no point in arguing. He didn't really want to pick a fight, but if Joe couldn't see a good thing when it was right in front of him, then maybe there was something wrong with his brain after all. Still, that was their lookout.

Joe did up his last button. 'And have a think about what I said, Billy. Dad's got all the details. They could use someone like you.'

Billy sighed. Being an ARP warden didn't have the glamour of a fighter returning from the front line and was unlikely to win him any female attention, but it might be better than nothing. 'All right, Joe,' he promised. 'I'll do that.'

★ ★ ★

'Sorry I'm a bit late.' Joe hated not turning up on time and had rushed the short distance from pub to café, only to find that Alice had got there before him anyway. She was seated at a table in the corner by the window, watching the world go by, a steaming mug of tea in front of her. She was wearing a bright patterned scarf he didn't think he'd seen before, but then again, he knew he didn't always notice such details. Mattie was always teasing him that he never spotted when she'd made something new on their old Singer sewing machine.

Alice looked up and smiled. 'Don't worry, I haven't been here long,' she said, tucking a wave of blonde hair behind her ear. 'I haven't ordered anything to eat, I thought I'd wait for you.'

Joe settled in the seat opposite Alice as Percy came over, apron tied tightly as ever around his waist.

'Same as last time?' Joe asked, his mouth suddenly dry as Alice's clear blue eyes held his own. He wondered if it was the scarf she was wearing that brought out their colour so vividly.

'Of course.' Alice grinned broadly, not aware of his slight discomposure. 'I've been looking forward to it all morning.' She raised her eyebrows. 'I wonder what they'll feed you in the Royal Navy?'

Joe shrugged, getting a grip on himself.

'Whatever they can get hold of, I should think. I get the feeling we'll be kept so busy that we'll be grateful for anything they put in front of us.' He lined up the HP Sauce in readiness, and Alice immediately moved the mustard pot closer to her.

'Yes, I feel like that sometimes when I get back from my rounds,' she said. 'I could eat a horse if I've been cycling from one end of the district to the other, going to and fro all day.'

'Isn't it quieter now that lots of the kiddies have been evacuated?' Joe wondered.

'You'd think so, but several of the ones who haven't left have gone down with whooping cough, which has kept us busy. I've spent more time teaching the mothers about avoiding dehydration than anything else these past few days, and telling all the other members of the family to wash their hands properly. Never easy when you don't have a tap inside the house.'

'No, I suppose not.' Joe shook his head. 'I can't really remember what it was like in our house before Dad got the water sorted out. We've always been lucky.'

'Me too,' Alice said. 'It wasn't until I started doing my Queen's Nurse training that I saw for myself the conditions some families have to cope with. Oh look, here come the sandwiches.'

Joe turned and caught the salty aroma of sizzling bacon, which made his mouth water. 'This will pep you up,' he said, eyes alight.

Both of them immediately set about demolishing the delicious sandwiches, Joe adding sauce to his, Alice a generous dollop of mustard. As she ate, she watched as a lock of Joe's neatly styled brown hair had slipped down over his eye and he unconsciously pushed it back into place again. It always did that, she thought, no matter how the rest of his tidy, Brylcreemed hair behaved. It made him seem boyish, in contrast to his usual steady-as-a-rock maturity.

Joe looked up, aware of her scrutiny. 'What are you looking at? Has a fly landed on my bonce or something?'

Alice laughed, 'No, you aren't attracting flies yet.' His eyes shone in amusement at her and for a moment the last thing on Alice's mind was her bacon sandwich.

'Ah, that's better.' Joe sat back in his seat and pushed the empty plate away as they finished. 'Now I feel ready for anything. Whatever the navy can throw at me, you name it.'

Alice pushed away her own plate with a sigh of satisfaction. 'What about something as difficult as transferring a library subscription? Did you bring the form?'

'Of course.' Joe reached inside his jacket pocket and brought out a sheet of paper and a pen. 'I've signed it already so you just have to put in your details and sign it. Then you take it back to the library and you're ready to go. Usually they'd want us to go together, but I explained I'd enlisted and wouldn't be able to do it, so they understood.'

'I see,' said Alice, casting her eyes over the form. It struck her how many changes there were going to be because of the war. She'd been prepared for the major disruptions — the children being evacuated, young men joining up — but now saw that the war would affect every single aspect of their lives, even down to this small matter of altering a library subscription. 'It's very kind of you to do this, Joe. I do appreciate it.'

'Think nothing of it,' he said, his eyes bright. 'No one in my family would have been interested, and it'll just go to waste if I'm away. I know you'll make good use of it.' He paused. 'I'll probably be gone by the time you go to see them and make it official.'

Alice met his gaze and held it. 'You're off that soon?'

He nodded. 'Wednesday this week. I only heard this morning, but that's when I'm to report for my initial training. I'm going down to Portsmouth.'

'Oh.' Alice didn't know how she felt about that. It suddenly seemed very soon, and having an actual day made it real. Somehow Joe had become part of the fabric of her life, their little get-togethers were now something she actively looked forward to, anticipated even. He'd become a good friend. 'Well, it'll be good to be by the sea, won't it? Fresh air — fresher than Dalston, that's for sure.' She felt she had to sound extra cheerful.

'I expect I'll see rather a lot of the sea,' he replied wryly. 'Don't you miss it? You're from Liverpool, aren't you?'

Alice sighed in acknowledgement. 'Yes, I do, but I knew that's what I'd have to give up to do my training down here. I miss the way the air tastes salty when the wind is blowing from the west, and the sound of the seabirds, that sort of thing. But I like it round here too.'

'Best place in England,' said Joe staunchly. 'I know I'm biased but you can't beat round here. I'm glad you've settled into the area. I'll miss it, I expect, but then they're bound to give me leave so I can come back and check how Ma and the rest of them are getting on, and what changes there are around the place.'

'All the Anderson shelters,' Alice suggested.

'Yes, ours is all kitted out now,' Joe said. 'Ma and Maisie have got it as comfortable as they can — they'd have family photos up on the walls given half a chance. But it won't all be about the war, will it? I mean, they're still planning to open that new cinema up in Clapton, war or no war. Not that it will be of any interest to you, though.'

Alice blinked in surprise. 'Won't it? Why not?'

'Well, I know you don't like the cinema,' Joe replied.

'Really? Who told you that?' Alice was confused.

'You did. You said you weren't interested in going to see *Jamaica Inn* and preferred to read the book.' It was Joe's turn to look baffled. 'Don't you remember? It's how we got talking about the library — come on, it wasn't that long ago. Have you changed your mind?'

Alice frowned and then began to laugh. 'Oh no, I see now. You've got the wrong end of the stick. I didn't want to go to the cinema then because I'd have been a proper gooseberry with Edie and Harry. Talk about being surplus to requirements. No, I thought I'd better keep out of the way as I could tell even then how much she liked him.' She paused. 'That was all it was. Otherwise I like the cinema very much, I just don't get the chance to go very often.'

Joe shook his head in exasperation at his own silly misunderstanding. 'I did wonder. I'd never met anyone who didn't like the movies. Well, there you are. I'm not a postman and you're not a stuck-up nurse.'

'No, I'm not,' said Alice very decisively.

'In that case, maybe you'd care to try out the Clapton Ritz with me once it is open, when I have leave?' Joe asked.

Alice almost gasped. Was Joe asking to walk out with her? But then she told herself that his expression hadn't changed, that he was teasing her, in the way he and Harry teased Mattie all the time. There was nothing else behind his invitation. There couldn't be, could there? All the same, she detected a warmth creep up her cheek. Surely it wasn't a blush?

'Yes, all right,' she said, the words were out of her mouth before she had time to stop them. 'That would be lovely.'

'It'll be something to look forward to when those seabirds wake me up with their screeching every morning,' he said, and again she wondered if she was mishearing the intention behind his words.

They both hovered for a moment, seemingly reluctant to say goodbye, but it was Joe who spoke first. 'I suppose I'd better get going, as I've a thousand things to do before Wednesday. Ma will need me back, so I had best be off.'

'Of course.' She stood and reached for her coat, but he got there first and helped her into it. She caught the warmth of his arm for a fleeting moment, and for a second wondered what it would be like to extend that brief touch, but told herself to stop reading too much into everything. He was just being polite, as she'd come to expect of him. They made their way to the café door.

'Well, I'm heading this way today,' Joe said, inclining his head away from the direction of the nurses' home.

'Then, goodbye for now,' Alice said, feeling a little caught on the hop at the speed of his departure. 'I hope your training goes well.' She smiled brightly up at him, hiding a little tremor of fear that he might be going into danger already. 'Promise me you'll look after yourself, Joe.'

'I will, don't you worry, and you do the same.' Then, before she could stop him, he swiftly bent forward, cupping her elbow in his hand, and gave her a light peck on the cheek. Alice caught the aroma of sandalwood and Pears soap as he leaned in towards her. 'Enjoy the library books,' he said as he walked away, giving her a wave, and then disappearing into the press of people out on a busy Saturday lunchtime.

Alice turned towards home, walking slowly, trying to work out what had just happened. Then she decided that she was just feeling churned up because of the stark reality of the war — all the changes, and the speed at which they were happening. Joe was just a friend. He would be away for far more time than he would be at home for the foreseeable future. 'Which is quite all right,' she said under her breath, 'because I'm not interested in him as anything other than as a friend, really I'm not.'

17

Gwen stopped Edith and Mary as they were about to go outside and fetch their bikes on Monday morning. 'Nurse Gillespie, Nurse Perkins,' she said formally, and the two young women exchanged looks, wondering what they might have done wrong.

'Yes?' Edith tried to be polite but she was itching to get going, as she had a full round ahead of her.

'You both have patients referred by Dr Patcham, don't you,' Gwen said, although it clearly wasn't a question. Dr Patcham had been practising in Dalston for over thirty years and just about every nurse had one of his patients on her round. He was very popular thanks to his kindly manner, and trusted by everybody who came to him.

'He won't be available for several weeks and so he has drafted in a locum,' Gwen went on. 'Therefore don't be surprised if you come across a Dr McGillicuddy. Just carry on as normal, and address your reports to him for the time being and not Dr Patcham.'

'Why, whatever's happened to him?' Mary asked. She had a soft spot for the doctor, who must have been nearing retirement age. 'I hope he's not been taken ill.'

'That's not for us to question,' Gwen said severely. 'Just do your work as you would usually do, but be prepared for a new doctor for a short while. Very well, off you go.' She turned and marched smartly back down the corridor towards the district room.

'Blimey, she's full of the joys of spring this morning,' grumbled Mary as she made her way to the bike rack. 'Surely it's only human to want to know what's up with the doctor. He's one of my favourites. He brought me ginger biscuits the last time he saw me, that's typical of him. I do hope there's nothing seriously wrong. If only it could have been Beastly Beasley instead.'

Edith shrugged and arranged her cloak so that it wouldn't catch in the bike chain as she got on. 'Maybe we'll find out more on our rounds,' she suggested. 'I'll try to see if anyone knows something. But I've got to go, I have a poor teenage boy with a tubercular hip and he needs to be seen as early as possible. I was afraid Gwen was going to make me late. Catch you later.' She hopped onto her bike and sped off before Mary could speculate any further.

★   ★   ★

Edith had no time to think about the old doctor as she tended her patient, a fifteen-year-old who needed careful nursing twice a day. By the time she had prepared the room, sorted out her sterile water and dressings, along with two pairs of forceps in a basin, made sure clean pyjamas were to hand and that the window of the tiny bedroom was shut, all her attention was on her work. She noted his temperature, respiration and pulse, as she would for any patient, and then followed the detailed routine of cleaning and bathing and dressing that his condition needed, all the while reassuring him and keeping him calm. She checked he had no bedsores on his pressure points, as the poor lad was bedbound and prone to them. Finally she tucked him into a freshly made bed, opened the window, and expertly cleared everything away in a hygienic manner. 'Right-o, Dennis, I'll see you next time,' she said breezily. 'I'll just go and have a chat to your mother. She's downstairs, isn't she?'

'That's right,' said Dennis, as cheerfully as he could, though he was already beginning to perspire with the effort. 'Thank you, Nurse.'

Edith shut his bedroom door, full of admiration for his bravery. He never complained, even though he must have been in constant discomfort at the very least. She sought out his anxious mother, and discussed what he was likely to have to eat for the day, suggesting a few improvements so that he had the best nutrition her limited money could stretch to.

'So he can have beef tea for his dinner.'

Edith agreed, pleased that things were going as well as could be hoped for.

'Yes, Doctor always says that's good for him,' Dennis's mother went on. She was a small, nervous woman, trying to hide the worry her son caused her every waking minute. 'Well, that's to say the old doctor. Did you hear what happened to him, Nurse?'

Edith paused in the fastening of her Gladstone bag. 'I'm not sure, Mrs Thomas,' she said cautiously. 'We've been told there's a locum for a little while, but that's all.'

'Oh, the poor doctor,' Mrs Thomas exclaimed, wringing her hands. 'It's this blasted blackout, that's what's to blame. Coming home from visiting his daughter on Saturday night, he was, and drove into a lamppost.'

'Goodness,' Edith said, taken aback. 'That sounds nasty.'

'He was ever so lucky. He didn't break nothing but I heard he's all shaken up. Hurt his head, all bruised he is, so they say.'

'That's terrible,' said Edith. 'Well, I'm to make my report to his temporary replacement, Dr McGillicuddy.'

'Strange name, ain't it,' Mrs Thomas remarked.

'Irish, I believe,' said Edith, wondering if the woman thought her own surname — Gillespie — was strange too.

'He didn't sound Irish,' Mrs Thomas said.

'Oh, have you met him?'

'Yes, he was ever so nice. He dropped round last night to make our acquaintance, fancy that. Young man, he is. Very dark hair, lovely kind eyes. He's good-looking too. You want to pay him a visit, nurse.' Mrs Thomas shook off her gloom and sounded almost teasing.

'Oh, that's of no interest to me,' Edith grinned back. 'I'm married to my work, you know.' She took her cloak off the back of the front door and wrapped it round her. 'I must be off, Mrs Thomas, but I shall see you later. Thank you for telling me about Dr Patcham.'

'Tell him get well soon from Dennis if you see

him,' the woman said, coming to the door to see her out.

★   ★   ★

Alice was the first back to the nurses' home at the end of the rounds and immediately went to the service room to make a hot drink. Gladys was there, cleaning the cupboard doors. 'Hello, Miss . . . I mean, Alice.'

Alice rubbed her cold hands together. 'Gladys, how are you? If I don't get a drop of cocoa soon I'm going to perish with the cold.'

Gladys moved out of the way so Alice could reach her shelf. 'You want to take your gloves with you. It's not summer any more. You're all out on those bikes — that wind will chill you to the bone, it will.'

'Good idea,' said Alice. 'Will you have time this evening to look at those exercises, Gladys? Have you managed to try them?'

Gladys put down her rag. 'Yes, I have. It was ever so hard to begin with but I reckon I've got the hang of some of it. It's when you put letters together that I get confused. They don't sound like what they ought.'

Alice nodded as she spooned out cocoa. 'I know what you mean. Letters don't make the same sound every time. You just have to learn the common words. But you'll find it easier as you go along.'

Gladys nodded seriously. 'I reckon you're right, Alice. Thank you ever so much. I got to do upstairs now but I'll see you later.' She flashed a smile, picked up her cleaning things and left, as Alice took her warm drink through to the seating area of the canteen.

The calm was broken as Mary whirled in, soon after followed by Edith.

'Well, I say. Have you seen him yet?' Mary pulled off her cap and her hair sprang free. 'The new locum doctor? I tell you, if I wasn't walking out with Charles, I'd make sure to make all my reports to him in person. He's a far cry from Dr Patcham, dear old soul that he is.'

'No, our paths didn't cross, but some of the patients told me about him,' said Edith. 'They all seemed to like him.'

'I should think so too. Seriously, how could you not? You'll have to find an excuse to meet him. He won't be here for long but he is a sight for sore eyes.' Mary raised her eyebrows. 'Temperatures will be raised across the district, that's my prediction.'

'Steady on, Mary,' laughed Alice. 'You'll make Charles jealous if he hears about it.'

'On no, he's no reason to be jealous, not really,' said Mary. 'In fact I'm seeing him later, just quickly, as he's off in a few days' time. He'll be going to and fro for a while so we must make the most of days when he's in town. I should go up and get changed. But I had to check to see if you've met the gorgeous Dr McGillicuddy.'

'Dr . . . McGillicuddy?' Alice echoed, setting down her cocoa.

Mary was too carried away with enthusiasm to notice the change in her friend's face. 'Yes, odd name, isn't it?'

'Irish,' said Edith automatically.

'But he's not Irish. He's from Liverpool,' said Mary. 'Toodle-pip, girls, I have to make myself beautiful for Charles.' She swirled out.

Edith looked at Alice. 'What's wrong?'

Alice shook her head, avoiding meeting Edith's eyes. She picked up her drink, put it down again, pushed it away. Suddenly the taste was less inviting. 'I . . . I might be wrong,' she began, her voice halting.

Edith sat down opposite her. 'It's the Liverpool connection, isn't it? Do you know him?'

Alice shrugged. 'I can't say. It's not such an unusual name up there — there are lots of Irish names, people who came from Irish families there.'

'And nothing wrong with that,' Edith said forcefully. She'd had a lifetime of teasing about her own name, and knew that her parents had sometimes found it hard to find a house to rent or proper employment.

'Exactly.' Alice sighed. 'But when I first started training back there, I did know a Dr McGillicuddy. He wasn't much older than me in fact — he'd just finished his own training. He was very good-looking; you couldn't help but notice it. All the nurses used to make excuses to be on his ward. It was quite funny really.'

Edith briefly shut her eyes. She had a horrible sense of where this conversation was leading — towards the one thing that Alice hardly ever spoke about.

'But you didn't, did you,' she said softly. 'You

weren't interested in Dr McGillicuddy.'

'No.' Alice gazed out of the window. 'I knew him quite well though, if it's the same person. You see . . . ' she paused and swallowed hard, as if to gather her strength to face the memory she'd tried so very hard to avoid. 'You see . . . he was Mark's best friend.'

There it was. She'd said the word. She'd named the man who had broken her heart. The young trainee doctor she'd first met on a night shift. After that moment she'd never spared anyone else a second glance, including the almost impossibly handsome Dr Dermot McGillicuddy.

'Oh, Alice.' Edith reached over and took her friend's hand. The hurt evidently still went deep. But now it looked as if she would have to suffer a daily reminder — or at least for as long as Dr Patcham remained out of commission.

'I'd better make an excuse to go to see him, get it over with rather than meet during the course of the rounds on the district,' Alice said, her voice whisper-thin. 'If he's going to talk to me about Mark then I'd rather it was at a time of my choosing. So I can be ready.'

'Good idea,' said Edith. 'Do you want me to come with you?'

'No,' said Alice at once, and then, realising it had come out too harshly, 'No, but thanks. I'd rather do it on my own. Get it over and done with.' She got up distractedly, gathering her things. 'I've got to see Gladys about her next lesson. I've got to go upstairs.' She wiped her cheek swiftly, but not so fast that Edith didn't see.

'Are you all right?' Edith was all concern.

Alice shook her head but spoke resolutely. 'Yes. Or I will be. Thanks, Edie — and you won't mention it to anyone, will you?'

'Of course not.'

'Then I'll try to see him first thing Monday. Get it over and done with.' Alice walked away, biting her lip, but knowing she had no choice. The most painful episode in her whole life was about to be ripped open again and somehow she had to get through it.

★ ★ ★

Never one to put off anything important, Alice presented herself at Dr Patcham's house on Monday morning, where there was a side door which led to the room he had turned into a surgery. It must once have been a sitting room and it still retained a rather grand appearance, with heavy wood panelling and beautiful cornices. The wallpaper was dark flock and the whole place would have been gloomy were it not for the big bay window which let in the autumn sunlight. In one corner stood an old wooden desk, and behind it sat a figure Alice would have recognised anywhere. Dr McGillicuddy hadn't changed a bit. He was bent over a pile of papers, which from where Alice was standing looked like nurses' reports.

'I'll be with you in a moment,' he said, not looking up, and Alice caught her breath at the familiar voice. She'd heard hardly any Liverpool accents since she left, and this made her at once homesick and wary.

He finished skimming the top report on the pile and placed it to one side, on another stack of papers. Then he sat back and his jaw dropped.

'Alice.'

She met his gaze. 'Hello, Dermot,' she said, pleased that her voice remained steady.

He rose to greet her and came halfway across the rich old gold carpet before changing his mind and holding out his hand, rather than giving her the hug that he would once have done. 'Fancy seeing you here,' he said, once he had got over the surprise. 'And you're a Queen's Nurse now.'

'Yes, that's right,' Alice said, fingering the badge at her neck. 'I came to London to train last year and then took up a post here in Dalston when I qualified.'

'Of course you left Liverpool, I remember that,' Dermot said, recovering quickly. 'I should have guessed it was you — I saw some reports from a Nurse Lake and the handwriting rang a bell but I didn't suppose it could be you. It would have been too much of a coincidence. Do sit down, what am I thinking of, forgetting my manners.' He gave her the broad smile that had sent all her colleagues' hearts a-flutter.

She took a seat on the beautifully carved oak chair opposite the desk, as he resumed his place.

'Yes, who'd have thought it,' said Alice quietly. She glanced down at her hands. 'One of the other nurses said she met the new locum and I realised it had to be you.'

242

'What are the odds, eh?' he said, still smiling, his voice light.

Alice couldn't keep up the small talk. 'I thought I should come. Better to see you now than to bump into you on the district, in front of a patient.'

Dermot shifted in his chair. 'I see.' He restacked his pile of reports to gather his thoughts.

'Why are you here? I mean, why have you left Liverpool?' she asked.

He frowned. 'I'm only here briefly. It wasn't planned, but when I heard what had happened to Ralph, I felt I had to help out,' he said.

'Ralph?' she echoed.

'Yes, Dr Patcham. He's an old friend of my godfather,' Dermot explained. 'I was staying with him in town this weekend on my way to Southampton, and Ralph's daughter rang him, in a bit of a state after the accident — you've heard about that? — and it seemed like fate. I don't have to be in Southampton until next month and so I said I'd take over, just for a few weeks, to give the old boy a chance to recover.'

'Why were you going to Southampton?' Alice wondered.

'I'm joining up. I'm going to be an army doctor.'

Alice sighed. Yet another way in which the war would affect the normal, everyday running of general life — the younger doctors would think of leaving the hospitals. 'Won't you still be needed back home?'

Dermot nodded sadly. 'It's a tough choice and

I thought hard about it, but I reckon on balance the army will need me more. Doctors of Ralph's generation can keep things going here, but when things start to heat up on the battlefront, that's where we younger ones will be vital. I felt I had to do it.'

Alice nodded in understanding. 'It's going to be difficult whichever way you choose, I should think.' She stood up and walked across to the bright window, with the shafts of sunlight full of dancing dust motes. She turned her back to Dermot as she asked, 'How is he?'

'Oh, Alice. You're still thinking of him.' Dermot's voice was heavy.

Alice nodded. 'Of course. Hard not to. You'd better tell me and get it over with. Don't worry, I'm not going to start crying or anything. It's all water under the bridge, but I'd like to know, for my own peace of mind.' She turned to face him and could see he was about to weigh up his words very carefully.

She had always liked Dermot, and felt lucky that she'd had a chance to get to know him without being overwhelmed by his looks, which in some ways were as much of a barrier as a draw. She'd heard all his friends tease him about giving up medicine and becoming a film star instead, but knew he was fiercely dedicated to his profession. He was a compassionate and skilled doctor and, if circumstances had been different, she would have been looking forward to working closely with him again for a few weeks. But there would always be the spectre of Mark between them.

'He's leaving Liverpool. He'll be in Southampton already,' Dermot told her. 'We talked it over for hours and he came to the same conclusion as me. He's joined up too. He felt it was the right thing.'

Alice turned away again as she said, 'Well, he would. He always wants to do the right thing.' This time she couldn't keep the bitterness from her voice.

'Alice.' Dermot's face suddenly looked weary. 'I know it was hard, but Mark thought it was for the best, you know that. It wasn't anything to do with you, how you were, it was circumstances beyond his control . . . '

'You don't have to make excuses for him,' said Alice quickly. 'He stuck to his principles and I always agreed with those, for all the use that turned out to be.' Then she recovered her composure. 'I shouldn't be surprised that he's joined up already. So many brave souls have done so.' For a fleeting moment Joe's image came into her mind but then it was superseded by a vision of Mark, and how he had looked when she had last seen him. That day when he'd told her how much he loved her but that they had no future together. He hadn't thought it was fair on her to ask her to wait when he had no idea of how long he would be away and what fate awaited him in Spain. The cause of the International Brigade was more important than their love. He was prepared to sacrifice his personal happiness for the greater good, and that meant she had to sacrifice hers as well.

'Alice, Alice.' Dermot rose and came across to

her. 'Don't upset yourself now.'

She stepped a little away from him, not wanting to resume their old familiarity. That brought back the sense of Mark being there with them. It was too sharply painful. She had to put up her guard, the one she'd built in those dark and despairing days after he'd left her and gone off to fight in the Spanish Civil War, so full of the high ideals that she couldn't help but come second to. 'I'm not upset, not really,' she said. 'I know it's all over and that's that. It's not that I want him back. I know he'll always put the cause first, and I admire him for his courage.'

'Yes, he's got a lot of that,' Dermot said. 'I only hope I have a quarter as much, when I come face to face with danger. You never know until you're tested, do you?'

Alice nodded. 'He's no coward, that's for sure. I was proud of that, even though it meant we had to part.' She subconsciously played with the badge at her throat again. 'So, how is he?'

'He's very well,' said Dermot, keeping his voice neutral. 'He was lucky not to be wounded out in Spain, and when he came back he took up his post at the hospital again. Said he couldn't believe how well equipped it was compared to where he'd been. He'd lost weight of course, but he's put it on again and is fighting fit now.'

'Good,' said Alice. 'He'll need to be, won't he.' She gazed down at her feet. 'Glad to know he's all right. Not that it makes a difference to me,' she said hurriedly. She didn't want Dermot going off to Southampton in a few weeks and telling Mark she was still pining for him. She had her pride.

'Anyway, thank you for seeing me.' She looked at her watch, a sensible plain one, not the delicate gold one Mark had once given her for Christmas. That was at the bottom of a drawer in her old bedroom in her parents' house. 'We're bound to come across each other over the next few weeks, and now that's cleared the air.' She gave him a bright smile even though she felt as if she was breaking inside with all the old memories resurrected.

Dermot know her too well to be fooled, but said nothing. He admired her, realising it had taken her own brand of courage to come here like this. He counted Mark as his best friend, closer even than his own two brothers, but thought that in this matter alone the man was a fool. How anyone could have won the heart of a woman as clever, clear-sighted and loyal as Alice Lake only to turn his back on her was completely beyond him. He only wished he had been half as lucky. While he was perfectly aware of his looks, the truth was that they brought him plenty of attention, but rarely of the sort he actually wanted. He had yet to find a true soulmate; and yet he had believed that was what Mark and Alice had found in each other. He had been proved sadly wrong.

'We will have plenty of patients in common if those reports are anything to go by,' he said now. 'I look forward to working with you again, Alice. Well, I'll have to get used to calling you Nurse Lake in front of everyone.'

'You will.' Alice brightened, cheered by the thought of working with someone whose abilities she knew she could trust without even having to think twice. 'I've got a professional reputation to maintain, I hope you realise.' She made to move towards the door.

'I don't doubt it for a minute,' he said, 'but I hope you have some free time? I'll be stuck in with my medical tomes otherwise. Shall we meet up after work this week?'

Alice nodded. Now she'd had this difficult conversation, she felt lighter. 'That would be lovely,' she said as he held open the surgery door. 'Thank you Dermot, for everything.'

18

'I do hate it when these blasted committee meetings go on late.' Fiona tied her scarf firmly around her neck as she and Gwen stepped out into the cool evening. 'If everyone was disciplined about it, they could have got through the agenda in half the time.' She shook her head. Wasting time and lack of discipline were two things she had little patience for. There was no avoiding the meetings, though. The nursing association was managed by the committee and so, as superintendent and deputy, Fiona and Gwen were accountable to them.

'Too many people enjoying the sound of their own voices,' Gwen agreed, hefting her shoulder bag into place, having retrieved her torch from it. She switched it on, making sure it was properly shielded to conform to the rules of the blackout. 'Still, that's that over and done with for a while.'

Fiona glanced up at her taller colleague. 'There's that to be thankful for at least, I suppose. Anyway they agreed to our main suggestions. That's something.' She was determined to look on the bright side, even though attending meetings was by far and away her least favourite part of the job. Now she was eager to get back to the nurses' home for a warming drink, after which she would probably sit up into the early hours, catching up with the never-ending paperwork.

Gwen pursed her lips. The suggestions would mean changes and she never liked that. 'Do you have any candidates in mind?' she asked. 'I'm assuming you do, or else you would never have mentioned the idea before the committee.'

Fiona nodded briskly. 'Naturally. You have to go into these situations well prepared, you know that. While I'm sure all our nurses could teach first aid perfectly adequately, it strikes me that some are far more suitable than others.'

Gwen snorted. 'We'll need to make sure they are steady and sensible. To my mind that rules out a fair few.'

Fiona laughed. 'Gwen, my dear, you're far too hard on them.'

Gwen shook her head. 'Not at all. Have you seen them this past couple of days? All this excitement about the new locum doctor. They're running around as if they've quite lost their heads. It's very unedifying.'

'Not all of them,' said Fiona. 'There are several who have steady boyfriends, fiancés even, and I'm pleased to say they have carried on as if nothing has happened. I was thinking of asking Edith Gillespie for a start.'

'Edith?' Gwen asked dubiously. She had never quite forgiven her for breaking curfew so defiantly.

'Yes, Gwen. She's settled down a lot over the summer,' Fiona stated. 'Her young man has just enlisted, you know. Teaching first aid might be just the thing she needs to take her mind off that. I've seen her work, and she's actually very good.'

'You must do as you think best,' said Gwen,

unable to keep the doubt from her voice.

'Exactly,' said Fiona. 'Also, we should ask Alice Lake, as she has a track record of teaching in the community. Her work with the school children made the difficult task of evacuating St Benedict's that much easier. And of course she's teaching Gladys to read in their spare time.'

'Is she?' Gwen came to a halt in surprise.

'Oh yes. They probably think I don't know about it. It's all very low key. But I caught Gladys looking at an exercise book at the weekend, and they've been huddled together a few times. I think it's excellent. I realise Gladys has kept her secret from everyone else, but this is the first time to my knowledge that she's felt confident enough to do anything about it. I find that very encouraging.'

Gwen smiled faintly. It never ceased to amaze her how her friend found the good in every situation. Here they were, facing war and all manner of dangers, and she was excited about their maid learning to read. In the greater scheme of things it didn't seem like much. Then she admonished herself for being mean-spirited. 'Yes, you'd have thought the poor girl would be dog-tired at the end of a long day, she works so hard around the home,' she acknowledged. 'Where she gets the energy to study on top of that, I do not know.'

'She has the incentive,' Fiona declared. 'We must find a way of rewarding that, when she's had a chance to come on a bit. We'll keep a weather eye.' She bustled along, filled with renewed energy herself, and Gwen had to

251

struggle to keep up.

They reached the front door of the home and Fiona swung it open. Her mind was on one thing only, and that was a nice cup of tea to warm her chilly hands on. 'We'll just get the kettle on . . .' she began, when the peace of the hallway was shattered by the insistent ringing of the telephone.

Gwen jumped. Even though she was used to it ringing in the daytime, it was still relatively new and it was unusual for it to sound after dark. A deep sense of foreboding told her this could not be good. She moved to reach for the receiver but, as ever, Fiona had reacted more quickly and got there first.

'Yes . . . yes, I see,' she murmured, while reaching for a notebook and pen with her other hand. 'Do you have any further details? That's a priority, of course . . . yes, not far at all. That will be perfectly all right, we will send somebody right away. Thank you, goodbye.' She put the receiver down again and sighed.

'Looks as if my bedtime drink will have to wait,' she said.

'Bad news?' Gwen asked. 'Is it serious?'

Fiona pulled a face. 'I don't know, but it could be. Another one of these blasted accidents thanks to the blackout. Honestly, it's causing more problems than leaving the lights on — I know I shouldn't say it. A young woman and her baby hit by a car that came off the road. It's Dr Patcham all over again, except this time pedestrians were involved. That was the ARP station, asking if we can get someone over there.

252

It's just back by the main road — we must have missed it by minutes. I'll go.'

'No, you need your tea after that meeting. I'll go,' Gwen insisted.

A voice spoke from the bottom of the stairs, which was in shadow.

'I'll go. I don't mind. You've both just got in.'

'Alice? Is that you?' Fiona called into the gloom.

Alice stepped into the light cast by the bulb nearest the telephone. 'Yes, and I heard what you just said. I've been in all evening and today's rounds weren't bad at all — I'm wide awake and won't sleep if I go to bed now anyway. My bag's all refilled. It won't take me a moment.' Without waiting for their reply she sped up the stairs to her room.

Fiona leant against the wall of the hallway, smooth from where scores of nurses had brushed by. 'Do you know what, Gwen, I'm inclined to send her,' she said reluctantly. 'Now we've come in from the cold, I don't mind admitting that it's just hit me I'm in need of a wee rest. Then I simply must attend to the administration I should have finished before we left. I honestly think she'll make a better job of it than either of us at this moment.'

Gwen nodded. 'You may well be right, Fiona. If Nurse Lake feels alert still then it makes sense to send her, as it is in the patients' best interests.'

Fiona nodded. 'I know. There's no room for false pride on an occasion such as this. We have to be confident that we send somebody who's up to the task, and I've no doubt that Alice will be.

Thank you, my dear,' she said, standing up straight again as the young nurse reappeared, Gladstone bag in hand. 'Make sure that you stay out of harm's way and come back as soon as you can. I'll be up, no matter what time it is, so come and report to me. You need to go to the main road, just by the big bakery — I'm sure you know where I mean.'

Alice shut her eyes for the briefest of moments. 'Yes, I do. It's by the junction of Jeeves Street.'

'That's the one,' said Fiona briskly. 'Right then, off you go.'

★ ★ ★

Kathleen had been hurrying along the pavement, trying to push the pram and hold her shielded torch steady at the same time. It was well nigh impossible, and she had to keep stopping to adjust her grip, which meant the journey took even longer than usual. As if sensing her anxiety, Brian began to grizzle, even though he was tucked up safe and warm against the evening's chill.

'Don't worry, we'll be home soon,' she sang out, trying to reassure him, but he could pick up his mother's real feeling behind the cheery words. He knew as well as she did that it was long past his bedtime and he wanted his cot and a feed.

Kathleen sighed as she swapped her torch from one hand to the other. She had never intended to stay out this late. She should have known better than to trust her mother. She hadn't seen her for ages, though, and so when she got a message that she'd be visiting her old friend Pearl who lived off Balls Pond Road, Kathleen had decided to join them. It was so much easier than getting the bus on the pram all the way down to her mother's unfriendly house.

They had got there just after teatime, so Pearl wouldn't feel obliged to offer them anything to eat. All the same, it had been over an hour before she was asked if she wanted as much as a cup of tea. By then Kathleen had been parched, as Pearl kept the house warmer than anybody she'd ever known, on account of her arthritis, which Kathleen now felt she knew enough to write a book about. Then Pearl and her mother had got out the sherry, and soon there was little sense to be had from either of them. Kathleen had declined, pointing out that she was still feeding Brian and it wouldn't be good for him.

'Oh, that old wives' tale,' her mother had snorted dismissively. 'It never done any of you any harm. That's typical of you, that is. Can't just have a bit of innocent fun, always got the long face to spoil the party.'

'Ma, that's not fair,' Kathleen had protested. 'I just like tea better than sherry.'

'Hark at her,' Pearl had said. 'Ain't that a shame, cos my Bertie got hold of a whole load of sherry and I'm nearly out of tea.' She cackled as she topped herself up.

Kathleen remembered Bertie, a boy who'd been a year or two ahead of her at school, and who'd been known as a bit of a bully. Nowadays

255

he had the reputation of someone who could get stuff off the back of lorries. Evidently that included sherry. She had glanced sadly at her mother, who looked like an older version of her but with thinning grey hair and a face set in lines of discontent. Kathleen always hoped they would get on better each time they met, but each time she was disappointed. She wondered why she bothered, and yet she couldn't stop trying. She clung to the belief that one day they would make up and have the same cosy relationship her mother seemed to have with the rest of her family.

'So how come you're out in the dark on your own on a night like this?' Pearl went on. 'Where's your Ray? Ain't he going to stop by to walk you home?'

'Oh, him. Wouldn't have thought he'd show his face round here,' her mother began, and so Kathleen cut her off before she could get stuck in to her favourite subject: how Ray was a waste of space and they never should have got married, but now they had it was up to Kathleen to cope with whatever disasters he brought upon them.

'Actually, no. He's in the Merchant Navy now,' she announced. She'd received a rare letter from him that very morning, informing her that he'd been officially transferred from his old ship to a Merchant Navy vessel, and so he was pleased to say he'd be getting regular wages. It was as if there had never been a row between them and he was going to behave like any normal caring husband. Kathleen had read it with a mixture of longing, disbelief, and relief.

256

Regular money but no Ray around the house — perhaps that was as good as she could ask for. Her heart still ached for the love and passion they had shared, but she couldn't risk him coming near Brian.

Her mother had perked up at that. 'Is he now? I never thought he had it in him, I don't mind admitting.' She turned to Pearl. 'How about your Bertie? When's he joining up, then?'

Pearl had bristled. 'He's in a valued job, he is. He's working all the hours God sends down the docks.'

Kathleen had had to stop herself from laughing. She could guess very well exactly what it was that Bertie was doing down the docks — tracking all the lorries so he could unload goods off the back of them on the QT. She wasn't surprised to hear he had no plan to enlist.

'Fit lad like him, they'd snap him up for one of the services,' her mother had gone on, deliberately needling her friend.

Kathleen could see that it was time to go. She didn't want to be around when the two older women started arguing. There was nothing her mother liked better than a good argument and they always left Kathleen with a headache that took days to shift. 'I'll be off,' she announced. 'Got to get Brian to bed.'

'All right then,' her mother had said, as if it wasn't ages since she'd seen her grandson. Kathleen supposed she had so many grandchildren it didn't matter to her whether she saw much of him or not. She tried her best to hide her hurt.

With nothing more than the lukewarm cup of tea inside her, she turned the big pram back up the main road and headed for home. The autumn wind cut through her thin coat. As she hadn't intended to be out this late, she hadn't thought to put on an extra layer. Stupid, she chided herself. She should have known better. Too late now.

She could just about make out the sign of the big bakery in the darkness, caught by the light of the moon coming out from behind a cloud. 'Nearly home,' she said to Brian, who gave a whimper. 'Won't be long, you'll see.' She was saying it as much for herself as for his benefit. She bent to tuck in a corner of blanket under his chin and didn't notice a car approaching at speed behind her. She was vaguely aware of a figure walking around the corner by the bakery, and was about to glance up to see if she knew who it was when everything started going very wrong.

★　★　★

Billy had been striding along, hands shoved deep into his coat pockets, fuming at the unfairness of the world. Here he was, fit and able, and walking as well as anybody else. How dare they say he'd hold up his comrades if he was forced to march for a day? He would bet he could carry a heavy pack better than most of them. He spent most of his working life hauling huge crates around the docks and hard graft came naturally to him. So why had they turned him down?

He barely slowed as he rounded the corner by the bakery, although its sign, flapping in the wind, brought to mind the taste of fresh bagels, which he loved. For a moment he was distracted. Tomorrow he could have some for lunch, if he was keen enough to get up early and take some with him. Maybe he'd have one with cream cheese and another with herring.

Then his attention was caught by a pair of headlights, weaving erratically and at great speed towards him. 'Silly bugger will get caught by the ARP,' he muttered, but then the lights illuminated a small figure coming along the main road. 'Oh my God, she's got a kiddie with her,' Billy breathed, as the approaching car veered wildly across the road, fortunately empty of other vehicles. 'What does he think he's doing, on a bleeding race track or something?' His first instinct was to get out of the way, but he could tell the woman hadn't yet realised what was going on just behind her. She had bent to attend to her child in the pram. He couldn't let her get mown down by this idiot. His urge to protect her was too strong and he sprinted towards her, only realising who she was at the last minute.

'Kath!' he shouted, moving faster than ever now he knew it was her. 'Get in — '

It was too late. The car's headlights rushed towards them, as the driver completely lost control and mounted the kerb. Billy had just time enough to push Kathleen, the pram and himself into a shop doorway before the impact hit them. The car's bonnet crumpled against the corner of the doorway. Billy had saved them

259

from the full force of the blow, but he could see that the pram was dented and Kathleen was bleeding. It took him another moment before he realised his own leg was crumpled beneath him and he was in agony. 'Kath . . . ' he gasped. 'Get the baby away . . . '

'Billy! Oh my God! Help me! Brian, come to Mummy, it's all right.' Kathleen, even through her injuries, was desperate to save the little boy, who was now wailing at the top of his voice, trapped in his ruined pram. Frantically she pushed back its hood, which wouldn't retract all the way but now hung at a strange angle, and scrabbled to get the baby out. Her arms seemed to be working, although she could see blood was pouring from somewhere. His little blanket would be beyond salvation, but that didn't matter now. She tugged at the corners of the thin mattress and managed to release his feet and then, after what felt like hours but was only a minute or two, she had Brian safe in her arms and she could get him away from the crashed car.

'Billy!' she called. 'Can you come over here? Come on, it's safe here.' She reached out her spare hand while the other clutched Brian to her as tightly as she could.

Billy groaned. 'It's me leg, Kath. I can't move me leg.' He tried to drag himself over to her but screamed in agony. It was no good. Now the rush of adrenaline had gone he couldn't propel himself any further. He hoped the car wouldn't go up in flames or he'd be a goner. 'You get further back, Kath!' he shouted.

Then there was a sound of running and a uniformed figure appeared. The ARP warden hurried towards them. 'What's happened here, then?' he called, at which there was movement from the car. The passenger door slammed open and a figure emerged, tousled and shaky but apparently not badly hurt. 'You come here and explain . . . ' the warden began, but the man pushed past him and began running away back down the main road before escaping by ducking down a side alley. The warden tutted but gathered himself to deal with the priorities. He took in the scene before him as best he could in the changing moonlight and the beam from the car's one undamaged headlamp. Quickly the warden assessed the dangers, as he'd been trained to do, peering in to the vehicle and noting the driver was still in there, before he moved to reassure the wounded pedestrians. 'Don't you worry,' he said in confident low tones that Kathleen found instantly comforting. 'We'll have you fixed up in no time.'

* * *

This was the scene Alice found when she arrived, breathless from pedalling as hard as she could into a headwind. For a moment she didn't recognise the young woman in front of her, blood pouring from a wound to her brow, but then her voice caught in her throat as she gasped, 'Kathleen?'

Kathleen turned her distraught face up to the nurse and cried aloud in relief. 'Nurse Lake,

Alice, oh, thank God it's you. Will you check Brian, make sure he's all right? He was in there . . . ' She pointed shakily to the crumpled pram.

Alice took a breath, knowing she must at all costs remain professional, although her immediate instinct was to reach for the baby. 'Let me just see what's what,' she said, as the ARP warden approached her. Swiftly he filled her in.

'My job's to see to the driver,' he said grimly.

'Is he hurt?' Alice asked.

'Hurt?' The ARP warden snorted. 'He doesn't seem to have anything major wrong with him. Not that he'd notice. He's drunk, that's what he is. Stinks of drink, he does.'

Alice's heart sank. It was her job to tend to everyone, regardless of who they were or what they'd done, but she found it hard to treat somebody who'd deliberately brought their woes upon themselves. Now her conscience was clear — she could see to the other casualties.

Quickly she checked little Brian who, apart from being frightened and cold, seemed pretty well all right. 'We'll put some Dettol on his scratches when we can get him somewhere warm and light,' she told Kathleen. 'Now let's see about you. That's a nasty cut to your forehead . . . but don't worry. They always appear much worse than they are, you know.' Quickly she dealt with the gash which, although bleeding profusely, was not deep and mercifully wasn't full of dirt or grit. 'If you can just hold that pad against your head with one arm and Brian can go in the other . . . there we are.'

There was a stone ledge to one side of the bakery entrance and Kathleen sank down onto it, her head ringing where it had been struck but full of relief that, despite the scare, neither she nor Brian had come off too badly. 'Now you got to see to Billy,' she croaked. 'He saved us, he did. We'd both have been goners without him, no doubt about it. Don't let anything happen to him, he's the last man who deserves that.'

Alice went across to the slumped figure who, now she came closer, she could tell was moaning softly. 'Billy?' she said steadily. 'Can you sit up? It's, Alice.'

The moans stopped as Billy half turned from where he had collapsed against the neighbouring shop, sitting up but with his legs out in front of him. One was at a strange angle and blood was forming a puddle on the paving slabs around him.

'It's me leg,' he explained, but Alice could see that for herself.

'Right, don't try to move,' she said. 'This is going to hurt a bit, and I'm sorry, but I need to see where that blood is coming from. Would you mind holding my torch?' The moonlight was too faint to see by, now they were in the shadow of the shop wall, and the one cracked headlight was pointing the other way. She retrieved her scissors from the Gladstone bag and neatly cut along the seam of his trouser leg, pulling back the material as gently as she could. 'Ah, I see. Well, I'll stem the bleeding, but you'll need to go to hospital to have this seen to. Looks like a clean break, as far as I can tell, but they'll sort you out. Just let me — '

'Aaaargh, bloody hell.' Billy couldn't hold back his agony as she slipped something under his leg and tied it firmly over his thigh. 'Sorry, Alice. Couldn't stop meself. Don't suppose you got a tot of rum on you? That'd help, I swear.'

Alice shook her head but smiled, guessing that if he could make a joke of it then there was hope for him. 'Against regulations, I'm afraid,' she told him. 'Worst thing you can do if you're in shock, as well, despite what you might have been told.'

'Shame.' Billy tried to smile. 'Is Kath all right? And the little 'un?'

'They're going to be just fine,' Alice assured him. She looked up at the rumble of an engine. 'This must be the ambulance. Stay as still as you can until they come to you with the stretcher — I must report to them on the state of your injuries right away.'

The ambulance driver pulled up behind the wreck of the car and he and his colleague swiftly got out. Alice gave them a quick summary, and they hastened to get Billy onto a stretcher while causing him as little pain as possible. 'And you'd better come with us too, ma'am,' said the driver, taking a good look at Kathleen's forehead. 'Can't be too careful with a bang on the head like that. Just to get you checked properly,' he added, seeing her look of dismay.

'But my boy,' Kathleen cried. 'He needs me, he wants feeding and it's way past his bedtime. I can't go, I'll be all right, it's just a scratch.'

'Ma'am, I really would advise — ' the driver began, but Alice interrupted.

'I'll take him,' she said. 'I'll bring him round to Mattie and Flo — they're just around the corner. He'll be safe there.'

Kathleen brightened. 'Would you, Alice? They're the only ones I'd trust him with, they're good as gold. They know what he likes to eat . . . ' She started to sob as all the events of the evening began to catch up with her. She was so glad her baby was safe, and if she was honest her head did hurt very badly.

The ARP warden stepped away from the car and back towards them. 'Did you say Mattie and Flo? Mrs Banham, you mean?'

'Well, yes,' said Alice.

'Stan Banham's on his way now,' the warden said. 'He's on duty tonight and has been called as backup. We didn't know what we'd find here. But I can deal with this young idiot. He's in no state to make a fuss, and the police can throw him in a cell for the night to sober him up. Then he can take his punishment.' His jaw set in anger, knowing the whole incident could have had a very different ending if the man whose leg had been broken hadn't been so brave. The young mother and baby would have been crushed and most probably killed.

It was only a few moments later that Stan arrived, his big presence instantly reassuring. 'My, my. What have we here. Kathleen, what have you been doing to yourself? And Alice too. Glad to see you here, though I dare say you'd rather be back in that nice nurses' home drinking cocoa.' His eyes sparkled with warmth in the intermittent moonlight.

'Fat chance of that,' Alice said wryly. She quickly told him what had happened, as the ambulance was ready to go.

'Coming, ma'am?' the driver called, holding open the back door. 'You come and sit in here in the warmth and keep your friend company. He could do with a familiar face.'

Even now Kathleen hesitated. 'But my baby . . . '

Stan stepped forward. 'Don't you worry about young Brian,' he said at once. 'He'll be safe with me. I'll even pop him inside my coat, then he'll be toasty as can be. Mattie will see to him, you know she will. I'll drop him off at home and then get back on my rounds. Sure you don't need me any more, Ted?'

The ARP warden shook his head. 'No, you get that child home. I got three of my own, I know what it's like,' he said kindly. 'Then this young lady can get back home too.'

Kathleen got unsteadily to her feet. She was shaking a little with the cold and the shock but thanked everyone heartily, watching as Stan buttoned Brian inside his big standard-issue warden's coat. 'I'll be off then,' she finished. At least she knew Brian would be well looked after, and in truth warmer and better fed than he would have been at home. Flo's kitchen was an oasis of comfort.

As she went towards the open back of the ambulance, she glanced at the wrecked car and the driver, still passed out drunk inside it. She gasped in sudden recognition. She hadn't seen him for ages but he'd been brought to mind

266

earlier today. The drink-addled driver who had nearly killed all three of them was none other than Pearl's precious son, Bertie.

19

'You all right, Edith?' asked Mary, breezing through the tables and chairs of the common room to her friend. 'You look a bit down in the dumps.'

Edith put down the letter she'd been reading and shrugged. 'Thanks, but I'm just tired. You know, the usual. Rounds finishing late, having to cycle in the dark and taking ages to get back. Now the nights are drawing in it seems even more difficult. Still,' she said, rousing herself, 'it's nothing really. I'll be all right once I get a good night's sleep.'

Mary leant over the back of the chair opposite. 'Oh, I do understand. It's exhausting, isn't it? And you must be missing Harry. Is that letter from him?'

Edith tucked a curl behind her ear and half wished she'd hidden the letter before Mary had come over. She didn't really want to talk about how much she was missing him. It was with her every day, sometimes a slow ache, sometimes so acute she could hardly breathe. Never mind all those soppy songs about moonlight and roses and love making the world go round. The everyday reality of it was just the opposite, and from this latest letter he had no idea of when he might be back.

'Yes, he's met some other soldiers who want to train as boxers, so he's setting up a sort of club,' she said. 'Only they haven't got anywhere to meet yet, so they just do exercises on the parade ground.'

Mary nodded, but her face betrayed that she wasn't at all interested in boxing. 'Jolly good,' she said. 'Anyway, I bet he'll be home before you know it.'

Edith wrinkled her nose. 'What do you mean?'

'Stands to reason,' Mary said. 'All that fuss about gas attacks over London, and us all having to be prepared to run to the refuge room at the sound of the siren, all those children being evacuated — and what's happened? Precisely nothing. It will all blow over in a jiffy, just you see if I'm right.'

'Really?' Edith found it hard to believe.

'Oh yes,' said Mary airily. 'Stands to reason. It's all been a big fuss over nothing.'

'Is that what Charles says?' asked Edith, quietly folding her letter away so that she could reread it later in her room in peace.

Mary pulled a face. 'Oh, he hates to talk about things like that. Says he spends all day discussing the war and so when he sees me he wants a change. Suits me. The last thing I want after a day washing wounds or changing bedpans is to hear about plans for fighting.'

'But what about petrol rationing?' Edith asked. 'Or restrictions on paper? Newspapers are going to get shorter for a start.'

'I hardly read them anyway,' Mary confessed. 'I'd rather listen to light music on the wireless. Who honestly reads papers from cover to cover?'

'Don't let Alice hear you say that,' Edith replied.

'Well, yes, but she's the only person I know,' Mary said. 'And as for petrol, it won't affect Charles because he's a staff officer and needs it for the good of the country. Which luckily includes taking me to restaurants.' She glanced at her watch and Edith noted it was a new one, with a delicate bracelet in woven gold. More benefits of knowing Charles, she supposed. 'Must be off, don't want to keep him waiting.'

'Have a lovely evening,' said Edith as she got up too. She didn't think she could bear another conversation, pretending everything was all right, when she felt so miserable inside. It wouldn't do to show that in public though. She would retreat to her bedroom and have a good cry, then she'd feel better.

From the doorway where she had been standing unnoticed, Gwen paused. She recognised the underlying sadness of Edith's expression, even if the girl's friend didn't. She was only too familiar with it and it would bring it all back if she wasn't careful. She fought off the waves of misery by remembering what Mary had said about the war being over soon. That girl — she was completely clueless. Anger surged through Gwen's veins. She'd met Miriam earlier, who'd told her that the Austrian family she'd had staying in her spare rooms had now left for Canada, but that another family would be arriving at the weekend. 'They're called Schmidt,' she'd said. 'Or at least, they are now. They had to change their name from a Jewish one to something safer but it isn't enough. They've got out while they could and have next to nothing, apparently.'

'How will you manage?' Gwen had asked, concerned for her friend.

Miriam had shrugged. 'We will,' she said shortly. 'We will have to.'

Gwen wondered if she should say something to Edith, but remembered that she herself had found such enquiries only made things worse, and so she walked down the corridor to check the district room was ready for whatever the morning might bring. She wondered if the young women around her really knew what they would be in for. How would they cope with the long haul of wartime? For she was as certain as she could be that this was just the beginning.

★ ★ ★

'Blimey, who's that?' Clarrie wondered, peering around the corner of the bar of the Duke's Arms. She unconsciously flicked her hair, catching the faintest trace of her Coty perfume, and smoothed her flared skirt. 'He hasn't been in here before, I'd have been sure to notice.'

Peggy tried to turn around but her friend stopped her. 'No, don't make it so obvious, he'll know we're watching. Try to see in the mirror over there.'

Peggy dutifully leant sideways, pretending she was adjusting the gilt buckle on her shoe, so that she could see the reflection of everyone on the other side of the room. 'Who . . . oh, I see who you mean. No, he's definitely new in town. Not that I'm interested, what with me being a married woman an' all.' She twisted the narrow band on the fourth finger of her left hand. It wasn't the most expensive ring by a long chalk, but Pete had promised her a better one when he could manage to buy it, maybe for their first anniversary. All their savings had gone now, but they'd had their wedding and all their family and friends had come to it, to toast the happy couple and wish them well on their lives together. The only problem was that they were now many miles apart.

'Have you heard from Pete this week?' Clarrie asked. 'Is he still in that training camp thingy?'

'I think so,' said Peggy. 'They won't let him say exactly what he's doing, so I have to fill in the blanks, but he sounds as if he's made a few friends and it's not too bad. Says the food isn't as good as mine though.' She smiled ruefully. When they'd planned their autumn wedding, many months ago, neither of them could have predicted being parted within a fortnight of the ceremony. Pete had agonised over leaving her, but couldn't sit idly by and watch his friends join up. Being newly married wasn't a good enough excuse. She'd cried bitter tears but then resolved to be proud of him and to paint on a bright face.

Both young women turned at a slight commotion at the side door. 'Billy!' Clarrie cried. 'Look at you, up and about again! Come over here, you can sit down all right, can't you?'

Billy grinned gratefully as he swung himself over to their table on his crutches. He was becoming quite skilled at getting around the place now, but he was glad to have the excuse to sit. He had half dreaded the prospect of standing at the bar with any of his remaining mates, but had forced himself to come out this evening, the first time since the accident. 'What are you having, Billy?' called the barman. 'I'll bring it over.'

'Let me get it,' said one of the men at the bar, who had once been Billy's neighbour. 'The man's a hero. Saved that woman and her kiddie, he did.'

'Cheers, Frank. I'll have a pint of the usual,' said Billy, trying not to beam like an idiot at the praise. Even though he had flat feet, he was still a hero after all. That was worth the pain in his leg, the heavy cast on it and the difficulty of everyday living. Now everyone would recognise he wasn't a coward.

Peggy obligingly shuffled around the table to make extra room so that Billy could sit with his leg outstretched and prop his crutches against the damask wallpaper. 'We heard all about it,' she said warmly. 'You could have died, Bill. You must have thought fast all right.'

Billy shrugged. The memory of that night was beginning to blur. 'I dunno about that,' he said, nodding happily to the barman bringing his pint. 'I just did what anyone would have done.'

'Not anyone,' said Peggy forcefully. 'You put yourself in danger to save Kath, we all know that.'

'How is she?' Clarrie asked. 'I haven't seen her down the market or anything.'

Billy sighed. The daft thing was, even though he'd been in agony, he'd had all that time with the woman he'd admired so fiercely for so long. She'd sat with him in the ambulance and waited with him in the hospital while his leg was reset and put in the cast, and she'd come home with him to make sure he was all right. She had barely flinched when her own wound was treated. If only things had been different. If only he'd had the nerve to tell her how he felt before that Ray Berry came along. Now it was too late and she'd married him, the lily-livered wastrel that he was. Yet in the hospital she had looked at him with such kindness, it was almost as if for that one evening she had been his.

He sighed again. No use dreaming about what wasn't going to happen. He raised his glass and took a welcome sip. 'I've missed this stuff,' he confessed, deliberately cheerful. 'Well, from what I heard, she's on the mend. I haven't been able to get out and see for myself, but that's what Stan Banham said. He's popped round to see me a few times. He recruited me for the ARP, you know.'

'Has he? Oh, you'll be good at that, Billy,' said Peggy. 'You'll tell us all to put our lights out but you'll do it with a smile on your face so we won't mind.'

Billy laughed. 'Maybe. Course I got to wait for my leg to get fully better before I can start. He'll make sure I know what's what, anyway.' He caught Clarrie's attention wandering to the other side of the bar. 'Here, Clarrie, am I boring you already?' he teased.

Clarrie smiled sheepishly at being caught out. 'No, course not. But — no, you won't be able to see from there. There's someone sitting at a table in the corner and I don't know who he is. Looks like a film star.'

'Oooh, she's come over all unnecessary,' giggled Peggy. 'It's true, Billy, there's a tall dark stranger and we haven't a clue who he is. Well, he might not be tall. He's sitting down.'

Billy twisted around, slowly so as not to fall and embarrass himself. 'Let's have a look and see what all the fuss is about. Peggy, aren't you ashamed of yourself, Pete's barely been gone a moment.'

'No harm in looking,' said Peggy.

'Ah,' said Billy, turning carefully back again. 'I couldn't tell you who that is, but I can tell you who he's with. It's the nurse who saved me that evening, Alice. Alice Lake.'

★ ★ ★

Alice didn't usually go out to pubs but she felt it could do no harm to sit in the lounge bar with Dermot. It was the third time they'd met up and his stay in Dalston was nearly over. At first she'd been nervous about seeing him, wary of unleashing all the old emotions about Mark, but now she could talk to him and not be haunted by images of how things used to be when they would go out as a threesome. The more she saw Dermot away from Liverpool, the more normal it felt. Also, they had plenty to discuss as they had several patients in common. They had been heatedly discussing the best way to treat someone with suspected emphysema who didn't

275

want to be treated, when she realised the medical details might not be well received by anyone close enough to overhear. She started to laugh. 'Sorry, that's all a bit grim,' she pointed out.

Dermot smiled back. 'Yes, I tend to forget and then get carried away,' he admitted. 'Anyway, he'll be your worry next week. Dr Patcham will be back in the saddle.'

'I'm glad he's feeling better,' said Alice.

'I'm sure some of his patients will be relieved,' said Dermot. 'The older ones look at me as if I'm just out of nappies. Some have even asked if I'm qualified. It takes a lot to win their trust.'

'Yes, they used to do that with me too,' Alice confessed. 'It was worse for Edith, she's younger than me and she's so small, they think she's still at school. Mind you, they only make that mistake once. They wouldn't dare repeat it — she stands for no nonsense.'

'So I've realised,' said Dermot. 'Did you mean her when you said another friend would meet us here?'

Alice shook her head. 'No, it's somebody else. You don't know her — it's a teacher from the local primary school. We always say we're going to see each other after work and somehow never do, so when I bumped into her in the street earlier, I thought I'd ask her along. You don't mind, do you?'

Dermot tutted. 'Of course not. What does she look like, in case I see her before you do?'

'Short brown curly hair, glasses,' Alice told him. 'She did say she might be late — she was asked to stay behind for a meeting and then her landlady gets terribly offended if she doesn't eat her evening meal. One reason why we haven't yet managed to meet up.' She glanced around, checking that she hadn't missed Janet coming in. Alice would not have cared to go into a pub on her own, even if she was meeting somebody, but Janet swore she wasn't in the least worried. 'If I was, then I'd never go out,' she'd said.

There was as yet no sign of the teacher, but she did notice the man in the other part of the bar, who caught her eye and got rather unsteadily to his feet. Alice tried to move across the floor to meet him, but he shook his head slightly as he determinedly wove over to the corner table. 'Billy, you're on your feet again,' she exclaimed. 'How's the leg?'

He grinned in the bright lights that lit the pub from every wall, making it feel cosy, with the blackout blinds adding to the effect. 'It's my first night back out on the town,' he admitted. 'It's mending nicely and that's down to you, that is. I wanted to come over to thank you — not sure that I managed it on the night. I was a bit distracted.' He smiled again.

'Billy, this is Dr McGillicuddy,' Alice said, realising she'd turned her back on Dermot and hastening to put that right. 'Dermot, this is Billy — I was one of the first on the scene when he had his accident.'

Dermot reached to shake hands, which Billy succeeded in doing only after propping one crutch against the neighbouring table. 'I heard about that — nasty business,' he said. 'Isn't the driver in jail now?'

Billy glanced over each shoulder. 'He was, but I dunno what happened, if they kept him in or what,' he said. 'His mates come in here sometimes, so I ain't asking no questions if you get my drift.'

Dermot nodded. 'Say no more. Alice, will you have another drink?'

Alice nodded. It was warm in the busy pub. 'Lemonade again, please.'

'Billy?'

Billy shook his head. 'No, I've got one in and I don't think I should have too many. I'll overbalance and that won't do, will it, Nurse?'

'Certainly not,' said Alice, mock-sternly, and they both laughed. Dermot moved off to talk to the barman and Billy grew solemn.

'I mean it, I am very grateful for what you done,' he said, awkward now.

Alice shrugged it off gracefully. 'It's my job. I did what any nurse would have done.'

'That's as maybe. Kath was glad it was you, though. It makes a difference. Sorry, I didn't mean to interrupt.'

'You're not . . . ' Alice began, but he had picked up his other crutch and was making his way back to the other side of the pub before she could explain.

Billy was concentrating hard on not toppling over but his mind was whirring. Maybe he had got it wrong. He'd teased Joe about his friendship with Alice even before he'd met her, convinced his friend was going to great lengths if there really wasn't any romance in it. Joe had denied it flatly, and now here was Alice with a doctor whose good looks had reduced Clarrie to a giggling jelly.

'Tell us, then!' she said now as Billy got back to his seat. 'Don't keep us on tenterhooks. Who's that man?'

Billy laughed and made small talk for as long as it took him to drain his pint. However, when another old acquaintance offered to buy him another, he declined. It hit him how tired he was and that maybe he wasn't as improved as he'd claimed. 'I'd best be off,' he told the others.

'I won't be long myself, Pete's mum don't like me staying out late,' Peggy said. 'She's kind and everything, but she's a bit old-fashioned like that.'

'Fair enough,' said Billy, hobbling on his crutches to the door. 'See you around, girls.' He paused to hold the door open for a woman in a dark brown overcoat with a shrewd expression on her face, but he didn't wait around long enough to notice that she went to join Alice and Dr McGillicuddy at their table.

* * *

'Janet! Good to see you.' Alice got up as her friend reached them. 'We've finally managed to meet each other out of work hours.'

'Well, this is cosy,' said Janet, looking around the place appreciatively. 'I've often been past but never come in — nobody I know comes here. Thank you for inviting me.'

Alice made the introductions and Janet nodded pleasantly at Dermot, but then launched into conversation with Alice, almost ignoring him. The meeting she'd attended earlier in the evening had raised the question of combining some schools, now that so many pupils had been evacuated, and yet they had begun to see a drift back into the city of families fed up with their billets, or who didn't take to country living. 'It could be chaos,' groaned Janet. 'Nobody actually knows how many children we will have by next term. It's very disruptive to their education, and to the school's organisation.'

Dermot sat back in his chair, slightly surprised. He wasn't used to being sidelined. Almost without exception, every woman upon meeting him for the first time would register his appearance even if she didn't say anything. It was a fact of life, and it was one reason he enjoyed Alice's company so much — she was 100 per cent just a friend. Yet here was a woman who barely acknowledged him, so consumed was she by her concerns.

After the initial shock he found he was enjoying himself. It wasn't often that he could sit back and watch people without getting drawn in. Because of his profession, he was always being asked for advice, but these two young women had no such need. Alice obviously knew the school and the other teachers well and was offering suggestions about class sizes.

'Oh, and I meant to ask you,' she went on. 'Do you think we could use the school hall after hours for first-aid classes? We've begun them in the church hall but it's freezing in there. We can't teach people how to roll up bandages if they

280

can't feel their fingers.'

'Good point.' Janet paused to draw breath. 'I'll ask, shall I?' Finally she turned to Dermot. 'I'm so sorry, I've just totally monopolised the conversation. That was very rude — I was just so incensed by some of my colleagues who seem to have no idea what all this is doing to the children's ability to learn.'

'So I can see,' said Dermot. 'Well, you must be thirsty. Please allow me to buy you a drink.'

'Lemonade?' Alice asked.

Janet pulled a face. 'That stuff is for summer picnics. I'd prefer something a bit stronger. Whisky and soda please.'

Dermot raised his eyebrows but then stopped himself. He was fond of that very drink himself, so why should he judge anyone else for asking for it? It was a highly unusual request from a woman, but that wasn't his business. 'Whisky and soda it shall be,' he said, rising to his feet once more. As he stood waiting at the bar, he watched Alice and Janet, deep in animated conversation, and felt a pang of regret that he would be going so soon. Just when things were getting interesting.

20

'You were doing really well there, Gladys,' said Edith as they both left the school hall. Janet had successfully persuaded the governors to let the first-aid classes move to St Benedict's and Gladys had signed up for them. Her reading was coming on in leaps and bounds, thanks to the lessons she was having with Alice, and she had felt confident enough to ask if she could come along.

'I know I can't follow all of the instructions on the packets of the bandages and that sort of thing, but I can understand some of them,' she'd explained.

Now Gladys tugged her scarf more tightly around her neck and smiled. 'Thank you, I really enjoy it,' she said gratefully to Edith. She was unused to compliments, as she had rarely received any before going to work at the nurses' home. 'Some of it I know already from listening to you all talk when you get back from on the district, but some of it is new. I never liked learning at school because I wasn't there very often and it was all so difficult, but this is different.'

'Glad to hear it,' Edith replied. 'It could come in very useful. Brrrr, it's growing very cold now, isn't it?'

'It'll soon be Christmas,' Gladys said. 'Will you be going back to your family?'

'No, I shouldn't think so,' said Edith, wondering if her mother would even notice if she stayed away. 'Patients will still need tending to, Christmas or no Christmas. I'm happy to do the rounds, specially if other nurses want to go and celebrate with their families.'

Gladys nodded. 'That's kind of you, that is.'

Edith shrugged. 'I really don't mind.' She had hoped Harry would be home and they could celebrate together, but he hadn't been told either way yet. That was all she cared about.

'Miss Dewar always organises nice things to make it all special,' Gladys told her. 'We decorate all the downstairs rooms and have crackers and proper Christmas cake and turkey. Maybe we'll have a carol concert again.'

Edith smiled. 'Oh, I love singing carols. I do hope it happens this year. Let's ask her once we get back.'

Gladys nodded and looked wistful. 'I love to listen but I always found it hard to learn the words. I never did much singing.' She brightened. 'Maybe this year I can read some of the song sheets, though. I'm going to have a go.'

'You should, you really should,' said Edith, shoving her gloved hands into her cloak pockets for warmth. 'I've heard you humming around the place as you work — I bet you've got a good voice. We'll help you.'

* * *

Stan Banham had been on early ARP duty and was making his way home in the bitter chill, looking forward to some of the hot soup Flo had promised to have waiting for him when he got back. He was fed up with some of the excuses people gave him about why they had left a light showing. Their cat had broken the blind. They didn't think it counted if it was for only a short time. There hadn't been any raids or gas attacks and so it didn't matter. It made the usually phlegmatic Stan fume with annoyance. He didn't like resorting to threats, but tonight he'd had to tell one man that he would fine him if he didn't stick to the regulations. It was enough to try the patience of a saint. The only good thing was that Billy was finally fit and able to get around without crutches, and so he would be accompanying Stan on his next shift, to get to know the job.

He could see his breath in the cold night air as he puffed out his bad temper. Then the heat of the house greeted him as he opened his front door. He hung up his heavy greatcoat, feeling the cares of the day recede.

Mattie came running down the stairs as he was doing so. 'Have you heard?' she cried. 'No, you won't have, of course not.'

'Heard what?' Stan asked, pushing open the kitchen door, catching the aroma of the soup. Chicken and mushroom, if he wasn't much mistaken. His mouth watered at the prospect.

'Ma will tell you,' Mattie replied, following him into the room.

Flo beamed at them from the dining table,

which was covered in her sewing. 'Take a look at this!' she exclaimed. She fished in the large front pocket of her apron and brought out a letter. 'This will warm the cockles of your heart! Mattie, pour your father some of the soup.'

Stan reached across and took the letter and instantly recognised the handwriting as that of his oldest child. Quickly he skimmed it and broke into a broad smile. 'Oh, that is good news,' he breathed. 'Joe's coming home for Christmas. What could be better?' He looked up and met his wife's happy gaze. Their eyes exchanged the message that neither of them had been willing to speak out loud: that they had feared for his safety ever since he had left. Even though people were calling it a phoney war, they both knew that there had been skirmishes, and that the navy had been involved. Joe had moved from his training base to a ship and they had had no means of knowing where he was or what he was doing.

'We'll have to have a proper Christmas dinner,' said Flo. 'We'll make it the best yet. I've got my turkey on order from the usual old fellow down Ridley Road but I'll tell him to get me a bigger one and then we could ask those nice nurses over too. Oh, if only Harry could be here.'

Mattie passed her father a bowl of the steaming soup and cut him some bread to go with it. Stan nodded in thanks. 'That might be asking too much, love,' he said gently. 'I know you want us all to be together but we must count our blessings that even one of our boys will be back. That's a miracle on its own.'

Mattie sat down at the table with a thump. 'I

don't expect Lennie will get leave either. I really wanted him home for Gillian's first Christmas, but I don't think he will be. Surely they'd have let him know by now.'

'You don't know that,' said Stan comfortingly. 'They probably can't tell some soldiers until the last minute. We'll make sure Gillian has a wonderful time, whatever happens.'

Mattie nodded. 'I know. I just miss him, that's all. Anyway, dwelling on it won't change anything. Pass me some of that mending, Ma, I might as well give you a hand.'

'Yes, your young eyes can see better than mine in the gaslight,' said Flo, picking up a shirt that was missing two buttons and handing it to her daughter. Her mind was racing ahead to what she would buy at the market tomorrow. If Joe was coming home, she'd make it the most marvellous festive season ever.

★ ★ ★

'Good heavens, what on earth is that?' Mary asked, leaning over the banister and gazing down into the ground-floor hallway. 'Come and look at this.' Alice and Edith craned their necks to see what was going on, as a man in a brown overall came into view, hauling one end of something dark and bulky.

Consumed by curiosity they raced downstairs, halting as Fiona Dewar came out of her office. For a moment Edith thought they would be told off for running.

'Good morning,' the superintendent said, her

bright eyes twinkling with merriment. 'I presume you've seen our new arrival.'

Alice nodded. 'We have — or rather we've seen something, but we're not sure what it is.'

'That's what we were going to find out,' added Edith.

Fiona clasped her hands in front of her. 'I can put you out of your misery, then. It's a piano.'

'Gosh, really?' Mary was delighted. 'Can anyone try it? I'd love to have a go.'

Fiona beamed at her. 'That is very good news indeed. I confess we have accepted this as a gift without knowing if anybody could actually play. I never got past the scale of C major, myself, and am always impressed by anyone who knows what they're doing.'

The three nurses followed her down to the ground floor, where the piano was being shunted into the common room. 'Where d'you want it, missus?' asked the taller of the two men trying to move it. 'Over against that wall?'

Fiona paused to consider. 'In the middle of the wall, I think. Then everyone can gather around it. If we need to swing it round we will have room for that too, if lots of people want to come to the concert.'

'Concert?' asked Mary.

'Why, yes, I thought we'd have a wee carol concert,' Fiona said cheerfully. 'Nothing like a good sing to put us in the festive mood. Excellent, Mary, you can be the accompanist. Edith, you don't look terribly surprised,' she added shrewdly.

Edith shook her head. 'That's because Gladys

287

told me you had one last year. I hoped we'd have it again this year too. I'm so glad. I love singing carols.'

Fiona glanced at her watch. 'Dear me, I must be away. Another committee meeting calls. But you must all write down your favourite carols and then Mary can start practising. You might like to know that it's Gwen we have to thank for this.'

'Gwen?' asked Mary.

'Why, yes. Her good friend had to make more room in her house and needed to get rid of this lovely piano, and she thought of us. So make sure you thank her the next time your paths cross.'

★   ★   ★

Alice was sitting on her bed that evening, carefully slitting open a letter with her paperknife. She looked at its delicate mother-of-pearl handle and sighed. It had been a birthday present from her parents. She knew she ought to write to them and explain why she hadn't put in for leave this Christmas, and maybe even try to squeeze in a visit to them either just before or just after the day itself. They would understand that many nurses had to work over what were holidays for most other people.

She drew out the sheet of paper. It was from Joe, saying he would be home for Christmas. Alice gave a small smile. That was one more reason not to go back to Liverpool. She ran her eyes over the rest that he had written. He was sure that both she and Edith would be welcome at Jeeves Street for Christmas dinner, if they had no other plans. 'That's very generous,' she murmured to herself. She didn't like accepting hospitality without being able to return the favour, and she couldn't very well invite the Banhams to the canteen downstairs, or try to cook for them using the limited facilities in the service room. Then the idea came to her: she could ask them to the carol concert. Fiona had told everyone that guests would be welcome, the more the merrier.

Joe asked about what books she had borrowed from the library, and she grinned, knowing that she had made good use of the subscription. She'd kept a note of what she had taken out, along with what she'd thought of each title, almost as a good-luck insurance that he would be back to discuss them with her. Her favourite so far had been by P. G. Wodehouse, his sunny style providing a perfect antidote to a long day of demanding work. That got her thinking — perhaps she could buy Joe a book as a Christmas gift. Something to make him laugh on those long voyages at sea.

There was no mention of Harry being able to join them. Alice knew that Edith had received plenty of letters from him and hadn't said anything about him returning either. She was sure her friend would want to go round to the Banhams' for the festive meal though; to feel welcomed by his family whether or not he was there. How sad it would be for Edie and Harry not to be able to spend their first Christmas together. Then again, so many would be in the same boat: husbands separated from wives, sons and daughters from parents, fathers from children. Edith and Harry were one couple among thousands.

Perhaps if she wrote now, the letter would reach Joe before he came home. Alice hunted around for her fountain pen, another gift from her parents. Writing a letter always felt better when using a really nice pen. Alice tried to picture where Joe would be when he opened it, but wasn't sure if he was on shore or at sea, as he could give little away and his news would already be out of date. She gave a low sigh, and hoped he was warm and safe, wherever it was.

★   ★   ★

Kathleen hurried along the narrow gap between the busy market stalls. Ridley Road teemed with people seeking festive bargains, and she would have loved to have had the time to stop and gaze at what was on offer. Today, though, she was in a rush, as she had to get back to Brian. Now they didn't have the big pram, shopping had become a quick dash to grab the basic necessities. Not wanting to presume too much on Flo and Mattie's kindness, she had left the baby with one of her elderly neighbours, who had moved in to Jeeves Place at the end of the summer. She seemed friendly enough and had had five children of her own, but Kathleen could tell Brian wasn't comfortable with her. Still, beggars couldn't be choosers.

She stopped, despite herself, in front of a tempting display of tangerines, glossy dark green leaves nesting against the bright orange peel. 'Get yer Christmas fruit 'ere!' called the stallholder, winking at her. 'Don't delay, buy it today. Who knows when we'll have any more? Don't let Hitler spoil yer Christmas!'

Kathleen reached for her purse. It was such a small indulgence, and surely she should have something in the house as a treat. Brian would like the juicy taste for a start, and the vitamins would be good for him. Even though she could scarcely afford anything extra, she made up her mind.

'I'll have just a small handful,' she said. 'It'll brighten the place up.'

'That's the spirit,' said the stallholder, grabbing a brown paper bag and tipping some of the fruit into it. 'Here you go, miss.'

Kathleen paid and was just tucking the bag into her shopping basket when a small woman in a moth-eaten headscarf pushed against her. 'All right for some, buying in the fancy stuff I see,' the woman hissed.

Kathleen whirled around. It was Pearl.

'That's not . . . I mean I'm not . . . ' Kathleen stuttered to a halt, silenced by the sheer hatred coming in waves off the shorter woman.

'Suppose you're all set for a lovely Christmas,' Pearl went on. 'At least you got your son at home with you. That's more than I have. I got to spend it on my own without the comfort of family, and it's all your fault.'

Kathleen couldn't believe her ears. '*My* fault?

How is it my fault?'

'If you hadn't have been there, then they wouldn't have called no police,' Pearl said, her eyes bright with anger. 'Now my Bertie is locked up just when I need him. Without you, he'd have got away like what his mate did.'

Kathleen was lost for words. She knew that if she hadn't been there then the car would have hit the wall even harder — its speed had been broken when it slammed into Billy's leg, caught her on the head and crushed the pram. However, Pearl didn't look as if she was in the mood to listen to reason.

'I hope you have a very happy Christmas, knowing that I'm all on my own and suffering,' she spat, before turning on her heel and plunging into the crowd.

Kathleen found she couldn't move. Her whole body started to shake, from the horrible shock of it and the blatant unfairness of the accusation. She'd always known Pearl had a poisonous side and only put up with her because her mother seemed to like her — or at least, enjoyed arguing with her. This was the first time she'd been directly in the line of attack though. She forced her feet to shuffle forward, heading unsteadily to the vegetable stall, where she had to make her money go even further now she'd splashed out on the tangerines, but she couldn't think straight. What vegetable was it she'd planned to buy — carrots or parsnips?

She couldn't stop trembling and felt like bursting into tears. Biting her lip, she cast around for somewhere to get out of the crowd, to gather her thoughts. She didn't want to break down in public, but she was so tired. Keeping going day after day was exhausting. Ray's money wasn't going as far as she'd thought it would. On some days she longed for him to come back, hold her in his arms and tell her everything would be all right. On others the very thought of him coming near her again, or worse, coming near to Brian, terrified her.

There was an alcove to the side of the butcher's stall and she ducked into it, relieved to be out of the way of everyone pushing and shoving, the overwhelming racket of stallholders' cries, general chatter, wheels of delivery carts being manoeuvred along the paving stones, protests of small children being dragged along by their mothers. Gradually she stopped shaking. This wouldn't do, she told herself firmly, she had to get a grip. Brian depended on her. Without a father to rely upon, with precious little help from her own family, it was still all down to her. How she envied Mattie sometimes — good old Lennie, who sent home regular money and adored his daughter, and that big, happy, welcoming family all around her. Kathleen longed to be a part of something like that. No matter how kind they were, she knew she was an added extra, not really central to them. It wasn't the same.

For a moment Billy's face came to her mind's eye. How happy he had been when she'd sat with him in the hospital that terrible evening. He hadn't even seemed to mind the broken leg. He was a good man through and through. She'd been stupid. She'd ignored him and been swept off her feet by Ray, won over by a handsome face and charming manners, unable to see what lay behind them. 'Well, you messed that up all right, my girl,' she muttered to herself.

A hand touched her arm — not Pearl's vicious grip, but a lighter, friendly pat. 'Hello, Kathleen,' said a woman's voice.

Kathleen turned and saw it was Edith. She slumped in relief. 'Edie! What are you doing here? Why aren't you at work?'

'I'm between visits,' said Edith, straightening her hat. 'As you can see. I went to visit a young woman complaining of stomachache, and found she was actually in labour, and she had no idea. So I had to arrange for a proper midwife to come instead.'

'I bet you could deliver a baby,' said Kathleen loyally.

'Well, I've been around quite a few births, including plenty of brothers and sisters, but I'd have to do an extra qualification to be a proper midwife,' explained Edith. 'I was thinking of it, but then war broke out so I didn't pursue it. I still might, we'll have to see. But anyway, I don't have another patient for half an hour, so I thought I'd chance it and come here to see if there are any decorations we can use in the canteen for the carol concert.'

Kathleen's expression grew puzzled. 'What carol concert?'

Edith's hand flew to her mouth. 'Oh no, didn't you get the message? We're having one at the home and you're invited. We sent a note to

Harry's family. I just assumed you'd hear from them.'

Kathleen shook her head. 'I thought maybe I should try not to rely on them so much, so I haven't been round for a few days. When is the concert?'

'Tomorrow evening — early, though, so it wouldn't affect Brian's bedtime,' Edith told her.

Kathleen frowned doubtfully. 'Would it be all right to bring him? I bet he'd love it — he likes music when Flo has the wireless on. But won't people get cross if he cries? My ma can't stand it if we go anywhere and he starts. I do understand if you'd rather he didn't come.' Her heart caught in her chest as she braced herself for disappointment. She loved singing carols — they always brought back memories of happier times, in a warm classroom with school friends. 'He might get in the way — probably better if I don't come.'

Edith all but stamped her foot. 'Stuff and nonsense. He won't be in the way. Anyway,' she grinned broadly, 'isn't that the whole point of Christmas? Celebrating the arrival of a baby boy? Without that there'd be no Christmas at all, so you bring him along. If anyone complains, they can damn well come to me about it.'

21

Gladys surveyed the common room in the pale early morning light, noting all the places that would need special attention. She rolled up her sleeves and picked up her dustpan and brush, humming as she did so. She didn't care that she would have to work extra hard to get the place into its usual tidy state after last night's concert. Some of the nurses had stayed late downstairs to begin the clearing up, but there was still a lot to do, all made extra tricky because of the many decorations festooning the walls, lights and furniture. It didn't matter one jot to her.

She had been a success and people had praised her singing. It was the first time that anything like it had ever happened to her, and at first she hadn't really taken it in. If she'd ever tried to sing at home her mother had told her to pipe down before she woke one of the young ones. So she'd all but stopped. Now, though, she'd learnt the words of the carols, with a fair bit of help from Edith and Alice, and had truly put her heart into all the ones she loved. Then Gwen, of all people, who'd been sitting in front of her, had turned around and nodded with approval. 'That was very good,' she'd said quietly, as the concert hadn't even finished.

The superintendent herself had come over at the end, and praised her. 'I couldn't help noticing what a lovely voice you have, Gladys my dear,' she'd said in her usual brisk tone. 'You've been hiding your light under a bushel!'

Gladys had blushed furiously but had managed to stammer a shy reply of thanks. Then, even better, Mary had come over. Everyone could see Mary was properly musical as she had played the piano all evening, and not got a note wrong, even in the very fast carols such as 'Ding Dong Merrily on High'. Mary had laughed in delight and said it was wonderful to have a fellow musician in the room. Gladys had almost melted on the spot, she was so happy. Now, as she swept, dusted and polished, she recalled that wonderful warm feeling and broke into a smile. Perhaps she didn't have to be the quiet mouse at the back for the rest of her life. Maybe, just maybe, things were changing at last.

★　★　★

Alice hadn't really expected Joe to be back in time for the carol concert, and so she couldn't claim she was disappointed when he hadn't shown up with the rest of the Banhams. Then Flo had taken her aside so they could hear each other properly and said she'd just found out that he would be back tomorrow and he wanted to keep his promise about the new Ritz. 'He said you'd know what he meant,' Flo had continued dubiously. 'All sounds a bit cloak and dagger to me.'

Alice had understood at once. 'It isn't really. He didn't get a chance to go to that new cinema up in Clapton before he left for his training and said we'd go when he got leave.'

'That'll be it, then,' said Flo. 'He left word to see you there at seven o'clock. I don't know how he's getting home, so I can't promise he'll be back in time to come to call for you. Will you be all right? I hate to think of anyone out in the blackout, really I do.'

'We're all used to it now,' Alice had said staunchly. 'Edith and Mary might want to come along, so there's no need to worry.'

Now she made sure she'd buttoned her warmest cardigan against the winter chill and that her torch was properly shielded with the regulation layers of tissue paper before leaving her bedroom to meet the other two nurses. She'd debated whether to wear her pale pink shirt with its pretty broderie-anglaise collar, but changed her mind and chose something better suited to keeping out the cold. Yet even if it was Joe she was meeting, and though she doubted he would have any interest in how she looked, somehow she still wanted to take care of her appearance.

'Sure you don't mind me tagging along?' asked Mary as she emerged from her own room. 'Only Charles has been called away at short notice, and I don't even know if I'll see him before Christmas.' She pulled a face. 'I do hope he manages to get back. I've got him a lovely silk tie as a present.'

Alice knew Mary hated sitting alone in her room, especially if her friends were out enjoying themselves. 'Don't be silly, you aren't tagging along,' she said. 'I told Joe's mother that you and Edie might be there.'

Edith was already waiting for them at the front door, torch in hand, and so they set off together.

True to his word, Joe was waiting on the pavement in front of the cinema. Alice was surprised by how pleased she was to see him, and her face broke involuntarily into a huge smile. In the dimness of the blackout it was hard to tell if he'd changed much, but she could see he too was smiling broadly as he caught sight of the three of them hurrying along towards him.

She came to a stop just before reaching him. 'Hello, Joe.' Now she was closer she was sure he looked a little different — maybe it was the way he was standing. His face seemed leaner, his shoulders broader. Or was it a trick of the faint light?

'Alice.' She caught her breath as he stepped towards her and they regarded each other, still smiling for a moment, before he turned to encompass the others. 'And Edith and Mary too. How good of you all to come. I wasn't sure my message had got to Ma, but I needn't have worried.'

'Let's get inside out of this cold,' suggested Mary, shuddering dramatically for effect. 'I can scarcely feel my feet. I do hope it's nice and warm in there.'

'Bound to be, I shouldn't wonder,' said Joe, holding open the grand door at the entrance. 'They say it's got all mod cons, with some fancy air system that means it'll be protected even in a raid. So we're in the safest place this evening.'

'Bit of a way to come if there's a raid on Dalston,' muttered Edith to Alice under her

299

breath. 'Still . . . ' She gazed around at the art deco details. 'Not bad, I'll give it that.'

Quickly they bought their tickets and found their seats in the circle, Joe waiting for the three of them to get settled before taking the final place in the row. Alice sat next to him. She had taken off her coat and could feel the warmth of his arm against hers, through the wool of her cardigan. She wondered if his arm seemed more muscly than before.

The Pathé news came on and she sat up a little straighter, just as Joe shifted too. Mary and Edith remained slumped comfortably in their seats, not as interested.

'Everyone thinks that nothing's going to happen because there haven't been any raids yet,' murmured Alice. 'But I don't think we can presume that.'

Joe drew in his breath sharply. 'Absolutely not. This is the calm before the storm. Don't you go forgetting your gas mask. Everyone has to stay vigilant, don't let anybody persuade you otherwise.'

'Don't worry, we've all brought them with us,' Alice reassured him, tapping her foot against the case that was resting on the floor. She accidentally brushed against the side of his big shoe and quickly moved away again.

'Glad to hear it,' he said, glancing sideways at her and grinning.

She couldn't tell if he was teasing her about touching his shoe and decided to ignore that idea, fixing her eyes firmly on the screen. The closing music came and then the theme of the main show began. Edith and Mary instantly became more alert, and Mary produced a bag of toffees from her handbag.

'Psst, pass them along,' she hissed, and Alice obliged, offering them to Joe and then relaxing back, determined to enjoy the film.

★ ★ ★

Joe pushed open the door to the Duke's Arms and stepped into the welcome brightness of the bar room. He was just in time for last orders. The nurses had had to hurry back to the residential home in order to meet the ten o'clock curfew, but he was too full of energy to go straight home, even though he knew his parents would still be up. He told himself he'd have one pint and go back to tell them how the evening had gone.

'The usual, Joe?' the barman called out, and Joe smiled at the offer. How he'd missed this place. There had been decent pubs near where they'd trained, but once on board ship there had been little opportunity to do anything as normal as have a few drinks with his mates. He had found it hard at first to make the change, to adapt to the routines and discipline, and he knew some of his comrades had found it far harder. Still, he wasn't going to pass up the chance to revisit his old haunts now he was back for a few days.

Gratefully he raised his glass and took a welcome sip of proper beer, savouring the foamy head and bitter taste of hops. He sighed aloud in satisfaction. One thing life on board had taught him, and that was to treasure the short moments of pleasure when they came, as you could never be sure when the next one would arise. He caught the eyes of some familiar faces along the bar, friends of his father, and a couple of them raised their own glasses to him in greeting.

It was a shame there hadn't been more time to talk earlier in the evening. He hadn't consciously realised it, but he'd been mentally rehearsing conversations he'd wanted to have with Alice, about what she'd read since he'd been gone, what life was like now the war was fully underway, how she thought everything was going. He valued her opinions — she didn't just echo what she'd seen in the papers or heard on the wireless, but always thought for herself. He had caught himself thinking over the last few weeks of the way her eyes lit up when she talked about something important, the way she smiled when she agreed with what he said, the way those eyes of hers looked at him so directly. There was no getting round it: he'd missed her far more than he thought he would. However, there hadn't been an opportune moment to speak to her on her own. She had had to rush off immediately after the main feature had finished, even though Edith had joked that she could get them back in through the broken fence. Joe smiled to himself. That would suit Edith all right but he couldn't see Alice doing it — she was too steady for that sort of escapade. He could think of no excuse to delay her, especially as all three of them would have to be fresh for their demanding work the next day.

Never mind, they would spend Christmas together at his house. He could take his time, find the right moment to speak to her then.

He was sure she would love Flo's special dinner. His mouth watered at the prospect of his mother's roast turkey with all the trimmings. His parents had quietly given up hope that Harry would make it back in time to join them, although Mattie still held on to the belief that Lennie would somehow appear. He hadn't wanted to disabuse her of the notion. After all, who wouldn't want their husband home to share their child's first Christmas?

Then someone clapped him on the back. 'Welcome home, Joe!' He turned and saw it was Billy.

'Billy! How are you?' Joe took in the sight of his old friend, who had been in a state of despair last time he'd seen him. There was no trace of that desperation now. 'I heard about the accident. How is the leg?'

Billy shuffled. 'Oh, you know. The odd twinge now and again, but pretty well good as new. Fancy another?' He tipped his head to indicate Joe's glass.

'Oh . . . ' Joe remembered his resolution to have just the one and then go home. But here was the man who'd saved Kathleen and little Brian, so he couldn't turn him down. 'Just a half, then.'

Billy got in his order just as the barman prepared to call time. 'Cheers,' he said. 'I been hearing some of what you've been up to from your old man. You know I'm in the ARP with him now, don't you?'

Joe nodded. 'Pa said. But I hadn't realised you were fit enough to start yet.'

'Yes, been doing it a couple of weeks now,' said Billy with pride. 'You got to be careful how you go; some folk take against you before you've had a chance to explain what you're on about, so you can't go flying off the handle. Your pa is the expert, though, I'm learning everything from him.'

Joe could well believe it. He wouldn't have fancied challenging people in their own homes, but he could imagine that his father was exactly the sort of person who could be calm but forceful when required. Billy was in good hands.

'It feels like ages since I was in here, but it's only been a few months,' Joe mused.

'I know what you mean, though.' Billy took a sip of his beer. 'When I was laid up it felt like a lifetime. Drove me mad, it did, when I couldn't go nowhere. Then I managed to get about a bit on me crutches. Once I got the hang of it, this was one of the first places I came.'

'I bet,' said Joe.

Billy smiled as he remembered that evening, when everyone had fallen over themselves to congratulate him. That was a sweet memory. Then another detail from that evening came back to him.

'Saw that nurse friend of yours in here as a matter of fact,' he said.

'Edith, you mean? Harry's girl?' Joe knew that Alice wasn't a great one for going to pubs.

Billy shook his head. 'No, the other one, the tall one with the blonde hair. She was there at the accident. Alice.'

'Oh?' Joe was surprised.

'Yes, that's right,' said Billy, recalling more of the evening. 'She was having a drink with this bloke I never seen before. Looked like a film star, he did. You should have heard Clarrie going on, you know what she's like at the best of times, but this fellow really got her going. Thought she was going to pass out, I did.'

'Really?' Joe set down his half pint.

'Funny, it was. Then I went over and said hello, like you do, and your friend introduced us. He's a doctor, so that puts him out of Clarrie's league I reckon.'

'Maybe.' Joe wanted to leave it there but couldn't quite manage to do so. 'Clarrie joined you, then?'

'Oh, no.' Billy drained his own glass. 'I didn't want to interrupt. Looked as if they had a lot to say to each other, they did. Thick as thieves, you could say. So I left them to it, went home not long after, and tell you the truth the beer hit me hard after being off it so long.'

Joe suddenly had an urge to get out of the pub and away from the conversation. The thought of Alice on an evening out with this doctor fellow . . . Joe knew there was nothing between himself and Alice but the thought of it hit him in the gut. 'I know the feeling,' he said, finishing his drink quickly. 'Can't be doing this every night. I'd better get back to my folks.'

'Give them my best and I'll see your pa

tomorrow,' Billy said as his friend picked up his coat and put it on.

Joe drew his collar up around his face for the short walk back to Jeeves Street, keen to hide his expression from any passers-by. He was sure the disappointment would show on his face. So, Alice had a doctor friend who looked like a film star. Why hadn't she mentioned that if there was nothing more to it? Then again, why would she have done? That was her business. Thick as thieves, moreover. He sighed, then berated himself. He shouldn't be at all surprised. Somebody like Alice was bound to have somebody special, and if the war had separated them then there was no reason at all for him to have come up in what brief conversations the two of them had had since getting to know one another. But the fact that he was a doctor, and looked like a film star . . . Joe told himself to get a grip. He had been sitting on his feelings for Alice, not truly being honest with himself about them, but Billy's news had come as a shock. What a fool he'd been. Alice saw him as a friend, nothing more, and now she had a new chap. This doctor, whoever he was, was a very lucky fellow. The country was at war and there was no time to dwell on a silly idea that would never come to anything. He didn't have that sort of relationship with Alice at all. They were — and it looked as if they would have to continue to be — simply friends. Joe was just going to have to accept it.

22

Mattie added the finishing touches to her Sunday best frock: a neat red patent belt with a carefully polished gilt buckle, and a delicate brooch in the shape of a bird, with a red jewel for an eye. She knew it wasn't a real ruby but it didn't matter. Lennie had given it to her last Christmas and that was what counted. She rubbed it with her finger. Perhaps it would work like a charm and bring him home. He was cutting it fine, though. Word had come through yesterday that Harry would be able to make it back at the last minute, but there was still no news from Lennie. Now it was Christmas morning and there was a lot of work to get through before they could all sit down and eat.

Before that, though, she had to see to Gillian. The baby was lying in the middle of the bed, which was really too wide for the room that Mattie had called her own since she was a little girl herself. However, once she had married Lennie and it had been decided it was not worth them renting a home of their own as he would be away so often, her parents had used some of their small pot of savings to buy them a proper double bed. It fitted, but only just, without much space for anything else. Gillian's wooden cot was wedged into the alcove where the wardrobe used to be; the wardrobe was now outside on the landing. The dressing table was snug against the window. If Mattie got out of bed too quickly she often banged her hip on the corner of it.

However, it was a small sacrifice if it meant she could still live with her parents. One day she and Lennie would have their own house, but she was in no rush. Sometimes she dreamt about it, how there would be space for everything they needed, how she would decorate the place and make it homely for him, but realistically she knew that was all a long way off.

'Let's put you in your lovely new frock Granny made you,' she said, reaching down and tickling Gillian, who chuckled and waved her chubby arms in the air. Mattie tugged on the fine cotton dress edged with bias binding, added a little cardie she had knitted from wool left over from one of her own, and then topped off the outfit with a large towelling bib. 'All right, I know it doesn't look as beautiful as your new frock but I know what you are like,' Mattie said dryly as she hoisted her daughter into her arms. 'We're going to have you looking lovely at dinner if it's the last thing I do. Then if Daddy comes he can see how pretty you are.'

'Da-da-da,' said Gillian.

'Yes,' said Mattie with determination. 'Daddy. He might come. We just have to keep hoping.'

★   ★   ★

Flo was already making headway with the preparations, and the kitchen window had steamed up thanks to the bubbling pans on top of the range. Gillian obligingly allowed herself to

308

be put to sit up in the cot and Mattie turned her attentions to the vast mound of potatoes.

Joe emerged from the back kitchen with an enamel bowl full of peeled carrots. 'Look what they've taught me in the navy,' he said with a straight face. 'No swimming lessons yet but I'm a dab hand at peeling vegetables.'

'Get away with you,' said Mattie, but her voice betrayed her pleasure at being teased once again by one of her brothers. She'd missed that since they'd gone.

'Good,' said Flo. 'Plenty of parsnips to be getting on with. You take them back through there and keep out of our way.'

Joe knew better than to disobey his mother, and promptly retreated with a fresh load of root vegetables.

There was a sound from the front of the house, and Mattie jumped in anticipation, but then dropped her shoulders as she remembered that Kathleen had promised to arrive early and help out. Sure enough, her friend came into the kitchen, balancing a bag in the crook of each arm while carrying Brian, who was squirming around to see what all the excitement was about.

Kathleen set the little boy down on the rug out of the way, hung up her coat and set to work, chopping the carrots Joe had just peeled. Flo turned on the wireless and found a carol service and they all joined in while the pans bubbled merrily away and the aroma of roast turkey grew stronger. Stan was briefly allowed near the kitchen counter to make himself some toast for a late breakfast, as he had been on duty the night before, but he was then shooed into the parlour to read an out-of-date newspaper that he hadn't yet had a chance to open.

This meant he was first to see Alice and Edith coming down Jeeves Street, and he ushered them in before they could knock at the door. Mattie's head flew around as she caught the movement of someone coming into the kitchen unannounced, then doused her hopes once more when she realised that it wasn't Lennie letting himself in with his key. She rushed to welcome the guests, but not before she caught Edith's eyes raking the room for the one face she wished to see above all others. She'd be on tenterhooks, waiting for Harry to arrive.

Joe came through with his big bowl of parsnips and nodded politely to Alice. He was determined not to let his new knowledge about her doctor friend show. He gallantly took her coat, and Edith's, and moved to the outer hall to find hooks for them. The place was filling up.

Flo glanced around the room once more, checking everything was going to plan, and then stealthily slipped into the parlour. Stan looked up from the old newspaper.

'Just checking that the presents we got for Edith and Alice are under the tree with the rest,' she breathed. 'Yes, good, all in place. We'll open them after we've eaten.'

Stan nodded in approval.

'We should be ready in about ten minutes,' Flo went on. 'Stan, what are you looking at? What's wrong — is it my hair?'

'No,' he said, rising to his feet, 'but I can hear

footsteps on the pavement. It might be our Harry.'

Flo took a deep breath. 'We've got to give the young ones the best day that we can, so that whatever happens in the future they have this to remember.'

Stan caught her hands as she came towards him. 'I know,' he said, looking into her eyes with an expression that conveyed how much she meant to him. He wasn't one for fancy speeches and so he just gave her hands an extra squeeze. 'I know.'

They stood still for a few moments, before two figures passed the parlour window before stopping at the front door. Flo waited for the sound of a key in the lock, but Stan was already heading for the hall, eager to see his younger boy — boxing champion or not, he'd always be a boy to him. Yet instead of one familiar figure there were two. Harry and Lennie.

Flo cried out in delight, which brought Mattie running to see what the matter was. Within a second she was in Lennie's arms and he was twirling her around, or as well as he could in the crowded hall. Mattie squealed in pleasure. 'I knew you'd come. I knew it,' she kept repeating, her arms tight around his neck. Finally he set her down. 'Come and see Gillian,' Mattie urged. 'She said Da-da this morning. She knew you were coming too.' Swiftly she touched her hand to the bird brooch as they went into the kitchen.

Harry followed them, Flo laughing behind him. 'Good timing as ever, son,' she chuckled.

311

'The turkey's ready in ten minutes. You've just got time to wash your hands.'

Harry turned back to her just before going into the warm room. 'I will, Ma, I will. But there's something else I have to do first.' He stepped through the doorway and instantly his eyes found the person he'd been waiting to see. There she was, in the dress that he knew she kept for best, as pretty as he'd remembered her, her face now alight with joy and disbelief.

'Harry,' Edith said, slowly rising from the dining table, setting down a half-folded napkin. Then, more loudly, 'Harry! Harry, you're back at last!'

Then she was in his arms and half laughing, half crying, aware that everyone was looking at them but not really giving a fig. The one wish she had made for Christmas had come true and she didn't care who knew it.

★　★　★

The turkey and trimmings demolished, the pudding and cake almost finished, Stan surveyed the room and nodded in satisfaction. This was what he loved: a home full of family and friends. This was what he had worked hard for all his life and what he sought to protect on the cold evening shifts on his ARP rounds, never complaining when people argued with him, turning the other cheek to their protests and insults. It was water off a duck's back to him anyway. This room, here and now, was what really counted.

'How about a little tot of whisky for those that want it?' he suggested, rising to his feet. 'Help that pudding go down a treat, it will.'

Joe brightened at the idea. 'Don't mind if I do.'

Lennie looked hesitant but Mattie said, 'Don't worry, I'll have her,' and reached for their daughter, expertly avoiding the carrot-covered hands and then firmly wiping them on a napkin. 'You have a wee dram, you know you like it.'

'Then I will. Thanks.' Lennie happily accepted a small glass, and Harry did too.

'Suppose you prefer rum, now you're in the navy?' he gently goaded his big brother.

Joe was too relaxed to rise to the bait. 'Not a bit of it. Doesn't matter what's in the glass, it's the company that counts, that's what I reckon.'

Flo nodded approvingly.

'That wasn't what you said when Pete gave us a taste of his dad's poteen,' Harry reminded him. 'You were among friends then but you said it was the worst thing you'd ever tasted.'

Joe pulled a face at the memory. 'It was, too.'

'I hope you aren't comparing my fine whisky to that workshy old codger's moonshine,' Stan protested.

Joe laughed. 'He wouldn't dare.' He raised his glass. 'To the cook and her helpers. Thanks, Ma. That was as good a Christmas dinner as we've ever had.'

Flo could have burst with pride and happiness.

★   ★   ★

'Put that down, Joe — you've nearly knocked it over once already.' Alice laughed as he carefully set down one of the precious china cups on the edge of the draining board. She wondered if he was under the influence of one too many top-ups of whisky. His eyes were brighter than usual, though still dark and quizzical.

'Quite right. Ma would have my guts for garters if I smashed one now,' he agreed, backing away a little from where she was doing her stint at the washing up. The daylight had faded and the gas lamp was lit, throwing its glow over the small room.

Alice shook soapsuds from her hands and repositioned the delicate cup with its pattern of crimson leaves on a cream background in a safer place. Then she resumed washing the rest of the crockery, conscious of Joe watching her. He seemed more intense than usual. Alice thought back to his peck on the cheek when they said goodbye before his posting and that smell of sandalwood and soap.

'Shall I start drying yet?' he asked after a while.

Alice shook her head, unsure whether she could trust him not to drop something. 'I think we've used up all the clean tea towels,' she said. 'There are couple drying out now over by the oven but they won't be ready for a while. So you are off the hook.'

'Who said I wanted to be let off the hook?' he said and gave a look she couldn't quite decipher.

Alice gave a little laugh, and the thought occurred to her that it seemed the most natural thing in the world, to be making domestic small talk with him like this, in his mother's back kitchen. She began to hum a soft tune, working her way methodically through the plates and saucers, then the cups. Joe picked up the melody and joined in.

'I didn't know you were a Glenn Miller fan,' Alice said in surprise, realising she'd been singing 'Moonlight Serenade'. Somehow she'd imagined Joe would like more serious music.

Joe shook his head. 'Well, there are a lot of things you don't know about me, Alice Lake. I am capable of a bit of sophistication every now and then, even though I'm not a doctor or anything fancy like that.' He said it with a half-smile, but all at once she was aware of a shift in the atmosphere in the little back kitchen.

'Is there something wrong, Joe?' Alice was suddenly unsure of herself.

'Nothing's wrong Alice,' he said gently. 'But it's hard to get to know someone properly over a library book.'

'I don't know what you mean.' When she turned to face him properly there was an intense look in his eyes that she was certain she hadn't seen before. She could feel her pulse rate increase and took a quick breath, her hands felt clumsy and she dropped the tea towel.

Joe looked into her eyes for a moment then bent to pick it up, handing it back to her. His face was softer now, the brief tension gone. 'Don't mind me, Alice. I must be drowning in all that Christmas spirit.'

'A little goes a long way,' she said, making light

of it, but aware there was something else behind his half-joking words. She met his gaze. He held it and then took a small step towards her, his eyes never leaving hers. She could feel the heat from his body, he was so close, but she didn't step away. For a moment neither of them moved.

There was a clatter from the doorway and Edith came in with a tray of plates covered in the crumbs from the Christmas cake. 'Alice! You should have said, you must be nearly out of hot water by now. I'd have helped.' Her eyes took in the fact that Joe was standing so close to her friend, but he moved away as she approached. 'You helping out, Joe? That's what we like to see.' She flashed him a smile.

Joe recovered and was back to his affable self. 'I tried, I really did, but Alice insisted all the towels were too wet, so I've been keeping her company.'

'That's right,' said Alice, a shade too quickly.

Edith put the tray down on the counter. 'Have you seen the time, though? Harry says he'll walk me, us, home soon, if you like. You're on duty tomorrow, aren't you?'

Alice wiped her hands on the apron she'd borrowed from Mattie, a bold red gingham one with patch pockets. 'Yes, I said I'd do the morning round, as several of the others want to spend Boxing Day with family.'

Joe raised his eyebrows. 'No rest for the wicked.'

Alice smiled ruefully. 'Just because it's Christmas doesn't mean people aren't sick. I won't do a full day, but there's the teenager with TB who'll need a visit first thing as usual.'

Edith nodded. 'And he's such a sweetheart, he really is. Anyway, I'm going back to the parlour. Coming?'

'All right, said Alice, and made her way into the brighter main kitchen and into the warm parlour, fragrant with the scent of rich fruit cake. Whatever Joe had intended to say or do in that brief moment was lost forever — Alice was puzzled, had she imagined it, surely Joe just thought of her as just a friend — wasn't that what they were? But this time, Alice wasn't so sure . . .

★ ★ ★

'Don't wait up for me,' Edith breathed, as Alice opened the heavy front door to the nurses' home. 'I'm just going to take one extra walk around the block with Harry.' Harry was waiting at a polite distance by the gate, but Alice could tell the young couple were keen to be alone. She couldn't blame them. He had told them on the way back that he had only three days' leave. Edith would be desperate to spend as much time as possible with him, and yet she had to work too. Alice couldn't begrudge her friend her night-time walk.

'Rather you than me, it's freezing,' she said with a smile.

'Doesn't matter,' said Edith confidently, 'Harry will keep me warm. Here, will you take this?' She handed Alice a bag holding the presents she had been given by the Banhams: a bright knitted scarf, cleverly made by Mattie, who'd managed to decorate it with a pom-pom fringe, and a little box from Harry, which Edith had opened with a gulp of delight. It contained a delicate silver necklace with a locket. 'So you can put my picture in it,' he'd said cheekily, and Edith had played along, pretending to tap him on the shoulder, saying 'Don't make assumptions.' But she'd whispered to Alice as they had reluctantly put on their coats in the snug hallway at Jeeves Street that she'd be finding the right picture as soon as she could.

'Have fun, then.' Alice took her friend's bag and waved at Harry from the doorstep. 'Night, Harry. Thank your mum again from me.' She could barely make him out in the blackout, lit only by starlight.

'Night,' he called back, as Edith ran to his side and took his arm. Alice swung closed the big front door. It wouldn't do to be caught out by the ARP warden who'd been unlucky enough to draw the Christmas night shift. She made her way upstairs, with her own present tucked under her elbow.

They were all so kind. She sighed. One of the disadvantages of being an only child was that you never got to spend a big family Christmas. Her parents had always given her carefully chosen presents — often books — but there had been no jolly carol singing, or whisky-fuelled versions of 'Roll Out the Barrel', or a happy mixture of different generations. Briefly her thoughts flew to Mark, wondering if he was in a cold barracks or even a tent somewhere over in France. She prayed he was safe, at least, and had managed some kind of celebration. Last Christmas she had been in pieces, wounded beyond belief at his decision that they must separate. She had thought that she would never get over it. Yet tonight, if she was honest, the pain had faded a little. It was not gone completely — but when there was so much else going on in the world, her doomed love felt small in the overall scale of things. And if not the same kind of romantic love, today she had been shown wonderful warmth and friendship, which was something you just couldn't buy.

'Time for bed,' she told herself. There was still one more present to be unwrapped. She held it tightly as she went upstairs to her room, and sat down on the bed to open it. Joe had pressed it into her hands just before she left Jeeves Street, and now she carefully pulled back the paper. Inside was a book, a collection of P. G. Wodehouse short stories. He knew her well, she realised, turning the first page, only to find an extra touch — a four-leafed clover nestling in the margin. She ran her finger over its dry shape, wondering what were the odds of this happening — since she had bought a book for Joe, and in it she too had tucked a four-leafed clover.

* * *

Mattie started as a door banged in the darkness. It took a moment before she remembered what day it was. For a fleeting second she thought the

319

war hadn't happened and she was safe in Lennie's arms on one of his usual leaves. Then it all came flooding back. She shifted slightly and the bed gave a creak.

'Whassappenin,' Lennie murmured.

'Nothing, go back to sleep,' said Mattie softly. 'Just a door.'

'Bet that'll be Harry,' said Lennie. 'He went to walk the nurses home and never come back. He'll have been with that one he's sweet on, I bet you any money.'

Mattie gave a quiet giggle. 'I dare say you're right. She's lovely, though, is Edith. She don't let him get away with nothing.'

'Bout time he met his match,' Lennie agreed. He turned so that he could cuddle Mattie properly, then paused and listened carefully. He could just about catch the steady snuffle of Gillian's regular breathing from the cot in the corner. 'Hey, do you think she's sleeping?'

Mattie half sat up and cocked a practised ear. 'Yep, she's gone off. She'll be out for the count until dawn now, then she'll start protesting till we let her in the big bed.'

'Dawn? So, for hours?'

'That's right.'

'Good,' said Lennie, gently pulling her down so he could put his arms around her properly. 'It's time I showed you how much I've missed you.'

'Oh Lennie, what are you like?' Mattie breathed, but she turned in his warm arms and held her face up to be kissed in the soft moonlight that filtered in from the edge of the blackout blind. This Christmas had turned out to be everything she had wished for, and more.

23

The bitter winds of January whistled through Ridley Road market, and the stalls shook with the force of them. The awnings fluttered and the sharp breezes whipped round the corners of the alleys, making chilly tunnels. Kathleen wished she had been able to fit a thicker jumper under her coat, but she needed to be able to button it up all the way from the hem to the collar if she was to keep in the slightest bit warm. She took off her glove to pull the last of her coppers from her purse to pay for the cheapest cut of meat and, even in that short time, her fingers turned blue.

Still, the good thing was that Brian was cosy in his new pram. It was even better than the one that had been destroyed in the accident. Harry had dropped into his old place of work while he was on leave over Christmas, and one of his former colleagues happened to mention that his sister had taken her kids to be evacuated but had left the pram behind as they'd nearly outgrown it anyway. Harry was on to it like a flash. The man hadn't even wanted any money for it as it was getting in the way, and so Harry had brought it home the very same day.

A swift dust, thorough clean and polish later, and it was good as new. It was easier to push than the old one and had a bigger shelf to carry shopping underneath. Kath was delighted with it. It meant she didn't have to rely on her old neighbour for babysitting — the woman was all right, but not exactly full of the joys of spring. Kath had never known anyone to have such a variety of minor illnesses and complaints — every day it was something different. She was willing to bet she heard about more maladies than Edith and Alice combined.

Shivering, she tucked the well-wrapped meat into her shopping bag and turned to manoeuvre the pram back to the main road. Even though she wouldn't be able to buy any fruit today, she still paused to wave at the kind stallholder, who waved back and called out, 'How's the boy today?'

'He's doing well, he had a lovely Christmas,' she called back, and the man broke into a wide smile.

Kathleen tried not to worry that the government had now announced that some food would now be rationed. You couldn't just go out and buy butter, bacon, ham or sugar any more. Perhaps that would mean everyone got a fair share, she thought, but she dreaded not having the choice of sugar in her tea. It was all very well for the likes of Flo, who never took it anyway. She and plenty of others like her looked forward to it as a bit of a treat.

'Ere, mind where you're going with that thing, your wheel nearly had me foot off.'

Kathleen jumped back, startled. She'd been so deep in thought that she hadn't really noticed

323

the angry little woman straight in front of her, though she could have sworn the pram's wheels were nowhere near her feet. Of course, it had to be Pearl. Kathleen tried to dismiss the uncharitable thought that her mother's friend had deliberately stepped out into the path of the pram so she would have cause to complain.

'H-hello,' she began hesitantly.

Pearl humphed. 'Saw your ma last night. She reckons she's seen more of me than what she has of you recently, and it being the season of goodwill too.' Her pinched little face twisted in malicious triumph.

'That's not true,' Kathleen protested, feeling her face blush red despite the cold. 'We went and saw her for Boxing Day and for New Year's Day too.' She didn't add that both occasions had been miserable affairs, with her mother finding fault in everything she did, whether it was the presents she brought along or how she held the baby. Kathleen had been glad to leave each time, conscious that she'd only gone round out of a sense of duty. It made the contrast with the Banham household all the sharper.

'Fine sort of daughter you are,' Pearl continued, her voice piercing. 'Leaving your poor old ma lonely like that.'

Hardly, thought Kathleen, not when her other siblings were close by and so much more in favour than she herself was. Besides, her mother would never be truly lonely as long as there was a sherry bottle within reach. That was her favourite companion of all.

'Nice to bump into you again,' said Kathleen

324

unconvincingly, trying to push the pram past the vicious little woman without actually touching her.

Pearl lifted her chin with a snort of disbelieving contempt. 'Hah. That's as maybe. Still, I'm surprised you aren't hurrying home to your husband,' she spat.

Kathleen stopped in her tracks. 'What do you mean?' she demanded. 'My Ray's in the Merchant Navy now, doing his bit. He couldn't get home for the holidays — they can't let them all have leave, you know,' she added with a sense of self-righteousness. Never mind that Ray hadn't sent so much as a card to her and Brian. He probably hadn't been in port at all. She thrust to the back of her mind his behaviour the last time he'd been home, and clung to the thought that he'd mended his ways and was at sea, serving his country as all right-thinking young men were.

'Oh, my mistake, then,' said Pearl loftily. 'Only I could have sworn someone said he was home around New Year's, hanging out down the pubs by the docks. You know, the really rough ones. The Dog and Whistle, for a start. Don't suppose he thought it would be somewhere you'd want to go. Maybe fancied a night out with his mates — was that it?'

'I don't know what you're talking about,' said Kathleen, now very hot and bothered. 'He'll be on board the merchant ship halfway to Canada by now, I shouldn't wonder. Of course he can't tell me exactly where he's been or where he's going — that wouldn't be right.'

'Very patriotic, I'm sure,' sneered Pearl. 'But my Bertie was sure it was him.'

'Bertie?' Kathleen repeated.

'Oh, didn't I say? They let him out. Sent him back to his dear old mum after all.' Pearl's eyes lit up with spite. 'He's hardly likely to forget what Ray looks like, is he, now? He's not going to confuse a night out down the docks with any others, seeing as he hasn't been able to go down the pub for ages, on account of him being behind bars for nothing at all.'

Kathleen had had enough. 'I must be going,' she said firmly.

Pearl stepped back but not before she'd let out a loud cackle. 'Yes, you do that. Run off, like you always do. No wonder Ray didn't want to go back to your place. Bet he won't find a warm welcome there, will he? Perhaps he's found a warmer one elsewhere.' She cackled again as Kathleen, ears burning with shame, pushed the big pram away from the stalls and down to the High Street. Hateful old woman, stirring up trouble as usual. She wouldn't pay her a blind bit of notice. It was all a parcel of lies.

★ ★ ★

'Darling, we were so glad you could come home at last,' said Mrs Lake, Alice's mother, as she passed the small plate of little cakes across the table to her daughter. 'Here, have one of these. I made them specially.'

'Oh, Mum, you shouldn't have,' said Alice, protesting weakly but aware of how rare these treats would be in future. Already there were rumours that sugar would be plentiful only if you had very deep pockets or knew the right people.

'Yes, she was up until late making sure they turned out right,' said her father, his eyes full of concern for his only daughter. 'No, you help yourself and don't worry about us, we won't go hungry. You're the one who has to keep up her energy.'

'I hope they don't work you too hard,' said her mother, patting anxiously at the turtleneck of her lilac sweater. A small, neat pearl necklace hung just below it.

Alice shook her head and smiled at them reassuringly. She knew in her heart that the workload, demanding though it was, wasn't the only reason she had avoided coming home for so long. She had dreaded coming back to the city where her heart had been so broken, and knew her parents, while wanting only the best for her, would feel obliged to bring up the subject of Mark. At least now she didn't run the risk of bumping into him. Knowing that loved ones all over the country were being separated by the rigours of war, she had decided she must brave the long train journey north to Liverpool, the place of her birth, which in truth she would always think of in some way as home. Stepping onto the platform at Lime Street had brought a wave of nostalgia, the familiar tang of the Mersey always present underneath all the other traces of a bustling city, the cry of the sea birds distantly wheeling above.

Now she was back in Sefton Park, in her

parents' house, in which she had lived for most of her girlhood. She could hardly remember moving in, she'd been so young. All the big decisions of her life had been made here or, more precisely, in the little blue-papered room upstairs which overlooked the carefully tended back garden. To stay on at school when she turned fourteen, unlike some of her classmates who couldn't wait to get out into the wider world. To take her Higher Cert. To study to become a nurse — and the eventful choice of the teaching hospital where Mark was working. To leave Liverpool after their break-up, to move to London. A lifetime of key moments in one bedroom.

The house was comfortable rather than luxurious, although Alice couldn't ever remember going without. Her parents hadn't been young when they'd married and had had to wait for a few years before she came along, which meant that they were fairly well set up by the time she was old enough to notice such things. Her father was a civil servant — was one still, although in the many long months since she'd last seen him, he'd grown a little greyer at the temples, a little stiffer in his movements. His eyes were still kind, though, and they crinkled at the corners in testament to his good humour.

Glancing around she could see that the furniture was a little more worn, the paintwork just that bit more tired. The old walnut sideboard which had belonged to her grand-mother had a few more scratches on it which the polish didn't quite hide. Her parents would be

328

getting old soon and she was taken aback by the realisation. When she'd left, only about a year ago, she'd still felt like a dependent daughter, even though she was a fully qualified nurse by then. Six months of further training followed by the challenging work of a district nurse had changed all that. Now she could see the beginnings of their need to be looked after themselves. Maybe not for a long while — but their positions had begun to be reversed, without her noticing until now.

'How do you find your accommodation?' asked her mother, still with some anxiety. 'What about the other nurses? Have you made friends?'

Alice nodded as she nibbled on the light sponge bun. 'This is delicious, Mum. Nobody down there can cook like this.' Even as she said it, she felt a pang of disloyalty, remembering Flo's fruit cake. But Flo's food was hearty, made to satisfy the appetites of her big family, especially her tall sons and husband. They would have demolished the delicate buns in one fell swoop. 'Like I said in my letters, I'm still billeted with Edith, the one who I trained with when I first moved down. And there are plenty of others as well.' She described the inhabitants of Victory Walk, from fearsome and energetic Fiona to modest Gladys, lately beginning to emerge from her shell. Now she was hundreds of miles away, Alice realised how much affection she held for them, even the noisy ones who'd just moved in to the rooms below. They made her smile — they reminded her of Edith when they'd first met.

Mrs Lake relaxed a little. 'It certainly sounds

329

as if you've found your feet,' she said. 'Of course we can't help but worry. London is bound to be a target if the war gets worse.'

Alice eyed her mother sadly. 'It's when, not if, Mum. But I'll be as safe there as I would be up here. You know the Mersey docks will be high on their list.'

Her father nodded gravely. 'She's right, my dear. Still no flies on you, eh, Alice? Yes, with so much of the country's supplies coming in across the Atlantic, our docks will be lucky to escape an attack at some point. That's if the merchant ships have managed to dodge the U-boats out at sea.'

Mrs Lake paled a little. She had always avoided talk of politics and international affairs and had fervently hoped her daughter would grow out of her interest in such matters. She could see that hadn't happened yet.

'Yes, reports of what's been going on in Scotland and Heligoland are just the beginning, I'd say,' said Alice, keen to hear her father's view. She had relied on him when growing up for a level-headed outlook on the world, and was relieved to find they were still of similar mind.

'More cake?' said her mother, passing the plate again. 'Do try the butterfly bun, darling. You used to love them. You were pretty good at making them, actually. Do you ever get a chance now?'

'Not really,' said Alice, licking a smear of butter-cream icing from her finger and feeling like a little girl again.

Mrs Lake leant forward to press home her

advantage and divert the course of the conversation while her daughter's mouth was full. 'And have you met any nice doctors down in London?' she asked. 'It must be full of suitable young men, a city that size.'

Alice sighed and shook her head. 'Really, Mum, you know I'm not interested.'

'So you say,' said her mother, who had never quite believed this.

'Well, do you remember Dr McGillicuddy? He was passing through and was a locum in our district, just for a very short while in the autumn,' she said, more to placate her mother than anything.

'Oh yes, how could I not remember him? Such a good-looking lad.' Her mother sat up, animated again. 'Wasted as a doctor — no, don't look at me like that. I know medicine is a noble profession but really, somebody that handsome, he could be on the stage or whatever he wanted.'

Alice raised her eyebrows. 'He is doing what he wants, Mum. He wanted to be a doctor and now he is one. He's gone to join the army, the British Expeditionary Force in France.'

'Has he now?' said her father. 'Very brave man, in that case.' He looked directly at his daughter. 'And what of Mark, then? They were best friends too, weren't they?'

Alice glanced down at her plate and then raised her gaze again. 'Yes, they were. Mark's gone with the BEF as well. They're both army doctors. So I expect they'll be in the thick of it in no time at all.'

Mrs Lake nodded and then plunged ahead.

'Well, that's very decent of them, and no doubt it's Liverpool's loss. But you know what I think, darling. He was a nice young man but a little bit on the intense side.'

'Mum!' Alice couldn't stop herself from exclaiming aloud.

'No, hear me out. I know how sad you were about him, and I'm not blaming anyone. But you mark my words. There are other fish in the sea, and I know you didn't want me to say that before you left, but I'm saying it now. You can do better, my love, and you will.'

Alice fought to contain the rush of emotion that washed over her. How could her mother be so insensitive? She had dreaded this very conversation. Mark had been everything to her. He hadn't been some foolish crush. Their love had been real and she had been unable to believe it was truly over. Her mother had seen all this at first hand — how could she say such things?

Her mother reached out and gently touched her hand. 'You can't bottle it up forever, darling,' she said quietly. 'You think we don't see what you're going through, but we do. We're delighted that you've thrown yourself into your work, and admire you tremendously for it. Just don't lose sight of that young girl you used to be who knew how to have fun. She's still in there somewhere.'

Alice stared at the white tablecloth, willing herself not to well up. She wouldn't cry. She'd built a hard shell around her heart and it had served her well this last year, enabling her to get on with her work, her career, and generally to get up in the mornings and carry on. She couldn't let it crack. She might never make it back on the train if she did.

Hesitantly she rose. 'I'll just go and powder my nose,' she said, using her mother's timeworn phrase, and all but running from the room.

Upstairs she shut the door to the small bathroom and perched on the edge of the bath, unable to stop the tears from flowing. Her shoulders shook with long-held-in emotion as the sorrow she'd tried to push away for so long burst forth, and her eyes smarted as she rubbed them red. Her whole body trembled with the pain of it. It was like it had all happened only yesterday, and she remembered how she had done just this, barred herself in her parents' bathroom, where nobody would see her. She didn't want to share the agony with anyone. It was her grief, and it was private.

Slowly the worst of the tears passed and she sank exhausted onto the padded top of the little wooden box where her mother kept the spare towels. She could smell the familiar scent of her mother's favourite lily-of-the-valley talcum powder. Wearily she wiped her raw eyes. This was what she had feared: coming home reawakening the sharp hurt of the past, combined with her parents' conviction that all she needed was a replacement young doctor for all to be right again. Slowly she breathed out, trying to regain some kind of control over her tumult of emotions. This was so unlike her. If any of her colleagues could see her now, they wouldn't recognise her. Well, except Edith.

A thought occurred to her that Edith had

laughed when she'd first described her childhood home. The idea of growing up with an inside bathroom had struck her friend as incredible. Edith's family had shared one outside toilet between everyone else living in the block of back-to-back terraced houses, and had managed with one cold tap in their back kitchen, and even that was thought of as a luxury. Alice had never had to endure such privations. Of course, in the hospitals where they'd first studied and now in the nurses' home, hygiene was paramount and they were never without such facilities — but for some of the nurses it had all been a novelty.

Alice buried her face in a thick cream towel and recognised her mother's favoured washing powder, Persil. Despite herself, she laughed. She'd missed that smell. The nurses' home used something else and she didn't have a say in the matter. Maybe she could ask her mother to wash all the clothes she'd brought up for the short stay and then she could take the smell of them back down with her.

Eventually she stood up. She felt better. Quickly she splashed her face with cold water and tried to improve her puffy red eyes. When she'd done as much as she could, she steeled herself to walk back downstairs.

Her mother was waiting in the hallway outside. As soon as she saw her daughter she opened her arms and enveloped her in a warm hug. 'Darling, we didn't mean to upset you,' she said.

Alice nodded against her mother's shoulder. They were about the same height, as her mother preferred court shoes with medium heels, whereas Alice hardly ever wore anything other than a low heel at the most. 'I know,' she said. 'I'm sorry. I'm better now.'

Her mother paused a moment. 'Don't ever feel sorry,' she said at last. 'There's no shame in falling in love. It's not your fault it all went wrong. Believe me, we hated seeing you suffer like that and we were glad you had your work to fall back on. We're so proud of what you do. But promise me you won't let losing Mark ruin your life.' She stepped back a little. 'Life is for living, Alice. I know you find it hard to credit, but your father and I were once young too. We remember what it's like. We just want to see you happy.'

Alice nodded. 'I know, Mum. It's been hard but I really think I'm on the mend. I was nervous about coming home but I'm glad I did.'

Mrs Lake gave a big smile. 'That's the spirit, my love. We're glad you came back too. We understand why you didn't before, and all that matters is that you're here now.' She tucked her arm into her daughter's. 'So let's go back to your father and finish off those cakes.'

24

Fiona hurried along the corridor to her office, as fast as she could without actually running. There seemed to be more and more to do these days. Constant committee meetings of various kinds demanded her presence. Rotas always needed changing, and the two new recruits to the district required supervising until they had settled in. Two nurses had moved out — one to get married, and one to join up as an army nurse and work in France. Primrose and Belinda had joined the North Hackney nurses' home at New Year, fresh from their Queen's Nurse training. She was tempted to delegate keeping an eye on them to Gwen, but was aware that maybe understanding the young wasn't her deputy's strongest suit. Gwen had instantly decided the pair were flighty and made no secret of it.

Fiona sighed. In addition to all that, it was colder than she could ever recall in London, as bad as her native Scotland. The Thames had frozen over. It had played havoc with travel arrangements. She would have to sanction extra money towards fuel; she couldn't have her nurses getting cold on top of everything else they endured, mostly without complaint.

'Well, at least it will keep transmission of infection down,' she muttered as she reached her office door. She paused as she could hear the sound of someone singing 'Over the Rainbow' from inside. She smiled and reprimanded herself for being so gloomy. There was always something to be grateful for, and Gladys finding her voice was one.

She opened the door and the singing abruptly ended. 'No, carry on, carry on,' Fiona said hastily. 'Don't let me stop you. It cheers me up to hear you, Gladys.'

Gladys, who had been cleaning the bookshelves, beamed. 'Thank you, ma'am.' She bobbed a little curtsey and Fiona frowned.

'No need for that, my dear. But as you've stopped, tell me, when is Alice Lake due back, do you know?'

Gladys nodded. 'She went to visit her folks, ma'am, and they're up in Liverpool, it's ever so far. Then she had to call us on the telephone to say the trains weren't running because of the weather and she'll be back tomorrow instead.'

Fiona nodded. She had feared as much. 'That's a shame, but nothing to be done about it. We'll just have to manage without her.'

Gladys rolled up her duster in her hand. 'Miss Edith said she'd help me with my reading later.'

'That's kind of her,' said Fiona. 'You're coming along nicely, Gladys. Don't think I haven't noticed. You work a full day here and then you study all evening. Well done.' She paused. 'Actually, can you ask Edith to come up here, if she's downstairs? Her shift should be over by now. Mary, too, if you see her. They haven't done anything wrong, I just need to ask them a favour.'

Gladys bobbed again, pink with delight at the praise. 'Of course, ma'am.'

Mary shook her hair and sighed. 'What do you make of that, then?'

Edith shrugged as she took down the cocoa powder from the top shelf. 'Suppose we'd better have this without sugar.' She pulled a face. 'It's not so bad, is it? Just keeping an eye on the new nurses while they settle in? I think Fiona didn't want to seem heavy-handed and that's why she didn't ask Gwen. She thought it would be better coming from us as we're at the same level as they are.'

Mary passed her two cups. 'Must we really do without sugar? I can't get used to it. Perhaps Charles can get hold of some. Or what about Harry's friends? Doesn't Billy work down at the docks? I bet he could manage it.'

'Mary!' exclaimed Edith, shocked. 'You can't do that. That's illegal. You'd get Charles in awful trouble. I can't ask Billy, he'd lose his job.'

Mary's face twisted. 'I know, I know, but cocoa without sugar! It's too bad. It tastes like mud.'

Edith frowned. 'Well, do you want it or not? I'll have yours if you don't.' Sometimes Mary exasperated her — the young woman had obviously never gone without and wasn't used to making any kind of compromise. Edith could easily remember times when any cocoa at all, made just with water and very weak, would have been a great treat.

'Oh, go on, then.' Mary gave way without too much of a struggle. 'You didn't answer my question properly. What do you think we're meant to do? We won't go on visits with them, will we?'

Edith carefully spooned an equal amount of powder into the two cups. 'No, Primrose and Belinda are qualified Queen's Nurses, they don't want us breathing down their necks. We'll just be here to advise them a bit from our experience of the district. Neither of them comes from round here so it'll take a while before they know their way about. Look at me, I'm a Londoner, but it still took me ages.' She added a little water, made a paste and then topped it up with hot water and a dash of milk. 'Here you are.'

Mary accepted it and managed to take a sip without pulling a face. She didn't mean to offend her friend by implying she wasn't grateful, and it was better than nothing. 'Anyway they'll probably be all right, won't they? They most likely won't need us to do anything other than show them where to park their bikes.'

It turned out they needed a little more than that. Their first few cases weren't too bad, or at least nothing beyond what they'd come across in their training, and if they were taken aback by the conditions in which some of their patients lived, they didn't say. So it was a shock for them to hear what Alice had had to deal with on the day after she got back, frazzled by the travel delays and hoping for a straightforward round to welcome her back. It wasn't to be.

★ ★ ★

Alice had set out on what sounded as if it would be a routine visit to a family living in a cramped house a few streets away, off Cricketfield Road. She had known there was a pregnant young woman in the household, but not when she was due to give birth; the call had originally been to visit the grandmother and change a dressing on her injured leg. The old woman was sitting huddled by the meagre fire in the kitchen and complaining about all and sundry. Nothing was right for her. Then she started on about her granddaughter. 'She's no better than she should be, that one,' she spat, as Alice tried to calm her so that the bandage could be fastened properly.

Alice tried to ignore the vicious comments; it wasn't her business to become involved in family squabbles. She was keen to leave the house as soon as possible. It had smelt badly of damp, and the fire, such as it was, wasn't drawing properly. So the room was smoky, with every surface grubby with soot and dust. She knew it was her duty to give general advice about hygiene as well as treating a specific condition, but had the distinct feeling her words would fall on deaf ears here.

It wasn't until the old woman paused to catch her breath that Alice became aware of a thin wailing from upstairs. It sounded frail and desperate all at the same time. The old woman dismissed it when asked what it was, but something told her she should investigate and, despite the grandmother's protests, she made her way upstairs, with dread in her heart even as she attempted to keep her cool and cheerful professional demeanour.

The scene she discovered was the saddest she'd experienced in her whole career. A very young girl lay on the bed, white-faced and sweating, panting for breath, and in her arms lay a baby so pale it was almost blue. The room was freezing, the grate empty, and the bed had only a pitifully thin blanket over it, so it was no good for warmth at all.

Before Alice could even properly establish what was going on, the baby's feeble cries petered out. She immediately went into the routine that had been so well instilled into them during training that it was almost automatic, going through every effort to resuscitate the tiny child, but it was no use. It had been too weak to begin with.

She felt painfully inadequate as she was forced to answer the unspoken question in the young girl's eyes. The child was dead and there was nothing to be done to save it. Alice belatedly checked: a little boy, its life over before it had really begun. It was no more than a couple of weeks old.

Slowly she drew the full story from the girl, who claimed she was seventeen, although Alice doubted it.

'Back last spring, I met this lad who'd come to the area looking for work,' the girl said in a near-whisper. 'He got himself taken on in the gas-mask factory and found lodgings nearby. At first he was nice, bought me bars of chocolate, even got me a bunch of flowers once. Nobody ever done that before. That was the evening he took me down Hackney Downs, and I know it was wrong what we done, but he was so kind and said he loved me and if I loved him back then I'd let him . . . you know.' She paused to gasp for breath, her forehead glistening with sweat. 'It took me ages to realise I hadn't had me monthlies, but he'd sworn it would all be all right and he'd make an honest woman of me, so I wasn't that worried. I believed him. More fool me.'

Alice could have guessed what was coming next.

'The moment war was declared he disappeared. Haven't heard a dicky bird from him since. I tried to hide me bump, that's when I couldn't get rid of it drinking gin and having a boiling hot bath, but after a while it was no good. Gran was furious and said I had to stay indoors or the family would be shamed. I didn't have no choice so I agreed, still thinking he might send word, but he didn't.

'Just after New Year I caught that flu what was going around and couldn't shake it off. Nobody would call a doctor for me. Even when one come to see Gran, they made me stay upstairs. Anyway, there is no hiding it and now it's too late.'

Alice's heart had ached for the girl. If only she had known, there were places she could have gone to have her baby, whether she was married or not. The Mother's Hospital would have taken her, but the girl hadn't heard of the place, even though it was nearby.

Alice thought the situation couldn't have been

more grim, but she was wrong. When the girl's father had turned up, things had gone from bad to worse, as he was drunk.

'You get out of here now,' he'd snarled, his face close to Alice's, his breath reeking of cheap spirits. 'This is my house and I say what goes. We don't need the likes of you do-gooders stickin' yer oar in.' For a moment Alice thought he was going to hit her, but she had stood her ground.

'I've been called in here to treat your mother's injury, and once a nurse is invited into a house it is her duty to help the family where appropriate,' she insisted. 'I can't just ignore your daughter and the death of her baby.'

'Course you can, it's no more than either of them deserve,' the man scoffed. 'We'll get rid of it and say no more about it. You ain't seen nothing.'

Alice knew she risked making him angrier but she couldn't agree. 'I'm afraid that just won't do,' she told him.

Again, she thought he might hit her as he stood swaying in front of her, but then with a grunt he turned, walking out of the half-rotten front door and slamming it behind him. She allowed herself a moment's pause, doing her best not to shake now the immediate danger had passed. Then she picked up her bag, knowing she would have to begin the sad procedures to notify the authorities of an infant death.

'It wasn't that so much that upset me,' Alice said, once she had eventually made it back to Victory Walk and given in to the urgent need to tell the others about the afternoon she'd just had. 'It was the look on the girl's face when she realised the baby had died. I'll never forget it. I know lots of people will say it was for the best, that it never stood a chance, but if they'd seen her face . . . '

Primrose and Belinda listened to the whole desperate tale with expressions of increasing horror. 'How do you manage to do it?' Primrose breathed. 'I'd have run away. I don't think I could stand it.'

Edith nodded and gently touched her shoulder. 'I know what you mean, but when it comes to the point, you wouldn't. It can be shocking at first, that young girls have babies out of wedlock like that, and some people would probably say the same thing — the baby is better off dead and the mother can get on with her life. It's not that simple when you see it first-hand, though. It's a tragedy, no matter where it happens — and all the more so when you realise it needn't have happened at all.'

Primrose nodded in acknowledgement. 'Thank you, Alice. For telling us, I mean.'

Alice sighed. 'Well, thanks for listening. It helped to tell someone. That poor, poor girl.'

Belinda rose. 'It's late, Primrose. We should turn in. Another day's shift beckons.'

Primrose exhaled deeply. 'And you have to go back there and see to that horrid old woman's bandage. She doesn't deserve it, I wish she'd just rot away for being so cruel.'

Edith cocked her head at her new colleague. 'You don't mean that, really.'

Alice got up as well. 'The thing is, she's had a

tough life — anyone can see that. I'll sort her out tomorrow and I'll see to the girl's flu too, not that she'll care after what's happened.'

'But you can make her comfortable,' Edith pointed out.

'Yes, I'll do my best.' Alice managed a smile. 'Thanks again for listening, for understanding. Hope I haven't put you off. It's not always like that.' She turned and headed for the door.

Edith watched as the two new nurses followed her, knowing how hard it would have been for them to realise that next time it might be them dealing with such a situation. But it was a lesson well learned. It didn't help to sugar-coat what they would be up against. Perhaps they thought that, having completed their training, that was the hardest bit over and done with. The truth was, it was only just beginning.

25

'Is that your bike, then?'

Alice braked quickly to avoid the small figure who'd stepped out in front of her as she was returning to the nurses' home. She was still on duty but had run out of boracic lint in her Gladstone bag, despite having repacked it only that morning. But it was just one of those things: every patient today had seemed to need it. She couldn't afford not to have it available but she didn't have time to stop to chat either.

However, the little girl wasn't going to give in so easily. 'How do you keep your balance? Can I have a go?'

Alice sighed and shook her head. 'No, Pauline. It's far too big for you, and really heavy.'

That only made Pauline more determined. 'I'm very strong, Nurse. Everyone says so. Look, I'm like Popeye.' She rolled back the sleeve of her baggy jumper and flexed her little arm. Alice noted she wasn't wearing a coat, despite the bitter weather.

Reluctantly she dismounted. 'You'll need to grow a lot taller before you can ride this,' she pointed out. 'Your legs have to reach the ground when you're sitting on the saddle. Otherwise you won't be able to get on or off, or stop safely.'

'Pity,' said Pauline. 'I fancied having a go.'

'Sorry, you can't. Not today, and not for a long while, I'm afraid. Besides, it's for work, not for fun,' Alice told her seriously. 'Anyway, why aren't you at school?'

Pauline sniffed. 'I'm going there now, ain't I,' she said. 'I'm just a bit late, that's all. I had to see to me gran.'

'You're more than a bit late,' Alice replied. 'It's nearly lunch time. They'll be worried about you. Miss Phipps will be wondering if you're sick.'

Pauline shook her head. 'They won't know. It's all different now. When everyone left they changed the classes and I was still with Miss Phipps, and that was good cos I like her. But now loads and loads of kids are coming back cos there weren't no bombs after all. Just like me gran said there wouldn't be. So we all got to change again. Nobody knows who's meant to be where. Me gran says they don't know their arse from their elbow, scuse me, Nurse.'

Alice frowned. Then again, the little girl was only repeating what someone else had said and she'd probably heard far worse. 'That must be quite confusing,' she said. When she'd last seen Janet Phipps, the teacher had said that children were beginning to trickle back from their various billets, as parents felt there was little risk and that the whole thing had been a mistake, an overreaction. Alice hadn't realised that more and more had returned.

'It must be nice to have your friends around you again,' she suggested. 'What was your special friend called — Dotty, wasn't it? Is she back?'

Pauline's face fell. 'No, she ain't come back yet. Me gran says she won't cos her mum's too lily-livered to come back herself. I wish she

347

would, I miss her something awful.'

'So who do I know who has come back, then?' asked Alice.

Pauline's eyebrows went up. 'Bleedin' George, that's who.'

Alice tutted. 'That's not a nice thing to say, Pauline.'

'To be fair though, Nurse, his ma calls him that as well,' Pauline said. 'I heard her when she come to collect him from school last week.'

'Doesn't matter.' Alice swung back onto her bike. 'You'd better hurry along now. Say hello to Miss Phipps from me.'

'If I even sees her,' said Pauline gloomily, but she obediently turned and began walking in the direction of St Benedict's, dragging her feet.

★   ★   ★

'Nurse Adams! A word with you, please!' Gwen called when she noticed the tall new nurse hanging her cloak up.

Belinda turned around and smiled in friendly greeting, but the expression froze on her face when she realised that the deputy superintendent was bearing down on her looking extremely stern. She had heard from her new colleagues that this woman had a bit of a reputation but as yet hadn't found out why.

Gwen didn't wait for the young woman to speak. 'I had cause to inspect the district room after you left it earlier this morning, and I have to say that it was a disgrace. Packets of bandages were left out, the spare jars of Vaseline hadn't

348

been put back and there was actually a spillage. A spillage, Nurse Adams. Copper sulphate, all over the surface of one of the tables. Need I remind you how important it is that the district room is kept in immaculate order?'

Belinda blanched. 'N . . . no,' she said, casting her gaze to her feet.

'It is of paramount importance. Paramount,' Gwen went on. 'Not only for reasons of hygiene, which are self-evident, but out of consideration to your fellow nurses. They must all be able to find what they require to replenish their bags at a moment's notice. Sometimes they will have to do this with hardly any time to spare. They simply cannot risk turning up at a patient's home only to discover some vital piece of equipment is missing.' She paused to check that the new nurse was taking in what she was saying. 'If any one of us leaves the district room in anything other than pristine condition, we put patient safety in jeopardy. That must never happen. Do you understand me, Nurse Adams?'

'Y . . . yes,' whispered Belinda, pushing her thick black hair out of her eyes.

'Very well. Don't let me have to speak to you about this again,' Gwen finished.

'No. No, of course not.' Belinda could feel herself blushing. She hated the way her skin betrayed her every emotion, and knew she would be glowing like a beetroot. Pointless to say that she hadn't spilled the copper sulphate or left the Vaseline out. Admittedly the room had been a little untidy when she'd gone in and she hadn't taken the time to put it right, as she was close to being late for her first appointment with a new mother. But she could tell Gwen was on her high horse and saying anything would only get another nurse into trouble. That was if the deputy superintendent even believed her.

She leant against the wall in relief as Gwen turned on her heel and briskly walked back upstairs.

Mary appeared from the district room doorway. 'Blimey, what did she want?' she asked.

Belinda told her. 'She didn't even ask if it was me,' she said, the injustice of it beginning to annoy her. 'I know I'm new but I wouldn't do that. We were told over and over again in our training that we were to keep the district room clean and tidy.'

Mary's hand flew to her face. 'Oh no. Oh, I am so sorry. I think it must have been my fault.'

'Your fault?' Belinda looked at her colleague in amazement. Mary had bent over backwards to be helpful to her and Primrose as newcomers, and they thought the world of her. She found it hard to believe that their mentor would do such a thing.

'Yes, well, sort of,' said Mary ruefully. 'I was restocking my bag before going off to see one of Dr Patcham's patients — have you met him yet? He's an old sweetie, we all love him — and then someone called me from the common room so I stepped away for all of five minutes. Then I went back in and put everything back in its place. Even the beastly copper sulphate. It's too bad you went in there after me and Gwen thought it was you. Shall I go and confess?'

Belinda shook her head. 'No, what's the point? She's said her piece. It would only get you into trouble as well. Really, don't. Thank you for telling me though.'

Mary shrugged her shoulders. 'I am sorry you caught it from her like that. Don't take it personally. She's like it with everyone. Come on, have you got time for a cup of tea? Don't let her ruin your day. If you get into that habit you'll be miserable for most of your time here, as you don't usually get a cheerful word from the woman. Nobody knows why, but there we are.'

'Yes, all right.' Belinda still wasn't completely sure how long it would take to get to her next set of visits but she was fairly confident she wouldn't be late. Anyway, she deserved a cuppa. Really, that Gwen could take all the joy out of a day.

★　★　★

Gwen pursed her lips as she flicked through a set of patient notes in her file. She'd had a vague hope that because of the war the new intake of nurses would be more conscientious, but she could see that she had been sadly mistaken. This latest pair were showing all the characteristics she'd come to expect from the younger members of her profession: lack of attention to detail, sloppiness, general indiscipline. What went on during those training courses she dreaded to think.

Perhaps they still thought they were safe, in their cocoon of a cosy home with everything provided, three good meals a day, comfy

351

accommodation, few domestic duties. There had been no gas attacks or raids as yet, and she knew the widespread opinion was that everything would soon be over with hardly anyone suffering a scratch. Yes, there had been a few casualties, but so far they'd been far away: Scotland, or far out at sea. In London more people had been injured because of accidents in the blackout than anything else.

Gwen knew they wouldn't escape so easily. She had been to Miriam's house at the weekend and met her latest arrivals. Now not only did her friend have the Schmidts from Vienna living with her, but another young couple from Germany, also Jews, also fleeing while they still could, bringing with them only what they could carry. The Goldbergs had been used to a life of comfort, as he had been an engineer and she had studied to be a scientist. Now they were reduced to living in what had been Miriam's music room, before she'd got rid of the piano.

Despite that, they were cheerful, relieved to have got away, hopeful of getting their parents out once they'd found somewhere more permanent to live. They had entertained everyone with stories about what Berlin had used to be like before the days of the Nazis, glossing over what had happened in the years just before their departure. Gwen had found herself laughing along with them, enjoying their company, and only afterwards did she pause to reflect on what had really occurred to make them take such a drastic step, leaving everything behind.

Miriam's son Max was still in New York. 'Of course I want to see him, more than anything,' she'd confessed, as she and Gwen stood in her kitchen making dark, strong coffee for all the guests. She'd fussed over the silver coffee pot, the aroma bitter and pungent, which Gwen could not get used to. 'I miss him more than I ever thought I would, and he's a grown man now. Funny, isn't it?' She turned to put some spoons on a tray. 'But Jacob and I have asked him to stay there. Not just for the business. We hope he can arrange for some of these good people to find jobs or houses; anything to get them away from Hitler and to new lives.'

'It's a lot to ask of a young man,' Gwen had pointed out.

Miriam had nodded, and in the glow cast by the kitchen lamp, Gwen could see the large shadows under her friend's eyes, almost like bruises. 'It is, but he's not alone. This young lady friend of his has influential family. They will help. It's more important he does that than see his old mother.'

Gwen had tried to cheer her up. 'Not so old. Steady on, we're the same age.'

Miriam had smiled ruefully. 'Exactly.'

Now Gwen slammed shut her file, exasperated yet again by the way the young nurses failed to realise what was happening virtually under their noses. As for that Belinda, well, she'd have to keep an extra-special eye on her. Just when she had thought some of the others had begun to settle down, in came trouble once more. She'd simply have to redouble her efforts to maintain

353

standards and strict discipline in the home. The world might be going to hell in a handcart, but that didn't mean this one establishment in the East End had to do the same.

26

The big freeze of winter slowly gave way to the first signs of spring. Still the expected raids didn't come, and even more children came back to their homes as their parents thought it was better to keep the families together. Dotty was one of the few from St Benedict's who stayed away.

The British Expeditionary Force continued its activities on the Continent and letters arrived home with regularity. Mattie watched the letterbox like a hawk, eagerly awaiting news from Lennie. He wasn't a great letter writer, even she had to admit that, but it was enough to know that he was alive and safe and thinking of her and Gillian. That was all she needed. Harry also wrote when he could, nearly always with news of how his boxing training was going. Joe's letters were longer but less regular, as they knew he wasn't always in a position to find a postbox, being at sea much of the time — not that he could say exactly where he was. The government had begun to stress the importance of not giving away any potentially important information, reminding everyone that careless talk cost lives.

The rattle of the letterbox brought Mattie running into the hall one morning in March,

355

and to her delight there was something from Lennie, with his big round handwriting showing clearly on the envelope. She rushed back into the warmth of the kitchen clutching it tightly. Flo was bent over the pile of mending which never seemed to grow any smaller, but seeing what Mattie was brandishing, she perked up at once.

'Shall I make us a cup of tea while you read that, and then you can tell me how he's getting on?' she offered, getting to her feet.

Mattie wrinkled her nose. 'I don't think I fancy one right now,' she said. 'You have one though. I'll put the kettle on, don't you get up.'

Flo sank gratefully back down. 'Thank you, love.'

Mattie plonked herself down at the big table and eagerly ripped open the envelope. Her eyes scanned the sheets of paper — Lennie's writing took up so much room that he always used more than one even when he didn't have much to say — quickly checking that he was basically all right before treating herself to rereading it all again slowly.

'Well?' asked Flo, almost as keen as Mattie to hear the latest. She was very fond of her son-in-law, who was so different to her own two boys, and knew that his marrying Mattie was the best possible thing for both of them. They were devoted to each other and to their darling daughter.

Mattie grinned happily and then pushed herself out of her seat to make the tea. Again she pulled a face at it. 'I don't know why, I'm right

356

off tea at the moment,' she commented as she brought it over to her mother. 'Not like me at all.'

Flo took a sip. 'No, you're usually the first to make a cuppa. Maybe you're coming down with something?'

'Perhaps.' Mattie sat down again and took up the sheets of paper. 'So, anyway, here's what's happening in France. They've got a new billet which is warmer than the last one. He's getting good use out of those socks I knitted him. The food isn't very good. They went into the nearest village and he tried the local stuff but he didn't like it. He says they all smelled of garlic for days after. He wishes you were there to make them a proper cake.'

Flo nodded approvingly. 'That's only right,' she said.

'He's bumped into someone who's keen on boxing and who was in the same camp as Harry for a bit just after Christmas, and they all reckon he's got the makings of a champion . . . I shan't tell him that or he'll be even more big-headed than usual.'

Flo tutted gently, as Mattie shouldn't have been rude about her brother like that, but it was a fair comment. Harry had many qualities but false modesty wasn't one of them.

'He says they spend a lot of time cleaning their weapons and practising marching. Oh well, at least he'll be fit next time he's back. He doesn't say when that might be, though.'

Flo put down her cup. 'That stands to reason, love. They probably don't know themselves. It'll

357

all depend on how things go over there, you know that.'

Mattie sighed. 'Yes, but I miss him.' She paused for a moment and then tucked the letter back in its envelope. 'He sends his love. That's about it. I'll go and put this with the rest before I lose it.'

As she climbed the stairs to her bedroom, where she kept all the letters in a special box so that Gillian could read them when she was older, the thought occurred to her that she was more tired than usual. Perhaps she really was coming down with something. That would be a nuisance, as there was always so much to do around the house now that Joe and Harry weren't there to share the heavier tasks and her father seemed to be on constant ARP duty. She'd have to buy a bottle of tonic, or maybe consult Edith. She brightened at that idea. She would walk over to the nurses' home and leave a message to see if she fancied meeting up.

★ ★ ★

Edith had just had a letter from Harry and was more than happy to share most of the contents with his sister. 'I haven't got long, as I need to take my watch to be mended after work,' she explained, 'but I'd love to drop in and see you all. I'm sure Harry will write to tell you about his match himself, but your parents will want to know how well he's doing.'

Mattie nodded, proud of her talented boxer brother, despite what she'd said earlier.

Edith looked at her friend as they walked along the side street, with Gillian being pushed along in her pram. The little girl was making cooing noises, singing to herself. There was something different about Mattie but she couldn't quite make out what. Mattie had said she'd felt unusually tired recently but there was something else going on.

Edith struggled for a way to phrase it, and then just came out with it. 'Are you all right, Mattie, other than being tired and missing Lennie, of course? I just thought there was something about you — I can't put my finger on it.'

Mattie nodded. 'I did wonder if I was coming down with a bug or something like that, but I don't know anyone who's had anything wrong with them recently.' She swung the pram expertly down the kerb, across the mouth of a narrow alley and up the other side onto the pavement again.

Edith frowned. Then she paused a moment as an idea took hold. She did a quick calculation in her head and then broached the subject. 'Look, you can tell me to mind my own business, but is there any chance you might be pregnant?'

Mattie gasped and almost steered the pram into a wall. 'Blimey, Edith, I don't . . . no, hang on.' The possibility hadn't occurred to her — Lennie had been home for such a brief stay, although they'd made as much of the time together as they could. Besides, it only took once, didn't it? She thought hard. 'Do you know, Edith . . . well . . . come to think of it, I don't know if I've had my monthlies since Christmas. I had them just before and Ma had to make me raspberry leaf tea, they were so bad, but now you mention it . . . ' She halted as the realisation hit home. 'I could be. You're right, I could be. That would explain why some things taste funny, wouldn't it? I thought I was going off tea and couldn't understand it. But if that's why — that's wonderful, I must write to Lennie straight away.'

'Early days yet,' Edith cautioned. 'Maybe wait until you're sure — you don't want to get his hopes up only to find it's a mistake.'

'Yes, good point,' said Mattie distractedly, her mind whirring. Could she have made a mistake, forgotten the dates? And yet she was sure Edith had hit the nail on the head. She remembered how she'd been with Gillian, how sick she'd felt for a while. That hadn't happened this time, or not yet, for which she was grateful, but she recalled her mother saying pregnancies weren't necessarily all the same.

'Come on, let's go and speak to your mother,' Edith said, almost as if she'd read Mattie's mind. 'This is so exciting, Mattie. Imagine, a little brother or sister for Gillian.'

'I know, I know.' Mattie could feel a bubble of joy rising inside her. 'She'll be thrilled, they all will be. I feel like dancing, I'm so happy.' Impulsively she threw her arms around her friend. 'A new baby! Even though there's a war on, it's the best news ever.'

Edith hugged her back. 'I'm so pleased, Mattie. It's just what we need.' Her expression grew solemn. 'Even though there's all of that going on, this will give us something to look forward to. A reason to hope.'

★ ★ ★

The news spread in no time at all. It was as if everybody was eager for a reason to be cheerful, to counteract the misery of being separated from loved ones or the restrictions of rationing. Mattie waited until she reckoned she was four months along and then wrote to Lennie, not wanting him to hear it from anyone else first. By then she was certain. The familiar signs she recognised from her first pregnancy told her that; soreness, tiredness, some sickness, but thankfully nowhere near as bad as it had been when she was carrying Gillian. To her relief she found she was able to carry on with her daily round of tasks and didn't need to overburden Flo with extra chores. Not that Flo would have minded. She was thrilled at the prospect of another grandchild. 'We've enough love to go round, that's for sure,' she'd said.

Clarrie and Peggy dropped in to congratulate Mattie on a bright late April afternoon. It was so warm that Mattie dragged out some kitchen chairs so that they could sit in the back garden and make the most of the sunshine. Gillian toddled unsteadily between them, her face showing her grim determination to master this new skill of walking.

'She's growing, isn't she,' said Peggy wistfully.

'Be a bit odd if she wasn't,' said Clarrie, who didn't dote on children the way Peggy did. Still, she held out her arms to catch the little girl when it looked as if she might fall.

'Wants to run before she can walk, that one,' said Mattie, laughing at the child's attempts to make it all the way across the yard in one go without holding on to anything.

'Wonder where she gets that from?' Clarrie teased. 'Do you think you're having a boy or a girl, Mattie? Do you want one of each?'

Mattie shook her head. 'I don't mind one bit. As long as it's healthy, that's all I ask.'

'What about Lennie?' Clarrie pressed. 'I bet he'll want a boy.'

Mattie shrugged. 'He's so pleased, he says he doesn't mind either. He loves Gillian to pieces and doesn't care that she's not a boy. He wrote to say he couldn't believe it for ages, that he was going to be a dad again. He's so excited. I wish he was here to see her growing and to meet the new one, whenever he or she arrives.'

Clarrie stood up. 'I've left my bag inside. I brought some lemonade — shall I fetch some glasses? I know where they are, so you stay right where you are, Mattie, and take it easy.'

'All right,' said Mattie, half thinking to protest that she didn't need pampering, but then deciding she quite liked it.

Peggy watched her friend go inside, as she sat on the edge of her chair and twisted her hands in her lap.

Mattie gazed at the blue sky through the branches of next-door's old apple tree, which they'd managed to grow in the corner of their yard. The leaves made patterns against the sky and for a moment she could have fallen asleep, it was so peaceful. It didn't seem possible that armies were lining up to fight across the Channel, and she wondered if it was as sunny where Lennie was right now. Pushing herself more upright, she carefully loosened her waistband as far as she could. Soon she'd have to start wearing different clothes. She still had her old maternity smocks somewhere, although Gillian had been born during the winter and the material they were made of might be too heavy. She wondered if she could buy some new.

'Penny for 'em,' she said to Peggy.

Peggy tried to smile.

Mattie looked more closely at her friend. 'Peggy, whatever is it? Is something the matter?'

Peggy started nervously, almost as if she'd forgotten where she was. Her smile faltered and she bit her lip. She glanced back over her shoulder, as if to check that Clarrie wasn't returning with the cool drinks, and then she could contain herself no longer.

'Oh, Mattie. I'm so sorry. I'm happy for you, I really am, but . . . but . . . ' A bout of sobbing overcame her and Mattie drew her own chair closer so that she could take her friend's hand.

'Tell me,' she said, quietly but firmly. 'You can tell me anything, you know that.'

Peggy shook her head forlornly. 'I'm jealous of you, that's what it is. Pete and I so wanted to have a baby, and just before Christmas I thought we were going to. I had all the signs, you know, stopping my monthlies, being sick in the morning. I almost wrote to him to tell him but

I'm so glad I didn't.' She paused and drew out her hanky from the sleeve of her light knitted cardigan. 'Then, when it was really cold — you know, when the river froze over? — it all went wrong and I began to bleed. I was so frightened, I didn't know what was happening. I didn't want to tell Pete's mum cos she's all right most of the time but she don't half take over given a chance. So I went round to Ma's and she got me to lie down but it didn't help. She explained to me I'd lost the baby. Said it had happened to her between me and my sister, that it's the same for lots of people but hardly anyone says.'

Mattie's heart flew to her mouth, a sick feeling of dread coming over her at the thought of it. If she lost this baby she would be heartbroken. It was a living link from her to Lennie, a proof that he had been home and that he loved her. Peggy must have felt the same — and her not long married too.

'Oh, Peggy, I'm so sorry,' she said. 'You must have felt terrible. Are you all right — did you see a doctor?'

Peggy nodded. 'Then I was afraid he would send one of the nurses we know to check on me, but it was somebody else. I just didn't want anyone to know. It was so cold out, and dark all the time, it made me even more miserable. I didn't even see Clarrie. I don't think she'd understand, and I wasn't going to tell you, I didn't want you to think about such things.'

Mattie frowned. 'Don't worry about me. I'm glad you said something, otherwise it would be eating you up inside. You'll just have to make extra sure to have another as soon as possible when Pete gets back.'

Peggy nodded. 'Yes, that's what I think too. I didn't at first, I was scared there was something wrong with me, but Ma said it's more common than we know. So I won't tell him in case he gets worried, and what good would that do? He's most likely got enough to worry about.'

A clinking of glasses announced Clarrie's return, and Mattie moved back to her original spot beneath the apple tree. Clarrie came through and set the tray down on the raised stone step Flo had had put in so she could reach one end of the washing line. She caught sight of her friend's red eyes.

'You all right, Peggy?' she asked.

Peggy nodded. 'It's just a touch of early hay fever, came on all sudden,' she insisted, and refused to meet Mattie's gaze.

27

'I don't know what's wrong with Charles lately,' Mary pouted as she propped her bike in its slot in the rack. It was the end of a busy shift and she was fed up. 'It's too bad. He's cancelled me again, and we were due to go to a matinee on Saturday afternoon. I was going to get my hair done and everything.' She shook her hair free from her cap as if to emphasise the point.

Edith made a face in sympathy. 'He's probably busy with whatever's going on in Belgium. Isn't he quite a big cheese behind the scenes?'

'Obviously not big enough or he could get somebody else to do his work for him,' Mary snapped. 'What does he expect me to do, sit mooching around on my lonesome until Tommy Trinder comes on the wireless with *In Town Tonight*? Sorry, Edith, I shouldn't take it out on you. You'll have had a busy week as well.'

Edith sighed as she secured her own bike in place. That was putting it mildly. On Tuesday she'd visited a woman in her late forties, who at first had been too shy to explain what the matter was. She wouldn't say a word until her children had left the room, and even then she kept her voice low. 'I don't want my husband to come home from work and hear me, he won't like it,' she'd said, a tremor in her voice.

366

Edith had waited, smiling encouragingly, until the woman screwed up her courage to explain. 'I'm bleeding a bit where I shouldn't. You know. I'm past all that, have been for a couple of years, but now it's begun again, only not like before.'

Edith had nodded, not wanting to alarm her patient but needing to know the details. She gently asked the necessary questions before telling her that she should see a doctor as soon as possible. 'I can go with you, if you'd prefer,' Edith had offered.

'I don't like to bother him, I'm probably being silly,' the woman had protested. 'It's a nuisance more than anything as I never know when it's going to happen.'

Edith knew that such symptoms could be caused by any number of things, but that one explanation was potentially serious. 'It's Dr Patcham, isn't it?' she said. 'He won't mind. He'd rather you came and had your worries laid to rest than ignore something unusual. We'll go together, shall we?'

Finally the woman had agreed, and two days later Edith had accompanied her to see the genial old doctor, now back to full fitness after his accident six months ago. He had listened carefully, and examined her, and didn't think she was wasting his time at all. He had sent her home with instructions to come back for a special clinic after the weekend, and then he had taken Edith to one side. 'I'm afraid this could be cancer of the uterus,' he said gravely. 'Do you know what her circumstances are?'

Edith had sighed. 'I was half expecting that

but hoping you'd say something different. She's got three school-age children and a husband who works. I haven't met him.'

'So you don't know how he would deal with a potentially sick wife?'

'No, but she didn't want him to know about it,' Edith remembered. 'I am not sure if that simply means she was embarrassed or that he'd react badly.'

'Well, my dear Nurse Gillespie, you might be required to lend your support to this poor woman if my fears prove to be correct,' he'd said.

This was what had been uppermost in Edith's mind as she'd parked her bike, and Mary's complaints about Charles had rather fallen on deaf ears. Edith churlishly thought that at least her boyfriend was in London, safe for now in his desk job, unlike Harry, facing who-knew-what in France somewhere. He'd triumphed in his first army boxing tournament, and she was proud of him for that, but she'd rather a thousand times that he was home safe. She shook her head. No point in wishing for what couldn't be.

★   ★   ★

'Did you hear the news?' Alice greeted them as they entered the common room. 'We've got a new prime minister. Winston Churchill's taking over from Neville Chamberlain.'

'Oh,' said Mary, still too cross about Charles's behaviour to think about anything else.

Alice frowned, as it was the most important thing to happen for ages, in her opinion, but having to realise that not everyone was as keen on such matters as she was.

'Right, well, that's good, isn't it?' asked Edith, who had gathered that lots of people thought Churchill was the right man to lead the war effort. 'He'll take us to victory, won't he?'

'If anyone can,' said Alice, with as much hope in her voice as she could manage. She'd picked up worrying indications in the newspapers that things weren't going well, and couldn't help wondering what was going on, particularly for all the young men they knew fighting in France. As for Joe, she had no idea where he was at the moment, as his letters gave little away and arrived so infrequently it was hard to guess what he was doing. She wasn't sure what she felt about that. For some reason she thought about his safety more than she'd expected to. 'Shall we listen to the wireless?'

'I'm going to have a cup of tea and then I'm going upstairs,' said Mary flatly, heading off to make her drink.

Edith pulled a face. 'Don't ask her,' she warned Alice. 'She's like a bear with a sore head. Charles is too busy to take her out at the weekend and she's fed up.'

'I dare say he's got other things on his mind,' suggested Alice.

'Just what I said. Honestly, I'm going to run out of patience with her soon,' confessed Edith. 'When she's got him nearby and Harry's all the way over in France, I just want to scream. I miss him so much. Sorry, I didn't mean to be so bad-tempered, it's been one of those weeks.'

'I know.' Alice gave her friend a hug. 'Let's do something nice at the weekend, go to the cinema or a concert if there's one on.'

'That's a good idea. Let's do that,' Edith agreed, trying to sound cheerful, although she'd have given a lifetime of concerts for one night out with Harry. 'We could check the paper. Where is it?'

Alice smiled. 'It's over in the corner, where Gladys left it.'

That really did brighten Edith up. 'Isn't it good that she can read it now?' she said. 'She might be ready to go on that Civil Nursing Reserve course soon. Well done, Alice, that was down to you.'

'You helped,' Alice pointed out. She picked up the local newspaper and flicked through the pages. 'There's a George Formby film on at the Regal, how about that?'

'Yes, all right.' Edith knew that would cheer her up. 'Let's see if Mary wants to come along too,' she added generously. 'Might take her mind off the dashing captain.'

★   ★   ★

Mary enjoyed the George Formby film despite herself, and by a miracle on Sunday afternoon Charles somehow found time to take her out after all. The next week Edith accompanied her worried patient to the specialist clinic, where following a pelvic examination it was found that she did not have cancer after all. Edith took her home and then went to see Dr Patcham again.

He admitted he was mightily relieved, as he'd heard on the grapevine that the husband was a notorious drinker and he would have had grave cause for concern if he had been left to cope with a sick wife and three young children. 'So there's much to be thankful for,' he said.

Edith tried to hang on to his words, and she repeated them to Alice when they sat down for their evening meal of corned beef and mashed potatoes. Alice nodded, keeping to herself the fears which were increasing day by day. She knew it made no difference, but she now read every newspaper she could find, as well as listening to news bulletins on the wireless. It seemed as if all was far from well in France and the Low Countries. The BEF was not succeeding as they'd hoped.

As the days went by her dread grew, and yet she carried on with her work, sharing with Edith the nursing of Dennis, the teenager with TB they'd both become so fond of, patching up a child who'd run into the road in front of a bus and was lucky to have avoided hospital, helping out at the ongoing first-aid classes, and even finding time for a quick cup of tea with Janet Phipps, who was worn to a frazzle by all the changes at St Benedict's. The weather grew warmer and the May evenings grew lighter, the blossom appeared on the trees and the birds sang loudly. If she could only have ignored the papers and wireless, she could have convinced herself that all was well with the world.

All was far from well, and towards the end of the month it became clear that the BEF was losing ground. It was eventually ordered to withdraw towards the port cities. What followed then was something few of them would ever forget. The army had retreated as far as it could and congregated in a French town by the name of Dunkirk.

28

Stan swung open the kitchen door and inhaled the delicious smell of one of his wife's stews. So far rationing hadn't stopped Flo producing tasty meals, and he wished above anything he could sit down and join his family at the table right now.

'Sorry, love,' he said as Flo turned to greet him. 'This is a flying visit. I've got to cover someone's shift tonight.'

Flo frowned. 'But you worked last night. Surely they can't expect you to go on patrol every night. That's not right.'

Stan came across to her and put his hands on her shoulders. 'I know, love, but it's an emergency. I'm covering Billy's shift.'

Mattie pushed open the back door and came in from the garden, overhearing her father's remark. She stopped dead in her tracks, on the threshold between the back kitchen and kitchen proper. 'Why? Whatever's happened to Billy? Is something wrong?'

Stan looked at his daughter and gave a heartfelt sigh. 'Have you heard the news on the wireless at all?'

Mattie shook her head. 'We've just had the music on. Singing along helps the housework get done quicker.'

Stan nodded in understanding but he had to

tell them what was going on. 'I'm afraid it's not good news from France. Hitler's got our boys on the run, and they're going to try to evacuate the whole army. That's where Billy's gone.'

Mattie turned and called into the back garden: 'Kath, you'd better get in here and listen to this.' She rested her hand protectively over her stomach, which was just beginning to show its new bump.

Kathleen ran in, wiping her hands on her cotton frock, followed by Gillian and Brian, both now much steadier on their feet. Their hands were covered in sand, as Stan had recently built a tiny sandpit for them. Kathleen made them wait in the back kitchen where she could clean them up at the sink.

'What's happened?' she asked in a voice full of foreboding.

Stan repeated what he'd said and went on to explain that all available small ships and even little boats were crossing the Channel to join the rescue. 'Billy knew some lads down the docks who could get hold of an old boat,' he said steadily. 'They thought it was their duty to go, even though they haven't sailed beyond the mouth of the Thames for years. Billy says she's seaworthy and they needed an extra hand, so I told him I'd cover his ARP shift. That young man is a hero, whether or not he's actually in the armed services.'

Kathleen's face went white. 'Billy's doing that? But he can't swim. He never learned, he told me.'

Flo came across and put her arm around

Kathleen's shoulders, which had started to shake. 'Don't take on, Kathleen. He won't need to swim. He'll just have to do what the others tell him, pull on a rope or whatnot.'

Kathleen nodded slowly. 'I hope so, I really do.' Yet again it struck her that she'd overlooked Billy's qualities too easily. He'd set off with no hesitation to save others and with no thought for his own safety. That was typical of him.

Mattie shut her eyes and swayed a little. 'Oh God, I hope he finds Lennie. I do hope he finds him and brings him home. Don't let Lennie be hurt. I couldn't stand it. Not my Lennie.'

Flo let go of Kathleen and hugged her daughter. 'Hush, Mattie. We don't know Lennie's there at all.'

'Or Harry!' Mattie cried, all her exasperation and irritation at her brother's annoying ways forgotten at the prospect of his being injured, or worse. She looked at Stan and realised this was exactly what had been on his mind too. 'He's in France, we know he is.'

'Sit down, my love.' Flo quickly pulled a chair from the table and helped Mattie lower herself onto it. 'We don't know anything for sure. Worrying won't help. We have to be strong, for the children. Chin up, my girl. Don't let Gillian see you cry. We don't want her upset as well.'

Mattie nodded dumbly.

'I'll make you a sandwich, Stan, to take with you, and you can have your stew at whatever time you get back,' Flo said, while Kathleen busied herself tidying up the children, who hadn't understood what was going on but had picked up on the atmosphere and realised the adults weren't happy. Hastily she held each of them up to the sink and washed their grubby hands, singing a nursery rhyme under her breath to soothe them.

Stan took the cheese and pickle sandwich that Flo had hastily wrapped in greaseproof paper and tucked it into his inner pocket. 'Thanks, love. Right, I'd best be off. I'll bring back as much news as I can but don't be surprised if we don't hear anything for a while. Try not to give in to worry when we don't know what's really gone on.'

He quickly gave Flo a peck on the cheek and was gone.

Mattie stared at the door. 'Now what do we do?' she breathed.

Flo came and sat beside her. Her heart was leaden but she tried to inject as much hope into her voice as she could. 'I'm afraid we wait.'

*   *   *

They waited like so many others in cities, towns and villages across the country. Everyone was desperately hoping that their loved ones had survived and were unhurt; nobody could say when they would know for sure. In Victory Walk, the nurses went about their business as usual, but many did so with heavy hearts. Edith was far from the only one to fear the worst while hoping for the best. She rode her bike to her regular roster of patients and managed to talk sensibly to a few new ones, yet largely with her mind

376

elsewhere. She was relieved that she hadn't had to break bad news to anyone; if the woman she had recently seen had been diagnosed with cancer and her difficult husband had caused problems, Edith doubted she would have been able to cope.

Fiona Dewar somehow knew what the matter was, in the way that she seemed to know most things about her charges' personal lives, and kept an eye on Edith, making sure she wasn't overburdened with new cases or required to do too many extra activities, unless she volunteered for them. Others could teach the first-aid course, for a start.

Alice watched over Edith like a hawk, keen to protect her as far as she could in this agonising period of not knowing. She also waited anxiously for news of Dermot and Mark; Dermot had written a few letters since he'd left London, just so that she knew they were both all right. She had no idea if their being doctors would have meant they were safer or not. What she did know was that neither of them was likely to run away from a fight.

She had no idea if Joe might have been caught up in the evacuation. His whereabouts were a mystery. There was no real reason why he would contact her, either, but she hoped for his sake and his family's that he was safe, somewhere, wherever it might be. That image of him in the back kitchen at Christmas kept coming into her mind, and that sensation that he was there was something between them, something he wanted to say or do or was troubling him. She realised she very much wanted to find out what it might have been, all the while banishing the little voice that taunted her: 'Maybe there won't be a next time.' She had to stay optimistic, for Edith's sake.

Mary had immediately ceased her complaining about Charles when she understood what he had most likely been doing, frantically planning the army's defence in France and the Low Countries. She also apologised to Edith for being thoughtless, thoroughly ashamed that she'd gone on and on about the captain's unavailability when Harry and his comrades had been facing heaven knew what dangers. 'He'll be fine,' she tried to assure her friend. 'If any Germans come near him he'll punch them on the nose and knock them out.' Edith had tried to smile back, knowing the remark was well meant, but she doubted Harry would be able to get away so easily.

Gladys took to surreptitiously clearing up after Edith, going far beyond the boundaries of her job, because she didn't want Edith to feel bad when she forgot to wash her mug or put away the cocoa. Gladys was fiercely fond of Edith, as one of the two nurses who had taken steps to help her when she'd finally admitted to being unable to read. Her loyalty to Edith and Alice was unshakable. Woe betide any of the others who made a thoughtless comment about Edith's sudden absent-mindedness.

Even Gwen relented from her usual remorseless drive for perfection in all fields, not taking Edith to task when she put things away wrongly in the district room or hung up her cloak on somebody else's peg. Edith didn't notice but Alice did and was quietly amazed. Of course, if it had been a major mistake with a patient put at risk, that would have been a different matter. But Edith held herself together when on her rounds, and so Gwen for once cut her some slack.

★　★　★

Kathleen lifted Brian into his pram and set off to try to buy meat. She left early, as every kind was rationed now and she knew she faced the prospect of queuing at several different shops if she wanted to come home with the meagre portion her coupons allowed. First she tried for ham, but that had sold out. Then she went to another shop she'd registered at in the hope they would have bacon, but there was none of that either. The third shop, nearly all the way up to Stamford Hill, had just received a delivery of sausages, and had some fresh eggs too, so even though she'd had to walk further than usual she came back with enough for several meals, along with aching shoulders from pushing an increasingly heavy Brian.

'You sit there,' she said, propping him on her bed and making a little wall with her pillows to try to keep him still while she unloaded her shopping. 'Here's your rabbit — tell him about the morning you've had.' She hummed to herself as she put the eggs on a high shelf, well away from curious little hands.

That done, she turned to the bucket of baby clothes she'd put to soak before leaving the house.

379

The weather was warm and a gentle breeze was blowing — perfect for a bit of laundry. She could rinse them through, peg them out in the tiny back yard and then they might be ready to iron by teatime. Keeping up with Brian's clothing was a ceaseless task — he never had much spare as he grew too fast, but she took pride in ensuring he was always clean, with a spare set of clothes always tucked into the bottom shelf of the pram in case of accidents. She had begun to put aside anything he'd grown out of that wasn't worn too thin in case it came in useful for Mattie's new baby. It was another chance to give something back to the generous Banhams.

She checked the collar of a little green shirt to see if it needed mending, and then carefully rinsed it out and set it in her washing basket. She was so engrossed in the task that she almost missed the knock on the door. Brian looked up from playing with his rabbit, his face expectant, as in his limited experience it was usually Mattie, and that meant Gillian as well.

Mattie, however, usually let herself in immediately after knocking. Kathleen dried her hands on a threadbare towel by the sink and went to see who it was. Standing there was a boy of about fourteen in the uniform of the General Post Office, his bike propped precariously by her doorstep. 'Mrs Berry?' he asked. 'Mrs Ray Berry?'

'Yes,' said Kathleen automatically, and on this fine sunny morning it didn't occur to her what this might mean. Her first worry was whether she had enough loose change to tip the telegraph boy.

He pushed his flopping fringe out of his eyes and handed her a telegram. 'This is for you, missus.'

Still it hadn't dawned on her that these few moments would alter everything. 'Thank you,' she said, squinting a little at the dazzling sun which had just come out from behind a small high cloud. 'Wait there, I've got some pennies indoors.'

The boy's face grew concerned. 'Think you should read it, missus.'

Kathleen smiled politely and popped back inside to her clay pot of coppers, which she kept on the top shelf and tried not to touch except for emergencies. 'Here you are, for your trouble,' she said, making no move to read the message.

'Thank you, missus.' The boy had no time to hang around and was off away down Jeeves Place to find his next port of call.

Kathleen shivered despite the warmth and stood in the doorway, her back against the jamb, suddenly extremely aware of all the sights and sounds around her — the familiar street, the open windows of her neighbours' houses, the caw of birds, the squeal of the buses' wheels from the High Street. The smell of dinner being cooked by the woman upstairs drifted down, a not very appetising chicken pie. Kathleen involuntarily wrinkled her nose, then took the plunge and read the telegram.

Regret inform you Ray Berry lost
at sea 29 May 1940 . . .

381

Slowly she read it again. The words seemed to be moving around and she couldn't focus properly. Lost? Was that . . . ? He couldn't be. Ray was never lost for anything. But here it was in black and white. In a daze, she dragged herself over to the table and sank down, her hand shaking as it held the bit of paper.

Her head swam at the realisation that Ray was dead. Her husband, no matter what had passed between them. No more Ray. It wasn't possible. Even when she'd hated what he'd done to her and how he'd treated Brian, even when he'd run off and not bothered to let her know where he was, she'd never imagined that she wouldn't see him again. There was always the thought — half longed for, half dreaded — that he could turn up at any time.

Brian would be without a father now. She glanced across to where he'd half rolled off the bed but was still clutching his beloved rabbit, chattering quietly in nonsense language to it. If only Ray had appreciated his lovely son. Now he never would. She would have to raise him alone and somehow tell him about what sort of man his father had been, without letting her bitterness show. She sighed. She'd tackle that when the need arose. Thinking about it was beyond her right at this moment.

★ ★ ★

Kathleen went through the rest of the day on autopilot. She finished rinsing the clothes and hung them out in the tiny back yard to dry. She brought them in and ironed them. She made herself one slice of toast and poached one of the eggs to put on top of it, telling herself she still had to eat, and then forced it down although she had no appetite. Brian dozed off for his afternoon nap. She sat in the one comfy chair and watched the world go by in Jeeves Place. Mrs Coyne left with her shopping basket on her arm. After a while she came back again. Kathleen had no idea how much time had passed.

At last she lit the gas lamp and tucked her son firmly into his cot, gently easing away the toy rabbit he liked to clutch as he fell asleep. She didn't want him trying to eat its ears — as she'd caught him doing last week — and choking. One day she would have to wash it, but then he would probably object as it would smell of Rinso laundry soap, and so she kept putting it off.

She watched the rise and fall of his chest as he breathed slowly, making little snuffling noises. She wondered if he would look like his father. That might be no bad thing; at least Ray had been handsome. Then again, if he hadn't been so good-looking she might not have fallen for him and that would have been a blessing. On the other hand, she wouldn't have had Brian. Nothing was ever simple. As long as he didn't take after his father in terms of character . . . That would be up to her, to set him on the right path.

She jumped as there was a soft knock on the door. It wasn't exactly late, but she was still wary as she approached the door, her stomach churning because of what had happened the last time anyone had come knocking. 'Who's there?' she called.

'Don't worry, Kath,' replied a familiar male voice. 'It's only me.'

'Billy!' she cried, flinging the door wide open. A rush of emotions assailed her, as she realised the shock of today's news had made her forget that Billy was missing. 'You're safe. You made it back.' Swiftly she drew him in, holding on to his arm. 'Come on in, sit down, I'll make us a cuppa,' she went on, remembering her manners.

'You don't have to, only if you're having one, Kath,' he said, eyes bright at the sight of her. 'Just thought I should pop round and show you I'm alive and in one piece. You don't mind, do you?'

Kathleen tried to keep her voice steady but didn't quite succeed. 'Don't be silly. We've been going out of our minds with worry. I'm just relieved to see you.'

He caught sight of her as the gas light shone fully on her face. 'Here, Kath, hang on. What's wrong?'

She turned her back to him, wringing her hands, almost unable to say the words. Once she spoke them out loud, there would be no going back. It would all be real. She took a deep breath. 'Ray's lost at sea.'

For a moment Billy couldn't say anything. He took a step towards her. 'Oh, Kath.' He could tell she didn't want him to come any closer. 'Kath, are you all right?'

She wouldn't meet his gaze but turned her

face to the ceiling. 'Yes. No. I don't know. It's too much to take in. Look, I'll make that tea, it'll help.'

'No.' He went as if to move towards the kitchen. 'I'll do it, I know where you keep it all . . . '

'Stop, Billy. Really. I want to do it.' There was comfort in small routines, she'd learnt that this afternoon. Swiftly she boiled the kettle again and set out an extra cup, putting fresh leaves into the pot rather than reusing the ones from earlier in the day as she would have done if she'd been alone. 'But tell me about how you got back. At least you're home in one piece, after we thought you might be a goner.' She set the battered tray down on the table.

Billy shook his head. 'No, takes more than a few pot shots from Jerry to get rid of me.'

Kathleen's hand flew to her mouth. 'What, did they shoot at you? Oh my God. Are you all right, are you hurt?'

He shook his head again and sat down on the hard wooden chair, as she perched on the edge of the armchair. 'They shot at all the little boats. Trying to put holes in them so they'd sink, I suppose. Well, they never managed it. Our boat, the *Molly May* she was, she lasted all the way back to Limehouse. We didn't know if she'd make it; she struggled a bit and she was low in the water as we packed her so tight, but she did us proud.'

Kathleen smiled despite herself. 'You're talking like a sailor, Billy.'

Billy wiped his hand over his face. 'Nah, one

thing I realised on that trip was what real sailors are like — how they can handle a boat, the tricky situations they can get themselves out of. I admired them, I don't mind telling you. We just went where we was put.'

'And did you rescue many soldiers, Billy? What was it like?'

Billy's expression clouded over. 'I don't want to tell you the details, Kath, I don't want the boy to overhear,' he said. 'It was like a nightmare. I don't ever want to see anything like it ever again. Those poor men. Boys, some of them. Terrible, it was.' He paused for a moment, remembering. Then his tone changed. 'But we got lots of them off the beach there, thousands. You know what, it was a big success. Everyone is saying so. We took dozens and dozens back with us — crowded as anything, it was, but we got them home safe. A couple were hurt bad, but with my ARP training I knew what to do to staunch the blood from their wounds. Then they got took straight to hospital when we reached Blighty.' He stopped to take a breath. 'And then we turned around and went back and did it all over again.'

'Oh, Billy.' Kathleen's face was full of concern.

'You should have seen the *Molly May*,' he continued. 'She was a beauty. It was like she knew she was on a rescue mission, she darted in there quick as you like, for all she was an old girl.'

Kathleen steeled herself to ask the next question. 'Don't suppose you saw anything of Lennie? Or Harry? Or Pete?'

Billy shook his head. 'No, I never. Is there no news of them?'

'No. Not yet, anyway.'

Billy refused to be daunted. 'We shouldn't give up hope, Kath. There were so many men there, you can't imagine. It'll take ages for it all to be sorted out, it stands to reason. They could be in some town on the south coast or down in Kent somewhere, unable to get a message back home. You never know. It was a huge operation, blimey, I never seen so many men together in one place. Made me proud to be British, it did, that we could save so many of our boys and come back like we did.'

'Of course.' She poured the tea and didn't stint on the milk, even though she was low on her ration. She added a heaped teaspoon of sugar to Billy's. To hell with being careful. His return was something to celebrate.

'I'm so glad you made it back, Billy,' she said, passing him his cup, her voice full of emotion. 'You were so brave to go off like that. Everyone thought so.' Her hand brushed against his as he reached for the cup, and he caught her gaze.

'It weren't nothing more than all the others were doing,' he said thickly. 'I couldn't have lived with meself if I hadn't done it. But I'm glad you think I'm brave. Means a lot to me, that does.'

Kathleen cleared her throat. 'I do think so, Billy. I really do.' For two pins she would have crossed the mean little room and thrown her arms around him. But she couldn't.

Even though she could read in his eyes plain as day what he felt for her, and if she was honest she'd known that for a while, she could do nothing about it. She had just lost her husband. Whatever sort of husband he had been, she had to respect him if only as the father of her child. She had loved him once with a deep and all-consuming passion, and knowing they would never share that again cut her deeply. How had she ever fallen for fickle, vicious Ray's good looks over Billy's quiet reliability? But she had, and couldn't undo what she'd done so foolishly. If she gave in to the urge to welcome him back now, the guilt would haunt her for the rest of her life. She must not. 'I do, Billy,' she said again.

'And you're brave too, Kath. We all think so.' He regarded her seriously. 'If you need anything, you make sure to come to me. I'm sorry you've been left like this, sorrier than I can say, but you've got good friends. Just you remember that.'

29

Word of the events at Dunkirk soon spread. There were plenty of stories like Billy's, small acts of great bravery all adding up to a triumph in the face of defeat. Even though it was a retreat, everyone celebrated the ingenuity of the rescuers, old and young, who had given little thought to their own safety but had battled across the Channel to do their duty. Newspapers carried articles portraying the courage that had brought home so many of the soldiers, and the mood of the country was buoyed by the tales of escape against the odds. If the army could engineer an escape like this when up against the might of the Nazi war machine, what else might it achieve once it had found time to recover and regroup? What could have brought the nation to its knees turned out to have the opposite effect, and spirits were running high.

The man who ran the newsagent's closest to Victory Walk, Mr Cooper, brought out copies of several papers he'd kept back for Alice, knowing she would collect them at the end of the day. 'Here you are, Nurse,' he said as she came through the door, the brass bell heralding her arrival. He could see she had propped her bicycle next to the plate-glass window outside — the handlebars were visible through the criss-cross of brown tape he'd put up in case of explosions. 'I knew you'd want to have these.'

'Thank you! Yes, these are headlines to keep, aren't they,' she said, reaching for the papers and flicking through the opening pages.

'Our brave boys lost the battle but won the day,' Mr Cooper declared, giving his wire-rimmed glasses a quick polish on the sleeve of his brown overall.

Alice nodded, digging out her purse. 'You're very kind to have put these aside for me,' she said warmly.

'Think nothing of it,' Mr Cooper hastily replied. He was proud to have so many of the nurses as regular customers. They were respect-able young women and of course it never hurt to know a nurse, as you never knew what would happen in times like these. Even so, today he wasn't going to give in to such thoughts. What could have been a disaster had turned into a triumph to savour.

★   ★   ★

The sun had almost set over Victory Walk when Stan made his way along to the far end, to the nurses' home. He stood for a moment before its imposing front, the immaculate big navy-painted door with the highly polished brasswork. Looking up he could see that some of the attic rooms had their windows open. He remembered Edith saying that she and Alice were on the top floor, and how much they liked it because of the views, despite the effort of climbing the extra flight of stairs. She wasn't going to like what he had to say now though.

Fiona Dewar opened the door when he knocked, being on the way out herself. 'Mr Banham!' she exclaimed. 'Now don't tell me you're here to discuss an infringement of the rules. We keep our blackout blinds in top order, I'll have you know.' Her friendly greeting petered out when she took in how haggard his face appeared. She had been at several committee meetings with him and had always been struck by how young he looked compared to how old she guessed he really was. Now he had suddenly aged twenty years and his pallor was grey under his weather-beaten face.

'Ah.' She quickly recognised the likely reason for his visit. 'You've come to find Edith Gillespie, then?'

He nodded briefly.

'Would it help to talk to her in a private room?' she asked.

He nodded, almost unable to speak, and then mastered his emotion. 'Yes. Thank you. That would be best.'

Fiona turned around. 'Follow me. We shall go to my office, where you won't be disturbed. This way.' She walked swiftly down the hallway, pausing at the foot of the stairs as she caught sight of Gladys coming out of the cloakroom. 'Ah, Gladys, just the person I wanted to see. Will you find Edith, please, and send her to my office? And then ask Alice Lake to go there after about ten minutes. Don't tell anyone else yet. Good, off you go.' She nodded briskly. 'This way, Mr Banham.'

★　★　★

391

Alice was on her way to the mysterious summons when she heard the cry from behind the closed office door. It was almost like that of an animal — an animal in agonised distress. Forgetting the rule about never running, she plunged down the corridor and threw open the door, knowing this was no time to stand on ceremony.

Stan stood at the window, staring out, wiping his face with his hand, his shoulders hunched over and looking worse than she had ever seen him. Here was a man who could do consecutive night shifts, go to work in the daytime and still find time for his family, but now it seemed as if all his steady energy had been taken from him. He was the picture of exhausted grief.

Curled up on the matron's sofa was Edith, huddled into a ball, and the sounds issuing from her were barely human. Alice took in the scene and her heart plummeted. It could mean only one thing.

Hurriedly she went to Edith and flung her arms around her. 'Shush, shush,' she said, more to soothe her friend than in any belief that she would stop crying. If the cause was what Alice thought, then Edith had every reason to cry her heart out. Alice rocked the smaller woman to and fro, rubbing her back, as if she were a little child in need of comfort. Finally, after what felt like an eternity, Edith's cries turned to sobs and then gulps. 'Harry,' she gasped eventually. 'He's gone. Harry's gone.'

'Oh no.' Alice couldn't bite back the words, even if it was what she had known deep inside on first opening Fiona's door. Nothing else but the

392

loss of one of his fine sons would have reduced Stan Banham to his current state. Nothing but the loss of her soul-mate would have turned Edith into this sorrowful wreck, unable to stand or barely speak.

Stan cleared his throat. 'Well, technically, he's missing,' he said, still staring out of the window, his eyes on the horizon. 'Nobody can say for sure. But . . . but it's likely. That he's dead, that is.' A spasm passed across his face.

'I'm so sorry.' Alice felt how inadequate the words were. She couldn't think of anything better though. She was sorry — profoundly, deeply sorry for Stan and Flo, and Mattie and Joe, and most of all for Edith, who had fallen so hard for the handsome young boxer, who seemed to have the world at his feet. It was beyond her imagination to think he would never stride into the Jeeves Street kitchen again, or whisk Edith off for a night-time walk after the cinema, or let loose his easy laugh as he played with his niece. It was just unthinkable, and she hardly knew him compared to the other two people in the room. What a waste of such promise. 'It was a difficult time over in France, that's what they're saying,' she added, as if that would make it any better.

Stan nodded, still scanning the rooftops. 'That's right. Our Harry's one of many.' He cleared his throat. 'Mattie's husband Lennie — he's been taken prisoner. At least we know that for certain. Also, their friend Pete — did you know him? — he's been killed, and someone saw, so at least his young wife has the comfort of certainty.'

Alice closed her eyes in shock. Lennie, a prisoner of war — just when Mattie had the joy of another baby to look forward to. How brutally unfair. And Pete — she struggled to remember him, but knew he was one of the gang of old friends who seemed to have stuck together since schooldays, another testament to the strong bonds of friendship the Banham siblings had such a talent for. The family had taken a welter of shocks all in one go.

'And Ray's dead,' said Edith suddenly. 'Kathleen's husband. Good.'

'Edith, you can't — ' Alice began, but her friend spoke over her, her eyes bright with abrupt fury.

'Good riddance and I mean it. He beat her up, Alice, you know that. He left her with no money and went gadding off and hated their lovely baby. He didn't deserve her and I'm glad she won't have to put up with him any more. There, I've said it. Not like . . . not like . . . ' She gave way to tears again. 'He was the most loving man, he was so caring and strong and looked after me like nobody's ever done or will do again, and I loved him to bits. We were going to . . . were going to . . . it doesn't matter. We'll never do it now.'

Alice nodded sadly. Edith had never spoken directly of her plans with Harry, but anyone could see the two of them were no flash in the pan. It wasn't just Harry she had lost — it was their whole future together too.

Stan slowly tore his gaze from the almost-dark sky and faced them. 'I have to be going,' he said.

'I'm on duty this evening.'

Alice gasped. 'Surely they won't expect you to work your shift on a day like this? Won't you be better off at home with everyone there?'

Stan shook his head. 'I don't mind what they expect. *I* expect me to turn up. The need to protect our streets doesn't go away because of one piece of terrible news. So many families will be in a similar situation. We can't all miss our shifts.'

Alice nodded, impressed by his solid determination. Here was someone who would not buckle under the weight of despair. 'Shall I see you out?' she offered.

Stan shook his head. 'No. You stay here with Edith. She needs you more. I can find the way, don't worry.'

'Give my love to Flo and Mattie,' said Alice bleakly, as the man she had always thought of as a rock took himself slowly but with dignity from the room.

The little golden carriage clock on the mantelpiece ticked away the minutes, and after a while Alice wondered if Edith had fallen asleep. She shook her gently. 'Hey, are you awake? You should go up to bed. I'll bring you something up if you like.'

Edith groaned. 'I'm awake. I wish I wasn't. Then this might all be a bad dream and I could fool myself it hasn't happened. But it has.'

'It has,' agreed Alice, wishing with all her heart it was not so. 'Come on, let's get you up to your room. You can't stay here, you really can't.'

Edith sighed so deeply that she might have

been a hundred years old. 'I know. Give me a moment. My legs feel so heavy, they don't want to move.' She slowly swung them off the couch but she could scarcely stand.

Alice rose and helped her friend up. 'Lean on me, that's right. Look, I'll go and find Gwen or write a note for Fiona, saying you'll miss work tomorrow.'

At this, Edith suddenly straightened. 'No, don't do that. I'm not missing my rounds.'

Alice looked at her. 'Don't be silly, you should take the day off, nobody would blame you in the slightest.'

Edith stood her ground. 'You heard what Stan said. We can't all lay down tools when we get bad news. There's too much of it. We'd crumble. I don't intend to let everyone down.' She met Alice's gaze. 'Harry would expect nothing less. He never ducked out of anything. So I shall do it for him, and that's all there is to it, and don't try to persuade me otherwise.' Her head came up proudly.

'Then you'd better get some sleep,' said Alice firmly, and led her from the room.

★ ★ ★

Alice reached for the cocoa. It was late. Edith had finally climbed into bed and she'd agreed to a warm drink to send her off to sleep, and so Alice had gone downstairs and was making a cup for both of them. She went about making the drink automatically, her mind still numb from the shocking news.

396

The building was quiet, as everyone else must have turned in for the night. She was relieved, as she didn't know if she could explain what had happened without breaking down, and she didn't want to do that. It wouldn't help.

She dug around in a cupboard and found a small tray. Its handles were lightly chipped but replacing it would not be a priority now. The home had more than that to be concerned about. As long as it was big enough for two cups of cocoa, she didn't mind anyway.

As this stray thought occurred to her, she realised there were footsteps approaching. Gwen came into the small service area, her face serious. 'Ah, Nurse Lake. Alice. I assume that second cup is for Edith?'

Alice nodded. 'Yes, she — '

'It's all right,' Gwen interrupted. 'You don't have to explain. I saw Fiona on her way out and she told me Mr Banham had come round and what sort of state he was in. We put two and two together — were we correct? Edith's young man has been lost at Dunkirk?'

Alice shut her eyes for a moment. 'Yes. Well, he's missing. But his father said we should assume the worst.'

Gwen nodded briefly. 'Why not bring the drinks up to my room, and I will give you something else for Edith to help her sleep.' She left, and Alice had little option but to follow.

Gwen's room was on the first floor, at the opposite end of the corridor to Fiona's office, and would have had a view over the back yard if the blackout blind hadn't been in place. Alice glanced around, observing that it was a large space, with room for a table and two chairs as well as a bed, easy chair, small desk, chest of drawers and a wardrobe. It also had the luxury of its own hand basin.

Gwen switched on a standard lamp in the corner, its fringed shade swaying a little as she did so. 'Set your tray down here, Alice, and do take a seat for a moment.'

Alice did as she was asked, taking in the comfort of the room. She wondered for how long Gwen had been here, to make it so homely. It was unlike any of the other rooms in the place, with its extra cushions and shelves of framed photos.

Gwen took a seat opposite her at the little table and folded her arms as she leant back. 'I'm very sorry to hear about Edith's loss. Well, your loss too — you knew the young man in question, didn't you? I can see from your face that you did.'

Alice nodded. 'Yes. We met him nearly a year ago, not long after we moved in here. He and Edith hit it off immediately and that was that. They suited each other so well.' She came to a halt, afraid that she could not go on. She glanced sideways and her eye was caught by the photographs arranged in a line.

Gwen saw what she was looking at.

'Well, my dear, I am full of sympathy for what she will be going through right now, and in the days to come,' she said sadly. 'Believe me, I know what it is like. You think your world has come to an end. You think your heart will never mend.

And yet, life goes on. While it might not be the life she would have hoped for, it will go on in some shape or form.'

Alice turned back to face the older nurse and was surprised by her expression, unlike anything she'd seen before. They were all used to Gwen being stern, strict and sometimes downright unforgiving, but this was something different. In spite of her sadness, she wondered what it might be.

Gwen sighed. 'I am fully aware what you all think of me,' she began, and ploughed on even when Alice tried to protest. 'Much of that is inevitable; I am many years older than most of you, and am in a position of seniority. It is my duty to maintain standards and I will continue to do that, no matter what the cost. I don't look for friendships with the new recruits, I simply expect professional behaviour. But I was young once.' She inclined her head towards the shelf of photographs, some of which were faded. 'I qualified just as the Great War got underway. We nurses saw much pain and suffering in those years. We also knew what personal loss was like.'

Alice's eyes grew dark. 'Those young men in the pictures?' she asked, hardly daring to believe she was asking such a question of the fearsome deputy.

'Indeed.' Gwen nodded. 'Two of them are — were — my brothers. Edgar and Walter. Neither survived the Somme.'

'I see,' said Alice, recognising what it must be costing Gwen to talk about this. No wonder she was so grave. 'And — and the other young man?

The one standing up?'

Gwen shifted position in her chair. 'Ah. Well, that is Wilfred. Captain Wilfred Holmes. He didn't survive either.' She looked away, and Alice could see the older woman's eyes brightening with unshed tears, even now so many years after the event. 'We were to be married. He was killed just one month before the war ended. It seemed so cruel, that he nearly made it. But there was nothing to be done.'

Alice stayed silent. There was nothing she could say that Gwen wouldn't have heard before. The handsome young man gazed out of the picture, the very image of bravery, his confident demeanour indicating what good company he would have been, his pride in his uniform evident even from this distance.

'So.' Gwen got to her feet and went to her desk, reaching to a ledge above it and retrieving a bottle, and then a glass. 'That's why I know what it's like, how Edith is feeling. People will tell her that time cures all ills, but in my experience it doesn't so much as cure them as change them, so that they slowly become more bearable. Her work will help. But in the meanwhile, here's some sherry, in case it does the trick in the short term.'

Alice's eyes widened in surprise. She knew Edith would have the occasional glass of the stuff but hadn't expected Gwen to have a supply of it.

Gwen gave a small smile. 'Don't be thinking I sit here on my own sipping this every evening, Nurse Lake. It's very much for special use, or emergencies, which by my reckoning is what this evening is. Don't let me detain you further, or your cocoa will be cold, but I wanted to give you this for her, just in case it is of use. And do tell her she can speak to me at any time, as I am only too aware what it's like.'

Alice rose, took the bottle and glass and added them to her tray. 'Thank you. I will tell her. Oh, and I forgot to say before, she's determined to go on her rounds tomorrow, no matter what.'

Gwen pressed her lips together in approval. 'That's for the best. She'll be needed, no matter how she feels inside. Nurse Gillespie has proved herself to be an asset to our establishment, no matter what reservations I initially held about her.' She opened her door so that Alice could pass through carrying the little tray. 'Good night, Alice. Look after your friend.'

'I will.' Alice nodded in acknowledgement of the unexpected kindness. Edith might be going through the worst night of her life but she would not be alone.

30

Edith was as good as her word. She rose the next morning, ate a very hurried breakfast and then set off on her bike, hardly speaking to anyone but with a face etched with determination. She had managed a few hours' sleep thanks to the mixture of cocoa and sherry, and had no desire to hang around the home.

Alice was fastening her cloak before leaving herself when the telephone rang. Knowing this would most likely be a request for an urgent appointment, she picked up the Bakelite receiver. 'Victory Walk nurses' home, how may I help you?' She reached for the pencil and notepad that were always kept alongside the telephone so that no messages ever went astray, fully expecting it to be a member of the public or one of the regular local doctors.

Instead, a distant voice said over a crackly line: 'Alice? Is that you?'

Alice gasped. 'Joe! Where are you?'

There was a cough from the other end of the line. 'Look, I know your line isn't for social calls but I won't be long — in fact I can't be. I have just a few minutes spare while in port, and I wanted to see how you were, and that you'd heard the news.'

Alice glanced around, but there was nobody else in the hallway for once. All the nurses knew they were not to take or make personal calls except in an extreme emergency — and yet, wasn't this close to being one? Especially after what Gwen had said last night, she couldn't bring herself to tell Joe to ring off. She found she didn't want to either.

'Yes, we've heard,' she said quietly. 'Your father came round yesterday evening.'

A brief silence fell on the other end of the line. 'How was he?' Joe asked, his voice thick with emotion.

'Bearing up,' Alice assured him. 'He wanted Edith to hear it from him, not from a rumour. Then he was off to do his ARP shift. He wouldn't miss it.'

Joe exhaled loudly. 'No. No, he wouldn't. And Edith — how is she?'

Alice felt a sob rising in her throat and choked it down again. 'She's heartbroken, of course. I think they'd been planning a future together and hadn't announced anything yet. But she's gone off this morning to her first patient, same as usual — she won't take time off.'

'That's good.' Joe sighed. 'That's what Harry would have wanted. He thought the world of her, you know. God knows he was no stranger to women but, once he met her, he changed. You're right, he wanted to marry her. They just didn't get around to telling us all, they thought it was too soon.'

'They thought they'd have all the time in the world,' Alice breathed, her heart constricting again at the unfairness of it. It occurred to her that not only had Joe lost his brother — he'd also lost his best friend. The two of them had understood each other so well, despite their many differences. He would have to face the future without him now.

'And how about you, Alice?' Joe asked, his voice full of obvious concern despite the bad line. 'How are you coping in the middle of all this?'

Alice tried to laugh. 'Don't worry about me, Joe. I'm all right.' She could imagine his face, anxious about his family and clouded with sorrow, but still with that strong resolve to do his duty.

'I wish I could be there with you,' he said suddenly, and she was reminded of that moment at Christmas when the air had seemed to change between them. 'With all of you,' he amended hastily. 'But I can't.' Joe paused and Alice sensed again that he was about to say something, so she waited.

Joe's next words came out quickly before she could speak. 'Billy told me he saw you out with your boyfriend, the doctor. It's nice you've got someone special, but can we still be friends, Alice, look out for each other?'

Alice now realised what Joe must have thought. 'Dr McGillicuddy is an old friend of mine, from Liverpool. It's not like that at all,' she said, strangely happy to be able to reassure him.

'But I thought . . . Billy said he looked like a matinee idol.' He laughed.

Alice laughed, 'He might well do, but some things are more important than that.'

'And what's important to you, Alice?' Joe asked, and Alice knew instinctively what he meant, without him needing to spell it out. She knew she had to choose her words carefully; Joe meant a lot to her and she didn't want to hurt his feelings or give him the wrong impression.

'Friendship. I need a friend, Joe, a good one like you.'

She could on hear the crackle of the line and in the silence she worried that Joe had gone. 'Are you still there, Joe?' she asked anxiously.

'I'm still here, Alice, because I need a friend too. We can be that for each other, in these uncertain times, can't we?'

Alice smiled into the phone. 'We can. I'd like that. More than anything.'

'It's a deal, Alice. Look, I can't tell you where I'm going but I'd better get back to the ship now. You'll write, won't you? Let me know how Edith gets on — and how you are.'

At that moment, Alice wanted to be there for Joe more than anything else in the world. She couldn't make up for Harry's death but she could be the one he came to when he wanted comfort, or to share a story, or just to say hello. She was suddenly desperate that he should know this, that he wouldn't feel so alone out on the seas, or wherever his duty took him. 'I'll go to see your family soon too,' she promised. 'Look after yourself, Joe. I'll be thinking of you all the time. I'll keep the lucky clover safe, and maybe that'll help you to sail safely and come home in one piece.'

'I will,' he said staunchly. 'And I've got your lucky clover too. Look after Edith, won't you? Well, of course you will. And then as soon as I can I'll come home to you. Until then, we'll carry on. I'd better go. Goodbye for now, Alice.'

'Goodbye, Joe.' The line went dead at the other end and she replaced the receiver in its cradle.

She knew her first patient would be expecting her soon but she needed a second to gather her thoughts. What a year it had been. Moving to Dalston, meeting the Banhams, war breaking out, and now Joe, and maybe something more — but was she ready for what was coming next? Yet she knew she had come on in leaps and bounds as a district nurse, confident that she could now cope with most situations, maintaining a calm and efficient composure no matter what she encountered on her rounds. She realised she might have to draw on that in the months to come, not knowing what they would all have to face. Then again, if Edith had the willpower to do so, even when in the depths of sorrow, she herself must face the challenges ahead.

They would manage; that was what they did. Her head went up and she touched the Queen's Nursing Institute badge that she wore so proudly at her throat. The sun was shining, the air was warm, and she picked up her Gladstone bag, took it to her bike and tucked it into the basket, ready to pedal off on her day's round.

Quarterdeck

JULIAN STOCKWIN

Quarterdeck

Hodder & Stoughton

First published in Great Britain in 2004 by Hodder and Stoughton
A division of Hodder Headline

A CIP catalogue record for this title is available from the British Library
Trade Paperback ISBN 0 340 83218 5
Hardback ISBN 0 340 83217 7

Typeset in Garamond by Palimpsest Book Production Limited,
Polmont, Stirlingshire

Printed and bound by
Clays Ltd, St Ives plc

Hodder Headline's policy is to use papers that are natural, renewable and recyclable products
and made from wood grown in sustainable forests. The logging and manufacturing processes
are expected to conform to the environmental regulations of the country of origin.

Hodder and Stoughton Ltd
A division of Hodder Headline
338 Euston Road
London NW1 3BH

In recent memory of Lieutenant Chris Walklett, RN
A true heart of oak

Prologue

A clock ticked loudly in the silence. The three commissioners, experienced sea captains all, stared implacably at the candidate, waiting for his answer.

Acting Lieutenant Thomas Kydd had every reason to feel the terror that froze his bowels: failure at this examination would see him stripped of his temporary rank and returned ingloriously to his old shipmates.

'Er, well, I would—'

'Come, come, sir! An easy enough question your certificate of service claims sea-time in *Artemis*, a crack frigate as ever I've seen. You must have seen a flying moor above a dozen times.'

It was unfair: here in this august Navy Office board-room he was being asked to describe one of the most risky manoeuvres, dropping anchor at speed and sailing on to the full scope of the cable, then letting go another before falling back on the two anchors. Black Jack Powlett of the *Artemis* would never have chanced his vessel so, Kydd thought indignantly, then took a deep breath. 'Coming boldly up t' the anchorage, I, er, would range both cables out on the gundeck

– veering parties double-banked, o' course – an' at m' furthest on, let go th' best bower. Then—'

'You do not feel it prudent to double bitt your cable first, sir?' the first commissioner interjected.

Then the second came in: 'And we have heard nothing of setting this bower a-cockbill in readiness.'

'That is, if your ship has not yet a trick stopper or similar,' the first added smugly.

Kydd forced his mind to an icy resolve. 'Aye, sir – I may have omitted t' say that in getting the anchor off the bows it is first necessary . . .'

It seemed to satisfy. He dared a glance at the third member of the board, who sat hard-faced and silent, Captain Essington, the captain of *Triumph* in which he had served at the bloody battle of Camperdown.

'Passing to navigation,' the first commissioner said flatly.

Kydd's anxieties returned: he had learned his skills at the hands of a merchant-service sailing master who had taught him a plain yet solid understanding of his craft, but Kydd knew that the Navy liked arcane descriptions and definitions.

'We'll begin with basic understanding, Mr Kydd. What is your conceiving of a great circle?'

'Er, the plane o' the equator when projected fr'm the centre on to a tangent plane becomes a straight line—'

'Thank you. The workings of an azimuth altitude will be familiar enough to you, no doubt – then clarify for me the correction of the right ascension of the mean sun, if you please.'

Kydd struggled, but could see frowns settling, glances exchanged. Failure was now more than a possibility and a cold dread stole over him. If only they would ask—

'Mr Kydd, you are aboard a two-decker.' It was Essington, leaning forward. Kydd shifted position to face him directly.

There was no trace of compassion in the man's eyes. 'Shall we say in the Caribbean? You are scudding before a regular-going hurricane and you sight land – dead to loo'ard. You throw out both bowers.' The other commissioners looked at Essington with curiosity. 'They carry away, one after the other. Only a sheet anchor is left to you to prevent the ship being cast ashore. Detail your actions, if you will, sir, to forestall a wreck and grievous loss of life.' He leaned back, unnerving Kydd with his stare. His fellow captains held back in surprise as Essington finished acidly, 'And shall we have a coral bottom?'

Kydd cast about for something to say, the right action to take in such an extreme situation – but then it dawned on him: he had been in exactly this plight in the old *Trajan*, and himself had been the one to pass keckling to preserve their last anchor, called as lee helmsman by the master himself. 'Aye, sir,' he said crisply. 'First we need t' ride out the blow. A coral bottom means we'll have to pass a deal of keckling aroun' the first two or three fathom of cable above the anchor clinch, and then . . .' Those desperate hours off the unknown island were burned into his consciousness: that endless night, the screaming hurricane, the cold dawn and the fearful danger of their action in clawing off. It steadied him, the simple recounting of fine seamanship. 'But to make an offing will be hard, an' we must wait f'r the wind to shift a point or two, but then we must take our chance, and only one chance it is. Show small canvas, and at th' right time cut the cable an' run f'r the open sea.'

The commissioners nodded, expressionless. 'I think that's enough, gentlemen, do you not?' Essington said.

Kydd held his breath. There was mumbled conferring, more frowns. Was it possibly more than coincidence that Essington had brought forward that particular circumstance? As if he had particular knowledge of his past and . . .

3

'Where are your certificates?'

They were asking for attestations to his 'Sobriety, Obedience, Diligence and Skill in the Profession of a Seaman'. Kydd handed over the journals and documents in a floodtide of hope: if he had failed, why would they be wasting time on the formalities?

The journals were leafed through, but they had been meticulously kept for years and it seemed the certificates of age and rated service appeared acceptable. His heart leaped: the last hurdle was being overcome.

'If my reckoning is correct, we have a difficulty.' One of the commissioners held the original, if somewhat crumpled, certificate of service from Kydd's first ship, *Duke William*. 'From this, it does seem that Mr Kydd is, according to regulations, one year short of the requirement for sea-time.'

Kydd had known of this deficiency, but had prayed that the regulations would not be applied rigorously. Horatio Nelson himself had been promoted to lieutenant before time, but if a commissioner of the board wished to make an issue of it little could be done.

Essington took the paper, then looked up with a tigerish smile. 'Yes – but this is worthless! It is in error! I distinctly recollect when Captain Caldwell was removed from *Royal Billy* to *Culloden*. I rather fancy we would get a different date were we to ask him directly. As it is, Captain Caldwell is now in the West Indies, admiral of the Leeward Squadron if my memory serves. I doubt he is to be troubled on this trivial matter.'

His manner quelled all discussion. The other commissioners gathered up the papers and returned them to Kydd. 'Well, it seems we are of one mind. Our recommendation will go forward to the Navy Office that for the good of the service you shall be confirmed in rank to lieutenant. Good day to you, sir.'

4

Chapter 1

The Portsmouth Mail made good speed on the highway south from London. Inside, it smelt pungently of leather and old dust, but Thomas Kydd did not care: it would take a great deal more than this to subdue his growing excitement.

After the examination, Kydd had spent some days in Yarmouth, where *Tenacious* had been taken out of commission for battle repairs, and had prevailed upon the naval outfitter in the matter of a splendid lieutenant's uniform, determined to go home on leave in a handsome manner.

He stared out at the tranquil winter country scene of soft meadows and gnarled oak trees. This was England at last, his hearth and home after so many years away. The postillion's long horn blared, and he leaned out of the window. It was Cobham – Guildford was not far away. He glanced at his friend sitting next to him. 'An hour, Nicholas – an hour only, an' I'll be seein' m' folks again!'

Renzi had been quiet since London, his withdrawn, ascetic expression discouraging talk. He nodded politely and smiled, then looked away.

Heaven only knew what he was thinking about. Their years together had been full of perils and adventure, but Renzi's friendship had brought Kydd an insight into learning, and respect for the riches of the mind. And now they were returning to where their long adventure had started.

Yet again Kydd brought to memory how he had last left home, when he and Renzi had stolen away back to sea, to *Artemis*, the famous frigate, after founding a school to secure his family's livelihood. There had been a world voyage that had ended in shipwreck, rousing times in the Caribbean, adventures in the Mediterranean. It seemed half a lifetime, but it was only four years or so. Here he was, just twenty-five, and . . .

The coach jerked to a stop, and the horses were changed for the last stage to Guildford. The door swung open, and a young lady was handed up, her tall bonnet catching on the roof sill. She settled opposite in a rustle of pale-blue silk, her eyes downcast.

An older gentleman followed, acknowledged Kydd and Renzi, then sat beside her. The ostler offered a hot brick in worn serge, which the man manoeuvred under the young lady's feet. 'Thank you, dear Papa,' she said demurely, snuggling her hands into a muff.

The man favoured a belly-warmer, which he settled inside his long coat. 'Uncommon cold for this time o' year!' he grunted.

Long inured to conditions far worse, Kydd caught Renzi's amused but discreet sideways glance. 'Er, I'm sure y'r right.'

The girl looked up, and noticed their uniforms. 'Oh!' she said prettily, her hand at her mouth. 'You're sailors!'

The man coughed irritably. 'They're officers, m'dear, naval officers, not sailors, d'ye see?'

'It is what I meant to say, Papa. Pray, sirs, were you in that dreadful battle of Camperdown? I have heard that it was quite the most shocking fight this age!'

The man clicked his tongue in exasperation, but Kydd's heart swelled with pride. Their coach still bore laurel branches from the helter-skelter celebrations of only a week or so ago.

'Indeed, this is so, Miss, and you will understand how truly weary we are, that we yearn for the blessings of peace and solitude for a period . . .' Renzi said quietly.

'Of course, sir, please do forgive me.' Her eyes rested briefly on Kydd. Then she turned determinedly to stare out of the window.

Kydd felt a pang of irritation, but understood that Renzi was sparing him idle chat so that he could enjoy the antici-pation of his homecoming.

The mention of Camperdown, his first big fleet action, brought back emotions that were still too raw and recent, images of the nightmare of the great mutiny at the Nore and its sequel; his mind shied away from them and instead concentrated on the incredible fact that he had been pro-moted on the field of battle and officially confirmed. He was now Lieutenant Kydd! It was still too heady a thought, so he let his mind return to the excitement of his home-coming.

The coach jolted over the infamous potholes at Abbotswood: Guildford Town was now minutes away. Almost too quickly, the square, grey-stone Elizabethan grammar school passed on the left, and the town proper began, familiar buildings at the top of the high street. The post-horn's baying echoed off the almshouse opposite Holy Trinity, drawing mildly curious glances from the townsfolk.

Clattering over the old cobbled road, they passed under the big clock, and the driver tooled the mail-coach through the narrow black and white half-timbered entrance of the Angel posting-house.

Kydd and Renzi left their bags with the obsequious landlord, then emerged on to the high street and turned left, past shops and alleys well known to Kydd. The reek and colour of the town, the bustle and shouts, the passing tide of people all seemed to advance like a dream.

Some glanced curiously at the two men, others with admiration. Self-conscious, Kydd waited for someone to recognise him, but perhaps the dark blue, white and gold of his handsome uniform put paid to that. He saw Betty, the fishmonger's attractive daughter, who stopped and stared in shock at the sight of him. Kydd doffed his brand-new cocked hat.

They reached the red-brick church of Holy Trinity, and turned off past the glebe cottages to Schoolhouse Lane, as it was now known. There was no mistaking the little naval school ahead: a huge blue ensign floated above for all the world to see – the flag under which Kydd had fought at Camperdown. And as they drew near they could hear a muffled chanting on the air: '. . . three sevens are twenty-one, four sevens are twenty-eight, five sevens . . .'

They stepped into the tiny quadrangle, two King's officers returned from the sea. A youngster emerged at the run from a classroom and teetered to a halt. He whipped off his cap and shrilled, 'I'll fetch th' bo'sun, if y' please, sir!'

Jabez Perrott emerged out of the building and stumped importantly towards them. His eyes widened, and he gasped, 'Be buggered! It's Master Kydd, be gob!'

Kydd opened his mouth, but Perrott, reddening with pleasure, grabbed for his silver call and emitted a piercing blast. Then, in a lower-deck bellow that had not softened with the years, he roared, '*Aaaaall* the hands! *Haaaands* to muster – clear lower deck, ye swabs! *Haaaands* to muster!'

Children boiled out of the classrooms, screeching in delight at the antics of their strict boatswain.

'Mr Perrott! *Mr Perrott!* What *are* you doing?'

Kydd recognised the voice and, holding back tears, advanced to meet his mother.

'Oh! Tom! It's you! M' darling boy, it's you! And you've...' The rest was lost in a fierce embrace that went on and on, knocking his hat askew.

'Mother! So long...'

Kydd's father had aged: his form was stooped and his eyes sightless. Nevertheless, he bore himself nobly in the black breeches of a headmaster. 'Er, is that you, son?'

'It is, Walter!' his mother said, as the old man moved uncertainly towards Kydd, holding out his hand. Kydd took it, then hugged him.

'Walter, Tom is an officer!' She looked anxiously to Kydd for confirmation – the idea was so enormous.

'Aye, Mother, it's "Lieutenant Kydd, Royal Navy" you must call me now, or I'll clap ye all in irons!' He spoke loudly so his father would make no mistake about what he was hearing.

'Carry on, sir?' Perrott said to Kydd, touching his hat.

'Er, please do,' said Kydd.

'Ship's comp'ny, ahoy! I'll have yez in two lines afore the mast – let's be havin' ye!' he bawled at the children. They shuffled eagerly into line. 'Now, we dips our colours t' a pair o' 'eroes 'oo has jus' come back 'ome fr'm such a battle as never was, an' we're going t' show how much we admires 'em!'

Lieutenants Kydd and Renzi stood solemnly to attention as 'God Save The King' and 'Rule Britannia' were sung enthusiastically by the wide-eyed youngsters.

A piercing squeal on the boatswain's call brought quiet,

and the colours were dipped reverently to half staff. With great dignity Perrott turned to face Kydd, removing his hat. Taken by surprise, Kydd raised his own cocked hat, at which the colours rose again.

'Silence!' Perrott thundered at the awed children. 'Now, Lootenant Kydd will talk t' you about y' dooty.'

Kydd managed to splutter a few words: 'Y'r duty is . . . steadfast in all weathers . . . courage at the cannon's mouth . . . King and country.'

It seemed to be enough. An eager child broke ranks and held up his hand. 'Please, sir, I want t' be a sailor – how do I be a sailor?'

Soon a pink-faced Kydd was mobbed by shouting boys.

'Pipe down, y' scurvy crew, 'n' listen to the l'tenant!' growled Perrott happily.

Kydd glanced across at his mother, who was bursting with pride, and knew there was only one thing to do. He turned to his father and touched his hat. 'Cap'n, sir, permission f'r liberty ashore t' both watches!'

'Oh, er, liberty?' his father stuttered. 'Yes, yes, er, Lieutenant Kydd. A half-holiday to, er, all hands!' The children screamed with delight and poured out of the school, leaving a dazed, happy Kydd family standing in the quadrangle.

'I shall withdraw at this point, if I may,' Renzi said quietly.

'No, no, Mr Renzi,' Mrs Kydd insisted. 'You must stay an' tell us where you have been on the sea – you'll both have such tales, I do declare!' She turned to Kydd. 'Now, I'll ask Mr Partington to spare us his room for you – he can stay with his friend Jonathan. For Mr Renzi . . .' She trailed off. Then she resumed stiffly: 'But, then, now Thomas has a reputation, he'll want t' have his own establishment.'

His mother's words could not hide the essence of the

matter, the brutal truth, and Kydd felt a chill at the passing of his simple life. He saw her colouring: she had understood that her son was no longer hers. From now on, society events and invitations would firmly distinguish between the Kydds.

'We shall stay at the Angel,' Renzi said softly. 'Then we will take modest lodgings in town.'

Kydd mumbled agreement.

'Well, then, that's settled,' his mother said bravely. 'It's for the best, o' course. Come inside an' take a posset – you must be frozen after y'r journey.'

As he cradled a mug of hot curdled milk at the kitchen table Kydd listened to the flow of prattle from his mother, felt the quiet presence of his father and caught the curious flash of the maid's eyes. His own kept straying down to his uniform, the blue and gold so striking. Who could guess what the future might hold now? A deep sigh escaped him.

He heard the approaching *tap, tap* of footsteps. His mother smiled. 'Ah, that must be Cecilia – she'll be so surprised to see you!'

The last time he had seen his sister was in a wrecked boat in the Caribbean. He recalled her mortal terror as they had fought for their lives against the sharks. What would she think of him now?

'She's done very well with Lord an' Lady Stanhope, Thomas. Quite the lady companion she is now,' Mrs Kydd said proudly. 'And don't go quarrellin' with her, if y' please, you know how it upsets your father.'

The outside door rattled, and Cecilia's voice echoed down the passageway. 'Father – what *is* going on? I saw quantities of your boys on the street and . . .' Her voice died away as the two men rose to their feet. She looked from face to face, incredulous. 'Thomas? You . . . you . . .'

Kydd awkwardly held out his hands. 'Ye're doin' well, Mother says—'

Suddenly her expression softened to a deep tenderness, and she seized her brother in a fierce hug. 'Oh, Thomas! I've so missed you!'

He felt her body heaving, and when she looked at him again he saw the sparkle of tears. His own voice was gruff with emotion as he said, 'Sis – y' remember in th' boat—'

She stopped him with a finger on his lips and whispered, 'Mother!' Then she let him go, crossed to Renzi and placed a generous kiss on both his cheeks. 'Dear Nicholas! How are you? You're still so thin, you know.'

Renzi replied politely, and Cecilia turned back to her brother. 'Thomas and Nicholas are going to take chocolate with me at Murchison's and tell me all their adventures, while you, Mother, prepare such a welcome for this wandering pair!' she announced. Her eyes widened. 'Gracious me – and if I'm not mistaken in the particulars – Thomas, you're a . . .'

'L'tenant Kydd it is now, Cec,' he said happily.

The evening meal was a roaring success. Kydd became hoarse with talking and Renzi was quite undone by the warmth of his welcome. Cecilia could not get enough of Kydd's descriptions of the Venice of Casanova, even above his protestations that the danger of their mission meant he was hardly in a position to discourse on the republic's attractions.

Distant thumps and a sudden crackle sounded outside. Cecilia clapped her hands. 'The fireworks – I nearly forgot! Tonight we'll see your Admiral Onslow – he is to be a baronet, and is now resting at Clandon with his brother the earl. It's

12

said he'll make an address from the balcony of the town hall! Gentlemen – I wish to attend! I shall be with you presently.' She swept away imperiously to appear shortly afterwards in a pelisse at the height of fashion: lemon silk, lined and faced with blue. She looked at them both with the suspicion of a pout. 'And who will be my gentleman escort?'

Kydd hesitated, but instantly Renzi bowed deeply and offered his arm. 'May I observe that I find Mademoiselle is in looks tonight?' he said, with the utmost courtly grace.

Cecilia inclined her head and accepted his arm. They went outside and, without a backward glance at Kydd, moved off down the lane, Cecilia's laughter tinkling at Renzi's sallies.

Kydd watched them helplessly. His sister had changed. There was not a trace of childhood chubbiness left: her strong features had developed into strikingly dark good looks and a languorous elegance. Her position with Lady Stanhope had allowed her to find an easy confidence and elegance of speech that he could only envy; he followed them, trying to look unconcerned.

Crowds pressed everywhere, while excited chatter and the smell of fireworks hung on the air. People held back respectfully. Kydd was not sure whether it was in recognition of them as gentlefolk or because of the Navy uniform. Closer to the torch-lit balcony the throng was tightly packed and they had to remain some distance back.

Cecilia kept Renzi's arm, but pulled Kydd forward, attracting envious looks from other ladies. 'Oh, I'm so proud of you!' she exclaimed, her voice raised above the excited babble of the crowd. She smiled at them both, and Kydd felt better.

'It was th' admiral gave me m' step, Cec – there in th' great cabin o' *Monarch*.' Kydd paused, remembering the scene. 'But it were Cap'n Essington put me forward.'

A deep thumping came from the other side, further down

the high street: the Royal Surreys called out to do duty on this naval occasion. Thin sounds of fife and trumpet rose above the hubbub, strengthening as they approached. Then, with a pair of loud double thumps on the bass drum, it ceased.

The crowd surged below the balcony and settled into a tense expectation. Torchlight illuminated upturned faces, caught the sparkle of eyes, the glitter of gold lace. At the signs of indistinct movement within, a rustle of anticipation arose and the mayor emerged on to the balcony in his best scarlet gown and tricorne, resplendent with his chain of office. 'M' lords, ladies an' gennelmen! Pray silence for the mighty victor o' the great battle o' Camperdown, our own – Adm'ral Onslow!'

The genial sea officer Kydd remembered stepped out on to the balcony. A furious storm of cheering met him, a roar of wholehearted and patriotic acclaim. Onslow, in his full-dress admiral's uniform, sword and decorations, bared his head and bowed this way and that, manifestly affected by the welcome.

Kydd watched him turn again and again to face all parts of the crowd. At one point he thought he had caught the admiral's eye, and wondered if he should wave back, but there was no sign of recognition.

The noise subsided, and Onslow moved to the front of the balcony. He fumbled in his coat, and withdrew a paper. He hesitated, then put the paper back, straightening to a quarterdeck brace. 'M' lord mayor an' lady – citizens of Guildford!' he began. 'I thank ye for your fine and loyal address followin' the action off Camperdown. But I must make something very clear to ye. An admiral doesn't win battles, the seamen do. An' I cannot stand here tonight without I acknowledge this before you all! Over there t' larb'd! Yes, those two men, ahoy! Be s' good as to join me and show y'selves! These are two of your true victors o' Camperdown!'

'Thomas – go!' Cecilia squealed, when it became obvious whom the admiral had singled out. The crowd shuffled and fell back.

Onslow was waiting for them and shook their hands warmly. 'A fine thing t' see ye both,' he rumbled, his keen eyes taking in their new uniforms. 'Let's out an' give 'em a sight, then you'll honour me with y' presence at the presentation.'

They emerged together on the balcony to a roar, Kydd waving awkwardly, Renzi bowing. Kydd's eyes searched out Cecilia. She was shouting something to him, waving furiously, and his heart swelled.

'A capital choice,' Renzi said, removing his coat and standing in waistcoat and breeches. 'It seems we shall be waiting out *Tenacious*'s repair in a tolerable degree of comfort.' He settled into a substantial high-backed chair.

Kydd rubbed his hands before the fire. The agent had left, and they had taken on this half-mansion below the castle for a reasonable sum. The owner had apparently instructed that officers in His Majesty's service could rely on his patriotic duty in the matter of a lease. Not only that but, agreeably, they could share the services of domestic staff with the adjoining residence, which, as it was inhabited by an old lady, should be no trial.

Kydd looked around him with growing satisfaction, albeit tinged with trepidation. The rooms were not large, but were bigger than anything he had lived in before. He'd always known that the heart of the home was the kitchen, but here it seemed that this elegant room had taken its place.

The walls were a soft sage colour, the broad, generous sash windows were hung with muslin and festoon curtains, and stout druggets lay beneath his feet instead of oiled floorcloths. The furniture was reassuringly old-fashioned and sturdy. He turned again to the fire with its plain but well-proportioned marble surround and mantelpiece, and felt an unstoppable surge of happiness. 'Two or three months, d'ye suppose?' he mused, recalling the savage wounds *Tenacious* had suffered.

'I would think so.' Renzi sat sprawled, his eyes closed.

'Nicholas, th' sun is not yet above th' foreyard, but I have a desire t' toast our fortune!'

Renzi half opened his eyes. 'Please do. You will not find me shy of acknowledging that it is these same fates that determine whether one should die of a loathsome disease or—'

'Clap a stopper on it, brother!' Kydd laughed. 'I'll go 'n' rouse out somethin' we c'n'—'

'I think not.'

'Why—'

'Pray touch the bell for the servant.'

'Aye, Nicholas,' Kydd said humbly. He found the well-worn but highly polished silver bell and rang it self-consciously.

'Sir?' A manservant in blue, with a plain bob wig, appeared.

Renzi pulled himself upright. 'Should you unlock my grey valise you will find a brace of cognac. Pray be so good as to open one for us.'

'Certainly, sir,' the man said, with a short bow, and withdrew.

Kydd tried to look unconcerned and toasted his rear until the servant returned bearing a gilt tray.

'*À votre santé*,' Renzi said.

'*À votter sonday*,' Kydd echoed awkwardly. The brandy burned a passage to his empty stomach.

Renzi stood up, raising his glass to Kydd. 'Our present fortune. May this indeed be a true augury of our future.'

'Aye, an' may we never find th' need t' deny our past ever,'

Kydd responded. 'Nicholas. M' true friend.' He looked side-ways at Renzi and, seeing he was attending politely, pressed on: 'I've been a-thinkin' – you don't care if I say my mind?'

'My dear fellow! If it were any other I would feel betrayed.'

'Well, Nicholas, this is all more'n I could ever hope for, somethin' that can only happen if – if y'r destiny is written somewhere, I reckon. So I'm takin' this chance wi' both hands! I'll give it m' rousin' best copper-bottomed, double-barrelled, bevel-edged try, I will!'

Renzi nodded. 'Of course, brother.'

'So this is what I have t' do.' Kydd took a determined pull on his brandy. 'I've seen y'r tarpaulin officer come aft through the hawse, a right taut son o' Neptune. Ye sees him on watch on th' quarterdeck an' it puts y' heart at ease. But, Nicholas, I don't want t' be a tarpaulin officer. They're stayin' l'tenants all their days, fine messmates I'm sure, but who should say – plain in their habits. The other officers step ashore t'gether while they stays aboard 'n' makes friends wi' a bottle.'

He glanced down at the glass in his hands. 'I want t' be a reg'lar-built King's officer and gentleman, Nicholas, an' I asks you what I c'n' do to be one o' them.'

Renzi's half-smile appeared. 'If this is your wish, Tom – yet I'll have you know there is no shame in being one of nature's gentlemen . . .'

'If y' will—'

'Ah. All in good time, dear fellow. This does require a mort of reflection . . .'

It was all very well for Kydd to ask this of him, even if what he said was perfectly reasonable – but in truth the job was nigh impossible. Renzi's eye covertly took in Kydd's figure: instead of a fine-drawn, willowy courtliness there were strong shoulders and slim hips standing four-square; rather than a distinguished slender curve to the leg, his knee-breeches betrayed sculpted musculature. And in place of a fashionably cool, pale countenance there was a hearty oaken one, whose open good humour was not designed for societal discretion. And yet he was undoubtedly intelligent: Renzi had seen his quick wits at work. But Kydd would have to learn to value politeness and convention – not his strongest suit. Then there was his speech – Renzi squirmed to think of the sport others would make of him behind his back. The probable course of events, then, would be for Kydd to retreat into the comfort of bluff sea-doggery, and thereby exclude himself from gentle-born society. But this was his particular friend: he could not refuse him.

'Mr Kydd, as now I must call you, this is what I propose.' He fixed him with a stare. 'Should you choose this path then I must warn you that the way is arduous. There's many a chance to stumble. Are you prepared for a hard beat to wind'd?'

'I am.'

'And there are, er, matters you must accept without question, which are not, on the face of it, either reasonable or explicable. Do you undertake that you will accept from me their necessity without question?'

Kydd paused. 'Aye.'

'Very well. I will give you my full assistance in your worthy endeavour, and if you stay the course, for you may indeed wish to yield the race at any point –'

'Never!'

'– then I in turn agree to assist in your elevation into society.'

Kydd flushed. 'I won't shame ye to y' friends, if that is y'r meaning.'

'That was not my meaning, but let us make a start.' He reached for the cognac and filled Kydd's glass. 'There is a beginning to everything, and in this it is the understanding that for a gentleman it is appearances that define. Politeness, the courtesies due to a lady, these are held at a value far above that of courage out on a yard, true saltwater seamanship. It is unfair, but it is the world. Now, in the matter of the courtesies, we have . . .'

Kydd persevered. He was aware that Renzi's precepts were introductory only and that there lay ahead a challenge of insight and understanding far different from anything he had encountered before. The morning lengthened, and by the time Renzi had reached the proper use of euphemisms Kydd was flagging.

They heard the rap of the front-door knocker. 'I'll go,' Kydd said, rising.

'You shall not!' Renzi's words stopped him, and he subsided into his chair.

The manservant entered with a small silver tray in his gloved hands and went pointedly to Renzi. 'Are you at home, sir?'

Renzi picked up a card. 'I am to this young lady, thank you.'

'Very well, sir.'

As the servant left, Renzi shot to his feet. 'Square away, Tom – it's your sister!'

Cecilia entered the sitting room, eyes darting around. 'Er, you're welcome, Cec,' Kydd said, trying vainly to remember his morning exercises in civilities.

She acknowledged Renzi with a shy bob. 'Mother said – such a silly – that men are not to be trusted on their own in a domestic situation. How insulting to you!'

'I do apologise, Miss Kydd, that we are not dressed to receive. I hope you understand.'

'Nicholas?' Cecilia said, puzzled, but then her expression cleared. 'But of course – you're standing on ceremony for Thomas's sake.' She looked at her brother fondly.

Kydd smouldered.

Cecilia, ignoring him, crossed to a candlestand and delicately sniffed the nearest. 'Well, it's none of my business, but I can't help observing that unless you have means beyond the ordinary, beeswax candles must, sadly, be accounted an extravagance. Tallow will be sufficient – unless, of course, you have visitors.' She crossed to the windows and made play of freeing the shutters. 'You will be aware how vital it is to preserve furniture from the sun.'

'We c'n manage,' Kydd growled. 'An' I'll thank ye to keep y'r household suggestions to y'rself.'

'Thomas! I came only out of concern for your—'

'Cec, Nicholas is tellin' me the right lay t' be a gentleman. Please t' leave us to it.'

'Indeed!'

'Dear Miss Kydd, your kindness in enquiring after our situation is handsomely done,' said Renzi, 'yet I feel it is probably a man's place to impart to another the graces of a gentleman.'

Cecilia hesitated. 'That's as maybe, Mr Renzi, but there is another purpose to my visit. You appear to have forgotten that a naval uniform will not answer in all appearances in polite society. I came merely to offer my services in a visit to the tailor.'

At the tailor's Cecilia was not to be dissuaded. She quickly disposed of Kydd's initial preferences. A yellow waistcoat, while undoubtedly fetching, was apparently irredeemably vulgar: dark green, double-breasted was more the thing; she conceded on the gold piping at the pockets. Buff breeches, a rust-coloured coat, and for half-dress, a *bon de Paris* with discreet gold frogging would be of the highest *ton* – she was not sure about the lace.

'An' what's the reckonin' so far?' Kydd had done well in prize money in the Caribbean, and after Camperdown there would be more, but this must be costing a shocking sum.

Cecilia pressed on relentlessly. A dark blue frock coat was essential, in the new style with cut-away skirts that ended in split tails for an elegant fall while horse-riding – it seemed frivolous to Kydd, who was more used to a sensible full-skirted warmth. A quantity of linen shirts was put in train, and material for a cravat was purchased that Cecilia insisted only she might be trusted to make.

Kydd rebelled at pantaloons, long breeches that could be tucked into boots. Knee breeches were what he would be seen in – no one would mistake him for a damned macaroni.

The tailor, gratified at patronage by those so recently in the public eye, promised that he would bend his best efforts to have them delivered soon. Kydd was then escorted to the bootmaker and, finally, to the premises of Henry Tidmarsh, hosier, hatter and glover, where he found for himself a dashing light-grey brimmed hat with a silver buckle.

As Kydd tried on hats, Renzi came up beside Cecilia. 'Quite a transformation,' he murmured.

'Yes, Nicholas,' agreed Cecilia, keeping her voice low, 'but I fear he will be thought a coxcomb if his dress is not matched by his manners.'

She turned to him, her hand on his arm. 'Dear Nicholas, I know you are trying your best, but Thomas can be very stubborn if he chooses. Do bear him with patience, I pray.'

'Of course. But the hardest for him will undoubtedly be his articulations – his speech damns him at once.'

Cecilia touched his arm. 'Is there anything, perhaps, that I can do?'

Renzi's thoughts had taken quite another course. She was no longer the ingenuous girl-child he had known from before. Cecilia was a desirable, self-possessed woman, who would be an ornament to any social gathering. 'Er, this is possibly something we could discuss together, should you be at leisure.' He felt a flush rising at the implication of the words.

'Why, Nicholas!' Cecilia said gaily. 'If I didn't know you more, I'd be obliged to consider you importunate.' She flashed him a smile, and turned her attention to her brother's fancy in hats.

Although he was now entitled to do so, Kydd could not indulge in the wigs that he had learned to make in his apprenticeship: the comet, the royal bird, the long bob – even the striking Cadogan puff – were now no longer fashionable. He would wear nothing, simply a neat black ribbon to hold back his hair at the nape of the neck. Hair-powder was taxed, so it would be quite understood if he left his hair as nature intended.

True to his word, the tailor delivered his work in only three days, and Kydd stood before the full-length bedroom mirror, regarding himself doubtfully. A generous cut on the waistcoat avoided any tense wrinkling resulting from muscle-play beneath, but the buff breeches seemed to cling indecently close. However, if he had to appear in public, this was not a bad beginning, he thought. He gazed down approvingly at the white stockings and buckled shoes, then whirled once about.

'Glad to see you in spirits, brother,' came from behind him.

'Aye, what must be . . .' said Kydd, adjusting a cuff. 'Are ye ready, Nicholas?'

'Ah!' Renzi waved a finger.

'What? Oh! I meant t' say, are you prepared, Mr Renzi?'

'Then let us sally forth on the world.'

Renzi was in brown, a complete dark brown, with breeches, coat and even waistcoat in the colour, relieved only by the cream gush of his cravat and the stockings. In the manner of a Romantic he sported a broad-brimmed dark hat worn at a rakish angle.

It was the first time Kydd had used an ebony cane. As they passed along Chapel Street it felt awkward to the hand, whether he swung it at each pace to click on the ground or twirled it about. He fought down a sense of fakery, but after the second time a passer-by made way respectfully for him he felt happier.

They passed under the big clock in the high street – the beadle outside the town hall touched his hat to them – turned down a side-street and entered a dingy doorway.

'Might I present M'sieur Jupon? He is engaged to be your dancing master.' A short but fierce-eyed man swept down in the most extravagant leg to Kydd, then straightened, fixing him with a challenging stare.

'Er, pleased t' meet ye,' Kydd stuttered, and essayed a jerky bow. Jupon and Renzi exchanged glances.

'M'sieur Jupon will instruct you in the graces of movement and courtesy, and you will attend here for one hour daily until you have mastered the elements.'

'Ah, Mr Kydd, you're not boardin' your ship now, sir. Do try a little *grace* in y'r movements.' The voice of the lady horse-master carried effortlessly across the ring. She could well be relied on to hail the foreyard from the quarterdeck in a blow, Kydd thought.

The horse, however, had sensed his innocence, swishing its tail and playing with its bit. Its eyes rolled in anticipation while Kydd struggled to heave himself up, staggering one-footed in a circle.

Renzi dismounted and came across. He checked the girth and yanked on the stirrup. 'Ah, the stablehand is having his amusement. You'd have your knees round your ears with this! We'll ease away – so.' The stirrups descended, the horse quieter under Renzi's firm hand. He slapped the horse familiarly on the rump. 'Look, here's a tip. Make a fist, and touch the stirrup bar up here. Now swing the iron up under your arm, and the right length for you will be when it just touches the body.'

Kydd swung up nervously into the saddle, suddenly finding himself at a great height. The horse snorted and tossed its head. He felt that it was biding its time before wreaking some terrible revenge.

'So we seem t' have made up our mind to go ridin' at last.' A sarcastic bellow came across the ring to him. 'We start wi' the walk.'

The horse plodded in a circle, and Kydd's confidence grew.

'Back straight, Mr Kydd.' He forced his spine to rigidity and completed another circle. 'Jehosaphat Moses! Keep y'r back supple, Mr Kydd. Let y'r hips rock *with* the horse, sir!'

The trot was more to his liking with its brisk motion, but the horse whinnied with frustration at the tight rein and Kydd eased it a little.

A gate was opened into a larger field, and Renzi began to canter. Kydd followed behind, feeling the thud of hoofs through the animal's frame and hearing snorts of effort coming from the great beast beneath him. It was exhilarating, and he relaxed into it. The horse seemed to sense this and responded with a more fluid, faster motion.

'Well done, Mr Kydd!' he heard. '"Collected an' light in hand", we say.'

As he turned he saw the woman pull out a large fob watch. 'To me!' she demanded impatiently.

Kydd felt the horse respond to his signals with knee and reins and suddenly was reluctant to finish for the morning. Impulsively, he clapped his knees to the beast's barrel-like sides. After a brief hesitation the horse responded and broke into a gallop. Instinctively Kydd acted as he would aloft, his standing crouch that of a topman leaning forward to hand a billowing sail. The horse stretched out down the length of the field. Now wildly excited, Kydd caught a glimpse of figures staring at him as he thundered past. The wind tore through his hair, the din of hoofs and the animal's rhythmic movements beat on his senses.

A gnarled wooden fence spread across his vision. As they hurtled towards it, Kydd considered an emergency turn to larboard. Far behind him a faint bellow sounded: 'Bridge y'r reins! Bridge your *reins*!' but he was too far gone. The horse threw itself at the rails. There was a momentary muscular tensing, a lunge into space, then all was quiet for a heartbeat before the beast landed with a mighty thud and a jerk.

Kydd stayed aboard as the horse raced away through nondescript winter-brown bracken and into the woods beyond. It hesitated in mid-stride, then swerved on to a woodland path, Kydd ducking to avoid whip-like branches.

He became aware of hoofbeats out of synchrony with his own, and indistinct shouting. He guessed it would be Renzi following, but dared not look behind. He shot past a gaping greenwood forager, then reached a more substantial lane across their path.

The horse skidded as it negotiated a random turn, but the

mud slowed it, and the gallop became less frantic. It panted heavily as it slowed to a trot. Renzi caught up and grasped the reins. 'How are you, brother?'

Kydd flashed a wide grin. 'Spankin' fine time, Nicholas, s' help me,' he said breathlessly, his face red with exertion.

Renzi hid a grin. 'And what has happened to your decorum, sir?'

'Oh? Aye, yes. Er, a capital experience, sir.'

They rode together for a space. The lane widened and a small cottage came into view ahead. 'Do dismount, old fellow, and ask directions back,' Renzi suggested. Gingerly, Kydd leaned forward to bring his leg across the saddle, but in a flash he had toppled backwards into the black winter mud, still with one foot in a stirrup.

The horse stamped and rolled its eyes as Kydd got ruefully to his feet and trudged down the garden path to the door.

It was answered by a stooped old man with alert bright eyes. Before Kydd could speak, he smiled. 'Ah, Master Kydd, I do believe? Thomas Kydd?'

'Aye, y'r in the right of it,' Kydd said. 'That is t' say, you have th' advantage of me, sir.'

The man feigned disappointment. Kydd's face cleared. 'O' course! Parson Deane!' It seemed so long ago that, as a boy, he had taken delight in going to the lakeside with the old man and his dog after duck. 'I hope I find you in health, sir,' he said. The parson glanced up at Renzi, who was still mounted. 'Oh, sir, this is Mr Renzi, my particular friend. Mr Renzi, this is the Rev'nd Deane.'

Renzi inclined his head. 'My honour, sir. Our apologies at this intrusion, we merely seek a more expedient way back to our *manège.*'

Deane's face creased in pleasure. 'I shall tell you, should

you come inside and accept a dish of tea while Thomas tells me where he's been spending his days.'

They left the horses to crop grass outside the garden fence and went into the parson's house. Deane looked at Kydd keenly, clearly enjoying his sparse recital of his impressment and subsequent adventures. 'So now you're an officer?'

Kydd grinned boyishly. 'L'tenant Kydd!' he said, with swelling pride.

'Then you are now, in the eyes of the whole world, a gentleman. Is this not so?'

It seemed appropriate to bow wordlessly.

Deane contemplated Kydd for a long moment. 'Do you stop me if I appear impertinent,' he said, 'yet I would later remember this moment with shame were I not to share with you now my thoughts concerning your station.'

'It would be f'r my advantage, Mr Deane.' He couldn't resist a quick glance of triumph at Renzi – after all, he had remembered the polite words – but Renzi responded with a frown. Obediently Kydd turned all his attention to the old man.

'It seems to me that the essence of a gentleman is to be found in his good breeding, his impeccable civility to all, including his servants. "Manners maketh man," as the Good Book teaches us. Outer manners reflect inner virtue.'

Renzi nodded slowly. 'The worthy Locke is insistent on this point,' he murmured.

'It is never quite easy for the young to acquire the civil virtues,' the parson continued. '"*Quo semel est imbuta recens, servabit oderem testa diu,*" was Horace's view, and by this you should understand . . .'

Kydd stirred restlessly in his armchair. 'Gettin' to be a gallows' sight more'n a man c'n take, Cec, all this'n.'

Cecilia affected not to hear. Kydd glanced at her irritably. 'I mean, how much o' this is going to stand by me at sea?'

'That's better,' Cecilia said demurely, but laid down her book. 'Now I'm sure the other officers will be polite and well bred, so you must be the same.'

Kydd snorted.

Renzi sighed. 'You have still three issues of the *Gentleman's Magazine* to digest, to my certain knowledge,' he said accusingly.

'And a *Spectator*,' Cecilia chimed in. 'How can you keep a lady entertained at table without you have small-talk to share?'

She looked at Renzi in mock despair, then brightened. 'Mr Renzi, have you seen our castle? The merest ruin, I'll grant, but of an age indeed. Mama will be persuaded to come – she knows all the history.'

'I'm wore out,' said Mrs Kydd, finding a wooden bench overlooking what remained of the castle keep. 'You two have a good look roun' by y'rselves.'

Cecilia was agreeable, and Renzi took her on his arm for the stony path winding about the castle mound. The winter sun had a fragile brilliance, contrasting colour bright with grey and brown tints.

'It grieves me to say it, but Thomas did not shine at the tea-party in any wise,' he opened. He was uncomfortably aware of her touch – it had been long years since last he had enjoyed polite female company, and Cecilia was now a beauty.

'Yes – the silly boy, sitting there like a stuffed goose while the ladies made sport of him. I despair, Nicholas, I really do.'

Renzi assisted Cecilia past a perilous rock. She flashed him a look of gratitude, then dropped her eyes, but her hold on his arm tightened.

'Miss Kydd . . .' began Renzi thickly, then stopped. With

his own feelings about her far from clear was it fair – was it honourable? – to engage her affections?

'Yes, Nicholas?' she said, smiling up at him.

He pulled himself up. 'I was. . . Your mother confides that you have secured the liveliest trust in your position with Lady Stanhope.'

'I have been very fortunate,' she said gravely. Then a smile broke through. 'You've no idea how many of the highest in the land I've seen. Lady Stanhope requires I attend her at all her routs and I'm sure it's only to find me a husband.'

'And—'

'Don't be a silly, Nicholas. I'm sensible of my fortune in this and, I do declare, I'm not ready to forsake it all now for the tedium of domestic life.' She tossed her head, eyes sparkling.

After another few paces she turned to him with a troubled expression. 'Thomas – he. . .'

He knew what concerned her: her brother would find himself first ridiculed and later shunned if he could not hold his own in company. 'Time is short, I agree. Do you not think that we are obligated to press him to enter in upon society in a more formal degree?'

Cecilia bit her lip, then decided. 'A dinner party! Now, let me see. . . We have the pick of Guildford, of course, a hostess would die to entertain a brace of heroes from Camperdown, but I rather feel that at this stage Thomas would not welcome the public eye too warmly.' She thought for a moment, then said, 'I know – I'll speak with Mrs Crawford, advise her that after such a dreadful battle Thomas relishes nothing better than a small, intimate gathering. I'll be seeing her on Thursday and shall speak to her then.'

'Splendid,' responded Renzi. It would indeed be a suitable

occasion for Kydd, if he could overcome his timidity in august surroundings. He beamed approval at Cecilia.

'Er, Nicholas,' she said off-handedly, 'something that I keep forgetting to ask. It's just my ill-bred curiosity, but you've never mentioned your own people.' She stopped to admire a singularly gnarled small tree.

'My own? Well . . . shall I say they're just an old country family of Wiltshire whom I haven't attended as assiduously as I might?'

Kydd sat motionless at the bare table, listening while Cecilia explained and cautioned, his expression hard but in control.

'No, Thomas, it just will not do. We do not enter like a herd of goats to feed. First to take their places are the ladies, and they will occupy one end of the table. When they are seated the gentlemen proceed – but, mark this, in strict order. They will be placed at the table in the same succession.'

Cecilia's eyes flicked once to Renzi, then turned back to Kydd.

Kydd's face tightened, but he kept his silence.

'Now, Mrs Crawford always dines *à la française*, as you know, Thomas, and allows promiscuous seating so a man may sit next to a lady, though some find this too racy for the English taste, and in this . . .'

Renzi's sympathy was all too transparent. 'I do rather think that Tom is more a man of daring and action, dear sister. This posturing must be a disagreeable strain for such a one.'

'Nevertheless, he shall require his manners wherever he may be,' Cecilia said coldly. 'A gentleman does not put aside his breeding simply for the perils of the moment. Now, please attend, Thomas.'

*   *   *

'Miss Cecilia Kydd, Mr Thomas Kydd and Mr Nicholas Renzi!' blared the footman.

The babble of conversations faded: it was common knowledge that the two guests now arrived had suffered in the legendary October clash off the Dutch coast, and it had been said that they had chosen tonight to resume their place in polite society. There were many curious rumours about these officers, but no doubt before the night was over the details would have been made clear.

A wave of determined females advanced, led by the hostess, and the groups dissolved in a flurry of introductions.

'Enchanted,' said Mr Kydd, making a creditable but somewhat individual leg to a gratified Mrs Crawford.

'Do say if you become too fatigued, Mr Kydd,' she said, eyeing his broad shoulders. 'You'll find us in the utmost sympathy with your time of trial.'

'That is most kind in ye, dear Mrs Crawford,' the handsome sailor-officer replied gravely.

She turned reluctantly to the other one, a sensitive-looking, rather more austere gentleman, and, reclaimed by her duty, murmured politely.

They sat down to dinner under the golden glitter of chandelier and crystal, to polite approbation at the first remove.

'May I help you t' a portion of this fine shott, Miss Tuffs?' said Mr Kydd, politely. The young lady on his left, nearly overcome at being noticed by one of the principal guests, could only stutter her thanks, tinged with alarm at the resulting pile of roast piglet generously heaped to occupy the whole plate.

'Sir, this toothsome venison demands your immediate attention. Might I . . .' The red-faced gentleman to the right would not be denied, and placed a satisfying amount on Mr Kydd's plate.

'Your servant, sir,' said Mr Kydd, inclining his head.

It was clear that the middle-aged woman across from him was set on securing his attention. 'The weather seems uncommon blowy for the time of year,' she said.

Mr Kydd thought for a moment, and replied politely, 'It's a saying ashore only, Mrs Wood, "When the wind is in the east, 'tis no good to man nor beast." And by this is meant that in the winter season we often shiver in th' winds o' Tartary from the east. Now, at sea we bless this wind, Mrs Wood, for it is a fair wind for our ships down-channel and . . .'

Fully satisfied in the matter of explanations, Mrs Wood retired to contemplate, at which Mr Kydd turned his attention to the red-faced gentleman. '*Gentleman's Magazine*'s interestin' this week – says about your electric fluid invented by Mr Volta all comes from frog legs in the end,' he remarked bravely.

The man shook his head slowly in amazement. 'Now, that's something I never knew,' he said at length. A look of barely concealed satisfaction suffused Mr Kydd's face as he looked up the table to where Mr Renzi sat quietly, nodding slowly.

A footman obliged with claret. 'Wine with you, sir!' Mr Kydd said happily, with all the joyous relief to be expected of one having passed through a personal trial and not been found wanting. 'I give you Lady Fortune, an' may she always be one!'

Chapter 2

'Aye, 'ere she comes, capting,' the inn porter said, indicating the gig under sail coming around Garrison Point. He held out his hand for a promised sixpence and left them to it, their chests and other impedimenta in a pile on Sheerness public jetty while they waited for the boat from *Tenacious*.

Kydd's heart bumped. This was the day he had been looking forward to these several months while *Tenacious* was under repair, the most important day of his life, the day he joined his ship confirmed in his rank, a King's officer. The day or so aboard after Camperdown didn't really count – he could hardly remember anything of the brute chaos and towering weariness in the wounded ship limping back to Sheerness.

The coxswain, a midshipman, cautiously rounded into the wind twenty yards off. Two seamen brailed up and secured the sail for a pull under oars the final distance to the jetty steps. It was not what Kydd would have done: the breeze, although fluky, was reliable enough for an approach under sail alone.

As the boat glided alongside, the sailors smacked the oars across their thighs and levered them aloft in one easy movement, just as Kydd had done in the not so distant past. His eyes passed over the boat and the four seamen, as he recalled the old saying, 'You can always tell a ship by her boats.' Was caution a feature of this ship, he wondered.

The sailors seemed capable, long-service able seamen economically securing the sea-chests and striking them into the centre of the boat, but Kydd sensed darting eyes behind his back as they took the measure of the new officers.

He and Renzi assumed their places in the sternsheets, at leisure while the midshipman took the tiller. The boat bobbed in the grey North Sea chop and Kydd's new uniform was sprinkled with its first salt water. He tried to keep his face blank against surging excitement as they rounded the point to open up the view of the Nore anchorage – and his ship.

She was one of a straggling line of vessels of varying sizes moored in this transitory anchorage to await different destinies. A wisp of memory brushed his consciousness: it was at the Nore that he had been taken as a bitter victim of the press gang, so long ago now, it seemed.

He glanced back to the scatter of dockyard buildings, the low fort, the hulks, and a pang of feeling returned for Kitty Malkin, who had stood with him during the dark days of the Nore mutiny. She had uncannily foretold his elevation, and that she would not be a part of it. Other memories of the time came too, dark and emotional. The red flag of mutiny, the spiralling madness that had ended in savage retribution and shame. Memories he had fought hard to dim.

Kydd crushed the thoughts. He would look forward, not back, take his good fortune and move into the future with it. The phantoms began to fade.

'She's storing,' Renzi said, as if reading something in his face.

'Er, yes, those are powder hoys alongside, she's ready t' sail,' Kydd muttered, his eyes fixed on the approaching bulk of *Tenacious*. The foretopmast was still on deck for some reason but her long commissioning pennant flew from her masthead. Repairs complete, she now stood ready in the service of her country.

A faint bellow from the ship sounded over the plash of the bow wave. The bowman cupped his hand and bawled back, 'Aye, aye!' warning *Tenacious* that her boat was bearing naval officers, who would expect to be received as the custom of the sea demanded.

The midshipman again doused sail and shipped oars for the last stretch. Kydd resolved to attend to the young gentleman's seamanship when the opportunity arose. The boat bumped against the stout sides and the bowman hooked on. Kydd held back as Renzi seized the handropes and left the boat. Although their commissions bore the same date, he was appointed fourth lieutenant aboard, and Kydd, as fifth, would always be first in the boat and last out.

The ship's sides were fresh painted, the thick wales black, with the lines of guns set in natural timber, smart in a bright preparation of turpentine and rosin. A strong wafting of the scent mixed pleasingly with that of salt spray.

Above, a boatswain's call pierced the clean, winter air. Kydd was being piped aboard a man-o'-war! He mounted the side steps: his eyes passed above the deck line to the boatswain's mate with his pipe on one side and two midshipmen as side-boys on the other. He touched his hat to the quarterdeck when he made the deck, and approached the waiting officer-of-the-watch. 'Lieutenant Kydd, sir, appointed fifth l'tenant.'

For a moment he feared this officer would accuse him of being an impostor, but the man merely smiled bleakly. 'Cutting it a trifle fine, don't you think?' he said, then turned to the duty quartermaster and ordered the chests swayed inboard. Renzi came to stand with Kydd.

'Captain Houghton will want to see you immediately, I should think,' the officer-of-the-watch said.

'Aye aye, sir,' Kydd replied carefully, conscious of eyes on him from all over the busy decks. He remembered little of her from the exhausted hours he had spent aboard after the battle, fighting to bring the damaged vessel to safe harbour, but all ships had similar main features. He turned and went into the cabin spaces aft.

Renzi reported first. There was a rumble of voices; then the door opened. 'Seems pleasant enough,' he whispered to Kydd.

Kydd knocked and entered. The captain sat behind his desk facing him, taking advantage of the wan light coming through the stern windows. He was glowering at a paper.

'L'tenant Kydd come aboard t' join, sir.'

'Don't sit,' the captain said heavily. 'You're to hold yourself ready to go ashore again.'

'But, sir, why?'

'You are owed an explanation, I believe,' Houghton said, looking at Kydd directly. 'I've been given to understand that your origins are the lower deck, that is to say you have come aft through the hawse, as the expression goes.'

'Er — aye, sir.'

'Then this must be to your great credit, and shows evidence, no doubt, of sterling qualities of some kind. However . . .' he leaned back in his chair, still fixing Kydd with hard, grey eyes, '. . . I am determined that *Tenacious* under my command shall have a loyal band of officers of breeding, who will be able to represent the ship with, um, distinction, and who may be relied upon in the matter of courtesy and gentle conduct.

'You should understand that it is no reflection on yourself personally, when I say that I am applying to the commissioner to have you replaced with a more suitable officer for this vessel. There is no question in my mind that your services will be far more valuable to the service perhaps in a sloop or gunboat, not in a sail-of-the-line.' He stood. 'In the meantime you may wish to avail yourself of the conveniences of the wardroom. Carry on, please.'

Kydd stuttered an acknowledgement and left. He felt numb: the swing from exhilaration to the bleakness of rejection was as savage as it was unexpected.

The mate-of-the-watch waited on the open deck. 'Sir?' Kydd's chest and personal possessions lay in a small heap.

'Leave 'em for now.' Kydd felt every eye on him as he went below to the wardroom. The only inhabitant was a marine captain sitting at the table, pencilling in an order book. He looked up. 'Some sort o' mistake,' Kydd mumbled. 'I'm t' be replaced.'

'Oh, bad luck, old trout.'

Kydd took off his coat and sat at the other end of the table. As desolation built, he tried to subdue the feeling of homelessness, of not belonging in this select community. He got up abruptly and, pulling himself together, stepped out on deck. He had seen Renzi with a party forward getting the topmast a-taunt. Renzi would have no problems of breeding with this captain, and later he must find his friend and bid him farewell.

The officer-of-the-watch caught sight of Kydd and turned with a frown. Some waiting seamen looked at him with open amusement. Face burning, Kydd returned to the wardroom.

It was half-way through the afternoon and the marine captain had left. A young wardroom servant was cleaning the table. 'Ah, sorry, sir, I'll leave,' he said, collecting his rags.

'No, younker, carry on,' Kydd said. Any company was better than none.

He looked about. It was a surprisingly neat and snug space with louvred cabin doors looking inward to the long table along the centreline and the fat girth of the mizzen mast at one end. The bulkheads and doors were darkly polished rich mahogany, and at the other end there was plenty of light from the broad stern windows – even the privacy of a pair of officers' quarter galleries. She would be an agreeable ship for far voyaging.

This old class of 64s were surprisingly numerous – still probably near thirty left in service – and were known for their usefulness. As convoy escorts they could easily crush any predatory frigate, yet at a pinch could stand in the line of battle. In home waters the mainstay of the major battle fleets was the 74, but overseas, vessels like *Tenacious* were the squadron heavyweights.

Kydd's depression deepened as he wandered about the wardroom. On the rudder head he found a well-thumbed book, *The Sermons of Mr Yorick*. Raising his eyebrows in surprise he found that it was instead a novel by a Laurence Sterne, and he sat to read. Half-way into the first chapter and not concentrating, he heard a piping of the side and guessed that the captain had returned with news of his replacement.

Word was not long in coming. A midshipman pelted down and knocked sharply. 'Lootenant Kydd? Sir, cap'n desires you wait on him.'

On deck the officer-of-the-watch looked at him accusingly.

His chest and bags, obviously a hindrance, had been moved to the base of the mainmast. 'Be getting rid o' them soon,' Kydd said defiantly, and went inside to see the captain.

This time Houghton stood up. 'I won't waste our time. We're under notice for sea, and there's no officer replacement readily at hand. I see you will be accompanying us after all, Mr Kydd.'

A leaping exultation filled Kydd's thoughts. Then a cooler voice told him that the explanation for his change of fortune was probably the inability of the commissioner's office to change the paperwork in time – an officer's commission was to a particular ship rather than the Navy as a whole, and could not easily be put aside.

'I'll not pretend that this is to my liking, Mr Kydd,' the captain continued, 'but I'm sure you'll do your duty as you see it to the best of your ability.' He stared hard at Kydd. 'You are the most junior officer aboard, and I need not remind you that if you fail me then, most assuredly, you will be landed at the first opportunity.'

'I will not fail ye, sir.'

'Umm. Quite so. Well, perhaps I'd better welcome you aboard as the fifth of *Tenacious*, Mr Kydd.' He held out his hand, but his eyes remained bleak. 'Show your commission and certificates to my clerk, and he will perform the needful. My first lieutenant has your watch details and you will oblige me by presenting yourself on deck tomorrow morning for duty.'

Excitement stole back to seize Kydd as he stood in the wardroom supervising his gear being carried down. His cabin was the furthest forward of four on the larboard side, and he opened the door with trepidation: only a short time ago this had been officers' private territory.

It was small. He would be sharing his night-time thoughts with a gleaming black eighteen-pounder below, and his cot, triced up to the deckhead for now, ensured that he could never stand upright. He would have to find room for his chest, cocked-hat box, sword, personal oddments and books. A cunningly designed desk occupied the forward width, taking advantage of the outward curve of the ship's side. He pulled at its little drawers and wondered which dead officer had unintentionally left it behind for others.

The gunport was open. At sea it would be closed and then the cabin would be a diminutive place indeed, but he had been in smaller. He tried the chair at the desk. It was tiny, but well crafted to fit into such a space, tightly but comfortably enfolding his thighs. He eased into it and looked around. Spartan it might be, but it was the first true privacy he had ever experienced aboard ship. His eyes followed the line of intersection where the bulkhead met the overhead beams. The thin panels were slotted: at 'beat to quarters' this entire cabin would be dismantled and struck down in the hold below. Over the door he noticed a ragged line of colour, where a curtain had once been fastened to cover the door space; he could have the door open and still retain a modicum of privacy.

It was adequate, it was darkly snug – and it was his. He went to his chest and rummaged around. Carefully stored at the bottom was his commission. Undoing the red silk ribbon he unfolded the crackling parchment and read it yet again.

By the Commissioners for executing the Office of Lord High Admiral of Great Britain . . . Lieutenant Thomas Kydd . . . we do appoint you Lieutenant of His Majesty's Ship the *Tenacious* . . . strictly charging the Officers and all the Ship's Company. . . all due Respect and Obedience unto you their said Lieutenant . . .

Kydd savoured the noble words.
It concluded sombrely:

Hereof nor you nor any of you may fail as you will answer to the contrary at your peril. And for so doing this shall be your Warrant . . .

It was signed Evan Nepean, secretary to the Admiralty, and the date of seniority, 20 January 1798, with the scarlet Admiralty seal embossed to the left. This single document would figure prominently for the rest of Kydd's life, defining station and position, rank and pay, authority and rule. He creased it carefully and put it away. A deep breath turned into a sigh, which he held for a long time.

He turned and found himself confronting a black man. 'Tysoe, sir, James Tysoe, your servant,' he said, in a well-spoken tone.

Kydd was taken aback, not that Tysoe was black but at the realisation that here was proof positive of the status he had now achieved. 'Ah, yes.' He had had a servant in the gun-room before, but this was altogether different: then it had been a knowing old marine shared with all the others; here the man was his personal valet. 'Do carry on, if y' please,' Kydd said carefully.

Tysoe hesitated. 'I think it were best, sir, should I stow your cabin.'

'Thank ye, no, I'll take care of it,' Kydd said, with a smile. There was nothing too personal in his possessions, but the thought of a stranger invading his privacy was an alien notion.

'Sir, I can do it,' Tysoe said softly. Something in his voice told Kydd that he should let the man go about his business. Then he realised that, of course, Tysoe needed to know the location of everything if he was to keep his master well clothed and fettled.

'Well, just be steady with the octant,' Kydd admonished him.

'Lieutenant Kydd, I believe!' Renzi chuckled as he entered the wardroom.

Kydd's heart was full, but he was still unsettled by his unfortunate welcome to the ship and could only manage, 'Aye, do I see Lieutenant Renzi before me?'

Renzi dumped a number of well-used order books on the table. 'Well, my friend, it does seem this is a task it would be prudent to begin immediately, if not earlier.'

Regulations. Orders. Directions. Covering every possible situation. Each in careful phrasing ensuring that every subordinate in the chain of command would be in no doubt that if any disagreeable situation arose it would not be the fault of his superior.

From the Admiralty:
Article: The Captain is to demand from the Clerk of the Survey a book, with the inventory of the stores committed to the charge of the Boatswain and Carpenter. . .

Article: If any be heard to curse or blaspheme the name of God, the Captain is strictly required to punish them for every offence by causing them to wear a wooden collar . . .

Article: The Lieutenant is expected that he do provide himself with the necessary instruments, maps and

42

books of navigation, and he is to keep a journal according to the form set down and at the end of the voyage shall deliver copies thereof signed by himself into the Admiralty and Navy Offices . . .

Article: No commander shall inflict any punishment upon a seaman beyond twelve lashes upon his bare back with a cat of nine tails, according to the ancient practice of the sea . . .

The commander in chief of the North Sea Fleet had his own instructions – from the timing of the evening gun when at anchor, to conduct when in sight of the enemy – all in all a dizzying succession of domestic detail, mixed with grave admonitions to duty.

Kydd sensed movement outside.

'Well, now, if I'm not mistook, here's our fourth and fifth lootenants!' It was a pleasant-faced young officer, rubbing his hands with cold.

'Ah, Thomas Kydd, sir, at your service.'

'Well, then, my dear sir, I am your humble and obedient Gervase Adams, third of this barky – was junior luff in *Raven*, sadly no more.' Kydd shook hands, grateful for the friendliness.

Adams turned to Renzi. 'Give you joy of your step, Renzi,' he said formally, holding out his hand. Renzi had served for a small time in *Tenacious* as master's mate: he'd been part of the ship's company at Camperdown. Kydd realised that they assumed his origins to be a senior midshipman promoted, not someone from forward, as he was.

Adams looked over Kydd's shoulder at the books. 'This is what you should be boning up on, m' boy.' He tapped one marked 'Captain's Orders'. 'This owner is new to me, but if

43

he's running to form he'll expect you to have it by heart in a day – "This is the word of the Lord: hear ye and obey!"'

There was a knock at the door and Adams crossed to answer it. 'L'tenant Kydd! Seems first luff has need of the solace of your company at this time.'

Kydd hesitated, partly out of concern for the reception he would receive from the captain's deputy, partly out of confusion as to where to go. He knew the first lieutenant's cabin would be here in the wardroom, the largest one to starboard and right in the stern, but it was unoccupied.

'In harbour he sets up shop in the coach next to the captain's cabin, you'll find.' Adams paused. 'Bryant the Beatific. The men call him Bull – last ship a frigate, and he wants his own command so bad it stinks. I'd steer small with him, Kydd, to be sure.'

'Sit, sir.' Bryant finished his scrawling. 'So, Mr Kydd, you're the fifth and junior. I've put you with Mr Bampton as second officer-of-the-watch until you can prove yourself. And I'll have you know, sir, that if you don't – and that damn soon – I'll see you broke. That I promise. Understand?'

'Sir.'

He consulted his paper. 'And you'll take the afterguard, where you're under my eye.' He looked up. 'Heard you came aft the hard way – and heard else – you'll not be shy in a fight an' I like that. Now, you bat square with me, and you'll do. Right?'

'Aye, sir.' Kydd was not sure what he was implying, and answered cautiously. The man, with his aggressive, out-thrust jaw and direct, almost angry manner, unsettled him.

'Ah, yes – and you'll be signal lootenant, o' course.'

'But, sir, I—'

44

'Then you'll learn, damn it, like we all did!' Bryant snapped. 'You've got a signal midshipman, Rawson, and two steady hands on the bunting. Do y' want a wet nurse as well?'

'I'll do m' duty right enough.' Kydd felt himself reddening.

Bryant eased back in his chair. 'Let's see. You were entered as a landman in 'ninety-three, then shipped in *Artemis* frigate around the world, did a few years in the Caribbean and came back a master's mate. Earned their lordships' approbation in the late mutiny at the Nore, and didn't disgrace yourself at Camperdown.' He slapped the papers back into their pack. 'I'm sure you'll do your duty, Mr Kydd.' He rose. 'Now, keep station on me – it's a new wardroom, we need to make our number to each other.'

The long table was laid with a starched white cloth and silver was much in evidence. It was close on four o'clock, supper time; aboard ship it was always taken considerably earlier than on land.

Kydd lost Bryant in a swirl of officers as old friends warmly greeted each other and new ones respectfully made themselves known. Renzi was deep in conversation with a plainly dressed man who had a curiously neat and sensitive face. Kydd made to cross to him, but a glass was thrust into his hand, and Adams's pleasant face appeared. 'A tincture with you, m' friend,' he said, leaning back while a seaman politely plied a bottle. The wine was deep and red, and eased Kydd's trepidation.

'Your very good health, sir,' Kydd said. Adams smiled, then turned to an older lieutenant, but before he could speak, Bryant, attended by a steward, took the head of the table, his back to the stern windows.

'We sit now,' warned Adams, and led Kydd quickly to the

opposite end of the table, to one side of the thickness of the mizzen mast growing up at the end. Then he swung round deftly and sat opposite.

A buzz of talk arose. Bryant roared down the table, 'Wine with you, Mr Kydd!'

The table fell quiet and Kydd caught covert glances in his direction. He tried to gather his wits. 'C-confusion to the French!' he called, raising his glass to Bryant. The words seemed weak and theatrical after the hearty oaths of seamen.

The marine captain raised his glass and declaimed drily, 'And to ourselves – as no one else is likely to concern themselves with our welfare.'

'Damn right!' Bryant said vigorously, and drank deeply, then held up his empty glass. Talk began again, but Bryant banged a spoon on the table. 'Gentlemen!' he demanded loudly. 'Today sees *Tenacious* with her company of officers complete. We're in commission, and we'll be rejoining the North Sea Fleet very shortly. I believe it's not too soon to make our acquaintance of each other.'

Kydd could hear a bottle being opened out of sight as he positioned his glass. He was grateful to the wine for settling his apprehensions.

'I'm your premier. My last ship was *Thetis*, thirty-eight, in the Indian Ocean, where we saw not much o' the French worth a spit. I hope to see some better sport before long.' He pitched his voice to the older lieutenant. 'Now you, sir.'

'Bampton, second luff, only officer surviving after Camperdown. Served two years with the North Sea Fleet in *Tenacious* before,' he added drily.

'Ah, was you at the Nore mutiny?' the marine wanted to know.

'Yes.' Kydd froze. 'And no. I was set ashore by the muti-

46

nous villains – but had the pleasure later of seeing 'em at a yardarm.' He gave a thin smile and sipped his wine.

Bryant's gaze slipped to Adams, who took up his cue. 'Gentlemen, you see before you one Gervase Adams, relict of the *Raven*, eighteen, fir-built and cast ashore. Take heed all ye who would place Baltic fir before good British oak . . .'

'And?'

Renzi's manner was perfect: his easy affability brought approving grunts from around the table. He raised his glass in Kydd's direction. 'Might I bring forward my particular friend Thomas Kydd, whom you see before you as junior aboard, but whose shining parts his modesty forbids him to mention. His actions in thwarting a fearful case of barratry while still a child of the sea is well remarked, and I owe my continued existence to his acting forcefully in a curious circumstance on an island in the Great South Sea. He it is who conned the longboat in the Caribbean that preserved Lord Stanhope, and in all, gentlemen, we must conclude that Mr Kydd be truly accounted a favoured son of Neptune!'

Bryant rumbled loudly, 'Hear him!'

Kydd reddened, and mumbled something. The table remained silent.

'That may be so,' exclaimed Adams, 'but be advised, Kydd, it's the custom of the service that if you've been around the Cape of Good Hope you're entitled to one foot on the table. If you've doubled Cape Horn, both feet on the table, but nothing entitles you to spit to wind'd!'

There was warmth in the easy laughter that followed the old saw. Kydd had no idea that there was such a fraternity in the officers in their wardroom, and he longed to be truly one of them.

Introductions continued. The marine turned out to be a

Captain Pringle, with a well-polished line in wardroom wit. It seemed that later a brand-new lieutenant of marines would also grace the ship.

Renzi's new friend was a Mr Peake, a quietly spoken and erudite gentleman who would be their chaplain, and completing the company, further along, was one not in uniform but wearing a comfortable green-striped waistcoat. He announced himself laconically as Pybus, the ship's surgeon.

The wardroom dissolved into talk and laughter, and a violin out of sight behind the mizzen mast began a soft piece Kydd did not recognise. At the same time the smell of onion soup filled the air, and silently a bowl appeared before him. Simultaneously, a number of covered dishes arrived.

'Kydd, dear fellow, may I assist you to some of these fresh chops?' Adams said, as Kydd finished his soup. 'Sadly, we shan't see their like again, I fear, before we next make port.'

Behind the chair of each officer stood a seaman or marine to wait at table; Tysoe was at the back of Kydd. Adams waited until he had withdrawn to see to Kydd's glass. 'That old blackamoor you have there, come down in the world since he was *valet de chambre* to Codrington, who, you might recollect, died of an apoplexy in our very great cabin.' He leaned forward. 'You don't have to stay with the old fellow – ask Pringle for a marine, they know the sea service.'

Kydd looked round at the other servants. There was none who appeared to be above thirty; Tysoe had substantial grey in his bushy hair. Having seen the scrimmages that sometimes took place as servants jostled to see their masters' needs met first, he had his doubts that Tysoe would hold his own. But something about the man's quiet dignity touched Kydd. There were advantages to youth, but different ones with maturity and, besides, were they

48

not both outsiders? 'Er, no, I'll keep Tysoe,' Kydd answered.

He saw the glow of contentment in the others as his eye roved over the animated officers. Eddying talk rose and fell, then lulled. He heard Bampton call down to him, his voice studied and casual: 'Kydd, something or other tells me you're no stranger to the lower deck. Can this be right?'

Bryant frowned. The table fell quiet, and faces turned to Kydd.

He took a deep breath. 'True, very true, sir. I was untimely taken up as a pressed man and, unable t' run, I find myself still here.'

Awkward grins surfaced, and Pringle murmured to the table in general, 'That won't please the owner – not by half, it won't.'

Bampton persisted: 'Was this not alarming? For your family is what I mean.'

'Damn it all!' Bryant exploded, glaring at Bampton. 'We were promised figgy duff – where the devil is it?'

It was a pearly calm winter's day when Kydd appeared for duty on the deck of the man-o'-war, a King's officer. After their pressed men had been claimed and come aboard, the ship's company would be mustered by open list into divisions and Kydd would see his men for the first time.

A hoy from the receiving ship came alongside in a flurry of flapping canvas and shouted orders. Kydd continued to pace the quarterdeck, the arrival of pressed men not his concern. Out of sight, in the waist below, the first lieutenant would be setting up to receive them, rating the seamen by their skills and consigning the rest – landmen – to the drudgery of brute labour.

Kydd felt contentment at the thought that within a week

or so this deck would be alive and heeling to the stern winds of the open ocean.

Renzi fell into step beside him.

'Nicholas! How did y' sleep?' Kydd's own experience had not been of the best. Alone in the dark, he had tried to keep the thoughts that surged through him under control. The cot, a square-sided canvas frame suspended from the deckhead, was comfortable, but he had not realised that bedding was his own responsibility, and were it not for Tysoe's silent intercession, he would have gone without.

'Well, it must certainly be admitted, our elevation to society in this watery world has its distinct attractions.' Renzi wore an indulgent smile, which triggered a jet of frustration in Kydd. After his own experiences, it was galling to see Renzi take to his new life so easily.

'It is agreeable, perhaps, but today we get th' measure of our men,' he said impatiently. Adams was on the opposite side of the deck, deep in conversation with a master's mate, and also appeared anxious to be started.

'Mr Kydd?'

He turned to see a dignified older man in plain uniform. The man touched his hat. 'Hambly, sir, sailing master.'

'Good morning, Mr Hambly,' Kydd replied. A full master, Royal Navy, paying his respects, the highest professional being in Kydd's universe before. The man's steady look had a quality of appraisal, cool judgement.

'Thought I'd make y'r acquaintance, sir.' Before Kydd could speak, he continued, 'Mr Jarman is m' friend.'

Kydd remembered the master of the topsail cutter *Seaflower*, who had patiently taught him the elements of navigation and whose octant he now used, pressed on him after his famed open-boat voyage.

'A fine man, Mr Hambly,' Kydd said sincerely. 'I owe him much.'

The master smiled slowly, touched his hat to Kydd, then Renzi, and left.

A double strike on the bell sounded forward: this was the time for the officers to repair to the great cabin where the shape of things to come would now become apparent.

'Gentlemen, be seated.' The captain remained standing, staring out of the stern windows. 'I won't keep you long,' he said. 'It is my intention to conclude the fitting of this vessel for sea as soon as possible. I desire that today you shall muster the people by open list, and prove your divisions. The first lieutenant has assured me he has now a complete watch and station bill.'

Bryant nodded emphatically, then glanced around at the officers meaningfully. There had been frantic work by his writer and clerks the previous night.

Houghton continued sternly, 'He wishes that this shall be advised to all hands – with a view to shifting to sea routine within a small space of days. The quarters bill will be posted this evening, I am assured.' He withdrew a silver watch. 'Shall we say, divisions at five bells?'

'Mr Lawes?' Kydd addressed the only master's mate among the group of about twenty men.

'Aye, sir.'

'Pleased t' see you,' Kydd said, touching his own hat at Lawes's salute. He turned to survey the men drawn up on the poop deck. Most of his division, the able seamen, landmen and idlers, would still be below for these first proceedings. 'Our petty officers, Mr Lawes?'

'Sir.'

These men were the hard centre of his division, the ones in local charge of the seamen at masts, yards and guns. They would also be at his right hand when his division was tasked for special duty, whether the boarding of a prize or the cutting out of an enemy – and they would be looking directly to him for their lead.

'This is Mr Rawson, signal midshipman.' It was the previous day's coxswain of the ship's boat, Kydd remembered.

'And Mr Chamberlain, midshipman.' He was absurdly youthful, thought Kydd, observing his curls and slight build, yet he knew this boy had a status and duties that placed him well above the hardiest able seaman.

'Samuel Laffin, bo'sun's mate . . .' Dark-featured and oddly neat in his appearance, on his hat he wore a ribbon with '*Tenacious*' in gold lettering.

'Henry Soulter, quartermaster.' Kydd recognised a natural deep-sea mariner, and warmed to his softly spoken ways.

And there were others, whom he knew he should remember – petty officers of the fighting tops, quarter gunners, petty officer of the afterguard – and rarer birds, such as captain of the hold, yeoman of the powder room and the carpenter's mates. In all, he would have a fair proportioning of the five hundred-odd of *Tenacious*'s company, such that most of the skills of a man-o'-war would be at hand if Mr Kydd's division was called away as a unit.

Kydd stepped forward and braced himself to address them: they would be expecting some words to set the tone. 'Ye'll find that I play fair, but I expect the same from you all. You know I come fr'm before the mast, that's no secret, but chalk this in y'r log – I know the tricks, an' if I see any of 'em, I'll be down on ye like thunder.

'I like a taut ship. If y' see an Irish pennant, send a hand t' secure it. If the job's not finished b' end of watch, stay until it's done. And look after y'r men! If I see you warm 'n' dry on watch while a man has a wet shirt, I'll have ye exchange with him.'

He felt their eyes on him, and he knew what they were thinking: how would all this translate to action, or was it mere words? Would he leave it to them, the senior hands, to deal with things on the spot so long as the objective was achieved, to administer justice in the time-honoured ways of the sea? In effect, would their status be properly acknowledged?

'Y' have your lists?' Each petty officer would have the watch and station details of every man he was responsible for, and Lawes would have a master list. After today there would be no excuse for any seaman not to know where he should be in every circumstance foreseeable by experience and necessity.

'Mr Lawes, I shall inspect my division in one bell.'

The territory allotted for mustering Mr Kydd's division was the after end of the main deck. His men assembled in order, three rows on each side facing inboard, their ditty bags of clothing at their feet. There was controlled bedlam as watch and stations were explained, noted and learned, friendships discovered between those of like watch and part-of-ship, and new-rated petty officers got to grips with their duties.

Kydd paced quietly down the middle. He could leave it to Lawes to muster the men and report when ready while he eyed them surreptitiously.

A Royal Navy warship was divided into as many divisions as there were officers. In this way each man could claim the ear of his own officer for complaint, requests and someone to speak for him at a court-martial. It was a humane custom of the Navy, but it required that the officer was familiar with his men.

But the men had other allegiances. Apart from the specialist artisans, the idlers, the crew was divided into two watches for routine working of the ship – starboard and larboard watches. These would in turn be divided into parts-of-ship – the fo'c'sle, maintop, afterguard on the quarterdeck and so on. As officer-of-the-watch, Kydd would therefore be certain to meet his men in another guise.

If there was a break in routine, as when a ship came to her anchor or took in sail for a storm, each man had his own particular post of duty, his station. Whether this was up at the main yard fisting canvas, or veering anchor cable when 'hands for mooring ship' was piped, he had to close up at his station or risk the direst punishment.

Now, before *Tenacious* faced the open sea, was the time to establish that the ship's company was primed and ready for their duty.

'Sir, division ready f'r your inspection,' said Lawes cautiously. He was an older master's mate and Kydd suspected that his origins were also from before the mast.

They stepped forward together to the front row. The sailors looked ahead vaguely, but Kydd knew he was under close scrutiny. In the future he could be leading them into the hell of a boarding, the deadly tensions of a night attack in boats – or seeing them spreadeagled on a grating under the lash.

'You, sir, what's your name?' The grog-blotched skin, rheumy eyes and flaccid ditty bag were a giveaway.

'Isaac Hannaford, s' please yer, sir.'

'And?'

The man's eyes shifted uneasily. 'Can't rightly recolleck,' he finally answered.

'First o' starb'd, sir, afterguard,' Lawes said heavily.

'Let's see y'r clothing, then, Hannaford,' Kydd said. The ditty bag was upended to reveal a forlorn, unclean assortment. 'Mr Lawes, what's in this man's list?'

'Sir, shirts, two, stockings, four.' Hannaford was an old hand and knew the ropes – but he had sold his clothing for illicit grog.

'Come, now, Hannaford, you're an old haulbowlings. Can't you see, without kit, you're not going t' be much use to the barky?' There was no use waiting for an answer, and he rounded on Lawes. 'To see th' purser for slops, t' make up his list.' It would be stopped out of his pay; whether that would have any effect was doubtful. 'And each Sunday t' prove his kit to the petty officer of his watch.'

As Lawes scrawled in his notebook Kydd passed to the next man. 'Thorn, sir.' Kydd nodded and moved on.

He stopped at a fine-looking seaman, so tall that he stood stooped under the deckhead. 'Haven't I seen you afore now? Was it . . . *Bacchante*, the Med?'

''Twas, right enough, sir,' the man said, with a surprised smile. 'But you was master's mate then – no, I tell a lie, quartermaster as was. Saw yez step ashore in Venice, I remembers.' At Kydd's expression he hurried to add, 'An' it's William Poulden, waist, sir, second o' larb'd.'

Kydd decided he would see if he could get this good hand changed from the drudgery of being in the waist with the landmen to something more rewarding.

He stopped at a shy-looking youngster with a stye on one eye. 'What's y'r station for reefing at th' fore?'

'Ah – fore t' gallant sheets 'n' clewlines, sir,' the boy said, after some thinking.

'Hmmm.' This was a topman – he should have been quicker to respond. 'And mooring ship?'

'T' attend buoy an' fish tackle,' he said instantly. Kydd knew that the quick reply was a guess. No topman would be left on the fo'c'sle while taking in sail. 'Mr Lawes, this man c'n claim his tot only when he knows his stations. And he sees the doctor about his eye.'

The rest of his division seemed capable. He noted the odd character eyeing him warily – but he would see their quality soon enough when he stood his first watch.

A distant call sounded from forward, a single long note, the 'still'. The captain was beginning his rounds.

'Straighten up, then! Mr Lawes, see they toe the line properly, if you please.' The rows shuffled into line, to Kydd's eyes their alert and loose-limbed bearing infinitely preferable to the perfect rigidity of a line of soldiers.

He saw the captain approach, accompanied by the first lieutenant, looking under pressure, with the captain's clerk and Pringle. Kydd whipped off his hat and prepared for inspection, but the captain managed only a rapid glance, a nod at Kydd and a few words with Lawes before he passed to the gundeck below.

The officers assembled for sail drill had no indication of the captain's mind when he appeared from his cabin. His fixed expression could mean disappointment at the quality of the men he had seen earlier or satisfaction with the relative ease with which *Tenacious* had been manned.

In any event, now would be the time that reputations were won or lost, weakness and strengths revealed, not least of which would be that of the captain himself, as he reacted to the success or otherwise of the morning's evolutions.

Kydd felt the tension. His eyes met Renzi's and provoked a slow half-smile as both turned to face their captain.

'Loose and furl by mast and watch. I shall not want to exercise further today – but if we are not striking topmasts within the space of three days . . .'

Already at his station on the quarterdeck, Kydd watched the other officers move to the fo'c'sle, main deck and forward of the main mast.

'Larb'd watch o' the hands – *haaaands* to stations for making sail!'

Two hundred seamen raced to their stations, the fore, main and mizzen shrouds black with men heading for the tops; others ran to the pin rails at the ship's side and the massive square bitts at the base of each mast, around which hung a complex maze of ropes.

Along the deck men hurried to the belaying points for important lines running aloft, braces, halliards, sheets. Petty officers pushed and bullied the hapless landmen into their places, showing no mercy to the slow-witted. It all seemed so straightforward now, but Kydd recalled his first daunting experiences at tailing on to a rope, in the old 98-gun *Duke William* in these very waters.

When the muttering, cursing and murmuring had settled, the captain lifted his speaking trumpet. 'Foremast, loose all sail to a bowline.'

Adams, clearly tense and waiting for the start, instantly lifted his head and blared up, 'Lay aloft, royal yardmen! Lay aloft . . .'

'Belay that!' Houghton's face was red with anger, and the hard edge in his voice carried forward. 'Brace around, damn it, lay the yard first, you fool!'

Adams's command had been a mistake. Firmly anchored,

and with but one mast with sail abroad, there was no opportunity to use another mast, with sails backing, to balance the
forces. His order would have seen the ship move ahead and
strain at her moorings.

Crimson-faced, Adams stood down his men at the halliards, shifting them to the forebraces, and brought the yards
round, as he should have done before sending the men aloft
to set the sail.

Kydd knew his turn would come.

The exercise went on. At the foremast, sail cascaded down
at the volley of commands, to hang limply forward. Minutes
later, men returned to the yards, this time to furl the sail to
a seamanlike stow. Houghton said nothing, his furrowed brow
evidence of the direction of his thoughts.

'Mainmast, loose all sail to a bowline,' Houghton ordered.
He was staying with the larboard watch and moving along
the masts: Kydd, at the mizzen, would be facing his test so
much the earlier. Would his petty officers be reliable enough
on the job, up there on the mizzen top? There was no chance
that he himself would ever again be up there with them, to
see their work, intervene if needed, chase down laggards . . .
It took an effort of will to remain aloof and outside the real
action, merely to direct in general – but at the same time the
responsibility was his alone.

'Mizzen, loose all sail to a bowline!'

Kydd turned instantly.

'Lay aloft an' loose mizzen tops'l!'

No point in going through the orders in detail from the
deck, when the captain of the mizzen top was perfectly
capable of taking charge on the spot. Kydd wheeled around
and snapped, 'Let go brails and vangs – man the clew outhaul and out spanker!' The mizzen did not have a course

spread on the cro'jack to worry about, but it did have a mighty fore and aft sail, the spanker, and this with not only a lower boom but a substantial gaff that had to be bodily raised apeak.

'Get those men movin', the maudling old women!' he threw irritably at the petty officer of the afterguard in charge of the halliard crew on deck. This was no time to be cautious, here directly under the captain's eye.

The mizzen topsail yard was nearly hoisted. Kydd bit his lip, but the sail came tumbling down at just the right time. He had been right to trust the men in the top.

'Lay aloft – loose t' garns'l!' Men swarmed up the higher shrouds, while below the topsail was settled. With the sail hanging down limply as it was, Kydd had foreseen the need to haul out the foot forward, and used the old trick of untoggling the top bowlines from their bridles and shifting them to a buntline cringle.

He stole a quick glance at Houghton. The captain stood impassive, waiting.

The topgallant set, it was then just the mizzen royal – and the gaskets came off smartly at just the time the spanker gaff reached its final position. Kydd judged that there would be no need on this occasion for play with a jigger at the spanker outhaul, and simply waited for the motion to cease.

'Start the halliards b' a foot or two,' he warned the afterguard – they had unwisely belayed fully before the order.

Sheepishly they threw off the turns, but Kydd was startled by a blast of annoyance from the captain. 'What the devil are you about, Mr Kydd? Not yet finished?'

The sprightly sound of 'Roast Beef of Old England' on fife and drum echoed up from the main deck. The men had already taken their issue of grog and gone below for the high point of their noonday meal, leaving the deck to the officers and indispensables of the watch. As they returned to work, to part-of-ship for cleaning, Kydd thankfully answered the call and made his way to the wardroom.

The table was spread, wine was uncorked and splashing into glasses; expressions were easing after the morning's tensions. Laughter erupted at one end of the table and the fragrance of roast pork agreeably filled the air.

'Your good health, brother!' Renzi grinned at Kydd over his glass: he had done tolerably well at the main mast that morning, avoiding the captain's wrath at the last moment by quick-thinking at the braces.

'Thank ye – and yours, old friend,' Kydd replied. There was a lot to think about, not the least of which was his standing in this world, so utterly different from that of the seaman.

An insistent tinkling intruded into his thoughts. It was the second lieutenant, tapping his glass with a spoon. 'Gentlemen, may I have your attention?' He waited until the talk died. 'I don't have to tell you that we shall soon be rejoining the fleet, which means, of course, that we shall need to provision against some months at sea.'

He looked pointedly at Kydd. 'There are some who are victualled "bare Navy" but have nevertheless seen fit to accept the hospitality of this mess.' Mystified, Kydd turned to Adams, who merely raised his eyebrows. 'This is neither fair nor honourable. But be that as it may, in my humble post as mess caterer, I have calculated that we shall need to consider the sum of fifty pounds per annum as a minimum subscription.'

'Preposterous! That's more'n five poun' a head!' Bryant's glass trembled in mid-air. 'What do we get for that?'

Bampton heaved a theatrical sigh. 'The mess commensal wine by quarter cask is half a pint a day, captain to dinner once a month. We lay in the usual cheeses, barrel oysters, tea and raisins, other conveniences for the pantry, such as cloves, pickles, ginger and the like, and when we consider breakages in glasses and dishes . . .'

Kydd thought of the seaman's broadside mess, with its square wooden plates and pewter tankards, the men using their own knives. There was little that could be considered breakable, and even the petty officers carried few crockery items in their mess racks. He decided to lie low while discussions raged about the mess subscription. He himself was not pressed for money and he had taken the precaution of appointing an agent. The Caribbean prizes had long yielded their bounty, but Camperdown was promising not only a medal but gun money in surprising degree.

'That's settled, then.' Bampton made a pencil note and sat back. 'We agree to subscribe the sum of five guineas per head. The officers' wine store is near empty, and with the usual allowance I believe you shall find room for four dozen apiece – you will be laying in your own cabin stores, of course.

'Now, it is usual to empower the mess caterer to go ashore on the wardroom's behalf. I shall do so in Yarmouth, and will expect one guinea in advance from each officer.'

Chapter 3

Over the next few days the rumble and squeak of gun trucks was a never-ending background to shipboard life. Not content with exercising the company of *Tenacious* at ship drill, their captain had a quarter gunner and his four gun-crews in turn hard at work from dawn to dusk.

Houghton had been on a gun-deck in the long-drawn-out battle of the Glorious First of June. 'Different ships, different long-splices,' was the saying before the mast: some captains were particularly keen on appearances, others favoured the niceties of seamanship. With this one it was gunnery, Kydd had realised quickly.

Then the awaited sailing orders came. Within minutes Houghton had summoned his officers to his cabin. 'I have here the Admiralty's instructions – and I have to say, they are not what I was expecting.' Houghton lifted his eyes from the paper, enjoying the suspense. 'Indeed not. It would seem that their lordships believe that after Camperdown the North Sea Fleet may be safely reduced, and therefore we are to be sent to join the North American station.'

Excited talk broke out. 'Sir, if we should fit foreign, then . . .' The first lieutenant needed details. Not only did there have to be a wholesale hold-restowing but there would, no doubt, be official impositions, from carrying mails to chests of specie for a garrison, to prickly passengers and returning prisoners.

'Now where in Hades do we find real foul-weather gear in Sheerness?' Pringle muttered. 'Gets cold as charity in Halifax.'

'Quite,' agreed Houghton, 'but we shall touch at Falmouth for a convoy. If my memory serves, there is adequate chandlery servicing the Atlantic packets. I'd advise you all to wait and procure your cabin stores there.'

'You've been to Halifax, sir?'

'I have. But not since His Highness took up his post.'

'Sir?'

'His Royal Highness Prince Edward. Our only overseas possession to boast a prince of the blood. Quite turned society on its head, I've heard.' Houghton stood up. 'Gentlemen, may I remind you there is not a moment to be lost? The first lieutenant will provide a list of actions that will result, I trust, in our being under way for the Downs in two days.'

'*Haaaands* to unmoor ship! *Aaaall* the hands! All hands on deck!' Although expected, the order brought a rush of excitement at the first move in putting to sea for a voyage of who knew how long.

A smack poled away from the sides of the ship, the tender now released from its workaday fetching and carrying. Her crew waved up at the big two-decker flying the Blue Peter at the fore masthead. She was outward bound to foreign parts, to mysterious worlds across the oceans, while they remained at home.

Kydd stood easy on the fo'c'sle, waiting with his party to bring the anchors to final sea stowage. Decks below, in the fetid gloom, the capstans would be manned and the fearsome job of winning her anchors would be acted out. Thankfully, this was not his concern.

The soft green of the land held a tinge of melancholy: how long before he would see these shores again? What adventures lay waiting? Just a brief stop in Falmouth to pick up the convoy, then he might be looking on his native England for the last time – deaths by disease and accident far exceeded those from enemy action.

Kydd's thoughts were interrupted by a swirl of muttering from his men as they watched a fishing-boat putting out from the shore. Under every stitch of sail, and heeled to her gunwales, it was making directly for *Tenacious*. Kydd went to the deck-edge and saw it come to clumsily at the side-steps. A redcoat stood up, swaying, and started waving and shouting.

The man obviously wished to board, but the side-ropes were no longer rigged. Kydd could hear shouting as a number of sailors gathered at the ship's side. A rope was flung down, knocking the man to his knees. The fishermen fashioned a bowline on a bight and passed it under the man's arms and, to barely muffled laughter, he was hoisted spinning and kicking aboard *Tenacious*. His baggage followed quickly. This would be the long-expected junior marine officer, Kydd guessed, but when he looked next, both marine and baggage had disappeared.

He glanced up. The men aloft were at their place – the cast would be to larboard, and his men deployed accordingly. Bampton waited at the gangway, watching Kydd with disdain. But with a clear hawse and the tide not yet on the make, Kydd was confident he knew what to do.

Over the bow, the starboard cable curved down into the grey-brown sea, the anchor buoy bobbing jauntily seventy feet ahead. From the low hawse hole the twenty-two-inch cable gradually tautened, a heavy shuddering settling to a steady passing inboard.

Checking yet again that the cat and fish falls were led properly along the deck, Kydd watched the anchor buoy inching towards the ship until the buoy boat grappled it. The process grew slower the steeper the angle of cable, until at last it was up and down.

'Short stay,' he growled at a seaman, who whipped up a white flag. The quarterdeck at the other end of the ship now knew that the anchor was ready to be tripped from the seabed. It would be essential to loose sail the instant this happened, the ship under way and therefore under control immediately; otherwise she would simply drift with the wind.

All waited in a tense silence. Kydd looked over the fat beakhead. The cable had stopped passing in, and he could imagine the savage struggle taking place at the capstan.

Suddenly the cable resumed its movement and Kydd sensed the ship feel her freedom. 'She's a-trip,' he snapped. The man's arm came down. With anchor aweigh *Tenacious* was now no longer tethered to the land. She was at sea.

Houghton's voice sounded through the speaking trumpet. Sail dropped from yards and staysails jerked aloft. He was taking a chance that the remainder of the cable would be heaved in and the anchor duly catted by the powerful tackle before the ship got too much way on. Kydd looked over his shoulder down the deck; when he saw Houghton's challenging figure, he knew he must not fail.

The first ripple of water appeared about the stem at the same time as the inches-thick anchor ring broke surface.

'Stoppers!' roared Kydd. It was now a race to uncouple the anchor from the cable and heave it clear of the water before the wake of the ship established itself. 'Hook on!' He leaned over the side to see. Men were furiously passing the stoppers on the cable, which would then be ready for hauling in at the hawse. He wheeled round, and cannoned into the second lieutenant, winding him.

'Have a care, damn you, sir!' Bampton said venomously.

'Aye, sir.' Kydd burned; the officer had no right to be there in a difficult operation for which he had no responsibility. The situation was well in hand: on hearing the 'hook on' the quick-witted fo'c'sle party had, without orders, taken the strain and begun hauling vigorously on the big cat-fall. Kydd had seen Poulden's leadership in this and blessed his recommendation to have the seaman transferred from the waist.

The squealing of sheaves stopped as the anchor rose to the projecting cathead. 'Well there, the cat.' It had done its duty by hoisting the anchor out of the sea. He turned back to the side and called down: 'Pass th' ring-painter – get that stopper on fast!' The three and a half tons of forged black iron was now being buffeted by passing waves.

There was a problem with the stoppering, the ropes passed to restrain the great weight of the cable. A hundred pounds in every six feet, it was a slithering monster if it worked free. Another fo'c'sleman swung round the beakhead to help, but with the vessel now under way and a frothy bow-wave mounting, the situation was getting out of control.

'Poulden!' Kydd barked. 'Get down an' get the fish-tackle on.' The tall seaman dropped to the swaying anchor and, balancing on its arms like a circus acrobat, took the fish-tackle and applied it firmly below the inner fluke.

Kydd's early intervention enabled the anchor to be hauled

up sideways out of the race of water while the crossed turns at the cable were cleared away.

'Walk away with the fish, y' sluggards!' Kydd ordered, satisfied. He had been right: *Tenacious* was a sea-kindly ship, her regular heave on the open sea reminiscent of a large frigate, even if there was more of the decorum of the mature lady about her.

Kydd lingered on the fo'c'sle after the party had secured. The hypnotic lift and crunch of the bows was soothing and he closed his eyes for a moment in contentment – but when he opened them again he saw four seamen looking at him resentfully.

Straightening, he took off his hat, the sign that he was there but not on duty, and left; it was their fo'c'sle and the men off watch had every right to their relaxation. He no longer belonged there: he had left their world and entered a higher one, but in its place did he now have anything that could provide the warmth and companionship he had enjoyed before?

On the way back, as he passed the belfry, there was a sharp clang: seven bells of the forenoon watch. Until safely anchored once again there would always be, for every hour of the day or night, a full complement of hands taking care of the ship, keeping watch and ward over their little community in the endless wastes of ocean.

Kydd was due to go on duty with Mr Bampton as officer-of-the-watch and himself as second. He made his way to the quarterdeck, where the captain held conference with the first lieutenant. They paced along the weather side, deep in conversation, while Kydd waited respectfully on the leeward.

At ten minutes before the hour Bampton mounted the main companion to the deck. He was in comfortably faded sea rig, with the modest gold lace allowed a lieutenant bleached to silver. A few months at sea would have Kydd's brand-new blues in the same way. Kydd was at his post early, and he said peevishly, 'I thought to see you below, Mr Kydd.'

'Sir.' Kydd touched his hat.

'No matter. Pray keep station on me, and don't trouble to interrupt, if you please.' Bampton waited impatiently for the captain to notice him. 'Sir, to take the deck, if you please.' Kydd heard the captain's wishes passed – course and sail set, special orders.

'I have the ship, sir,' Bampton said formally, and thereby became commander *pro tem* of HMS *Tenacious*. His eyes flickered to Kydd, then he turned to the mate-of-the-watch. 'I'll take a pull at the lee fore-brace,' he said, 'and the same at the main.' He looked up, considering. 'Send a hand to secure that main t'gallant buntline – and I mean to have all fore 'n' aft sail sheeted home in a proper seamanlike manner, if you please.'

He turned on his heel and paced away down the deck. Kydd didn't know whether to follow or stay at attention. He compromised by taking a sudden interest in the slate of course details stowed in the binnacle. 'Nobbut a jib 'n' stays'l jack,' he overheard the quartermaster's low growl to his mate, and saw no reason to correct the observation.

It was a hard beat down Channel, a relentless westerly heading them and the brood of merchant shipping that was taking advantage of the company of a ship of force. They clawed their way tack by tack, driven by the need to make Falmouth and the convoy on time.

The wind strengthened, then fell and eased southerly, allowing a tired ship's company to shape course past the Eddystone, albeit in an endless succession of rain squalls.

The master put up the helm and bore away for Falmouth. As the yards came round and the wind and seas came in on the quarter – a pleasant lift and pirouette for him, a lurching trial for the landmen – Kydd looked ahead. He'd never been to Falmouth, the legendary harbour tucked away in the craggy granite coast of Cornwall. It would be the last stop in England before the vastness of the Atlantic Ocean.

The master stood hunched and still, raindrops whipping from his dark oilskins and plain black hat. This man held a repository of seamanship experiences and knowledge that even the longest-serving seaman aboard could not come close to: he could bring meaning and order into storm, calms, and the unseen perils of rock and shoal.

Kydd moved up and stood next to him. 'My first visit t' Falmouth, Mr Hambly,' he said. 'I'd be obliged should you tell me something of the place.'

The head turned slowly, eyes cool and appraising. 'Your first, Mr Kydd? I dare say it won't be y'r last while this war keeps on.' He resumed his gaze forward. 'A fine harbour, Falmouth, in the lee of the Lizard, and big enough for a fleet. At the beginning o' last year, you may recollect the great storm – 'twas then four hundred sail sheltered f'r three weeks in Falmouth without we lost one. Fine port, Mr Kydd.'

'Then why doesn't we have the Channel Fleet there instead of Plymouth?'

The master's expression cracked into a smile. 'Why, now, sir, that's a question can't concern an old shellback like me.'

'Th' hazards?'

'No hazards, sir, we have nine mile o' ten-fathom water inside, Carrick Roads, and no current more'n a knot or two . . .'

The coast firmed out of the clearing grey rain, a repelling

blue-black only now showing here and there a tinge of green. To larboard of them the great promontory of the Lizard thrust into the Channel. The hurrying seas had changed direction and were now heading in the same direction as *Tenacious*.

Hambly pointed to a jumble of broken coastline: 'The Manacles.' Kydd had heard of their reputation. 'An' here is where you'll find the great sea wrack and th' bloody sea dock,' Hambly added. 'Seaweed, in course.'

'The bottom?'

'Grey sand, mixed wi' bits o' shell and brown gravel, but as soon as y' finds barley beards or cornets, think t' turn up th' hands an' shorten sail.' When approaching a coast in fog or other murk the only indication of its proximity was a change in the appearance of what was brought up in the hollow base of the hand lead-line armed with tallow. To Kydd this was singular – these tiny sea mites had been born and died deep in the bosom of the sea. The first time they met the light of this world was when they were hauled up by a seaman, to convey the means of preserving the life of half a thousand souls. Held in thrall, Kydd stared over the grey seascape.

'And it's here you'll fin' the sea grampus – an' the baskin' shark, o' course. As big as y' longboat, he is, but as harmless as a sucking shrimp—'

'Mr Hambly,' Bampton cut in sharply from behind. 'Be so kind as to attend your duties – we're but a league from St Anthony's.'

'Aye aye, sir,' Hambly said calmly, and crossed to the binnacle in front of the wheel. He picked up the traverse board and deliberately matched the march of its pegs with the scrawled chalk of the slate log, then looked up at the impassive quartermaster. 'Very good, son,' he said, and resumed his vigil forward.

An occluding head of land opened to an indentation and the smaller sail accompanying them began to converge on the same place. 'St Anthony's,' Hambly murmured, as the headland, fringed with white, pulled back to reveal an opening in the lowering coastline no more than a mile wide. On the western side was the stark, squat, greyish-white of a broad castle turret. 'Pendennis, an' Falmouth lies beyond.'

He turned to the officer-of-the-watch. 'Tops'ls will suffice, sir.'

By this time the captain had appeared on deck, but he made no attempt to relieve the officer-of-the-watch.

'Bo'sun, all hands on deck, pipe hands to shorten sail.' Kydd wondered at Bampton's order: to his eyes there was no urgency – the watch on deck were quite capable of taking in the courses one by one.

The calls pealed out and men tumbled up from below to take in the big lower sails. 'Keep the men on deck, if you please,' Bampton ordered.

'You'll beware Black Rock,' Hambly warned Bampton. 'A pile o' broken rocks squatting athwart th' entrance, right in our course.' He pointed to a flurry of white around a mound of black right in the centre of the harbour entrance.

'Which side, Mr Hambly?' Bampton asked.

'The eastern, sir, deepest channel.'

'A point to starboard,' snapped Bampton. The quartermaster spoke quietly to the helmsman, who set the bowsprit pointing off to starboard of the gloomy black whaleback.

'Not as you'd say difficult,' Hambly said. 'You sees Black Rock at half-tide, and on th' overflow you c'n be sure there's three fathom over the bar within.'

A coastal brig, sailing at the same rate, converged on the eastern passage with *Tenacious*. Both vessels were before the wind; they drew closer. The smaller vessel seemed to ignore their presence.

The captain snatched up the speaking trumpet from its bracket. 'The brig ahoy, sheer off. Bear away, this instant!' A ship-of-the-line was far too ponderous to play games.

'He means to head us through,' Houghton exclaimed in disbelief. 'You villains! Bear off! You must give way to a King's ship, damn you!'

Houghton stalked forward, eyeing the menace of Black Rock ahead. 'Give him a gun, forrard!' he roared. A six-pounder on the fo'c'sle banged out. The gunsmoke was borne away in a body through the entrance, but the brig paid no heed, her main yard dipping and swaying closer and closer to their own lower rigging. 'We take the eastern channel, let that villain choose the west,' Houghton snapped. The brig's shallower draught would allow him the passage.

'Aye aye, sir. Lay Black Rock close to larb'd, and hold your course,' Bampton acknowledged.

Just two hundred yards from Black Rock the brig diverged to the other side of the danger. The seaweed-covered rocks were now in close detail. All eyes followed the rogue vessel still under full sail plunging past the hazard.

'Sir!' the helmsman called urgently. Unable to release the wheel he indicated vigorously with his head. With all attention on the brig they had not noticed two fishing smacks close-hauled under fore and aft sail, crossing their bows to leave harbour. They shot into view from behind St Anthony's Head to starboard. Seeing the brig they changed their minds and tried to go about, floundering in stays dead ahead.

Bampton's mouth opened – but closed again. The channel

was only a few hundred yards wide, with Black Rock to one side and the high headland of St Anthony to the other. It didn't take much imagination to see that, running downwind as they were, backing or dousing sail to stop their way was impossible – even if this was achieved *Tenacious* would probably slew helplessly round to cast up on shore. The smacks were doomed.

'Helm a-larb'd,' Hambly calmly told the man at the wheel. 'Keep with th' land a cable or so.'

'No. . .' Bampton hesitated. He could not utter the words of contradiction that would firmly sheet home to him responsibility for the next few minutes.

The master kept his eyes ahead, his face tranquil. *Tenacious*'s bows slowly paid off towards the rain-dark coast towering so near to starboard. Individual tumbling rock formations could be made out, seagulls perched on them watching the big ship curiously. The swash of their wake, the slat and creak of shipboard noises were loud in the silence.

They'd avoided the smacks, but another danger presented. Sprawled across their track was a new headland, with a round castle prominent on its heights, but Hambly kept his course.

'Should you—'

Hambly did not deign to notice Bampton.

Kydd saw the problem. If they could not come hard round their only other action to starboard was to head ignominiously into a creek just opening up. He held his breath, then felt the first puff of a playful easterly coming down the creek . . . Depth of water close to, local winds – the master had known!

The edge of their sails shivered and Hambly said, over his shoulder, 'We'll brace up, I believe.'

As they did so, Kydd saw that, without any movement at

the helm, the ship's bow swung safely away from the shore.

'Aye, the set of th' ebb,' Hambly said and, unexpectedly, smiled. HMS *Tenacious* found her course again and came to anchor in the spacious expanse of Carrick Roads and Falmouth.

Kydd hugged his boat-cloak around him as the officers' gig left the shelter of the ship's side, sails to a single reef. He pulled his hat tighter and smiled weakly at Renzi through spats of spray. A straggle of low buildings along the shore-line, Falmouth was a small town tucked away just inside the western headland, around from the ruined Pendennis Castle.

Inside the harbour, clusters of smaller ships were moored close before the town, but the majority of shipping, assembling for the convoy, crowded into Carrick Roads – a mass of merchant ships of all kinds and destinations, with boats under sail or oar criss-crossing the waters.

'Fish Strand,' Renzi told the coxswain, as they approached the town. The gig headed past the anchored vessels for the tiny quay. 'Return before dusk, if you please,' he ordered, and the two friends stepped ashore.

'If you should desire a restorative . . .' The First and Last on Market Street seemed to meet the bill – with a jolly tavern-keeper and roaring fire in the taproom to accompany their hot spiced rum.

'Fish Strand?' Kydd said, cupping his toddy.

'Indeed. Mr Pringle assures us that somewhere about here we'll find all we need to preserve the soul in the wilderness of Nova Scotia.' Renzi pulled a battered guinea from his pocket. 'And it seems that I should return with a proof suitable for a diminutive midshipman against Boreas's worst.'

Lieutenants did no watches in harbour: this was a duty for

master's mates and midshipmen. Kydd acknowledged that it was very satisfactory to be free to go ashore as the spirit moved, and he was privately relieved to be away from the atmosphere in the wardroom.

A grey-haired man of some quality entered the alehouse. He saw the two naval officers and inclined his head, then signalled to the pot-boy and came across. 'Good afternoon, gentlemen. Do I see officers of that fine two-decker in the roads?'

'You do, sir,' Renzi answered. 'Lieutenants Kydd and Renzi of His Majesty's Ship *Tenacious*, at your service.'

'Greaves, Lawrence Greaves. And your noble vessel is bound for North America?'

'She is.'

'Ah! Then you will be our guardian angel, our protector of this "trade", perhaps?' Greaves was clearly no stranger to sea passages – a 'trade' was the common maritime term for a convoy. 'May I sit with you?' he asked. 'My wife and I will be embarked on the *City of Sydney* for Halifax.' The pot-boy hovered. 'The same? Or would you prefer wine?' The grey was confined to his side-whiskers, and his eyes were genial. 'Your first visit?'

'It will be,' Kydd admitted, 'but I'll wager this is not *your* first, sir.'

'No indeed. I'm commissioner for lands in Halifax, as it happens, returning to my post.'

'Then, sir, it puzzles me t' know why you don't take the packet service – it's much the faster,' Kydd said, seeing a smart brigantine with the Blue Peter at her masthead through the tavern window.

'No mystery, my friend. My wife is no sailor and insists on the conveniences of a larger vessel, and for me, I much prefer the comforting presence of one of His Majesty's men-o'-war about me. Do you know much of these packets?'

'Not a great deal, sir, but that they do carry inviolable protections against the press,' said Renzi.

'Well, then, the post-office packet, small but fast, the mails of the kingdom are entrusted to these, and not only that but passengers and specie – bullion for treasury interchange. They risk tempest and privateers to make a fast passage, and I ask you to conceive of the value to a merchant of receiving his letter-of-credit by reply within fifteen weeks of consigning his petition to an Atlantic crossing.'

Kydd murmured an appreciation, but Greaves leaned forward. 'A nest of villains, sir! They carry the King's mails, but should they spy a prize, they will not scruple to attack at risk of their cargo – and worse! Even under the strictest post-office contract, they weigh down their vessel with private freight to their common advantage. And should this not be enough, it is commonly known that while the post office will recompense them for a loss at sea to an enemy, profit may just as readily be won from the insurances.'

A crack of gunfire drew their attention to the brigantine. Her Blue Peter was jerking down, with vigorous activity at her foredeck windlass. 'Ah, yes, she'll be in Halifax two weeks before us – if the privateers let her . . .'

Kydd put down his glass. 'Mr Greaves, have you any suggestions f'r preserving body 'n' soul in Halifax? We've heard it can be grievous cold at times.'

'Why, yes, but you'll be paying over the odds here, you'll find. Pray wait until Halifax and you will quickly acquire an embarrassment of stout gear. Shall we raise a glass to the success of our voyage?'

*   *   *

'Just curious,' Kydd said, as they strolled down the sea-smelling streets of Falmouth, the keening herring gulls raucous along the seafront, clouds of them swooping on the boats landing fresh-caught fish.

'Then if you must, here is one such.' With a pang, Kydd reflected that this was like the old days, when he and Renzi had been carefree sailors wandering together in sea-ports around the world.

Outside the shop a large signboard announced, 'The Falmouth Bazaar, Prop. James Philp: Stationer, Perfumer, Patent Medicines and Dealer in Fancy Goods to the Falmouth Packet Service.'

The interior was odorous with soaps and perfumery, an Aladdin's cave of massed fabrics, baubles and necessaries, the tawdry and the sublime; no passenger facing the prospect of more than a month at sea would lack for suggestions of what to include in their baggage.

The shopkeeper approached them. 'If I c'n be of service to you gennelmen?' he said, gripping his lapels.

'You have a fine range o' stock,' Kydd said, fingering a lace shift of unusual stoutness.

'We have indeed,' said the shopkeeper. 'And what, may I enquire, might interest you?'

Further into the store Kydd saw a couple looking curiously their way. 'What do y' have for the run t' Halifax?' he asked.

'Leather an' velvet reticules, purse-springs, clarionets o' superior tone, dissected maps, Pope Joan boards wi' genuine pearl fish, ivory walkin' stick with sword—'

'Aye, that will do,' said Kydd, ignoring the ingratiating tone. 'I'll think on it.'

The two left, then turned on to Killigrew Street where they came across Bampton. Kydd lifted his hat politely.

'Mr Kydd,' he responded archly. 'I admire your *sangfroid*.'

'Sir?'

'There is a convoy assembling to sail tolerably soon, and you see fit to linger ashore at your pleasure, when as signal lieutenant you know there is a convoy conference to conduct. You must be confident it will not sail this age.'

'Convoy conference?'

'Why, of course! A signal lieutenant, do you not read your standing orders?' His sniff of disdain incensed Kydd. 'Flagship of the escort, and the first lieutenant has not a staff for signals? I shouldn't wonder that at this moment he has the ship in a moil, looking for her signal lieutenant.'

Hardly a flagship, thought Kydd, as he left the first lieutenant's cabin. Just two men-o'-war: the ship-sloop *Trompeuse* and the six-pounder brig *Viper*, both near hidden by the increasing numbers of merchant ships assembling in Carrick Roads.

Bryant had not been searching for him. He seemed mildly surprised that the new signal lieutenant had cut short his run ashore to hurry back on board. Papers for the ship's masters had not yet been completed, and in any event Houghton had not yet indicated his wishes in the matter of the signal codes to be used in the convoy.

Loyally, Renzi had returned on board with Kydd, and joined his friend as he headed for the upper deck. 'Are we to panic, do you think?' he murmured.

'Not as who should say. But t' play the ignoramus does not sit well wi' me.'

'What are—'

'You'll see!'

*　　*　　*

78

With a bored look on his face, the duty master's mate was standing by the main shrouds with his telescope of office. He was clearly taken with the idea Kydd put to him. 'Bo'sun's mate! Desire midshipman Rawson to present himself on the quarterdeck.'

'Mr Rawson,' said Kydd, to the wary youth, 'your boat-handling, I'm sorry t' say, is not of the standard we expect aboard a sail-o'-the-line, and a flagship, at that.'

Rawson mumbled something, but Kydd clapped him on the shoulder. 'But don't ye worry, lad, today you an' I will go a-sailing together and you could learn something t' your advantage.'

Renzi looked at him curiously, but Kydd went on, 'An' then you shall show me what y' know of signals.'

For the rest of the forenoon Kydd took away the twenty-five-foot gig and a boat's crew, and in his turn Rawson discovered what it was to sail. Under Kydd's patient direction, and in the brisk winds of the roads, the lug foresail and mizzen were dipped and backed, brailed and reefed while Rawson found how to read a wind, to give best to a squall, and when to ship washstrakes.

While the boat plunged between the anchored mer-chantmen, Kydd hid his apprehension: before long he would have to stand alone on the quarterdeck taking command as a full officer-of-the-watch in a major warship.

The afternoon saw a changed Rawson, respectful, increas-ingly confident and ready to fall in with Kydd's wishes.

'We shall rig for signalling, if y' please.'

'Sir?'

'For exercise, hands to stations f'r signalling,' Kydd repeated firmly.

'Aye aye, sir,' Rawson said hastily. It took some time to

find the other signal midshipman and four seamen, and just as long to find the little table for the signal log.

'Are we ready?' Kydd checked on his signals crew – Rawson and three of the seamen at the flag-locker, and his own midshipman messenger with another.

'Sir.'

'Then we shall begin. Mr Rawson, please t' change places with y'r young friend, I want you on hand. Now, ye see *Trompeuse* lying there fine t' larboard. We're senior, and will want to have her responding to our motions. I've spoken with her commander, he is persuaded t' exercise his own signals crew, so we will play the admiral.'

The flag locker was set snugly across the taffrail, right at the after end of the raised poop-deck, handy for the mizzen peak signal halliards. The locker had dozens of neat miniature doors, each with a brightly painted image of a flag.

'Have you a list of these, b' chance?' Kydd asked casually.

Rawson brought over a dog-eared pocketbook. 'This belonged to the last signal l'tenant – he didn't survive Camperdown – and now it's yours.' It was a handwritten notebook of useful information gleaned from the *Fighting Instructions* and other sources.

'Sir, in the front here we have our flags. This is the code of Admiral Howe that we carry, and it's just numbers – 'ought to nine. We have some others, the "affirmative", the "preparative" an' that, but it's best you see 'em in action. All we do is look in this part of the signal book and we have codes for two hundred and sixty signals, spelled out by number.'

He glanced at Kydd doubtfully, and continued, 'So if we want to tell our ships "Break through the enemy line and engage 'em from the other side", then we look up in the headings, find the signal, and it's twenty-seven, which we hoist.'

'Seems clear enough — but what if we want t' tell them to stay about all together? How do we let 'em know when t' put the helm down?'

'Ah, that's easy. The order is hoisted up so all c'n see it. Then when they all say they're ready, we pull it down sharply, which is the signal. Or we can use the preparative flag if the admiral wants to give us time t' get ready.'

'But what if we want t' do something that doesn't have a code in the book? What do we then?'

Rawson scratched his head. 'Can't send it,' he admitted. So that was the reason, Kydd realised, for the many occasions he had known when his ship had laboriously come up within hail of a senior, and the two ships had rolled along together while angry communications took place by speaking trumpet.

He tried not to think of the impossibility of doing this in the smoke and violence of battle and took up the little signal book again. 'So, let's amuse *Trompeuse*. I see here I can order her to open fire on th' closest enemy — so let's be having it. I find the code here . . .'

'Er, begging your pardon, Mr Kydd, but we hoists *Trompeuse*'s pennant first so he knows the signal is for him, which we finds here.'

At the flag locker a yellow and blue pennant was taken, deftly toggled to the signal halliard, then sent soaring aloft. On another halliard the two-flag code was hoisted close up.

Kydd waited for a reaction. A red and white pennant jerked aloft from the brig. 'The answering pennant,' crowed Rawson. 'They see and will obey!'

Their own signal brought down, one made its way up the mast of the little ship. Rawson dived for the book.

'Nine-seven-one – "I have to report there has been undue mortality in my rats."' At Kydd's expression he explained gleefully: 'It's a sign means they could have fever aboard!'

The evening grog issue cut short their sport, and Kydd went below with the signal book. The system seemed rational enough but he could foresee problems. What if the wind was gusting *towards* them from a ship? It would set her flags end-on. And in any kind of battle, with its vast amount of powder-smoke, flags would be invisible.

'So signals is the life for you?' Adams said.

'Seems t' be all plain sailing to me. And is a mort better than chokin' on smoke in the gun-deck!'

Adams adjusted his cravat. It was an open secret that a certain landlady was bestowing her favours liberally, under certain expectations not unconnected with Adams's solitary visits ashore. 'Pray don't be too cocksure, dear chap,' he said, with feeling. 'A reputation can be destroyed by false bunting just as easily as putting a ship ashore.'

Kydd smiled, but closed the book. He felt reasonably secure in his knowledge of signals and, despite Bampton's acid words, surely there could not be much more to add that he needed to say to a crowd of merchant seamen. With the ship about to sail, it made sense to sup on the fat of the land while they could. 'Nicholas! I have a fancy to step ashore again, are you interested?

'Falmouth?' Renzi ruminated, hiding a smile. 'This is the Valubia of Virgil – you have probably overlooked that passage in *The Aeneid* describing Falmouth. Let me see: "*Est in recessu longo lo cus; insula portum. . .*" it goes, as I remember. You will recognise the Dryden too: "Where vale with sea doth join into its purer hands; 'twixt which, to ships commodious Port is shown—"'

'Sir!' It was a small midshipman at the door. 'The captain, sir, desires Mr Kydd to attend on him before he lands, should it be convenient.'

'The convoy instructions have arrived, Mr Kydd,' Houghton grunted. His clerk scratched away to one side, a sizeable pile of paper mounting beside him.

'Sir.'

'And the convoy will sail in two days.' Houghton looked up at him. 'I am senior officer and I will be calling a conference of ships' masters for tomorrow afternoon at two. You will attend, of course, and will probably wish to prepare. My clerk, when he's finished, will disclose to you my private signals and wishes in respect of the escorts.

'Mark my words, I mean to brook no insolence from the master of any merchant vessel, and I will have obedience. I want you to make this quite plain.'

'Aye aye, sir,' Kydd said, turning to go. 'And may I have a convoy signal list?'

Houghton started in annoyance. 'Of course not! Have you forgotten they are secret? The losing of just one such can lead our convoy into ambuscade, the loss of millions, disgrace to our flag. All are accounted for, sir, and are now under guard – I'm surprised you see fit to ask such a thing.'

It was a shock: first, the level of secrecy to which he was now privy, but second, that he had not given it much thought. Simple courage and seamanship were no longer the only things that would matter in the future.

Houghton grunted. 'Very well. You may study a signal list in the lobby while Mr Shepheard is working. Any notes you take will be kept by him also. That is all, Mr Kydd.'

*   *   *

83

His heart sank; the mass of detail about fleet signals was exhaustive. Once under way and at sea each ship would be an island, unreachable except for these signals. Kydd leafed through the orders for distinguishing signals and vanes, then the instructions on to the formation of the convoy; it would apparently be a multi-column square advancing over the ocean. The name of each ship was filled in and assigned a number, which turned out to be its column and row position, and the three escorts were positioned around them, *Tenacious*, with a tiny flag added to her name, in the van.

The bulk of the details however, was taken up with resolving problems before they occurred. He turned more pages in dismay. Even putting to sea in good order required special flags to be hung out from odd places about the ship. A red and white weft at the mizzen peak indicated that a ship wished to speak, probably for some urgent concern; a signal of 492 required the unfortunate ship concerned to hoist a yellow flag and steer straight for an enemy in a warlike manner, imitating the action of a warship.

It went on: Kydd's eyes glazed. He began to resent the implied assumption that a naval officer could do anything at a moment's notice, and tried not to think of what he had to face in less than a day. Was it possible to get to grips with so much in that time?

Marines at the landing pier clashed to present arms when Captain Houghton stepped out of the boat, and more lined the way along Arwenack Street to the Customs House where the conference was due to take place.

With their marine guard Kydd paced along stoically behind Houghton and his first lieutenant, lugging the padlocked bag of signal instructions and trying to ignore the curious glances of the townsfolk. At the Customs House, a big, square-looking stone building with a brace of captured French cannon at the entrance, they were met by a prosperous-looking individual wearing an old-fashioned tricorne hat. 'Cap'n Houghton? Raddles, Collector o' Customs. Welcome to Falmouth, an' your convoy gentlemen are a-waitin' within.' They passed inside along a musty-smelling passage. 'Been here before, sir?' Without waiting for an answer he went on, 'The long room is where they meets mostly.'

They entered a large room with barn-style beams and imposing, floor-length windows. It was noisy, as some hundreds of plainly dressed and weatherworn seamen were present. The babble died as they entered, and those standing in groups moved to take chairs.

Kydd followed Houghton up the aisle to the front, conscious of heads turning. There was a small lectern, a chalkboard and a table. Just three chairs, facing the hundreds seated, waited.

Houghton took the centre chair and Kydd the left. Bryant was on the right. The talking died away. The collector introduced the officers briefly with a bow and a gesture, then left.

The captain wasted no time. He stepped up to the lectern and fixed his glare on the audience. 'I am senior officer of the escorts. On this voyage you will have ships of force with you, and need fear nothing from the French, as long as you sail agreeable to the plan. Runners will not be tolerated unless arrangements are in hand. Do I make myself clear?'

Kydd knew that runners were individual ships that tired of the slower speeds of a convoy and struck out ahead alone. They were taking a chance and were on their own, but stood to gain a lot when theirs was the first cargo landed.

'We have a favourable wind and I intend to proceed tomorrow forenoon with the tide. If you have any objections to the sailing plan you may see me in *Tenacious* up to six hours before we weigh. Otherwise I will take it that you agree to its provisions and will abide by them.' He gripped the sides of the lectern. 'Have you any questions? No?' A restless stirring went through the meeting. Houghton relaxed his stance. 'Lieutenant Kydd here will present the sailing plan and explain the signals.' Kydd felt a moment of panic, but remembered to nod and smile under the scrutiny of so many eyes. He had a deep sense of responsibility that so many merchant seamen were putting their trust in the Navy.

'Then it is only left for me to wish you fair winds and a successful voyage. Good day, gentlemen.'

To Kydd's relief, Houghton and the first lieutenant strode together down the aisle and left. He had no wish for his performance to be seen by anyone from *Tenacious*. Aware of a rustle of expectation he moved to the lectern and stood before the sea of stony faces. 'L'tenant Kydd, signal lieutenant in *Tenacious*.'

His voice came out thin and unconvincing. 'I want t' talk to you about our convoy to Halifax an' Newfoundland,' he said, trying to toughen his tone. 'And especially the conduct o' your ships when given direction by th' escorts. My captain has particularly asked me to—'

'So what if we can't agree wi' your *direction*, young feller?' A hard-faced man towards the front had risen to his feet. 'The King's service knows aught o' what worries us, so why should we do *everythin'* you tell us? Eh?'

Kydd stuttered a weak reply.

Another master got up, more to the back, but his voice boomed out effortlessly. 'Tell us, Mr Lootenant Kydd, truly now, have ye ever crossed the Atlantic in a blow? Come on, son, don' be shy! When it's blowin' great guns 'n' muskets, squalls comin' marchin' in a-weather, lee gunnels under half th' time. Have ye?'

'Er, myself, I'm no stranger t' foul weather.'

'Good. Then you'll be able t' tell us how in Hades we c'n spy all your flags an' numbers in a fresh blow an' all!' The two captains sat down to a murmur of agreement.

In front of him were experienced seamen who had been to sea before he was born and whose sea wisdom cast his own into pale insignificance. Kydd saw that Bryant had returned, and was standing at the end of the hall, listening to him. 'Should ye not make out our signal, y' keep the answering pennant at the dip,' he went on hesitantly. He saw some leaning forward, straining to hear. 'If th' weather—'

Bryant marched up the aisle, grim-faced. Kydd yielded the lectern to him.

'I'm L'tenant Bryant, first o' the *Tenacious*,' he began, challenging them with his tone and glowering at them individually. 'L'tenant Kydd is my assistant.' He flashed a dispassionate glance at Kydd. 'Now we have a convoy to get under way afore noon tomorrow, so no more nonsense, if y' please. Any who wants to argue with a King's ship knows what to expect.'

He took a wad of instructions and held them up. 'As you all know, this is how we conduct our convoy. As usual I'll start at th' beginning, remembering all you've been told about keepin' this under lock 'n' key.

'Convoy assembles in Falmouth Roads, outside the harbour. Each ship t' rig their coloured vane to fly at the fore or main, accordin' to the instructions, not forgetting your number good and plain on each stern-quarter. Order o' sailing and first rendezvous, you should have by you, before we leave.'

Bryant leaned forward on the lectern. 'Now, here's a thing. My captain's a right Tartar, he is, a hard horse driver who's always on our necks. He's your senior officer now, so I advise you all t' spread what canvas you need to keep the convoy closed up an' all together.' He allowed that to sink in, then went on, 'Signal code for the convoy is in two parts, and provision is made . . .'

The presentation continued. Kydd stood awkwardly beside Bryant, resentful yet admiring of his easy competence.

Then the conference drew to a close and a line of merchant captains came forward to sign the register and take custody of their convoy instructions. They left to return to their ships; the Blue Peter would soon be at each masthead.

Kydd picked up his gear, avoiding Bryant's eye. He was startled to hear him give a quiet laugh. 'They falls out o' the line of sailin', you know what we do? Give 'em a shot in the guts! Sets 'em into a more co-operative frame of mind, it does.'

Bryant helped Kydd heap paper rubbish into the bag; this would later be burned. 'But the biggest threat we can use is to report 'em to Lloyds,' he continued. 'They show stubborn, we tell Lloyds, an' then they have to explain to their owners why their insurance premiums just doubled.' Before Kydd could say anything, Bryant had consulted his watch and stalked off.

Chapter 4

'God blast his eyes!' Houghton's fists were clenched and he shook with fury. 'I'll see this rogue roast in hell! Hoist his number on the lee fore halliard and give him another gun.'

The signal for 'lie to, and await orders before proceeding' still flew from *Tenacious*'s mizzen peak together with *Lady Ann*'s distinguishing number. It was inconceivable that the shabby timber ship could not understand the need to form up the convoy properly before their voyage began. She seemed intent on heading off into the general distance, vaguely bound for the west, despite the plain sight of so many other ships hove to with brailed-up canvas waiting for the remainder of the convoy to issue out from the inner anchorage.

Kydd marvelled at the sight in front of him: 148 ships, large and small, a vast mass of vessels filling the wide bay. Bustling between them were the two smaller escorts. The whole scene was an expression of economic strength – and vulnerability. If Britain could preserve this great stream of trade goods arriving and leaving the kingdom, her survival was assured. If not, the end of this cataclysmic war would not be far off.

At last *Lady Ann* slewed and hove to, but her actions had meant *Tenacious* had moved well out of station and had to heave round back to the assembly points. Her captain was fuming, his officers on edge, and the ship's company thoroughly bad-tempered.

The last of the joiners came through the harbour entrance, past Black Rock and into the open sea. 'Convoy will proceed,' roared Houghton, glaring at his signal lieutenant as though it was all his fault.

Kydd found the place in the signal book, and hastily shouted the hoist to those at the taffrail flag-locker. Flags were bent on, soaring up the halliards as the thump of their fo'c'sle gun drew attention to them.

'Have they acknowledged yet?' snapped Houghton.

Kydd had his telescope up, trying to locate *Trompeuse* and *Viper*, just two sail among so many.

'Well?'

Kydd saw the three gunboats of the port's standing force, which had been detached to see the convoy to sea and were temporarily under Houghton's command, but he could not spot the low, half-decked, two-masted craft.

'Good God! Do I have to—'

'*Viper* acknowledges, sir.' It was Bampton at the officer-of-the-watch's telescope.

'And *Trompeuse*,' Kydd added, finding the small ship-sloop. Then he spotted the vessel sliding into the line of sight from behind a bulky salt-carrier, a red and white pennant at her signal halliards. 'A gunboat answers, sir.'

Houghton took a deep breath. 'Then hoist and execute for pennant ships, damn your eyes!'

Rawson already had the signal bent on and swooping up the rigging where it fluttered gaily for several minutes then jerked down. One by one, from random places in the milling ships, trusted merchant vessels followed the lead of *Tenacious* and hoisted a yellow triangular flag above an unmistakable red-and-white square – the Halifax convoy.

First *Tenacious*, then the pennant ships marking leading positions in the convoy purposefully set their bowsprits to the open Atlantic, and a pattern formed after them. Ship after ship fell into column, jockeying with shortened sail into their order of sailing; men-o'-war chivvied and snapped at the heels of the laggardly, and the vast fleet headed away from the land. The gunboats returned to port.

Well before they had left the outer Falmouth Roads and laid the deadly Manacles to starboard, the signal for escorts to take station was made. *Tenacious* led the convoy, she and her consorts on the windward side of the mass of shipping – the best position to drop down quickly on any of their charges if they were attacked.

'*Viper* to leave the stragglers and come up to station,' Houghton ordered testily. 'Never know what's waiting for us out there.' The inevitable late starters would have to catch up as best they could. One lumbering merchantman was caught flat aback when avoiding another, and Kydd could see its helpless gyration through his glass as it gathered stern-way and turned in reverse in obedience to the last helm order.

A grey-white wall of drizzle approached silently. In the westerly wind the craggy loom of the peninsula to starboard was no threat. But when they reached its end, the notorious Lizard, they would leave its shelter and face whatever the Atlantic Ocean could bring.

'Damn!' Bampton cursed. The light rain had reached them

and was beginning a damp assault. While Houghton kept the deck no one dared go below, and all had to suffer coats heavy with wet and rivulets of cold water wriggling down their necks. The captain stood aggressively as the rain ran down his face. Kydd's crew shivered and clutched their coats but none dared ask to leave the deck.

Suddenly Houghton started. 'Who has the watch?'

'I, sir,' responded Bampton.

'I shall be in my cabin.' Houghton wheeled round and left. Other officers followed his example and went below, but Kydd knew he must stay so he moved down from the exposed poop-deck. Bampton called for his watch-coat and Kydd his oilskins, but then the rain ceased and the wind resumed a chill buffeting.

Kydd used his signals telescope to survey the slow-moving convoy. Once they made the open sea beyond the Lizard they would spread more sail for best speed, but if the stragglers could not make up the distance before they met the friendless ocean they would be in trouble.

In the main they were closing manfully, but a small gaggle were now miles astern locked together. Kydd shuddered with the cold and lowered the telescope. But something made him raise it again. The larger of the stopped vessels had one corner of her main course drawn up to the yard, a peculiar action at sea. He steadied the glass, leaning back with his elbow braced on his chest to see better. There was activity, but it was not co-ordinated.

Straining to make it out, he waited for a spasm of shivering to subside and concentrated on the other vessel. Something about her — she was not low in the water. 'Sir!' he said loudly. 'Seems the stragglers are being taken!'

'What?' said Bampton incredulously. He brought up his

big telescope. 'Are you mad? That's nothing but a parcel of lubberly merchantmen got in a tangle!'

'But the main course! It's up to—'

'What are you babbling about, Mr Kydd? She still flies her pennant. The other vessel has her vane a-fly – leave them to it, I say.'

'Sir, should we not send *Viper* down to 'em?'

'And put her to loo'ard and having to beat back just when we make the open sea? I'm surprised at your suggestion, Mr Kydd, and can only ascribe it to your, er, lack of experience in these waters.'

The captain appeared from the cabin spaces. 'Ah, Mr Bampton. All's well?'

'Yes sir.'

'Th' stragglers are bein' snapped up f'r prizes!' Kydd blurted out.

'What? Give me that,' said Houghton, taking Kydd's telescope.

'I'm sorry, sir – Mr Kydd's enthusiasm sometimes exceeds his experience and—'

'Why do you say that?' Houghton snapped at Kydd.

'Main course. It's goosewings now, but that would be so if they only had time to haul one clew up to the yard, not both, and if the lubbers hadn't yet loaded the signal guns or shipped aprons against the rain, they—'

Bampton broke in, 'What are you wittering about, Kydd? Those vessels have their numbers hoisted. They have not hauled down their colours or signalled distress – they're in a god-awful mess. I've seen it many times before, and so will you.'

Houghton's telescope steadied. '*Viper* and *Trompeuse* to close and investigate,' he bawled to the poop-deck.

He rounded on Bampton. 'Mr Kydd knows his signals –

"Haul up your main course and two guns to weather" is the signal for the approach of strange sail. They must have been caught napping by some damned privateer disguised as one of our ships, who knows our procedures and that our attention is all ahead.'

Trompeuse hurried back along the convoy, keeping to the windward edge. *Viper* angled off downwind.

The master came up to watch developments but remained silent.

'What *is* that idiot in *Viper* up to?' Bampton said.

Kydd had his own ideas about why the gun-brig had clapped on all sail away to the east, well to leeward of the action, but kept his silence.

Tysoe arrived with Kydd's oilskins and a warm jersey, which Kydd struggled into under his waterproofs.

'*Sail hoooo!*' The masthead lookout's hand was flung out to seaward. As the Lizard opened up to the westward a respectable-sized frigate under easy sail close inshore came into view.

'No colours,' growled Houghton, 'but we know what she's up to. Quarters, Mr Bampton.'

Then *Tenacious* heard the heart-stopping thunder of the drums in anger for the first time this voyage. Kydd's post in battle was at the signals; he had but to send for his sword and see to the lead-lined bag ready for sinking secret material should the need arise.

'She thinks t' fall on the convoy while the escorts are to loo'ard dealing with the brig – they wouldn't guess a ship o' force was waiting for 'em,' the master said. With grim satisfaction Kydd spared a glance astern.

The enemy must have seen events swing against them, for both the hapless goosewinged merchantman and the anonymous brig loosed sail hurriedly and swung about – but it was too late. The reason for *Viper*'s move had become clear. She was now squarely between the enemy and his escape.

'Spankin' good sailin'!' Kydd burst out. With *Trompeuse* now coming down fast from one direction and *Viper* well placed in the other, the end was not really in doubt.

The smoke of a challenging shot eddied up from *Viper*, the ball skipping past the enemy and her prize. The two came briefly together, probably to recover crew, before one broke out French colours and crammed on all sail to try to make off, leaving the other with ropes slashed and drifting help-lessly. So close to Falmouth there would be no trouble recov-ering the abandoned prize.

As the brig attempted to pass *Viper*, she made a perfect target for raking fire and *Viper* did not waste it. When the smoke of her broadside cleared, the brig had already struck her colours. Jubilation rang out on *Tenacious* from the deck below, and satisfied smiles were to be seen on the quarter-deck.

But as *Tenacious* thrust towards her, the frigate shied away and bore south-east, towards the distant French coast. When she had drawn away, and *Tenacious* stood down from quar-ters, Kydd saw that the convoy was now much closer together, and in impeccable formation.

As one, the argosy rounded the Lizard, taking Atlantic rollers on the bow in explosions of white, hauling their wind for the south-west, the wanly setting sun and the thousands of miles that lay ahead.

'Your health, Mr Kydd!' The surgeon leaned forward, as usual in his accustomed evening-wear of a worn green waistcoat. He had an odd, detached way of regarding people, part earnest, part sardonic.

'Thank ye, Mr Pybus,' Kydd answered, 'It's always a pleasure t' have a doctor wishing me good health.'

The wardroom was abuzz with chatter. Besides the charge of anticipation that a new voyage always brought, there was the tension of getting the convoy to sea – and their first brush with the enemy.

'Sharp of His Nibs to spot the wolf among the sheep,' said Pringle, helping himself to another cutlet.

Adams leaned across for the asparagus. 'Did hear that you helped him to a conclusion, Kydd?' he said, and when his eyes flicked towards the head of the table, Kydd guessed that the story of his *contretemps* with Bampton was now common knowledge.

'Always like t' help when I can,' he said cautiously. Bampton was talking with the purser, but Kydd occasionally caught his eyes straying to himself.

Louder, Adams went on, 'To the devil with modesty, old fellow, tell us, what put you on to him?'

'Er, his lee clew t' the course was—'

'Speak up, dear chap, we're working to wind'd!' To make her offing of Wolf's Rock in the night, the ship's taut rigging was causing the length of her hull to creak in noisy protest.

'I said, with only one clew to the yard an' the chance her guns were yet not primed, she'd be tryin' t' let us know she was in trouble and could not. If she had her vanes an' colours correct, seems to me she was surprised, and then th' boarders let all stand to make us think she was a vessel retirin' back to Falmouth.'

He grinned. 'But then I thought t' take a look at her draught – a brig, outward bound, an' sittin' high in th' water! Stands to reason—'

'You didn't tell me that!' Bampton's voice cut through the

talk, which quickly died away. 'If I'd known what you saw!'

It was on the tip of his tongue to remark that with his bigger telescope Bampton was better placed to see the same thing, but Kydd remained guarded. 'Ah, in fact, there was not really time enough t' tell it.'

Bampton held rigid.

The next morning the land was gone. There was just empty sea and the convoy. In loose columns, they bucketed through the long heaving swells from the west, substantial Hudson Bay traders with fine passenger cabins, hardy vessels headed for the Newfoundland cod fishery, slab-sided timber ships that would return with precious masts for the dockyards of the kingdom. And impoverished immigrants crammed among supplies for the settlements.

The night-time shortening of sail now became a resetting of plain sail to reach maximum speed of the slowest. A tedious schedule of hauling and loosing was necessary to adjust speeds; the leading-edge ships had to be reined in while slower ones, which had slipped to the back during the night, were bullied into lengthening their stride.

Routine was only re-established mid-morning when *Tenacious* was free to go to quarters for exercise of the great guns. After an hour or more of hard work the welcome sound of the tune 'Nancy Dawson' drifted up from the main-deck, announcing grog and dinner for the hands.

But first, on an open deck nearly deserted of seamen, the officers gathered on the quarterdeck for the noon-day sight. Every officer performed the duty, including the midshipmen, but only the 'workings' of the lieutenants were pooled for reliability.

This would be Kydd's first occasion as an officer, for

although since those years in the Caribbean he had known how, it was now that his contribution would be a valid element in the navigation of a King's ship.

He readied his octant, an old but fine brass and ebony instrument, by setting the expected latitude down to the tangent screw. This would shorten the time needed to do a fine adjustment in the precious seconds of a meridian altitude. Next, he took the precaution of finding his 'height-of-eye' on the quarterdeck. There was an appreciable correction to be made – from there the distance to the horizon of a ship-of-the-line was a full seven miles.

Cradling his instrument Kydd took his place, feeling the long swell come in fine on the bow in a heave down the length of the ship. He estimated it at no more than twelve feet, which meant another correction to height-of-eye. Then, like the others, he trialled the sun – close, but some minutes to go.

He was aware of the helmsman behind him, silently flicking the wheel to catch a wave, glancing up at the weather leech of a sail, then resuming his blank stare ahead. Kydd knew what he was thinking – the wielding of sextants, the consulting of mysterious figures in the almanac marked out an officer from a common seaman.

He lifted the octant again: the reflected lower edge of the sun was getting near the horizon. Kydd waited patiently, shifting the vernier with delicate twists of the tangent screw. Then it was time, the sun was at its highest altitude: reflected by the octant, its image kissed the line of the horizon.

'Stop,' he called, his voice mingling with the others. The time to a second was recorded by a master's mate: this was the exact instant of local noon along this line of longitude, the meridian. By the elevation of the sun above the earth, the distance along that line from the equator, the latitude, could be found, and where the two intersected would be the ship's position.

He lowered his instrument and, through habit, glanced into the binnacle: at noon on the meridian the sun was exactly due south so this was a good time to check the compass.

In the wardroom the table filled quickly with paper and books. Kydd jotted down his octant reading, returned the instrument to its case, and found his *Moore's Nautical Almanac*. In practised sequence he entered the tables, applied the corrections and neatly summarised his workings, his final latitude and longitude boldly there for all to see.

'Thank you, gentlemen,' the master said, collecting the workings. They agreed within a minute or so, but Kydd's was the closest of all to Hambly's own.

'Mr Kydd.' The captain was standing on the weather side of the quarterdeck.

'Aye, sir,' Kydd replied, moving quickly to him.

'As you must be aware,' he said gruffly, 'with four watch-keeping officers, having a second officer-of-the-watch forces them to watch on, watch off. The first lieutenant has asked that the ship's officers now move to single watches.'

'Sir.'

'Therefore you will oblige me by assuming your own watch,' he said drily. 'Should you feel unsure in *any* situation, you will call me at once. Do you understand?'

'Instantly, sir.'

'Carry on, please, Mr Kydd.'

The last dog-watch was nearly over when Kydd appeared by the wheel to take the next watch. In the early night-darkness the men stood about quietly, their faces eerily lit from beneath by the dim light of the binnacle lamp.

'Mr Bampton,' Kydd said in greeting.

The second lieutenant grunted, and turned to look at Kydd. 'Course sou'west b' south, courses are in to topsails one reef, last cast of the log five and a half knots.' He glanced once at the dark, near invisible sea, speckled prettily with golden pricks of lanthorn light where the convoy sailed on quietly through the night.

'Convoy still seems to be with us, carpenter reports nine inches in the well, we have two in the bilboes.' These unfortunates would spend all night in leg irons until hauled before the captain in the morning, but it was necessary to pass on the information. In the event that the ship was in danger of foundering they must be released.

'You have the ship, I'm going below. If you get into a pother, *don't* call me. Good night.'

It was done. A momentary rush of panic, then exultation. The man standing on the quarterdeck in command, around whom the world that was HMS *Tenacious* would revolve, was Thomas Paine Kydd.

A duty quartermaster held out the chalk log. The watch always started with a clean slate and Kydd took it, his notations of course and sail now holy writ to be transcribed later to the master's log. He heard the quartermaster murmur the heading to the new hand on the wheel, then saw him squint at the compass before returning to report, 'Sou'west b' south, Brown on the wheel, sir.' Much as Kydd himself had done not so very long ago.

The figures dispersed, leaving the new watch in possession of the deck. Kydd's midshipman messenger was behind him, and the mate-of-the-watch with his boatswain's mate stood to leeward, waiting for orders. The rest of the watch were at different positions around the deck under their station captains, for now Kydd, as an officer, could never treat with them directly.

Eight bells clanged forward. It was the first watch, and in accordance with practice, the ship went to evening quarters. Mess-decks were transformed as ditty bags were taken down, benches stowed below, mess-traps placed in racks and the hinged table removed. Once again the broad space reverted to its true purpose – a gun-deck with martial rows of heavy cannons.

At the guns, the fighting tops and in the waist of the ship, men stood ready. It was a time to muster them, to ensure they knew their place in combat intimately, and also it was an opportunity for the seamen to learn about those in authority over them. But this did not concern Kydd, who maintained his watch from on high over them all.

Quarters over, the men were released. Hammocks were piped down from their stowage in the nettings around the bulwarks and slung below. In the same hour the space passed from a dining room to a ship of war and then a dormitory. The ship changed from a busy working place to a darkened domain of slumber.

It was a clear night with the wind steady on the beam. Kydd stepped inside the cabin spaces to the lobby, where a small table bore a chart. It was now his duty to think of the bigger picture. A seaman before the mast simply accepted that a course was set to a compass heading. Beyond that, it was of no interest to someone who could have no say in his destiny, but who at the same time did not have to worry about it.

Kydd lowered the dim lanthorn so its soft golden light was enough to see their pencilled course pricked out. They were heading mainly south with the Canary current to avoid the strong trade westerlies, and to pick up later the countervailing seasonal north-easterlies in a swing across the width of the ocean.

Kydd stepped out on deck again. He had been in countless

night watches and been comforted by the nocturnal sounds: the slaps and dings of ropes against masts, sails occasionally cracking with a high-spirited flourish, the never-ceasing spreading groan and creak of timbers, the ghost-like susurrus of wind in the lines from aloft – all had been a soothing backdrop before. Now its character had changed. Any number of hazards might lie in wait to challenge his still untutored judgement, a started strake even now spurting black water into the depths of the hold, a wrung topgallant mast tumbling to sudden ruin, a sleepy merchant ship yawing across their bows . . .

'Lawes, prove the lookouts!' It sounded more urgent than he meant.

In response to his mate-of-the-watch's hail came answering cries of 'Aye aye!' from around the deck.

Kydd moved along the weather gangway, thumping on ropes. If they gave a satisfying hard thrum they were well taut, but a dead feel under his fist meant a job for the watch on deck. He returned by the lee gangway, looking up at the pale expanse of sail. They drew well, but there was no compelling need for speed, locked in as they were to the speed of the convoy. He had no wish to be known as a 'jib and staysail jack', always trimming yards and canvas to the annoyance of the night watch.

Back on the quarterdeck, the ship's easy motion was reassuring, the stolid presence of the helmsman and quartermaster companionable, and his tense wariness subsided.

The master-at-arms came aft from the main hatchway with a midshipman and corporal. 'All's well, sir, an' lights out below,' he reported.

'Very good. Carry on, please,' Kydd said, echoing the words of the countless officers-of-the-watch he had known. The master-at-arms touched his hat, leaving them to their solitude.

The accustomed tranquillity of a night watch began to settle – bringing a disengagement of mind from body, a pleasant feeling of consciousness being borne timelessly to reverie and memories.

Kydd pulled himself together. This was not the way an officer-of-the-watch should be, with all his responsibility. He turned and paced firmly to the mainmast and back, glaring about.

The night wore on. It was easy sailing: he could hear the monotone of one of the watch on deck forward spinning a yarn. There was a falsetto hoot and sudden laughter, but for him there would be no more companionable yarns in the anonymous darkness.

He spun on his heel and paced slowly back towards the binnacle, catching the flash of eyes in the dimness nearby as the quartermaster weighed the chances of a bored officer-of-the-watch picking fault with his helmsman. Reaching the binnacle Kydd glanced inside to the soft gold of the compass light. Their course was true. All along the decks, lines bowsed taut. What could go wrong?

His imagination replied with a multitude of possible emergencies. He forced them away and tried to remain calm, pacing slowly to one side of the deck. Low talk began around the wheel. It stopped when he approached again. Could they be discussing him? Years of his own time at the wheel told him that they were – and anything else that might pass the hours of a night watch.

Oddly comforted, he made play of going to the ship's side and inspecting the wake as if he was expecting something, but his senses suddenly pricked to full alertness – there were sounds that did not fit. He spun round. An indistinct group of men lurched into view from the main hatchway. Even in the semi-darkness he could see that two were supporting a third, slumped between them. Another followed behind.

He recognised the voice of the boatswain but not those of the other men, who were moaning and arguing. Kydd hurried to the light of the binnacle. 'Yes, Mr Pearce?' he snapped at the boatswain.

The moaning man was lowered to the deck in a sprawl. 'Fetch the corporal with a night-lanthorn,' Kydd snapped, 'and ask the doctor to—'

'Sir,' Pearce began heavily, 'Ord'nary Seaman Lamb, sir, taken in drink in th' orlop.'

'What's this, y' useless skulker? Think t' swill out o' sight, do you?' Kydd spat venomously.

The violence of his anger shocked him and he knew he had overreacted. He pulled himself together. 'What's y'r division?'

'L'tenant Adams, sir,' Lamb said thickly, touching his forelock in fear.

'Said it's his birthday, sir.'

The white face of the offender stared up at Kydd from the deck. Lamb struggled to stand but fell back.

Kydd could easily picture what had happened. With typical generosity his messmates had plied him with illicitly hoarded rum in celebration. He had staggered down to the orlop to sleep it off, then had the misfortune to encounter the boatswain on his rounds.

Kydd's sympathies swung to the lad. Life on the lower deck in the cold north Atlantic was not pleasant and seamen looked for any kind of release – generally rum.

But there was no real escape. A ship of war that might in minutes find itself yardarm to yardarm with an enemy was no place for a drunken hand at the guns. Kydd's duty was plain. 'Sleeps it off in irons, t' front the captain in the forenoon.' Houghton would have no mercy and tomorrow there would be pain and suffering at the gangway.

Kydd turned his back and paced away. He had no stomach for any scenes of pitiful begging but there were only muffled gasps and grunting as the young sailor was hauled away.

'Bring him forward.' Houghton stood rigid, his lips clamped to a thin line, his hands behind his back as Lamb was brought before the lectern.

'Take orf that hat!' growled the master-at-arms. The youth's thatch of hair ruffled in the wind that buffeted down over the half-deck. His open face was set and pale, but he carried himself with dignity.

On one side of the captain Kydd attended for the prosecution, on the other was Adams. 'Well?' snapped the captain, turning to Kydd.

'Sir, Ordinary Seaman Lamb. Last night at six bells o' the first watch the boatswain haled this man before me under suspicion o' drink.' Caught by the boatswain, prostrate with drink before the officer-of-the-watch, there was not the slightest chance of denial. But the grim ritual of the trial must be completed.

'And was he?'

Kydd's answer would be the boy's condemnation. 'He — he was incapable.' He had had as much chance of avoiding those words as Lamb had of escaping the lash.

'I see. Mr Adams?'

'Sir. This lad is young. It was his birthday and his shipmates plied him with grog in celebration but, sir, in his youth and inexperience he was unable to resist their cajolery. It's nothing but youth and warm spirits—'

'This is of no account! At sea there is no excusing a

man-o'-war's man being found beastly drunk at any hour, when paid by the King to hold himself in readiness to defend his country! Have you anything to add as witness to his character?'

'Er, Lamb is a willing hand. His ropework is admired by all in the maintop. And, er, he volunteered into *Tenacious* and is always forward in his duty . . .'

The captain glanced once at Adams, then fixed Lamb with a terrible stare. 'Have you anything to say for yourself, you rogue?'

Lamb shook his head and bit his lip. 'Then I find you guilty as charged. Two dozen!' Lamb went white. This was savage medicine, quite apart from the theoretical limit of a dozen strokes allowed a captain at sea.

'*Haaands* lay aft to witness punishment – *aaaall* the hands.' Boatswain's mates strode about above- and below-decks with their piercing silver calls, summoning witnesses to justice. As would be the way of it from now on, Kydd remained out of sight below in the wardroom, avoiding conversation until the word was passed down for the final ceremony.

'Officers t' muster!' squeaked a messenger at last. Solemnly, the officers left the wardroom and made their way up to the quarterdeck. There, the gratings were rigged, one lashed upright to the half-deck bulkhead and one to stand on. The ship's company were mustered ready, a space of open deck, then a sea of faces stretching forward. Kydd avoided their gaze, moving quickly up the ladder to the poop-deck.

The captain stalked forward to the poop-rail, much as Kydd had seen so many times before from the opposite side, looking up as a foremast hand. Now, with the other officers, he stood squarely behind him, seeing only the back of his head. Blackly, he saw that his view of proceedings was obscured by the break of the poop, and that therefore on all those occasions before, the officers must have seen nothing of the lashes and the agony.

Marines stood to attention at the rails, a drummer-boy at the ready. Lamb stood before his captain, flanked by the powerful figures of two boatswain's mates. A brief rattle of the drum brought a subdued quiet.

'Articles of War!' barked Houghton. His clerk passed them across. "'Article two: All persons in or belonging to His Majesty's ships or vessels of war, being guilty of drunkenness, uncleanness or other scandalous actions, in derogation of God's honour, shall incur such punishment . . . as the nature and degree of their offence shall deserve.'"

He closed the little book. 'Carry on, boatswain's mate.'

The prisoner was led over to the gratings and out of sight, but Kydd – flogged himself once – needed no prompting to know what was going on. Stripped and lashed up by the thumbs, Lamb would be in a whirl of fear and shame and, above all, desperately lonely. In minutes his universe would narrow to one of pounding, never-ending torment.

Kydd had seen floggings by the score since his own, but this one particularly affected him.

The drum thundered away, then stopped. Kydd's skin crawled in anticipation of that first, shocking impact. In the breathless quiet he heard the unmistakable hiss of the cat, then the vicious meaty smack and thud as the body was driven against the gratings. A muffled, choking sob was all that escaped – Lamb was going to take it like a man.

There was a further volleying of the drum; again the sudden quiet and the sound of the lash. There was no sound from Lamb. It went on and on. One part of Kydd's mind cried out – but another countered with cold reason: no-one had yet found a better system of punishment that was a powerful deterrent yet allowed the offender to return to work. Ashore it was far worse: prison and whipping at the cart's tail for a like offence – even children could face the gallows for little more.

The lashing went on.

The noon sight complete, the officers entered the wardroom for their meal. 'Your man took his two dozen well, Gervase,' Pringle said to Adams, as they sat down. He tasted his wine. 'Quite a tolerable claret.'

Adams helped himself to a biscuit. 'I wonder if Canada rides to hounds – 't would be most gratifying to have some decent sport awaiting our return from a cruise. They've quite fine horseflesh in Nova Scotia, I've heard.'

'Be satisfied by the society, old chap. Not often we get a chance at a royal court, if that's your bag.'

'Society? I spent all winter with my cousin at his pile in Wiltshire. Plenty of your county gentry, but perilously short of female company for my taste.'

Conversation ebbed and flowed around Kydd. As usual, he kept his silence, feeling unable to contribute, although Renzi had by degrees been drawn up the table and was now entertaining Bryant with a scandalous story about a visit to the London of bagnios and discreet villas. Pringle flashed Kydd a single veiled glance and went on to invite Bampton to recount a Barbados interlude, leaving him only the dry purser as dinner companion.

The afternoon stretched ahead. Kydd knew that Renzi had come to look forward to dispute metaphysics with the erudite chaplain and had not the heart to intervene. Having the first dog-watch, he took an early supper alone and snapped at Tysoe for lingering. Melancholy was never far away these days.

He went up on deck early, and approached the master. 'Good day to ye, Mr Hambly.'

'An' you too, sir.'

'Er, do you think this nor' easterly will stay by us?'

'It will, sir. These are the trades, o' course.' Hambly was polite but preoccupied.

'I've heard y' can get ice this time o' the year.'

The master hesitated. 'Sir, I have t' write up the reckonings.' He touched his hat to Kydd and left.

At four he relieved Bampton, who disappeared after a brief handover. Once more he took possession of the quarterdeck and the ship, and was left alone with his thoughts.

An hour later Renzi appeared. 'Just thought I'd take a constitutional before I turn in,' he said, 'if it does not inconvenience.' He sniffed the air. 'Kydd, dear fellow, have you ever considered the eternal paradox of free will? Your Oriental philosopher would have much to say, should he consider your tyrannous position at the pinnacle of lordship in our little world . . .'

Kydd's spirits rose. There had been little opportunity so far to renew their old friendship, and he valued the far-ranging talks that had livened many a watch in the past. 'Shall ye not have authority, and allow a false freedom to reign in bedlam?' he said, with a grin, falling into pace next to Renzi.

'Quite so, but Mr Peake advances an interesting notion concerning the co-existence of free will in the ruled that requires my disabusing the gentleman of his patently absurd views.' He stared out pensively to leeward.

Kydd stopped dead. Bitterness welled and took focus. Renzi stopped, concerned. 'What is it, brother? Are you—'

'Nothing!' Kydd growled, but did not resume his walk. 'May I—'

'Your ven'rable Peake is waiting – go and dispute with him if it gives you s' much pleasure!' Kydd said bitterly.

Renzi said softly, 'There is something that ails you. I should be honoured were you to lay it before me, my friend.'

It was not the time or place – but Kydd darted a glance around the quarterdeck. No one was watching. He looked across to the conn team at the wheel and caught the quarter-master's eye, then pointed with his telescope up the ladder to the poop-deck. The man nodded, and Kydd made his way with Renzi up on to the small deck, the furthest aft of all. It was not a popular place, dominated as it was by the big spanker boom ranging out from the mizzen mast and sometimes activity in the flag-lockers at the taffrail. They were alone.

Kydd stared out over the wake astern, a ragged white line dissolving to nothing in the distance, ever renewed by their steady motion and the noisy tumbling foam under their counter. His dark thoughts were full but refused to take solid form, and he hesitated. 'Nicholas. How c'n I say this? Here I stand, an officer. *A King's officer!* More'n I could dare t' dream of before. And it's – it's not as it should be . . .'

Renzi waited patiently, gazing astern.

Kydd continued weakly, 'Y' see, I don't *feel* an officer – it's as if I was playin' a role, dressin' up for the part like a common actor.' The frustrations boiled up and he gulped with emo-tion. 'I know th' seamanship, the orders an' things but – Nicholas, look at me! When the others talk t' each other, they're talkin' to the squire, the gentry – their father is lord o' the manor of some fine family, they talk of ridin' with the hounds, calling on the duke in London, what's the latest gossip . . .' His voice thickened. 'And me, what can I talk about at table without I open m' mouth and be damned a yokel?'

Renzi murmured encouragement. Paradoxically, this made it all the worse for Kydd, and his frustration took a new path. 'It's easy enough f'r you. You've been born into it,' he said bitterly, 'lived that way all y'r life. This is why you can talk y'r horses an' estates 'n' politics with the others. And have you thought how it is f'r me? I sit there sad as a gib cat, hearin' all this jabber and feelin' as out of it as—'

The carpenter interrupted them with his report and Kydd processed the information mechanically. Twenty-four inches in the well: if he left it, the night watch would have to deal with it, manning the big chain pump with all its creaking and banging, rendering sleep impossible for the watch below. He'd see to it before he left the deck.

Renzi spoke quietly: 'Tom, do you consider awhile. We all have had to learn the graces, the manners and ways of a gentleman. It's just that we've had much longer than you to learn. You see? You *will* learn in time, then—'

'Be damned!' Kydd choked. 'Do ye take me f'r a performing monkey? Learn more tricks and bring 'em out in company? Is this how to be a gentleman?'

Renzi's face set. 'You're being obnoxious, my friend,' he said softly.

'An' I'm gettin' sick o' your word-grubbin' ways! You're no frien' if all you can say is—'

Renzi turned on his heel. 'Nicholas! I – I didn't mean t' say . . .' Renzi stopped. Kydd's hand strayed to his friend's shoulder but there was no response: Renzi merely turned, folded his arms and looked coldly at him. 'I've been thinkin' a lot, Nicholas. About who I am, is the short of it.' He lifted his chin obstinately. 'Afore now I've been proud t' be a man-o'-war's man. Life f'r me has been simple an' true. Now I've gone aft it's all gone ahoo. I've lost m' bearings – an' all my friends.'

'Do I take it that you still wish to be an officer?'

Kydd looked away for long moments. 'Nicholas, you may account me proud or stubborn – but I will not be a tarpaulin to pity f'r his plain ways. An officer left t' one side when it comes to society an' promotion. Gentlemen officers laugh at the poor sot behind his back – gets a-fuddle wi' drink ashore 'cos he don't know what t' say. I'd rather be cream o' the shit than shit o' the cream, damn it.'

Renzi winced. 'You may regret turning your back on fortune.'

'Did I say I was? I just don't know, is all.'

Renzi coughed gently. 'Possibly I am in no small measure to blame in this, dear fellow, but still I feel there is only one logical course, and one you seem to have already rejected. For as long as it will take, you must apply your best and most sincere endeavours to fitting yourself out for a gentleman officer – in look, word and deed. Then, and only then, you may take your rightful place in society, my friend.'

At Kydd's moody silence Renzi insisted on an answer. 'I'll think on it,' was all he could achieve.

They were heading north to where the Labrador current from the icy fastness of the polar region met the unseen river of warm water driving up from the Caribbean, the Gulf Stream. Such a confluence was highly likely to result in the navigator's nightmare: fog.

Ahead there were several days of slow sailing across the mouth of the great St Lawrence before they made the shallower waters of the Grand Banks, then the doubling of Cape Race for St John's and landfall.

The Halifax-bound leaver division of the convoy had

parted, and now the convoy was mainly smaller ships, bringing out supplies for the important cod fishery, with some larger vessels who would touch at St John's before making south for the United States. Kydd knew them all by sight now, and it would be strange after a month and a half of ocean travelling when their familiar presence was no longer there.

With the wind dropping all the time, the seas lost their busy ruckling of the long, easy swell. There was hardly a gurgle or a splash from the ships' languorous sliding through the grey water. Quite different from the fetid heat and glassy calms of the doldrums, this was simply the removal of energy from the sea's motion.

A sudden cry came from the masthead lookout. '*Saaail hoooo!* Sail t' the nor'ard, standin' towards!'

A distinct stir of interest livened the decks. This was much too early for the sloops and gunboats of St John's they were to meet, and a single sail would be bold to challenge a ship-of-the-line.

'My duty to the captain, and I would be happy to see him on deck,' the officer-of-the-watch, Adams, told his messenger, but it was not necessary. Houghton strode on to the quarter-deck, grim-faced.

'You'd oblige me, Mr Kydd, should you go aloft and let me know what you see.'

Kydd accepted a telescope from Adams and swung up into the rigging, feeling every eye on him. His cocked hat fell to the deck as he went round the futtock shrouds – he would remember to go without it next time – and to the main top-mast top, joining the lookout who politely made room for him.

'Where away?' Kydd asked, controlling his panting. Breaking the even line of the horizon was a tiny smudge of paleness against the grey – right in their path. He brought up the telescope. It was difficult to control: even in the calm sea the slow roll at this height was sufficient to throw off the sighting. He wedged himself against the topgallant mast, feet braced against the cross-trees, then got his first good look at the pale pyramid of sail head on. His heart jumped. The glass wandered and the small image blurred across.

'What do you see?' Houghton bellowed from below.

Kydd swept the telescope to each side of the pyramid. Nothing. Tantalisingly he caught brief glimpses of it, now getting sharper and larger, but there was never enough time to fix on it. He prepared to lean over to hail the deck, then noticed wan sunlight shafting down close to it. He would give it one last try.

A glitter of light moved across the sea towards it. He raised his telescope – and saw it transformed. 'Deck *hooo*! An ice island!'

The whole incident had gone unnoticed by the convoy, for the height-of-eye of *Tenacious*'s lofty masts ensured she saw it well before any other, but all were able to take their fill of the majestic sight as they passed hours later. Up close, it was not all pure white: there were startling pale blues, greens and dirty blotches – and such a size! There was an awed silence along the decks as men came up to stare at the silent monster from the frozen north.

The wind died, leaving a lethargic swell and the ship creaking and groaning under a dull, pearly sky. While Houghton paced up and down in frustration, Kydd noticed one of the larger vessels of the convoy far to the leeward edge. As with all ships, her sails hung lifeless from her yards but for some reason she had none on her foremast, not even headsails. 'Odd,' he mused to the master. Then a signal jerked hastily aloft from her mizzen peak halliards. Without wind to spread the flags it was impossible to make out the message, but there was clearly activity on deck.

'Damn the fellow!' Houghton snapped. Virtually dead in the water, there was little *Tenacious* could do to investigate further.

'I thought so,' the master said, seeing the dead white of a fog-bank advancing stealthily in eddying wreaths that hugged the sea surface and eventually engulfed the ship in a blank whiteness. The muffled crump of two guns sounded from somewhere within the white barrier; in conjunction with the flags this was the agreed signal for distress.

Houghton stopped. All eyes turned towards him. They could not lie idle if there were souls in need of them.

'Away launch, if you please, Mr Pearce.' He paused to consider. 'A bo'sun's mate and ten men, and we'll have two carpenter's mates in with 'em – and pass the word for the surgeon.'

He looked about the deck and caught Kydd's eye. 'See what all the fuss is about, Mr Kydd. If the ship is at hazard of foundering and our men can save her, do so. Otherwise advise her master in the strongest terms that a King's ship is not to be troubled in this way.' Kydd knew perfectly well why he had been selected for this duty – as the most junior officer, he would be the least missed if he were lost in the fog.

As the yardarm stay tackles were hooked on to the boat Houghton added, 'Take an arms chest too, Mr Kydd.' Some of the ships carried convicts for the defensive works in St John's.

Kydd went to his cabin and found his sword, part of the uniform and authority of a naval officer when boarding a strange vessel. Tysoe helped fasten the cross strap and buckle on his scabbard sling. 'Nothing but a merchantman all ahoo.'

Kydd chuckled at the sight of his grave expression.

'Get a boat compass,' Kydd told Rawson, as he came back on deck. Seamen tumbled into the big launch, then helped sway down the arms chest; there was no point in shipping mast and sails in the flat calm.

Rawson returned with a small wooden box with a four-inch compass set in gimbals. Kydd had the bearing of the hapless vessel and checked that the indication with the boat compass was good. This was handed down, and he watched Rawson go aboard the launch, correctly wearing his mid-shipman's dirk. Kydd then went down the side, last to board.

'Take the tiller, if y' please,' Kydd told Rawson, taking his place in the stern-sheets. The surgeon sat patiently on the opposite side. 'Why, Mr Pybus, you haven't any medicines?' he said, seeing no bag or chest.

'Oh? You know what it is then I must treat? Wounds, in-flamed callibisters, one of a dozen poxes? I tried to persuade these brave fellows to load aboard my dispensary entire but. . .'

Houghton called down loudly from the ship's side: 'I'll thank you to lose no time, Mr Kydd!'

'Aye aye, sir,' Kydd threw back. 'Get moving!' he muttered to Rawson.

'Fend off forrard,' Rawson ordered. 'Out oars – give way, together.' Kydd gently wedged the compass into the bottom of the boat, careful to ensure there was no iron near. Their lives might depend on it.

The men stretched out. It was a good three miles to pull but conditions were ideal: not any kind of sea and the air was cool and dry – it might be different in the fogbank. Kydd saw that Thorn, the stroke oar, was pulling well, long and strong and leaning into it. He was a steady hand with a fine gift for ropework. Further forward was Poulden, who, Kydd vowed to himself, he would see as a petty officer in *Tenacious*.

Rawson stood with the tiller at his side, his eyes ahead. 'Mr Rawson,' Kydd said quietly, 'you haven't checked your back bearing this last quarter-mile.'

The youth flashed an enquiring glance astern at the diminishing bulk of *Tenacious*, and looked back puzzled.

Kydd continued mildly, 'If we're runnin' down a steady line o' bearing, then we should fin' that where we came from bears exactly astern. If it doesn't, then . . .' At the baffled response Kydd finished, 'Means that we're takin' a current from somewheres abeam. Then we have t' allow for it if we want to get back, cuffin.' He had been checking surreptitiously for this very reason.

The white blankness of the fogbank approached and suddenly they left a world with a horizon, a pale sun and scattered ships, and entered an impenetrably white one, where the sun's disc was no longer visible, its light wholly diffused and reduced to a weak twilight. Men's voices were muffled and a dank moisture lay on everything as a tiny beading of slippery droplets.

They pulled through the wreathing fog-smoke, Kydd making certain of their course – its reciprocal would lead them back to their ship. Paradoxically the heavy breathing of the men at the oars sounded both near yet far in the unpleasant atmosphere that was weighing heavy on his sleeves and coat and trickling down his neck from his hat.

'Sir?' Poulden cocked his head intently on one side. 'Sir! I c'n hear a boat!'

'Oars!' snapped Kydd. The men ceased pulling. 'Still! Absolute silence in the boat!' They lay quietly, rocking slightly. It was long minutes of waiting, with the cheerful gurgle and slap of water along the waterline an irritating intrusion. Men sat rigid, avoiding eyes, listening.

Then there *was* something. A distinct random thump, a bang of wood against wood and a barely synchronised squeaking, which could only be several oars in thole pins or rowlocks — and close.

It was probably innocent, but what boat would be abroad in these conditions without good reason? The sound faded, but just as Kydd was about to break the silence it started again somewhat fainter — but where? The swirling clammy white was a baffling sound trap, absorbing and reflecting, making guesses of direction impossible.

Kydd felt a stab of apprehension. 'Break out the arms — I'll take th' tiller. Quickly!' he hissed.

The wooden chest emptied quickly. Cutlasses were handed along with a metallic slither, one or two tomahawks, six boarding pistols. Kydd saw that they were ready flinted and prayed that the gunner's party had them loaded. He drew his sword. The fine-edged weapon, which had seemed so elegant, now felt flimsy and insubstantial beside the familiar broad grey steel of a cutlass.

He laid the naked blade across his knees and experimentally worked the tiller. Rawson fingered his dirk nervously, but the surgeon lolled back with a bored expression. He had no weapon and, in reply to Kydd's raised eyebrows, gave a cynical smile.

Waiting for the men to settle their blades safely along the side, Kydd held up his hands for quiet once more. In the breathless silence, a drip of water from oars, the rustle of waves and an occasional creak were deafening. Kydd concentrated with every nerve. Nothing.

He waited a little longer, automatically checking that their heading remained true, then ordered quietly, 'Oars, give way, together.' The men swung into it and the bluff-bowed launch got under way again.

In one heart-stopping instant a boat burst into view, headed directly for them. In the same moment Kydd registered that it was hostile, that it was a French chaloupe, and that it had a small swivel gun in its bow.

His instincts took over. 'Down!' he yelled, and pulled the tiller hard over. The swivel cracked loudly – Kydd heard two shrieks and felt the wind of a missile before the bow of the enemy boat thumped heavily into their own swinging forepart. French sailors, their faces distorted with hatred, took up their weapons and rose to their feet in a rush to board.

The launch swayed as the British responded, snarls and curses overlaid with challenging bellows as they reached for their own weapons in a tangle of oars and blood. Pistols banged, smoke hung in the still air. One Frenchman collapsed floppily, his face covered with blood and grey matter; another squealed and dropped his pistol as he folded over.

It was the worst form of sea warfare, boat against boat, nothing but rage and butchery until one side faltered.

An arm came out to grasp the French gunwale and pull it alongside. A tomahawk thudded across the fingers, which tumbled obscenely away. 'Get th' bastards!' Kydd roared, waving his sword towards the enemy.

The boats came together, oars splintering and gouging, enemy opponents within reach. The furious clash and bite of steel echoed in the fog. Kydd's sword faced a red-faced matelot flailing a curved North African weapon. The smash of the blade against his sword numbed Kydd's wrist, but the man triumphantly swept it up for a final blow, leaving his armpit exposed. Kydd's lighter steel flashed forward and sank into the soft body. The man dropped with an animal howl.

There was an enraged bellow and a large dark-jowled man shouldered his way into his place, a plain but heavy cutlass in his hand. His face was a rictus of hatred and his first lunge was a venomous stab straight to the eyes. Kydd parried, but the weight of the man's weapon told, and Kydd took a ringing blow to the side of the head.

The man drew back for another strike. He held his weapon expertly, leaving no opening for Kydd. The next blow came, smashing across, and Kydd's awkward defence did not stop a bruising hit above his hip. He felt cold fear – the next strike might be mortal.

As the man stepped on to the gunwale he cunningly swept a low straight-arm stab at Kydd's groin and, at his hasty defence, jerked the blade up for a lethal blow to Kydd's head. Kydd's sword flew up to meet it, an anvil-like ringing and brutish force resulting in the weapon's deflection – and a sudden lightness in his hand.

Kydd looked down. His sword had broken a couple of inches from the hilt. The man gave a roar of triumph and jumped into the launch. Kydd backed away, flinging the useless remnant at him. Jostled by another fighting pair the man stumbled before he could land his final stroke. Kydd cast about in desperation and saw a bloodied cutlass lying in the bottom of the boat.

He wrenched it up, in the process taking a stroke from the Frenchman aimed again at the head, but Kydd's blade was now a satisfying weight in his hand and he'd kept the blow from landing. Fury building, he swung to face his assailant. The man paused, taken aback by Kydd's intensity.

Kydd went on to the attack with the familiar weapon. He smashed aside the man's strikes, landing solid, clanging hits. In the confined space it could not last. As he thrust the broad blade straight for the belly, Kydd brought one foot forward to the other. The man's cautious defence was what he wanted.

As the man readied his own thrust, the spring in Kydd's heel enabled him to lunge forward inside the man's own blade, the cutlass drawing a savage line of blood on one side of his head.

The man recoiled, but met the side of the boat and fell against it. Mercilessly Kydd slashed out, his blade slithering along the top of his opponent's to end on the man's forearm. The Frenchman's cutlass fell as he clutched at his bloody wound.

'*Je me rends!*' he shouted hoarsely. Kydd's blade hovered at the man's throat, death an instant away. Then he lowered it.

'Down!' he snarled, gesturing. 'Lie down!' The man obeyed. The blood mist cleared from Kydd's brain and he snatched a glance around him. As quickly as it had started the brutal fight was ending. In the launch the three or four Frenchmen who had boarded were dead or giving up, and the bulk of the British were in the chaloupe, forcing back the remainder. The end was not far away.

'Tell 'em t' lie down!' he yelled. 'Don't let the bastards move an inch!'

High-pitched shouts came from the French boat; they were yielding. Kydd felt reason slowly return to cool his passions. He took a deep breath. 'Secure the boats t'gether,' he ordered, the bloodstained cutlass still in his hands.

His body trembled and he had an overpowering urge to rest, but the men looked to him for orders. He forced his mind to work. 'Poulden, into th' Frogs' boat and load the swivel.' The petty-officer gunner was nowhere to be seen — he'd probably not survived.

While Poulden clambered over the thwarts and found powder and shot, Kydd looked around. There was blood everywhere, but he was experienced enough in combat to know that just a pint looked mortal. The wounded men were being laid together in the widest part of the launch as Pybus climbed back in. When he caught Kydd's eyes on him, he defiantly handed over a tomahawk – bloodied, Kydd noted.

At Poulden's call, the French were herded weaponless back into their chaloupe and the swivel brought round inside to menace the boat point-blank. 'Hey, you, Mongseer!' Kydd's exasperated shout was lost on the sullen men in the boat. He turned to his own boat. 'Any o' you men speak French?'

The baffled silence meant he would have to lose dignity in pantomime, but then he turned to the midshipman. 'Rawson! Tell 'em they'll be hove overside if they make any kind o' false move.' Let him make a fool of himself.

Kydd realised he was still clutching his cutlass, and laid it down, sitting again at the tiller. His hip throbbed and his head gave intermittent blinding stabs of pain; it was time to return to *Tenacious* and blessed rest. He would secure the Frenchy with a short towline; they could then row themselves close behind under the muzzle of the swivel. He would send another three men to stand by Poulden.

Pybus was busy with the men in the bottom of the boat. 'So, we go home,' Kydd said, searching around for the compass. 'Now do ye remember what course . . .'

Ashen-faced, Rawson held out a splintered box and the ruins of a compass card. With an icy heart Kydd saw that their future was damned. The wall of dull white fog pressed dense and featureless wherever he looked, no hazy disc of sun, no more than a ripple to betray wave direction. All sense of direction had been lost in the fight and there was now not a single navigation indicator of even the most elementary form to ensure they did not lose themselves in the vast wastes of the Atlantic or end a broken wreck on the cold, lonely Newfoundland cliffs.

Kydd saw the hostility in the expressions of his men: they knew the chances of choosing the one and only safe course. He turned to Rawson. 'Get aboard an' find the Frenchy's compass,' he said savagely.

The midshipman pulled the boats together and clambered into the chaloupe. In the sternsheets the man Kydd had bested held up the compass. Rawson raised his hand in acknowledgement, and made his way aft. Then, staring over the distance at Kydd with a terrible intensity, the Frenchman deliberately dropped the compass box into the water just before Rawson reached him.

Disbelieving gasps were followed by roars of fury, and the launch rocked as men scrambled to their feet in rage. 'We'll scrag the fucker! Get 'im!' Poulden fingered the swivel nervously: if they boarded he would no longer have a clear field of fire.

'Stand down, y' mewling lubbers!' Kydd roared. 'Poulden! No one allowed t' board the Frenchy.' He spotted Soulter, the quartermaster, sitting on the small transverse windlass forward. 'Soulter, that's your division forrard,' he said loudly, encompassing half the men with a wave. 'You're responsible t' me they're in good fightin' order, not bitchin' like a parcel of old women.'

'Sir?' The dark-featured Laffin levered himself above the level of the thwarts from the bottom boards where he had been treated for a neck wound.

'Thank 'ee, Laffin,' Kydd said, trying to hide his gratitude. If it came to an ugly situation the boatswain's mate would prove invaluable.

'We'll square away now, I believe. All useless lumber over

the side, wounded t' Mr Pybus.' Smashed oars, splintered gratings and other bits splashed into the water.

'Dead men, sir?' There was a tremor in Rawson's voice.

Kydd's face went tight. 'We're still at quarters. They go over.' If they met another hostile boat, corpses would impede the struggle.

After a pause, the first man slithered over the side in a dull splash. His still body drifted silently away. It was the British way in the heat of battle: the French always kept the bodies aboard in the ballast shingle. Another followed; the floating corpse stayed with them and did not help Kydd to concentrate on a way out of their danger. The fog swirled pitilessly around them.

'Is there any been on th' Grand Banks before?' Kydd called, keeping his desperation hidden.

There was a sullen stirring in the boat and mutterings about an officer's helplessness in a situation, but one man rose. 'I bin in the cod fishery once,' he said defensively. Kydd noted the absence of 'sir'.

'Report, if y' please.' The man scrambled over the thwarts. 'This fog. How long does it last?'

The man shrugged. 'Hours, days – weeks mebbe.' No use, then, in waiting it out. 'Gets a bit less after dark, but don't yez count on it,' he added.

'What depth o' water have we got hereabouts?' It might be possible to cobble together a hand lead for sounding, or to get information on the sea-bed. He vaguely remembered seeing on the chart that grey sand with black flecks turned more brown with white pebbles closer to the Newfoundland coast.

'Ah, depends where we is – fifty, hunnerd fathoms, who knows?'

There was nowhere near that amount of line to be found in the boat. Kydd could feel the situation closing in on him. 'Er, do you ever get t' see th' sun?'

'No. Never do – like this all th' time.' The man leaned back, regarding Kydd dispassionately. It was not his problem. 'Y' c'n see the moon sometimes in th' night,' he offered cynically.

The moon was never used for navigation, to Kydd's knowledge, and in any case he had no tables. There was no avoiding the stark fact that they were lost. There were now only two choices left: to drift and wait, or stake all on rowing in a random direction. The penalty on either was a cold and lengthy death.

'We got oars, we get out o' this,' muttered one sailor to stroke oar. There were sufficient undamaged oars to row four a side, more than needed; but the comment crystallised Kydd's thinking.

'Hold y'r gabble,' Kydd snapped. 'We wait.' He wasn't prepared to explain his reasons, but at the very least waiting would buy time.

The fog took on a dimmer cast: dusk must be drawing in. Now they had no option but to wait out the night. Danger would come when the cold worked with the damp of the fog and it became unendurable simply to sit there.

In the chaloupe the French sat tensely, exchanging staccato bursts of jabber – were they plotting to rise in the night? And now in the launch his men were talking among themselves, low and urgent.

He could order silence but as the dark set in it would be unenforceable. And it might cross their minds to wait until it was fully dark, then fall upon Kydd and the others, claiming they had been killed in the fight. The choices available to

125

Kydd were narrowing to nothing. He gripped the tiller, his glare challenging others.

For some reason the weight of his pocket watch took his notice. He'd bought it in Falmouth, taken by the watchmaker's claims of accuracy, which had been largely confirmed by the voyage so far. He took it out, squinting in the fading dusk light. Nearly seven by last local noon. As he put it back he saw derisive looks, openly mocking now.

Night was stealing in – the fog diffused all light and dimmed it, accelerating the transition, and soon they sat in rapidly increasing darkness.

'All's well!' Laffin hailed loyally.

'Poulden?' Kydd called.

'Sir.' The man was fast becoming indistinct in the dimness.

As if to pour on the irony the dull silver glow of a half-moon became distinguishable as the fog thinned a little upward towards the night sky. If only . . .

Then two facts edged from his unconscious meshed together in one tenuous idea, so fragile he was almost afraid to pursue it. But it was a chance. Feverishly he reviewed his reasoning – yes, it might be possible. 'Rawson,' he hissed. 'Listen to this. See if you c'n see a fault in m' reckoning.'

There was discussion of southing, meridians and 'the day of her age' and even some awkward arithmetic – but the lost seamen heard voices grow animated with hope. Finally Kydd stood exultant. 'Out oars! We're on our way back, lads.'

They broke free of the fogbank to find the convoy still becalmed, and away over the moonlit sea the silhouette of a 64-gun ship-of-the-line that could only be *Tenacious*.

A mystified officer-of-the-watch saw two man-o'-war boats

hook on as the missing Kydd came aboard. At the noise, the captain came out on deck. 'God bless my soul!' Houghton said, taking in Kydd's wounds and empty sword scabbard.

'Brush with th' enemy, sir,' Kydd said, as calmly as he could. 'Compass knocked t' flinders, had to find some other way back.'

'In fog, and at night? I'd be interested to learn what you did, Mr Kydd.'

'Caused us quite some puzzling, sir, but I'll stake m' life that Mr Rawson here would be very pleased to explain th' reasoning.'

Rawson started, then said smugly, 'Oh, well, sir, we all knows that f'r any given line o' longitude – the meridian, I mean – the moon will cross just forty-nine minutes after the sun does, and falls back this time for every day. After that it's easy.'

'Get on with it, then.'

'Well, sir, we can find the moon's southing on any day by taking the day of her age since new, and multiplying this by that forty-nine. If we then divide by sixty we get our answer – the time in hours an' minutes after noon when she's dead in the south, which for us was close t' eight o' clock. Then we just picked up our course again near enough and—'

Houghton grunted. 'It's as well Mr Kydd had such a fine navigator with him. You shall take one of my best clarets to the midshipmen's berth.' Unexpectedly, the captain smiled. 'While Mr Kydd entertains me in my cabin with his account of this *rencontre*.'

Chapter 5

The Newfoundland convoy was now safely handed over off St John's, along with *Viper* and *Trompeuse*, the ship signalling distress in the fog missing, presumed lost. *Tenacious* hauled her wind to sail south alone to land her French prisoners and join the fleet of the North American station in Halifax.

As they approached there was a marked drop in temperature; chunks of broken ice were riding the deep Atlantic green of the sea and there was a bitter edge to the wind. Thick watch-coats, able to preserve an inner retreat of warmth in the raw blasts of an English winter, seemed insubstantial.

Landfall was made on a low, dark land. It soon resolved to a vast black carpeting of forest, barely relieved by stretches of grey rock and blotches of brown, a hard, cold aspect. Kydd had studied the charts and knew the offshore dangers of the heavily indented rock-bound coast flanking the entrance to Halifax.

'I'm advising a pilot, sir,' the master said to the captain.

'But have you not sailed here before?' Houghton's voice

was muffled by his grego hood, but his impatience was plain: a pilot would incur costs and possibly delay.

Hambly stood firm. 'I have, enough times t' make me very respectful. May I bring to mind, sir, that it's less'n six months past we lost *Tribune*, thirty-four, within sight o' Halifax – terrible night, only a dozen or so saved of three hundred souls . . .'

While *Tenacious* lay to off Chebucto Head, waiting for her pilot, Kydd took in the prospect of land after so many weeks at sea. The shore, a barren, bleached, grey-white granite, sombre under the sunless sky, appeared anything but welcoming. Further into the broad opening there was a complexity of islands, and then, no doubt, Halifax itself.

The pilot boarded and looked around curiously. 'Admiral's in Bermuda still,' he said, in a pleasant colonial drawl. 'Newfy convoy arrived and he not here, he'll be in a right taking.'

Houghton drew himself up. 'Follow the motions of the pilot,' he instructed the quartermaster of the conn.

With a south-easterly fair for entry, HMS *Tenacious* passed into a broad entrance channel and the pilot took time to point out the sights. 'Chebucto Head – the whole place was called Chebucto in the old days.' The ship gathered way. 'Over yonder,' he indicated a hill beyond the foreshore, 'that's what we're callin' Camperdown Hill, after your mighty victory. Right handy for taking a line of bearing from here straight into town.'

Running down the bearing, he drew their attention to the graveyard of *Tribune*. Up on rising ground they saw the raw newness of a massive fortification. 'York Redoubt – and over to starb'd we have Mr McNab's Island, where the ladies love t' picnic in summer.'

The passage narrowed and they passed a curious spit of

land, then emerged beyond the island to a fine harbour several miles long and as big as Falmouth. Kydd saw that, as there, a southerly wind would be foul for putting to sea, but at more than half a mile wide and with an ebb tide it would not be insuperable.

Tenacious rounded to at the inner end of the town, there to join scores of other ships. Her anchors plummeted into the sea, formally marking the end of her voyage.

'Gentlemen,' Houghton began, 'be apprised that this is the demesne of Prince Edward, of the Blood Royal. I go now to pay my respects to His Royal Highness. I desire you hold yourselves ready, and when the time comes, I expect my officers to comport themselves with all the grace and civility to be expected of a King's officer in attendance on the civil power.'

The wardroom took the orders with relish. Every port had its duties of paying and returning calls; some were more onerous than others, with entertainments that varied from worthy to spirited, but this promised to be above the usual expectation.

For Kydd it would be high society as he had never dreamed of. Receptions, royal dinners, lofty conversations. All grand and unforgettable. But would he be able to carry it through like a true gentleman? Just how could *he* strut around as though born to it? It was daunting – impossible.

Soon the wardroom and spaces outside became a beehive of activity with servants blacking shoes, boning sword scabbards, polishing decorations, and distracted officers finding deficiencies in their ceremonials. The ship, however, lay claim to attention first: dockyard stores brought from England were hoisted aboard lighters and taken in charge, and a detachment of the 7th Royal Fusiliers came aboard to escort the regimental pay-chest ashore.

Fore and aft, *Tenacious* was thoroughly cleaned down, then put in prime order: the cable tiers were lime whitewashed, brickdust and rags were taken to the brasswork, and cannon were blackened to a gloss with a mixture of lamp-black, beeswax and turpentine. Bryant took a boat away and pulled slowly round the ship, bawling up instructions that had the yards squared across exactly, one above the other.

Then the first invitations came. The captain disappeared quickly, and Pringle, who had old friends in Halifax, vanished as soon as he was decently able, accompanied by Lieutenant Best. The others prepared to find their own way ashore.

'Spit it out, man!' Adams demanded. The note handed in by a messenger was addressed to Renzi, who gravely announced to the wardroom that it seemed both himself and Lieutenant Kydd were invited to the home of the commissioner for lands, Mr Lawrence Greaves.

'Ah, as this eminent gentleman no doubt wishes to honour *Tenacious* in the proper form,' said Adams smoothly, 'it would be seemly, therefore, that a more senior officer be present. As it happens, gentlemen, I shall be at leisure . . .'

The boat landed them next to the careening wharf where a carriage waited. The stone steps of the landing-place were reasonably dry, but when they moved forward the hems of their boat-cloaks brushed the snow-mush.

On leaving the dockyard area they turned north, away from the town, and had their first glimpses of a new land. Kydd marvelled at the rugged appeal of the snow-patched raw slopes, the countless spruce and jack-pine – and the silence.

At their destination a gravel track led to a mansion, and

as they drew up their Falmouth acquaintance came to the door. 'This is most kind in you,' Renzi said, with a bow. 'May I present Lieutenant Gervase Adams, sir, who cannot be denied in his desire to learn more of your remarkable realm.'

Greaves acknowledged him with a bow and slight smile. 'Calm seas and a prosperous voyage indeed, gentlemen. Your brisk action at the outset of our voyage has been particularly remarked.'

They settled inside by the large fire. 'Calibogus?' Greaves offered. At the puzzled looks he smiled, 'A Nova Scotian cure for the wind's chill – spruce beer stiffened with rum. I believe we will have King's calibogus, which is taken hot, and is a sovereign remedy.'

Mrs Greaves joined them. 'To an English eye, our country may appear outlandish, gentlemen, but to us it is an Arcadia indeed,' she said proudly.

'With the fisheries to bring wealth and substance to your being,' Renzi replied.

'The cod kingdom you will find in the north, in Newfoundland. Here we glory in trade – you have seen our convoys, hundreds of ships and sailing almost every month . . .'

'Such a crowd of shipping – all from Nova Scotia?' Adams asked, puzzled.

'Ah, no, sir,' Greaves said. 'This is the trade of the North American continent – not only Canada but the United States as well. The seas are alive with privateers and other vermin, and without a navy of their own Cousin Jonathan likes to consign his goods here for safe passage across the ocean.'

Renzi rubbed his hands as the generous pinewood fire blazed, warming and cheering. 'This is spring,' he ventured. 'I believe in truth it may be said your winter is worse?'

'It can be a sad trial at times,' Greaves replied, 'but when the snows come and the great St Lawrence freezes a hundred miles from bank to bank, Halifax with its fine harbour is always free for navigation.'

His wife added gravely, 'Last winter was dreadful, very severe. Our roads were impossible with ice and snow and we ran uncommonly short of the daily necessaries – the Army could get no beef and the common people were being found frozen in the street! Goodness knows how the maroons survive.'

In his surprise Kydd forgot himself and interjected, 'Maroons – you mean black men fr'm Jamaica?'

'Yes! Can you conceive? They were in rebellion and given settlement here. It quite touches my heart to see their poor dark faces among all the snow and icy winds.' Kydd remembered his times in the West Indies as Master of the King's Negroes. Could even the noble and powerful Juba have survived in this wilderness?

'To be sure, m' dear!' Greaves said. 'Yet in their Maroon Hall you will see some of our best workers, and you remember that when they were offered passage back to Africa, only a few accepted. In my opinion they're much to be preferred to that homeless riff-raff on the waterfront.'

Adams stirred restlessly and leaned forward. 'The Prince. How do you find having a prince o' the blood among you all?'

'A fine man. He has done much for Halifax, I believe.'

'Did not King George, his father, send him here into exile, and is he not now living in sin with his mistress Julie?'

'We do not speak of such matters,' Greaves said coldly. 'When His Royal Highness arrived, this place was raw and contemptible. Now it has stature and grace, with buildings worthy of a new civilisation, and is strong enough I fancy to secure all Canada from a descent.'

'Sir, I didn't mean . . .'

'Do you care to see the town, perhaps? We have time to make a visit and return for dinner.'

'You are very obliging, sir.'

Halifax consisted of one vast rampart, an imposing hill overlooking the harbour. It sloped down to the shoreline, with a massive fortification dominating the crest – the citadel with its enormous flag. There, the party stepped out to admire the view. Greaves had provided fur coats against the chill bluster of the winds, which under lead-coloured skies intermittently drove icy spicules of snow against Kydd's skin. He shivered at the raw cold.

Around them was broad open ground, cleared to give the citadel a good field of fire. The vegetation emerging from snow-melt was bleached a drab light-brown and mud splashes showed where others had walked before. But the view was impressive: the expanse of harbour below stretched out in the distance, the sea a sombre dark grey. Model-like ships lay at anchor, black and still. And the rugged country, blanketed by the monotonous low black-green of subarctic forest, extended like a dark shadow as far as the eye could see.

Kydd caught Renzi's eye. His friend was rapt: 'This is a land like no other!' he breathed. 'One we might say is in perpetual thrall to the kingdom of the north. There is an unknown boreal fastness here that lies for countless miles to the interior, which has its own bleak beauty that dares men . . .'

Greaves smiled as they tramped back to the carriage. 'You could not be visiting us at a worse time of the year,' he said, 'after the snow, and before the green-up. You may find it hardly credible, but in no more than a month there will be delicate blooms of wild pear, and trees all along Argyle Street that will surprise you with the green of old England.'

Just below the citadel the first buildings began, substantial, stone structures that would not have been out of place in England. The air was chill and raw but smoky from countless fires that promised warmth and company. 'Now, there's a sight!' Adams said, with satisfaction, as they reached the town proper. Houses, shops, people, all the evidence of civilised living. The streets were rivers of mud and horse-dung but everywhere there were boardwalks to protect pedestrians' feet.

After weeks of familiar faces at sea, the variety of passers-by seemed exotic: ladies with cloaks and muffs picking their way delicately, escorted by their gentlemen; a muffin man shuffling along in sharp contrast to a pig-tailed ranger, half-Indian, with cradled long rifle and bundle. To Kydd's surprise sedan chairs toiled up the steep slope, a sight he had not seen since his youth.

'We do tolerably well in the matter of entertainments,' Greaves murmured. 'May I mention the Pontac, a popular coffee-house with quite admirable mutton pies, or Merkel's, if tea and plum cake is more to your taste?' At Adams's expression he added drily, 'And, of course, there is Manning's tavern, which is well remarked for its ale and respectability.'

'Sir, there is a service you may do us,' Renzi said. 'If you could indicate a chandlery or such that is able to outfit us in the article of cold-weather clothing . . .'

'That I can certainly do, and close by, at Forman's — you shall need my advice, I suspect.' The emporium in question was well patronised, and they were met with curious looks from weather-worn men and capable-looking women. An overpowering smell lay on the air.

'Sea gear, if you please,' Greaves told the assistant.

'Goin' north?' The broad Canadian twang was noticeable against Greaves's more English tones.

'He means to Newfoundland and the Arctic. Would this be so, do you think?'

'Not in a sail-of-the-line, I believe.'

'Well, Capting, here in Forman's we has somethin' fer all hands. Aloft, it's tarred canvas th' best, but there's many prefers their rig less stiff sort o' thing, uses boiled linseed oil instead. An' regular seamen on watch always takes heavy greased homespun under their gear as well.'

He swung out a set of what seemed to be heavy dark leather gear. 'Norsky fishermen swear by this'n.' Selecting an impossibly sized mitten, he added, 'Boiled wool, then felted – you don't fear fish-hooks in the dark wi' this!'

Watching their faces for a reaction, he chose another garment. 'Er, you gents are goin' to be more satisfied wi' these, I guess.' The jacket was of heavy cloth, but much more flexible. However, with every proud flourish he made, a rank animal miasma arose, catching at the back of the throat. 'See here,' the assistant said, opening the garment and revealing pale, yellowish smears along the seams. 'This is guaranteed t' keep you warm 'n' dry. Prime bear grease!'

Forewarned by *Lady Jane* schooner, Halifax prepared for the arrival of the North American Squadron from its winter quarters in Bermuda. As if in ironic welcome, the morning's pale sun withdrew, lowering grey clouds layered the sky with bleak threat and tiny flakes appeared, whirling about the ship. Kydd shuddered. Obliged to wear outer uniform he had done his best to cram anything he could find beneath it, but the spiteful westerly chilled him to the bone.

Long before the squadron hove in sight, regular thuds from the outer fortresses marked its approach. Six ships in perfect line finally emerged around the low hump of George's Island, indifferent to the weather.

'*Resolution*, seventy-four,' someone said, pointing to the leading ship's admiral's flag floating high on the mast. The rest of the conversation was lost in the concussion and smoke of saluting guns as the two biggest ships present, *Resolution* and *Tenacious*, acknowledged each other's presence, then deigned to notice the citadel's grand flag.

Just as her first anchor plunged into the sea the flagship's launch smacked into the water, and sails on all three masts vanished as one, drawing admiring comments from *Tenacious*'s quarterdeck.

Kydd tensed, aware of a warning glance from Bryant standing next to the captain, but he was ready. In *Resolution*, the white ensign at her mizzen peak descended; simultaneously, in *Tenacious*, the huge red ensign of an independent ship on its forty-foot staff aft dipped. In its place, in time with the flagship, a vast pristine white ensign arose, signifying the formal accession of the 64 to the North American Squadron.

The snow thickened, large flakes drifting down endlessly and obscuring Kydd's sight of the flagship. If he should miss anything . . .

A three-flag hoist shot up *Resolution*'s main; Kydd anxiously pulled out his signal book, but Rawson knew without looking. "'All captains!'" he sang out gleefully, almost cherubic in his many layers of clothing.

Kydd hurried down to the quarterdeck but Houghton had

anticipated the summons and was waiting at the entry port, resplendent in full dress and sword. His barge hooked on below the side-steps and, snowflakes glistening on his boat-cloak, he vanished over the side.

Duty done, *Tenacious* settled back to harbour routine. The snow began to settle. Deck fitments and spars, brightwork and blacked cannon, all were now topped with a damp white.

As expected, 'All officers' was signalled at eleven. Boats put off from every English man-o'-war in the harbour to converge on the flagship; the officers were in full dress and sword, with a white ensign to denote their presence.

It was the pomp and majesty of a naval occasion, which Kydd had seen many times before but from the outside. He stood nervously with the others as they were welcomed cordially by the flag-lieutenant on the quarterdeck and shown below by a serious-faced midshipman.

The great cabin of *Resolution* extended the whole width of the deck; inside a large, polished table was set for dinner with crystal and silver. Kydd, overawed by the finery, took an end chair.

Next to him a lieutenant nodded amiably, and Kydd mumbled a polite acknowledgement. The hum of conversation slackened and stopped as Vice Admiral of the White, George Vandeput, commander-in-chief of the North American Squadron, came into the cabin.

The massed scraping of chairs was deafening as the officers rose, murmuring a salutation. 'D'ye sit, gentlemen,' he called, finding the central chair. He whirled the skirts of his frock coat around it as he sank into it, and beamed at the company.

'I'd be obliged at y'r opinion of this Rhenish,' he said

affably, as decanters and glasses made their appearance.

Kydd's glass was filled with a golden wine that glittered darkly in the lanthorn light. He tasted it: a harder, mineral flavour lay beneath the flowery scent. Unsure, he sipped it again.

Vandeput looked down the table but most officers remained prudently noncommittal. Renzi sat three places along, holding his glass up to the light and sniffing appreciatively. 'A fine workmanlike Rheingau,' he said, 'or possibly a Palatinate, though not as who should say a Spätlese.'

The cabin fell quiet as several commanders and a dozen senior lieutenants held their breath at a junior lieutenant offering an opinion on his admiral's taste in wine, but Vandeput merely grunted. 'Ah, yes. I feel inclined t' agree – a *trocken* it is not, but you'll excuse me in th' matter of taste. Its origin is a Danish prize whose owner seemed not t' value the more southerly whites.'

Renzi nodded and the admiral shot him an intent look, then steepled his fingers. 'Gentlemen, f'r those newly arrived for the season, a welcome.' He held attention while he gazed around the cabin, recognising some, politely acknowledging others. 'We have some fresh blood here following our famous victory at Camperdown so I'm taking the opportunity t' meet you all. The North American Squadron – often overlooked these days, but of crucial importance, I declare. The convoy of our mast-ships alone justifies our being. Where would the sea service be without its masts and spars? An' half the world's trade flows through this port, including the West Indies, of course.'

Kydd was transfixed by the glitter of the admiral's jewelled star, the gold facings of his coat, the crimson sash, which were grand and intimidating, but Vandeput's pleasant manner and avuncular shock of white hair set him almost at his ease.

'Therefore our chief interest is in the protection of this trade. I rather fancy we won't be troubled overmuch by French men-o'-war – rather, it's these damn privateers that try my patience. Yet I would not have you lose sight of the fact that we are a fleet – to this end I require that every ship under my command acts together as one, concentrating our force when ordered, and for so doing you signal lieutenants shall be my very nerves.'

A rustle of amusement passed around the table: the flagship's smartness was well marked and life would not be easy for these junior officers.

'We shall be exercising at sea in company as opportunities arise. I commend my signal instructions to you, with particular attention to be given to the signification of manoeuvres. My flag-lieutenant will be happy to attend to any questions later.

'I wish you well of your appointment to the North American Squadron, gentlemen, and ask that you enjoy the entertainment.'

A buzz of talk began as the doors swung wide and dishes of food were brought in. Kydd was about to help himself to the potted shrimps when the stout officer next to him half stood over the biggest salver as its cover was removed. 'Aha! The roast cod. This is worth any man's hungering. Shall you try it, sir?'

The fish was splendid – buttery collops of tender white, and Kydd forgot his duty until the officer introduced himself: 'Robertson, second of the *Acorn*. Damn fine cook our admiral has, don't y' know?'

'Kydd, fifth o' *Tenacious*.' He hesitated, but Robertson was more concerned with his fish, which was vanishing fast. '*Acorn* – the nine-pounder lying alongside?'

'Is her,' Robertson agreed. 'I suggest only the chicken pie afore the main, by the way. Ol' Georgie always serves caribou, an' I mean to show my appreciation in spades.'

'May I?' Kydd had noticed the disappearing fish and was pleased to have remembered his manners so far as to help him to a handsome-sized slice of cold chicken pie. The Rheingau was perfectly attuned to the cold food and his reserve melted a little. 'Nine-pounder frigate – hard livin' indeed.'

'Aye,' Robertson said, his mouth full, 'but better'n a ship-of-the-line.'

'And how so?'

'Prize money, o' course. Ol' Georgie's no fool – sends us out all the days God gives after anything that floats, French, Spanish, Scowegian – even American, if we can prove she has a cargo bound for the enemy. If it's condemned in court, cargo 'n' all, then shares all round.'

The rumours of caribou were correct, and to the accompaniment of a good Margaux, the dark flesh was tender with an extraordinary sweet wild meat flavour. Kydd sat back, satiated. Renzi was toying with a breast of spruce partridge while deep in serious talk with an older, lean-faced officer.

Kydd stole a look at the admiral: he was genially in conversation with a hard-looking officer to his left. Kydd wondered at the simple fact that he himself was sharing a meal with such august company.

'Wine with you, sir!' It was the officer opposite, who had not said much before.

Kydd held his glass forward. 'Prize money b' the bucket-full!' he toasted.

The other seemed restless. 'That would be fine, sir, but while we're topping it the sybarite, others are fighting. And by that I mean winning the glory. There's no promotion to be gained by lying comfortably at two anchors in some quiet harbour – only in a right bloody battle.' He held up his wine to the light and studied it gloomily. 'To think it – we've been thrown out of the Med since last year, there've been descents on Ireland, and at home I hear Pitt has admitted the collapse and destruction of the coalition and none else in sight. We stand quite alone. Can things be much worse? I doubt it.'

Kydd said stoutly, 'I'm come fr'm the Caribbee and I can tell you, we've been takin' the French islands one b' one, and now the Spanish Main is ours. And who c'n doubt? The Mongseers have reached their limits, baled up in Europe tight as a drum. To the Royal Navy, gaol-keeper! And may she lose the keys!' But the officer remained grave and quiet. Kydd frowned. 'Do ye doubt it, sir?' The wine was bringing a flush, but he didn't care; he seemed to be holding his own in this particular conversation.

With a weary smile the officer put down his glass. 'I cannot conceive where you have been this last half-year that you have not in the least understood the motions of the French Directory – intrigues at the highest, or at the point of a bayonet, they have now secured the subjugation or acquiescence of the whole of the civilised world.

'They are arrogant, they care not who they antagonise, for in every battle they triumph, whole nations kneel at their bidding, and for what purpose? While these lie beaten, they have a mighty general, Buonaparte, who is ready to venture forth on the world! Mark my words, before this year's end there will be such a bursting forth by the French as will make the world stare!'

He leaned back in his chair and resumed his wine, looking reprovingly at Kydd. Deliberately, Kydd turned back to Robertson, who was now engrossed with the task of picking at a pretty corner dish. 'Sweetbreads?' he mumbled, and offered the dish.

Kydd took one and tried to think of an intelligent remark to make. 'The Americans'll be amused at our troubles wi' the French,' he said hopefully.

Robertson raised his eyebrows. 'Ah, not really, I think.' He looked at Kydd curiously. 'You must know they've done handsomely out o' this war – being neutral an' all, I mean. Can trade with any and all, if they can get away with it, o' course.'

Kydd's blank look made him pause. 'How long've you been made up, then?' he asked directly.

'Just this January,' Kydd answered warily.

'Then I'd clap on more sail an' get as much o' this business hoisted aboard as you can. You're boarding officer an' take in a fat merchantman that the court decides is innocent, expect to explain yourself to the judge in damages!' He grinned broadly and turned to a pyramid of syllabubs.

The warm glow of the wine fell away. These men were of a different origin, brought up from the cradle with discernment, education, the talk of politics continually around them. How could he conceivably claim to be one of them? Kydd stole a look at Renzi, holding forth elegantly on some exemplary Greek, then at the admiral, listening with his head politely inclined to a fine story from a young lieutenant, and finally at the officer opposite, who was now yarning with his neighbour.

Kydd closed the door of his cabin. There was nobody in the wardroom, but the way he felt he did not want to see another face. His experience of the previous night had left him heart-sick, unable to deny any longer that trying his hardest was not enough: he just did not belong in this society. He was a deep-sea sailor, true, but as an officer he was a fish out of water; talk of fox hunting and the Season was beyond him, the implications for his acceptance by them only too clear.

He knew well what was in store: others who had 'come aft by the hawse' had found their place – as a tarpaulin officer. Known in the Navy as characters, they were bluff, hard on the men they knew so well and had no pretensions to gentility or learning. Utterly reliable at sea, they were outcasts in polite social situations, and usually took refuge in hearty drinking. As for promotion and ambition, improbable.

Was this his fate? He had tasted the sweets of a higher life with Renzi – their leisurely talking of philosophers and logic under a tropic moon, the dream-like times in Venice, the dinner with Renzi's brother in Jamaica had been a taste of what should be, but now . . .

Thought of his friend brought with it a wave of desolation. Renzi was in his element now, clearly headed for the highest levels and thoroughly enjoying his change of fortune. He had aided Kydd as much as he could, teaching him the forms and appearances, but there was no help for it. This was not a matter of learning the ropes, it was breeding.

His depression deepened: logic would say – and Renzi was a servant to logic – that in truth his friend no longer needed a sea companion to lighten his intellectual existence and ease his self-imposed exile. Now Renzi had the chaplain to dispute with whenever he felt inclined, Kydd thought bitterly. All told, perhaps it would have been more merciful if Kydd had never known another existence – had never encountered Renzi, even.

He felt despair and flung open the door for Tysoe. When his servant did not immediately appear he roared his name.

Tysoe arrived, his hands showing evidence that he had been at work boning Kydd's best shoes. He wore a perfectly composed expression. 'Sir?'

'Fetch me one o' my clarets.'

Tysoe's eyes flickered. 'Will that be two glasses, sir?'

Kydd coloured. 'No, damn y'r eyes – just th' one!'

When it came, he snatched bottle and glass, slammed his door, then splashed the wine into the glass, hands shaking with emotion. He drank hard, and it steadied him. He stared morosely at the ship's side in his tiny cabin, forcing himself to be calm. 'Tysoe! Another bottle an' you can turn in f'r the night,' he shouted.

It was obvious now. There was only one cause for his despondency: loneliness. An outsider in the wardroom, he was cut off from the rough, warm camaraderie before the mast that he knew so well. Now he had no one. And Renzi would be moving on soon, probably taken up as a flag-lieutenant.

The second bottle was half-empty already, but Kydd's pain was easing. He allowed the warm memory of Kitty to return: she had stood by him during the terrible days of the Nore mutiny – she had a strength he'd rarely seen in a woman. With her, he might have . . . There was a lump in his throat and he gulped another glass. If only she were here, if only . . .

He stared at the glass in his hand. Already he was turning into what he dreaded to be – a tarpaulin officer. Through self-pity he was sliding down the same slope as they all must have: to find acceptance they had turned themselves into a patronised caricature, then found a steady friend in the bottle.

'God rot me, but I'll not be one.' His harsh croak in the confined space startled him. He seized the bottle and pushed it away. So shameful was the thought that he lurched to his feet and threw open the door, clutching the bottle by its neck. The wardroom was still deserted, all others no doubt gone ashore together.

'Tysoe!' he called. The man came quickly and silently and Kydd knew why: he had conceived it his duty to stand by his master while he got helplessly drunk, then tumble him into his cot.

The realisation hurt Kydd: it bore on his spirit that others would now be making allowances for him, and he stiffened. 'If ye'd like the res' o' the wine . . .' He awkwardly held out the bottle. 'I shan't need any more.'

Renzi was not at breakfast but Kydd found him later in the day in his cabin. 'The admiral plans to visit his realm in Newfoundland,' he said, 'and for some unaccountable reason he wishes me to accompany him. A vexation – if you remember I planned to join the Shiptons for whist.' He seemed preoccupied. 'There will be no sea exercises with the admiral in Newfoundland counting his cod, dear fellow. If you can bear to leave your signal books, why do you not see more of the country? You really should get away more.'

Kydd murmured something, watching his friend rummaging in his chest.

Renzi looked up, shamefaced. 'I'd be obliged should you lend me a shirt or two, Tom – there will be a quantity of social occasions in Newfoundland, I've heard.' A surge of feeling surprised Kydd with its intensity as he fetched them, but he said nothing. A stubborn pride still remained, which would not allow him to burden Renzi with the problem.

Renzi left with a hasty wave. Pringle emerged from his cabin the picture of military splendour, a pair of pigskin gloves in one hand, a swagger stick in the other. He noticed Kydd, gave a noncommittal grunt, then he, too, strode away. Servants came to clear the afternoon clutter, looking at Kydd warily. There was nothing for it but to retire to his cabin.

Pride would not let him inveigle himself into another's invitation – besides, he might find himself in a situation that would end in his making a spectacle of himself again. He burned with embarrassment at the recollection of his conversation at table. What could they think of an officer as crassly ignorant as any foremast hand?

The wardroom was clear again; he paced about, morose. A book lay on the rudder-head. He wandered over idly and pulled it out: *Observations on the Current War, by an Officer of Rank.* It was full of maps and diagrams, painstakingly hatched with tiny lines and minuscule lettering. It covered in great detail every military campaign of the war so far.

He had never had an interest in the interminable to and fro-ing that seemed to be the lot of the Army, but this book had an introductory treatment for each theatre of war, which sounded robust and useful. His spirits rose a little. This at least was something constructive he could do – learn some facts to ward off assumptions of ignorance.

It was a workmanlike book, and the treatment was clear and direct but, even so, talk of why the Duke of York had considered the Austrian Netherlands worth a hopeless campaign was baffling, mainly because it assumed a degree of familiarity with the political background that he did not have.

He persevered, going to each introduction in turn and stitching together a basic understanding on which he could hang his facts. Yet as he did so, he found his attention held by the implications of what he was reading: armies and trade – expressions of a nation's economic strength, but vulnerable to the quixotic twists of fate and man's plotting.

It was a new experience for Kydd. He read on until a fundamental realisation stole over him. He set down the book and stared into space. Until now he had unconsciously thought of his ship as a boundary to his world. He could step ashore in foreign parts and see sights impossible for most, but he could always return to his snug little world and sail away. There, the dangers of the sea and the malice of the enemy were reality.

Now it was all changed. Events in one part of the world could reach out and touch an officer, have grave military and legal consequences if a wrong decision was made. They might conceivably damn his career or even cause an international incident. In essence, an officer dealt with the wider world; the common seaman did not.

'Mr Kydd!' Bryant's bellow reached effortlessly from the quarterdeck to the fo'c'sle where Kydd had taken refuge from the marines drilling loudly on the poop-deck under an enthusiastic Lieutenant Best.

Hastily Kydd made his way aft. 'I've been called away, damn it, an' just when we're due a parcel o' new men. Should be coming aboard this hour. Bring 'em aboard, if y' please, and take all the able-bodied but, mark this, send all the rubbish back – we don't want 'em, right?'

'Aye aye, sir. Are they pressed men?'

'Not all. We've got a press warrant out, but most o' these are merchant jacks, tired of winterin', and odd sods off the streets. We can be satisfied with a dozen. I'll rate 'em when I get back this afternoon.' Bryant jammed on his hat and stalked off.

Kydd warned off a duty midshipman to desire the surgeon to hold himself in readiness, the purser to his slops and the boatswain to provide a holding crew. It was a well-worn routine: the need for men in any man-o'-war was crucial. Even if the ship was in first-class shape, battle-ready and stored, it was all a waste without men to work her. Kydd had no misgivings about what had to be done to achieve this.

'A King's Yard boat, sir,' Rawson reported. The dockyard launch made its way out to them and, as it neared, Kydd leaned over the side to see what was being brought. Looking up at him were a scatter of winter-pale faces, some listless, others alert, some sunk in dejection. A stock collection – the seamen among them would show immediately: they would have no trouble with the side-steps and bulwark.

The mate-of-the-watch took charge. It would not be seemly for Kydd to appear until the men were inboard and assembled; he disappeared into the lobby.

It seemed so long ago, but into his mind, as clear as the day it had happened, came his own going aboard the old battleship *Duke William* as a pressed man, the misery, homesickness, utter strangeness. Now these men would face the same.

'New men mustered, sir.'

Kydd tugged on his hat and emerged on to the quarterdeck, aware of all eyes on him. They were bunched together in a forlorn group near the mainmast. 'Get them in a line, Mr Lawes,' he ordered.

A more odd assortment of dress was difficult to imagine. Bearskin hats and well-worn animal-hide jackets, greasy-grey oily woollens and ragged trousers, even two with moccasins. More than one was stooped by ill-nourishment or age. Some, the ones standing alert and wary, with blank faces, carried well-lashed seaman's bags.

'I'll speak t' them now, Mr Lawes.'

The shuffling and murmuring stopped. He stepped across to stand easily in front of them, waiting until he had their eyes. 'My name's L'tenant Kydd. This is HMS *Tenacious*. We're a ship-of-the-line an' we're part of the North American Squadron, Admiral Vandeput.'

Stony stares met him. The men were clearly resigned to a fate known to some, unknown to others.

'C'n I see the hands o' the volunteers?' A scatter of men signified. 'You men get th' bounty in coin today, an' liberty later t' spend it. The rest . . .' Kydd continued: 'When this war started, I was a pressed man, same as you.' He paused for effect. It startled some, others remained wary. 'Rated landman in a second rate. An' since then I've been t' the South Seas in a frigate, the Caribbean in a cutter and the Mediterranean in a xebec. I've got a handsome amount o' prize money and now I'm a King's officer. So who's going t' say to me the Navy can't be th' place to be for a thorough-going seaman who wants t' better himself?

'Now, think on it. Should y' decide to serve King George and y'r country you could end up th' same. Give your names t' the first lieutenant as a volunteer this afternoon and tell him y' want to do well in the sea service o' the King and he'll give ye a good chance.'

Kydd turned to Lawes. 'Carry on, these men. Stand fast that one an' the two at the pinrail – we'll send 'em back. Rest go below to see the doctor.' The men still had their eyes on Kydd, one in particular, a thick-set seaman, who lingered after the others.

'Good haul, I think.' It was Bryant, watching them leave. 'Surly-looking brute, the last. Shouldn't wonder if he's shipped for some very good reason.'

The sun at last became visible through a pale cloud cover, a perceptible warmth on the skin, and Kydd's spirits rose. Ashore, he could make out a different green from the sombre green-black of the boreal forest, and he thought that the country might seem quite another in summer.

The captain left with the first lieutenant to call on the officers of York Redoubt, and a young lady whom Adams had taken up with demanded his constant presence. For now, Kydd decided, he would continue his acquaintance with war's wider canvas.

This time he prepared to take notes. Sitting at the wardroom table, his back to the stern windows, he picked up his book and resumed reading. He discovered that the thousand-year republic of Venice had been sacrificed in a cynical exchange between France and Austria and that the Corsican Napoleon Buonaparte must now be considered England's chief opponent.

It was truly astonishing how much of momentous significance to the world had happened since he had gone to sea — and to think that he had been unknowingly at the heart of these events. The evening drew in, the light faded, but he had found another book, more dog-eared and harder-going, which purported to be a treatment of the economic consequences of a world at war, and he set to.

He felt a small but growing satisfaction: this was one positive course he could take, and it was shaping into a workable aspiration in life. If he could not be a natural-born officer, at least he would be an informed one.

He became aware of a figure standing and looked up. It was Tysoe, cupping a small peg lamp that glowed softly with a clear, bright flame. 'Thank 'ee, Tysoe – but does Mr Hambly know I have his lamp?' It was charged with spermaceti oil and used only for painstaking work at the charts.

'Sir, he will be informed of his generous assistance to you when he returns aboard.'

Kydd inclined his head to hear better. 'Er, what seems t' be afoot on the upper deck?' There had been odd thumpings and occasional cries, but nothing the mate-of-the-watch could not be relied on to deal with.

Tysoe bent to trim the lamp. 'The hands, sir. They wish to dance and skylark.' Kydd nodded. There were men aboard, visiting from other ships, the weather was clear and it would be odd if there was not some kind of glee going in the fo'c'sle. He laid down his book. Perhaps he should cast an eye over the proceedings.

Darkness had fallen, but it was easy to make out activity on the foredeck by the light of lanthorns hung in the rigging. A hornpipe was being performed beside the jeer bitts of the foremast. Kydd wandered forward unnoticed. The seaman was skilled, his feet flashing forward to slap back rhythmically, the rigid body twirling in perfect time, while his upper body, arms folded, remained perfectly rigid and his face expressionless.

The fiddler finished with a deft upward note and, with a laugh, took a pull at his beer. 'Ben Backstay!' The call was taken up around the deck, and eventually a fine-looking seaman from another ship stepped into the golden light and struck a pose.

> 'When we sail, with a fresh'ning breeze,
> And landmen all grow sick, sir;
> The sailor lolls with his mind at ease,
> And the song and can go quick, sir.
>   Laughing here,

Quaffing there,
Steadily, readily,
Cheerily, merrily,
Still from care and thinking free
Is a sailor's life for me!'

The violin gaily extemporised as cheers and roars delayed the next verse. There was no problem here: these were the core seamen of *Tenacious*, deep-sea sailors whose profession was the sea. They were the heart and soul of the ship, not pressed men or the refuse of gaols.

With a further burst of hilarity the singer withdrew to receive his due in a dripping oak tankard, and Kydd turned to go. Then a plaintive chord floated out, it hung – and a woman's voice sounded above the lessening chatter. 'Sweet Sally, an' how her true love Billy Bowling was torn fr'm her arms an' pressed.' A blonde woman, standing tall and proud, continued, 'Sally's heart's near broken, she can't bear t' be parted – so she disguises as a foremast jack 'n' goes aboard that very night.' Kydd moved closer: the woman resembled his lost Kitty.

'Aboard my true love's ship I'll go,
And brave each blowing gale;
I'll splice, I'll tack, I'll reef, I'll row,
And haul with him the sail;
In jacket blue, and trousers too,
With him I'll cruise afar,
There shall not be a smarter hand
Aboard a man-o'-war.'

Her voice was warm and passionate. Talk died away as she sang on. Kydd's mind took him back to other ships, other

153

ports – and evenings such as this with his shipmates – when he'd had not a care in his heart.

She finished, but the memories she had aroused came on him in full flood, stinging his eyes. He became aware that faces were turned towards him, conversations dying away. A woman moved protectively towards her man and the expressions became dark, resentful.

Poulden came across. 'Sir?' he demanded suspiciously.

These men had every right to their territory, little enough in a ship of war. And he had no right – he did not belong. 'Er, just came t' hear the songs,' he said weakly. 'Rattlin' good singing, lads,' he added, but it fell into a silence. 'Please carry on,' he said, louder.

The men looked at each other, then the seaman who had sung 'Ben Backstay' got to his feet and stood purposefully under the lanthorns. He muttered an aside to the violinist and clutching a tankard launched loudly into:

> 'To our noble Commander
> His Honour and Wealth,
> May he drown and be damn'd—'

Singer and violinist stopped precisely in mid-note and looked at Kydd. Their point made, the duo continued:

> '—that refuses the Health;
> Here's to thee Billy, honest an' true;
> Thanks to the men who calls them his crew
> An' while one is drinking, the other shall fill!'

A girl sprang into the pool of light. 'A sarabande!' she called. But Kydd had left.

Chapter 6

'Well, I wish you joy of your voyage, gentlemen –
unhappily I have a court-martial to attend and therefore shall not be with you.' There was no mistaking the
smug satisfaction in Bampton's tone. In the normal run of
events the inbound convoy would have been met by one
or two of the hard-working frigates, but this one was trans-
porting the lieutenant-governor of New Brunswick and his
family to take up his post and *Tenacious* had been deemed
more suitable.

It seemed to Kydd that he was the only one looking forward to the sea time. The weather had been miserable these
past few days, cold and blustery, and although they would
only be out a day or so at most, the general consensus was
that it was an ideal time to snug down in harbour until better
conditions returned.

Kydd had long ago realised that he was a 'foul-weather jack'
– one of those who revelled in the exhilaration and spectacle
of stormy seas, racing clouds and the life-intensifying charge
of danger. In this short voyage he knew they would probably

not face a full-blown tempest but the thought of a lively experience at sea lifted his spirits.

Tenacious and *Ceres*, a 32-gun frigate belonging to the Newfoundland Squadron, proceeded to sea together. With the cliffs of Chebucto Head abeam, they braced up for the hard easterly beat to rendezvous with the convoy.

The weather was freshening: their bows met foam-streaked waves at an angle, dipping before them, then rearing up to smash them apart in explosions of white. Standing aft, Kydd felt the sheeting spray in his teeth. With canvas taut as a drum, weather rigging harping to the wind's bluster, and, far on their beam, *Ceres* swooping and seething along under small sail, he was happier than he had been for some time. There would be no problems with the enemy – any rational privateer would have long since scuttled southwards until the weather improved. No prize could be boarded in this.

By afternoon they had not sighted the convoy; almost certainly it had been delayed by the poor weather. Houghton, on the quarterdeck in oilskins slick with spray, obviously had no plans to return to port and at the end of the day they shortened sail and kept enough way on the ship to head the easterly. It showed signs of veering, which had the master muttering anxiously to Houghton. At midnight they wore to the south and at the end of the middle watch took the third leg of a triangle to approximate their dusk position again.

A cold dawn brought no improvement in the weather, just the same streaming fresh gale and lively decks a-swill with water. There was no sign of the convoy but *Ceres* had stayed with them and by mid-morning there was a flutter of colour at her peak halliards: the convoy had been sighted.

Widely scattered, the ships were struggling to stay together – it was a miracle that they were even within sight of each other after so many thousands of miles of ocean. Without a convoy plan Kydd had no idea how many there should be, but a quick count enabled him to report what must be a sizeable proportion to the captain when he appeared on deck.

'We're looking for *Lord Woolmer*, she's carrying the new lieutenant-governor,' Houghton said brusquely, 'an ex-Indiaman. Be so good as to apprise the lookouts and report to me when she's in sight.'

Ships of all kinds laboured past, converging on the rendezvous position; some showed obvious signs of storm damage. Towards the rear a battered sloop appeared, oddly out of shape with a truncated fore topmast, but bent on coming up with *Tenacious*.

'Heave to, please,' Houghton ordered, as he took the officer-of-the-watch's speaking trumpet and waited. The sloop barrelled up to leeward and backed her headsails. Close by, the little vessel's appalling motion was only too apparent – she was bucking in deep, jerky movements, bursts of spray sheeting over the small huddle at the wheel.

'Where – is – *Lord* – *Woolmer*?' Houghton called.

A figure in the sloop made his way to the shiny wet shrouds and aimed a speaking trumpet. Kydd could hear thin sounds from it, but not make out what was said. The sloop showed canvas enough for it to ease in, its exaggerated bucketing so much the more pitiable as it lurched closer alongside.

'*Woolmer* – sprung mainmast – left her at fifty-five twenty west – running down forty-three north . . .'

At that longitude she was considerably to eastward of her course; somewhere in the stormy grey of the Atlantic she had encountered a squall that had nearly taken her mainmast by the board. She would have fished the mast with capstan bars and anything to hand, then been grateful for the easterly, which at least would have her heading slowly but surely for Halifax.

Looking down from the deck of *Tenacious*, Kydd felt for the sloop commander. Without a soul to ease the decision out there in the lonely ocean he had needed to weigh the consequences of standing by the injured vessel with her important cargo or resume his watch over the convoy. His presence was proof of the hard resolution he had made: to him the value to England of the merchant ships had out-weighed that of one big ship and her passenger.

The sloop sheeted home and thrashed away after her convoy. Houghton turned to the master. 'Mr Hambly, all sail conformable to weather. I believe we shall lay on the larb'd tack initially, with a view to returning to starb'd and inter-secting our forty-three north line of latitude somewhere about fifty-seven west longitude.'

Much depended on the weather. *Lord Woolmer* was heading westwards as close as she could stay to a known line of lat-itude. If *Tenacious* sailed along the same line in the opposite direction they should meet. The problem was that the wind was dead foul from the east – in difficult conditions *Tenacious* would need to tack twice to intersect the line at the prob-able furthest on of the other ship. And *Woolmer* herself would be finding it hard to be sure of her latitude without sight of the sun for days at a time.

Kydd went below to find a dry shirt. He was watch-on-deck for the last dog-watch and wanted to be as comfortable as possible; there would be no going below later. As he came back up the companionway he saw the master, face set grimly, entering his tiny sea cabin. 'Do ye think th' easterly will hold?' Kydd asked, wedging himself against the door for balance. The hanging lanthorn cast moving shadows in the gloom.

'See this?' Hambly tapped the barometer, its vertical case on gimbals also a-swing. His face seemed old and more lined in the dim light. 'Twenty-nine 'n' three fourths. These waters, as soon as we gets a drop more'n a tenth of an inch below our mean f'r the season, stand by. An' we've had a drop o' two tenths since this morning.'

He checked the chart again and straightened. 'North Atlantic, even at this time o' year, it's folly to trust. It wouldn't surprise me t' see it veer more southerly, an' if that's with a further drop we're in for a hammering.'

Kydd turned to go, then asked, 'You'll be about tonight, Mr Hambly?'

'I will, sir,' said the master, with a tired smile.

In the last of the light the foretop lookout sighted strange sail. It was *Lord Woolmer* with no fore and aft canvas from the main or anything above her course. She put up her helm to run down on *Tenacious*, and Kydd could imagine the relief and joy aboard. With luck they would be safe in Halifax harbour in two or three days and the story of their crossing would be told in the warmth and safety of their homes for months to come.

By the time the ship had come up with *Tenacious* it was too dark for manoeuvres, so they waited until the big, somewhat ungainly merchantman pulled ahead then fell in astern, three lanthorns at her fore-yard to comfort the other ship, whose stern lanthorns were plainly visible.

The morning brought the south-easterly that the master had feared; the wind had strengthened and the barometer dropped. It was time for even a well-found ship like *Tenacious* to take the weather seriously.

Houghton did not waste time. 'Mr Pearce, Mr Renzi, we'll have the t'gallant masts on deck.' The jibboom was brought in forward. Aloft, all rigging that could possibly carry away to disaster was doubled up, preventer braces, rolling tackles put on the yards, slings, trusses – nothing could be trusted to hold in the great forces unleashed in a storm.

Anchors were stowed outboard – they would be of crucial importance should land be seen to leeward – and were secured against the smash of seas on the bows with tough double ring painters and lashing along the length of the stock.

The rudder, too, was vital to safeguard: a relieving tackle was rigged in the wardroom and a spare tiller brought out. It would need fast work to ship a new one – Rawson could be trusted in this, or to rouse out a portable compass and align its lubber-line to the ship's head for use if the tiller ropes from the wheel on deck broke. The relieving tackle would then be used to steer.

On each deck a hatchway forward and aft ventilated the space through gratings. These now were covered with strong canvas and fastened securely with battens nailed around the coaming. Seas breaking aboard might otherwise send tons of water into the ship's bowels.

The most feared event in a storm was a gun breaking loose: a big cannon might smash through the ship's side. The gunner and his party worked from forward and secured them; each muzzle seized like an ox to the ringbolt above the closed gunport, with double breechings and side frappings. Finally, on deck, lifelines were rigged fore and aft on each side of the masts, and on the weather mizzen shrouds a canvas cloth was spread to break the blast for the helm crew.

Tenacious was now snugged for a blow. Kydd hoped that the same was true for the merchantman. What would probably be of most concern to her captain was the state of his noble passengers. However splendid their appointments, their cabins would now be a hell on earth: the motion would be such that the only movement possible would be hand to hand, their only rest taken tied into a wildly moving cot, their world confined to a box shaken into a malodorous, seasick chaos.

The ships plunged on into the angry seas. Aboard, muscles wearying of the continual bracing and staggering along the deck, eyes salt-sore in the raw cold and the streaming wet, Kydd made a circuit of the deck looking for anything that could conceivably fret itself into a rapidly spiralling danger. He checked little things, that the drain-holes of the boats were kept open, their deck-gripes bar-taut, spare spars under them lashed into immobility. When he stripped off in the damp fug of the wardroom, he could see his own concern reflected in others' eyes, and Renzi wore a taut expression.

He pulled on wool: long undergarments, loose pullovers. Anything to keep out the sapping cold of the streaming wind.

This was no longer an exhilarating contest with Neptune, but something sinister. The first feelings of anxiety stole over Kydd – there was a point in every storm when the elements turned from hard boisterousness to malevolence, a sign that mankind was an interloper in something bigger than himself, where lives counted for nothing.

Back on deck Kydd had no need to check the compass to see that the wind had veered further: the angle of the treble-reefed topsails was now much sharper. If it continued much past south they stood to be headed, prevented from making for Nova Scotia to the west, no more than two days away.

Kydd could just make out a few words as he approached Houghton, who was talking to the master under the half-deck near the wheel: '. . . or lie to, sir.' Hambly pointed out over the foam-streaked seas. Beneath the wind-scoured waves a swell, long and massive, was surging up. And it came from the south-west, a portent of the great storm that had sent it.

Kydd glanced at the merchantman. They were but two days from port. So near, yet – Houghton had no authority over her and, indeed, if he had it was difficult to see how any meaningful signal could be made.

'The monster crosses our way, sir, and I'm not sanguine of th' chances of a wounded ship in a real North Atlantic storm,' continued the master.

'We stay with *Lord Woolmer*. That must be our duty,' Houghton said abruptly.

Within the hour *Woolmer* began to turn – away from the wind.

'She's scudding!' said Houghton.

'No, sir, I do believe she wears.' The ship continued round, slowly and uncomfortably, until she had come up on the opposite, starboard tack where she held a-try about four points from the wind.

'I thought so!' Hambly said, against the bluster of the wind at the edges of the half-deck. 'He's seen enough of the western ocean t' know that if there's a turn f'r the worse, the shift will come out of somewheres close to th' north, and wants to get his staying about over with now.' It also meant that *Woolmer* had given up hope of making it through to Halifax and now lay to under storm canvas, going very slowly ahead, waiting out the storm. Kydd's heart went out to the passengers, who must be near to despair: storms could last weeks.

Tenacious was set to edging round to conform, and together the two vessels endured. By midday the seas had worsened and the wind's sullen moan had keened to a higher pitch, a dismal drone with whistling overtones. The swell had increased and the depth between each crest became a dismaying plunge and rise.

Kydd had experienced Caribbean hurricanes, but this was of a different quality: the cold at its heart gave it a unique dark malice. Like the other officers, Kydd stayed on deck. At noon they took stale bread and cold tongue, biscuit and anchovies, then resumed their vigil.

Suddenly, a mass of panic-stricken men burst up from the after hatchway, spilling on to the deck, falling over themselves to be out. A chill stabbed at Kydd. A seaman shouted hoarsely, 'Gotta loose gun!'

Bryant dropped his food and raced for the hatchway, shouting to Kydd, 'A dozen micks – now!'

Because of the weather the hammocks had all been stowed below in the lowest deck. Kydd stood in the hatchway, snatching a dozen men to a halt. 'Down t' the orlop – we'll go under.' He plunged recklessly down the hatchway, praying they would follow. As he passed the level of the gun-deck he had a brief glimpse of a squat black creature crouching for the kill. He hurried on.

Finally in the orlop he paused to allow his eyes to adjust; then he set the men to work. In the wildly heaving gloom hammocks were passed up while Kydd cautiously entered the deserted gun-deck. The gun stood out brazenly from the ship's side. The muzzle lashing had pulled its ringbolt from rotten wood and some weighty motion of the ship had subsequently caused the iron forging of the breeching tackle on one side to give way. The big cannon had swung out and, held by a few stranded ropes, was all but free.

Bryant stood to one side with a crew of seamen armed with handspikes. Kydd signalled to the first men to come up.

'Stand your ground!' the first lieutenant roared, at the men hesitating at his back. The whites of their eyes showed as they fearfully hefted their handspikes and waited for the order.

When Kydd's men had temporarily stopped the beast with hammocks thrown in its path, Bryant's would hurl themselves on it with the handspikes in an attempt to overturn it.

Tenacious rose to a wave and fell to starboard. It was all that was needed; the remaining ropes parted with a dull *twang* and the twenty-four-pounder trundled across the deck, accelerating as it went. The men threw themselves back at the sight of the unrestrained rampage while the cannon hurtled at the opposite side. Then the deck heaved the other way. The gun slowed and stopped, trickling back and forth in a grotesque parody of a bull-fight as the ship hesitated at the top of a roll. The next headlong charge might be the last.

'Er, can we help?' Lieutenant Best, accompanied by half a dozen marines, stood uncomprehending and hesitating at the hatchway.

'No! Get 'em away.' Kydd appreciated his courage but a crowd was not needed – only a handful of daring, active seamen. He glanced behind him: Chamberlain, the midshipman, with the agility of youth, Lamb, a spry topman, Thorn, steady and quick – he had enough.

'Each a mick, an' follow me – rest, wait until we has it cornered, then move in fast.' He seized a trussed hammock for himself and moved forward, feeling the eyes of Bryant's crew on him.

Tenacious's bows rose to a comber. The deck canted up and the cannon suddenly rolled – towards him. Kydd threw the hammock before it and flung himself to one side. It thrust by, skidding on the hammock and fetched up against the mainmast with a splintering crash.

'Chamberlain – here! Lamb 'n' Thorn, get in behind it!' He spotted Best, still hovering. 'Get out of it,' he snarled, and pushed the crestfallen officer away.

They must close in at whatever risk: Bryant's crew could do nothing until the beast was stopped and then they had seconds only. The next few minutes would see heroes – or death. Warily he approached the cannon, trying to gauge the seas outside.

The bows began to rise again and he tensed, but the downward motion of the cannon abruptly changed course as the wave angled under her keel, and it rumbled headlong towards the ship's side and where Best stood, paralysed with horror.

It happened very quickly: a fatal wavering and the two-ton monster caught him, snatched him along, and slammed against another – a choking squeal and a brief image of spurting blood, limbs and white bone. Best's body was flung to the deck.

Yet his sacrifice was the saving of the ship. Caught in the gun's small wheels his body caused the cannon to slew and stop. Kydd hurled his hammock in its path. Others threw themselves at it, Bryant's crew with handspikes levering furiously, frantically.

They had won.

Shaken, Kydd needed the open decks. *Lord Woolmer* lay to a mile or so away, taking seas on her bows in explosions of white, pitching and rolling under her scraps of sail.

Hambly was standing by the main shrouds, looking up at the racing dark clouds and the torn seascape. On seeing Kydd, he shouted, 'We're takin' it more from the west, I fear.' The rest of his words were snatched away by the wind's blast.

'And this means?' Kydd had not heard Houghton approach behind them. Hambly wheeled round, then respectfully accompanied them to the shelter of the half-deck.

'Sir, it means the centre o' the storm is placin' itself right in our path. We'll be down t' bare poles at this rate – we should really bear away an' scud instead of lyin' to. There's no hope this storm is goin' to blow itself out, sir.'

Kydd wondered whether the real reason *Woolmer* was hanging on was the reluctance of her captain to deny his passengers hope of a harbour and surcease. To scud was to abandon all attempts even to hold a position and simply fly before the violence, but this was to turn about and be blown back over the miles they had won at such cost.

'I understand, Mr Hambly, but we stay with them.'

Conditions were deteriorating and it was hard to keep them in sight: the air was filled with stinging spray, the motion of the ship becoming a shuddering heave as the seas grew more confused.

The hours wore on. Kydd imagined what it must be like for the people of *Woolmer*: an indescribable nightmare, endlessly protracted.

After midday *Woolmer* finally submitted to fate and made the decision to scud. It would be touch and go: the swells issuing from the storm centre were now more than forty feet high, higher even than the lower yards, and clawed into white streaks by the pitiless wind. They had left it perilously late. To fall off the wind, then run before it they must first pass through the most dangerous time of all – broadside to the powerful seas.

Tenacious stood by while *Woolmer* began to turn, all aboard holding their breath. Her captain had clearly planned his turn away from the wind, for the small sail left on main and mizzen vanished at exactly the same time as her headsails mounted. The leverage told, and the ship, plunging and rocking like a fractious horse, began putting her bow downwind, faster and faster. A rampaging comber burst on her side, checking her movement, but with the appearance of square sail on her fore – loosed by some heroic topmen aloft – *Woolmer* completed her turn. Rolling drunkenly at first she settled to her new track.

'A princely piece of seamanship as ever I've seen, and with an injured mast!' exclaimed Houghton. Kydd quietly agreed: it had been well done indeed.

'At least they has no worry o' being pooped,' said Hambly, eyeing the stately East Indiaman's high stern. With a following sea there was always the danger of a giant wave overtaking and crowding on to her deck to sweep everything before it.

'That's not m' worry,' Kydd said – seared on his memory was fighting the helm of a similar-sized vessel in the Great Southern Ocean, the frigate *Artemis* on her way round Cape Horn.

Hambly looked at him, troubled. 'What's that, sir?'

'No matter.' Kydd could not voice the fears that had been triggered by the memory.

Houghton broke in decisively: 'I'm going to scud under fore-topmast stays'l and a close-reefed fore tops'l. Mr Hambly?'

'Aye, sir.' Hands went to their stations, Kydd on the poop at the mizzen. The reefed driver was brought in and all sail aft disappeared, released seamen sent to the main deck. *Tenacious* began her turn, experiencing the same vertiginous rolls before she, too, was round with the hard wind at her stern.

Barely set on her course, *Tenacious*'s fore topsail split and was instantly transformed to streaming ribbons. 'I'll have a quick-saver on that,' Houghton shouted at the hurrying boatswain, ordering the replacement topsail and a pair of ropes to be crossed over the sail to prevent it ballooning forward.

Then, there were cries of horror. No more than half a mile away, Kydd saw *Woolmer*, her silhouette dark against the white of the spindrift, strangely misshapen. Her weakened mainmast had given way under the wind pressure: it had splintered and fallen in ruin over the side.

While *Tenacious* watched, agonised, the inevitable happened. The crew were unable to cut away the substantial wreckage in time and it acted as a drag to one side. *Woolmer* yawed. Pulled to one side she was at the mercy of the onrushing water, which pushed her further broadside. Kydd's fears had come to pass: with no ability to come back on course she was forced right over on her beam ends, and the giant seas fell on the helpless vessel. *Lord Woolmer* capsized in a smother of wreckage, her long hull a glistening whale-like rock for a time before she disappeared altogether; lords, ladies and common seamen gone for ever.

'Mr Hambly,' said Houghton, in an unnatural voice, 'the best course for us?'

Hambly tore his eyes away from the scene and pulled himself together. 'Er, to the suth'ard would keep us fr'm the centre. . . We scuds afore the westerly, that's undoubted, until we can show canvas and come about – there's nothing more we c'n do, sir.'

Alone, *Tenacious* fought the sea, men moving silently in a pall of disbelief, senses battered by the hammering wind. For all of twenty hours the ship ran before the tempest until, in the early hours of the next day, the master judged it possible to set square sail on the main and thereby edge closer to the wind. By evening the winds had moderated to the extent that at last *Tenacious* could ease round more westward, towards the now distant Halifax.

But the storm had one last trial for the old ship. By degrees the wind shifted north and the temperature fell. The first whirling snowflakes came, then snow squalls that marched across the seas with dark, brassy interiors bringing intense cold.

It got worse. Ice covered shrouds, sails, decks, freezing exposed faces. It stiffened wet ropes to bars that seamen, with frozen fingers in wet gloves and feet in agony with the cold, had to wrestle with to coil.

Even breathing was painful: Kydd bound a cloth round his face but it soon clogged with ice as moisture froze. Below, the wardroom stank of damp wool, bear-grease and the hides used in foul-weather gear. No one spoke: it was too much effort. Renzi sat with his head in his hands.

On Kydd's watch the wind moan increased, the pitiless blast buffeting him with its fearsome chill. He hugged himself, grateful for his moose-hide jacket, and thought of the hapless men in the fo'c'sle. In the scrappiest clothing against the numbing chill they had to muster on watch day and night, working, enduring.

Hambly came over. 'Shall have t' take in the main tops'l,' he said, looking significantly at Kydd. They had been fortunate until now that they carried the same square sail, close reefed fore and main topsails, but the wind had increased again.

Kydd stared up at the straining sail. There was no question, the ship was over-pressed in these conditions and must be relieved – he could feel it in her laboured response to the helm. He was officer-of-the-watch and the responsibility was his, not the master's.

But there was the deadly glitter of ice on the shrouds, in the tops and along the yards: how could he send men aloft in the almost certain knowledge that for some there would be a cry, a fall and death?

His eyes met Hambly's: there was understanding but no

compassion. Without a word Kydd turned and made his way down to the main deck where the watch on deck shivered, hunkered down in the lee of the weather bulwarks.

They looked up as he descended, their faces dull, fatigued, and pinched with cold. He paused. How could he order them to go aloft into a howling icy hell? Perhaps some rousing speech to the effect that the ship, they themselves even, depended on them taking their lives into their hands and going aloft? No. Kydd had been in their place and knew what was needed.

His face hardened. 'Off y'r rumps, y' lazy swabs. I want th' main tops'l handed, now.' They pulled themselves slowly to their feet. Their weary, stooped figures and bloodshot eyes wrung his heart.

'Lay aloft!' he roared. Every man obeyed. Kydd allowed a grim smile to surface. 'An' there'll be a stiff tot f'r every man jack waiting for ye when you get back. Get moving!'

For two hours, ninety feet above Kydd's head, the men fisted the stiff sail in a violently moving, lethal world. Fingernails split and canvas was stained with blood, tired muscles slipped on icy wood and scrabbled for a hold, minds retreating into a state of numbed endurance.

And for two hours, Kydd stood beneath, his fists balled in his pockets, willing them on, feeling for them, agonising. That day he discovered that there was only one thing of more heroism than going aloft in such a hell: the moral courage to order others to do it.

For two more days *Tenacious* fought her way clear of the storm, which eventually headed north, increasing in malevolence as it went. On the third day the Sambro light was raised – and, after a night of standing off and on, HMS *Tenacious* entered harbour.

Chapter 7

'Damn! That cursed tailor will hound me to my grave,' groaned Pringle. The mail-boat had arrived back from the dockyard and the wardroom sat about the table opening letters and savouring news from home.

Adams, clutching six, retired to his cabin but Bampton slipped his into a pocket and sipped his brandy, balefully watching the animation of the others.

Kydd was trying to make sense of his borrowed *Essays on Politesse Among Nations,* despairing of the turgid phraseology; his restraint in matters social, and sudden access of interest in literature, was generally held to be owing to some obscure improving impulse, and he was mostly left to it.

'You don't care for letters, Mr Kydd,' Pybus said, with acerbity. He had received none himself, but was still scratching away lazily with his quill.

Kydd looked up and saw that there was indeed one letter left on the table. 'For me?' He picked it up. 'From m' sister, Doctor,' he said. She wrote closely, and as usual had turned the page and written again at right-angles through the first to be frugal in the postage.

'Well?' demanded Pybus.

But Kydd was not listening.

Dear Thomas – or should I say Nicholas as well? I do hope you are keeping well, my dears, and wrapping up warm. The willows are budding early along the Wey here in Guildford and . . .

The words rushed on, and Kydd smiled to picture Cecilia at her task. Her evident concern for them both warmed him but her admiration for him as an officer in the King's Navy sparked melancholy.

A hurried paragraph concluded the letter:

. . . and Father says that it would be of service to him should you enquire after his brother Matthew. You remember they came to some sort of a misunderstanding an age ago, and his brother sailed to Philadelphia? Papa says that was in 1763. Since then we have heard nothing of him, except that in the War for Independence he was a loyalist and went north with the others to Halifax in about 1782. Thomas, it would so please Papa to know that he is alive and well – do see if you can find him!

Of course, his uncle: an adventurer in this wilderness land, carving a future for himself – or perhaps he was a successful trader, even a shipowner in the profitable Atlantic trade routes.

'News?' Pybus said drily.

'Oh, aye. Seems it could be m' uncle is here, Doctor, in Halifax. Who would credit it?' A Kydd ashore, possibly one who had achieved eminence in society and was highly thought of in the community. For the first time in a long while he felt a rush of excitement. 'I do believe I'm t' visit him today.'

'Kydd – Mr Matthew Kydd.' It was strange uttering the words. There were not so many Kydds in the world that it felt anything other than his own name.

The man he had stopped considered for a moment. 'Can't say as I've heard of the gentleman, sir,' he said finally. 'You may wish to try Linnard's the tailors. You'll understand they know all the gentry hereabouts.' But Kydd was tiring of the chase. It was becoming clear that his uncle was far from being a notable in Halifax. It had been foolish of him to imagine that one of modest origins could have pretences at high office – but this did not mean that he had not secured a lesser, well-respected place in society.

He toiled up the street, a curious mix of fine stone edifices and shoddy clapboard buildings, but it was not practical to think of entering and asking at random: there had to be a more efficient way. An idea came to him. He would contact Mr Greaves, the commissioner for lands. If his uncle was in any form a landowner he would know him. Kydd brightened as he savoured the effect on his uncle of receiving a card out of the blue from a Lieutenant Kydd shortly about to call.

The land registry was a stiff walk well to the south, and Kydd set out along Barrington Street, past the elegance of St Paul's Church. A line of soldiers was marching up and down on the large open area to his right, and when Kydd approached, the young officer in command halted his men and brought them to attention, then wheeled about and saluted. Kydd lifted his hat to him, which seemed to satisfy. With a further flourish of orders the soldiers resumed their marching.

Then an unwelcome thought struck. Supposing his uncle

had fallen on hard times or was still a humble tradesman? It would make no difference to him – but if Greaves thought he was of lowly origins it might prove embarrassing . . . He would move cautiously and find out first.

'To be sure, a Kydd,' murmured the clerk, at the desk of the weathered timber structure near the old burying ground. 'There was one such, resident of Sackville Street, I seem to recall, but that was some years ago. Let me see . . .' He polished his spectacles and opened a register. 'Ah – we have here one Matthew Kydd, bachelor, established as trader and landowner in the year 1782, property on Sackville Street . . . Hmmm – here we have a contribution to the Sambro light, er, the usual taxation receipts . . .'

It was certainly his uncle. At last! How would he greet him? He had never met the man: he had sailed from England well before Kydd had been born. Should it be 'Uncle Matthew' or perhaps a more formal salutation?

'. . . which means, sir, we have nothing later than the year 1791.'

Kydd's face dropped. 'So—'

'We find no evidence at all for his continued existence after then. I'm sorry.'

'None?'

'No, sir. You may wish to consult the parish books of St Paul's for record of his decease – there was fever here at the time, you understand.'

'Thank ye, sir.' Kydd made to leave, but another clerk was hovering nearby.

'Sir, you may be interested in this . . .' They moved to the other end of the office. 'My wife admired Mr Kydd's work,' he said, 'which is why she bought this for me.' It was a handsomely carved horn of plenty, taking bold advantage of the twisted grain of the wood, and supported at the base by a pair of birds. 'You will understand that time is on our hands in the winter. Mr Kydd used to occupy his in carving, which I think you will agree is in the highest possible taste . . .'

Kydd stroked the polished wood, something his own near relative had created: it felt alive.

'Yes, those birds,' the clerk mused. 'I confess I have no knowledge of them at all – they're not to be seen in this part of Canada. But Mr Kydd always includes them in his work. It's a custom here, a species of signature for claiming fine work as your own.'

'But I recognise it well enough,' Kydd said. 'This is y'r Cornish chough, sir. And it's the bird you find in the coat-of-arms of our own Earl Onslow of Clandon and Guildford.'

The man looked back at him with a bemused kindliness, but there was nothing more to learn here. Kydd emerged into the day: he was not yet due back aboard so his hunt would continue.

But at St Paul's there was no entry for Matthew Kydd, in births, deaths or marriages. A whole hour of searching in the gloom of the old church sacristy yielded only two entries in the tithe-book, and a smudged but tantalising reference to banns being called.

A mystery: at one time he had existed, now he did not. It was time to face the most unsatisfactory result of all: his uncle was not in Halifax but somewhere else in Canada – or, for that matter, he could be anywhere. And it explained why no one seemed to know of a Kydd in Halifax. He would regretfully conclude his search and write to his father accordingly.

'If you'd be so good, Tom . . .' Adams seemed anxious, but it did not take much imagination to grasp why he would want to absent himself from church that Sunday morning.

'I trust she's so charming you hold it of no account that you put your immortal soul to hazard?' Kydd said. The captain had made it plain that he wanted an officer from *Tenacious* at the morning service on Sundays, and it was Adams's turn.

Kydd had no strong feelings about religion, although he enjoyed the hearty singing of the grand old hymns. With his Methodist upbringing he was inured to sitting inactive for long periods.

Army officers with ladies on their arms swept into the church. Other ranks waited respectfully outside and would crowd in later. Kydd took off his hat and made his way inside, settling for an outside seat in a pew towards the front, nodding to the one or two other naval officers scattered about.

A pleasant-faced woman sat down next to him and flashed him an impish smile. 'There, my dear,' said the stern, stiffly dressed man by her, settling a rug about her knees.

'Thank you,' she said, and as soon as it was seemly to do so, turned to Kydd and whispered, 'I don't think I've seen you here, sir.'

'Lieutenant Kydd of the *Tenacious*,' he whispered back, unsure of the etiquette of the occasion.

'Mrs Cox. Your first visit to Halifax, Lieutenant?'

The church was filling fast but the front pew was still decorously empty.

'Yes, Mrs Cox. Er, a fine place f'r trade.'

'Indeed. But when I was a little girl it was a horrid place, believe me, Lieutenant.' She smiled again.

There was a damp, penetrating cold in the cavernous interior of the church, barely relieved by two fat-bellied stoves smoking in corners. Kydd shivered and wished he had brought a watch-coat.

Mrs Cox fumbled in her muff. 'Here you are, Lieutenant,' she said, proffering a silver flask. 'Get some inside and you won't feel the cold.' It was prime West Indian rum. At his ill-concealed astonishment she pressed it on him. 'Go on – we all have to.' Aghast at the thought of drinking in church, Kydd hesitated, then, red-faced, took a pull, but as he lowered the flask he saw an august personage and his lady sweeping up the aisle.

Crimson with embarrassment, Kydd froze. With a gracious inclination of her head, the woman smiled and continued. Kydd handed back the flask and settled for the service, trying not to notice the distracting stream of servants bringing hot bricks for the feet of the quality in the front row.

Outside, after the service, when they passed pleasantries, Kydd remembered that Mrs Cox had been born in Halifax. Impulsively he asked, 'I wonder, Mrs Cox, can you remember less'n ten years ago, a gentleman by the name of Kydd, Matthew Kydd?'

She considered at length. 'I can't say that I do, Lieutenant. A relation?'

'My uncle – I'm tryin' to find him.'

Mr Cox pulled his ear as if trying to recall something. 'Er, there was a gentleman by that name, I think – recollect he was in corn and flour on Sackville Street. Fine-looking fellow.'

'That's him,' said Kydd.

A look of embarrassment flashed over Cox's face. 'Ah.' He gave a warning glance to his wife, whose hand flew to her mouth.

'Then I'm truly sorry to tell you . . . he is no more,' Cox said quietly.

Kydd swallowed.

'Yes. In about the year 'ninety – or was it 'ninety-one? – he went to Chignecto with his partner looking out prospects, but unhappily was mortally injured by a bear.'

'I remember. It was in the newspaper – such a dreadful thing,' Mrs Cox added. 'It never does to disturb them in their sleep, the brutes.'

Cox drew himself up. 'I'm grieved that your search has led you to this, sir. I do hope that the remainder of your time in Halifax will be more felicitous. Good day to you, Lieutenant.'

As was usual for officers in harbour, Kydd's duties were light and he felt he owed it to his father to gather the circumstances of his brother's demise. Possibly he had family, a widow. He would get the details from the newspaper and pass them on.

The *Halifax Journal* office was on Barrington Street, not far from Grand Parade, and the man inside was most obliging. 'Yes, indeed, I remember the story well. A fine man, come to such a fate. Uncle, you say. I'll find the issue presently. If you would be so good . . .'

On a table near the compositing desk Kydd learned the sad details of his uncle's death. He had gone to Chignecto, on the other side of Nova Scotia, exploring prospects in muskrat and beaver. His business partner, an Edward Gilman, had accompanied him, but of the two who had set out, only one returned: Gilman. He had buried his friend and partner at the edge of the wilderness by the sea, then brought back the news.

Judging by the upset expressed in the newspaper, Matthew Kydd had been a man of some substance and standing and was sorely missed. Kydd leafed idly through the rest of the paper.

Out in the street he determined that before he wrote to his father he would find Gilman, ask what kind of man his uncle was, find out something about his end.

Sackville Street was just round the corner, steep and colourful with timber dwellings and shops; some were worn and weathered, others painted brown and yellow or red and white. He found a corn factor with a faded sign telling him that this was Gilman's establishment. There was no mention of 'Kydd'.

He went into the dusty office, where he was met by a suspicious-looking clerk. 'May I speak with Mr Gilman?' Kydd asked.

'Concernin' what?'

'That's my business,' Kydd said.

The man hesitated, clearly baffled by Kydd's naval uniform. 'Mr Gilman,' he called. 'Gennelman wants t' see you.'

Kydd had the feeling of eyes on him. Eventually a hard-looking man appeared, his face showing distrust. 'I'm Gilman. Yes?'

'I think y' knew Matthew Kydd?'

Gilman tensed but said nothing.

'You were with him when he was killed by a bear?'

'You're English,' Gilman said slowly.

'He was m' uncle, came t' Canada in 'seventy-eight.'

Gilman's expression altered slightly. 'I weren't with him. That was my pap.'

The man must have lost his youth early in this hard country, Kydd reflected. 'I'd be much obliged if he could talk with me a little about m' uncle,' he said.

'He can't.' At Kydd's sharp look he added, 'He's bin buried. In the Ol' Burying Ground.'

'Do you remember Matthew Kydd?'

'No.' It was flat and final.

Pybus was unsympathetic. 'Chasing after long-lost relatives is seldom a profitable exercise. Now you have the task before you of communicating grief and loss where before there was harmless wondering. Well done, my boy.'

Kydd sharpened his pen and addressed himself to the task. How to inform his father that his brother was no more, and had met his end in such a hideous way? The plain facts – simply a notification? Or should he spare his father by implying that his death was from natural causes? Kydd had never been one for letters and found the task heavy-going.

He decided to wait for Renzi's return. There was no urgency, and Renzi could readily find words for him, fine, elegant words that would meet the occasion. He put aside his paper and went up on deck.

The master had a telescope trained down the harbour. 'D'ye see that schooner, sir? Country-built an' every bit as good as our own Devon craft.'

Kydd took the telescope. 'Aye, not as full in th' bow, an' has sweet lines on her.'

He kept the glass on the vessel as Hambly added, 'An' that's because of the ice up the St Lawrence, o' course. They'll ship a bowgrace in two or three weeks, when the ice really breaks up. Nasty t' take one o' them floes on the bow full tilt, like.'

The approaching vessel stayed prettily and shortened sail preparatory to anchoring, Kydd watching her. She was a new vessel, judging by the colour of her sails and running rigging. He shifted the view to her trim forefoot, pausing to admire her figurehead – a Scottish lass holding what appeared to be a fistful of heather, a striking figure in a streaming cloak with a pair of birds at her feet.

Birds? He steadied the telescope and, holding his breath, peered hard. He kept his glass on the barque as she glided past. There was no mistake, they were Cornish choughs.

'I'll be damned!' Kydd said softly. Then he swung on Hambly. 'Tell me,' he said urgently, 'do y' know which yard it was built this'n?'

'Can't say as I does.' Hambly seemed surprised at Kydd's sudden energy. 'There's scores o' shipyards up 'n' down the coast, most quite able t' build seagoin' craft o' this size.'

It might be a coincidence – but Kydd felt in his heart it was not. 'The yawl ahoy,' he hailed over the side to *Tenacious*'s boat's crew, then turned back to Hambly. 'I'm going t' see that schooner, Mr Hambly.'

The master of the *Flora MacDonald* did not want to pass the time of day with a lieutenant, Royal Navy. His cargo was to be landed as soon as convenient, and although an impress warrant was not current, who could trust the Navy? However, he did allow that the schooner was new and from St John's Island in the great Gulf of St Lawrence, specifically, the yard of Arthur Owen in New London.

Was it conceivable that his uncle had survived and was now working as a ship-carver on an island somewhere on the other side of Nova Scotia? It made no sense to Kydd. Why hadn't his uncle returned to take up his business? It was coincidence, it had to be.

But he knew he would regret it if he did not follow up this tantalising sign. A quick glance at a chart showed St John's Island no more than a couple of days' sail with a fair wind and if Canso strait was free of ice.

Although *Tenacious* was required in port by the absence of

the admiral and his flagship, activity aboard was light, and there was no difficulty with his request for a week's leave.

It was probably only someone continuing his uncle's particular carving signature, but the expedition would be a welcome change and would give him a chance to see something of Canada. He asked Adams if he wished to come, and was not surprised at his regrets – his diary was full for weeks ahead. Kydd was going to adventure alone.

Vessels were making the run to the newly ice-free St John's Island with supplies after the winter and Kydd quickly found a berth, in a coastal schooner, the *Ethel May*. Wearing comfortable, plain clothes, he swung in his small sea-bag.

The beat up the coast was chill and wet, but the schooner's fore and aft rig allowed her to lie close to the north-easterly and she made good time; Cape Breton Island, the hilly passage of Canso strait, then the calmer waters in the gulf, and early in the morning of the second day they closed with St John's Island.

It was a flat, barely undulating coastline with red cliffs and contrasting pale beaches. The dark carpet of forest was blotched in places with clearings, and even before they gybed and passed the long narrow sandspit into New London Bay Kydd had seen signs of shipbuilding – gaunt ribs on slipways, timber stands, distant smoke from pitch fires.

In the sheltered waters the schooner glided towards a landing stage with a scatter of tidy weatherboard buildings beyond. 'Where y' bound?'

'Owen's yard,' Kydd answered.

The skipper pointed along the foreshore. 'Around th' point, one o' the oldest on St John's.' He pronounced it 'Sinjuns'.

'Thank ye,' Kydd said, feeling for coins to put into the man's outstretched hand. It had been a quick trip, and sleeping in a borrowed hammock in the tiny saloon was no imposition.

Kydd pushed past the crowd and the buckboard carts that had materialised on the schooner's arrival, hefted his sea-bag and set out.

The road was slush and red mud that the passing inhabitants seemed to ignore. Women wore old-fashioned bonnets and carried large bundles, their skirts long enough for modesty but revealing sturdy boots beneath. Men passed in every kind of dress; utility and warmth took first place over fashion. All looked at Kydd with curiosity – few strangers came to this out-of-the-way place.

The buildings were all of a style, mainly timbered, with high, steeply sloping roofs; the fields were wooden-fenced, not a stone wall in sight. English hamlets had lanes that meandered over the countryside; here there were bold straight lines in everything from settlements to roads.

The shipyard was not big: two slipways and a jetty, a blacksmith's shop and buildings presumably housing the workforce. Kydd tried to keep his hopes in check but he felt a thrill of anticipation as he approached one of the half-built hulls. 'Is this Mr Owen's yard?' he hailed shipwrights at work high up on staging.

'It is,' one called.

'Th' one that built the *Flora MacDonald*?'

'The very same.'

'Could y' tell me if you've heard of a Mr Kydd – Matthew Kydd?' blurted Kydd.

'Can't say as we heard any o' that name on th' island, friend.'

'I'd like t' meet the ship-carver who worked on her figurehead, if y' please,' Kydd said.

'We don't do carvin' in this yard. Ye'll want Josh Ellis.'

Ellis ran a small business in town. Kydd found the shop and a well-built man of about thirty came to the counter. 'I'd like t' speak with Mr Ellis,' Kydd said.

'That's me.'

He was obviously not old enough to be his uncle; Kydd tried to hide his disappointment. 'Did you work the figure-head o' the *Flora MacDonald*, Mr Ellis?'

'*Flora MacDonald*?' he reflected. 'That's right, I remember now, pretty little schooner from Arthur Owen. Do ye wish one for y'self?'

'Fine work,' Kydd answered carefully. 'Did ye carve the birds an' all?'

'I did.'

'What sort o' birds are they, then?'

'Well, I guess any ol' bird, nothin' special.'

'Nobody told you how t' carve them?'

'What is it y' wants? Not a carving, I figure,' Ellis said, defensive.

'I'm sorry if I offended – y' see, those birds are special, Cornish choughs. You only find 'em in England an' they're rare.'

Ellis said nothing, watching Kydd.

'An' they remind me of m' uncle. You find 'em on the coat-of-arms of our earl, in Guildford.' There was still no response. 'I came here because I thought I'd find out somethin' of him – Kydd, Matthew Kydd.'

'No one b' that name on the island, I c'n tell y' now.' He folded his arms across his chest.

Kydd saw there was no point in continuing. The whole thing looked like coincidence, and if there was anything more he could not think why. 'Well, it was only a fancy. I'll wish ye good day, sir.'

*   *   *

184

He decided to head back to his ship. The landing-stage was close, but there were no vessels alongside and it was deserted. He hesitated, then made for the small general store in the main street to enquire about a passage back to Halifax.

'None I knows of t'day.' The shopkeeper stroked his jaw. 'Could be one's goin' t'morrow or the next – we don't have a reg'lar-goin' packet, only traders.'

Kydd lumped his bag on the counter. 'Seems I'm stranded. D'ye have an inn, b' chance?'

'No, sir,' he said with amusement, 'but y' might try Mrs Beckwith. Her husband were a seagoin' gentleman.'

'Yes indeed,' said Mrs Beckwith. 'I have a room fit fer a adm'ral, bless ye. Stow yer dunnage an' tonight I'll bring alongside as fine a line o' vittles as'll stick t' yer ribs.'

Kydd decided to walk off his expectations; the letter was waiting to be written when he returned to *Tenacious* and he was in no rush to begin it. Besides, the tranquillity of this strange land was appealing: tiny shoots of green were now appearing at the sunny edges of fields, even flowers peeping up through winter-bleached grass. The silence stretched away into the distance. It could not have been more remote from war and the striving of nations.

'So far fr'm the Old Country,' Mrs Beckwith said, as the dinner was brought in by a well-built young man. 'Oh – this is Mr Cunnable, he boards wi' me too.'

'Er, yes. That is, it's a long way t' England.'

'Mr Kydd, help y'self. This is our salt cod, an' we got a pile more o' them potatoes. Now, would ye mind tellin' me, how do th' ladies in London Town have their hair this year?

Heard tell, high style well powdered 'n' greased over y'r pads is quite past.'

'Thank you, Mrs Beckwith, salt cod will be fine with me. Er, the ladies o' quality I think now are windin' it up and fixin' it to the top of their heads. This is damn fine fish even if I do say so. But these leaves, I can't recollect we have any of them in England.'

'Sour dock an' sheep sorrel. Gives winter vittles a mort more flavour. So you're a Navy officer! Then y' must've been to some o' them great balls an' banquets with our Prince Edward! They do say they're goin' to change the name o' this island after him.'

'We've only been here a short while, an' our admiral is away in Newfoundland, but I'm sure we'll be invited soon.' Kydd lifted his glass; in it was a golden brown liquid, which he tasted gingerly. It was a species of ale, with an elusive tang of malt and spice.

'Seed-wheat wine – made it m'self. Tell me, Mr Kydd, in England do they . . .' She paused, frowning, at a knock on the door. ''Scuse me.'

Kydd nibbled at what appeared to be a peppery-flavoured dried seaweed and listened to Mrs Beckwith's shrill voice rising, scolding, and another, quieter. She returned eventually, flushed and irritable. 'It's very wrong t' disturb ye, Mr Kydd, but there's a woman here wants t' see you an' won't go away.'

Kydd got up. 'She's Irish,' warned Mrs Beckwith. 'If y' like, shall I ask Mr Cunnable t' set the dog on her?'

'No, no. I'll come.'

A woman in a shawl hung back in the darkness and spoke quietly: 'Good evenin' to yez, sorr – an' you're the gennelman just come ter the island an' asking after his uncle?'

'Yes, that's right.'

'Then I'm t' tell ye, if tomorrow at noon y' comes with me, you'll meet someone as knows what happened t' him.'

The next day, dressed economically, she was waiting motionless down the road. Kydd saw that, despite her lined face, she held herself proudly. Without a word she turned and walked away from the town.

Where the river shoreline came close she turned down a path. It led to the river and a birchbark canoe with an Indian standing silently by it. The woman muttered some words and the Indian turned his black eyes on Kydd and grunted.

The canoe was much bigger than he had imagined, twenty feet long at least, and made of birch bark strips. There were cedar ribs as a crude framework and seams sewn with a black root. It had half a dozen narrow thwarts and Kydd was surprised to see it quite dry.

In the middle part, a good five feet across, there was a mound of baggage. 'If ye'd kindly get in like this, sorr,' the woman said. She leaned across the canoe until she held both sides, then, transferring her weight, stepped in neatly and sat. 'Be sure t' stand in th' very middle,' she added.

Kydd did as he was told, sitting behind her in the front part. The Indian shoved off, swung in, and began to ply his paddle in a powerful rhythm that quickly had them out in the river and gliding along rapidly. He worked silently, his face set like stone, and the woman did not offer any conversation.

They left cleared land behind, dark green anonymous forest stretching away endlessly on both sides. Eventually the Indian ceased paddling, then spun the canoe round and grounded it at the forest's edge.

'Nearly there,' the woman said. They left the Indian to follow with the baggage and took a footpath into the trees. Kydd felt as if the forest was closing in; with its hard green conifers uniformly shaped to shed snow, unknown cries and sudden snapping in the undergrowth, it was utterly different from the soft deciduous woodland of England. Kydd thought of his uncle, killed by a bear that had burst from the trees, and was afraid. Why had he agreed to this madness?

Suddenly he glimpsed the dark blue of water, and a grey spiral of smoke. 'Here!' the woman said happily, as they came upon a cluster of log cabins in a patch of land leading down to the sea. She called, and a man appeared. He stood on the porch of one of the largest cabins, a big man, long-haired and with a deep chest; he wore moose-hide worked with porcupine quills.

'My husband Joseph Bourne, sorr.'

The man shook hands with Kydd, looking at him keenly. Kydd felt the strength and hardness in his clasp. 'I hear you knew my uncle, Matthew Kydd, Mr Bourne,' Kydd said.

'Very close t' me, he were,' Bourne said at length, in a deep Canadian burr. 'Come inside, sit y'self down.'

The cabin was snug and warm with a steeply sloping cedar-shingle roof; the logs chinked smoothly on the inside. Skins and two bear hams hung from the high beams. Woven Indian matting decorated the walls and a pair of long guns was crossed above the fire. It smelt pungently of smoke and human living.

Two rocking chairs faced the fire, and the men sat together. 'M' wife got t' hear of you in town,' he said, in a voice both soft and slow. 'Thought I could help.'

Kydd murmured something, conscious of the man's look.

'You're fr'm the old country,' Bourne said. 'Fr'm what part do ye hail?'

'Guildford, which is in Surrey.'

'Very pretty, I heard.'

'Mr Bourne, ye said you'd tell me of m' uncle Matthew,' said Kydd.

'All in God's good time, friend,' Bourne said, and leaned round his chair. 'Colleen, c'n you fetch us a jug o' beer, darlin', and some moose jerky? Our guest's come a long way t' be here. Now, y'r uncle Matthew.' He collected a long pipe and tobacco pouch from the chimneypiece above the fire. 'Need t' think,' he said, as he stuffed the bowl and got a light from the fire. When he had it going to satisfaction, he started: 'He came t' Nova Scotia fr'm the Colonies in 'seventy-eight – wanted no truck wi' revolutions an' that. Set himself up in business, an' did well for hisself. Then got destroyed by a bear in Chignecto country.'

Kydd tried to hide his irritation – that much he already knew, and if the man simply wanted company . . . 'Sir, it would oblige me greatly, should you—'

'His wife died in Halifax o' the fever. Had three bairns, all taken. That was in 'eighty-four.' He drew long on his pipe, staring into the fire. 'After that, well, I guess he took a dif-f'rent slant on life. Got inta business, corn tradin' an' such. Did well, laid out silver in the right place an' got him a gov-'ment contract f'r the Army, set up in Sackville Street, noticed by th' governor . . . but never remarried.'

'What kind o' man d'ye think he was?'

Bourne poured from a stone jug into colourful pottery tankards and offered one. From the woodsy taste, Kydd recognised it as spruce beer – it had a compelling bitterness and he decided it was an acquired taste.

'A straight arrow, I reckon. Hard worker but . . .'

'Mr Bourne?'

'But I'm thinkin' he weren't so happy, really.' He lapsed again into an introspective silence.

Kydd coughed meaningfully and asked, 'I have t' ask if you know anything about his bein' taken by the bear. Was it . . . quick?' His father would want details.

Bourne puffed once more, then said quietly, 'Who wants t' know?'

'Why, he had an elder brother who's my papa. They parted years afore I was born, some sort o' misunderstanding. M' father's gettin' frail an' hoped t' be reconciled. Now I have to write t' him, you understand.'

Bourne got to his feat, crossed to the fire and knocked out his pipe on a log. He turned, but did not resume his chair, looking at Kydd with an unsettling intensity.

Then his gaze shifted; his wife was standing rigid behind Kydd, staring at her husband. His eyes returned to Kydd. 'You're a smart lad. What d' they call ye?'

'I'm Thomas – Tom Kydd.' He looked steadily at the older man. 'An' do I call ye Uncle?' he added softly.

In the stillness the hardwood fire snapped and spat, sending up fountains of red sparks. For a long time Bourne held his silence, until Kydd thought he had not heard. Then he spoke. 'I guess you do that,' he said.

'Come, lass, sit by we,' Kydd's uncle said, after composure had been regained and whisky had been downed. She moved over and sat on the floor, close.

'I'm goin' t' tell ye the whole nine yards, Thomas – Tom. It's a long ways fr'm here to Guildford, so don't go makin' judgements before you've heard me out. I told ye no lie. About seven, eight year ago I weren't happy. Ye might say I was miserable. I got t' thinkin' about life 'n' all, and knew I

190

was a-wastin' the years God gave me. So I did somethin' about it. Simple, really. I did a deal with m' partner – Ned Gilman, right true sort he were. I spelled out t' him that if he said I was took by a bear, an' let me start a new life, I'd let him have the business. We shook on it, an' I guess that's it – here I am.'

'Just – gave him th' business?'

'I did. But he suffered for it!' His face wrinkled in amusement. 'Folk said th' bear tale was all a story – that really he'd murthered me an' left me t' rot, while he came back alone 'n' claimed th' business.'

Kydd remembered the hostility his enquiries had met and now understood. 'Will ye leave y'r bones here, d'ye think?' It was a far, far place, England, where ancient churches and the old ways comforted, with graveyards, ceremony and mourning at life's end. What was there of that in this raw land?

'Tom, you don't know this land, y' never lived here. It's hard, break-y'r-heart bad at times, but it's beautiful – *because* it's so hard.'

He stood up suddenly. 'Come wi' me.' He strode to the door and out into the gathering dusk. The sun was going down in a display of soft lilac and grey; a mist hung over the still waters and the peace was only broken by the secret sounds of nature.

'See there? It's a land so big we don't know how far it is t' the other side. It's new an' raw, open to all – the west an' the north is all waiting, mile on mile o' country without it's seen a man. But that's what I want, t' be at peace. M' heart is here, Tom, where I c'n live like God means me to.'

Kydd saw his face light up as he spoke. 'How d' ye live? Y'r carving?'

Turning to him the older man spoke quietly but firmly. 'T' you, I'm a poor man. I ask ye to think of what I have here – all m' time is my own, all of it. This place is mine, I built it m'self as I want it. And yes, I carve – in winter y' has a lot o' time, an' what better than t' create with y'r own hands?'

He chuckled. 'Y' saw the choughs. I didn't think t' see anyone fr'm old Guildford here. But it keeps me in coin enough t' meet m' needs.' He threw open a door to a side cabin. In the gloom Kydd could see huge figures: griffons, mermaids, solemn aldermen and long, decorative side panels. The odour of fresh-carved timber chips was resinous and powerful. 'The yards 're startin' for th' year. They'll be wantin' the winter's work now.'

They trudged back to the main cabin. A train-oil lamp was burning inside, intensifying the shadows, while the smell of beef pie and potatoes eddied about.

'Now, m' lad, how's about you tell me about Guildford an' y'r folks?'

Kydd talked of the old country, of the stirring changes that had resulted from this final great war with the French, the school they had bravely started, the appearance of various little ones in the family. At one point Kydd stopped, letting the stillness hang, then asked carefully, 'We were told there was a misunderstanding with my papa, Uncle. Was it s' bad you remember it t' this day?'

His uncle guffawed loudly. 'Was at first, but then I hears after she married someone else anyhow. Didn't seem right t' start up writin' again so . . .'

The evening was a great success. Colleen brought out a hoarded jar of blueberry wine and, in its glow, stories of old times and old places were exchanged long into the dark night.

'So you've never regretted it?'

'Never!' His hand crept out to take hers. 'In Halifax they'd never let an Irish woman in t' their society. I'd always be tryin'. Here we live content the same as man 'n' wife, an' here we stay.'

The fire flared and crackled, the hours passed and the fire settled to embers. Eventually Kydd yawned. 'Have t' return to m' ship tomorrow,' he said, with real regret.

His uncle said nothing, staring into the fire. Then he took a deep breath. 'Seems y' have a teaser on y' hands, m' boy.'

'A problem?'

'Yes, sir. Now, consider – you've seen me, alive 'n' well. You have t' decide now what ye say to y'r father. The world knows I was killed by a bear. Are you goin' to preserve m' secret an' let it stand, or will ye ease his human feelings 'n' say I'm here?'

'I – I have t' think on it,' was all Kydd could find to say.

His uncle gave a slow smile. 'I'm sure ye'll know what t' do.' His gaze on Kydd was long – and fond.

'Wait here,' he said, and went outside.

While he was gone, Kydd's thoughts turned to his father. Where was the mercy in telling him that, according to the world, his brother was no more? Or, on the other hand, that his brother was alive and well but had turned his back on society, preferring a pariah woman and a vast wilderness?

There was just one course he could take that would be both merciful and truthful. He would say that, according to the records, his uncle Matthew had lived in Halifax doing well until 1791 but had then moved somewhere else in the immense country of Canada. In this way at least his father would remain in hope.

The door creaked open and his uncle returned with an object wrapped in old sacking. 'You're goin' to be the last

Kydd I ever sees,' he said thickly, 'an' I'm glad it were you. See here—' He passed across the sacking. It contained something heavy, a single, undistinguished black rock. But, breaking through it in several places, Kydd saw a dull metallic gleam. Gold. Astonished, Kydd took it, feeling its weight.

'Fell down a ravine years ago, goin' after a animal, an' there it was. But it's no use t' me – I bring that t' town an' in a brace o' shakes it'll be crawlin' with folks grubbin' up th' land an' fightin'. Never bin back, leave th' rest in the good earth where it belongs. But you take it – an' use it to get somethin' special, something that'll always remind ye of y'r uncle Matthew in Canada.'

Chapter 8

Seamen were hoisting in heavy stone bottles of spruce-beer essence. Admiral Vandeput considered the drink essential to the health of his squadron.

'I'll sweat the salt fr'm your rascally bones – sink me if I don't.' The squeaky voice of a midshipman was unconvincing: he had a lot to learn about the handling of men, Kydd thought, and turned away irritably. He put his head inside the lobby. Adams had promised to relieve him, but was nowhere to be found. Kydd returned impatiently to the quarterdeck. The seamen had finished their work and all of the wicker-covered jars were below at last.

The last man of the work party was still on deck, slowly coiling down the yardarm tackle fall. There was something disquieting about this thick-set seaman: Kydd had seen him come aboard with the new men and several times he'd noticed the man looking his way with a significant cast.

Kydd paced forward. The man glanced over his shoulder at him and turned his back, busying himself with his task. When Kydd drew near he straightened and turned, touching his forelock. 'Mr Kydd, sir,' he said, his voice not much more than a low rasp.

Surprised, Kydd stopped.

'Sir, ye remembers me?'

There was an edge of slyness to his manner that Kydd did not like. Was he a sea-lawyer perhaps? But the man was only a little shorter than Kydd himself, powerfully built, with hard, muscular arms and a deep tattooed chest: he had no need of cozening ways on the mess-deck.

The man gave a cold smile. 'Dobbie, petty officer o' the afterguard,' he added, still in a low tone.

Kydd could not recall anyone by that name. The midshipman popped up out of the main-hatchway but saw them together and disappeared below again. 'No, can't say as I do,' Kydd replied. Unless the seaman had something of value to say to an officer he was sailing closer to the wind than a common sailor should. 'I don't remember you, Dobbie – now be about y'r duties.'

He turned to go, but Dobbie said quietly, 'In *Sandwich.*' Kydd stopped and turned. Dobbie stared back, his gaze holding Kydd's with a hard intensity. 'Aye – when you was there. *I* remembers ye well . . . sir.'

It had been less than a year ago but the *Sandwich* was a name Kydd had hoped never to hear again. She had been the mutineers' flagship and at the centre of the whirlwind of insurrection and violence at the Nore. It had climaxed in failure for the mutiny and an end to the high-minded attempt to complete the work begun at Spithead. Many sailors had paid with their lives. Kydd had joined the mutiny in good faith but had been carried along by events that had overwhelmed them all. But for mysterious appeals at the highest level he should have shared their fate.

'Dick Parker. Now there was a prime hand, don' ye think? Saw what was goin' on, but concerns hisself with the men, not th' gentry. Sorely missed, is he.'

Kydd drew back. Was Dobbie simply trying to ingratiate himself, or was this a direct attempt at drawing Kydd into some crazy plot? Anxiety and foreboding flooded in. Either way this had to be stopped.

'Enough o' this nonsense. Where I came from before I went t' the quarterdeck is no concern o' yours, Dobbie. Pay y'r respects to an officer an' carry on.' Even in his own ears it rang false, lacking in authority.

Dobbie looked relaxed, a lazy smile spreading across his face. Kydd glanced uneasily about; no one was within earshot. 'Did ye not hear? I said—'

'Me mates said t' me, "An' who's this officer then, new-rigged an' has the cut o' the jib of the fo'c'sle about 'im?" What c'n I say?' Dobbie was confident and as watchful as a snake. 'I keeps m' silence, 'cos I knows you has t' keep discipline, an' if they catches on that you is th' Tom Kydd as was alongside Dick Parker all the time—'

'What is it ye want?' Kydd snapped.

Dobbie picked up the end of the fall and inspected its whipping, then squinted up at Kydd. 'Ah, well. I was wonderin' – you was in deep. Not a delegate, but 'twas your scratch what was clapped on all them vittlin' papers, I saw yez. Now don't y' think it a mort strange that so many good men went t' the yardarm but Mr Tom Kydd gets a pardon? Rest gets the rope, you gets th' King's full pardon 'n' later the quarterdeck.' The lazy smile turned cruel. 'We gets t' sea, the gennelmen in the fo'c'sle hear about you, why, could go hard f'r a poxy spy . . .'

Kydd flushed.

Dobbie tossed aside the rope and folded his arms. 'Your choice, Mr Tom Kydd. You makes m' life sweet aboard – I'm a-goin' t' be in your division – or the fo'c'sle hands are goin' to be getting some interestin' news.'

'Damn you t' hell! I didn't—' But Dobbie turned and padded off forward.

Kydd burned with emotion. It was utterly beyond him to have spied treacherously on his shipmates as they had fought together for their rights. He was incapable of such an act. But the men of the fo'c'sle would not know that. Dobbie was one of them, and he was claiming to have been with Kydd at the mutiny and to have the full story. Unable to defend himself in person, Kydd knew there was little doubt whom they would believe.

The consequences could not be more serious. He would not be able to command these men, that much was certain; the captain would quickly recognise this and he would be finished as an officer. But it might be worse: a dark night, quiet watch and a belaying pin to the head, then quickly overside . . .

And the wardroom – if they believed he owed his advancement to spying and betrayal, what future had he among them?

It was incredible how matters had reached such a stand so quickly. He would have to move fast, whatever his course. The obvious action was to submit. It had definite advantages. Nothing further would happen because it was in Dobbie's interest to keep his leverage intact. And it would be simple: Kydd as an officer could easily ensure Dobbie's comfortable existence.

The other tack would be to brazen it out. But Kydd knew this was hopeless: he would be left only with his pride at not yielding to blackmail, and that was no choice at all.

He yearned for Renzi's cool appraisal and logical options: he would find the answers. But he was in Newfoundland. Kydd was not close to Adams and the others: he would have to face it alone.

His solitary, haunted pacing about the upper deck did not seem to attract attention, and two hours had passed before he found his course of action.

Kydd knew the lower deck, is strengths and loyalties as well as its ignorance; its rough justice and depth of sentiment could move men's souls to achieve great things – or stir them to passionate vindictiveness. He would now put his trust in them, an unshakeable faith that he, even as an officer, could rely on their sense of honour, fairness and loyalty.

The afternoon ebbed to a pallid dusk, and the hands secured, then went below for grog and supper. Kydd waited until they were in full flow. Then he went down the after hatchway to the gun-deck and paused at the foot of the ladder.

The mess-tables were rigged and the usual warm conviviality of a meal-time, enlivened by rum, rose noisily from the tables between the rows of guns. A few curious looks came his way, but in the main seamen were more interested in the gossip of the day and he was ignored.

Methodically, he removed his cocked hat. Then he took off his lieutenant's uniform coat and laid it carefully over his arm. By this time he had the attention of the nearest, who looked at him in astonishment.

He paced forward slowly, and with terrible deliberation. One by one the tables lapsed into an amazed silence, which grew and spread until the whole gun-deck fell into an unnatural quiet and men craned forward for a better view.

Kydd continued his walk, his face set and grim, eyes fixed

forward in an unblinking stare. He was either right to trust – or he had lost everything. He passed the great jeer capstan, the mighty trunk of the mainmast, the main hatch gratings, his measured tread now sounding clear and solemn.

He halted abreast the fore capstan, his eyes still fixed forward. Slowly his gaze turned to one side: Dobbie sat, transfixed, at the mess by number-five gun. Kydd marched over. Not a man moved. He held Dobbie with his eyes, dropping his words into the silence. 'I'll be waiting for ye – the Mizzen tavern. At two, tomorrow.' Then he wheeled about and began the long walk back down the silent gun-deck.

In the privacy of his cabin Kydd buried his face in his hands. As an officer there was no question of how to deal with a slur on one's honour: a duel was the inevitable result. Dobbie was not a gentleman, therefore Kydd could not demean himself in calling him out. But this was a matter for the lower-deck: different rules applied. By now the news would be already around the ship. It was too late for him to back away – and also for Dobbie.

Dobbie was big and a bruiser, well used to a mill. Kydd could take care of himself, but this was another matter. Of a surety he would be the loser, in all probability suffering a battering and disfiguring injury. But the result would be worth it. Never more would any man question his honour or integrity: Dobbie's word would be hollow against that of a man who had set aside the power and privileges that were his by right to defend his honour in the traditional way.

Kydd had no fear of it coming to the ear of the captain – or any other officer, for that matter. It would be common currency on the mess-decks and every seaman and petty officer would know of it, but it was their business and, as with so many other things, the quarterdeck never would hear of it.

He slept well: there was little to be gained in brooding on hypothetical events of the next day and in any case there was nothing he could do about it now that events had been set in train.

As he moved about the ship there were surreptitious looks, curious stares and a few morbid chuckles. He went below to find his servant. 'Er, Tysoe, there is something of a service I want you t' do for me.'

'Sir, don't do it, sir, please, I beg,' Tysoe said, with a low, troubled voice. 'You're a gentleman, sir, you don't have to go mixing with those villains.'

'I have to, an' that's an end to it.'

Tysoe hesitated, then asked unhappily, 'The service, sir?'

'Ah – I want you to find a fo'c'sle hand who c'n lend me a seaman's rig f'r this afternoon. Er, it'll be cleaned up after.'

'Sir.' But Tysoe did not leave, disconsolately shuffling his feet. 'Sir, I'm coming with you.'

'No.' Kydd feared he would be instantly discovered and probably roughed up: he could not allow it. 'No, but I thank ye for your concern.'

There was a fitful cold drizzle when Kydd stepped into the boat, which gave him an excuse to wear a concealing oilskin. Poulden was stroke; he had gruffly volunteered to see Kydd through to the Mizzen tavern, but made determined efforts not to catch his eye as he pulled strongly at his oar.

They landed at King's Slip. Without a word, Kydd and Poulden stepped out and the boat shoved off. The waterfront was seething with activity and they pushed through firmly to Water Street.

It was lined with crude shanties and pot-houses; raw weathered timbers abuzz with noise, sailors and women coming and going, the stink of old liquor and humanity in the air. A larger hostelry sported a miniature mast complete with upper yards, jutting out from a balcony. 'The Fore, sir,' said Poulden, self-consciously. 'We has three inns; the Fore, the Main, 'n' the Mizzen, which, beggin' yer pardon, we understands t' be respectively the wildest, gayest an' lowest in Halifax.' Hoisted on the Fore's mast was the sign of a red cockerel, a broad hint to the illiterate of the pleasures within.

Kydd's heart thudded, but he was angry with Dobbie — not so much for trying such a scheme but for the slur on Kydd's character. His anger focused: whatever the outcome of the next few hours he would see to it that he left marks on Dobbie.

They swung down a side-street to see a crowd of jostling men outside an entrance with a small mizzen mast. 'Sir, gotta leave ye now.' Poulden returned the way he came, leaving Kydd on his own. His mouth dried. Screeches of female laughter and roars of appreciation at some unseen drunken feat filled the air. As a young seaman he'd been in places like this, but he had forgotten how wild and lawless they were.

'There he is! Told yer so!' Heads turned and Kydd was engulfed with a human tide that jollied him inside, all red faces and happy anticipation. A black-leather can was shoved at him, its contents spilling down his front. 'No, thank ye,' he said quickly, thrusting it away.

Women on the stairs looked at him with frank curiosity, some with quickening interest at his strong, good looks. A hard-featured seaman and two others tried to push through. 'Gangway, y' scrovy bastards, an' let a man see who it is then,' he grumbled.

'Akins, Master o' the Ring. I have t' ask, are ye Lootenant Kydd an' no other?' The taphouse broke into excited expectancy at Kydd's reply. He recognised both of the others: Dean, boatswain's mate of *Tenacious*, standing with brutal anticipation, and Laffin, petty officer of the afterguard, wearing a pitying expression. There were others from *Tenacious*, their images barely registering on Kydd's preternaturally concentrated senses.

'Are ye willing t' stand agin Bill Dobbie, L'tenant, the fight t' be fair 'n' square accordin' t' the rules?' There was a breathy silence. Bare-knuckle fighting was brutal and hard, but there were rules – the Marquess of Queensberry had brought some kind of order to the bloody business.

'Aye, I'm willing.'

The pothouse erupted. 'Fight's on, begob, an' me bung's on Dobbie.'

This was going to be a legendary match to be talked of for years. The crush was stifling, but Laffin cleared the way with his fists and they passed through the damp sawdust and sweaty, shoving humanity to the sudden cool of the outside air. It was a small inner courtyard with rickety weathered buildings on all four sides. In the centre, sitting on a standard seaman's chest, was Dobbie.

Kydd stopped as the significance of the chest crowded in on him. This was not going to be a fight according to Queensberry's rules: this was a traditional way of the lower deck to settle the worst of grudges – across a sea-chest. They would sit facing each other over its length, lashed in place, to batter at each other until one yielded or dropped senseless.

To back away now was impossible. He had to go through with it. He took in Dobbie's deep chest and corded arms.

His fists were massive and strapped up with darkened, well-used leather. There was no doubt that Kydd was in for heavy punishment.

The men and women in the courtyard were shouting obscene encouragement to Dobbie, urging him to take it out on an officer while he had the chance. A hoot of laughter started up at the back of the crowd and Kydd's servant was propelled to the front.

'Tysoe!'

'Sir, sir—' He had a bundle clutched to his chest, and his frightened eyes caught Kydd's. 'I came, sir, I – I came—'

'He's come t' drag Tom Cutlass home after, like,' chortled Dean. It was the first Kydd had heard of any lower-deck nickname – from the desperate time fighting in the boat when his sword had broken and he had taken up a familiar cutlass. Strangely, it strengthened his resolve.

'Don't worry, Tysoe, I'll see ye right!' Kydd said forcefully, above the crowd.

The laughter died as the men sensed the time had come. Kydd looked directly at Dobbie, who returned the look with a glittering-eyed malignity. 'Get on wi' it, yer sluggards!' screamed one woman, her cries taken up by the baying circle of men. Scowling, Akins turned to Kydd. 'Get y'r gear off, then, mate.'

Kydd pulled off his shirt, feeling the icy cold wind playing on his bare torso. There was a stir of amazed comment as the stretched and distorted scars criss-crossing his back were recognised for what they were: a relic of the long-ago agony of lashes from a cat-o'-nine-tails at a grating. The women's screeches diminished and the crowd subsided.

Laffin produced cords and Kydd took his place at the other end of the chest, feeling the feral impact of Dobbie's presence, his heart racing at the carnage about to be wrought. The ropes cut into his legs, but his eyes rose to lock on Dobbie's.

'Are ye ready, gemmun?' Akins had no watch, no tools of a referee – this was going to be a smashing match. A thin, cold rain began, chilling Kydd's skin and running into his eyes, mixing with salt sweat, stinging and distracting. He raised his fists slowly, his heart hammering. Dobbie responded, holding his low for a first murderous punch, his pale, unblinking eyes locked on Kydd's.

Akins raised his arm, looking at each in turn. His eyes flickered once and the arm sliced down. 'Fight!' he yelled and leaped aside.

For one split second, Dobbie held Kydd's eyes, then cut loose with a bellow. 'No!' he roared, dropping his arms. 'Be buggered! I'll not do it!'

The crowd fell into an astonished silence, staring at Dobbie. He thrust his head forward, his fists by his side. 'Take a swing, mate – come on, make it a settler.'

Kydd, shaken but suddenly understanding, obliged with a meaty smack to the jaw, which rocked Dobbie. Laffin came forward with his knife and severed the ropes. Dobbie got to his feet. He shook his head and turned to the rowdy crush. 'Shipmates! Y' came t' see a grudge fight, an' I'm sorry I can't give yez one. See, this 'ere is Tom Kydd as I remember fr'm the Nore – I saw 'im stand alongside Dick Parker 'n' them in the mutiny when others were runnin' like rats. But I thought as 'ow 'e got 'is pardon by sellin' out his mates, an' I told him so.

'Mates, if y' wants a lesson in honour, Mr Kydd's yer man. Won't stand fer anyone takin' 'im fer a villain without 'e stands up fer 'isself, an' that's why 'e sees me 'ere – a duel, like. An

I 'ave ter say, I didn't reckon 'e'd 'ave the sand t' see it through, sling 'is mauley like a good 'un, 'im bein' an officer an' all.'

He turned back to Kydd and touched his forehead. 'I'd take it kindly in ye should y' shake m' hand, sir.'

A roar of wild applause burst out, going on and on, until Dobbie held up his arms. 'M' lads – I want yer t' unnerstand, this 'ere Kydd is one of us, but 'e's done good fer 'imself, an' that's no crime. An' I f'r one is going ter foller Lootenant Kydd.'

'All bets 'r off, gennelmen!' bawled Akins.

The press of spectators broke into riotous commotion. Kydd's comprehension of events rapidly disintegrated – he was being slapped on the back and idolised by dozens of drunken seamen. An unwilling Tysoe was plied with beer; women's gleeful painted faces danced before him; and Dobbie, now the centre of a throng of seamen, was telling the story of the great mutiny of the Nore.

Admiral Vandeput and his squadron returned three days later, joining *Tenacious* at her anchorage. Kydd was in the boat returning from the flagship, and could see Renzi waiting on the quarterdeck of *Tenacious*, and dared a brief wave. It was good to see his friend and the clouds lifted from his spirit.

Clutching the precious pouch of despatches and confidential signal information, Kydd hauled himself up the side and took Renzi's hand. 'I'd thought to see you flag-lieutenant b' now,' he said.

'Flag-lieutenant? Not if the present incumbent can help it.' Renzi chuckled drily. 'And while you've been in this Arcadia resting, I've been privy to secrets concerning the cod fishery that would stand you amazed, dear fellow.'

'You'll tell me of y'r secrets this very afternoon. You get y'r gear inboard while I get these t' Captain Houghton. I have it from on high that the adm'ral will want t' have his squadron to sea f'r exercises as soon as he's stored – that's t'morrow, I'll wager.'

'If it were at all possible, a light walk ashore among the spring blooms would be pleasant, Tom. Our admiral does not spare his minions, you may believe.'

The Dartmouth side of the harbour was speckled with green shoots and the ground was firming. They paced it out in the hesitant sunshine, feeling the country awake out of its winter retreat.

'A singular place, Newfoundland,' Renzi said, at length. 'At times I believed that the island should be entirely covered by curing fish, were it not that room has to be made for the vats of that monstrously malodorous fish oil.'

'Your secrets?' Kydd wanted to know.

'Nothing, really. It's a turbulent place that requires the admiral to show firm on occasion – the fisher gentry from Devon have it that Newfoundland is their personal fief, and deliver rough justice to those who say otherwise. You'd smile to hear the talk in an assembly at St John's – you'd swear it was Exeter or Bideford on market day.'

They walked on companionably. 'So, all has been uneventful in the meantime?' Renzi enquired.

Kydd hesitated. Renzi was the soul of discretion, but that was not the point at issue – his uncle had left the resolution of his problem to him alone: Should he involve his friend in a matter of family?

There was no question: he had been on his own for too long. 'Nicholas, the strangest thing – I met m' uncle f'r the first time not long since.' His tone made Renzi look at him sharply.

'Yes – m' father's brother, here in Canada.' Kydd went on to tell of his discovery and his quandary – and his decision neither to conform to the story of the bear nor to reveal his uncle's current whereabouts to his family.

'An admirable, even logical decision, Tom, and I honour you for it,' Renzi said sincerely.

They strolled on in the quietness at the edge of the forest. 'That's not all of the matter, is it, brother?' Renzi said, stopping and facing Kydd directly. 'I'd be honoured to share whatever it is that lays its hands on my friend.'

Kydd looked away, staring at the jack-pines carpeting the landscape, all seeming the same but when looked at separately every one an individual, uncountable thousands into the blue-grey distance. 'Nicholas, it doesn't answer. I have t' face it. I'm not t' be one of y'r deep-dyed, gentleman officers who knows their fox-hunting an' Seasons. I know seamanship an' navigation, not dancin' and talking to ladies.'

'Dear fellow, this—'

'When I got my step t' the quarterdeck it was hard t' believe. Then it seemed to me that there was no end t' it – captain of my own ship, even. But I know better than that now. The King's service needs l'tenants for sure, but only the *gentlemen* will find 'emselves promoted – an' I'm no gentleman, an' now I know it.'

'No gentleman? What nonsense—'

'Spare me y'r comfortin' words, Nicholas,' Kydd said bitterly. 'For my own good, I have t' hoist this aboard an' stop pining f'r what can't be, and that's that.'

'But it only requires you learn the marks of civility, the—'

'Is that *all* it is to be a gentleman, jus' know all the tricks? I don't think so.' Kydd fell silent, morosely kicking a pine cone.

'Do you despise gentlemen?' Renzi asked quietly.

Kydd flashed him a suspicious look. 'Not as who should say – they were born to it, that's their good luck . . . and yours,' he added, with a sardonic smile.

They walked on for a space, then Kydd stopped again. 'T' be honest, it sticks in m' gullet that I'm t' leave promotion to others – and I'm of a mind t' do something about it.'

'What?'

'Well, in a merchant ship they have no care f'r gentle ways – a berth as mate in an Indiaman would suit me right handsomely, one voyage a year out east, an' my own freight . . .'

'Leave the Navy?'

'And why not?'

Kydd obstinately avoided Renzi's gaze as his friend stared at him.

In a brisk south-easterly early next morning the North American Squadron put to sea for one week's exercising in the waters between Nova Scotia and the United States, the 74-gun HMS *Resolution* as flagship in the van, the seven ships a picture of grace and might.

In *Tenacious*, at the rear, the picture was more apparent than real: the file of ships that stretched ahead to the flagship in perfect line also obscured her signals, and the little fleet could not stretch to the luxury of a repeating frigate.

Despairing, Kydd hung out from the rigging to weather, trying to steady his big telescope against the thrumming in the shrouds and bracing himself to catch the meaning of *Resolution*'s signal flags end-on. They were clawing their way out close-hauled; if they were to end on an easterly course passing south of the Thrumcap they would have to pass through the wind's eye.

It was the admiral's choice, to tack about or wear round, and with the Neverfail shoal waiting ahead and the same unforgiving rocks under their lee that had claimed *Tribune* so recently. Tack or wear – put the helm down or up – it all depended on the signal that would be thrown out to the fleet in the next few minutes.

Captain Houghton stumped up and down the quarterdeck, nervous midshipmen scuttling along behind him, the master keeping a respectful distance to his lee. It was impossible to send the men to their stations until it was known the action to be taken, and they stood about the decks in uneasy groups.

Devil's Island, the most seaward part of Halifax, lay abeam: now there was no reason why they could not bear up – and then there was a tiny flutter of bunting on *Resolution*'s poop.

Kydd concentrated with his glass. A quick refresh from his pocket book had shown him that there was only one flag in the two hoists that differentiated 'tack' and 'wear' – a yellow diagonal on a blue background – and this was number three, 'tack'. If he just glimpsed that flag, he could ignore the rest and they would gain a vital edge. Houghton stopped pacing and faced Kydd. Around the ship men followed suit, every face turning towards him.

There! A cluster of flags mounted swiftly in *Resolution*'s rigging, their fluttering edges making the hoist nearly impossible to read – but Kydd's straining eyes had spotted the distinctive number three as the flagship's signal crew bent it on as part of the hoist. Before the flags had reached the peak he roared triumphantly, 'It's *tack*!'

Men raced to their stations; running gear was thumped on

the deck and faked for running, afteryards manned by the starboard watch and headyards the larboard, double manning for the greatest speed. The signal jerked down aboard the flagship – execute!

The wheel spun as the quartermaster at the wheel and his mate threw themselves at the task and *Tenacious*'s bluff bow began to move. At the waist, ropes' ends were out as the petty officers ensured the foresheet was let go smartly and the lee brace checked away. In growing excitement Kydd saw that of the file of ships only *Tenacious* herself at the rear and the flagship at the head had begun a swing round into the wind. His pride swelled at the evidence of his enterprise – they were well into their tacking about while in front, *Andromeda*, was still in line ahead.

'Helm's a-lee!' Big driving sails began shaking, the yards bracing round while the foreyards took the wind aback to lever her round. '*Mainsail haul!*' The ship passed slowly through the eye of the wind and all hands heaved and hauled with all their might to make the sails belly out comfortably on to the new tack. It was neatly done.

'Sir!' It was Rawson, tugging on his sleeve urgently. Kydd turned irritably. The midshipman pointed mutely at the line of ships: *Resolution* had tacked about as fast as they, but all the rest were still thrashing along on the old tack, not one even attempting to go about.

A feeling of growing apprehension crept over Kydd. Something was wrong. *Resolution* was now in plain view to weather, her entire beam to *Tenacious* instead of her stern – and as they watched, a flutter of bunting mounted at her main, the original signal. But ominously, there for the whole fleet to see was *Tenacious*'s pennant climbing brazenly aloft. A gun thudded out peremptorily for attention.

'What, in the name of God?' Houghton roared at Kydd. The admiral was telling the world that HMS *Tenacious* had blundered and should conform to his signal.

'It's tack, but *in succession*, sir,' Rawson whispered urgently, pointing to an entry in the signal book. It was the order to tack, sure enough, but the maddening additional flag at the end indicated that instead of turning into line like a file of soldiers, the admiral wanted the column of ships to reach a fixed point, then wheel round to follow him, thereby preserving their line ahead formation.

'Sir, the signal is "tack in succession". I – I'm sorry, sir . . .' Kydd's voice seemed thin and weak.

Houghton's chest swelled and his face reddened, but before the explosion another gun sounded impatiently from the flagship. There was nothing for it but public ignominy.

'*Haaands* to stations for staying!' *Tenacious* must obey the last order and come back to her original tack; her ship's company, feeling the shame and the entire fleet's eyes on them, took up their ropes again while Kydd stood mortified, face burning. *Tenacious* came ponderously about and tried to assume her old place at the end of the line – but by now the line itself was all but gone, preceding ships now having reached the fixed point and tacked round on to the new course.

Cursing, weary men picked up their ropes and prepared to haul round for the third time in a row. But when the due point was reached *Tenacious* had not picked up enough speed, and when the helm went down she headed up languidly into the wind – and stayed there, held in the wind's eye, in irons.

The master lunged over and took the helm, bawling at the men forward as the ship drifted astern, the hapless officer-of-the-watch nervously clutching his telescope and watching the captain, appalled. Kydd, with nothing to do, could only stand and suffer as the ship tried to regain her dignity.

Finally in her place at the rear of the line stretching away to the east, *Tenacious* settled down and Kydd turned to his captain, prepared for the worst – but yet another signal streamed out from *Resolution*. 'Fleet will heave to,' Kydd reported carefully. Main topsails were backed and way fell off. There had to be a reason why the whole squadron was coming to a stop.

'Flagship, sir – our pennant and, er, "Send a lieutenant."' The admiral wanted an official explanation from *Tenacious* for the recent display – and there would be no bets taken on who would go as the sacrifice . . .

Admiral Vandeput did not spare his squadron. Between Cape Sable and Cape Cod, seven ships sailed resolutely in formation, assuming tactical divisions by signal, running down invisible foes, shortening sail for battle. Curious fishing-boats were diverted by strings of flags run up the flagship's rigging, followed by instant animation aboard every vessel of the squadron – and the occasional gun for attention.

Kydd doggedly improved his acquaintance with the *Fighting Instructions* and attached signals, and when the squadron was ready to return to port several days later, he was fully prepared. 'Sir, vessels in the squadron to retire in order of sailing.' It was the return to Halifax. 'Signal to wear, sir,' Kydd added, as the flags broke at the masthead. This would see the ships turning on their heel and facing where they had been – but this time with *Tenacious* leading the squadron back to port.

Now was the time to show her breeding in the manoeuvre of going about completely, stern to wind. 'Brace in the afteryards – up helm!' The mizzen topsail began shaking, the main just full and the fore up sharp. *Tenacious* started her swing, the line of ships ahead commenced their wheel about. 'Lay y'r headyards square! Shift headsheets!' Her rotation brought the wind right aft, and the weather sheets were eased to become the lee. 'Brace up headyards – haul aboard!' Men laboured to get the tack hard in forward and the sheets aft as she came on to her new heading. *Tenacious* responded with a willing surge.

'Draw jib!' It was the last order before she settled on her new course, the sheets hauled aft to bring the headsails to a full tautness. The fo'c'slemen responded heartily, the thought of safe haven in Halifax just hours away lending weight to their hauling.

A crack as loud as a three-pounder gun came from far forward. The crew on the jibsheets fell to the deck, others crouched down and looked about fearfully. It was impossible to see what was happening from aft as the clews of the big courses effectively shut out the scene.

'Can't 'old 'er, sir!' bawled the helmsman, as *Tenacious* immediately fell off the wind and inevitably out of line. An incomprehensible hail came from forward, amplified by a breathless messenger. 'Lost our jibboom, sir!' he yelled, his voice cracking.

Houghton lifted his speaking trumpet. 'Douse the fore t'gallant instantly, d'ye hear?' He wheeled round, his face set. A volley of orders brought sail in, and way off the vessel. 'You know what to do, get forrard and bear a hand – now!' he snapped at Kydd. Rawson could be relied on to hoist the necessary 'not-under-command' general signal that indicated *Tenacious* was no longer in a position to obey her captain.

Kydd hurried forward. This was Renzi's part-of-ship: Kydd would take orders from him without question. He arrived at the scene to see a tangle of rigging from aloft – and a truncated bowsprit. A thumping from the lee bow and men staring down showed where the failed spar was now.

'Poulden, do you clap on the t'gallant bowline as well.' It was strange to hear the crack of authority in Renzi's voice, to see the gleam of hard purpose in his friend's eyes.

'Sir,' Kydd reported to the fourth lieutenant.

Renzi flashed a brief smile. 'Martingale stay parted, the jibboom carried away,' he said, flicking his eyes up to watch the progress of the jib downhaul, which was clearly being readied to hoist the spar back aboard. 'I'm sanguine we'll have it clear soon – it's to loo'ard, and I've taken the liberty to set the fore-topmast stays'l to make a lee while we see to the jib.'

The boatswain quickly had the experienced fo'c'slemen at work reeving a heel rope: the fifty feet of Danzig fir surging below was a formidable spar to recover aboard.

Renzi gazed intently at the descending downhaul. 'Mr Kydd, I'd be obliged if you'd inform the captain of our situation, that I've furled the fore t'gallant, but desire the fore t' gallant mast be struck.'

Kydd touched his hat, then hastened back to the quarter-deck.

Houghton listened sourly, his eyes straying to the line of ships passing by, beginning the evolution to heave to. 'Request Flag to pass within hail,' he said. The signals soared up rapidly, but even as they did, *Resolution* had put down her helm and closed.

Briefly, Houghton passed details by speaking trumpet to the admiral. There was little to discuss: *Lynx*, a 16-gun ship-sloop, was detached to stand by them while they repaired; the remainder sailed on to Halifax.

*   *   *

It was not an easy repair: even with a spare spar fortunately to hand, the stump of the jibboom had to be extracted from the bowsprit cap and sea-hardened heel ropes cut away. It was sheer bad luck that the bee-block seating the new jibboom to the bowsprit needed reshaping, and now with jib-stay and fittings to apply there was no chance they would complete by dusk.

The hours passed uncomfortably. Without steadying sail on the open sea *Tenacious* wallowed glumly all night, Cape Cod forty miles under her lee. Kydd had the morning watch: red-eyed and tired, he observed a grey dawn approach with *Lynx* far out to the southward but stoutly clapping on all sail. Thick mist patches persisted to the north in the calm seas, wisps reaching out occasionally to *Tenacious* with their clammy embrace.

As soon as there was light enough, work began on the jib-boom, and well before the wan sun had cleared the foreyard it was all but complete.

'What, in hell's name?' Houghton said, stopping his restless pacing. It was gunfire – to the north and not too distant, a distinct thud.

'At least twenty-fours, maybe thirty-twos,' growled Bryant, puzzled. Another flurry of thumps in the mist were heard.

Houghton looked nonplussed. 'This can only be the squadron – there's not another sail-o'-the-line at sea, unless. . .' He paused, then looked significantly at Bryant. 'Send *Lynx* to investigate with all despatch.' It was a disturbing mystery: guns of such weight of metal were only carried by line-of-battle ships.

Lynx disappeared into the light mist while *Tenacious* had her topsails set and drawing within minutes of her headsails being once more complete. As she began to gather way her mainsail was loosed and she picked up speed.

The royals of a ship showed above the mist, and *Lynx* burst into view, a signal at her main. 'Enemy in sight!' shouted Kydd from the poop, but the signal had been recognised at once.

'Clear for action!'

For the first time on the American side of the Atlantic *Tenacious* made ready for battle. The mist cleared slightly – giving a tantalising view of two dark shapes before it closed round them once more.

The urgent rhythm of 'Hearts of Oak' ceased as Bryant reported the ship cleared fore and aft; it was replaced by a long, solemn drum-roll. Quarters!

Kydd's sword banged against his legs as he raced up the poop-deck ladder – if this were a rogue enemy 74 and frigate escort they were in dire trouble.

'Make to *Lynx*, "take position one mile to windward", if you please,' said Houghton. Small fry had no business in the line when big ships met in combat.

Tenacious glided into the trailing mist, the wind now only a dying breeze. The masthead lookout hailed the deck. '*Deck hoooo!* Two ships, two points t' larboard, near ter five mile off!'

At Houghton's command Kydd exchanged the heavy signal telescope for the more handy glass of the officer-of-the-watch and swung up into the shrouds. He was clear of the mist by the main-top; there was no need to go further – and over there to larboard, protruding through the rumpled white upper surface of the fog, were the upper masts and tops of two vessels – ship rigged, as the lookout had said.

Kydd held the telescope against an upper shroud and gazed intently. Both were under sail but were hove to at an angle to each other. He steadied the glass and found the tricolour of France hanging limply on one, he couldn't tell for the other; certainly they were not ships-of-the-line. He swept once around the horizon, noting that the mist was clearing to patches around the enemy, and bawled down his report, then clambered back to the deck.

'What the devil? You saw no other vessels at all?' Houghton barked. They had unmistakably heard the gunfire of a ship of force.

'Sir, is it—' the master began, then the obscuring mist lifted, and some four miles away almost dead to leeward they saw the enemy.

'Damn my eyes if that ain't a frigate!' Bryant said, in wonder.

'An' that looks like one o' our merchant ships, sir,' interposed Hambly.

'Lay us to wind'd of the frigate, Mr Hambly,' said Houghton shortly. 'We'll look for that damned ship-o'-the-line later.'

Adams came up to stand beside Kydd. 'Can you just conceive,' he said, with a boyish grin, 'what discussions must be afoot on her quarterdeck? Just about to take a fat prize and a ship-o'-the-line, no less, sails out of the fog.'

Houghton said, over his shoulder, 'Mr Kydd, recall *Lynx* – to take station astern.' Aboard the Frenchman there would be something approaching panic: an additional ship in the equation, however small, meant double the worry for the unknown commander of the frigate, now making hasty sail.

'Stuns'ls, sir?' The south-easterly breeze was playful and light and they were bearing down slowly.

'No, Mr Hambly. We'll wait and see what he's going to try first.' If the frigate bore away downwind there would be every reason for stuns'ls but if she moved off on the wind

Tenacious could not follow until the awkward sails and their booms had been taken in.

With the rapt attention of the entire quarterdeck, the Frenchman's length foreshortened as her yards came round. 'She's running large,' said Bryant. It would be strange indeed if a frigate did not have the legs over a cumbersome ship-of-the-line in a stern chase and in a matter of hours she would be clean away.

The merchant ship, a large vessel with clean lines, ran up her colours as they approached. 'American?' Bryant took off his hat and scratched his head, glancing up at their own ensign as if for reassurance.

'Cousin Jonathan is a neutral – what *is* the Frenchy up to?' Adams murmured, as they passed the cheering merchant ship under full sail.

'If y' please, sir . . .' began the master.

'Mr Hambly?'

'If I'm not wrong, sir, that's not a National Ship – she's a heavy privateer. Slight in the build, maybe over-sparred, an' the size of her crew . . .'

'I think he's right, sir,' agreed Bryant, borrowing a telescope. The sea ahead was now free of mist and the chase, no more than a mile ahead, loosed all plain sail – but no stuns'l.

Houghton pursed his lips. To stand any chance of staying with the chase he must soon spread stuns'ls abroad – a canny captain of the 'frigate' would wait for the manoeuvre to complete, then put his own wheel over and go close-hauled, knowing that it would take some time for his pursuer to strike his stuns'ls and follow. But on the other hand, if they did nothing, the chase would draw ahead and disappear. 'Mr Hambly, be so good as to see how the chase goes.'

The sailing-master found his sextant and measured the angle from masthead to waterline of their prey. A few minutes later he repeated the action. 'We're dropping astern by as much as two knots, I fear, sir.'

'Not worth our trouble,' Adams said gloomily to Kydd. 'We spread more sail, so does she – an' I've yet to find any two-decker can stay with a frigate. She'll be hull down by sunset.'

The Frenchman was now visibly drawing away, disdaining even to set her own stuns'ls. Houghton took a telescope and trained it for a long time on the chase. Suddenly he snapped shut the glass. 'Pass the word to Mr Bampton and Mr Renzi – we will yaw, and on command they will pepper the rogue with a full broadside.'

The midshipman messenger touched his hat, expressionless. Even he knew that this was a last gesture after which the Frenchman could sail away over the horizon in peace. Houghton's action would hopelessly slow their advance in the light winds. The lad ran off smartly and from the rumbling Kydd could picture the long twenty-fours being run out, hand-spikes plied to make them bear as far forward as they could – and the talk around the guns as men peered out of open gunports to catch a sight of their target.

Houghton paced impatiently, waiting for the youngster to report back, his gaze fixed on the ship ahead.

Reported ready, it needed only the captain's order to complete their final, aggressive, act. Houghton gave a brief smile to the group on the quarterdeck, and said quietly to Hambly, 'Larboard, if you please.'

Tenacious sheered off slowly, giving the gun-captains time to lay their weapons, so when the order to open fire was given the guns crashed out almost together. Smoke rolled down lazily on their target and, seconds later, the sudden eruption of a forest of white splashes along the line of sight brought war-like roars from the gun-decks.

The wheel spun and, sluggishly, *Tenacious* traced her bowsprit back on target, and past. She steadied for a moment, and her opposite broadside thundered out across the calm seas. Again the gun-smoke, the close scatter of splashes – then the enemy's mizzen topmast fell in a graceful curve.

'Please, God . . .' breathed Adams. It was by no means a decisive hit, but the complete absence of square sail on the mizzen might be enough to hamper the vessel, allowing them to close and engage.

Activity died down as every man stared forward, willing the chase to falter, but it was not to be. Sacrificing his wounded topmast, trailing in the water alongside, the French ship ruthlessly cut it loose and continued on as before.

'O' course, she won't grieve over the topmast,' Kydd said, glumly. 'Going large, she c'n balance by tricing up the clew o' the mains'l one side. She knows all she has t' do is carry on and she'll lose us.'

'That may be so,' Adams said, 'but what happens when she wants to go by the wind? Close-hauled she'd be a cripple.'

'And why would she do that?' Bampton's acid comment from behind was nearly lost in a general growl of dismay at the sudden crump of gunfire and smoke issuing out from their quarry.

'She has stern-chasers,' Adams remarked soberly. These guns, which could fire straight aft into a pursuer when there was no opportunity to return fire, would be a sore trial. At the next salvo Kydd heard the crack of the guns and, moments later, felt the slam of the passage of one ball over their heads. Several officers ducked automatically, then rose shamefacedly.

'Marines, go below. Stand the men down into the waist, Mr Bryant,' Houghton ordered. Although these were only light six-pounders banging away, a hit would kill.

They kept up the chase for another twenty minutes, falling astern the whole while until the first lieutenant approached the captain. 'There's no profit in this, sir – we shall have to give him best, I fear.'

Houghton glared at him. 'Damned if I will! Observe – he cannot run to leeward for ever. On this course he stands to meet the Nantucket shoals off Cape Cod before long. He must choose then between hauling his wind and going east about the Cape to slip into the Gulf o' Maine, or an easier passage west but directly into United States waters.

'I want to box him into the coast. Therefore I shall desire Lynx to lie to his starb'd and persuade him that this is his better course.' The little sloop would thus stand between the enemy and a refuge in the wider reaches of the Gulf of Maine – but it would be a foolhardy move for the French captain to take on the little ship knowing that just one lucky hit from any of the sloop's sixteen six-pounders could deliver her straight into the clutches of the waiting bigger ship.

'Aye, sir.'

Houghton smiled for the first time. 'And when he has to bear away, he's under our lee and then we'll have him . . .'

In the early afternoon, the enemy was far ahead but, with Lynx faithfully to her starboard, the master was satisfied that they were irrevocably within the hook of the shoals, cutting off her escape to the east. 'Tides o' five knots or more around 'em. Steep too, so sounding won't answer and if fog comes, it's all up with the ship,' he added, with feeling.

The wind dropped further until it was a ghosting calm, favouring the smaller vessel, which glided a little further and out of range before ceasing movement. The three ships lay becalmed in the grey dusk.

Kydd came on watch: the position of the chase the same. In the night hours there was a choice for their quarry – to attempt a repair by the light of bunched lanthorns, or not show any betraying light and hope to steal away in the night.

She chose the latter: were it not for the quick-witted commander of *Lynx* she might have succeeded. As darkness closed in, the little sloop rigged a makeshift beacon for *Tenacious* of a cluster of lanthorns in a box beaming their light secretly in one direction only.

Through the night *Lynx* stayed faithfully with the enemy, her beacon trained; *Tenacious* lay back in the blackness. When the wind came up some time after midnight and the privateer captain made his move, Houghton knew all about it.

Coming round to the west, the Frenchman clearly wanted to put distance between him and his tormentor before he struck for the open sea, but dawn's grey light showed her the flat nondescript coast of an outlying island of New England to the north-east and two men-o'-war of the Royal Navy to seaward.

Houghton was on deck to greet the dawn, sniffing the wind's direction. 'We have him!' he said, with relish. 'He can't show much sail forrard with this wind abeam and no square sail aft – we can try for a conclusion before noon, I believe.' He looked at the group on the quarterdeck with satisfaction. 'It will be a good day's work for all today.'

Tenacious bore down, guns run out. With land to leeward and two English ships to weather, the Frenchman's only course was west, the wind veering more southerly. To maintain a reasonable westerly course it was necessary to balance fore and aft sail: with no mizzen topsail the logical thing was to reduce sail forward to compensate and accept a loss of speed.

However, from her cro'jack yard canvas appeared. It was not a sail-bearing spar but the French had lashed a sail along its length, loosed it and secured its clews. They had a drawing square sail aft. Kydd shook his head in admiration; admittedly the 'sail' blanketed the poop, silencing the chase guns, but she could keep ahead of her pursuers.

'I'm not concerned,' said Houghton, in tones that suggested he was. 'There's Long Island Sound ahead – he has to go about or he'll be trapped, so it's there we'll have *Lynx* waiting.'

Kydd's first sight of the United States, therefore, was the nondescript sandy scrubland of Block Island ahead, then the low, forested New England coast to the north.

'Sir, I must point out that these are American waters.' There was no response to Adams's concern, Houghton keeping his gaze on the fleeing ship ahead. 'They're well known to be jealous of their sovereignty, sir—'

'I know that, damn your blood!' Houghton said. But the Frenchman showed no signs whatsoever of putting down her helm and proceeded to pass Block Island, entering the closed length of Long Island Sound.

'They're mad! They've no way out – what do they—'

'Mr Hambly! Quickly! What's the distance across the widest entrance to the sound?'

'Er, to nor'ard – that's betwixt Matunuck and Sandy Point on th' island – and it's . . . seven miles.'

'We can do it. North about it is, Mr Hambly. Have a care you stay exactly mid-channel – the Americans claim one league from the low-water mark, which by my reckoning leaves just a mile breadth for our peaceful passage.'

'Aye aye, sir,' said Hambly, eyeing the Frenchman, who seemed to have no notion of such niceties.

Leaving Block Island to larboard, *Tenacious* entered the capacious arm of the sea; there could be no escape now – with both English ships to windward and able to close with the Frenchman if he turned back, it was only a matter of waiting.

'He's wasting time,' snorted Houghton, impatient.

'Sir, recollect: the French have been friends to the Americans since their support for them in the late war.' Renzi had come up from the gun-deck in curiosity.

Bryant sneered: 'Pah! Nonsense! They've seen how the French conduct revolutions and want no part of such roguery.'

'Then what is the meaning of his motions now?' Renzi answered quietly. The privateer had run up a huge tricolour, which streamed out to leeward and barely two miles ahead, and boldly put up his helm to pass through the mile-wide entrance to an inner expanse of water.

'One league, sir.'

'Yes, yes, I had not forgotten.' Houghton bit his lip as he eyed the scene. 'Take a cast of the lead. I believe we will anchor. One league off shore precisely.'

After one last look at the French privateer, just six miles away and, with calm impunity, preparing to berth in a tiny port, Kydd joined the others in the captain's cabin. Houghton was irascible. 'Ideas?'

'Cut 'em out!' Bryant's growl was instant. 'And be damned to any consequences. There's nought hereabouts but fisher-folk an' farmers – and the Americans have no navy at all that I've heard about.'

'True,' said Houghton, thoughtfully, 'but I'll remind you

that in law this must be construed as a combatant seeking refuge in a neutral port, and it would go ill with any who can be shown to violate it.'

'And who's to know? Cloth over our name on the stern, boat's crews at night and you can't make 'em out—'

'I honour the ardency of your spirit, Mr Bryant, but I fear this would provoke extremely.'

'Swimmers! Under cover o' dark, they go in with borers, sink the bugger where he lies—'

'Mr Bryant! I will not suffer such language! And, besides, they'll never pierce a copper-sheathed hull without fuss and noise.'

The cabin fell quiet until Renzi spoke. 'Under the assumption that the sympathies of the Americans must lie with the French, I rather feel they would not be over-nice in the laws applicable in cases of neutrality. We may find ourselves lying at anchor, waiting, for some considerable time. Therefore it would seem logical to sail away – with deep regrets, of course.'

Bryant snorted but could find no riposte.

'And while we dally, the admiral is deprived of a major unit of his fleet, which is nominally under his orders . . .'

Houghton grunted. 'Possibly, but consider – this privateer is big. Should we leave her to her foul plundering, she can take her pick of the largest prizes. We would certainly be held to account if we did not a thing.'

'But if you are unable to effect a solution, by reasons of *force majeure*, your course is chosen for you. We must give up.'

There was a lengthy pause. Then the captain said, 'We have stores only for days. An extended voyage was not contemplated. I have no choice.'

Bryant let out his breath like a punctured balloon. 'To sail.'

'Yes.' The captain's voice was final. But then he added, 'There is, however, one small chance.'

'Sir?'

'I will send an officer ashore to parley with the Americans. They can't object to that. Try to get 'em to see where their interests best lie, bit of law, that sort of thing. It's possible then that they'll throw the Frenchy out to where we'll be waiting for him.'

'A long shot, if I may say so, sir.' Pringle's languid voice came from the rear of the group of disconsolate officers. 'Did you have anyone in mind?'

'That is a matter that exercises me. If I send my first lieutenant there will undoubtedly be a confrontation, which is devoutly to be avoided.' Bryant's splutter was ignored. 'Any officer of eminence will confer too much consequence on the affair with the local authorities, whoever they may be in these backwoods.

'I rather feel that the name of Lieutenant Kydd suggests itself.'

Chapter 9

'Mr President, the Minister Plenipotentiary of Great Britain. Sir, the President of the United States.' The aide ushered Liston into the broad room, then departed.

'Robert, so kind in you,' said John Adams. He was standing by the tall marble mantelpiece and advanced with outstretched hand. 'Sit down, man.'

'Thank you, Mr President.' Liston took an armchair before the fire with a gracious inclination of his head. 'May I know if Rebecca is happy in Trenton? It's a wise precaution to depart Philadelphia before the sick season.'

'She is indeed, God bless her,' said Adams. In the absence of any others at this meeting, he poured the sherry himself. 'Your health, Robert.'

Liston waited, watching the President over the rim of his glass. Adams, a short, chubby man who looked like a country squire, was not to be underestimated. The two of them had seen much together of this new country's spirited political struggles and personally he wished it well, but this was not a social call. He had come in response to a diplomatic summons.

Adams set down his glass and steepled his fingers. 'This cannot be allowed to continue, this stopping and searching on the high seas. Congress and the people will not tolerate it. Your Navy provokes by its high-handed actions, whatever its rights in the matter. Impressing men from the very decks of United States merchant vessels – it's insufferable, you must understand, and now the British courts in the Caribbean are condemning United States merchant ships seized by the Royal Navy as prizes.'

Liston murmured an acknowledgement. It was an old problem, and there were well-rehearsed rejoinders, but he chose another tack. 'Mr President, this, I can appreciate, is your immediate concern – but you will understand that here we have a clash of belief and therefore law. You will have your country's position set in law – but we, sir, have had ours since the 1756 Rule of War and it is accepted by the world. Why then should we change it so?'

Adams picked up his glass and smiled. 'That is well known, Robert, because it favours the Crown so disproportionate.'

'And the French,' continued Liston evenly, 'with their demands of equipage and new decrees—'

'We will firmly abide by our treaty obligations of 1778.'

'Sir, the point I wish to make is that unless these three systems of law are brought to an expression of harmony, your country's trade is in continued jeopardy. It would seem therefore but natural that, if only to restore a balance in world affairs, a measure of amity be enacted between our two nations prohibiting these excesses – here I do not exclude the possibility of an alliance.'

'Against France? I think not. The country would never countenance it.'

'Sir, consider, the French have been all but swept from the

seas. What more practical way to safeguard your ships than have them watched over by the most powerful nation at sea, under flags in amity?'

'Minister, we shall look after our own. We have no need of a foreign power's intervention.'

'Without a navy?' said Liston gently.

'Sir, this discussion is concluded.' The President stood up. 'Have you any other matter you wish to lay before me?'

'Thank you, Mr President. While we are in an understanding, may I be so bold as to refer you to the intolerable actions of French agents in arming bands of Indians on the Canadian border?'

That night the minister made his excuses to his wife and retired to the little room where he was accustomed to gathering his thoughts and rendering them lucidly for his master. Another hand would cipher the despatches.

He tested the nib of his quill, his mind ordering events into neat aggregations, then analysis to their natural heads. It was the least that was expected by Lord Grenville, King George's noble and demanding minister for foreign affairs.

Liston considered carefully: he had been ambassador to the United States for Britain in all but name during many of those turbulent years following the revolution and had acquired a respect for the colonials that bordered on liking. They had followed up their revolution with a constructive, well-considered constitution, which had humanity at its core; the French, even with the American example, had resorted to blood and chaos in an age-old lust for world domination.

There would be no elaborate salutations: Lord Grenville wanted meat in his despatches, personal observations and opinions unfettered by the delicacies of diplomatic language.

The first subject? The likelihood of intervention by America in the titanic world struggle that was reaching its peak. In Europe there was not a single nation of significance, save England, that still stood against France. America remained outside the fight, and as a neutral she could afford to; she was profiting immensely by trading across the interests of the belligerents – there would be little to gain in taking sides.

Yet the French were growing confident, arrogant even, in their dealings. New decrees had been issued by a victorious Directory in Paris that required all merchant ships to carry papers covering their cargo signed by a French consul if they were to escape being taken as a prize of war. There was even talk of an out-of-hand condemnation if British goods of any kind were found aboard.

If the French had the means to enforce this at sea it would have a devastating impact on the Americans. Without a navy, they would have no choice but to bow to French demands. In the end, though, Paris would find it never paid to bully the United States.

But would the Americans see this as cause for war? Some were still sentimentally attached to the British, and others saw French power as a threat that needed balancing. But there were those who remembered France as an ally closely involved in the birth of their nation and would never sanction an aggressive act against her.

Liston sighed. In the end, as always, it came back to politics and personalities in this most democratic of nations. He respected the bluff President, standing four-square for his country, plain-spoken and direct, even with his resolute opposition to British influences, but making no secret of his loathing of the French regime.

But he was increasingly isolated: his party, the Federalists, were the patricians, old landowners staunchly in favour of central government – and generally took the British view. His opponents were the Republicans under Thomas Jefferson, who had no love for England and were mainly new money, naturalised immigrants and strongly pro-French.

The two parties were locked in bitter political strife, which Liston could perceive Adams was badly placed to handle. In this odd system his own Vice President, Jefferson, was leader of the opposing party and privy to who knew what murky political secrets. And he was gravely handicapped by the extremist Hamilton at his elbow, splitting his party and draining confidence from his administration.

It was a fevered time: mobs were marching at night, shattering windows; newspapers were full of wild rumour and acid attack. He wondered briefly what Adams would say if he told him that such was his concern, the great George Washington himself was in secret communication with London. From Pennsylvania a deputation had even demanded clarity on the matter of Mr Adams, son of the President, who was said to be betrothed to a daughter of the King of Great Britain and thereby for the same General Washington to hold the United States in trust for the King.

There was an even chance of an alliance – but as the French depredations increased so must the Americans' grudging tolerance of British measures at sea. If the Royal Navy could be induced to grasp the delicacy of their position, there was a chance . . .

With a large white flag streaming from a halliard, *Tenacious*'s pinnace sailed towards the shore, Lieutenant Kydd in the sternsheets, Midshipman Rawson at the tiller.

It was unfair: Kydd knew next to nothing about the United

States and even less about the international law with which he had been told to threaten the local authorities if they did not drive the French back to sea. He was dressed in civilian clothes and unarmed, in accordance with convention when visiting a neutral country. In fact, he had been obliged to don his best rig, the dark green waistcoat and rust-coloured coat that Cecilia had taken such pains to find in Guildford. He held his light grey hat with its silver buckle safely on his knees.

As the low, wooded coast drew closer, Kydd saw the masts and yards of the French privateer beyond the point; it was clear that she was securing from sea. Further in, he made out a timber landing area, and around it a scatter of people.

The sprit-sail was brailed up and lowered, the oars shipped. 'Head f'r the jetty,' he growled.

Only one of the figures seemed to wear any semblance of a uniform but a number carried what appeared to be muskets. Kydd braced himself: he was going as a representative of his country and he would not be found wanting in the article of military bearing.

A couple of hundred yards from shore Rawson put the tiller over to make the final run in. Suddenly there was the unmistakable report of a flintlock and a gout of water kicked up sharply, dead in line with the bow.

'Wha'? God rot 'em, they're firing on a white flag!' Kydd spluttered. 'Keep y'r course, damn you!' he flung at the midshipman.

The people ashore gesticulated and shouted. One levelled his gun in Kydd's direction. 'S-sir, should we—' hissed Rawson.

'Take charge o' y'r boat's crew,' Kydd replied savagely. Ashore the weapon still tracked Kydd and then it spoke. The bullet spouted water by the stroke oar, followed by a wooden thump as it struck the boat below where Kydd sat.

'Sir?'

'Keep on, damn y'r blood!' snapped Kydd. Even these ignorant backwoodsmen would know they'd be in deep trouble with their government if they caused loss of life by firing on a flag of truce.

More long guns came on target. There was a flurry of shouting, then the weapons were lowered slowly. Grim-faced, Kydd saw the waiting figures resolve to individuals.

'Garn back, y' English pigs!' yelled one, brandishing a rifle. Others took up the cry. Kydd told Rawson to hold steady and lay alongside. The shouting died down, but a dozen or more people crowded on to the jetty.

'Oars – toss oars,' Kydd told the midshipman.

The crowd grew more menacing, one man threatening them with a pitch-fork. The boat drifted to a stop. 'Bowman, take a turn o' the painter,' Kydd ordered. The boat nudged the timbers of the landing-stage; hostile figures shuffled to the edge.

Kydd stood up in the boat. 'I ask ye to let me land – if y' please.' Nobody moved. 'Then am I t' take it you're going to prevent by force the landing on the soil of the United States of America of a citizen of a nation, er, that you're not at war with?' It sounded legal, all but the last bit.

'We don' want yore kind here. Git back to yer ship or I'll give yez a charge o' lead up yer backside as will serve as y'r keepsake of Ameriky.'

'Get his rope, Jeb – we'll give 'em a ducking.' Hands grabbed at the painter, rocking the boat.

'Hold!' The crowd fell back to where a well-dressed man waited on horseback. He dismounted and walked to the jetty edge; malice hung about him. 'Can you not see you're unwelcome, sir?' he called evenly to Kydd.

'Am I so fearsome the whole town turns out t' oppose me?'

'You're an Englishman – that's enough for these good folk. And Navy too. There's many here who have suffered their ships taken as prize, youngsters snatched away by the press – they have reasons a-plenty, sir.' There were cries of agreement. 'Therefore I'd advise you to return whence you came.' He folded his arms.

Kydd lowered his head as though in resignation, but his eyes were busy measuring, gauging. He placed a foot on the gunwale, leaped across the gap of water, heaved himself over the edge of the jetty and ended up next to the man. 'I thank ye for your advice, sir, but as you can see, here I am, landed.' He dusted himself off. 'L'tenant Kydd, at your service, sir.'

The man's reply was cold. 'Schroeder. Christopher.' He did not hold out his hand.

Kydd bowed, and looked around at the crowd. 'I thank ye most kindly for my welcome, and hope m' stay will be as pleasant.' When it was clear there would be no interchange, he leaned over and ordered his crew to throw him up his single piece of baggage. 'Proceed in accordance with y'r previous orders, Mr Rawson,' he added, and the boat stroked away to sea.

He was now in the United States, and very much alone.

Kydd set off down the path into the village, which he knew by the chart was the tiny seaport of Exbury in the state of Connecticut. It was a pretty township, barely more than a village with square, no-nonsense wooden houses and neatly trimmed gardens – and, to Kydd's English eyes, unnaturally straight roads with their raised wooden sidewalks. It also had a distinct sea flavour: the resinous smell of a spar-maker, the muffled clang of a ship-smithy and what looked like a well-stocked chandlery further down the street.

Women carrying baskets stopped to stare at him. The men muttered together in sullen groups. 'Can you let me know where I c'n get lodgings?' he asked one, who turned his back. When he located the general store to ask, its keeper snapped, 'We'm closed!' and slammed the door.

Kydd sat down heavily on a bench beneath a maple tree. It was a near to hopeless mission, but he was not about to give up. He had no idea what had turned the town against him, but he needed lodgings.

A gang of rowdy youngsters started chanting:

> '...And there they'd fife away like fun
> And play on cornstalk fiddles
> And some had ribbons red as blood
> All bound around their middles!
> Oh – Yankee doodle, keep it up
> Yankee doodle dandy...'

Kydd missed the significance of the revolutionary song and, nettled by his politeness, the youths threw stones at him. Kydd shied one back, which brought out a woman in pinafore and bonnet. She glared at him, but shooed away the urchins.

He picked up his bag and set off towards the other end of town. As he passed the houses, each with their doors and windows all closed, a man stepped out on to his porch. 'Stranger!' he called sternly.

Kydd stopped. 'Aye?'

'You're the Englishman.'

'I am, sir – Lieutenant Thomas Kydd of His Majesty's Ship *Tenacious*.'

The man was thin and rangy, in working clothes, but had dignity in his bearing. 'Jacob Hay, sir.' Kydd shook his hand. It was work-hardened and calloused. 'Your presence here ain't welcome, Lootenant, but I will not see a stranger used so. If it's quarters ye're after, I'm offerin'.'

'Why, thank you, Mr Hay,' said Kydd, aware of several people muttering behind him. Hay glanced at them, then led the way into his house.

'Set there, Mr Kydd, while we makes up a room for ye.' Kydd lowered himself into a rocking-chair by the fire. 'Judith, find something for Mr Kydd,' he called, through the doorway. A young woman entered with a jug and a china pot. She did not lift her eyes and left quickly.

To Kydd, Hay said, 'There's no strong drink enters this house, but you'll find th' local cider acceptable.'

Kydd expressed his appreciation and, proffering some coins, added apologetically, 'I have t' tell you now, sir, I don't have any American money for my room.'

'Put it away, sir. That won't be necessary.' Hay pursed his lips and said, 'I don't mean t' be nosy, but can I ask what business is it y' have in Exbury? Somethin' to do with the Frenchy, I guess.'

'I – have to, er, enquire of the authorities what they mean t' do in the matter,' Kydd said cautiously.

'To do? Nothin' I guess. Frenchy is here t' fit a noo mizzen and be on her way, and that's all – we let him be.'

'It's the law, Mr Hay.'

'Law? No law says we has to send him out fer you to take in that two-decker o' yourn,' he said coldly.

'I have t' hear the authorities first, y' understands,' Kydd said. 'Who would that be, do ye think?'

Hay's coolness remained. At length, he said, 'That'll be Mr Dwight or Mr Chadwick. Selectmen fer Exbury.' Seeing the blank look on Kydd's face, he added, 'Magistrates, like. Call th' meetings, run th' constables.'

'I'd like to call on 'em, if y' please,' Kydd said politely.

'Time fer that after supper.' The aroma of fresh-baked bread filled the air. Hay sniffed appreciatively. 'An' if I'm not wrong we're havin' steamed clams.'

'. . . and may the Lord make us truly thankful. Amen.'

While Mrs Hay set about the dishes, Kydd tried to make conversation. 'M' first time in the United States. I have t' say, it's a good-lookin' country.' Hay regarded him without comment.

Kydd smiled across at Judith, who hastily dropped her eyes. He turned once more to Hay. 'I'd be obliged if ye could find your way clear t' tellin' me why I'm not welcome, Mr Hay.'

Hay's face hardened. 'That's easy enough. We live fr'm the sea by fishing 'n' trade. We're a small town, as ye can see, and when a ship is built an' vittled for tradin' there's a piece of everyone in her when she puts t' sea. Life ain't easy, an' when a family puts in their savin's it's cruel hard t' see that ship taken f'r prize by a King's ship an' carried into a Canadian port t' be condemned.'

'But this is because you've been caught trading with the French – the enemy.'

'Whose enemy?' Hay snorted. 'None of our business, this war.'

'And if the French beat us, then you don't think they're

going to come and claim back their American empire? They have most o' the rest of the world.'

Hay grunted. 'Eat y'r clams, Mr Kydd.'

The atmosphere thawed as the meal progressed. Eventually, after apple pie and Cheddar, Hay sat back. 'If you're goin' t' see a magistrate, make it Dwight.' He wouldn't be drawn any further and Kydd set off alone. At the substantial gambrel-roofed house, which Hay had previously pointed out, he was greeted by a short, tubby man wearing a napkin tucked round his neck.

'Er, I need t' see Mr Dwight.'

'Himself,' the man said, in a peculiar, rapid delivery. 'I guess you're the English officer. Am I right?'

'Aye, Lieutenant Kydd. Sir, pardon me if I seem unfamiliar with y'r ways, but I need t' find the authority here in Exbury – the public leader, as it were, in your town.'

Dwight raised his eyebrows, but motioned Kydd inside and closed the door. 'I'll shake hands with you in private, if you don't mind, L'tenant. Now sit ye down, and here's a little rye whiskey for your chilblains.'

Kydd accepted it.

'Sir, if you're lookin' for our leader, I guess I'm your man. Selectman o' Exbury. It's about as high as it goes, short o' the governor in Hartford. Now, how can I help you?'

'Sir, I come on a mission o' some delicacy. No doubt you're aware that a French privateer lies in your port –'

'I am.'

'– which we surprised in the fog in th' process of takin' a merchant ship of the United States goin' about its lawful business.'

'Don't surprise me to hear it, sir.'

'Oh?' said Kydd, prepared only for disbelief and scorn.

'Sir. Let me make my position clear. I'm known as a plain-speakin' man and I'll tell it straight.

'I'm a Federalist, same as the President, same as General Washington himself. I won't try your patience in explaining our politics. Just be assured we stand for the old ways and decent conduct, and we don't hold with this damn French arrogance and ambition. We're opposed by a bunch o' rascals who think t' sympathise with them on account of their help in the late war – saving y'r presence, sir.'

Kydd began to speak, but was interrupted. 'I said I'll speak plain, and I will. We've been taking insults to our flag and loss to our trade, and we'll not have it. There's going t' be an accounting, and that soon.

'But, sir, I'll have you understand, because we take the same view, this does not mean we're friends.'

Kydd gathered his thoughts and began again: 'What we seek, sir, is an indication how you mean to act.' As smoothly as he could, he continued, 'You have here a belligerent vessel seeking a neutral haven f'r repairs. According to international law, he must sail within two days. Do ye mean to enforce the law?'

Dwight sighed. 'Philadelphia is a long ways off – the law is as may be. Here, it's what the citizens say that counts.'

'Does this mean—'

'If I tried t' arrest the Frenchman with my two constables, I'd start a riot – *and* be thrown out of office. This town has just lost a ship t' the British and two lads to your press-gang. And I'd run smack dab against Kit Schroeder.'

'I believe I've met the gentleman,' Kydd murmured.

'Owns three ships and the store, knows how t' lift a cargo with all the right papers to see it past the British an' then on to a French port. There's most folks here do business

240

with him and don't want to see him interfered with, y' see.'

'So you're saying that there's nothing you c'n do? You mean th' Frenchy to lie alongside as long as he wants?' For the sake of local politics the privateer was to be left untouched; *Tenacious* would be forced to sail in a few days, releasing the vessel to continue her career of destruction. Resentment boiled up in Kydd.

Dwight held up a pacifying hand. 'Now, I didn't say there was *nothing* I could do. I'm a selectman an' you have come to me with a case. I'll be letting the governor in Hartford know – but that'll take some time with the roads as they is. However, I'm empowered to, and I will, issue a warrant for a town meeting to consider, um, whether the committee of public safety should take action to prevent there being a hostile action on our soil. Requiring the Frenchman t' take himself elsewhere, say. No promises, Mr Kydd, but you'll get to say your piece and—'

He broke off and cocked his head. Indistinct shouts sounded in the night, rhythmic thuds like a drum. Dwight crossed to the window and pulled the shutter ajar. 'Trouble,' he said, in a low voice. 'Republicans. Don't like you being here, I guess.'

Kydd peered out. Flickering torches were being borne along towards them, and in their light he saw marching figures, gesticulating, shouting.

'Had 'em here before, the wicked dogs. Here, lend me a hand, sir.' They moved over to each window and secured the folding shutters, the smell of guttering candles in the gloom of the closed room now oppressive.

A maid came from the rear, hands to her mouth. 'We'll be quite safe, Mary,' Dwight said, and pulled open a drawer. Kydd caught the glint of a pistol. 'They're only here 'cos they've had a skinful of Schroeder's liquor – they'll be away after they've had their fun.'

He eased open the shutter a crack. 'See that? They're wearing a tricolour cockade in their hats! Republicans do that so there's no mistake who it is they support.'

The noise grew close. A drum thudded in an uneven rhythm, while harsh shouts and laughter came clearly through the closed shutters. Suddenly there was a sharp thud and tinkling glass, then another. Dwight stiffened and swore. 'Breaking windows. I'll have Schroeder's hide – no need f'r this.'

But, as he had prophesied, the influence of drink faded and the small crowd dispersed. 'I'm truly sorry you've been inconvenienced, Mr Kydd,' Dwight said, with dignity, 'but in my country we value free speech above all things. Good night to ye.'

Kydd did not sleep well and was up at cockcrow, pacing along the single cross-street to get the stiffness from his limbs.

It did not take long for the gang of youngsters to find him and begin chanting again, but Kydd grinned broadly and gave them a cheery wave. They soon tired of the sport and darted away. After a few minutes one returned and took station next to him. Kydd guessed he was about ten.

'Are you English?' the boy blurted out.

'Aye. I come fr'm Guildford, which is in Surrey,' Kydd said.

'What's your ship's name?'

'Oh, she's His Britannic Majesty's sixty-four-gun ship *Tenacious*, an' I'm her fifth l'tenant, Kydd, so you have t' call me "sir"!'

'Yes, sir,' the boy said smartly. 'I'm Peter Miller.' They

walked on together. 'How do ye keelhaul a man, sir?'

'What? No, lad, we don't keelhaul sailors. We flog 'em, never keelhaul.' Kydd chuckled.

'Have you ever bin flogged, sir?' Peter asked, wide-eyed.

Kydd hesitated. It was not an admission he would make in polite company. 'Yes, a long time ago, before I was an officer.'

Peter nodded seriously. 'I want t' join the Navy like you, but my pap says we ain't got a navy,' he added defensively.

'We have Americans in the Royal Navy, lad. Ye could—'

'No, sir!' Peter said with spirit. 'I'll not serve King George. Er, that's any king a'tall, not just your king, sir.'

Kydd laughed, and the boy scampered off.

He reached the end of the street, turned the corner and found himself heading towards the French privateer alongside the commercial wharf. At the thought of seeing the ship at such close quarters he quickened his pace. There were idle onlookers standing about on the quay taking their fill of the novel sight; Kydd could see no reason why he should not be one of them.

A shout came from behind him. 'There he is – the English bastard! Come t' spy on our friends.' He recognised the voice of a hothead who had been at the boat. Several men hurried towards him, one hefting a length of paling wood; an authoritative-looking figure watched from the foredeck of the privateer. Kydd stiffened. There would be no help from the spectators by the vessel: they were too busy gawping and the few looking in his direction seemed disinclined to intervene.

Kydd stood his ground with folded arms. He knew he could probably make a good account of himself, but he would not be the first to make a move.

'Spyin' dog! Y' knows what happens t' spies?'

'Are ye as chuckle-headed as y' look? I'm no spy, skulkin' around. I've got just as much right t' take the air here as – as y'r Frenchy there.'

One of the bystanders came up. 'He's right, y' knows. Both furriners, stands t' reason y' can't pick one over the other.'

'Hold y' noise, Darby.' Schroeder strode across. 'You, sir!' he called at Kydd, standing aggressively between him and the ship. 'Will you account for your presence as an officer of a belligerent power at the lawful mooring-place of a ship of the opposing nation? Or shall it be spying?'

Kydd held his temper. 'No.'

Schroeder started. 'You're saying—'

'I said, "No", which is to say I do not have t' account to you or any man for what I'm about on m' lawful business on a public highway.'

Schroeder's jaw hardened, but Kydd looked past him to the privateer. Scores of men were pouring on to the wharf, scattering the onlookers.

Kydd waited. Surely they would not dare anything in broad daylight, before witnesses. But then they spread out in a line and moved towards him. Kydd tensed, the features of individual seamen resolving, alien chatter quietening to a purposeful advance.

Kydd stood firm. They came closer and stopped in front of him, undeniably seafarers, but with their sashes, floppy liberty caps and Mediterranean swarthiness, there was something distorted and menacing about them. They shuffled together to form a barrier, and when Kydd moved to go round it, they blocked his way again. Kydd spotted the figure on the foredeck and bellowed, 'Let me pass, y' villains!' The officer shrugged and called out an unintelligible stream of

French. It was stalemate: there was nothing for it but as dignified a retreat as possible.

Kydd stalked off, seething at being outwitted by the French. At the very least he had hoped to report back on the ship, her state for sea, guns, anything he could see. Now he would have to admit he hadn't been able to get close.

He forced his mind to focus on the situation and by the time he'd reached the cross-street he had a plan: he would see the other side instead. That implied a boat; the tide was on the make, which would allow him to drift past and take his fill of the scene.

Kydd found the young lads playing in the same place and he called across to Peter, 'A silver sixpence wi' King George's head on it should you tell me where I c'n hire a fishin'-boat.'

The dory was double-ended and handy. In borrowed oilskins, Kydd set the little boat drifting along, an unbaited line over the side.

The privateer, the *Minotaure de Morlaix*, was big. Work was going ahead on the mizzen, a new spar chocked up ready on the wharf, but there appeared to be no hurry. Kydd scanned the vessel: her clean lines meant speed but also implied limited sea-endurance, given the large crew.

His attention was caught by a peculiar break in the line of bulwarks with their small gunports. A whole section amidships had been lowered on hinges – inside Kydd glimpsed the astonishing sight of the black bulk of a long gun, mounted on some sort of pivot, another barely visible trained to the other side of the ship. But this was no ordinary gun: it was a twenty-four-pounder at least. The armament of a ship-of-the-line on a near frigate-sized vessel.

This must have been the origin of the sound of heavy

guns that had mystified *Tenacious* at sea earlier, and although there appeared to be only one on each side, it would be enough to terrorise any victim and certainly give pause to a similar sized man-o'-war; a grave threat let loose on the trade routes of the continent. It was sheer chance that had placed the only other ship-of-the-line in North America across the Frenchman's path.

After returning the boat and gear he walked back along the tree-lined road, deep in thought, but the only conclusion he could come to was the impossibility of his situation.

A man in an old-fashioned black tricorne hat stopped him. 'Are you Lootenant Kydd?'

'I am.'

'I'm a constable o' Exbury township,' he said importantly, 'an' I'm instructed by the selectmen to advise ye that a warrant fer a town meetin' has been issued concernin' you.'

'Ah – does that mean they wish me t' attend?'

The constable looked aghast. 'No, sir! Only citizens o' this town c'n attend a town meeting. Mr Dwight jus' wants ye to know that y'r matter is being looked into, is all.'

Kydd turned to go, but the constable pulled at his sleeve. 'Yon Frenchy is goin' – make sure an' be there as well, I'tenant. Th' meeting house is round the corner.'

People from all parts of the town were making their way to a small building whose lines reminded Kydd of the Methodist chapels of his youth. Several greeted him openly; others glared. Schroeder arrived in a carriage and was handed down by a black man. He ignored Kydd and waited; a little later a French officer arrived and the two fell into discussion.

Kydd found his eyes straying to the tall, elegant figure he recognised from the morning's events. By the inscrutable logic of war, he was being granted sight of the man who, as his king's enemy, was his duty to kill.

The discussion stopped. The two turned in his direction and Kydd felt the intensity of the Frenchman's glare across the distance; he hesitated, then withdrew his gaze. When he dared another look, they were walking away.

'All attendin' please enter!' bawled the constable. The late-comers and Schroeder entered, leaving Kydd and the Frenchman alone.

Should he follow the dictates of politeness that required he notice the man and introduce himself, or was there some form of defiance required that he had not the breeding to recognise? The Frenchman was tall, mature and had a lan-guid elegance in his mannerisms that made Kydd aware of his own origins. His feelings of inadequacy returned and he stared back at the man with dislike.

There were bad-tempered shouts from inside, then a head-to-head crescendo. The Frenchman looked across at Kydd and raised his eyebrows in a gesture of refined amusement, but Kydd was unsure of himself, wanting no part in any kind of engagement, and turned sharply away.

Unexpectedly the door to the meeting house opened and Dwight appeared. 'Gentlemen,' he called, looking carefully between them, 'the meeting recognises that this is an, er, irregular situation, and wishes you each t' state your case now.'

There was a hush in the audience, and heads turned as Kydd followed the Frenchman up the aisle. At the simple table at the front there was no provision for extra persons. 'We have t' ask ye to stand, if y' will,' Dwight said apolo-getically.

The rows of faces that looked back at Kydd seemed either

impassive or hostile, and anxiety rose in him at the thought of a public humiliation from the worldly Frenchman.

'Citizens o' Exbury, it's my duty to present – *Capitaine* Hercule Junon of the French ship *Minotaure.*' The French officer inclined his head graciously. 'An' this is L'tenant Kydd, of the English ship *Tenacious.*' Kydd inclined his head also, but feared the gesture had turned out as a nod.

'In view of Captain Junon bein' French as he is, and just to be fair, is there any man present can translate for him?'

Schroeder immediately stepped forward. 'I can.'

'Then let's begin. We have here a request from our English guest that it might be better to hear fr'm him direct. L'tenant?'

Kydd's palms moistened. He took a deep breath and turned to address the meeting. 'You have a French privateer alongside, here in Exbury. He has every right t' be here, to repair an' refit as he needs. But the law says he must leave in forty-eight hours. I request that th' United States do then enforce the law an' make sure he does. Er, that's all.'

There was a disturbance at the back of the hall and a distant voice shouted, 'Y' mean, send 'em out to just where y'r waiting for 'em?'

Another voice cut in, yelling at the first, and Dwight rapped sharply with his gavel. 'I'll have order in the meeting. Now, Captain Junon?'

There was an exchange in low voices, then Schroeder faced Kydd. 'Captain Junon understands L'tenant Kydd's duty in this matter and approves his spirit, but begs to be informed, what is this law of which he speaks? He has no knowledge of such a one.'

Kydd tried to remember Houghton's hurried words before he left. 'Ah, Captain Junon needs remindin' of the Rule of War of 1756. This specifies clearly—'

There was an urgent mutter from Junon, and Schroeder nodded impatiently. 'The Rule of War of 1756 is, of course, an English law and has had no jurisdiction in the United States after 1776 – and, since the lieutenant apparently requires educating, deals with the opening of trade to neutrals and really has no bearing whatsoever on this affair.'

Scattered titters came from the audience. Kydd stared back stubbornly, but could think of no rejoinder.

'And while we are discussing rules, by what laws do the British press men out of American vessels and take their ships prize on the high seas?' Junon allowed an expression of injured pride to appear while Schroeder pressed home his words. 'Are the British so careless of the sanctity of a nation's flag that they dare attempt to demand from the citizens of a neutral country—'

Kydd glared at Junon. 'I saw y'r ship firing on an American flag vessel not two days ago.'

A rustle of interest was interspersed with occasional shouts. Junon allowed it to die away before he made his reply to Schroeder. 'Regrettably there are occasions when Captain Junon's government requires him to confirm that a vessel is not conveying contraband – there are some whose conscience is not clear in this regard and attempt to flee. It is sometimes a necessity to deter.'

'And is this the action of a friend to America, I ask the captain?' Kydd said hotly, incensed at Junon's facile delivery.

A burst of clapping provoked angry shouts from another quarter and Dwight called for order again.

Kydd's face burned. 'We also have our treaty!' he lashed out. 'And in it—'

'Sir!' Schroeder called, in mock outrage. 'You must recall that yours was not a treaty of friendship – not at all. This was, dare I say it, the vanquished accepting terms from the victor!'

A storm of mixed protest and cheers broke out, obliging the constable to intervene. Dwight stood and waited for the uproar to diminish, then spoke firmly: 'Will the strangers now withdraw?'

Outside, Kydd paced rigidly, avoiding Junon's amused glances, as they waited for the meeting to come to a decision. It was not long before the hoots and shouts died away. After an interval the constable summoned them back.

'L'tenant, we have voted on the matter of your request,' Dwight said importantly. 'The township of Exbury has considered it, and as selectman I have to tell you your request is denied.'

Kydd's expression tightened, but he tried to put the best face on it, remembering to turn and bow to the people of the town.

'The business of this meeting is now concluded.'

The gathering broke up noisily and people streamed to the door. Dwight fiddled with his papers and, in a low voice, said to Kydd, 'I'm sendin' a rider to Hartford. This should be gov'ment business.'

Jacob Hay came forward with his hat in his hands. 'Jus' like t' say sorry it came out agin you, Mr Kydd, but as ye can see, the people spoke.' He put out his hand and Kydd could see that it was genuinely meant.

Outside, people were still in groups, some in animated discussion. Kydd could not remember when he had felt so isolated. A roar of laughter drew his attention: it was Darby, one of the hotheads of the morning's events at the French ship.

Kydd's blood rose as the man approached him. 'Y' lost

yer vote, then,' he said loudly. Kydd could not trust himself to reply, but then Darby clapped him on the shoulder and said, 'No hard feelin's? I'd take it kindly if you'd sink a muzzler with us, friend.'

Kydd could not think what to say, but a surging need for the release of a drink and the rough companionship of a tavern overcame his wonder at American generosity of spirit. 'Aye, I would,' he said, and allowed himself to be taken to the Blue Anchor. The weatherboard tavern was already alive with humanity, and Kydd began to feel better. There were odd glances at his clothing, but Darby loudly announced his presence. 'What'll ye have?' he asked genially.

'Er, a beer?'

'Beer? That's spruce, birch, sassafras?'

A nearby toper closed his eyes and chanted, '"Oh, we can make liquor t' sweeten our lips – of pumpkins, o' parsnips or walnut-tree chips."'

'Aye, well, it's the sassafras, then.'

It was the strangest-tasting brew. 'Er, what do ye mix with this'n?' Kydd inquired carefully.

'We don't *mix* anythin', Mr Englishman. That's straight beer, it is, bit o' y'r beet tops, apple skin, roots all boiled in, gives it taste, o' course.'

Kydd downed it manfully, then called for something different. Darby slipped a china mug across to him. 'Flip – now there's a drink f'r a man.' Kydd lifted the creaming brew doubtfully and was not disappointed at the strength of the rum that lay within.

'To th' American flag!' Kydd called.

There was a surprised roar and Kydd found faces turning his way. The reddest called across to him, 'Well, I can't drink t' your king, friend, but I can t' your good health.'

The drink was doing its work and Kydd beamed at his new friends. In the corner a pitch-pipe was brought out and after a few tentative whistles two young men launched into song.

'Come, join hand in hand, brave Americans all,
And rouse your bold hearts at fair Liberty's call;
No tyrannous acts shall suppress your just claim
Or stain with dishonour America's name!'

'Let's hear an English song, then!' Darby demanded, grinning at Kydd and shoving another flip across.

'I'm no sort o' hand at singin',' protested Kydd, but was overborne. He thought for a moment, recalling what had most stirred him in times past. 'Well, this is a sea song, shipmates, an' we sing it around the forebitts forrard – an' I warn ye again, I'm no singer.

'Come, all ye jolly sailors bold,
Whose hearts are cast in honour's mould;
While English glory I unfold
On board o' the Arethusa!'

He found his voice and rolled out the fine old words heartily. And as he sang his mind roamed over the times and places where he had enjoyed the company of true deep-sea mariners in this way, beside him his shipmates through the gale's blast and the cannon's roar, and in all the seas over the globe. As he never would experience again.

Tears pricked and his voice grew hoarse, but in defiance he roared out the final stanza:

'And now we've driven the foe ashore,
Never to fight with Britons more,
Let each fill a glass
To his favourite lass;
A health to the captain and officers true
And all that belongs to the jovial crew
On board o' the Arethusa!'

Something of his feeling communicated itself to the tavern: not a soul moved and when he finished there was a storm of acclamation. Even the pot-boy stood entranced and the tapster abandoned his post to stand agog.

'Ah, Mr Kydd – he'll have a whiskey o' your best sort, Ned,' one man said, and when Kydd had taken it, he raised his own glass and called, 'T' Mr Kydd an' his Royal Navy!'

The morning was a trial. With a throbbing head, he had to endure an icy, disapproving silence at breakfast. 'Guess you'll be on y'r way now,' Hay said meaningfully.

He left after breakfast for a walk in the cool morning to consider his situation. It was obvious that he must admit defeat. He would display the noon signal that would have the boat return to take him off.

At the end of the cross-street he went to turn down the road but, catching sight of the French privateer, he decided to go the other way. As he did so he caught a fleeting glimpse of a figure slipping out of sight. He frowned and continued, but stopped sharply and turned, to see the figure behind duck away again.

This might be a French agent on his trail or a crazed citizen seeking revenge on an Englishman – and Kydd was unarmed. He remembered the trees where he had met Peter.

He walked on rapidly and, at the end of the road, turned the corner, then sprinted towards them. He heaved himself up among the leaves and on to a branch overlooking the path by the road.

His shadower swung round the corner and stopped, looking baffled. He moved forward cautiously but did not appear armed. Kydd waited. The man increased his pace and came nearer, treading carefully. Kydd tensed and, when the man passed beneath, dropped on his shoulders. The two fell in a heap, but Kydd was faster and wrenched the man over, gripping his throat one-handed in restraint.

The man ceased struggling and stared up at Kydd, who slowly released his hold. 'Er, if you'd kindly let me up, I'll try to explain.' The voice was American, polite and apologetic.

'Do, if y' please.' Kydd had never heard a footpad so well-spoken, but did not drop his guard.

The man dusted himself off and smiled ruefully. 'My name's Jasper Gindler – Lootenant Gindler – and this kind of work is not t' my liking, I'll have you know.'

'Lieutenant – Army?'

'Navy.'

'Don't try t' gull me – the United States doesn't have a navy.'

The visitors had left. Liston climbed the stairs painfully to his private room, ruing the onset of age with its aches and pains, but he knew his duty.

He sat down and reached for paper, then selected a pen abstractedly. A woman's hand placed a glass of brandy by him, and her lips softly touched his hair. He twisted round, reached for her hand and kissed it tenderly. 'My dear,' he said softly.

His wife said nothing, just looked down at him for a long moment. Then she left, closing the door behind her.

Liston sighed and collected his thoughts.

In respect of the biggest question of the moment – would the United States enter the war against France – there was no answer . . . yet. Liston smiled grimly as he penned his appreciation of the difficulties faced by the beleaguered President.

Following the commercial success of the contentious Jay treaty of two years before, the French had retaliated by insisting on the letter of the law in their own treaty, which granted free passage to any vessel carrying a French *rôle d'équipage*. Now a vessel without it would be subject to seizure.

The consequences to the expanding trade of the young country had been nothing short of catastrophic. Liston picked up Pinckney's *Congressional Report on European Spoliation of American Trade* to refresh his mind on the figures.

It was staggering – worse even than the dire predictions of the fire-breathing Hamilton. In the Caribbean, worst hit, no less than three hundred ships had been taken and, counting the dangerous waters on the approaches to war-ravaged Europe since the Jay treaty, nearly a thousand American flag vessels had hauled down their colours and been carried into French ports; ship, cargo and crew.

Liston could barely credit that the proud Americans would submit to such intolerable and cynical actions by a so-called ally – but they had. President Adams had stoutly resisted all attempts by Liston and even his own party to be embroiled in a European war, whatever the provocation, but there had to be limits.

Even so, Liston could see his difficulty. The opposition Republicans were led by the astute and learned Jefferson, talked about as the next president, who would never allow him to declare war on an ally. In any case he did not have the means: he had only a few frigates that had been left part built after a brief alarm over Algerine pirates nearly half a dozen years ago.

Yet something had to give. In the last few months, insurance rates in the Caribbean had soared to an impossible 25 per cent of ship and cargo value.

The French were defeating whole nations; coalitions against them had crumbled and they were clearly about to break out of Europe to the wider world. It had made them arrogant and confident, but Liston felt that the latest act was beyond sufferance: envoys of the United States in Paris, attempting to negotiate an amelioration of French attitudes, had been met with a demand for two hundred thousand dollars as a pre-condition for any kind of talks.

This incitement to naked bribery had appalled the Americans, and when it had leaked out there had been outrage. For the first time it appeared President Adams would have to move – to declare war? And with what?

Liston dipped his pen and began to write.

Chapter 10

'May I correct you, sir? We *do* have a navy,' Gindler said, with an ironic smile, 'As of a week ago. Might I explain?'

It seemed that there had been congressional authorisation for a 'naval armament' since the Algerines trouble, but this had been a War Department matter of the time. Now Congress wanted the reality, and had therefore recently established a Department of the Navy to act like the British Admiralty and was to appoint a full secretary of the Navy.

'So, our navy is born.' Gindler had an engaging smile, but Kydd detected a harder layer beneath his cheery manner.

Kydd's head was still muzzy after his visit to the Blue Anchor, and he tried to concentrate. 'Y' don't just *say* you'll have a navy – you now have t' find ships, officers. How are y' going t' do that? And dockyards, victualling, slops . . .'

He looked at Gindler – and felt that this vigorous new country might just find some way. 'Wish ye well of it, Mr Gindler,' he said sincerely. Then he added, 'But I'd be obliged now, sir, if you'd explain what you were doing.'

'Certainly. I was spying on you, Mr Kydd.'

'Wha'?'

'We need to know what a British officer is doing on our soil, you'll agree?'

'Then why th' skulking about? It's no secret why I'm here.'

'Ah. This is not to do with your own good self, I do assure you. It has rather more to do with our democratic way, Mr Kydd. If the citizens of this town, living as they do in Connecticut, find out that I, as an agent of the federal government, am poking around in a matter they conclude is theirs, then I'll soon need a fast horse out of Exbury.'

'Oh? Have you got what you came for, then?' Kydd thought the whole thing sounded more than a little far-fetched.

'Shall we say, sir, that I'd rather like to be shaking hands with an English officer as he steps into his boat to return to his ship?'

'Aye. Well, thanks t' your citizens, the Frenchman lies here untouched an' my ship must sail away. Have no fear, you'll have y'r wish, Mr Gindler. At noon I throw out my signal and the boat will come to take me and my English carcass off.' He smiled wryly, then added, 'But do walk with me until then, an' tell me more of y'r plans for a navy.'

Kydd retrieved his baggage from Jacob Hay and stood with Gindler on the small jetty. *Tenacious* was approaching and would heave to on the three-mile line for a space while telescopes spied the shore for Kydd's signal. If there was none, she would fill, stand out to sea and return on the following day.

'If it's any consolation, my friend, it grieves me as much as it does you,' Gindler said, in a voice low enough not to be overheard by the ragged crowd that had come to see the defeated Englishman leave.

'Oh?' said Kydd bitterly. He was in no mood to be consoled.

Gindler was spared having to answer by the thud of hoofs. The constable hove into view and pulled up his horse. 'Mr Dwight sends 'is compliments an' hopes you can pay him a call before y' leaves.'

Kydd bit his lip. It was within half an hour of midday, and if he missed the time to display his signal flag, *Tenacious* would stand offshore for another day.

The constable leaned down. 'Noos!' he said hoarsely, and winked broadly.

Dwight was businesslike. 'It's none of your business, o' course, Mr Kydd, but you'll find out anyway – I've had word from the governor in Hartford, an' he takes his advice from Philadelphia. Seems they've had enough o' the Frenchies and I'm to serve an order on their captain that they've just twenty-four hours to quit United States territory.' He stuffed papers into a desk. 'I guess this means you'll be about y'r business then, Mr Kydd,' he added, holding the door open.

Kydd had minutes – if he could make his signal . . .

A wily captain like Junon could play it well; he would use all his twenty-four hours to fettle his ship for any circumstance. Then, no doubt, he would sail slowly and directly to the edge of territorial waters, luring *Tenacious* towards him. When the English ship was committed to his approach he would throw over his helm to one side or the other and, hoisting every possible sail, break out with his superior speed into the open sea.

Gindler was waiting curiously at the jetty. '*Minotaure* – she's t' sail within twenty-four hours,' Kydd said quietly, catching his breath, watching the main topsail of *Tenacious* brace sturdily around as she made to heave to.

'Well, now, you leave like a hero.'

'Perhaps not – I have t' think,' Kydd said, distracted. True, the *Minotaure* was forced to sea, but what was the use of this if the privateer could slip away past her pursuer? It was damned bad luck that their sloop, *Lynx*, would not yet have returned from alerting the admiral of *Tenacious*'s dispositions, for the two together had a chance of hounding *Minotaure* to her doom. Could anything be done?

Desperate times meant desperate measures: Kydd had heard of a drag-sail being used to reduce speed; a disguised ship would pretend dull sailing to lure a prey. Perhaps he could stay ashore and tie a sail secretly to *Minotaure*, slow her enough to catch. He soon realised that before the privateer had gone any distance her captain would want to know why she was slowing and discover the trick.

'Mr Kydd!' Gindler pointed out to sea where *Tenacious* was bringing round her main topsail yard.

Kydd pulled the red number-one flag from his pocket and hurried to the front of the gaggle of spectators, spread it wide and let it hang. His news would surely set the ship abuzz.

There appeared to be little activity on her quarterdeck: the daily run inshore had lost its novelty, no doubt. Then topmen began mounting the shrouds and in a smart display the main topsail came around and filling, at the same time as the main course was loosed – and *Tenacious* gracefully got under way for the open sea.

Kydd held the signal high in the forlorn hope that someone was looking back on the little township but, her sails sheeted home, *Tenacious* made off to the horizon amid the sniggering and laughter of the onlookers.

Kydd stood mortified. Not only was he left stranded but he had failed to pass on his vital news. Even if he could find a boat quickly no small craft could catch a big square-rigger in full sail. The only certainty was that *Tenacious* would return the next day.

And where could he lay his head that night? He knew he could not go back to Hay. 'Er, Mr Gindler, if y're familiar with this town, do you know of any lodgin' house?'

'No, sir, I do not. That is, I don't know of one fit for a gentleman.' He smiled. 'Come now, I can't have an English guest take back a poor notion of my country. You shall stay with me, Mr Kydd.'

'Why, Mr Gindler, that's very kind in you.'

Gindler patted him on the shoulder. 'And it keeps you safely under my eye . . .'

'I always try to make New England for the summer, a prime place to rest the spirit – and it is here that I stay.' It was a retired fisherman's cottage by the edge of the water, complete with its own boathouse.

'Do you fish, Mr Kydd? The halibut and cod here, fresh caught, will by any estimate grace the highest table in the land. We shall try some tonight.'

Kydd tried to take an interest, but his mind was full of the consequences of his inattention at the jetty. The only glimmer of hope was that if *Minotaure* made use of her full twenty-four hours, *Tenacious* would have returned in time to try to catch her prey.

'We shall have to make shift for ourselves, sir,' Gindler said apologetically. 'The hire of this cottage does not include servants.'

'Oh? Er, yes, of course, Mr Gindler.'

'This is American territory, Mr Kydd. Be so kind as to address me by my first name, Edward – that is, Ned.'

'Thank you, sir – I mean, Ned, and pray call me Tom.'

Kydd went out on to the little porch and stared out to sea. Gindler joined him with pewter tankards of cider and they sat in cane chairs.

'If you can believe it, you have my earnest sympathy, Tom,' he said. 'Damnation to the French!' he added.

'But aren't they y'r friends?' said Kydd, startled out of his dejection.

'They've caused us more grief and loss than ever you English did, curse 'em, and I have that from Secretary of State Timothy Pickering himself.'

Kydd's spirits returned. 'So it wouldn't cause you heartbreak to see this corsair destroyed.'

'No, sir. It would give me the greatest satisfaction.'

Kydd grinned savagely. 'Then let's get our heads together an' work out some way we c'n bring about that very thing.'

Gindler shook his head. 'We? Recollect, Tom, that this is the territory of the United States. Should I act against a ship of a neutral flag while she's lying in our waters I'd be hoist by both sides.'

'So I'm on my own again.'

'And I'm duty-bound to oppose any action against a neutral – especially in one of our ports, you'll understand.'

Kydd slumped in his chair.

'Tell me, Tom, are we friends?' Gindler asked.

Surprised, Kydd agreed.

'Then my scruples tells me it is no crime to help a friend. What do you think?'

An immediate council of war concentrated on one overriding thing: unless *Minotaure* could be slowed there was little chance that *Tenacious* could catch her.

'Then we're th' only possible chance,' Kydd said morosely.

'It seems that way. How about a drag-sail?'

'It would easily be discovered, soon as they put t' sea and felt its effect. Perhaps I could cut half through a brace or somethin' that will carry away at the right time,' Kydd said, more in despair than hope.

'With the barky alert and swarming with men? I don't think so.'

It seemed ludicrous to contemplate two men against a frigate-sized ship, but Kydd persevered. 'There is another way . . .' he pondered. 'To slow the Frenchy's one thing t' bring him to us, but there's his steering as well.'

'Steering? Helm and tiller ropes?'

'His rudder.'

'You do anything with that and he's sure to know just as quick.'

'Not so, if m' idea is sound.' It was years ago, but the image was as clear as yesterday. An English frigate careening at a remote island in the south Pacific Ocean – and, in the balmy oceanic winds, the crew scraping and cleaning the vast rearing bulk of the hull. He had been at work around the stern, over-awed by the hulking presence of the thirty-foot-high rudder at close quarters, and had gone to inspect its working.

'Ned,' Kydd said cautiously, 'may I quiz you on y'r under-standing of how rudders are hung?'

'By all means.'

'A pin – the pintle on the rudder, going through the eye of a gudgeon on the hull. Now I ask ye to agree this. At the last extremity o' the hull is the sternpost.'

'Yes, this must be so. The underwater run of the hull coming together in a fine upright sternpost.'

'And the rudder fits to th' sternpost with your gudgeons and pintles. Now I particularly desire ye to remark the gap between the forward edge of the rudder and the after edge o' the sternpost. The thickness of the rudder in a frigate would amaze you – it's every bit of a foot or more, as must be th' sternpost, and I mean t' thrust a wedge between them.'

'A magnificent scheme, but pray how will you apply this wedge?'

'Er, we'll discuss that part later. F'r now, we have to settle some details. First, th' gap is only an inch or two wide. No wedge this thick c'n stand the sea forces of a rudder. But – and this needs y'r verifying – there is a very suitable place. At th' point where the pintle meets the gudgeon the ship-wrights cut out a space in th' rudder below it, or else we cannot unship the rudder. This they call th' score.'

'And how big is your gap there?'

'Above six inches – so now we have two flat surfaces a foot long an' six inches apart. A wedge that size has a chance.' Kydd grinned boyishly. 'Just think, Ned, the Frenchy goes t' sea, sees *Tenacious* coming for him an' throws over his helm t' slip by one side, but his helm is jammed. Before he has time t' work out the trouble he's kind enough to deliver him-self straight to us.'

'Congratulations – but of course—'

'Well, yes, there is th' question of how t' get the wedge in there, I'll grant ye.'

'And what sort of ship goes to sea with jammed steering?'

'Ah, I've thought of that.'

'I'm gratified to hear it.'

Kydd gave a dry smile. 'This is callin' for something spe-cial, and here it is. We screw an eye into one end of th' wedge and secure a line to it, which is passed through our gap. If you tug on the line it brings the wedge whistling up an' smack into the gap. But it won't be us that's tugging . . .'

'I stand amazed. Who will?'

'Ah! Your old friend a drag-sail. It's only a small piece o' canvas rolled up and secured to the opposite end of the line, and when it opens it does the tugging.'

'How?'

'Well, we need the helm t' jam only at the right moment – so we must find a trigger to stream our drag-sail just at that time. And here it is – we bundle the canvas up with twine and when we want it to open an' start pulling the wedge we break the twine.'

'Which is . . .'

'Yes, well, this is a long piece of twine, and if you look f'r a discreet little pick-up buoy astern o' the Frenchy, then that's the end o' the twine.'

Gindler didn't say anything.

'Well?' asked Kydd anxiously.

'I can only . . . I have two objections.'

'Oh?'

'Who is going to affix the device? And who is going to find our wee buoy – maybe under gunfire?'

'I'll do both,' said Kydd solemnly, but he had no idea how.

The boathouse provided all they needed. A woodworking bench, try-plane, saws – it would be a straightforward enough task. Kydd blessed the time he had spent in a Caribbean dockyard working for a master shipwright.

'Ned, I want some good wood for m' wedge.'

Gindler fossicked about and, from a dark corner, dragged out what looked like a small salvaged ship frame, dark with age. 'This should suit. It's live oak, and very hard. Capital for hacking out a wedge.'

'Aye, well . . .'

'And it damn near doesn't float.'

'Done!'

The try-plane hissed as Kydd applied himself to the work, watched by an admiring Gindler. Indeed, the wood was extremely dense, and Kydd sweated at the task. Gindler had already found the twine and was snipping round a piece of dirty canvas; then he rummaged for a screw eye.

Kydd realised he needed to see the French ship again in the light. The big privateer still lay alongside the commercial wharf but with a renewed, purposeful air, loading sea stores and working at her rigging. As he looked across the little bay at her, it became clear that there was no easy way to get close: there were sentries on deck and quay, and the ship was alert.

Kydd scanned the shoreline: the wharf was set on timber pilings. If he could get among them . . . and there, at the end, he saw a spur of light grey rocks extending into the sea.

Back in the boathouse a lanthorn glowed. 'I believe I have a chance,' Kydd told Gindler.

'Yes, Tom. When will you go?' Gindler was indistinct in the evening shadows but his voice had an edge to it.

'It has t' be before midnight. The tide is on the ebb and her gunports'll fall below the level of th' wharf before then.' He picked up the neat piece of canvas Gindler had prepared. It was rolled tightly together with sailmaker's twine, to which a stronger line was securely fixed.

'How long will you have this?' The coil of light line seemed a lot but was probably only fifty feet or so.

'I think all o' that,' Kydd said. The longer it was, the safer the task of picking up the buoy and yanking the line. 'And th' last thing – our buoy.' He cast about for an object that would serve and found some duck decoys: one of the duck-

lings would suit admirably. He secured it to the light line –
and all was complete.

In the blackness of night they stood at the edge of the woods
where they were closest to the privateer and had a front-row
view of the ship. Lanthorns in her rigging cast bright pools
of light on to the wharf; figures paced slowly along the dockside. Work had ceased. This would not be the case if an early-
dawn departure was planned.

'Well, here we are,' Gindler whispered, 'and it's here that
we part, my friend. I cannot in all conscience go further, but
I'd like to shake the hand of a brave man.'

'Let's be started,' Kydd muttered. He tucked the precious
bundle of canvas and rope tightly under his arm and slipped
down to the water's edge, careful to stay in the shadows of
the spur of rock.

There he paused, safe for the moment, and listened to the
quiet chuckle and ripple of the calm evening sea. The ship
was over a hundred yards away – and when he stepped round
the spur there was a dozen yards of open beach before the
shelter of the wharf piling. For that distance he would be in
plain view of the ship.

The single thing in his favour was surprise. They might
expect a rush by an armed party, but never by a lone, unarmed
man. It was small comfort, but it also seemed the height of
absurdity to be going into battle against a heavily gunned
privateer armed only with a lump of wood and a piece of
dirty canvas.

In the shadow of the rocks he stripped down to his long
underwear and stockings, awkward and vulnerable. He laid
down his clothes carefully and stumbled over to the inky black
sea. He could not risk the forty feet of open beach; the only

alternative was to wade off into the outer blackness.

The water was fearfully cold and his heart nearly failed him. He forced himself to continue, his feet feeling the sharp stones and shells on the rocky bottom. Deeper he went – the cold biting into his legs then his waist, leaving him gasping for breath. Out past the end of the spur, the ship was now in plain view and as he turned to round the end he lowered himself into the numbing water to his neck. Past the rock, the bottom turned mercifully to the softness of mud and he leaned forward, shuddering with cold, pushing on parallel to the beach and praying he could not be seen.

Minotaure was bows to sea, her carved stern towards him. There was a light in the captain's cabin, a dim gold point through the mullioned windows. A couple of figures stood together on her after deck and Kydd could see the occasional red of a drawn pipe, but the rest was in shadow.

There was the odd scurry of unknown sea creatures at his feet, the stubbing of a toe against an invisible barnacled rock – and what seemed an eternity of knifing cold. At last he saw the edge of the wharf piling resolve out of the darkness.

Gratefully he entered the safety of the overhang with its concentrated sea odours and stood upright. A mistake. The tiny evening breeze was now a searching icy blast that stopped his breath. He lowered himself back into the water, which was almost warm by contrast.

Stumbling along in the darkness he passed between the heavily barnacled and slimy piles, clutching his bundle until he came abreast of the looming black vastness of the privateer. Turning towards it he moved forward and felt the slope of the sea-bed suddenly drop away. He pulled back in alarm. He was an awkward swimmer and, encumbered with his device, he could not possibly do other than move upright.

With a sinking heart he realised it was logical to build the wharf for larger ships where the water was deep enough for them to come close in – *Minotaure* would draw fifteen or twenty feet. Far out of his depth. His frozen mind struggled and he looked around wildly. Past the stern of the ship, tucked in just under the wharf edge he saw a low, elongated shape, a ship's side punt used by sailors to stand in as they worked their way down the hull caulking and painting.

He pulled the little raft towards him, hoisted his bundle in, and hanging off one end, he thrust out. The punt glided towards the black bulk of the ship's hull and finally bumped woodenly against it. Kydd's feet dangled in the freezing depths.

A mix of terror and elation washed over him at the physical touch of the enemy; he worked his way along the hull, sensing noise and movement within until he reached the curved overhang of the stern. Here he would be out of sight from above while he set his trap, but any boat coming down the other side of the hull would burst into view just feet from him without warning.

He took the bundle, his hands shaking as he prepared it. The motionless rudder was lost in the shadows but Kydd could hang on to the rudder chains and be guided down to it. He would have to work by feel. Near the waterline would be the lower hance, a projecting piece at the trailing edge of the rudder; with its hoisting ring plate he could not fail to find it. He felt the barnacle-studded fitting and pulled himself to it. The final act: to thread the line through the score, the inner gap.

He let his hands slide inwards. The pintle strap led to the pintle itself going through the gudgeon eye – and there was the score. A gap just below the waterline and big enough to put his whole fist through. Excitement surged through him.

All he had to do now was put the line through with the wedge one side and the rest the other.

He pushed the line through easily enough, then had to bend it on the wedge. His hands were numb but he fumbled it through the screw eye. But when he tried to tie a simple one-handed bowline his stiff fingers could not obey. He scrabbled at the line helplessly, aware that if he lost his hold on the wedge it would sink down for ever into the black depths. He couldn't *feel* anything! Nearly weeping with frustration he tried again and failed. Then, with one last effort, he rested his elbows on the edge of the punt, leaving both hands free. Clumsily he managed to manipulate the sodden line.

Letting the wedge hang free by its line he tested it, then let it sink slowly toward the sea-bed. Moving to the other side of the rudder he freed the bundle of canvas and let the pick-up buoy float away. The little bundle, weighted with a fishing lead, sank also, and all that was left of his night's work was a shabby little duckling floating nearby.

Gindler was waiting behind the rocky spur and when Kydd staggered up from the dark waters he threw a blanket round his frozen body and rubbed furiously. 'Mr Kydd, you're the maddest son-of-a-gun I've ever heard of!' he whispered. 'Now let's get something hot into you.'

It was King's calibogus, spruce beer stiffened with New England rum, a drink to which Greaves had introduced him; taken hot in front of the log fire, it was medicine indeed. While Kydd recounted his tale, Gindler threw clams and chunks of cod into a pot, with onion and bacon, and crushed biscuit for thickening, then let the mixture simmer and fill the snug cottage with an irresistible aroma.

'Er, do pardon me the liberty,' said Gindler, after the

chowder pot had been satisfyingly scraped empty, 'I can't help but observe that your character is so – different from your usual King's officer, Tom. You never hang back when there's a need to soil the hands, to bear a fist directly – and you speak plainer, if you understand me.'

'Aye, well, that could be because I come fr'm a different land. I came aft through th' hawse, as we say. But now I'm a gentleman,' he added doubtfully.

'You are indeed,' Gindler said sincerely.

'How about your folk, Ned?' Kydd asked, cradling another calibogus.

'My mother's family came over with the *Mayflower*,' Gindler said proudly. 'Settled in the north, near Boston. Pa runs a business . . .'

A grey day broke, and Kydd's sleepless night was over at last. Today would end in a flurry of gunfire and a captured privateer – or failure. Any one of those barbarous small rocks that had left his feet so sore could snag the line and part it, and they would be left with a useless end. So much could go wrong: even as they breakfasted, a crew member might look over the side of *Minotaure* and raise the alarm, and then it would be over before it started, or the ship might sail at dawn when *Tenacious* was not in the offing.

Kydd sat on the porch, brooding. 'What do ye say we take a walk through th' town? Perhaps we—'

'You must stay here, my friend. Your presence near the vessel at this time could be . . . unfortunate.' Gindler got to his feet. 'I will undertake a reconnaissance.'

He returned quickly. 'They're ready for sea near enough, but there's a little duck taken up residence under her stern.'

The morning dragged by; Kydd tried to learn a card game

but it quickly palled. In the end they sat on the porch and talked, eyes straying out to sea.

'I believe we must take position now,' Gindler said lightly. 'We have our smack ready at hand.'

The craft was not big but had a single mast stepped to a forward thwart, and with a light spritsail took the morning breeze with a will. In nondescript fishermen's gear Kydd and Gindler saw they were one of a handful of boats chancing the day for sea-bass.

The entrance to the inner sound was no more than a couple of miles across and the one league boundary a half-mile beyond. Gindler eased sheets and steered for the northern point.

'There she is!' cried Kydd exultantly. HMS *Tenacious* under topsails was calmly approaching from the north. All the players were now converging and it was only a matter of time before the final act.

Minotaure had to sail by noon; her captain was waiting for the last possible moment and, as a consequence, would have to face *Tenacious*. But he would have been told about the midday signal arrangement – why did he wait and risk the confrontation?

Then it dawned on Kydd. Junon was both confident and cool. He *wanted* the English ship to present herself: he knew he could out-manoeuvre the big ship and in this way could establish where she was and therefore be free of the threat of an unpleasant surprise later.

The privateer's fore topsail rose: she was about to proceed. Kydd's heart beat faster. Her headsails fluttered into life and, as he watched, her bow detached from the wharf. The French tricolour was lowered from her ensign staff but reappeared at her mizzen peak. Other canvas made its appearance and *Minotaure* stood out into the sound.

Her actions were not lost on *Tenacious* whose battle-ensign soared up to the mainmasthead in answer. Kydd pictured the frenzied rush to quarters and was torn between the desire to be back aboard his ship in action and the knowledge of what he had to do.

Tenacious stood squarely across the entrance at the edge of the boundary, heaving to in the slight winds, while the privateer advanced cautiously towards her under just topsails, not giving the slightest indication of which side she was going to pass.

Kydd's admiration for the coolness of the French captain increased as he noticed that the wind's direction had *Tenacious* hove to with broadside towards, normally a battle-winning raking position, but the bigger ship could not in any circumstances open fire into United States waters and certainly not risk shot ricocheting into the town. Therefore *Minotaure* could move forward in perfect safety.

'We need t' get under her stern,' Kydd growled. Gindler sheered the boat round and edged more into the sound, keeping safely to one side. The privateer drew nearer and Kydd visualised the wedge and the little bundle bumping over the mud of the sea-bed, hopefully then to stream out behind – or they might already have been torn off.

Kydd spoke, more to himself than to Gindler: 'When she makes her move, she'll loose sail t' crack on speed and only then choose her side an' put over her helm sharp. Therefore our signal will be when she looses more sail.' *Tenacious* would have little chance of reacting in time, being stationary in the water with only the chance of a fleeting shot as the faster vessel surged past.

The privateer came on, seeming immense from the little smack. Her upper decks appeared full of men and her gunports were open. Gindler eased away the sail and let the big ship come down on them, jockeying to be as near as possible.

'Wave at 'em!' Kydd said urgently. Answering waves appeared up at the deckline. They were very close now, every raw detail of her timbers and gun muzzles plain. Gindler put over his tiller and the boat spun about to face the same direction, jibbing and rolling in the side wake of the privateer. *Tenacious* was precisely dead ahead – still no indication. Kydd waved again, anxiety flooding him at the thought of what hung on the next few minutes.

Gindler jockeyed the boat about, slipping back until the stern-windows of the ship came into view then sidling up behind. 'The duckling, find th' duck!' Kydd gasped. They searched frantically astern of the ship – but there was no sign of a buoy.

'No!' Kydd cried harshly.

Gindler kept on behind the rearing stern then pointed. 'Th-there!' he whooped. Kydd leaned over and saw, in the roiling, bubbling wake, a jaunty duckling bobbing vigorously, much closer to the stern than he had planned.

'Get us in there, f'r God's sake!' he yelled hoarsely, careless of anything but the final task.

Hardening in the sheets Gindler brought the smack closer but startled faces appeared over the stern high above. 'Snag the bastard, quick!' he hissed. The boat was bouncing around in the uneven wake and the wind around the looming stern was fitful and chancy.

Clear and positive over the noise of the tumbling water came the sound of a boatswain's calls – to man yards and set sail. Kydd leaned far over the bow, reaching, scrabbling for the ducking. There would be no second chance now, and shouts were coming from above.

He touched the painted wood but it bounced out of reach then skittered back. He grabbed at it with the furthest extremity of his reach – he had it, pulled, but it jerked from his grasp. Kydd cried out in frustration.

The shouts above turned angry, demanding, dangerous. In despair he glanced back at Gindler, whose pale, set face took on a look of determination. He yanked on the sheets and the little boat responded, going right under the stern of the big ship. Kydd fell over the thwarts trying to keep with the buoy but at last he seized it in both hands.

Gindler instantly let out sheets and the smack fell back. Kydd was ready for it and crushed the little duck to him as the soaked line tautened unbearably – then fell slack. It was over.

Near sobbing with relief, Kydd fell back into the boat, still with the duckling clasped to his chest. He looked up – *Minotaure* was receding from them and, indeed, was loosing sail from every bare yard. She was still heading for *Tenacious* and waiting until the sails drew, gathering speed for the vital turn.

Kydd held his breath until it hurt – there was no sign, no hint that he had achieved anything: *Minotaure* was poised for her turn, all ready . . . and still no turn—

He had done it! Incredibly, unbelievably, it had worked! The privateer's steering had locked, to the bewilderment of her crew and now, as he watched, confusion and chaos over-took as orders for setting sail were reversed, panic and fear flooding in as the ship delivered herself into the arms of a ship-of-the-line.

It was over in moments. A disbelieving *Tenacious* had seen *Minotaure* come straight at her and sent a challenging ball under her bow. There was nothing any sane captain could do when brought to, helpless under the threat of the broad-side of a two-decker – her colours came down slowly and HMS *Tenacious* took possession of her prize.

Chapter 11

The President lifted another rose in his cupped hands and sniffed it. 'Perfect!' He sighed, raising his eyes to meet those of his new secretary of the Navy, Benjamin Stoddert. Then he straightened and said softly, 'I'm right glad you accepted, Ben.'

There was a moment of shared feeling. This was not the red-blooded hewing of a vision from the chaos of the revolution twenty years before: it was a time for hard-headed recognition of power and reality in a world at war.

'I fear we may be too late,' Stoddert said. 'It came all of a moil so quick, John.'

The lines in Adams's face deepened. 'I don't want war with the French – understand that of all things! I loathe their system and their arrogance, but I'll be doing anything I can think of to prevent an alignment of the United States with one party or the other.'

Stoddert followed Adams to the next rose-bush. 'Agreed – but we must stand up for ourselves. No one in this world will stand up for us.'

Adams straightened. 'Ben, I've abrogated the treaty we've had since 1778 with the French. I've swallowed insults from Jefferson about my reasons and finally pulled Congress into line. You have your navy. Leave it to me to take care of the rest of the world.'

'Yes, sir.' Stoddert saw no reason to dilute a response to French actions, but knew better than to debate Adams's moderate tactics. Besides which, Adams had a personal interest in the formation of this new navy: he had been the one to create the Continental Navy, the motley fleet of the revolution that had taken on the Royal Navy at sea. It had then been disbanded. This Federal Navy was going to be different, professional, and Stoddert had the honour of leading it into existence.

'You have your captains now.' It had been a fraught business, the few experienced men available vying for positions of seniority and honour.

'I have. Truxtun, Nicholson, Barry, of course, and the lieutenants.' It had taken the personal intervention of the ageing George Washington to settle the question of seniority.

'And the ships.' Converted merchantmen to begin with, six frigate-class vessels racing to completion: *Constitution*, *Constellation* and others.

'And your budget,' Adams said finally. Congress had voted it through, complaining bitterly at the cost of the new vessels, and the Republicans had fought against it as irrelevant to a continental power with no enemies, but now it was going to happen.

'Ben, be careful, my friend,' Adams said quietly. Both understood the political risks that were being taken. 'Well, I won't keep you.' He plucked his rose with a sigh, then turned back to Stoddert. 'One thing interests me. How will you forge a – a way of doing things, a spirit of the sea, if you will?'

Stoddert pondered. 'It seems to me we acquire it in the same way as we have our common law. We take what we want from the English and cast away the rest.' He pursed his lips. 'After all, it's the Royal Navy, the first navy of the age.'

The main sticking point was Gindler. He had begged Kydd not to mention his part, arguing that for him to have taken an active part in operations against a neutral might cause an international incident. But without Gindler's corroboration his account would not be believed – especially the latter stages, which would have been impossible without an accomplice. He could imagine the polite contempt with which his claim would be met at the wardroom table, seen as a shabby attempt to embellish his experiences. No – he could not risk that.

There was nothing for it but a bald statement of his treatment ashore, his urging of a town meeting and the final instructions from Hartford. He had reported as much verbally to the captain, who had generally approved his conduct, understanding his encounter with the odd notions of democracy obtaining ashore. It would take a lot to put the captain out of humour with such a prize meekly astern, and no doubt this report would be passed on to the admiral with suitably warm words.

Kydd was proud of what he had done and chagrined at having to keep it quiet – Renzi had agreed to go over the report for him before he handed it in, but afterwards Kydd had promised him such a tale as would keep him tolerably entertained.

Halifax had seen ships come and go in wartime, and this occasion was not noticeably different. *Tenacious* anchored in the bosom of the fleet, salutes were exchanged and Captain

Houghton, in sword and decorations, went aboard the flag-ship to make explanation of his prize – and the consequent accession to the admiral's own purse.

By return new fleet instructions were sent to her signal lieutenant, the effective date three days hence.

Kydd groaned with vexation. Signals and their meanings were a prerogative of the admiral commanding the station and were buried in the *Fighting Instructions*, detailed prescripts from the admiral for the precise manner in which he wished his ships to engage the enemy. Admiral 'Black' Dick Howe, who had brought the fleet mutiny at Spithead to an end the previous year, had done much to standardise operation of flag signals and Kydd saw that these from Admiral Vandeput were similar.

There were ten signal flags, than the preparative, and the substitute – pennants and wefts, differences of meaning depending on where hoisted, night signals, recognition pro-cedures, signals for individual ships, divisions, fleets. This was the system that had resulted from so much practice over years of sea warfare. It had gone into battle with Howe on the Glorious First of June; only the previous year Jervis had signalled Nelson at St Vincent, and Duncan had used it with such effect at Camperdown.

Now Lieutenant Kydd had inherited this accrued wisdom and must prove himself worthy of it. He took the signal pocketbook, which had been owned by his dead predecessor, as a model and with scissors and patience set about con-structing the *vade mecum* that would stay with him while he was a signal lieutenant.

The flag-lieutenant himself brought the summons: Lieutenant Kydd to wait on the admiral immediately. Kydd flinched when he recalled his previous summoning. What *could* be the reason now? It was astonishing. He was a mere lieutenant – and so many commanders would slay to be noticed by a commander-in-chief – and there was no apparent reason for it.

Kydd bawled at Tysoe in a fever of anxiety: only new stockings and faultless linen would answer. Decorations? He had none. Sword? The plain hanger he had bought in Halifax would have to do. He pulled on his breeches, watched by half the wardroom.

A gig was brought alongside and Kydd descended the ship's side and sat bolt upright in the sternsheets. The bowman cast off with an excess of flourishes and the midshipman in charge set the men to pulling smartly.

The flag-lieutenant led the way wordlessly to the great cabin. 'Lieutenant Kydd, sir.'

'Enter!'

Admiral Vandeput advanced to meet him. 'Well, now, is this the officer the fuss is all about?' He regarded Kydd keenly.

'Sir?'

The white-haired admiral spoke in an easy manner; this could not be a carpeting.

'Please sit, Mr Kydd.' He went round his desk and found a paper, while Kydd perched on the edge of an elegant Windsor chair. 'This is a most particular request, not to say direction, and it comes from Mr Liston. Our minister to the United States, that is – what you might call an ambassador.' He laid the paper on the table and Kydd glimpsed the cipher of the Court of St James at the top.

'In it he desires me to release an officer for a particular service to a foreign power – as you probably know, we have had officers seconded to the Swedish Crown, St Petersburg, other countries. This is not unusual. It is a little odd, though, that you have been named, and that you are so damn junior.' His quiet chuckle took the sting from his words. 'It seems the United States is conjuring up their own navy and they have asked Mr Liston for an observer from the Royal Navy, if possible a Lieutenant Kydd. He feels that it would be right at this time to be seen co-operating with a neutral nation.

'There! What do you think of that, Mr Kydd? You're noticed diplomatically.' His genial smile grew wider and he stabbed a finger at Kydd in emphasis. 'And I'd wager more went on ashore in that backwoods village than ever found its way into your report, hey-hey?'

'Er, sir, I—'

'Never mind. Whatever it was, you did right. Now, let's talk about what you'll be doing. They've got together two or three frigates — built 'em themselves, damn it — and I've seen the gunboats their Revenue runs. Calls 'em their 'treasury navy'. Now, you'll probably be shipping in one of their frigates — they're fitting out now. Your status will be supernumerary for the voyage — a passenger, any Christian would call it — and you won't be called upon to serve a gun if it comes to fighting.'

'Er, who will be their enemy, sir?'

'Well, that's a little difficult to say, but . . .' he tapped his nose '. . . I've been hearing that the French have overstepped their position, making hay with American trade, and they don't like it. In any event, they'll probably tell you about it themselves.

'Now, I know you'll comport yourself as a gentleman should, marks o' respect to all the proper persons, flags and so on. But I think what they're probably after is a correct steer on how things are done in our service. I don't see any reason why you can't tell 'em anything reasonable they want to know. Must be hard to start from nothing,' he reflected sombrely. 'You go in plain clothes, will be victualled by the, er, United States Navy, and I don't suppose you'll be away from us for long. There's a brig leaving for Philadelphia shortly – it's their capital, where our Mr Liston is expecting you. Good fortune, Lieutenant!'

Kydd took in the sights as the brig rounded Cape May for the long trip up the broad Delaware. This was quite a different land from rugged grey rock-bound Nova Scotia or even pretty, forested Connecticut. Here there was well-settled land on either bank, farming and orchards, settlements and roads. The sails of coastal shipping thronged the river as it narrowed towards the capital. Kydd was impressed. No mean colonial sprawl, Philadelphia was a fine city that stretched for miles along the river, as busy as any he had seen in England.

Kydd followed his baggage ashore and looked to see if someone was there to meet him. A ferry loaded noisily and a market stretched away into the distance, improbably occupying the middle of a wide road.

'Mr Kydd?'

He wheeled round. 'Aye?' he said cautiously.

A well-dressed young man inclined his head. 'Thornton, secretary of Legation.'

'How—'

'Please believe, it's not so hard a task to spy out a sailor, Mr Kydd.' He raised a beckoning finger and a coachman came for Kydd's baggage. 'So good in you to leave your wooden world at such short notice. His Excellency is returning from Mount Vernon and hopes to make your acquaintance tomorrow. I trust you'll find our accommodation congenial.'

With a growing sense of unreality Kydd boarded a high-wheeled carriage and the debonair Thornton pointed out the sights as they made Walnut Street at a fast clip. 'Minister Liston keeps unfashionable hours, I fear. Can you find it in you, dear fellow, to appear at nine tomorrow morning? It seems he's anxious to see you.'

'Of course.'

'Should you like theatre, I have tickets for this evening.'

'Thank you,' Kydd murmured, his head spinning with the pace of events.

'Mr Liston,' Thornton said softly, ushering Kydd into a small drawing room and closing the door noiselessly as he left.

'Ah, Mr Kydd,' said Liston, finishing a letter. 'Pray be seated, I won't be long.'

While Liston sanded and sealed the missive, Kydd had the feeling that he was under discreet observation.

'Very well. To business. You will be aware by now that this country has seen fit to begin the creation of a navy, arising from the grievous nature of the depredations of the French on their trade. For details of that you will no doubt have your professional sources.' He paused significantly. 'There are many elements of delicacy in this situation, and in a way I would wish that you were of a more elevated, senior character, but in this I am constrained by their very firm petition for your own good self to undertake this service. Therefore I will be plain. The United States has done us the signal honour of embarking on a characterisation of their navy that is in the greatest measure our own. This is gratifying to us, of course, as it presupposes an alignment of purpose consequent upon a convergence of practices. This, naturally, has put the French out of countenance, for the Americans have turned their back on their traditional ally in this.'

Liston paused, considering Kydd. 'And in this, as in all things, you will consult your honour as to how on foreign soil you will best conduct yourself in furtherance of your country's interests.'

Something in the smooth flow of words alerted Kydd and he listened warily. 'I will, sir, be assured.'

'Then if this is your prime motivation I can rely on your loyalty to the Crown?'

'Sir.'

'Then let me lay out the issues before you. You are in a unique position to allay the fears of your government on certain matters concerning the effectiveness of this armament . . .'

'Sir!' Kydd said tightly. 'You're askin' me to spy on th' Americans?' The warmth of a flush spread, but he did not care. Spies and betrayal, this was not how he saw his duty.

Liston's face tightened. 'Have a care, Lieutenant! Recollect you hold the commission of King George. And in it you have sworn certain loyalties that cannot so easily be cast aside. What I am asking is no more than any officer of honour is bound to do when on foreign territory, whether on parole or any other basis – simply to keep his eyes open.' The crack of aristocratic authority in his voice remained as he went on, 'And if I might remark it, you appear surprisingly deficient thereby in your understanding of the bounds of gentlemanly conduct.'

Kydd stiffened, then dropped his eyes.

Liston's tone softened: 'We're not asking you to report back on the number of ships and guns and so forth, if that is your scruple. It is something of far more significance. I desire that you will return to me with an opinion as to whether you believe the United States is determined in this matter, has resolved to establish an armed force of credibility, or is merely embarked on a ploy to deter the French.' He fixed his gaze on Kydd. 'And if you conceive that they are in earnest, your professional opinion as to their effectiveness at sea. In short, whether they can fight – should the world take notice.'

Kydd returned the gaze steadily. 'I will do that, sir.' It was not an act of spying: it was an opinion.

Liston relaxed a little. 'Then as we seem to have come to an understanding, would you care to join me for coffee? The American bean is generally accounted superior, and we have the remainder of this hour before your hosts make their appearance.'

Twenty minutes later there was a firm knock on the door. Thornton appeared, with an indistinct figure behind him. 'Sir, a gentleman for Mr Kydd.' It was Gindler.

Outside they shook hands gleefully. 'Well, this must be the strangest coincidence of the age,' laughed Gindler, but his knowing look gave the game away.

'So, what has the American Navy in store for poor Lieutenant Kydd?'

'Ah, the United States Navy is what we call it – you English will have reason to remember the Continental Navy of the revolution; this is now the Federal Navy but some take exception to the term.'

'Noted.'

'And you are now talking to L'tenant Gindler, third of the United States Frigate *Constellation*, Captain Truxtun, now fitting out in Baltimore.' He smiled wickedly. 'And *I* am talking to the mysterious supernumerary on our first voyage . . .'

Kydd laughed but his interest swelled fast. This was not to be a pettifogging political appointment but a real seagoing situation. 'When—'

'Not so fast, good sir. I'm instructed that our new secretary of the Navy wishes to make your acquaintance before we hazard the briny deep.'

'Do excuse this mare's nest of a room – my wife has not yet arrived in Philadelphia to take charge of my household.' Stoddert made ineffectual attempts to clear a space at one end of a plain table where a stout chair stood. His manner was distracted but his gaze direct as he greeted Kydd.

'Secretary Stoddert has only recently arrived in the capital,' Gindler murmured, standing clear of the welter of papers and furniture.

'Thank you, Lieutenant. Pray call on me before you leave Philadelphia. I may have something for Captain Truxtun.' Gindler bowed and left.

'Now, you are Lieutenant Kydd of the Royal Navy.'

'Sir.'

'And you must be wondering why you are here, not to say concerned.'

'Aye, sir,' Kydd said, uneasy at yet more attention from on high. Stoddert lowered himself into his chair. 'Then, first, the wider issue. We are in the process of creating our own navy. We have chosen to follow the example and traditions of the Royal Navy as a starting point for our own. It would be of the utmost value to us were an officer of that illustrious service to signify to us our success in this endeavour. As to why your own good self, Mr Gindler was good enough to render me a full and satisfying account of what transpired in Exbury – in confidence, of course. There can be no question that the United States is implicated in any way.'

'I understand, sir.'

'But more to our liking are Mr Gindler's remarks upon your character. Let me be candid, sir. The Royal Navy is a proud and ancient service, but there are many of its officers whose superior attitude is both lamentable and abhorrent to us as a nation. It is a trait that regrettably seems to appear more prominent with seniority, and this is why we have chosen to request a less senior officer.

'Mr Gindler tells us that your conduct ashore was circumspect and respectful to the feelings of the people even to the point of joining the merriment in a tavern – in short, sir, you have the common touch, which we as a people do prize so much.' Stoddert rose, gripping the edge of the table and wincing as he did so. At Kydd's concern he gave a low chuckle. 'Ah, this. A souvenir given me by the English at Brandywine Creek.'

He drew the chair to a more confiding proximity. 'Let me be frank, Mr Kydd. Your position as a King's officer in a warship of the United States Navy is anomalous, not to say irregular, and there are those who would put the worst construction on your presence. Therefore you are entered as a supernumerary on board, specifically a friend of the captain. You haven't yet the pleasure of an introduction to Captain Truxtun, but he will be advised of you, and will be encouraged to take full advantage of your knowledge and experience of the Royal Navy. I'm sure he will appreciate your assistance.' He leaned forward further. 'Before you go, I should like to make it very plain that on your return I would deeply appreciate your sincere appraisal of our efforts. Do you think this will be possible?'

'Sir.' Kydd felt resentment building at the way so many seemed to be treating him like a pawn in a higher game.

'Then, sir, it only remains for me to wish you God speed on your voyage. You will find Lieutenant Gindler waiting in the drawing room below.'

'Was all that necessary?' A figure moved out from behind a covered escritoire.

Stoddert closed the door. 'I think so. The military of any race should not be overburdened with considerations of politics.' At times Murray, his political agent, could be insensitive to the perceptions of others.

'Be that as it may, Mr Stoddert, you didn't warn him of the Republicans – he should have been told.'

'That we have an opposition in Congress so lost to honour they would stop at nothing to ruin our navy for crass political gain? Jefferson has done his worst to try to prevent America reaching for a sure shield against the world – how can I explain that to a man whose country continues to exist only because of her own power at sea? I cannot. In any case, this talk of subverting crews and so on is probably from unreliable sources and should be discounted. What most concerns me are my captains. A prickly, difficult bunch, Murray. Especially Truxtun.'

'A fighting captain,' Murray interposed strongly.

'Oh, indeed. But as a privateer. And pray bring to mind the fluttering in Congress there was during the English war, on hearing how he set John Paul Jones himself to defiance over some notion of which ship was to fly some pennant. Not one to be led easily – and too damn clever by half. Did you know he was once pressed by the Royal Navy?'

'Indeed?'

'But that's by the by. Here is my main hope for L'tenant Kydd. He has no interest in politics. He's a tarpaulin mariner and cares only for his ropes and sails. He must be intelligent, he wouldn't hold a commission else, so he'll be able to tell me exactly what I want to know...'

Nothing could convey better to Kydd the continental vastness of the country than the overland coach journey with Gindler to Baltimore. From as fine a four-horse conveyance as any in England, they admired the spring-touched verdancy of the deciduous woodland that had replaced the northern conifers, the glittering lakes, rivers and blue-washed mountains far into the interior.

At stops to change horses, Gindler added to Kydd's impressions: he pointed out that beyond the mountains to the west the land was wild, stretching for more than sixty degrees of longitude; an unimaginable distance, more than the Atlantic was wide, and no one knew what was within it. Unsettled by the effect of this enormity Kydd was glad when they met the cobblestones of Baltimore.

'She'll be lying in the Patuxent river,' Gindler said. 'We're nearly ready for sea.' There was no delaying: a fast packet on its way down the Chesapeake to Norfolk had promised to call at Patuxent and their ship.

The sight of naked masts and yards towering above the low, bushy point made Kydd's pulse quicken. The packet rounded the point into the broad opening of a river and there at anchor was the biggest frigate he had ever seen.

'A thing of beauty,' breathed Gindler. 'Don't you agree?'

Kydd concentrated as they neared the vessel. She was distinctive and individual; her lines and finish owed nothing to the conservative traditions of old-world shipwrights, and there was an alert purposefulness about her. There was much in her that a sailor could love. Nearly half as big again as the lovely *Artemis*, she seemed well armed. 'Twenty-fours?' he asked.

'Indeed! I'd like to see any frigate that swims try to come up against the old *Connie*,' Gindler said proudly.

'Old?' Kydd said wryly, observing seamen applying a tar mixture to the last remaining raw timber of the bulwarks.

'Well, I grant you she's newborn, but I have the feeling you'll be hearing from us in the future, my friend.' His glance flicked up to the flag with its stars and stripes and he added softly, 'I promise you that.'

Kydd had seen far too many ships fitting for sea to be concerned at the turmoil on deck. He followed Gindler aft to the captain's cabin. Gindler knocked and an irritable bellow bade them enter.

'Mr Kydd, sir,' said Gindler, and when the captain looked up in incomprehension he added, 'Our supernumerary.'

The captain's gaze swivelled to Kydd. Intelligent but hard eyes met his. Then the man grunted, 'Mr Kydd, y'r service,' and turned back to his papers. 'Berth him in the fourth loo'tenant's cabin. He won't be sailing,' he ordered, without looking up.

'Aye, sir,' said Gindler, and withdrew with Kydd.

Picking their way through men at blocks and ropework – some seaming canvas, others scaling shot – they headed for the after hatchway. 'I fear I must desert you now, Tom, duty calls. I'll take you to the wardroom, and I'm sure Captain Truxtun will want to see you when less pressed.'

'Welcome back, Lootenant!' a fresh-faced seaman called, with a grin, to Gindler and waved a serving mallet.

'Thanks, Doyle,' Gindler threw back. At Kydd's raised eyebrows he added, 'A mort of difference from a King's ship, I think. Remember, aboard here every man jack is a volunteer on wages and, as Americans, they're not accustomed to bending the knee.'

Kydd did not rise to the bait and privately wondered at their reliability in action when instant obedience was vital.

The wardroom was almost deserted. A black messman glanced at him curiously and left. Kydd looked about him. The raw newness had not yet been overcome to bring individuality. At the same time there was an alien air. The unfamiliar wood graining, the slant of the munnions – even the smell: striking timber odours, the usual comfortable galley smells subtly different, no waft of bilge.

He crossed to the transom seat. Reassuringly, it was still the repository of the ephemera of wardroom life and he picked up a Philadelphia newspaper, the *Mercantile Advertiser*. While he awaited Truxtun's summons he settled by the midships lanthorn and opened it. There was no ochre tax stamp and the paper was of good quality. He scanned the front page, which was given over to a verbatim setting out of a newly enacted statute. The next page, however, was vigorous and to the point: a growing feeling against the French gave colour to the local news and trade intelligence. Further inside there were advertisements and notices.

'Mr Kydd? Cap'n wants ye.' He folded the paper, tugged his waistcoat into position and followed the messenger, apprehensive at meeting those hard eyes again.

Truxtun was standing, his back to Kydd, staring broodily out of the windows of his cabin. He turned and gestured to a chair. 'Sit y'self down, Mr Kydd.' He himself remained standing.

'I'll be plain with you, sir. Mr Secretary Stoddert thinks to provide me with an aide who'll tell me how they do it in King George's Navy. I can tell you frankly I don't give a solitary hoot how you do things – this is the United States Navy and I'm captain o' the *Constellation*, and I'll do things the way I want.' His face had the implacability of a slab of oak. 'Therefore your presence aboard is a waste. For Ben Stoddert's sake, I'll carry you these few days, but I'll have you know, sir, that I'll be giving orders that no United States officer or crewman shall hold converse with you – I don't want 'em getting strange ideas agin mine about how a ship o' war should be run. I'd be obliged if you'd keep your views to yourself.

'In return, you're welcome to sit at vittles in the wardroom and the fourth's stateroom is yours. You'll know to keep out from under while the ship's being worked, and should we meet an enemy you'll stay below. Have I made myself clear, sir?'

It was going to be a hard time for Kydd. He was not introduced when the wardroom sat for dinner. He was passed the condiments when he asked, but none caught his eye. Desultory talk went on about progress in the final run-up to sea trials in the morning, a few lame attempts at humour – this was a wardroom that had not been long together but would coalesce around individuals as the commission went on.

In the morning he caught Gindler, now a taut-rigged lieutenant, about to go on deck. 'I'm sorry it has to be this way, Tom,' he said softly. He touched his hat and left for the nervous bustle above.

Kydd hesitated: he could see down the length of the deck

to the cable party readying the messenger; the tierers were moving down the hatchway for their thankless task at bringing in the cable.

He decided against making an appearance and returned to the wardroom. Although it was galling to be left in ignorance below decks, this was a first voyage with a new ship and a new company and he felt it was not altogether fair to witness the inevitable mistakes and dramas. He found a dog-eared copy of the *North American Review* and tried to concentrate, but the long tiller up against the deckhead began to creak and move as the man at the wheel exercised the helm. Then piercing calls from the boatswain and his mates told of the hoisting of boats, all suffused with the age-old excitement of the outward bound.

Rhythmic singing came from the men forward, and he felt a continual low shuddering in the deck that was, without doubt, the capstan at work. A sudden clatter and flurry of shouting would be a fall running away with the men while heavy thumps against the ship's side were the boats being brought in and stowed. The noises lessened until there was silence. They were ready to proceed.

Constellation's deck lifted and moved. In a deliberate sway it inclined to starboard, a heel that paused then returned and steadied to a definite angle, which had only one meaning: they were under sail and moving through the water.

Kydd threw down the newspapers – it was too much. He had to catch a glimpse of the sea. There were no stern windows in the wardroom, so the nearest place to see the ship's position was from the captain's cabin above.

He hurried up the companion and through the lobby. To the sentry loosely at attention outside the great cabin, he muttered, 'Have t' see out.' If he craned his neck, he could just glimpse the coastline of the Patuxent slowly rotating; a discernible wake was disturbing the water astern and the frenzied squeal of blocks could be heard even below decks.

He nodded to the marine and returned to the wardroom.

He knew vaguely that they should shape course south down Chesapeake Bay to the sea, but without sight of a chart he was in the dark. The angle of the deck lessened, then he heard another volley of faintly heard shouts, and there was a brief hesitation – they must be staying about.

At the right moment the tiller groaned with effort as the wheel went over but after some minutes there was no corresponding sway over to larboard. They had missed stays. Kydd cringed for the officer of the deck as the unmistakable bull roar of Truxtun erupted; he was grateful to be out of sight. He picked up the *Review* again and flicked the pages.

After an hour or so the motions were repeated but this time in a smooth sequence, the frigate taking up on the opposite tack. Again the manoeuvre and again an easy transition. Dare he emerge on deck? He waited for a space; the angle of heel increased gradually and he guessed that more sail was being loosed. Kydd could stand it no longer. He made his way to the aft companion and mounted the steps to the quarterdeck. In the tense scene, not a soul looked his way. Groups of men were at the bitts, the base of the masts, the forecastle, all looking aft to where Truxtun stood with folded arms, staring up at taut canvas.

'Stream!' he snapped, to the men at the taffrail. One held the reel of the log high while the log-ship, a triangular drag piece, was cast into the sea astern to uncoil the line from the drum. It hurtled out at speed and when the sand-glass had run its course a lanky midshipman called, 'Nip,' and then, 'Eleven knots an' a hair over.'

Truxtun's expression did not change. 'Not good enough. I'll have the lee stuns'ls abroad immediately.'

The spring breeze whipped the tops from the waves as Kydd edged his way behind Truxtun towards the wheel and binnacle. Under the unblinking eye of the quartermaster he got what he wanted – a sight of the compass. South-south-east, wind from the west with a touch of north in it. Ideal blue-water sailing for a frigate: no wonder Truxtun was letting her have her head.

They were passing a broad river mouth to starboard with small vessels of all kinds converging at the confluence. 'Potomac,' hissed the midshipman behind him.

'I beg y'r pardon?' Kydd said, taken off-balance.

'The river – Potomac.' He busied himself preparing the log for another cast.

'Thank ye,' Kydd said quietly.

With stuns'ls drawing and royals atop each mast, *Constellation* foamed ahead. It was remarkable for a new vessel to have achieved such speed so soon. The log went out and the excited midshipman yelled, 'A whisker less fourteen!' It was nothing short of extraordinary – and exhilarating. If Kydd was not to be an active participant at least he could enjoy the sensation.

Truxtun's eyes darting aloft, then aft, caught Kydd's eye. Kydd smiled broadly in open admiration. 'She goes like a racehorse!'

'Aye – like a Yankee racehorse!' But there was no rancour in his voice and his grim expression had eased. It would be a gratifying thing, thought Kydd, to be in command of a frigate that, with her twenty-four pounders, could outfight any other and, at the same time, run or chase as she chose.

* * *

In the darkness of late evening they came to single anchor in the shelter of Hampton Roads, within sight of the broad Atlantic. The wardroom was abuzz at the splendid showing of their ship and it seemed only right to invite their captain to a hearty dinner.

Kydd sat at the furthest remove from Truxtun's place of honour at the head, but he was grateful to be present, hearing the happy talk about him, seeing friendships being forged and strengthened that would stand by them all in the ocean voyages ahead.

The talk roamed over the chance of war with France, seeing *The Glory of Columbia* at the Chestnut Street theatre, the right way to treat a halibut – it was just the same as his own wardroom . . . but different.

The dishes came and went, and the cloth was drawn. Blue smoke spiralled to the deckhead, glasses were raised and confidences exchanged. The chatter rose and fell. Into a chance silence Gindler's voice was raised: 'Ah, Mr Kydd, you must have seen some sea service in your time. Pray tell us of it.'

Glances were shot at Truxtun but he gave no sign that he objected.

'Aye, well, I had th' good fortune to take a cruise around th' world,' Kydd said, thinking quickly. 'A frigate, nearly as fine as this.' He saw this was received well. 'Setting a parcel o' philosophers on a rock, an' keeping the cannibals in their canoes at bay . . .' He told them of the adventure, and when he concluded with the sad wreck of *Artemis* on the Azores, there was a general stirring of sympathy.

Midshipman Porter leaned forward and exclaimed, 'Have you b' chance seen action?'

'A little – Camperdown, which was where I got m' step.'

Kydd wouldn't be drawn on the experience and tried to move on to Venice, but Truxtun himself interrupted: 'Your fleet were in bloody mutiny before then.' A ripple of muttering showed that the dreadful events had been shocking news here as well. 'How did that affect you?'

The warmth of the evening fell away as he forced his mind to deal with the sudden release of memories. 'It – my ship mutinied, but I was not hurt.'

'Would you say the sailors had just cause?'

'At Spithead they had their reasons, and the Admiralty granted most and gave a pardon. But at the Nore. . .' He felt his face redden.

'Yes?'

'At the Nore, where I was, their cause was understandable but they went about it the wrong way.'

Truxtun growled, 'There's no treating with mutineers, ever.'

The next day a small convoy had yet to assemble, so the dark-featured First Lieutenant Rodgers was sent ashore to the settlement of Norfolk to open a recruiting rendezvous to bring in more volunteers. Kydd saw Truxtun hand him silver at the gangway, saying, 'Get some music going and grog for all hands – indulge their humour in a farewell frolic.' Rodgers grinned and went over the side.

From forward came the dull *blang* of scaling charges as they cleared the cannon of rust and debris. Men squatted on the foredeck as they made up paper cartridges for the small arms, while others had the hatches off for the last of the sea stores still coming aboard.

By the early afternoon activity had died away. But Truxtun was not satisfied. He beat to quarters, and for two hours had the great guns exercised. Big twenty-four-pounders given resplendent names by their gun crews, Thunderer, Volcano, Murderer, and all plied with ferocity and resolution.

That night Kydd did not sit down with the wardroom. Captain Truxtun had requested the pleasure of his company and he entered the great cabin with some apprehension, for they were alone. Through the stern windows Kydd could see dim specks of light on shore; a tawny gold issued from the windows of a vessel anchored nearby, prettily dappling the water.

They passed pleasantries while they took a simple meal, and the steward swiftly removed the dishes. Kydd's wariness grew with Truxtun's politeness. 'Do take a chair,' Truxtun said, gesturing to a comfortable one near the stern windows. He found a cedar box in his writing desk and drew out a cigar. 'Do you indulge, Mr Kydd?' At Kydd's declining he put it away again.

'You'll pardon me, Mr Kydd, but you're the darnedest Royal Navy officer I ever clapped eyes on.' His frank gaze was unsettling. 'I can tell a smart man when I see one. Don't have the airs of a King's man but I'll guess that's because you come from the people.' He pondered for a moment. 'So, do you hold it right to press men from under their own flag?'

'Sir, if these men are British they have a duty to—'

'They are American, sir.'

'They say they are.'

'They hold protections to prove it – and these are spat on by English officers.'

'Yes! Th' rate for an American protection by your consul in Liverpool is one guinea and no questions asked.'

Truxtun smiled. 'We each have our views.' The smile disappeared. 'It's insulting to our flag for our merchant ships to be stopped and submit to search on the high seas. What do ye think of that?'

'Sir, Britain is a small island,' he said carefully. 'Trade is all we have. To survive we have to protect it, and—'

'You're right – and damn wrong. Do you know that most of the trade out of Nova Scotia is your cargo in our bottoms, on its way to ports of the world only a neutral can reach? You stop an American and you sink your own trade.'

Kydd flushed. 'You asked for views – I don't know y'r details but this I do know: if you're doin' the same for the French you're makin' a hill o' money out of it.'

Truxtun's expression hardened, then a glimmer of a smile showed. 'Well, as to that . . .'

It was the first that Kydd had heard of the true extent of the French attacks on American shipping and Truxtun's tone left no doubt of his feelings. 'If we don't stand on our hind legs and fight 'em we deserve to be beat.'

He looked directly at Kydd. 'You're wondering why we don't declare war. So am I!' He glowered. Suddenly he got to his feet, crossed to his desk and abstracted a folded paper. 'I'll show you this,' he said, in an odd voice. 'It came in today.'

It was a single page, and bore the seal of the President of the United States. Kydd looked up in surprise. 'Don't worry, the whole world's going to know about this tomorrow,' Truxtun said heavily.

It began, 'Instructions to Commanders of Armed Vessels, belonging to the United States, given at Philadelphia in the twenty-second Year of the Independence of the said States . . .' Truxtun leaned over and stabbed a finger at the second paragraph. 'There!' 'WHEREAS, it is declared by an Act of Congress . . . that armed Vessels, sailing under authority or Pretence of Authority from the French Republic, have committed Depredations on the Commerce of the United States . . . in violation of the Law of Nations, and Treaties between the United States and the French Nation. . .' Truxtun snorted. 'And what must we do?' He tapped the last paragraph: 'THEREFORE, and in pursuance of the said Act, you are instructed and directed, to seize take and bring into any Port of the United States . . .'

'You see? It's on. A shootin' war against the French.'

Kydd stared in astonishment – everything had changed. 'But—'

Truxtun interrupted him: 'But it's not. We haven't declared war, the French haven't. What kind of peace is it that requires me to fire into a Frenchman on sight? Some sort of – of quasi-war?'

Kydd was in no doubt. 'Any kind o' war is fine. This is thumpin' good news – and c'n I say, sir, if we both have the same enemy then we must be friends.'

'No! No – I didn't say that. I didn't say that at all. We just has the same enemy, is the truth of it. I'll be doing my duty at sea and you'll be doing yours as you see it.' He took back the paper. 'If it's any clearer,' he said gruffly, 'I mean to say I hope we meet at sea one day – as equals, Mr Kydd.'

The convoy was finally ready to sail. Showers blustered in from the north in curtains of white, vivid against the sullen grey of the sky, and lines of foam-crested waves advanced seaward.

A sullen thump came from forward – the signal gun for departure; two cutters moved about the dozen merchantmen cajoling, threatening, shepherding. It was so similar to Kydd's sailing from Falmouth, yet there was a difference: the lift of a head, the ringing shouts of the petty officers, the brazen size of the flag at the mizzen peak, the length of the pennant at the mainmasthead. This was a unique experience: to be aboard the first frigate commissioned in the United States Navy, and the first to put to sea on a war cruise.

Kydd stood out of the way, to the side, buffeted by the wind and with rain dripping from his hat brim. He was in no mood to go below. Although he was a spectator, he knew that no one would forget the day: a navy brought in just months from nothing to one that could execute the will of the nation. From helpless acquiescence to a sea force that would now go against the country's enemy – and conceivably within hours.

He looked forward. Gindler strode ahead proudly, disdaining oilskins over his lieutenant's uniform. To starboard the square, lofty lighthouse of Cape Henry lay abeam. With *Constellation* in the lead, the convoy left the haven of Chesapeake Bay and sailed for the open ocean to the east and all that lay beyond.

Standing out to sea the frigate lifted to the swell, new men staggered to the businesslike roll, while others sniffed the wind as if eager to be out to sea – or was it in anticipation of bloody action? The merchant ships bunched together close to the American frigate: there had been talk ashore of a pair of big privateers lying in wait and self-preservation was a strong motive for keeping station.

The weather moderated as they made their offing, although *Constellation* needed only double-reefed topsails to stay with her labouring convoy. Kydd walked forward, keenly appreciative of the motion of a frigate once more and interested indeed in the weatherliness of the American.

After the sociability of the dinner he was now greeted with cautious nods and the occasional smile – even the intense Lieutenant Rodgers touched his hat to him at one point.

When the land had been sunk and a tossing wilderness of

empty ocean had been reached, the convoy dispersed, some to the Barbadoes, others to Dublin and London, thousands of miles of hard sailing with small crews, with the constant fear of sighting the sails of a predator. But *Constellation* was free now to soar.

'Mr Kydd.' Truxtun snapped, as though struck by a sudden thought. 'We shall be cruising south tomorrow.' The rest of the quarterdeck was listening intently. 'Therefore I believe it would be most expedient for you then to take your leave from this vessel. I shall stop a Philadelphia packet for your convenience, sir.'

Kydd had taken to standing beside the lee helmsman, willing the ship on, feeling her motion through the water, and turned in surprise. 'Er – why, of course, Captain.' It was a disappointment not to see the frigate at her best, and despite the circumstances of his passage, there was something about this ship and her crew . . .

In the dog-watches, as the ship shortened sail for the night, Kydd lingered on deck, then went below for his last dinner aboard the *Constellation*. He went to his accustomed place at the end of the table, but found a black steward there. 'If y' please, sah,' he said, and pointed to the head of the table, where all the American officers stood with glasses, grinning at him.

'Come 'n' set, Tom,' one called. Kydd did as he was asked, and took the chair normally occupied by the first lieutenant, bemused.

'Just wanted t' wish you God speed, Mr Kydd,' Rodgers said, proffering a glass.

Kydd took it and lifted it to them. 'Your very good health, gentlemen,' he called, touched beyond measure.

The group broke into warm conversation, and as dinner was brought he found himself talking as amiably as any. More wine, more dishes: Kydd felt a rush of feeling that came out as hot words of admiration for their fine ship, their spirit, their future.

He sat with flushed face and beamed at them all. No cool talk of the London season, not a word about fox-hunting or estates in the country, this was good sturdy conversation about horses, prospects of prize money, scandalous theatre gossip – here he could safely say his piece without fear of being thought a boor.

'Fr'm Kentucky, friend, you'll hanker after this . . .' Bourbon whiskey was added to the list of Kydd's American experiences.

'Did I ever tell ye of Gibraltar? Now there's a rare place, one thunderin' great rock . . .'

Happy and muzzy, he did not notice that Truxtun was in the wardroom until he suddenly saw him sitting at the other end of the table. He froze – but Truxtun raised his glass. 'Ye share the same forename as me, Tom, and I'd like to say that, should you find it in your heart to become an American, there could be a berth aboard *Constellation* if you choose.'

Kydd turned in to his tiny cot, unable to control his whirling thoughts. An American? Thomas Paine Kydd, citizen of the United States, gentleman of the land and lieutenant of the United States Navy? It was not impossible – he had no ties, no wife and family back in England.

Excitement seized him and his eyes opened wide in the darkness. Why not start a new life in a country where there did not seem to be any difference between gentleman and commoner, a nation that seemed to have so much land and so few people – opportunity unlimited?

But he held the King's commission. Would he be betraying his country in her time of need? What about other officers in foreign navies? Well, they had been allowed to resign their commissions to take service, and was there not one in the Russian Navy who was now a grand duke? And, above all, if he were in the American Navy he would be fighting the King's enemies even if it was under another flag.

And there were so many English seamen already serving – he had heard aboard *Constellation* the accents of Devon, the North, London. He could always be among his country-men if he felt lonely. They had made the choice, even if many had chosen desertion. Could he?

He tossed and turned until finally sleep came mercifully to claim him.

It seemed only minutes later when he jerked awake. He knew that he had heard a cannon shot and sat up. Almost imme-diately the urgent rattle of a drum beating to quarters set his heart hammering.

Kydd dropped clumsily out of his cot and reached for his clothing. Nearby, thumping feet sounded urgently. He strug-gled into breeches and shirt, flung on his coat and raced barefoot up the companion to the upper deck.

In the cold of daybreak, out of the thin drifting rain ahead, the dark shape of a ship lay across their path. *Constellation*'s helm was put up to bear away. Even in the bleak grey half-light it was plain that they had come upon a man-o'-war, a frigate, who had instantly challenged them.

'Get out of it, damn you!' Truxtun bawled, catching sight of Kydd. 'Get below!'

There was something about this enemy frigate – Kydd knew he had seen her before.

'Now, sir!' Truxtun bellowed.

It was the characteristic odd-coloured staysail, the abrupt curve of her beakhead. But where? Her colours flew directly away and were impossible to make out; the two signal flags of her challenge flickered briefly into life as they were jerked down and, her challenge unanswered, her broadside thundered out.

In the seconds that the balls took to reach them Kydd remembered, but before he could speak, Truxtun roared, 'Get that English bastard below, this instant!'

Shot slammed past hideously, gouting the sea and sending solid masses of water aboard. One slapped through a sail. Kydd urged Truxtun, 'Sir, hold y'r fire, for God's sake – she's a British ship!'

Incredulous, Truxtun stared at him. 'She fired on the American flag! She's got to be a Frenchman, damn you!'

'That's *Ceres* thirty-two, I'd stake m' life on it!' But how fast would *Ceres* take to reload and send another, better-aimed, broadside?

'An English ship!' Truxtun's roar carried down the deck and pale faces turned, then darkened in anger, menacing growls rising to shouts. 'I'll make 'em regret this! Mr Rodgers—'

'Do ye want war with England as well?' Kydd shouted. Livid, Truxtun hesitated.

'Hoist y'r white flag!'

'Surrender? Are you insane?'

'No – flag o' parlay.' All it needed was for one over-hasty gunner on either side and the day would end in bloody ruin.

For a frozen moment everything hung. Then Truxtun acted: 'White flag to the main, Mr Rodgers,' he growled.

*   *   *

'He'd better be coming with an explanation!' Truxtun snapped to Kydd, as a boat under a white flag advanced, a lieutenant clearly visible in the sternsheets.

'Sir, be s' good as to see it from his point o' view. His private signals have not been answered and as far as he knows there *is* no United States Navy with a ship o' this force. You have t' be a Frenchy tryin' a deception.'

Truxtun gave an ill-natured grunt and waited for the boat. When it drew near Kydd saw the lieutenant stand and look keenly about him as the bowman hooked on. As he mounted the side angry shouts were hurled at him by seamen, which Truxtun made no attempt to stop.

'Now, before I blow you out of the water, explain why you fired into me, sir,' Truxtun said hotly, as the lieutenant climbed over the bulwark.

He had intelligent eyes and answered warily, 'Sir, the reason is apparent. You did not answer my ship's legitimate challenge and, er, we have no information about an American frigate at sea. Our conclusion must be obvious.' Before Truxtun could answer, he added, 'And remembering we are under a flag of truce, sir, I believe I might respectfully demand that you offer me some form of proof of your notional status – if you please.'

'Be damned to your arrogance, sir!' Truxtun punched a fist towards the huge American flag above them. 'There is all the proof anyone needs!' Shouts of agreement rang out and seamen advanced on the quarterdeck. The lieutenant held his ground but his hand fell to his sword.

Kydd held up a hand and stepped forward. 'L'tenant, a word, if y' please.'

The lieutenant looked in astonishment at Kydd's bare legs, his civilian coat and breeches, soaked and clinging to him. 'Er, yes?'

Drawing him aside, Kydd spoke urgently. 'I'm L'tenant

Kydd of HMS *Tenacious*, supernumerary aboard. I have t' tell ye now, this is a United States frigate true enough, and no damn Frenchy.'

The lieutenant's disdain turned to cold suspicion. 'You'll pardon my reservations, sir,' he said, giving a short bow, 'but can you offer me any confirmation of your identity?'

Kydd pulled his wet coat about him: a great deal hung on his next words. 'Very well, I can do that,' he said softly. 'Off Devil's Island not a month ago, *Ceres* was there when *Resolution* hangs out a signal to tack – in succession. *Tenacious* makes a fool of herself. *I* was that signal lieutenant.'

The lieutenant stared, then smiled. 'I really believe you must be.'

He turned to Truxtun and removed his hat. 'Sir, you have my condolences that this unhappy incident took place, but cannot concede any responsibility. This will be a matter for our governments to resolve. Good day, sir.'

The furious Truxtun did not reply, glowering at the man as he solemnly replaced his hat and went down the side to his boat, followed by yells of defiance.

What if it had been *Tenacious* instead? Kydd's thoughts raced – a ship-of-the-line thundering out her broadside? How could two proud navies cruise the seas without it happening again? They were at war with the same enemy – that was the main point. All else was pride.

'Sir.' Truxtun drew a deep breath and Kydd went on quickly, 'Be so kind as t' honour me with a minute of y'r time – in private.'

Truxtun turned to Rodgers. 'Stand down the men.' He stalked over to Kydd and stared at him. 'Very well – and then, for your own safety, sir, I'm confining you to your cabin until you're off this ship.'

'Thank you, sir.' Kydd felt he was being carried forward in a rush of destiny that could not be stopped, yet his mind was protecting him from the enormity of what he was contemplating by an odd detachment from reality.

'If I might go t' my cabin for a moment.' He was back quickly and went with Truxtun into his great cabin, closing the door behind him.

'*One* minute.'

'Sir. Captain – this is a madness. We must fight t'gether, not each other. So I'm now going t' trust you with my honour, an' I know it's not going t' be misplaced.' He could read nothing in Truxtun's stony face.

'Sir.' He gulped as he felt in his coat and withdrew a small pocket book. 'Sir, this is a copy of our secret signals. If you are challenged by a British ship you may safely reply with the correct private signal of the day, here, and at night challenge and response, here.

'Take it, sir, an' I know you'll protect its confidentiality with your own honour.' If the enemy ever got hold of its secrets, the ships of the Royal Navy would be at their mercy.

Truxtun stared at the book and then at Kydd. 'God rot me, but you're a brave man, Mr Kydd,' he said softly. He took the book and slipped it into his own coat. 'It'll be safe with me.' He held out his hand. 'I hope you do not suffer for this, but what you've done . . .' He clapped his hand on Kydd's shoulder. 'An honour to know you, sir.'

Chapter 12

Kydd had been able to reassure Stoddert with what he had seen, and Liston had listened to his account of a new player on the world maritime stage with grave attention, accepting his considered opinion of the new navy as an effective force. But now Kydd must face his day of reckoning and his return to Halifax was charged with dread at how he would be received. He knew why he had acted as he did, but the Admiralty might regard it as no less than treason.

Leaving the deadly Sambro Ledges well to leeward, the packet he'd caught back finally rounded the grey rocks of Chebucto Head for the run in to Halifax harbour. He had been away only days but it seemed like months.

Soon Kydd was standing on Water Street pier. He knew exactly what he had to do. He left his baggage at the shipping office and hurried down to the watermen's steps to hire a wherry to take him to the flagship at anchor.

The officer-of-the-day quickly got rid of Kydd to the flag-lieutenant.

'I have to wait upon the admiral immediately,' Kydd said tightly.

'You have an appointment, of course.'

'I'm just this hour returned from th' United States.'

The officer snorted in contempt. 'Good God, Mr Kydd, you know better than to come aboard hoping the admiral is at leisure to see you. Leave your reasons with me and—'

'L'tenant, unless you take me t' Admiral Vandeput this instant, you'll rue it, an' that is my solemn promise.'

'Very well. Be it on your own head. What ship, you say?'

The officer knocked softly on the door to the admiral's day cabin. 'Lieutenant Kydd, sir, HMS *Tenacious*. No appointment, but he seems monstrous anxious to see you.'

Kydd entered.

The admiral was at his desk frowning, his secretary standing nearby with papers. 'Yes?'

'Sir, I have a matter of th' greatest importance.' Kydd's voice came out thickly.

Vandeput looked at him steadily, then glanced at his secretary. 'Go,' he snapped, then turned back to Kydd. 'You're back from America. What is it?'

It took but small minutes to convey the gist of his experiences, ending with the final, shocking clash. 'Therefore, sir, I saw that if it happens again there's chance f'r a mortal fight or . . .'

Vandeput's expression hardened. 'And then?'

Kydd took hold of all his courage. 'I gave Captain Truxtun m' own signal book, which has all th' private signals for your fleet.'

There was an appalled silence, then the admiral said softly, 'You're saying this American captain now has possession of all our secret signals?'

'Aye, sir,' said Kydd, trying to keep the tremor from his voice.

'Well done.'

'S-sir?'

'A good, officer-like solution, L'tenant. Always worried me, Americans at sea in a ship o' force sharing the same ocean without we have a form o' co-operation. The politicos won't go at it out o' pride, but now we've forced their hands. I can see how this can go further, Mr Kydd. As I say, well done, sir.'

Weak with reaction, Kydd swayed. 'Oh, I see it's been a fatiguing journey for ye, Mr Kydd,' the admiral said solicitously. 'Do sit, and I'll ring for a brandy.'

Kydd stared moodily at the town from the decks of *Tenacious*. He had been welcomed back by a newly respectful wardroom, but after a while conversations turned once again to the social scene. The whole town was mesmerised by the impending visit of the Duke of Schweigerei, elder son of the Archduke of Austria, which would climax in a grand reception and banquet given by His Royal Highness Prince Edward in the Duke's honour. In view of the importance attached to the country for its role in Pitt's coalitions, every officer would be expected to attend the glittering occasion.

Renzi had tried to be interested in Kydd's adventure, but he was clearly preoccupied with some personal matter, and Kydd found himself once more at a loose end. The seductive thought on his mind was of what might be – service in the new navy of a vigorous young land. No more would he hear of lords and estates, fox-hunting and the Season.

Kydd stirred uncomfortably and noticed the master, with a large notebook and folded chart, checking something over the side. 'Nothing amiss, Mr Hambly?' It was unusual to see the master at work on deck in harbour.

'Nay, sir, nothing t' worry you on,' he said. Then, seeing Kydd's interest, he explained further. It seemed that the new Admiralty hydrographic department had issued instructions to all sailing masters that anchorages they might from time to time visit should be surveyed by hand lead-line from a ship's boat with a view to verifying the accuracy of charts now in the course of preparation in England.

'A fine and proper thing,' said Kydd. Every mariner was at the mercy of his charts, whether dependable or false, and any endeavour that could lessen the fearful risks of navigation was a service to mankind. 'Where are you going t' start?'

'Why, Mr Kydd, it's kind in ye to enquire. I thought t' try the Bedford Basin – there, through the narrows, an' you'll find a fine body o' water twice the size of Halifax harbour there.'

A nearly perfect land-locked haven: a fleet could safely ride out a storm there. This was really worthwhile – an exercise of professional sea skills with a purpose. Kydd brightened. 'Mr Hambly, I'd like t' do some of this work m'self. Would you be s' kind as to show me on the chart?'

Kydd had chosen to begin his first line of soundings across the widest point of the basin to establish some sort of bottom profile. It was satisfying work, and congenial to the spirit. Real skill was needed to hold the octant laterally to establish the bearings ashore and provide the exact position of the pinnace. Poulden, in the bows, would send the hand-lead plummeting down, singing out in cadence the exact depth of water told by the marks. Kydd noted the time carefully; later, there would be work with tide tables to establish the true depth, corrected for the state of tide, then referenced to the chart datum.

Kydd was so engrossed in the work that, for a space, he

had forgotten his concern about the banquet. It had been heavily hinted at by Captain Houghton that every officer would not only attend but with a suitable lady. To those who had attained a degree of intimacy with the gentle reaches of Haligonian society it would be a matter of choice. For Kydd, who had not only been away but felt awkward and ill-at-ease in well-born company, it was a trial. He realised he would probably end up with the insipid daughter of the vicar, with whom he was on nodding terms, to the amusement of the more senior in the wardroom.

He forced his mind back to the task at hand. Surprisingly, their first traverse reached the twenty-fathom limit of a hand-lead less than a third the way across. Such deep water? Perhaps he should stay with the shoreline and first establish a forty-foot line of depth along it, this being of most interest to a big-ship navigator. It was not difficult to pick up the mark again, and astute reading of the characteristics at the edge of the shoreline soon had a useful number of forty-foot soundings carefully pencilled in. But for the unfortunate narrows at the entrance, restricting access to square-rigged vessels whenever the winds were in the north, it was spacious and deep enough to take the entire Channel Fleet at single anchor, an impressive body of water.

Something ashore caught Kydd's eye: a figure in white, standing, watching. He ignored it and continued with his work. They drew abreast; the figure was still there. As he watched he realised it was a woman, waving a handkerchief.

She waved again, an exaggerated movement. 'Someone wants t' speak, sir,' Poulden volunteered.

'Aye. Well, perhaps we should see what she wants. Oars, give way together.'

The boat headed inshore. The wooded slopes leading down

to the water looked immaculately cared for, and they saw the edge of a building peeping out from blossom-laden trees. Closer in, Kydd noticed a discreet landing-stage and headed for it. The woman made no move to descend to it, still standing and watching from her vantage-point.

Cursing under his breath, Kydd threw a rope ashore and pulled himself up to the little jetty. He was hardly dressed for meeting ladies in his worn sea uniform but he clambered up to where she was waiting.

'Yes, madam?'

'Oh. I was watching you, you see,' she said, her voice soft and prettily accented with French.

Kydd remembered himself and snatched off his hat. Dressed for the garden, she was in a white gown and be-ribboned straw hat. She was also strikingly beautiful, her large dark eyes adding an appealing wistfulness.

'And I thought 'ave you lost something – you look for it so long.' She seemed a touch older than him and had a dis-concertingly worldly-wise air.

'Not at all, madam. We conduct a hydrographical survey o' the coastline.' She was probably one of the sad band of royalist refugees who had settled in Nova Scotia, he conjec-tured, although apparently from a wealthy family. 'Oh, er, might I present m'self? L'tenant Kydd, Royal Navy.'

'*Enchantée*, Lieutenant.' Her bob coincided with Kydd's sturdy bow. 'Then you do not know me?'

'No, madam, er, you have th' advantage of me.'

She contemplated him, then said, 'I am Thérèse Bernardine-Mongenet and zis is where I live.' She gestured gracefully up the slopes.

At a loss, Kydd bowed again.

'I was taking refreshment in ze garden. Perhaps you would

care to take some lemonade wiz me, and tell me about your hydrog-cally, Lieutenant?'

Kydd accepted graciously: the boat's crew would be reliable with Poulden and would not object to an hour's leisure. They walked together up a winding path, past little summerhouses with gilded latticework and bells tinkling on their pagoda-like roofs. It was the most enchanting and sumptuous garden Kydd had ever seen. Atop a bluff overlooking the water, cunningly nestled among trees, there was a two-storey wooden mansion, vaguely Italian in style, and on the grass lawn below a cloth-covered table with jug and glass.

'A moment.' She summoned a maid and spoke rapidly in French to her, then turned back to Kydd. 'So, tell me what is it you are doing.'

Kydd was uncomfortable in his old uniform but he thawed at her warmth, and by the time the maid returned with another glass and a cake stand he was chuckling at her misapprehensions of the sea service. 'Rousin' good cakes,' he said, having sampled one of the tiny, lemon-flavoured shells.

'Ah, ze *madeleines*,' she said sadly. 'The old King Louis, 'is favourite.'

It did not seem right to dwell on past griefs, so Kydd said brightly, 'Have you heard? The Duke o' Shwygery is t' be honoured with a banquet, an' we're all invited to attend. Your husband will have an invitation, o' course?'

'I am not married,' she said quietly.

'Oh, I'm sorry, madam,' he said. 'Ah – that's not t' mean I'm sorry you're not married at all. I – er, please forgive...'

'Forgiven, M'sieur,' she said gently.

'Will I see you there?' he asked hopefully.

She looked at him steadily. 'I have not been invited.'

Kydd's heart went out to her, so elegant, beautiful and

serene. No man had begged her hand for the occasion, unwilling to risk the mortification of being declined – indeed, in the normal way he would never be noticed by a lady of such quality. It was so close to the event it was more than probable there would be no more offers forthcoming and she would be obliged to stay at home. Any gentleman . . . 'Madam, I am not engaged for the occasion. It would be my particular honour t' escort you, should ye be inclined.'

There was a fraction of hesitation, then she smiled. 'I would be delighted to accept, Lieutenant,' she murmured, and the smile moved to her eyes.

'What do ye think, Nicholas?' said Kydd, rotating in his new full-dress uniform coat. The white facings with gold buttons against the deep blue were truly magnificent and he looked forward to making his appearance in it.

'Dare I enquire, dear fellow, if you have a lady of suitable distinction marked out for the occasion?' Renzi asked doubtfully.

'I have.' Kydd was going to give nothing away before the night; all he had to do was take a ship's boat to the landing-stage, then make his way to the house. Thérèse had said she would find a carriage.

'It *is* at Government House,' Renzi stressed, 'and although we shall not be prominently seated you do understand we *will* be under eye, possibly of the Prince himself.'

'Thank you, Nicholas. I will try not to disappoint. And y'r-self?'

'I have my hopes, dear fellow.'

The day of the banquet arrived. Captain Houghton addressed his officers in the wardroom as to the seriousness of the occasion, the honour of the ship, the correct forms of address to the Prince and to an Austrian duke and duchess and the probable fate of any officer who brought shame to his ship.

Later in the day Tysoe jostled with others to begin the long process of bringing his officer to a state of splendour: a stiff white shirt topped with a black stock at the neck under the high stand-up collar of the coat, gleaming buckled shoes over white stockings, and immaculate tight white breeches. It had been shockingly expensive and Kydd had borrowed heavily against his future prize money from *Minotaure*, but he was determined to make a showing.

One by one the other officers departed, some to share carriages, others to walk up the hill. Renzi left, with a troubled glance at his friend.

Kydd trod the same path as before, the early-summer evening tinting the garden with a delicious enchantment. A footman waited and escorted Kydd to an open carriage. 'Madame will attend you presently,' he intoned.

Thérèse emerged and Kydd was left struggling for words: there must be few in Halifax who could possibly reach her heights of fashionable elegance. He took refuge in a deep bow as she came towards him in a full-length, high-waisted ivory gown, perilously low-cut and trimmed fetchingly in blue, her elaborate coiffure woven with pearls and a single ostrich feather sweeping up imperiously.

'*Bonsoir, mon lieutenant.* An' such a clement evening, *n'est ce pas?*'

With the footman holding open the door of the carriage, Kydd helped her up, her long gloved hand in his. It seemed so unreal, and all he could think of was that he must not let down Cecilia after all her patient tutoring on gentility.

The chaise lurched into motion, keeping to a sedate pace. Kydd sat bolt upright next to his lady. Thankfully, the grinding of the wheels made conversation an effort, and he concentrated on the journey, imagining the effect on his ship-mates when he and his lady were announced.

As they approached the town he was given a measure of what to expect by the reaction of passers-by. Some gaped, others pointed. Kydd swelled with pride – they must make a striking couple indeed. The carriage clattered along the streets and headed for a large building between two churches, illuminated in every window, and with the sound of fine music coming from within.

They drew up outside among the crowd of sightseers and Kydd was gratified once again by the impression he and his lady made. He bowed graciously this way and that, then has-tened to assist Thérèse down. He offered his arm, and they swept into Government House through a lane of gaping onlookers. His confidence soared.

Inside he glimpsed the levée room, packed with glittering personages in animated talk, jewellery sparkling in candle-light, and a military concert band in full flow in the corner. A bewigged major-domo at the door hesitated. 'Er, Madame Thérèse Bernardine-Mongenet,' Kydd said importantly – it had taken hours to learn, 'And L'tenant Thomas Kydd.'

The man looked petrified; possibly this was his first impor-tant occasion, Kydd thought. Nevertheless, he coughed and bawled resolutely, 'Lieutenant Thomas Kydd and – and Madame Thérèse Bernardine-Mongenet.' With her hand on his arm, Kydd stepped into the room. If only Cecilia could see him now!

Every face in the room turned towards them: conversa-tions died, the band's efforts faded uncertainly. Kydd's head was spinning. This was what it was to be in high society! 'You will introduce me?' Thérèse whispered.

Overflowing with happiness and with the broadest smile, Kydd turned to his left and approached the nearest group, who started with apprehension. He bowed deeply to the eld-erly gentleman and made a grand introduction. The man's wife curtsied, staring wide-eyed at Thérèse. Kydd moved on graciously, trying to think of suitable small-talk.

He knew he would never forget the night – or the effect of a truly beautiful woman on society. Around them con-versations stopped, then picked up again as they progressed down the room.

To the side, he saw Houghton staring at them as if at a ghost. Next to him stood Bampton, clearly in shock. 'My captain,' Kydd said happily to Thérèse, as they approached. Houghton seemed overcome at the introduction, gobbling something indistinct, but Thérèse, clearly delighted, bestowed on him special attention and offered her hand to be kissed. As he watched his captain grovel before a grand lady, Kydd believed the evening could promise nothing more satisfying.

Prince Edward stood in the centre of the room surrounded by aides-de-camp, courtiers and military men in gleaming reg-imentals. Kydd summoned every ounce of courage and led Thérèse over to him. 'Y'r Royal Highness, may I be allowed t' introduce Madame Thérèse Bernardine-Mongenet?' Thérèse's graceful curtsy was long held. 'An' myself, L'tenant Thomas Kydd, o' HMS *Tenacious*.' He bowed as low as he could.

'Lieutenant, tell me true, have you been in Halifax long?' The Prince had an aristocratically hard face; Kydd had heard stories of his unbending attitude to military discipline, his early-morning parades and merciless justice.

'Not long, Y'r Royal Highness, an' much o' that in the United States.'

'Oh. I see. Well, I wish you a pleasant evening, Mr Kydd.'

'Thank you, sir,' Kydd mumbled, remembering to back away. He had survived, and he turned to grin at Thérèse.

A fanfare of trumpets sounded from the other room, announcing the banquet. An immediate move was made towards the connecting door, but Kydd remembered to keep clear: as a junior officer he would certainly be bringing up the rear. He stayed to one side, nodding pleasantly to those whose eyes strayed towards him and Thérèse until eventually he judged it time to enter.

The room was huge. In the distance a long table was raised on a dais, the centre occupied by the Prince and honoured guests. Behind them two servants gently fanned the principal guests with enormous ostrich feathers, tastefully coloured in red, white and blue.

Lesser mortals occupied the long tables in rows from the front and, as he had suspected, he was shown to one near the rear. To his delight he saw Renzi seated there. Next to him was a voluble woman with pasty skin and a profusion of cheap jewellery who tugged incessantly at his sleeve. Renzi looked up at Kydd, and stared, stricken, at him as if the world had been turned upside-down.

Gleefully Kydd made his introduction, indicating to Thérèse that this was his particular friend, but when he made to seat his lady, he was interrupted by a courtier. 'Sir, His Royal Highness commands you and Madame to join him,' he murmured, discreetly indicating the Prince, who was beckoning.

Heart thudding, Kydd turned to Renzi and muttered his excuses. He wended his way with Thérèse through the tightly packed tables, feeling all eyes upon him, hearing animated murmuring following in their wake.

They mounted the dais and approached Prince Edward, who leaned back to speak. 'Ah, so kind of you to join us.' His eyes did not move from Thérèse as he continued, 'I don't think you've met *Hoheit Herzog* Schweigerei, his wife the

Herzogin Adelheid. Sir, Lieutenant Kydd and Madame Thérèse Bernardine-Mongenet.'

The evening proceeded. Over the wild duck Kydd found himself explaining sea service to the Prince; the saddle of mutton saw him recounting his American sojourn to the sharp-featured Duke. While he was helping Thérèse to another pompadour cream he looked out over the massed tables below them. Somewhere in the hazy distance Renzi, Captain Houghton and the rest were looking enviously to the dais at Prince Edward, Thérèse Bernardine-Mongenet – and Thomas Kydd.

At last the banquet drew to a close. The Prince rose, conversation stilled, and there was a sudden scraping of chairs as everyone stood up. One by one the members of the high table descended, following the Prince as he processed out affably, nodding to the bobs and curtsies as he passed. Looks of admiration and envy shot at Kydd, who smiled back lazily.

In the foyer the Prince turned to Kydd. 'Lieutenant, you will no doubt be returning to your ship. Pray do not stand on ceremony for Madame – I will personally see she returns home safely.' With a wry smile, Kydd bowed. 'And, Lieutenant, I will not forget your service to me this night!'

Thérèse looked at Kydd. She crossed to him and kissed him firmly on both cheeks. '*I* will not forget this evening. *Bon chance, mon ami.*'

They left. Kydd watched the Prince's carriage depart, Thérèse's last glance back and fond wave. The rest of the guests issued out noisily, and it seemed the whole of Halifax wanted to meet him, make his acquaintance, be seen with him. Captain Houghton appeared, staring wordlessly at Kydd and shaking his head slowly before he moved on; Adams came up and insisted on taking his hand. 'Damme if that wasn't the finest stroke of the age!' he said sincerely.

Finally Renzi emerged. Full of the deepest delight Kydd said casually, 'Then was she not a suitable lady?'

'Brother, we must walk for a spell.' Renzi did not bother to introduce the lady with him, who pouted at the slight. 'Into your coach, m'dear,' he said firmly. 'I shall follow.' When they were alone on the street Renzi turned to him. 'My dear fellow,' he began, then stopped. 'My dear chap. Where can I *begin*?' He paced about in frustration, ignoring the admiring glances passers-by were throwing at Kydd. 'In polite society – in the highest society – damn it all, what you did was either inspired deviltry or the purest ignorance! And all Halifax believes it the first.'

'Nicholas, you talk in riddles. If you're just envious—'

'Tom – if you must know, this is what you did. You invited the Prince's mistress to a banquet hosted by the Prince himself.'

'Thérèse – Julie?' Kydd fell back in dismay. The flush drained from his face. At the very least it was the ruin of his career, a spectacular end to his promising beginnings. After the exaltation of earlier it was agonising.

'Not at all.' Renzi struggled for the words. 'The world believes you knew that Julie appears at lesser occasions, the Prince having a particular taking for her, but at affairs of state – foreign potentates – she must not be seen. To the Prince's great pleasure you produced her for him at this occasion under the unimpeachable courtly pretence of not knowing her situation.'

He gave a low laugh. 'There must be many haughty matrons of Halifax who have been put sadly out of countenance tonight – but many more gentlemen whose admiration for you is unbounded. Just consider – you now have the ear and attention of a prince of the Blood Royal. You are made in society, you – you have but to claim the fruits of your cunning.'

*   *   *

'Where's Renzi?' It was late morning in the wardroom and he had still not appeared. Kydd had put it down to over-indulgence, but his friend's cabin was empty.

'Renzi? I do believe he must still be at Manning's tavern – he was well away when I saw him,' Pringle drawled.

A tavern? Kydd threw on his coat and clapped on his hat. In all the time he had known Renzi he had never once seen him in liquor. Surely he was not a spurned lover. The woman whom he had seen at the banquet? Impossible!

Manning's was often frequented by officers but Kydd could not find Renzi in the high-backed chairs of the taphouse or in any of the more secluded public rooms. Discreet enquiry yielded that he was still in his room and furthermore had sent for two bottles since midnight, and was unaccountably alone.

Disturbed, Kydd went up the stairs. Knocking at the door several times did not produce a result. 'Nicholas!' he called softly. 'I know you're there. Let me in, brother.'

About to knock again he heard Renzi's muffled voice, 'Thank you for your visit, but I'm indisposed. I shall return aboard – later.'

'If bein' tosticated is what ails ye, then it's a poor shab as won't see his friend.'

There was a silence, then a rattling, and the door opened. Kydd nearly laughed at the frowsy bleariness of his friend but kept a grave expression and entered. He sat in a chair next to the bed. 'Can I be of service to ye?' he asked neutrally.

Renzi glared balefully at him. Then he groaned and lolled back in the other chair. 'I'm all undone, I see. You shall have the truth of it – but first a drink.'

Kydd sat up, alarmed, but Renzi reached for the water pitcher on the dresser and up-ended it, gulping the water noisily. He wiped his mouth and tried to grin. 'Ah, let us say I have been the unwitting sport of Venus, the plaything of Cupid. In fine, I have to admit to being gulled in full measure.'

'Aye?' said Kydd, trying not to show his considerable interest.

'A charming nymph, a young sprig of society, whose name will be known in the highest reaches of Haligonian gentility, she it was who – who has refused me.'

'That – that woman at the banquet?' Kydd said, appalled.

'Not her,' said Renzi testily. 'A mere *quicumque vult*, a Cyprian taken up for the occasion. No – I speak of a young woman of grace and talents, a perfect specimen of spirited maid-enhood. I met her at the admiral's rout and since then have been seen in her company at many a polite occasion, a sparkling companion. Then, the sap unwonted rising high, I pressed my attentions on her, would not be denied . . .' He trailed off, staring disconsolately at the wall.

'And then?'

'It grieves me to say it, but she – she . . .'

'Yes?'

'It seems that the young lady is – how shall we phrase it? Of the Sapphic persuasion.' At Kydd's blank look he added wearily, 'This is to mean that she prefers the company of women to that of men, in all its forms.'

'Then—'

'Quite so. For her I have been but a toy, a necessary social ornament. It has been a – salutary experience.'

'Nicholas, I—'

'And is now most firmly a thing of the past,' Renzi concluded bleakly.

Kydd subsided. It explained Renzi's distraction, his absences.. And it was certain he would appreciate neither sympathy nor pity.

Renzi drew a deep breath and leaning forward said, 'Therefore we shall speak of your transmogrification.'

'My . . . ?' said Kydd carefully.

'You're clearly not fully aware of what has happened, and by that I do not mean simply your appearance with Madame Thérèse.' He held his head and closed his eyes for a space. 'Consider this: your action in bringing Julie to the banquet is seen as a very clever piece of theatre to bring yourself to the attention not only of society but of Prince Edward himself, a coup that has all Halifax abuzz.

'Now what that is telling the world is that you must be accounted a superior player in the arts of society, and it would go well with any who can boast your acquaintance. This is my wager with you – you'll have more invitations in the next week than you can possibly accept in a year.'

'But I don't—'

'Let me continue. This is a triviality, a vaporous nonsense compared to its true significance.' He took another pull at the water pitcher and, looking directly at Kydd, continued, 'Tom, dear chap, what is signified is that the forms of politeness, so well expressed by John Locke, however requisite in the salons and courts, must always yield to that of true character in polite company.

'*In vino veritas*, then. I was wrong. I freely admit it. You are your own man now, with a character and reputation that will only grow. You don't need airs and my clever words – and neither do you need to bandy empty talk about fox-hunting or the Season, for you've established a manly character of your own, which, dare I say it, is above such nonsense.

'My dear fellow – go forth and conquer. Know that you can match any gentleman for wit and reputation and at last take your place in society.'

Renzi closed his eyes. 'And leave me to die in peace.'

Kydd rose noiselessly and tiptoed away.

Renzi was right. Invitations arrived by the dozen for Lieutenant Kydd in the days that followed. At one point Captain Houghton came to him personally with a mumbled request that he grace an evening with him at the attorney general Uniacke's, known like Cunard for his four daughters, and a power in the land. Fortunately Kydd found his diary free for that night.

And Renzi was right about the other thing: the wardroom continued to talk country estates and Vauxhall Gardens, but when Kydd came in with an appreciation of the new United States Navy or a light observation on signals he was listened to respectfully, getting laughs in all the right places.

It was a heady discovery that he was free at last. Free of the demons of inferiority, the fear of being seen as socially gauche, the oaken-headed tarpaulin, an embarrassment. Now he could hold his own in any society.

'Nicholas, are you at liberty tonight? It would give me th' greatest pleasure to sup with you – at Pontac's at seven?'

Kydd was determined to do his friend proud. 'Do have more o' the roast lark, they're so particular in the cooking here,' he said. 'And I hope the Lafite is up to your expectations,' he added anxiously. He piled Renzi's plate high and insisted on pouring the wine.

Renzi was unusually silent, which Kydd put down to his recent experience. It needed all of an hour before he finally spoke his mind. 'There is an observation I feel obliged to make, Thomas, bearing as it does on our long friendship.' He weighed his words carefully. 'An unkind observer might remark

326

that in our lower-deck existence we had a peculiar need, one for the other. I – that in my term of exile there was one of intelligence, uncommon good sense and enquiring nature to lighten my durance. You – my trifles of philosophy and intellectual penetrations could enable you to rise above the limitations of your surroundings. That same observer could then say, in perfect truth, that those needs are now concluded. You have succeeded in all the accomplishments of gentility and the sea profession, so I am no longer needed.'

Kydd slammed down his glass. 'Stuff 'n' nonsense, Nicholas!' He saw Renzi's eyes glitter – it seemed it was costing him much to speak as he had.

'And I,' Renzi continued, with some difficulty, 'I have had my choice of wranglers in reason, the company of my peers in breeding, the sweets of society, but in cleaving to these it grieves me to recall how I have so shamelessly neglected our friendship – all for the sake of the evanescent. Is this then an end to our association? Logic is a stern mistress and pronounces that, with the extinction of need, we must necessarily part, go our own ways—'

'A pox on y'r damned logic!' Kydd said angrily. 'As a philosopher you're nothin' but a double-barrelled, copper-bottomed fool! Do ye think I don't still want you as a friend, share the laughs 'n' pains o' life, enjoy while we can? Raise up y'r glass, Nicholas, an' let's drink to friendship.'

Renzi lifted his head. A reluctant half-smile spread and he replied, 'I will – but this time it's a friendship of equals.'

Glasses clinked. When they had regained composure Kydd fumbled in his coat. 'Er, Nicholas, I'd value y'r opinion. Which o' these invitations do ye think we should accept?'

Author's Note

Aquestion I am often asked is how long does the research for each book take? That is a difficult thing to quantify because in some ways I suppose I have been unconsciously doing it all my life – during my time at sea absorbing the universals all mariners hold dear, and ingesting material from countless maritime books, both fiction and non-fiction, that I've been drawn to since a very early age.

The proportion of my time now devoted to research must come close to fifty per cent. But I have to say, it's an aspect of being a writer that I *particularly* enjoy.

Research for the Kydd series has provided an opportunity to go down many fascinating paths in search of some arcane fact or other – and this book has proved no exception. I found myself corresponding with Dr David Green at the USDA Forest Service about the specific gravity of swamp oaks; this enabled me to send Kydd on his night-time sabotage mission against the French frigate. A chance discovery of an old pilot book of Kydd's time in a Falmouth museum had me enquiring of the august Royal Institute of Navigation.

One of their members, Dr Mark Breach, confirmed the antique rule-of-thumb about the moon's meridian that saved Kydd and his boat crew in the fog.

And while on the subject of chance, what were the odds of my coming across a signal book actually belonging to a lieutenant on the North American station at exactly the time when Kydd learns his craft as a signal lieutenant? Retired Paymaster Commander William Evershed generously extended a loan of the precious family relic for me to study.

Research has enriched my life in another way, too. It has made me many new friends who also are irresistibly drawn to the sea. Two, in particular, have a special connection with *Quarterdeck*. I first met ship modeller Robert Squarebriggs when I visited Canada's Maritime Provinces in 2002. He shared his love of the boreal wilderness, and I hope in this book that I have done justice to his infectious enthusiasm for his native land. Tyrone Martin is an erudite scholar of the dawn of US Navy history, and a former captain of *Old Ironsides*. His many insights into this fascinating period will again be invaluable when Kydd returns to North America, which he assuredly will.

I feel some degree of guilt in not being able to acknowledge everyone I consulted in the process of writing this book, but they all have my deep thanks. However I could not omit mentioning the four wonderfully professional women in my life – my wife (and creative partner) Kathy, my literary agent Carole Blake, my editor Carolyn Mays, and my publicist Kerry Hood. Between them, they contrive to keep the hassles of the modern world at bay, allowing me to give full rein to my creative juices, ready for the next adventure . . .